THOMAS PYNCHON

THOMAS PYNCHON is known almost exclusively through his writing. In all other respects, he craves and guards his privacy. The public facts about his life are therefore few and far between. He was born in 1937 and attended Cornell University, where he published his first story, "Mortality and Mercy in Vienna," in EPOCH. Soon after leaving Cornell, he published three short stories— "Under the Rose," in NOBLE SAVAGE #3; "Entropy," in THE KENYON REVIEW; and "Low-Lands," in NEW WORLD WRITING #16—which earned him an immediate reputation among the narrow but intense circle of short story readers. His novel *V.* won the coveted William Faulkner Foundation First Novel Award in 1963. His second novel, *The Crying of Lot 49,* appeared in 1966. Since then he has published "The Secret Integration" in THE SATURDAY EVENING POST, and an essay of Los Angeles in THE NEW YORK TIMES MAGAZINE. *Gravity's Rainbow,* his third and most recent novel, was published in 1973 and won the National Book Award.

Bantam Windstone Books
Ask your bookseller for the books you have missed

Daddy —
    Somehow you need
to find time to read this
book. It's awesome.
    Merry Christmas '87

    Love,
        Dave

THOMAS PYNCHON

BANTAM BOOKS
TORONTO • NEW YORK • LONDON • SYDNEY • AUCKLAND

V.

A Bantam Book / published by arrangement with
Harper & Row, Publishers Inc.

PRINTING HISTORY

Lippincott edition published March 1963
2nd printing .... March 1963   3rd printing ..... April 1963
4th printing . . . June 1963

Bantam edition / March 1964

2nd printing .... March 1964	8th printing .... March 1973
3rd printing .... March 1967	9th printing . September 1973
4th printing ... October 1968	10th printing . December 1973
5th printing ... January 1970	11th printing .. February 1976
6th printing ..... April 1971	12th printing .. February 1977
7th printing ... October 1972	13th printing ... January 1978

14th printing ... September 1979
Bantam Windstone edition / September 1981
16th printing ... January 1983   17th printing ... June 1984

Windstone and accompanying logo of a stylized W are
trademarks of Bantam Books, Inc.

The author wishes to thank the editors of THE NOBLE SAVAGE
for permission to reprint portions of chapter three which
appeared originally (considerably altered) as a short story titled
"Under the Rose" in THE NOBLE SAVAGE 3, *published by*
World Publishing Company.

Bantam Books are published by Bantam Books, Inc. Its trade-
mark, consisting of the words "Bantam Books" and the por-
trayal of a rooster, is Registered in U.S. Patent and Trademark
Office and in other countries. Marca Registrada. Bantam
Books, Inc., 666 Fifth Avenue, New York, New York 10103.

contents

VVVVVVVVVVV
VVVVVVVVVV
VVVVVVVV
VVVVV
VVVV
VVV
VV
V

chapter one

*In which Benny Profane,
a schlemihl and
human yo-yo,
g e t s t o
an apo-
cheir*

V

I

Christmas Eve, 1955, Benny Profane, wearing black levis, suede jacket, sneakers and big cowboy hat, happened to pass through Norfolk, Virginia. Given to sentimental impulses, he thought he'd look in on the Sailor's Grave, his old tin can's tavern on East Main Street. He got there by way of the Arcade, at the East Main end of which sat an old street singer with a guitar and an empty Sterno can for donations. Out in the street a chief yeoman was trying to urinate in the gas tank of a '54 Packard Patrician and five or six seamen apprentice were standing around giving encouragement. The old man was singing, in a fine, firm baritone:

> Every night is Christmas Eve on old East Main,
> Sailors and their sweethearts all agree.
> Neon signs of red and green
> Shine upon the friendly scene,
> Welcoming you in from off the sea.
> Santa's bag is filled with all your dreams come true:
> Nickel beers that sparkle like champagne,
> Barmaids who all love to screw,
> All of them reminding you
> It's Christmas Eve on old East Main.

"Yay chief," yelled a seaman deuce. Profane rounded the corner. With its usual lack of warning, East Main was on him.

Since his discharge from the Navy Profane had been road-laboring and when there wasn't work just traveling, up and down the east coast like a yo-yo; and this had been going on for maybe a year and a half. After that long of more named pavements than he'd care to count, Profane had grown a little leery of streets, especially streets like this. They had in fact all fused into a single abstracted Street, which come the full moon he would have nightmares about. East Main, a ghetto for Drunken Sailors nobody knew what to Do With, sprang on your nerves with all the abruptness of a normal night's dream turning to nightmare. Dog into wolf, light into twilight, emptiness into waiting presence, here were your underage Marine barfing in the street, barmaid with a ship's propeller tattooed on each buttock, one potential berserk studying the best technique for jumping through a plate glass window (when to scream Geronimo? before or after the glass breaks?), a drunken deck ape crying back in the alley because last time the SP's caught him like this they put him in a strait jacket. Underfoot, now and again, came vibration in the sidewalk from an SP streetlights away, beating out a Hey Rube with his night stick; overhead, turning everybody's face green and ugly, shone mercury-vapor lamps, receding in an asymmetric V to the east where it's dark and there are no more bars.

Arriving at the Sailor's Grave, Profane found a small fight in progress between sailors and jarheads. He stood in the doorway a moment watching; then realizing he had one foot in the Grave anyway, dived out of the way of the fight and lay more or less doggo near the brass rail.

"Why can't man live in peace with his fellow man," wondered a voice behind Profane's left ear. It was Beatrice the barmaid, sweetheart of DesDiv 22, not to mention Profane's old ship, the destroyer U.S.S. Scaffold. "Benny," she cried. They became tender, meeting again after so long. Profane began to draw in the sawdust hearts, arrows through them, sea gulls carrying a banner in their beaks which read Dear Beatrice.

The Scaffold-boat's crew were absent, this tin can having got under way for the Mediterranean two evenings ago amid a storm of bitching from the crew which was heard out in the cloudy Roads (so the yarn went) like voices off a ghost

2

ship; heard as far away as Little Creek. Accordingly, there were a few more barmaids than usual tonight, working tables all up and down East Main. For it's said (and not without reason) that no sooner does a ship like the Scaffold single up all lines than certain Navy wives are out of their civvies and into barmaid uniform, flexing their beer-carrying arms and practicing a hooker's sweet smile; even as the N.O.B. band is playing Auld Lang Syne and the destroyers are blowing stacks in black flakes all over the cuckolds-to-be standing manly at attention, taking leave with rue and a tiny grin.

Beatrice brought beer. There was a piercing yelp from one of the back tables, she flinched, beer slopped over the edge of the glass.

"God," she said, "it's Ploy again." Ploy was now an engineman on the mine sweeper Impulsive and a scandal the length of East Main. He stood five feet nothing in sea boots and was always picking fights with the biggest people on the ship, knowing they would never take him seriously. Ten months ago (just before he'd transferred off the Scaffold) the Navy had decided to remove all of Ploy's teeth. Incensed, Ploy managed to punch his way through a chief corpsman and two dental officers before it was decided he was in earnest about keeping his teeth. "But think," the officers shouted, trying not to laugh, fending off his tiny fists: "root canal work, gum abscesses. . . ." "No," screamed Ploy. They finally had to hit him in the bicep with a Pentothal injection. On waking up, Ploy saw apocalypse, screamed lengthy obscenities. For two months he roamed ghastly around the Scaffold, leaping without warning to swing from the overhead like an orangutan, trying to kick officers in the teeth.

He would stand on the fantail and harangue whoever would listen, flannelmouthed through aching gums. When his mouth had healed he was presented with a gleaming, regulation set of upper and lower plates. "Oh God," he bawled, and tried to jump over the side. But was restrained by a gargantuan Negro named Dahoud. "Hey there, little fellow," said Dahoud, picking Ploy up by the head and scrutinizing this convulsion of dungarees and despair whose feet thrashed a yard above the deck. "What do you want to go and do that for?"

"Man, I want to die, is all," cried Ploy.

"Don't you know," said Dahoud, "that life is the most precious possession you have?"

"Ho, ho," said Ploy through his tears. "Why?"

"Because," said Dahoud, "without it, you'd be dead."

"Oh," said Ploy. He thought about this for a week. He calmed down, started to go on liberty again. His transfer to the Impulsive became reality. Soon, after Lights Out, the other snipes began to hear strange grating sounds from the direction of Ploy's rack. This went on for a couple-three weeks until one morning around two somebody turned on the lights in the compartment and there was Ploy, sitting crosslegged on his rack, sharpening his teeth with a small bastard file. Next payday night, Ploy sat at a table in the Sailor's Grave with a bunch of other snipes, quieter than usual. Around eleven, Beatrice swayed by, carrying a tray full of beers. Gleeful, Ploy stuck his head out, opened his jaws wide, and sank his newly-filed dentures into the barmaid's right buttock. Beatrice screamed, glasses flew parabolic and glittering, spraying the Sailor's Grave with watery beer.

It became Ploy's favorite amusement. The word spread through the division, the squadron, perhaps all DesLant. People not of the Impulsive or Scaffold came to watch. This started many fights like the one now in progress.

"Who did he get," Profane said. "I wasn't looking."

"Beatrice," said Beatrice. Beatrice being another barmaid. Mrs. Buffo, owner of the Sailor's Grave, whose first name was also Beatrice, had a theory that just as small children call all females mother, so sailors, in their way equally as helpless, should call all barmaids Beatrice. Further to implement this maternal policy, she had had custom beer taps installed, made of foam rubber, in the shape of large breasts. From eight to nine on payday nights there occurred something Mrs. Buffo called Suck Hour. She began it officially by emerging from the back room clad in a dragon-embroidered kimono given her by an admirer in the Seventh Fleet, raising a gold boatswain's pipe to her lips and blowing Chow Down. At this signal, everyone would dive for and if they were lucky enough to reach one be given suck by a beer tap. There were seven of these taps, and an average of 250 sailors usually present for the merrymaking.

Ploy's head now appeared around a corner of the bar. He snapped his teeth at Profane. "This here," Ploy said, "is my friend Dewey Gland, who just came aboard." He indicated a long, sad-looking rebel with a huge beak who had followed Ploy over, dragging a guitar in the sawdust.

"Howdy," said Dewey Gland. "I would like to sing you a little song."

"To celebrate your becoming a PFC," said Ploy. "Dewey sings it to everybody."

"That was last year," said Profane.

But Dewey Gland propped one foot on the brass rail and the guitar on his knee and began to strum. After eight bars of this he sang, in waltz time:

> Pore Forlorn Civilian,
> We're goin to miss you so.
> In the goat hole and the wardroom they're cryin,
> Even the mizzable X.O.
> You're makin a mistake,
> Though yore ass they should break,
> Yore report chits number a million.
> Ship me over for twenty years,
> I'll never be a Pore Forlorn Civilian.

"It's pretty," said Profane into his beer glass.

"There's more," said Dewey Gland.

"Oh," said Profane.

A miasma of evil suddenly enveloped Profane from behind; an arm fell like a sack of spuds across his shoulder and into his peripheral vision crept a beer glass surrounded by a large muff, fashioned ineptly from diseased baboon fur.

"Benny. How is the pimping business, hyeugh, hyeugh."

The laugh could only have come from Profane's onetime shipmate, Pig Bodine. Profane looked round. It had. Hyeugh, hyeugh approximates a laugh formed by putting the tongue-tip under the top central incisors and squeezing guttural sounds out of the throat. It was, as Pig intended, horribly obscene.

"Old Pig. Aren't you missing movement?"

"I am AWOL. Pappy Hod the boatswain mate drove me over the hill." The best way to avoid SP's is to stay sober and with your own. Hence the Sailor's Grave.

"How is Pappy."

Pig told him how Pappy Hod and the barmaid he'd married had split up. She'd left and come to work at the Sailor's Grave.

5

That young wife, Paola. She'd said sixteen, but no way of telling because she'd been born just before the war and the building with her records destroyed, like most other buildings on the island of Malta.

Profane had been there when they met: the Metro Bar, on Strait Street. The Gut. Valletta, Malta.

"Chicago," from Pappy Hod in his gangster voice. "You heard of Chicago," meanwhile reaching sinister inside his jumper, a standard act for Pappy Hod all around the Med's littoral. He would pull out a handkerchief and not a heater or gat after all, blow his nose and laugh at whatever girl it happened to be sitting across the table. American movies had given them stereotypes all, all but Paola Maijstral, who continued to regard him then with nostrils unflared, eyebrows at dead center.

Pappy ended up borrowing 500 for 700 from Mac the cook's slush fund to bring Paola to the States.

Maybe it had only been a way for her to get to America —every Mediterranean barmaid's daftness—where there was enough food, warm clothes, heat all the time, buildings all in one piece. Pappy was to lie about her age to get her into the country. She could be any age she wanted. And you suspected any nationality, for Paola knew scraps it seemed of all tongues.

Pappy Hod had described her for the deck apes' amusement down in the boatswain's locker of the U.S.S. Scaffold. Speaking the while however with a peculiar tenderness, as if slowly coming aware, maybe even as the yarn unlaid, that sex might be more of a mystery than he'd foreseen and he would not after all know the score because that kind of score wasn't written down in numbers. Which after forty-five years was nothing for any riggish Pappy Hod to be finding out.

"Good stuff," said Pig aside. Profane looked toward the back of the Sailor's Grave and saw her approaching now through the night's accumulated smoke. She looked like an East Main barmaid. What was it about the prairie hare in the snow, the tiger in tall grass and sunlight?

She smiled at Profane: sad, with an effort.

"You come back to re-enlist?"

"Just passing," Profane said.

"You come with me to the west coast," Pig said. "Ain't an SP car made that can take my Harley."

"Look, look," cried little Ploy, hopping up and down on

6

one foot. "Not now, you guys. Stand by." He pointed. Mrs. Buffo had materialized on the bar, in her kimono. A hush fell over the place. There was a momentary truce between the jarheads and sailors blocking the doorway.

"Boys," Mrs. Buffo announced, "it's Christmas Eve." She produced the boatswain's pipe and began to play. The first notes quavered out fervent and flutelike over widened eyes and gaping mouths. Everyone in the Sailor's Grave listened awestruck, realizing gradually that she was playing It Came Upon a Midnight Clear, within the limited range of the boatswain's pipe. From way in the back, a young reserve who had once done night club acts around Philly began to sing softly along. Ploy's eyes shone. "It is the voice of an angel," he said.

They had reached the part that goes "Peace on the earth, good will to men, From Heav'n's all-gracious king," when Pig, a militant atheist, decided he could stand it no longer. "That," he announced in a loud voice, "sounds like Chow Down." Mrs. Buffo and the reserve fell silent. A second passed before anybody got the message.

"Suck Hour!" screamed Ploy.

Which kind of broke the spell. The quick-thinking inmates of the Impulsive somehow coalesced in the sudden milling around of jolly jack tars, hoisted Ploy bodily and rushed with the little fellow toward the nearest nipple, in the van of the attack.

Mrs. Buffo, poised on her rampart like the trumpeter of Cracow, took the full impact of the onslaught, toppling over backwards into an ice-tub as the first wave came hurtling over the bar. Ploy, hands outstretched, was propelled over the top. He caught on to one of the tap handles and simultaneously his shipmates let go; his momentum carried him and the handle in a downward arc: beer began to gush from the foam rubber breast in a white cascade, washing over Ploy, Mrs. Buffo and two dozen sailors who had come around behind the bar in a flanking action and who were now battering one another into insensibility. The group who had carried Ploy over spread out and tried to corner more beer taps. Ploy's leading petty officer was on hands and knees holding Ploy's feet, ready to pull them out from under him and take his striker's place when Ploy had had enough. The Impulsive detachment in their charge had formed a flying wedge. In their wake and through the breach clambered at least sixty more slavering bluejackets, kicking, clawing, side-arming, bellowing uproariously; some swinging beer bottles to clear a path.

Profane sat at the end of the bar, watching hand-tooled sea boots, bell-bottoms, rolled up levi cuffs; every now and again a drooling face at the end of a fallen body; broken beer bottles, tiny sawdust storms.

Soon he looked over; Paola was there, arms around his leg, cheek pressed against the black denim.

"It's awful," she said.

"Oh," said Profane. He patted her head.

"Peace," she sighed. "Isn't that what we all want, Benny? Just a little peace. Nobody jumping out and biting you on the ass."

"Hush," said Profane, "look: someone has just walloped Dewey Gland in the stomach with his own guitar."

Paola murmured against his leg. They sat quiet, without raising their eyes to watch the carnage going on above them. Mrs. Buffo had undertaken a crying jag. Inhuman blubberings beat against and rose from behind the old imitation mahogany of the bar.

Pig had moved aside two dozen beer glasses and seated himself on a ledge behind the bar. In times of crisis he preferred to sit in as voyeur. He gazed eagerly as his shipmates grappled shoatlike after the seven geysers below him. Beer had soaked down most of the sawdust behind the bar: skirmishes and amateur footwork were now scribbling it into alien hieroglyphics.

Outside came sirens, whistles, running feet. "Oh, oh," said Pig. He hopped down from the shelf, made his way around the end of the bar to Profane and Paola. "Hey, ace," he said, cool and slitting his eyes as if the wind blew into them. "The sheriff is coming."

"Back way," said Profane.

"Bring the broad," said Pig.

The three of them ran broken-field through a roomful of teeming bodies. On the way they picked up Dewey Gland. By the time the Shore Patrol had crashed into the Sailor's Grave, night sticks flailing, the four found themselves running down an alley parallel to East Main. "Where we going," Profane said. "The way we're heading," said Pig. "Move your ass."

Where they ended up finally was an apartment in Newport News, inhabited by four WAVE lieutenants and a switchman at the coal piers (friend of Pig's) named Morris Teflon, who was a sort of house father. The week between Christmas and New Year's Day was spent drunk enough to know that's what they were. Nobody in the house seemed to object when they all moved in.

An unfortunate habit of Teflon's drew Profane and Paola together, though neither wanted that. Teflon had a camera: Leica, procured half-legally overseas by a Navy friend. On weekends when business was good and guinea red wine splashing around like the wave from a heavy merchantman, Teflon would sling the camera round his neck and go a-roving from bed to bed, taking pictures. These he sold to avid sailors at the lower end of East Main.

It happened that Paola Hod, nee Maijstral, cast loose at her own whim early from the security of Pappy Hod's bed and late from the half-home of the Sailor's Grave, was now in a state of shock which endowed Profane with all manner of healing and sympathetic talents he didn't really possess.

"You're all I have," she warned him. "Be good to me." They would sit around a table in Teflon's kitchen: Pig Bodine and Dewey Gland facing them one each like partners at bridge, a vodka bottle in the middle. Nobody would talk except to argue about what they would mix the vodka with next when what they had ran out. That week they tried milk, canned vegetable soup, finally the juice from a dried-up piece of watermelon which was all Teflon had left in the refrigerator. Try to squeeze a watermelon into a small tumbler sometime when your reflexes are not so good. It is next to impossible. Picking the seeds out of the vodka proved also to be a problem, and resulted in a growing, mutual ill-will.

Part of the trouble was that Pig and Dewey both had eyes for Paola. Every night they would approach Profane as a committee and ask for seconds.

"She's trying to recover from men," Profane tried to say. Pig would either reject this or take it as an insult to Pappy Hod his old superior.

Truth of it was Profane wasn't getting any. Though it became hard to tell what Paola wanted.

"What do you mean," Profane said. "Be good to you."

"What Pappy Hod wasn't," she said. He soon gave up trying to decode her several hankerings. She would on occasion come up with all sorts of weird tales of infidelity, punchings-in-the-mouth, drunken abuse. Having clamped down, chipped, wire-brushed, painted and chipped again under Pappy Hod for four years Profane would believe about half. Half because a woman is only half of something there are usually two sides to.

She taught them all a song. Learned from a para on French leave from the fighting in Algeria:

> Demain le noir matin,
> Je fermerai la porte
> Au nez des années mortes;
> J'irai par les chemins.
> Je mendierai ma vie
> Sur la terre et sur l'onde,
> Du vieux au nouveau monde . . .

He had been short and built like the island of Malta itself: rock, an inscrutable heart. She'd had only one night with him. Then he was off to the Piraeus.

Tomorrow, the black morning, I close the door in the face of the dead years. I will go on the road, bum my way over land and sea, from the old to the new world. . . .

She taught Dewey Gland the chord changes and so they all sat around the table of Teflon's wintry kitchen, while four gas flames on the stove ate up their oxygen; and sang, and sang. When Profane watched her eyes he thought she dreamed of the para—probably a man-of-no-politics as brave as anyone ever is in combat: but tired, was all, tired of relocating native villages and devising barbarities in the morning as brutal as'd come from the F.L.N. the night before. She wore a Miraculous Medal round her neck (given to her, maybe, by some random sailor she reminded of a good Catholic girl back in the States where sex is for free—or for marriage?). What sort of Catholic was she? Profane, who was only half Catholic (mother Jewish), whose morality was fragmentary (being derived from experience and not much of it), wondered what quaint Jesuit arguments had led her

10

to come away with him, refuse to share a bed but still ask him to "be good."

The night before New Year's Eve they wandered away from the kitchen and out to a kosher delicatessen a few blocks away. On returning to Teflon's they found Pig and Dewey gone: "Gone out to get drunk," said the note. The place was lit up all Xmasy, a radio turned to WAVY and Pat Boone in one bedroom, sounds of objects being thrown in another. Somehow the young couple had wandered into a darkened room with this bed in it.

"No," she said.

"Meaning yes."

Groan, went the bed. Before either of them knew it:

Click, went Teflon's Leica.

Profane did what was expected of him: came roaring off the bed, arm terminating in a fist. Teflon dodged it easily. "Now, now," he chuckled.

Outraged privacy was not so important; but the interruption had come just before the Big Moment.

"You don't mind," Teflon was telling him. Paola was hurrying into clothes.

"Out in the snow," Profane said, "is where that camera, Teflon, is sending us."

"Here:" opened the camera, handed Profane the film, "you're going to be a horse's ass about it."

Profane took the film but couldn't back down. So he dressed and topped off with the cowboy hat. Paola had put on a Navy greatcoat, too big for her.

"Out," Profane cried, "in the snow." Which in fact there was. They caught a ferry over to Norfolk and sat topside drinking black coffee out of paper cups and watching snow-shrouds flap silent against the big windows. There was nothing else to look at but a bum on a bench facing them, and each other. The engine thumped and labored down below, they could feel it through their buttocks, but neither could think of anything to say.

"Did you want to stay," he asked.

"No, no," she shivered, a discreet foot of worn bench between them. He had no impulse to bring her closer. "Whatever you decide."

Madonna, he thought, I have a dependent now.

"What are you shivering for. It's warm enough in here."

She shook her head no (whatever that meant), staring

11

at the toes of her galoshes. After a while Profane got up and went out on deck.

Snow falling lazy on the water made 11 P.M. look like twilight or an eclipse. Overhead every few seconds a horn sounded off to warn away anything on collision course. But yet as if there were nothing in this roads after all but ships, untenanted, inanimate, making noises at each other which meant nothing more than the turbulence of the screws or the snow-hiss on the water. And Profane all alone in it.

Some of us are afraid of dying; others of human loneliness. Profane was afraid of land or seascapes like this, where nothing else lived but himself. It seemed he was always walking into one: turn a corner in the street, open a door to a weather-deck and there he'd be, in alien country.

But the door behind him opened again. Soon he felt Paola's gloveless hands slipped under his arms, her cheek against his back. His mental eye withdrew, watching their still-life as a stranger might. But she didn't help the scene be any less alien. They kept like that till the other side, the ferry entered the slip, and chains clanked, car ignitions whined, motors started.

They rode the bus into town, wordless; alit near the Monticello Hotel and set out for East Main to find Pig and Dewey. The Sailor's Grave was dark, the first time Profane could remember. The cops must have closed it up.

They found Pig next door in Chester's Hillbilly Haven. Dewey was sitting in with the band. "Party, party," cried Pig.

Some dozen ex-Scaffold sailors wanted a reunion. Pig, appointing himself social chairman, decided on the Susanna Squaducci, an Italian luxury liner now in the last stages of construction in the Newport News yards.

"Back to Newport News?" (Deciding not to tell Pig about the disagreement with Teflon.) So: yo-yoing again.

"This has got to cease," he said but nobody was listening. Pig was off dancing the dirty boogie with Paola.

III

Profane slept that night at Pig's place down by the old ferry docks, and he slept alone. Paola had run into one of the Beatrices and gone off to stay the night with her, after

12

promising demurely to be Profane's date at the New Year's party.

Around three Profane woke up on the kitchen floor with a headache. Night air, bitter cold, seeped under the door and from somewhere outside he could hear a low, persistent growl. "Pig," Profane croaked. "Where you keep the aspirin." No answer. Profane stumbled into the other room. Pig wasn't there. The growl outside turned more ominous. Profane went to the window and saw Pig down in the alley, sitting on his motorcycle and racing the engine. Snow fell in tiny glittering pinpoints, the alley held its own curious snow-light: turning Pig to black-and-white clown's motley and ancient brick walls, dusted with snow, to neutral gray. Pig had on a knitted watch cap, pulled down over his face to the neck so that his head showed up as a sphere of dead black. Engine exhaust roiled in clouds around him. Profane shivered. "What are you doing, Pig," he called. Pig didn't answer. The enigma or sinister vision of Pig and that Harley-Davidson alone in an alley at three in the morning reminded Profane too suddenly of Rachel, whom he didn't want to think about, not tonight in the bitter cold, with a headache, with snow slipping into the room.

Rachel Owlglass had owned, back in '54, this MG. Her Daddy's gift. After giving it its shakedown cruise in the region around Grand Central (where Daddy's office was), familiarizing it with telephone poles, fire hydrants and occasional pedestrians, she brought the car up to the Catskills for the summer. Here, little, sulky and voluptuous, Rachel would gee and haw this MG around Route 17's bloodthirsty curves and cutbacks, sashaying its arrogant butt past hay wagons, growling semis, old Ford roadsters filled to capacity with crewcut, undergraduate gnomes.

Profane was just out of the Navy and working that summer as assistant salad man at Schlozhauer's Trocadero, nine miles outside Liberty, New York. His chief was one Da Conho, a mad Brazilian who wanted to go fight Arabs in Israel. One night near the opening of the season a drunken Marine had showed up in the Fiesta Lounge or bar of the Trocadero, carrying a .30-caliber machine gun in his AWOL bag. He wasn't too sure how he had come by the weapon exactly: Da Conho preferred to think it had been smuggled out of Parris Island piece by piece, which was how the Haganah would do it. After a deal of arguing with the bartender, who also wanted the gun, Da Conho finally triumphed, swapping for it three artichokes and an eggplant. To the mezuzah nailed up over the vegetable reefer and the Zionist banner hanging in back of the salad table Da Conho added this prize. During the weeks that followed, when the head chef was looking the other way, Da Conho would assemble his machine gun, camouflage it with iceberg lettuce, watercress and Belgian endive, and mock-strafe the guests assembled in the dining room. "Yibble, yibble, yibble," he would go, squinting malevolent along the sights, "got you dead center, Abdul Sayid. Yibble, yibble, Muslim pig." Da Conho's machine gun was the only one in the world that went yibble, yibble. He would sit up past four in the morning cleaning it, dreaming of lunar-looking deserts, the sizzle of chang music, Yemenite girls whose delicate heads were covered with white kerchiefs, whose loins ached with love. He wondered how American Jews could sit vainglorious in that dining room meal after meal while only halfway round the world the desert shifted relentless over corpses of their own. How could he tell soulless stomachs? Harangue with oil and vinegar, supplicate with heart of palm. The only voice he had was the machine gun's. Could they hear that, can stomachs listen: no. And you never hear the one that gets you. Aimed perhaps at any alimentary canal in a Hart Schaffner & Marx suit which vented lewd gurgles at the waitresses who passed, that gun was an object only, pointing where any suitable unbalance force might direct it: but which belt buckle was Da Conho taking a lead on: Abdul Sayid, the alimentary canal, himself? Why ask. He knew no more than that he was a Zionist, suffered, was confused, was daft to stand rooted sock-top deep in the loam of any kibbutz, a hemisphere away.

Profane had wondered then what it was with Da Conho and that machine gun. Love for an object, this was new to him. When he found out not long after this that the same thing was with Rachel and her MG, he had his first intelligence that something had been going on under the rose, maybe for longer and with more people than he would care to think about.

He met her through the MG, like everyone else met her. It nearly ran him over. He was wandering out the back door of the kitchen one noon carrying a garbage can overflowing with lettuce leaves Da Conho considered substandard when

14

somewhere off to his right he heard the MG's sinister growl. Profane kept walking, secure in a faith that burdened pedestrians have the right-of-way. Next thing he knew he was clipped in the rear end by the car's right fender. Fortunately, it was only moving at 5 mph—not fast enough to break anything, only to send Profane, garbage can and lettuce leaves flying ass over teakettle in a great green shower.

He and Rachel, both covered with lettuce leaves, looked at each other, wary. "How romantic," she said. "For all I know you may be the man of my dreams. Take that lettuce leaf off your face so I can see." Like doffing a cap—remembering his place—he removed the leaf.

"No," she said, "you're not him."

"Maybe," said Profane, "we can try it next time with a fig leaf."

"Ha, ha," she said and roared off. He found a rake and started collecting the garbage into one pile. He reflected that here was another inanimate object that had nearly killed him. He was not sure whether he meant Rachel or the car. He put the pile of lettuce leaves in the garbage can and dumped the can back of the parking lot in a small ravine which served the Trocadero for a refuse pile. As he was returning to the kitchen Rachel came by again. The MG's adenoidal exhaust sounded like it probably could be heard all the way to Liberty. "Come for a ride, hey Fatso," she called out. Profane reckoned he could. It was a couple hours before he had to go in to set up for supper.

Five minutes out on Route 17 he decided if he ever got back to the Trocadero unmaimed and alive to forget about Rachel and only be interested thenceforth in quiet, pedestrian girls. She drove like one of the damned on holiday. He had no doubt she knew the car's and her own abilities, but how did she know, for instance, when she passed on a blind curve of that two-lane road, that the milk truck approaching would be just far enough away for her to whip back into line with a whole sixteenth of an inch to spare?

He was too afraid for his life to be, as he normally was, girl-shy. He reached over, opened her pocketbook, found a cigarette, lit it. She didn't notice. She drove single-minded and unaware there was anyone next to her. She only spoke once, to tell him there was a case of cold beer in the back. He dragged on her cigarette and wondered if he had a compulsion to suicide. It seemed sometimes that he put himself

15

deliberately in the way of hostile objects, as if he were looking to get schlimazzeled out of existence. Why was he here anyway? Because Rachel had a nice ass? He glanced sidewise at it on the leather upholstery, bouncing, synched with the car; watched the not-so-simple nor quite harmonic motion of her left breast inside the black sweater she had on. She pulled in finally at an abandoned rock quarry. Irregular chunks of stone were scattered around. He didn't know what kind, but it was all inanimate. They made it up a dirt road to a flat place forty feet above the floor of the quarry.

It was an uncomfortable afternoon. Sun beat down out of a cloudless, unprotective heaven. Profane, fat, sweated. Rachel played Do You Know the few kids she'd known who went to his high school and Profane lost. She talked about all the dates she was getting this summer, all it seemed with upperclassmen attending Ivy League colleges. Profane would agree from time to time how wonderful it was.

She talked about Bennington, her alma mater. She talked about herself.

Rachel came from the Five Towns on the south shore of Long Island, an area comprising Malverne, Lawrence, Cedarhurst, Hewlett and Woodmere and sometimes Long Beach and Atlantic Beach, though no one has ever thought of calling it the Seven Towns. Though the inhabitants are not Sephardim, the area seems afflicted with a kind of geographical incest. Daughters are constrained to pace demure and darkeyed like so many Rapunzels within the magic frontiers of a country where the elfin architecture of Chinese restaurants, seafood palaces and split-level synagogues is often enchanting as the sea; until they have ripened enough to be sent off to the mountains and colleges of the Northeast. Not to hunt husbands (for a certain parity has always obtained in the Five Towns whereby a nice boy can be predestined for husband as early as age sixteen or seventeen); but to be granted the illusion at least of having "played the field"—so necessary to a girl's emotional development.

Only the brave escape. Come Sunday nights, with golfing done, the Negro maids, having rectified the disorder of last night's party, off to visit with relatives in Lawrence, and Ed Sullivan still hours away, the blood of this kingdom exit from their enormous homes, enter their automobiles and proceed to the business districts. There to divert themselves among seemingly endless vistas of butterfly shrimp and egg foo yung; Orientals bow, and smile, and flutter through summer's twilight, and in their voices are the birds of summer. And with night's fall comes a brief promenade in the street: the torso of the father solid and sure in its J. Press suit; the eyes of the daughters secret behind sunglasses rimmed in rhinestones. And as the jaguar has given its name to the mother's car, so has it given its skin-pattern to the slacks which compass her sleek hips. Who could escape? Who could want to?

Rachel wanted. Profane, having repaired roads around the Five Towns, could understand why.

By the time the sun was going down they'd nearly finished the case between them. Profane was balefully drunk. He got out of the car, wandered off behind a tree and pointed west, with some intention of pissing on the sun to put it out for good and all, this being somehow important for him. (Inanimate objects could do what they wanted. Not what they wanted because things do not want; only men. But things do what they do, and this is why Profane was pissing at the sun.)

It went down; as if he'd extinguished it after all and continued on immortal, god of a darkened world.

Rachel was watching him, curious. He zipped up and staggered back to the beer box. Two cans left. He opened them and handed one to her. "I put the sun out," he said, "we drink to it." He spilled most of it down his shirt.

Two more folded cans fell to the bottom of the quarry, the empty case followed.

She hadn't moved from the car.

"Benny," one fingernail touched his face.

"Wha."

"Will you be my friend?"

"You look like you have enough."

She looked down the quarry. "Why don't we make believe none of the other is real," she said: "no Bennington, no Schlozhauer's, and no Five Towns. Only this quarry: the dead rocks that were here before us and will be after us."

"Why."

"Isn't that the world?"

"They teach you that in freshman geology or something?" She looked hurt. "It's just something I know."

"Benny," she cried—a little cry—"be my friend, is all." He shrugged.

17

"Write."

"Now don't expect—"

"How the road is. Your boy's road that I'll never see, with its Diesels and dust, roadhouses, crossroads saloons. That's all. What it's like west of Ithaca and south of Princeton. Places I won't know."

He scratched his stomach. "Sure."

Profane kept running into her in what was left of the summer at least once a day. They talked in the car always, he trying to find the key to her own ignition behind the hooded eyes, she sitting back of the right-hand steering wheel and talking, talking, nothing but MG-words, inanimate-words he couldn't really talk back at.

Soon enough what he was afraid would happen happened—he finagled himself into love for Rachel and was only surprised that it had taken so long. He lay in the bunkhouse nights smoking in the dark and apostrophizing the glowing end of his cigarette butt. Around two in the morning the occupant of the upper bunk would come in off the night shift—one Duke Wedge, a pimpled bravo from the Chelsea district, who always wanted to talk about how much he was getting, which was, in fact, plenty. It lulled Profane to sleep. One night he did indeed come upon Rachel and Wedge, the scoundrel, parked in the MG in front of her cabin. He slunk back to bed, not feeling particularly betrayed because he knew Wedge wouldn't get anywhere. He even stayed awake and let Wedge regale him when he came in with a step-by-step account of how he had almost made it but not quite. As usual Profane fell asleep in the middle.

He never got beyond or behind the chatter about her world—one of objects coveted or valued, an atmosphere Profane couldn't breathe. The last time he saw her was Labor Day night. She was to leave the next day. Somebody stole Da Conho's machine gun that evening, just before supper. Da Conho dashed around in tears looking for it. The head chef told Profane to make salads. Somehow Profane managed to get frozen strawberries in the French dressing and chopped liver in the Waldorf salad, plus accidentally dropping two dozen or so radishes in the French fryer (though these drew raves from the customers when he served them anyway, too lazy to go after more). From time to time the Brazilian would come charging through the kitchen crying.

18

He never found his beloved machine gun. Lorn and drained-nervous, he was fired next day. The season was over anyway—for all Profane knew Da Conho may have even taken ship one day for Israel, to tinker with the guts of some tractor, trying to forget, like many exhausted workers abroad, some love back in the States.

After teardown Profane set out to find Rachel. She was out, he was informed, with the captain of the Harvard crossbow team. Profane wandered by the bunkhouse and found a morose Wedge, unusually mateless for the evening. Till midnight they played blackjack for all the contraceptives Wedge had not used over the summer. These numbered about a hundred. Profane borrowed 50 and had a winning streak. When he'd cleaned Wedge out, Wedge dashed away to borrow more. He was back five minutes later, shaking his head. "Nobody believed me." Profane loaned him a few. At midnight Profane informed Wedge he was 30 in the hole. Wedge made an appropriate comment. Profane gathered up the pile of rubbers. Wedge pounded his head against the table. "He'll never use them," he said to the table. "That's the bitch of it. Never in his lifetime."

Profane wandered up by Rachel's cabin again. He heard splashing and gurgling from the courtyard in back and walked around to investigate. There she was washing her car. In the middle of the night yet. Moreover, she was talking to it.

"You beautiful stud," he heard her say, "I love to touch you." Wha, he thought. "Do you know what I feel when we're out on the road? Alone, just us?" She was running the sponge caressingly over its front bumper. "Your funny responses, darling, that I know so well. The way your brakes pull a little to the left, the way you start to shudder around 5000 rpm when you're excited. And you burn oil when you're mad at me, don't you? I know." There was none of your madness in her voice; it might have been a schoolgirl's game, though still, he admitted, quaint. "We'll always be together," running a chamois over the hood, "and you needn't worry about that black Buick we passed on the road today. Ugh: fat, greasy Mafia car. I expected to see a body come flying out the back door, didn't you? Besides, you're so angular and proper-English and tweedy—and oh, so Ivy that I couldn't ever leave you, dear." It occurred to Profane that he might vomit. Public displays of sentiment often affected

19

him this way. She had climbed in the car and now lay back in the driver's seat, her throat open to the summer constellations. He was about to approach her when he saw her left hand snake out all pale to fondle the gearshift. He watched and noticed how she was touching it. Having just been with Wedge he got the connection. He didn't want to see any more. He ambled away over a hill and into the woods and when he got back to the Trocadero he couldn't have said exactly where he'd been walking. All the cabins were dark. The front office was still open. The clerk had stepped out. Profane rooted around in desk drawers till he found a box of thumbtacks. He returned to the cabins and till three in the morning he moved along the starlit aisles between them, tacking up one of Wedge's contraceptives on each door. No one interrupted him. He felt like the Angel of Death, marking the doors of tomorrow's victims in blood. The purpose of a mezuzah was to fake the Angel out so he'd pass by. On these hundred or so cabins Profane didn't see mezuzah one. So much the worse.

After the summer, then, there'd been letters, his surly and full of wrong words, hers by turns witty, desperate, passionate. A year later she'd graduated from Bennington and come to New York to work as a receptionist in an employment agency, and so he'd seen her in New York, once or twice, when he passed through; and though they only thought about one another at random, though her yo-yo hand was usually busy at other things, now and again would come the invisible, umbilical tug, like tonight mnemonic, arousing, and he would wonder how much his own man he was. One thing he had to give her credit for, she'd never called it a Relationship.

"What is it then, hey," he'd asked once.

"A secret," with her small child's smile, which like Rodgers and Hammerstein in 3/4 time rendered Profane fluttery and gelatinous.

She visited him occasionally, as now, at night, like a succubus, coming in with the snow. There was no way he knew to keep either out.

I V

As it turned out, the New Year's party was to end all yo-yoing, at least for a time. The reunion descended on Sus-

20

anna Squaducci, conned the night watchman with a bottle of wine, and allowed a party from a destroyer in drydock (after some preliminary brawling) to come aboard.

Paola stuck close at first to Profane, who had eyes for a voluptuous lady in some sort of fur coat who claimed to be an admiral's wife. There was a portable radio, noisemakers, wine, wine. Dewey Gland decided to climb a mast. The mast had just been painted but Dewey climbed on, turning more zebralike the higher he went, guitar dangling below him. When he got to the cross-trees, Dewey sat down, plonked on the guitar and began to sing in hillbilly dialect:

> Depuis que je suis né
> J'ai vu mourir des pères,
> J'ai vu partir des frères,
> Et des enfants pleurer . . .

The para again. Who haunted this week. Since I was born (said he) I've seen fathers die, brothers go away, little kids cry. . . .

"What was that airborne boy's problem," Profane asked her the first time she translated it for him. "Who hasn't seen that. It happens for other reasons besides war. Why blame war. I was born in a Hooverville, before the war."

"That's it," Paola said. "Je suis né. Being born. That's all you have to do."

Dewey's voice sounded like part of the inanimate wind, so high overhead. What had happened to Guy Lombardo and "Auld Lang Syne"?

At one minute into 1956 Dewey was down on deck and Profane was up straddling a spar, looking down at Pig and the admiral's wife, copulating directly below. A sea gull swooped in out of the snow's sky, circled, lit on the spar a foot from Profane's hand. "Yo, sea gull," said Profane. Sea gull didn't answer.

"Oh, man," Profane said to the night. "I like to see young people get together." He scanned the main deck. Paola had disappeared. All at once things erupted. There was a siren, two, out in the street. Cars came roaring on to the pier, gray Chevys with U. S. Navy written on the sides. Spotlights came on, little men in white hats and black-and-yellow SP armbands milled around on the pier. Three alert revelers ran along the port side, throwing gangplanks into the water.

A sound truck joined the vehicles on the dock, whose number was growing almost to a full-sized motor pool.

"All right you men," 50 watts of disembodied voice began to bellow: "all right you men." That was about all it had to say. The admiral's wife started shrieking about how it was her husband, caught up with her at last. Two or three spotlights pinned them where they lay (in burning sin), Pig trying to get the thirteen buttons on his blues into the right buttonholes, which is nearly impossible when you're in a hurry. Cheers and laughter from the pier. Some of the SP's were coming across rat-fashion on the mooring lines. Ex-Scaffold sailors, roused from sleep below decks, came stumbling up the ladders while Dewey yelled, "Now stand by to repel boarders," and waved his guitar like a cutlass.

Profane watched it all and half-worried about Paola. He looked for her but the spotlights kept moving around, screwing up the illumination on the main deck. It started to snow again. "Suppose," said Profane to the sea gull, who was blinking at him, "suppose I was God." He inched on to the platform and lay on his stomach, with nose, eyes and cowboy hat sticking over the edge, like a horizontal Kilroy.

"If I was God . . ." He pointed at an SP; "Zap, SP, your ass has had it." The SP kept on at what he'd been doing: battering a 250-pound fire controlman named Patsy Pagano in the stomach with a night stick.

The motor pool on the pier was augmented by a cattle car, which is Navy for paddy wagon or Black Maria.

"Zap," said Profane, "cattle car, keep going and drive off the end of the pier," which it almost did but braked in time. "Patsy Pagano, grow wings and fly out of here." But a final clobber sent Patsy down for good. The SP left him where he was. It would take six men to move him. "What's the matter," Profane wondered. The sea bird, bored with all this, took off in the direction of N.O.B. Maybe, Profane thought, God is supposed to be more positive, instead of throwing thunderbolts all the time. Carefully he pointed a finger. "Dewey Gland. Sing them that Algerian pacifist song." Dewey, now astride a lifeline on the bridge, gave a bass string intro and began to sing Blue Suede Shoes, after Elvis Presley. Profane flopped over on his back, blinking up into the snow.

"Well, almost," he said, to the gone bird, to the snow. He put the hat over his face, closed his eyes. And soon was asleep.

Noise below diminished. Bodies were carried off, stacked in the cattle car. The sound truck, after several bursts of feedback noise, was switched off and driven away. Spotlights went out, sirens dopplered away in the direction of shore patrol headquarters.

Profane woke up early in the morning, covered with a thin layer of snow and feeling the onset of a bad cold. He blundered down the ladder's ice-covered rungs, slipping about every other step. The ship was deserted. He headed below decks to get warm.

Again, he was in the guts of something inanimate. Noise a few decks below: night watchman, most likely. "You can't ever be alone," Profane mumbled, tiptoeing along a passageway. He spotted a mousetrap on deck, picked it up carefully and heaved it down the passageway. It hit a bulkhead and went off with a loud SNAP. Sound of the footsteps quit abruptly. Then started again, more cautious, moved under Profane and up a ladder, toward where the mousetrap lay.

"Ha-ha," said Profane. He sneaked around a corner, found another mousetrap and dropped it down a companionway. SNAP. Footsteps went pattering back down the ladder.

Four mousetraps later, Profane found himself in the galley, where the watchman had set up a primitive coffee mess. Figuring the watchman would be confused for a few minutes, Profane set a pot of water to boil on the hotplate.

"Hey," yelled the watchman, two decks above.

"Oh, oh," said Profane. He sneaky-Peted out of the galley and went looking for more mousetraps. He found one up on the next deck, stepped outside, lobbed it up in an invisible arc. If nothing else he was saving mice. There was a muffled snap and a scream from above.

"My coffee," Profane muttered, taking the steps down two at a time. He threw a handful of grounds into the boiling water and slipped out the other side, nearly running into the night watchman who was stalking along with a mousetrap hanging off his left sleeve. It was close enough so Profane could see the patient, martyred look on this watchman's face. Watchman entered the galley and Profane was off. He made it up three decks before he heard the bellowing from the galley.

"What now?" He wandered into a passageway lined with empty staterooms. Found a piece of chalk left by a welder, wrote SCREW THE SUSANNA SQUADUCCI and DOWN

WITH ALL YOU RICH BASTARDS on the bulkhead, signed it THE PHANTOM and felt better. Who'd be sailing off to Italy in this thing? Chairmen of the board, movie stars, deported racketeers, maybe. "Tonight," Profane purred, "tonight, Susanna, you belong to me." His to mark up, to set mousetraps off in. More than any paid passenger would ever do for her. He moseyed along the passageway, collecting mousetraps.

Outside the galley again he started throwing them in all directions. "Ha, ha," said the night watchman. "Go ahead, make noise. I'm drinking your coffee."

So he was. Profane absently hefted his one remaining mousetrap. It went off, catching three fingers between the first and second knuckles.

What do I do, he wondered, scream? No. The night watchman was laughing hard enough as it was. Setting his teeth Profane unpried the trap from his hand, reset it, tossed it through a porthole to the galley and fled. He reached the pier and got a snowball in the back of the head, which knocked off the cowboy hat. He stooped to get the hat and thought about returning the shot. No. He kept running.

Paola was at the ferry, waiting. She took his arm as they went on board. All he said was: "We ever going to get off this ferry?"

"You have snow on you." She reached up to brush it off and he almost kissed her. Cold was turning the mousetrap injury numb. Wind had started up, coming in from Norfolk. This crossing they stayed inside.

Rachel caught up with him in the bus station in Norfolk. He sat slouched next to Paola on a wooden bench worn pallid and greasy with a generation of random duffs, two one-way tickets for New York, New York tucked inside the cowboy hat. He had his eyes closed, he was trying to sleep. He had just begun to drift off when the paging system called his name.

He knew immediately, even before he was fully awake, who it must be. Just a hunch. He had been thinking about her.

"Dear Benny," Rachel said, "I've called every bus station in the country." He could hear a party on in the background. New Year's night. Where he was there was only an old clock to tell the time. And a dozen homeless, slouched on the wooden bench, trying to sleep. Waiting for a long-haul

24

bus run neither by Greyhound nor Trailways. He watched them and let her talk. She was saying, "Come home." The only one he would allow to tell him this except for an internal voice he would rather disown as prodigal than listen to.

"You know—" he tried to say.

"I'll send you bus fare."

She would.

A hollow, twanging sound dragged across the floor toward him. Dewey Gland, morose and all bones, trailed his guitar behind him. Profane interrupted her gently. "Here is my friend Dewey Gland," he said, almost whispering. "He would like to sing you a little song."

Dewey sang her the old Depression song, Wanderin'. Eels in the ocean, eels in the sea, a redheaded woman made a fool of me . . .

Rachel's hair was red, veined with premature gray, so long she could take it in back with one hand, lift it above her head and let it fall forward over her long eyes. Which for a girl 4'10" in stocking feet is a ridiculous gesture; or should be.

He felt that invisible, umbilical string tug at his midsection. He thought of long fingers, through which, maybe, he might catch sight of the blue sky, once in a while.

And it looks like I'm never going to cease.

"She wants you," Dewey said. The girl at the Information desk was frowning. Big-boned, motley complexion: girl from out of town somewhere, whose eyes dreamed of grinning Buick grilles, Friday night shuffleboard at some roadhouse.

"I want you," Rachel said. He moved his chin across the mouthpiece, making grating sounds with a three-day growth. He thought that all the way up north, along a 500-mile length of underground phone cable, there must be earthworms, blind trollfolk, listening in. Trolls know a lot of magic: could they change words, do vocal imitations? "Will you just drift, then," she said. Behind her he heard somebody barfing and those who watched laughing, hysterically. Jazz on the record player.

He wanted to say, God, the things we want. He said: "How is the party."

"It's over at Raoul's," she said. Raoul, Slab, and Melvin being part of a crowd of disaffected which someone had labeled The Whole Sick Crew. They lived half their time in a bar on the lower West Side called the Rusty Spoon. He thought of the Sailor's Grave and could not see much difference.

"Benny." She had never cried, never that he could remember. It worried him. But she might be faking. "Ciao," she said. That phony, Greenwich Village way to avoid saying good-bye. He hung up.

"There's a nice fight on," Dewey Gland said, sullen and redeyed. "Old Ploy is so juiced he went and bit a Marine on the ass."

If you look from the side at a planet swinging around in its orbit, split the sun with a mirror and imagine a string, it all looks like a yo-yo. The point furthest from the sun is called aphelion. The point furthest from the yo-yo hand is called, by analogy, apocheir.

Profane and Paola left for New York that night. Dewey Gland went back to the ship and Profane never saw him again. Pig had taken off on the Harley, destination unknown. On the Greyhound were one young couple who would, come sleep for the other passengers, make it in a rear seat; one pencil-sharpener salesman who had seen every territory in the country and could give you interesting information on any city, no matter which one you happened to be heading for; and four infants, each with an incompetent mother, scattered at strategic locations throughout the bus, who babbled, cooed, vomited, practiced self-asphyxia, drooled. At least one managed to be screaming all through the twelve-hour trip.

About the time they hit Maryland, Profane decided to get it over with. "Not that I'm trying to get rid of you," handing her a ticket envelope with Rachel's address on it in pencil, "but I don't know how long I'll be in the city." He didn't.

She nodded. "Are you in love, then."

"She's a good woman. She'll put you on to a job, find you a place to stay. Don't ask me if we're in love. The word doesn't mean anything. Here's her address. You can take the West Side IRT right up there."

"What are you afraid of."

"Go to sleep." She did, on Profane's shoulder.

At the 34th Street station, in New York, he gave her a brief salute. "I may be around. But I hope not. It's complicated."

"Shall I tell her . . ."

26

"She'll know. That's the trouble. There's nothing you—I—can tell her she doesn't know."

"Call me, Ben. Please. Maybe."

"Right," he told her, "maybe."

v

So in January 1956 Benny Profane showed up again in New York. He came into town at the tag-end of a spell of false spring, found a mattress at a downtown flophouse called Our Home, and a newspaper at an uptown kiosk; roamed around the streets late that night studying the classified by streetlight. As usual nobody wanted him in particular.

If anybody had been around to remember him they would have noticed right off that Profane hadn't changed. Still a great amoebalike boy, soft and fat, hair cropped close and growing in patches, eyes small like a pig's and set too far apart. Road work had done nothing to improve the outward Profane, or the inward one either. Though the street had claimed a big fraction of Profane's age, it and he remained strangers in every way. Streets (roads, circles, squares, places, prospects) had taught him nothing: he couldn't work a transit, crane, payloader, couldn't lay bricks, stretch a tape right, hold an elevation rod still, hadn't even learned to drive a car. He walked; walked, he thought sometimes, the aisles of a bright, gigantic supermarket, his only function to want.

One morning Profane woke up early, couldn't get back to sleep and decided on a whim to spend the day like a yo-yo, shuttling on the subway back and forth underneath 42nd Street, from Times Square to Grand Central and vice versa. He made his way to the washroom of Our Home, tripping over two empty mattresses on route. Cut himself shaving, had trouble extracting the blade and gashed a finger. He took a shower to get rid of the blood. The handles wouldn't turn. When he finally found a shower that worked, the water came out hot and cold in random patterns. He danced around, yowling and shivering, slipped on a bar of soap and nearly broke his neck. Drying off, he ripped a frayed towel in half, rendering it useless. He put on his skivvy shirt backwards, took ten minutes getting his fly zipped and another fifteen repairing a shoelace which had broken as he was tying it. All the rests of his morning songs were silent cuss words. It wasn't that he was tired or even notably un-

27

coordinated. Only something that, being a schlemihl, he'd known for years: <u>inanimate objects and he could not</u> live in peace.

Profane took a Lexington Avenue local up to Grand Central. As it happened, the subway car he got into was filled with all manner of ravishingly gorgeous knockouts: secretaries on route to work and jailbait to school. It was too much, too much. Profane hung on the handgrip, weak. He was visited on a lunar basis by these great unspecific waves of horniness, whereby all women within a certain age group and figure envelope became immediately and impossibly desirable. He emerged from these spells with eyeballs still oscillating and a wish that his neck could rotate through the full 360°.

The shuttle after morning rush hour is near empty, like a littered beach after tourists have all gone home. In the hours between nine and noon the permanent residents come creeping back up their strand, shy and tentative. Since sunup all manner of affluent have filled the limits of that world with a sense of summer and life; now sleeping bums and old ladies on relief, who have been there all along unnoticed, re-establish a kind of property right, and the coming on of a falling season.

On his eleventh or twelfth transit Profane fell asleep and dreamed. He was awakened close to noon by three Puerto Rican kids named Tolito, José and Kook, short for Cucarachito. They had this act, which was for money even though they knew that the subway on weekday mornings, no es bueno for dancing and bongos. José carried around a coffee can which upside down served to rattle off their raving merengues or baións on, and hollow side up to receive from an appreciative audience pennies, transit tokens, chewing gum, spit.

Profane blinked awake and watched them, jazzing around, doing handsprings, aping courtship. They swung from the handle-grips, shimmied up the poles; Tolito tossing Kook the seven-year-old about the car like a beanbag and behind it all, clobbering polyrhythmic to the racketing of the shuttle, José on his tin drum, forearms and hands vibrating out beyond the persistence of vision, and a tireless smile across his teeth wide as the West Side.

They passed the can as the train was pulling into Times Square. Profane closed his eyes before they got to him. They

28

sat on the seat opposite, counting the take, feet dangling. Kook was in the middle, the other two were trying to push him on the floor. Two teen-age boys from their neighborhood entered the car: black chinos, black shirts, black gang jackets with PLAYBOYS lettered in dripping red on the back. Abruptly all motion among the three on the seat stopped. They held each other, staring wide-eyed.

Kook, the baby, could hold nothing in. "Maricón!" he yelled gleefully. Profane's eyes came open. Heel-taps of the older boys moved past, aloof and staccato to the next car. Tolito put his hand on Kook's head, trying to squash him down through the floor, out of sight. Kook slipped away. The doors closed, the shuttle started off again for Grand Central. The three turned their attention to Profane.

"Hey, man," Kook said. Profane watched him, half-cautious.

"How come," José said. He put the coffee can absently on his head, where it slipped down over his ears. "How come you didn't get off at Times Square."

"He was asleep," Tolito said.

"He's a yo-yo," José said. "Wait and see." They forgot Profane for the moment, moved forward a car and did their routine. They came back as the train was starting off again from Grand Central.

"See," José said.

"Hey man," Kook said, "how come."

"You out of a job," Tolito said.

"Why don't you hunt alligators, like my brother," Kook said.

"Kook's brother shoots them with a shotgun," Tolito said.

"If you need a job, you should hunt alligators," José said.

Profane scratched his stomach. He looked at the floor.

"Is it steady," he said.

The subway pulled in to Times Square, disgorged passengers, took more on, shut up its doors and shrieked away down the tunnel. Another shuttle came in, on a different track. Bodies milled in the brown light, a loudspeaker announced shuttles. It was lunch hour. The subway station began to buzz, fill with human noise and motion. Tourists were coming back in droves. Another train arrived, opened, closed, was gone. The press on the wooden platforms grew, along with an air of discomfort, hunger, uneasy bladders, suffocation. The first shuttle returned.

29

Among the crowd that squeezed inside this time was a young girl wearing a black coat, her hair hanging long outside it. She searched four cars before she found Kook, sitting next to Profane, watching him.

"He wants to help Angel kill the alligators," Kook told her. Profane was asleep, lying diagonal on the seat.

In this dream, he was all alone, as usual. Walking on a street at night where there was nothing but his own field of vision alive. It had to be night on that street. The lights gleamed unflickering on hydrants; manhole covers which lay around in the street. There were neon signs scattered here and there, spelling out words he wouldn't remember when he woke.

Somehow it was all tied up with a story he'd heard once, about a boy born with a golden screw where his navel should have been. For twenty years he consults doctors and specialists all over the world, trying to get rid of this screw, and having no success. Finally, in Haiti, he runs into a voodoo doctor who gives him a foul-smelling potion. He drinks it, goes to sleep and has a dream. In this dream he finds himself on a street, lit by green lamps. Following the witch-man's instructions, he takes two rights and a left from his point of origin, finds a tree growing by the seventh street light, hung all over with colored balloons. On the fourth limb from the top there is a red balloon; he breaks it and inside is a screwdriver with a yellow plastic handle. With the screwdriver he removes the screw from his stomach, and as soon as this happens he wakes from the dream. It is morning. He looks down toward his navel, the screw is gone. That twenty years' curse is lifted at last. Delirious with joy, he leaps up out of bed, and his ass falls off.

To Profane, alone in the street, it would always seem maybe he was looking for something too to make the fact of his own disassembly plausible as that of any machine. It was always at this point that the fear started: here that it would turn into a nightmare. Because now, if he kept going down that street, not only his ass but also his arms, legs, sponge brain and clock of a heart must be left behind to litter the pavement, be scattered among manhole covers.

Was it home, the mercury-lit street? Was he returning like the elephant to his graveyard, to lie down and soon become ivory in whose bulk slept, latent, exquisite shapes of chess-

30

men, backscratchers, hollow open-work Chinese spheres nested one inside the other?

This was all there was to dream; all there ever was: the Street. Soon he woke, having found no screwdriver, no key. Woke to a girl's face, near his own. Kook stood in the background, feet braced apart, head hanging. From two cars away, riding above the racketing of the subway over its points, came the metallic rattle of Tolito on the coffee can.

Her face was young, soft. She had a brown mole on one cheek. She'd been talking to him before his eyes were open. She wanted him to come home with her. Her name was Josefina Mendoza, she was Kook's sister, she lived uptown. She must help him. He had no idea what was happening.

"Wha, lady," he said, "wha."

"Do you like it here," she cried.

"I do not like it, lady, no," said Profane. The train was heading toward Times Square, crowded. Two old ladies who had been shopping at Bloomingdale's stood glaring hostile at them from up the car. Fina started to cry. The other kids came charging back in, singing. "Help," Profane said. He didn't know who he was asking. He'd awakened loving every woman in the city, wanting them all: here was one who wanted to take him home. The shuttle pulled into Times Square, the doors flew open. In a swoop, only half aware of what he was doing, he gathered Kook in one arm and ran out the door: Fina, with tropical birds peeking from her green dress whenever the black coat flew open, followed, hands joined with Tolito and José in a line. They ran through the station, beneath a chain of green lights, Profane loping unathletic into trash cans and Coke machines. Kook broke away and tore broken-field through the noon crowd. "Luis Aparicio," he screamed, sliding for some private home plate: "Luis Aparicio," wreaking havoc through a troop of Girl Scouts. Down the stairs, over to the uptown local, a train was waiting, Fina and the kids got in; as Profane started through the doors closed on him, squeezing him in the middle. Fina's eyes went wide like her brother's. With a frightened little cry she took Profane's hand and tugged, and a miracle happened. The doors opened again. She gathered him inside, into her quiet field of force. He knew all at once: here, for the time being, Profane the schlemihl can move nimble and sure. All the way home Kook sang Tienes Mi Corazón, a love song he had heard once in a movie.

31

They lived uptown in the 80's, between Amsterdam Avenue and Broadway. Fina, Kook, mother, father, and another brother named Angel. Sometimes Angel's friend Geronimo would come over and sleep on the kitchen floor. The old man was on relief. The mother fell in love with Profane immediately. They gave him the bathtub.

Next day Kook found him sleeping there and turned on the cold water. "Jesus God," Profane yelled, spluttering awake.

"Man, you go find a job," Kook said. "Fina says so." Profane jumped up and went chasing Kook through the little apartment, trailing water behind him. In the front room he tripped over Angel and Geronimo, who were lying there drinking wine and talking about the girls they would watch that day in Riverside Park. Kook escaped, laughing and screaming "Luis Aparicio." Profane lay there with his nose pressed against the floor. "Have some wine," Angel said.

A few hours later, they all came reeling down the steps of the old brownstone, horribly drunk. Angel and Geronimo were arguing about whether it was too cold for girls to be in the park. They walked west in the middle of the street. The sky was overcast and dismal. Profane kept bumping into cars. At the corner they invaded a hot dog stand and drank pina colada to sober up. It did no good. They made it to Riverside Drive, where Geronimo collapsed. Profane and Angel picked him up and ran across the street with him held like a battering ram, down a hill and into the park. Profane tripped over a rock and the three of them went flying. They lay on the frozen grass while a bunch of kids in fat wool coats ran back and forth over them, playing pitch and catch with a bright yellow beanbag. Geronimo started to sing.

"Man," Angel said, "there is one." She came walking a mean, nasty-face poodle. Young, with long hair that danced and shimmered against the collar of her coat. Geronimo broke off the song to say "Coño" and wobble his fingers. Then he continued, singing now to her. She didn't notice any of them, but headed uptown, serene and smiling at the naked trees. Their eyes followed her out of sight. They felt sad.

Angel sighed. "There are so many," he said. "So many millions and millions of girls. Here in New York, and up in Boston, where I was once and in thousands more cities. . . . It makes me lose heart."

"Out in Jersey too," said Profane. "I worked in Jersey."

"A lot of good stuff in Jersey," Angel said.

"Out on the road," said Profane. "They were all in cars."

"Geronimo and I work in the sewers," Angel said. "Under the street. You don't see anything down there."

"Under the street," Profane repeated after a minute: "under the Street."

Geronimo stopped singing and told Profane how it was. Did he remember the baby alligators? Last year, or maybe the year before, kids all over Nueva York bought these little alligators for pets. Macy's was selling them for fifty cents, every child, it seemed, had to have one. But soon the children grew bored with them. Some set them loose in the streets, but most flushed them down the toilets. And these had grown and reproduced, had fed off rats and sewage, so that now they moved big, blind, albino, all over the sewer system. Down there, God knew how many there were. Some had turned cannibal because in their neighborhood the rats had all been eaten, or had fled in terror.

Since the sewer scandal last year, the Department had got conscientious. They called for volunteers to go down with shotguns and get rid of the alligators. Not many had volunteered. Those who had quit soon. Angel and he, Geronimo said proudly, had been there three months longer than anybody.

Profane, all at once, was sober. "Are they still looking for volunteers," he said slowly. Angel started to sing. Profane rolled over glaring at Geronimo. "Hey?"

"Sure," Geronimo said. "You ever use a shotgun before?"

Profane said yes. He never had, and never would, not at street level. But a shotgun under the street, under the Street, might be all right. He could kill himself but maybe it would be all right. He could try.

"I will talk to Mr. Zeitsuss, the boss," said Geronimo.

The beanbag hung for a second jolly and bright in the air. "Look, look," the kids cried: "look at it fall!"

chapter two

The Whole Sick Crew

V

I

Profane, Angel and Geronimo gave up girl-watching about noon and left the park in search of wine. An hour or so later, Rachel Owlglass, Profane's Rachel, passed by the spot they'd abandoned, on her way home.

There is no way to describe the way she walked except as a kind of brave sensual trudging: as if she were nose-deep in snowdrifts, and yet on route to meet a lover. She came up the dead center of the mall, her gray coat fluttering a little in a breeze off the Jersey coast. Her high heels hit precise and neat each time on the X's of the grating in the middle of the mall. Half a year in this city and at least she had learned to do that. Had lost heels, and once in a while composure, in the process; but now could do it blindfolded. She kept on the grating just to show off. To herself.

Rachel worked as an interviewer or personnel girl at a downtown employment agency; was at the moment returning from an appointment on the East Side with one Shale Schoenmaker, M.D., a plastic surgeon. Schoenmaker was a craftsman, and came high; had two assistants, one a secretary/receptionist/nurse with an impossibly coy retroussé nose and thousands of freckles, all of which Schoenmaker had done himself. The freckles were tattooed, the girl his mistress; called, by virtue of some associative freak, Irving. The other assistant was a juvenile delinquent named Trench who amused himself between patients by throwing scalpels at a wooden plaque presented to his employer by the United Jewish Appeal. The business was carried on in a fashionable maze or warren of rooms in an apartment building between First and York Avenues, at the fringes of Germantown. In keeping with the location, Brauhaus music blared over a concealed loudspeaker system continuously.

She had arrived at ten in the morning. Irving told her to wait; she waited. The doctor was busy this morning. The office was crowded, Rachel figured, because it takes four months for a nose job to heal. Four months from now would be June; this meant many pretty Jewish girls who felt they would be perfectly marriageable were it not for an ugly nose could now go husband-hunting at the various resorts all with uniform septa.

It disgusted Rachel, her theory being that it was not for cosmetic reasons these girls got operated on so much as that the hook nose is traditionally the sign of the Jew and the retroussé nose the sign of the WASP or White Anglo-Saxon Protestant in the movies and advertisements.

She sat back, watching the patients come through the outer office, not particularly anxious to see Schoenmaker. One youth with a wispy beard which did nothing to hide a weak chin kept glancing at her embarrassed from moist eyes, across a wide stretch of neutral carpeting. A girl with a gauze beak, eyes closed, lay slumped on a sofa, flanked by her parents, who conferred in whispers about the price.

Directly across the room from Rachel was a mirror, hung high on the wall, and under the mirror a shelf which held a turn-of-the-century clock. The double face was suspended by four golden flying buttresses above a maze of works, enclosed in clear Swedish lead glass. The pendulum didn't swing back and forth but was in the form of a disc, parallel to the floor and driven by a shaft which paralleled the hands at six o'clock. The disc turned a quarter-revolution one way, then a quarter-revolution the other, each reversed torsion on the shaft advancing the escapement a notch. Mounted on the disc were two imps or demons, wrought in gold, posed in fantastic attitudes. Their movements were reflected in the mirror along with the window at Rachel's back, which extended from floor to ceiling and revealed the branches and green needles of a pine tree. The branches whipped back and forth in the February wind, ceaseless and shimmering, and in front of them the two demons performed their metronomic dance, beneath a vertical array of golden gears and ratchet wheels, levers and springs which gleamed warm and gay as any ballroom chandelier.

Rachel was looking into the mirror at an angle of 45°, and so had a view of the face turned toward the room and the face on the other side, reflected in the mirror; here were time and reverse-time, co-existing, cancelling one another exactly out. Were there many such reference points, scattered through the world, perhaps only at nodes like this room which housed a transient population of the imperfect, the dissatisfied; did real time plus virtual or mirror-time equal zero and thus serve some half-understood moral purpose? Or was it only the mirror world that counted; only a promise of a kind that the inward bow of a nose-bridge or a promontory of extra cartilage at the chin meant a reversal of ill fortune such that the world of the altered would thenceforth run on mirror-time; work and love by mirror-light and be only, till death stopped the heart's ticking (metronome's music) quietly as light ceases to vibrate, an imp's dance under the century's own chandeliers. . . .

"Miss Owlglass." Irving, smiling from the entrance to Schoenmaker's sacristy. Rachel arose, taking her pocketbook, passed the mirror and caught a sidelong glance at her own double in the mirror's district, passed through the door to confront the doctor, lazy and hostile behind his kidney-shaped desk. He had the bill, and a carbon, lying on the desk. "Miss Harvitz's account," Schoenmaker said. Rachel opened her pocketbook, took out a roll of twenties, dropped them on top of the papers.

"Count them," she said. "This is the balance."

"Later," the doctor said. "Sit down, Miss Owlglass."

"Esther is flat broke," Rachel said, "and she is going through hell. What you are running here—"

"—is a vicious racket," he said dryly. "Cigarette."

"I have my own." She sat on the edge of the chair, pushed away a strand or two of hair hanging over her forehead, searched for a cigarette.

"Trafficking in human vanity," Schoenmaker continued, "propagating the fallacy that beauty is not in the soul, that it can be bought. Yes—" his arm shot out with a heavy silver lighter, a thin flame, his voice barked—"it can be bought,

Miss Owlglass, I am selling it. I don't even look on myself as a necessary evil."

"You are unnecessary," she said, through a halo of smoke. Her eyes glittered like the slopes of adjacent sawteeth.

"You encourage them to sell out," she said.

He watched the sensual arch of her own nose. "You're Orthodox? No. Conservative? Young people never are. My parents were Orthodox. They believe, I believe, that whatever your father is, as long as your mother is Jewish, you are Jewish too because we all come from our mother's womb. A long unbroken chain of Jewish mothers going all the way back to Eve."

She looked "hypocrite" at him.

"No," he said, "Eve was the first Jewish mother, the one who set the pattern. The words she said to Adam have been repeated ever since by her daughters: 'Adam,' she said, 'come inside, have a piece fruit.'"

"Ha, ha," said Rachel.

"What about this chain, what of inherited characteristics. We've come along, become with years more sophisticated, we no longer believe now the earth is flat. Though there's a man in England, president of a Flat Earth society, who says it is and is ringed by ice barriers, a frozen world which is where all missing persons go and never return from. So with Lamarck, who said that if you cut the tail off a mother mouse her children will be tailless also. But this is not true, the weight of scientific evidence is against him, just as every photograph from a rocket over White Sands or Cape Canaveral is against the Flat Earth Society. Nothing I do to a Jewish girl's nose is going to change the noses of her children when she becomes, as she must, a Jewish mother. So how am I being vicious. Am I altering that grand unbroken chain, no. I am not going against nature, I am not selling out any Jews. Individuals do what they want, but the chain goes on and small forces like me will never prevail against it. All that can is something which will change the germ plasm, nuclear radiation, maybe. They will sell out the Jews, maybe give future generations two noses or no nose, who knows, ha, ha. They will sell out the human race."

Behind the far door came the thud of Trench's knife practice. Rachel sat with her legs crossed tightly.

"Inside," she said, "what does it do to them there. You

alter them there, too. What kind of Jewish mother do they make, they are the kind who make a girl get a nose job even if she doesn't want one. How many generations have you worked on so far, how many have you played the dear old family doctor for."

"You are a nasty girl," said Schoenmaker, "and so pretty, too. Why yell at me, all I am is one plastic surgeon. Not a psychoanalyst. Maybe someday there will be special plastic surgeons who can do brain jobs too, make some young kid an Einstein, some girl an Eleanor Roosevelt. Or even make people act less nasty. Till then, how do I know what goes on inside. Inside has nothing to do with the chain."

"You set up another chain." She was trying not to yell. "Changing them inside sets up another chain which has nothing to do with germ plasm. You can transmit characteristics outside, too. You can pass along an attitude . . ."

"Inside, outside," he said, "you're being inconsistent, you lose me."

"I'd like to," she said, rising. "I have bad dreams about people like you."

"Have your analyst tell you what they mean," he said.

"I hope you keep dreaming." She was at the door, half-turned to him.

"My bank balance is big enough so I don't get disillusioned," he said.

Being the kind of girl who can't resist an exit line: "I heard about a disillusioned plastic surgeon," she said, "who hung himself." She was gone, stomping out past the mirrored clock, out into the same wind that moved the pine tree, leaving behind the soft chins, warped noses and facial scars of what she feared was a sort of drawing-together or communion.

Now having left the grating behind she walked over the dead grass of Riverside Park under leafless trees and even more substantial skeletons of apartment houses on the Drive, wondering about Esther Harvitz, her long-time roommate, whom she had helped out of more financial crises than either could remember. An old rusty beer can lay in her path; she kicked it viciously. What is it, she thought, is this the way Nueva York is set up, then, freeloaders and victims? Schoenmaker freeloads off my roommate, she freeloads off me. Is there this long daisy chain of victimizers and victims, screwers and screwees? And if so, who is it I am screwing.

She thought first of Slab, Slab of the Raoul-Slab-Melvin triumvirate, between whom and a lack of charity toward all men she'd alternated ever since coming to this city.

"What do you let her take for," he had said, "always take." It was in his studio, she remembered, back during one of those Slab-and-Rachel idylls that usually preceded a Slab-and-Esther Affair. Con Edison had just shut off the electricity so all they had to look at each other by was one gas burner on the stove, which bloomed in a blue and yellow minaret, making the faces masks, their eyes expressionless sheets of light.

"Baby," she said, "Slab, it is only that the kid is broke, and if I can afford it why not."

"No," Slab said, a tic dancing high on his cheekbone—or it might only have been the gaslight—"no. Don't you think I see what this is, she needs you for all the money she keeps soaking you for, and you need her in order to feel like a mother. Every dime she gets out of your pocketbook adds one more strand to this cable that ties you two together like an umbilical cord, making it that much harder to cut, making her survival that much more in danger if the cord ever is cut. How much has she ever paid you back."

"She will," Rachel said.

"Sure. Now, $800 more. To change this." He waved his arm at a small portrait, leaning against the wall by the garbage can. He reached over, picked it up, tilted it toward the blue flame so they both could see. "Girl at a party." The picture, perhaps, was meant to be looked at only under hydrocarbon light. It was Esther, leaning against a wall, looking straight out of the picture, at someone approaching her. And there, that look in the eyes—half victim, half in control.

"Look at it, the nose," he said. "Why does she want to get that changed. With the nose she is a human being."

"Is it only an artist's concern," Rachel said. "You object on pictorial, or social grounds. But what else."

"Rachel," he yelled, "she takes home 50 a week, 25 comes out for analysis, 12 for rent, leaving 13. What for, for high heels she breaks on subway gratings, for lipstick, earrings, clothes. Food, occasionally. So now, 800 for a nose job. What will it be next. Mercedes Benz 300 SL? Picasso original, abortion, wha."

"She has been right on time," Rachel said, frosty, "in case you are worrying."

"Baby," suddenly all wistful and boyish, "you are a good woman, member of a vanishing race. It is right you should help the less fortunate. But you reach a point."

The argument had gone back and forth with neither of them actually getting mad and at three in the morning the inevitable terminal point—bed—to caress away the headaches both had developed. Nothing settled, nothing ever settled. That had been back in September. The gauze beak was gone, the nose now a proud sickle, pointing, you felt, at the big Westchester in the sky where all God's elect, soon or late, ended up.

She turned out of the park and walked away from the Hudson on 112th Street. Screwer and screwee. On this foundation, perhaps, the island stood, from the bottom of the lowest sewer bed right up through the streets to the tip of the TV antenna on top of the Empire State Building.

She entered her lobby, smiled at the ancient doorman; into the elevator, up seven flights to 7G, home, ho, ho. First thing she saw through the open door was a sign on the kitchen wall, with the word PARTY, illuminated by pencil caricatures of the Whole Sick Crew. She tossed the pocketbook on the kitchen table, closed the door. Paola's handiwork, Paola Maijstral the third roommate. Who had also left a note on the table. "Winsome, Charisma, Fu, and I. V-Note, McClintic Sphere. Paola Maijstral." Nothing but proper nouns. The girl lived proper nouns. Persons, places. No things. Had anyone told her about things? It seemed Rachel had had to do with nothing else. The main one now being Esther's nose.

In the shower Rachel sang a torch song, in a red-hot-mama voice which the tile chamber magnified. She knew it amused people because it came from such a little girl:

> Say a man is no good
> For anything but jazzing around.
> He'll go live in a cathouse,
> He'll jazz it all over town.
> And all kinds of meanness
> To put a good woman down.
> Now I am a good woman
> Because I'm telling you I am
> And I sure been put down
> But honey, I don't give a damn.
> You going to have a hard time

40

Finding you a kind hearted man.
Because a kind hearted man
Is the kind who will . . .

Presently the light in Paola's room began to leak out the
window, up the air shaft and into the sky, accompanied by
clinking bottles, running water, flushing toilet in the bathroom. And then the almost imperceptible sounds of Rachel
fixing her long hair.

When she left, turning off all the lights, the hands on
an illuminated clock near Paola Maijstral's bed stood near
six o'clock. No ticking: the clock was electric. Its minute
hand could not be seen to move. But soon the hand passed
twelve and began its course down the other side of the face;
as if it had passed through the surface of a mirror, and
had now to repeat in mirror-time what it had done on the
side of real-time.

II

The party, as if it were inanimate after all, unwound like a
clock's mainspring toward the edges of the chocolate room,
seeking some easing of its own tension, some equilibrium.
Near its center Rachel Owlglass was curled on the pine floor,
legs shining pale through black stockings.

You felt she'd done a thousand secret things to her eyes.
They needed no haze of cigarette smoke to look at you out
of sexy and fathomless, but carried their own along with
them. New York must have been for her a city of smoke, its
streets the courtyards of limbo, its bodies like wraiths. Smoke
seemed to be in her voice, in her movements; making her
all the more substantial, more there, as if words, glances,
small lewdnesses could only become baffled and brought to
rest like smoke in her long hair; remain there useless till
she released them, accidentally and unknowingly, with a
toss of her head.

Young Stencil the world adventurer, seated on the sink,
waggled his shoulderblades like wings. Her back was to him;
through the entrance to the kitchen he could see the shadow
of her spine's indentation snaking down a deeper black
along the black of her sweater, see the tiny movements of
her head and hair as she listened.

She didn't like him, Stencil had decided.

41

Queen? or
bis

"It's the way he looks at Paola," she'd told Esther. Esther of course had told Stencil.

But it wasn't sexual, it lay deeper. Paola was Maltese.

?

Born in 1901, the year Victoria died, Stencil was in time to be the century's child. Raised motherless. The father, Sidney Stencil, had served the Foreign Office of his country taciturn and competent. No facts on the mother's disappearance. Died in childbirth, ran off with someone, committed suicide: some way of vanishing painful enough to keep Sidney from ever referring to it in all the correspondence to his son which is available. The father died under unknown circumstances in 1919 while investigating the June Disturbances in Malta.

On an evening in 1946, separated by stone balusters from the Mediterranean, the son had sat with one Margravine di Chiave Lowenstein on the terrace of her villa on the western coast of Mallorca; the sun was setting into thick clouds, turning all the visible sea to a sheet of pearl-gray. Perhaps they may have felt like the last two gods—the last inhabitants—of a watery earth; or perhaps—but it would be unfair to infer. Whatever the reason, the scene played as follows:

MARG: Then you must leave?

STEN: Stencil must be in Lucerne before the week is out.

MARG: I dislike premilitary activity.

STEN: It isn't espionage.

MARG: What then?

(Stencil laughs, watching the twilight.)

MARG: You are so close.

STEN: To whom? Margravine, not even to himself. This place, this island: all his life he's done nothing but hop from island to island. Is that a reason? Does there have to be a reason? Shall he tell you: he works for no Whitehall, none conceivable unless, ha, ha, the network of white halls in his own brain: these featureless corridors he keeps swept and correct for occasional visiting agents. Envoys from the zones of human crucified, the fabled districts of human love. But in whose employ? Not his own: it would be lunacy, the lunacy of any self-appointed prophet. . . .

(There is a long pause, as the light reaching them through the clouds weakens or thins out to wash over them enervated and ugly.)

STEN: Stencil reached his majority three years after old Stencil died. Part of the estate that came to him then was a number of manuscript books, bound in half-calf and warped by the humid air of many European cities. His journals, his unofficial log of an agent's career. Under "Florence, April, 1899" is a sentence, young Stencil has memorized it: "There is more behind and inside V. than any of us had suspected. Not who, but what: what is she. God grant that I may never be called upon to write the answer, either here or in any official report."

MARG: A woman.

STEN: Another woman.

MARG: It is she you are pursuing? Seeking?

STEN: You'll ask next if he believes her to be his mother. The question is ridiculous.

Since 1945, Herbert Stencil had been on a conscious campaign to do without sleep. Before 1945 he had been slothful, accepting sleep as one of life's major blessings. He'd spent the time between wars footloose, the source of his income then, as now, uncertain. Sidney hadn't left much in the way of pounds and shillings, but had generated good will in nearly every city in the western world among those of his own generation. This being a generation which still believed in The Family, it meant a good lookout for young Herbert. He didn't freeload all the time: he'd worked as croupier in southern France, plantation foreman in East Africa, bordello manager in Greece; and in a number of civil service positions back home. Stud poker could be depended on to fill in the low places—though an occasional mountain or two had also been leveled.

In that interregnum between kingdoms-of-death Herbert just got by, studying his father's journals only by way of learning how to please the blood-conscious "contacts" of his legacy. The passage on V. was never noticed.

In 1939 he was in London, working for the Foreign Office. September came and went: it was as if a stranger, located above the frontiers of consciousness, were shaking him. He didn't particularly care to wake; but realized that if he didn't he would soon be sleeping alone. Being the sociable sort, Herbert volunteered his services. He was sent to North Africa, in some fuzzily defined spy/interpreter/liaison capacity and seesawed with the rest from Tobruk to El Agheila, back through Tobruk to El Alamein, back again to Tunisia. At the end of it he had seen more dead than he cared to again. Peace having been won he flirted with the idea of resuming that prewar sleepwalk. Sitting at a café in Oran frequented largely by American ex-GI's who'd decided not to return to the States just yet, he was leafing through the Florence journal idly, when the sentences on V. suddenly acquired a light of their own.

"V. for victory," the Margravine had suggested playfully.

"No." Stencil shook his head. "It may be that Stencil has been lonely and needs something for company."

Whatever the reason, he began to discover that sleep was taking up time which could be spent active. His random movements before the war had given way to a great single movement from inertness to—if not vitality, then at least activity. Work, the chase—for it was V. he hunted—far from being a means to glorify God and one's own godliness (as the Puritans believe) was for Stencil grim, joyless; a conscious acceptance of the unpleasant for no other reason than that V. was there to track down.

Finding her: what then? Only that what love there was to Stencil had become directed entirely inward, toward this acquired sense of animateness. Having found this he could hardly release it, it was too dear. To sustain it he had to hunt V.; but if he should find her, where else would there be to go but back into half-consciousness? He tried not to think, therefore, about any end to the search. Approach and avoid.

Here in New York the impasse had become acute. He'd come to the party at the invitation of Esther Harvitz, whose plastic surgeon Schoenmaker owned a vital piece of the V.-jigsaw, but protested ignorance.

Stencil would wait. He'd taken over a low-rent apartment in the 30's (East Side), temporarily vacated by an Egyptologist named Bongo-Shaftsbury, son of an Egyptologist Sidney had known. They had been opponents once, before the first war, as had been Sidney and many of the present "contacts"; which was curious, certainly, but lucky for Herbert because it doubled his chances of subsistence. He had been using the apartment for a pied-à-terre this last month; snatching sleep between interminable visits among his other "contacts"; a population coming more and more to comprise sons and friends of the originals. At each step the sense of "blood" weakened. Stencil could see a day when he would only be tolerated. It would then be he and V. all alone, in a world that somehow had lost sight of them both.

Until such time there were Schoenmaker to wait for; and Chiclitz the munitions king and Eigenvalue the physician (epithets characteristically stemming from Sidney's day though Sidney had known neither of the men personally) to fill up the time. It was dithering, it was a stagnant period and Stencil knew it. A month was too long to stay in any city unless there were something tangible to investigate. He'd taken to roving the city, aimlessly, waiting for a coincidence. None came. He'd snatched at Esther's invitation, hoping to come across some clue, trace, hint. But the Whole Sick Crew had nothing to offer.

The owner of this apartment seemed to express a prevailing humor common to them all. As if he were Stencil's prewar self he presented to Stencil a horrifying spectacle.

Fergus Mixolydian the Irish Armenian Jew and universal man laid claim to being the laziest living being in Nueva York. His creative ventures, all incomplete, ranged from a western in blank verse to a wall he'd had removed from a stall in the Penn Station men's room and entered in an art exhibition as what the old Dadaists called a "ready-made." Critical comment was not kind. Fergus got so lazy that his only activity (short of those necessary to sustain life) was once a week to fiddle around at the kitchen sink with dry cells, retorts, alembics, salt solutions. What he was doing, he was generating hydrogen; this went to fill a sturdy green balloon with a great Z printed on it. He would tie the balloon by a string to the post of the bed whenever he planned to sleep, this being the only way for visitors to tell which side of consciousness Fergus was on.

His other amusement was watching the TV. He'd devised an ingenious sleep-switch, receiving its signal from two electrodes placed on the inner skin of his forearm. When Fergus dropped below a certain level of awareness, the skin resistance increased over a preset value to operate the switch. Fergus thus became an extension of the TV set.

The rest of the Crew partook of the same lethargy. Raoul wrote for television, keeping carefully in mind, and complaining bitterly about, all the sponsor-fetishes of that industry. Slab painted in sporadic bursts, referring to himself as a Catatonic Expressionist and his work as "the ultimate in non-communication." Melvin played the guitar and sang liberal folk songs. The pattern would have been familiar—bohemian, creative, arty—except that it was even further re-

45

moved from reality, Romanticism in its furthest decadence; being only an exhausted impersonation of poverty, rebellion and artistic "soul." For it was the unhappy fact that most of them worked for a living and obtained the substance of their conversation from the pages of Time magazine and like publications.

Perhaps the only reason they survived, Stencil reasoned, was that they were not alone. God knew how many more there were with a hothouse sense of time, no knowledge of life, and at the mercy of Fortune.

The party itself, tonight, was divided in three parts. Fergus, and his date, and another couple had long retreated into the bedroom with a gallon of wine; locked the door, and let the Crew do what they could in the way of chaos to the rest of the place. The sink on which Stencil now sat would become Melvin's perch: he would play his guitar and there would be horahs and African fertility dances in the kitchen before midnight. The lights in the living room would go out one by one, Schoenberg's quartets (complete) would go on the record player/changer, and repeat, and repeat; while cigarette coals dotted the room like watchfires and the promiscuous Debby Sensay (e.g.) would be on the floor, caressed by Raoul, say, or Slab, while she ran her hand up the leg of another, sitting on the couch with her roommate —and on, in a kind of love feast or daisy chain; wine would spill, furniture would be broken; Fergus would awake briefly next morning, view the destruction and residual guests sprawled about the apartment; cuss them all out and go back to sleep.

Stencil shrugged irritably, rose from the sink and found his coat. On the way out he touched a knot of six: Raoul, Slab, Melvin and three girls.

"Man," said Raoul.

"Scene," said Slab, waving his arm to indicate the unwinding party.

"Later," Stencil said and moved on out the door.

The girls stood silent. They were camp followers of a sort and expendable. Or at least could be replaced.

"Oh yes," said Melvin.

"Uptown," Slab said, "is taking over the world."

"Ha, ha," said one of the girls.

"Shut up," said Slab. He tugged at his hat. He always wore a hat, inside or outside, in bed or dead drunk. And

George Raft suits, with immense pointed lapels. Pointed, starched, non-button-down collars. Padded, pointed shoulders: he was all points. But his face, the girl noticed, was not: rather soft, like a dissolute angel's: curly hair, red and purple rings slung looped in twos and threes beneath the eyes. Tonight she would kiss beneath his eyes, one by one, these sad circles.

"Excuse me," she murmured, drifting away toward the fire escape. At the window she gazed out toward the river, seeing nothing but fog. A hand touched her spine, exactly in that spot every man she ever knew had been able to find, sooner or later. She straightened up, squeezing her shoulder-blades together, moving her breasts taut and suddenly visible toward the window. She could see his reflection watching their reflection. She turned. He was blushing. Crew cut, suit, Harris tweed. "Say, you are new," she smiled. "I am Esther."

He blushed and was cute. "Brad," he said. "I'm sorry I made you jump."

She knew instinctively: he will be fine as the fraternity boy just out of an Ivy League school who knows he will never stop being a fraternity boy as long as he lives. But who still feels he is missing something, and so hangs at the edges of the Whole Sick Crew. If he is going into management, he writes. If he is an engineer or architect why he paints or sculpts. He will straddle the line, aware up to the point of knowing he is getting the worst of both worlds, but never stopping to wonder why there should ever have been a line, or even if there is a line at all. He will learn how to be a twinned man and will go on at the game, straddling until he splits up the crotch and in half from the prolonged tension, and then he will be destroyed. She assumed ballet fourth position, moved her breasts at a 45° angle to his line-of-sight, pointed her nose at his heart, looked up at him through her eyelashes.

"How long have you been in New York?"

Outside the V-Note a number of bums stood around the front windows looking inside, fogging the glass with their breath. From time to time a collegiate-looking type, usually with a date, would emerge from the swinging doors and they would ask him, one by one in a line down that short section of Bowery sidewalk, for a cigarette, subway fare, the price of a beer. All night the February wind would come barreling down the wide keyway of Third Avenue, moving right over them all: the shavings, cutting oil, sludge of New York's lathe.

Inside McClintic Sphere was swinging his ass off. His skin was hard, as if it were part of the skull: every vein and whisker on that head stood out sharp and clear under the green baby spot: you could see the twin lines running down from either side of his lower lip, etched in by the force of his embouchure, looking like extensions of his mustache.

He blew a hand-carved ivory alto saxophone with a 4½ reed and the sound was like nothing any of them had heard before. The usual divisions prevailed: collegians did not dig, and left after an average of 1½ sets. Personnel from other groups, either with a night off or taking a long break from somewhere crosstown or uptown, listened hard, trying to dig. "I am still thinking," they would say if you asked. People at the bar all looked as if they did dig in the sense of understand, approve of, empathize with: but this was probably only because people who prefer to stand at the bar have, universally, an inscrutable look.

At the end of the bar in the V-Note is a table which is normally used by customers to put empty beer bottles and glasses on, but if somebody grabs it early enough nobody minds and the bartenders are usually too busy anyway to yell at them to get off. At the moment the table was occupied by Winsome, Charisma and Fu. Paola had gone to the ladies' room. None of them were saying anything.

The group on the stand had no piano: it was bass, drums, McClintic and a boy he had found in the Ozarks who blew a natural horn in F. The drummer was a group man who avoided pyrotechnics, which may have irritated the college crowd. The bass was small and evil-looking and his eyes were yellow with pinpoints in the center. He talked to his instrument. It was taller than he was and didn't seem to be listening.

Horn and alto together favored sixths and minor fourths and when this happened it was like a knife fight or tug of war: the sound was consonant but as if cross-purposes were in the air. The solos of McClintic Sphere were something else. There were people around, mostly those who wrote for Downbeat magazine or the liners of LP records, who seemed to feel he played disregarding chord changes com-

48

pletely. They talked a great deal about soul and the anti-intellectual and the rising rhythms of African nationalism. It was a new conception, they said, and some of them said: Bird Lives.

Since the soul of Charlie Parker had dissolved away into a hostile March wind nearly a year before, a great deal of nonsense had been spoken and written about him. Much more was to come, some is still being written today. He was the greatest alto on the postwar scene and when he left it some curious negative will—a reluctance and refusal to believe in the final, cold fact—possessed the lunatic fringe to scrawl in every subway station, on sidewalks, in pissoirs, the denial: Bird Lives. So that among the people in the V-Note that night were, at a conservative estimate, a dreamy 10 per cent who had not got the word, and saw in McClintic Sphere a kind of reincarnation.

"He plays all the notes Bird missed," somebody whispered in front of Fu. Fu went silently through the motions of breaking a beer bottle on the edge of the table, jamming it into the speaker's back and twisting.

It was near closing time, the last set.

"It's nearly time to go," Charisma said. "Where is Paola."

"Here she comes," said Winsome.

Outside the wind had its own permanent gig. And was still blowing.

chapter three

*In which Stencil, a
quick-change artist,
does eight
imperson-
ations*

V

As spread thighs are to the libertine, flights of migratory
birds to the ornithologist, the working part of his tool bit to
the production machinist, so was the letter V to young Stencil. He would dream perhaps once a week that it had all
been a dream, and that now he'd awakened to discover the
pursuit of V. was merely a scholarly quest after all, an adventure of the mind, in the tradition of *The Golden Bough*
or *The White Goddess*.

But soon enough he'd wake up the second, real time, to
make again the tiresome discovery that it hadn't really ever
stopped being the same simple-minded, literal pursuit; V.
ambiguously a beast of venery, chased like the hart, hind
or hare, chased like an obsolete, or bizarre, or forbidden
form of sexual delight. And clownish Stencil capering along
behind her, bells ajingle, waving a wooden, toy oxgoad. For
no one's amusement but his own.

His protest to the Margravine di Chiave Lowenstein (suspecting V.'s natural habitat to be the state of siege, he'd
come to Mallorca directly from Toledo, where he'd spent a
week night-walking the alcázar, asking questions, gathering
useless memorabilia): "It isn't espionage," had been, and
still was, spoken more out of petulance than any desire to
establish purity of motive. He wished it could all be as re-

one among a repertoire of identities

spectable and orthodox as spying. But somehow in his hands the traditional tools and attitudes were always employed toward mean ends: cloak for a laundry sack, dagger to peel potatoes; dossiers to fill up dead Sunday afternoons; worst of all, disguise itself not out of any professional necessity but only as a trick, simply to involve him less in the chase, to put off some part of the pain of dilemma on various "impersonations."

Herbert Stencil, like small children at a certain stage and Henry Adams in the *Education*, as well as assorted autocrats since time out of mind, always referred to himself in the third person. This helped "Stencil" appear as only one among a repertoire of identities. "Forcible dislocation of personality" was what he called the general technique, which is not exactly the same as "seeing the other fellow's point of view"; for it involved, say, wearing clothes that Stencil wouldn't be caught dead in, eating foods that would have made Stencil gag, living in unfamiliar digs, frequenting bars or cafés of a non-Stencilian character; all this for weeks on end; and why? To keep Stencil in his place: that is, in the third person.

Around each seed of a dossier, therefore, had developed a nacreous mass of inference, poetic license, forcible dislocation of personality into a past he didn't remember and had no right in, save the right of imaginative anxiety or historical care, which is recognized by no one. He tended each seashell on his submarine scungille farm, tender and impartial, moving awkwardly about his staked preserve on the harborbed, carefully avoiding the little dark deep right there in the midst of the tame shellfish, down in which God knew what lived: the island Malta, where his father had died, where Herbert had never been and knew nothing at all about because something there kept him off, because it frightened him.

One evening, drowsing on the sofa in Bongo-Shaftsbury's apartment, Stencil took out his one souvenir of whatever old Sidney's Maltese adventure had been. A gay, four-color postcard, a Daily Mail battle photo from the Great War, showing a platoon of sweating, kilted Gordons wheeling a stretcher on which lay an enormous German enlisted man with a great mustache, one leg in a splint and a most comfortable grin. Sidney's message read: "I feel old, and yet like a sacrificial virgin. Write and cheer me up. FATHER."

51

Young Stencil hadn't written because he was eighteen and never wrote. That was part of the present venery: the way he'd felt on hearing of Sidney's death half a year later and only then realizing that neither of them had communicated since the picture-postcard.

A certain Porpentine, one of his father's colleagues, had been murdered in Egypt under the duello by Eric Bongo-Shaftsbury, the father of the man who owned this apartment. Had Porpentine gone to Egypt like old Stencil to Malta, perhaps having written his own son that he felt like some other spy, who'd in turn gone off to die in Schleswig-Holstein, Trieste, Sofia, anywhere? Apostolic succession. They must know when it's time, Stencil had often thought; but if death did come like some last charismatic bestowal, he'd have no real way of telling. He'd only the veiled references to Porpentine in the journals. The rest was impersonation and dream.

I

As the afternoon progressed, yellow clouds began to gather over Place Mohammed Ali, from the direction of the Libyan desert. A wind with no sound at all swept up rue Ibrahim and across the square, bringing a desert chill into the city.

For one P. Aïeul, café waiter and amateur libertine, the clouds signaled rain. His lone customer, an Englishman, perhaps a tourist because his face was badly sunburned, sat all tweeds, ulster and expectation looking out on the square. Though he'd been there over coffee not fifteen minutes, already he seemed as permanent a landscape's feature as the equestrian statue of Mohammed Ali itself. Certain Englishmen, Aïeul knew, have this talent. But they're usually not tourists.

Aïeul lounged near the entrance to the café; outwardly inert but teeming inside with sad and philosophical reflections. Was this one waiting for a lady? How wrong to expect any romance or sudden love from Alexandria. No tourists' city gave that gift lightly. It took—how long had he been away from the Midi? twelve years?—at least that long. Let them be deceived into thinking the city something more than what their Baedekers said it was: a Pharos long gone to earthquake and the sea; picturesque but faceless Arabs;

52

monuments, tombs, modern hotels. A false and bastard city; inert—for "them"—as Aïeul himself.

He watched the sun darken and wind flutter the leaves of acacias round Place Mohammed Ali. In the distance a name was being bellowed: Porpentine, Porpentine. It whined in the square's hollow reaches like a voice from childhood. Another fat Englishman, fair-haired, florid—didn't all Northerners look alike?—had been striding down rue Chérif Pacha in a dress suit and a pith helmet two sizes too large. Approaching Aïeul's customer, he began blithering rapidly in English from twenty yards out. Something about a woman, a consulate. The waiter shrugged. Having learned years back there was little to be curious about in the conversations of Englishmen. But the bad habit persisted.

Rain began, thin drops, hardly more than a mist. "Hat fingan," the fat one roared, "hat fingan kahwa bisukkar, ya weled." Two red faces burned angry at each other across the table.

Merde, Aïeul thought. At the table: "M'sieu?"

"Ah," the gross smiled, "coffee then. Café, you know."

On his return the two were conversing lackadaisically about a grand party at the Consulate tonight. What consulate? All Aïeul could distinguish were names. Victoria Wren. Sir Alastair Wren (father? husband?). A Bongo-Shaftsbury. What ridiculous names that country produced. Aïeul delivered the coffee and returned to his lounging space.

This fat one was out to seduce the girl, Victoria Wren, another tourist traveling with her tourist father. But was prevented by the lover, Bongo-Shaftsbury. The old one in tweed—Porpentine—was the macquereau. The two he watched were anarchists, plotting to assassinate Sir Alastair Wren, a powerful member of the English Parliament. The peer's wife—Victoria—was meanwhile being blackmailed by Bongo-Shaftsbury, who knew of her own secret anarchist sympathies. The two were music-hall entertainers, seeking jobs in a grand vaudeville being produced by Bongo-Shaftsbury, who was in town seeking funds from the foolish knight Wren. Bongo-Shaftsbury's avenue of approach would be through the glamorous actress Victoria, Wren's mistress, posing as his wife to satisfy the English fetish of respectability. Fat and Tweed would enter their consulate tonight arm-in-arm, singing a jovial song, shuffling, rolling their eyes. . . .

Rain had increased in thickness. A white envelope with a

crest on the flap passed between the two at the table. All at once the tweed one jerked to his feet like a clockwork doll and began speaking in Italian.

A fit? But there was no sun. And Tweed had begun to sing:

> Pazzo son!
> Guardate, come io piango ed imploro ...

Italian opera. Aïeul felt sick. He watched them with a pained smile. The antic Englishman leaped in the air, clicked his heels; stood posturing, fist on chest, other arm outstretched:

> Come io chiedo pietà!

Rain drenched the two. The sunburned face bobbed like a balloon, the only touch of color in that square. Fat sat in the rain, sipping at the coffee, observing his frolicking companion. Aïeul could hear drops of rain pattering on the pith helmet. At length Fat seemed to awake: arose, leaving a piastre and a millième on the table (avare!) and nodded to the other, who now stood watching him. The square was empty except for Mohammed Ali and the horse.

(How many times had they stood this way: dwarfed horizontal and vertical by any plaza or late-afternoon? Could an argument from design be predicated on that instant only, then the two must have been displaceable, like minor chess pieces, anywhere across Europe's board. Both of a color though one hanging back diagonal in deference to his partner, both scanning any embassy's parquetry for signs of some dimly sensed opposition—lover, meal-ticket, object of political assassination—any statue's face for a reassurance of self-agency and perhaps, unhappily, self-humanity; might they be trying not to remember that each square in Europe, however you cut it, remains inanimate after all?)

They turned about formally and parted in opposite directions, Fat back toward the Hotel Khedival, Tweed into rue de Ras-et-Tin and the Turkish quarter.

Bonne chance, Aïeul thought. Whatever it is tonight, bonne chance. Because I will see neither of you again, that's the least I can wish. He fell asleep at last against the wall, made drowsy by the rain, to dream of one Maryam and tonight, and the Arab quarter....

Low places in the square filled, the usual random sets of

criss-crossing concentric circles moved across them. Near eight o'clock, the rain slackened off.

II

Yusef the factotum, temporarily on loan from Hotel Khedival, dashed through the failing rain, across the street to the Austrian Consulate; darting in by the servants' entrance.

"Late!" shouted Meknes, leader of the kitchen force. "And so, spawn of a homosexual camel: the punch table for you."

Not a bad assignment, Yusef thought as he put on the white jacket and combed his mustaches. From the punch table on the mezzanine one could see the whole show: down the decolletages of the prettier women (Italian breasts were the finest—ah!), over all that resplendent muster of stars, ribbons and exotic Orders.

Soon, from his vantage, Yusef could allow the first sneer of many this evening to ripple across a knowledgeable mouth. Let them make holiday while they could. Soon enough the fine clothes would be rags and the elegant woodwork crusted with blood. Yusef was an anarchist.

Anarchist and no one's fool. He kept abreast of current events, always on lookout for any news favorable to even minor chaos. Tonight the political situation was hopeful: Sirdar Kitchener, England's newest colonial hero, recently victorious at Khartoum, was just now some 400 miles further down the White Nile, foraging about in the jungle; a General Marchand was also rumored in the vicinity. Britain wanted no part of France in the Nile Valley. M. Delcassé, Foreign Minister of a newly-formed French cabinet, would as soon go to war as not if there were any trouble when the two detachments met. As meet, everyone realized by now, they would. Russia would support France, while England had a temporary rapprochement with Germany—meaning Italy and Austria as well.

Bung ho, the English said. Up goes the balloon. Yusef, believing that an anarchist or devotee of annihilation must have some childhood memory to be nostalgic about by way of balance, loved balloons. Most nights at dreams' verge he could revolve like the moon about any gaily-dyed pig's intestine, distended with his own warm breath.

But from the corner of his eye now: miracle. How, if one believed in nothing, could one account . . .

A balloon-girl. A balloon-girl. Hardly seeming to touch the waxed mirror beneath. Holding her empty cup out to Yusef. Mesikum bilkher, good evening; are there any other cavities you wish filled, my English lady. Perhaps he would spare children like this. Would he? If it should come to a morning, any morning when all the muezzins were silent, the pigeons gone to hide among the catacombs, could he rise robeless in Nothing's dawn and do what he must? By conscience, must?

"Oh," she smiled: "Oh thank you. Leltak leben." May thy night be white as milk.

As thy belly . . . enough. She bobbed off, light as cigar smoke rising from the great room below. She'd pronounced her o's with a sigh, as if fainting from love. An older man, solidly built, hair gone gray—looking like a professional street-brawler in evening dress—joined her at the stairs. "Victoria," he rumbled.

Victoria. Named after her queen. He fought in vain to hold back laughter. No telling what would amuse Yusef.

His attention was to stray to her now and again throughout the evening. It was pleasant amid all that glitter to have something to focus on. But she stood out. Her color—even her voice was lighter than the rest of her world, rising with the smoke to Yusef, whose hands were sticky with Chablis punch, mustache a sad tangle—he had a habit of unconsciously trimming the ends with his teeth.

Meknes dropped by every half-hour to call him names. If no one happened to be in earshot they traded insults, some coarse, some ingenious, all following the Levantine pattern of proceeding backward through the other's ancestry, creating extempore at each step or generation an even more improbable and bizarre misalliance.

Count Khevenhüller-Metsch the Austrian Consul had been spending much time in the company of his Russian counterpart, M. de Villiers. How, Yusef wondered, can two men joke like that and tomorrow be enemies. Perhaps they'd been enemies yesterday. He decided public servants weren't human.

Yusef shook the punch ladle at the retreating back of Meknes. Public servant indeed. What was he, Yusef, if not a public servant? Was he human? Before he'd embraced political nihilism, certainly. But as a servant, here, tonight, for "them"? He might as well be a fixture on the wall.

But that will change, he smiled, grim. Soon he was day-dreaming again of balloons.

At the bottom of the steps sat the girl, Victoria, center of a curious tableau. Seated next to her was a chubby blond man whose evening clothes looked shrunken by the rain. Standing facing them at the apices of a flat isosceles triangle were the gray-headed man who'd spoken her name, a young girl of eleven in a white shapeless frock, and another man whose face looked sunburned. The only voice Yusef could hear was Victoria's. "My sister is fond of rocks and fossils, Mr. Goodfellow." The blond head next to her nodded courteously. "Show them, Mildred." The younger girl produced from her reticule a rock, turned and held it up first to Victoria's companion and then to the red face beside her. This one seemed to retreat, embarrassed. Yusef reflected that he could blush at will and no one would know. A few more words and the red face had left the group to come loping up the stairs.

To Yusef he held up five fingers: "Khamseh." As Yusef busied himself filling the cups, someone approached from behind and touched the Englishman lightly on one shoulder. The Englishman spun, his hands balling into fists and moving into position for violence. Yusef's eyebrows went up a fraction of an inch. Another street-fighter. How long since he'd seen reflexes like that? In Tewfik the assassin, eighteen and apprentice tombstone-cutter—perhaps.

But this one was forty or forty-five. No one, Yusef reasoned, would stay fit that long unless his profession demanded it. What profession would include both a talent for killing and presence at a consulate party? An Austrian consulate at that.

The Englishman's hands had relaxed. He nodded pleasantly.

"Lovely girl," the other said. He wore blue-tinted spectacles and a false nose.

The Englishman smiled, turned, picked up his five cups of punch and started down the stairs. At the second step he tripped and fell; proceeded whirling and bouncing, followed by sounds of breaking glass and a spray of Chablis punch, to the bottom. Yusef noted that he knew how to take falls. The other street-fighter laughed to cover the general awkwardness.

57

"Saw a fellow do that in a music hall once," he rumbled. "You're much better, Porpentine. Really."

Porpentine extracted a cigarette and lay while smoking where he'd come to rest.

Up on the mezzanine the man with the blue eyeglasses peeked archly from behind a pillar, removed the nose, pocketed it and vanished.

A strange collection. There is more here, Yusef guessed. Had it to do with Kitchener and Marchand? Of course it must. But— His puzzling was interrupted by Meknes, who had returned to describe Yusef's great-great-great-grandfather and grandmother as a one-legged mongrel dog who fed on donkey excrement and a syphilitic elephant, respectively.

III

The Fink restaurant was quiet: not much doing. A few English and German tourists—the penny-pinching kind whom it was never any use approaching—sat scattered about the room, making noise enough for midday in Place Mohammed Ali.

Maxwell Rowley-Bugge, hair coiffed, mustaches curled and external clothing correct to the last wrinkle and thread, sat in one corner, back to the wall, feeling the first shooting pains of panic begin to dance about his abdomen. For beneath the careful shell of hair, skin and fabric lay holed and gray linen and a ne'er-do-well's heart. Old Max was a peregrine and penniless at that.

Give it a quarter of an hour more, he decided. If nothing promising comes along I shall move on to L'Univers.

He had crossed the border into Baedeker land some eight years ago—'90—after an unpleasantness in Yorkshire. It had been Ralph MacBurgess then—a young Lochinvar come down to the then wide enough horizons of England's vaudeville circuits. He sang a bit, danced a bit, told a number of passable barnyard jokes. But Max or Ralph had a problem; being perhaps too daft for small girls. This particular girl, Alice, had shown at age ten the same halfway responses (a game, she'd carol—such fun) of her predecessors. But they know, Max told himself: no matter how young, they know what it is, what they're doing. Only they don't think about it that much. Which was why he drew the line at sixteen or

58

so—any older and romance, religion, remorse entered like blundering stagehands to ruin a pure pas de deux.

But this one had told her friends, who became jealous—one at least enough to pass it on to the clergyman, parents, police—O God. How awkward it had been. Though he'd not tried to forget the tableau—dressing room in the Athenaeum Theatre, a middle-sized town called Lardwick-in-the-Fen. Bare pipes, worn sequined gowns hung in a corner. Broken hollow-pasteboard pillar for the romantic tragedy the vaudeville had replaced. A costume box for their bed. Then footsteps, voices, a knob turning so slow . . .

She'd wanted it. Even afterward, dry-eyed among a protective cordon of hating faces, the eyes had said: I still want it. Alice, the ruin of Ralph MacBurgess. Who knew what any of them wanted?

How he had come to Alexandria, where he would go on leaving, little of that could matter to any tourist. He was that sort of vagrant who exists, though unwillingly, entirely within the Baedeker world—as much a feature of the topography as the other automata: waiters, porters, cabmen, clerks. Taken for granted. Whenever he was about his business—cadging meals, drinks, or lodging—a temporary covenant would come into effect between Max and his "touch"; by which Max was defined as a well-off fellow tourist temporarily embarrassed by a malfunction in Cook's machinery.

A common game among tourists. They knew what he was; and those who participated in the game did so for the same reason they haggled at shops or gave baksheesh to beggars: it was in the unwritten laws of Baedeker land. Max was one of the minor inconveniences to an almost perfectly arranged tourist-state. The inconvenience was more than made up for in "color."

Fink's now began a burst into life. Max looked up with interest. Merrymakers were coming across rue de Rosette from a building which looked like an embassy or consulate. Party there must have only now broken up. The restaurant was filling rapidly. Max surveyed each newcomer, waiting for the imperceptible nod, the high-sign.

He decided at last on a group of four: two men, a small girl and a young lady who like the gown she wore seemed awkwardly bouffant and provincial. All English, of course. Max had his criteria.

He also had an eye, and something about the group disturbed him. After eight years in this supranational domain he knew a tourist when he saw one. The girls were almost certain—but their companions acted wrong: lacking a certain assurance, an instinctive way of belonging to the touristic part of Alex common to all cities, which even the green show their first time out. But it was getting late and Max had nowhere to stay tonight, nor had he eaten.

His opening line was unimportant, being only a choice among standard openers, each effective as long as the touches were eligible to play. It was the response that counted. Here it came out close to what he'd guessed. The two men, looking like a comedy team: one fair and fat, the other dark, red-faced and scrawny, seemed to want to play the gay dog. Fine, let them. Max knew how to be gay. During the introductions his eyes may have stayed a half-second too long on Mildred Wren. But she was myopic and stocky; nothing of that old Alice in her at all.

An ideal touch: all behaved as if they'd known him for years. But you somehow felt that through some horrible osmosis the word was going to get round. Wing in on the wind to every beggar, vagrant, exile-by-choice and peregrine-at-large in Alex that the team of Porpentine & Goodfellow plus the Wren sisters were sitting at a table in the Fink. This whole hard-up population might soon begin to drift in one by one, each getting the same sort of reception, drawn into the group cordially and casually as a close acquaintance who had left but a quarter of an hour before. Max was subject to visions. It would go on, into tomorrow, the next day, the next: they would keep calling for waiters in the same cheery voices to bring more chairs, food, wine. Soon the other tourists would have to be sent away: every chair in the Fink would be in use, spreading out from this table in rings, like a tree trunk or rain puddle. And when the Fink's chairs ran out the harassed waiters would have to begin bringing more in from next door and down the street and then the next block, the next quarter; the seated beggars would overflow into the street, it would swell and swell . . . and the conversation would grow to enormity, each of the thousands participating bringing to it his own reminiscences, jokes, dreams, looninesses, epigrams . . . an entertainment! A grand vaudeville! They'd sit like that, eating when hunger came, getting drunk, sleeping it off, getting drunk again. How would it end? How could it?

Victoria

She'd been talking, the older girl—Victoria—white Vöslauer gone perhaps to her head. Eighteen, Max guessed, slowly giving up his vision of vagrants' communion. About the age Alice would be, now.

Was there a bit of Alice there? Alice was of course another of his criteria. Well the same queer mixture, at least, of girl-at-play, girl-in-heat. Blithe and so green . . .

She was Catholic; had been to a convent school near her home. This was her first trip abroad. She talked perhaps overmuch about her religion; had indeed for a time considered the Son of God as a young lady will consider any eligible bachelor. But had realized eventually that of course he was not but maintained instead a great harem clad in black, decked only with rosaries. Unable to stand for any such competition Victoria had therefore left the novitiate after a matter of weeks but not the Church: that with its sadfaced statuary, odors of candles and incense, formed along with an uncle Evelyn the foci of her serene orbit. The uncle, a wild or renegade sundowner, would arrive from Australia once every few years bringing no gifts but his wonderful yarns. As far as Victoria remembered, he'd never repeated himself. More important perhaps, she was given enough material to evolve between visits a private back of beyond, a colonial doll's world she could play with and within constantly: developing, exploring, manipulating. Especially during Mass: for here was the stage or dramatic field already prepared, serviceable to a seedtime fancy. So it came about that God wore a wideawake hat and fought skirmishes with an aboriginal Satan out at the antipodes of the firmament, in the name and for the safekeeping of any Victoria.

Now Alice—it had been "her" clergyman, had it not?—she was C of E, sturdy-English, future mother, apple cheeks, all that. What is wrong with you Max, he asked himself. Come out of that costume box, that cheerless past. This one's only Victoria, Victoria . . . but what was there about her?

Normally in gatherings like this Max could be talkative, amusing. Not so much by way of paying for his meal or kip as to keep fit, retain the fine edge, the knack for telling a good yarn and gauging his own rapport with the audience in case, in case . . .

He could go back into the business. There were touring companies abroad: even now, eight years aged, eyebrow-line

61

altered, hair dyed, the mustache—who'd know him? What need for exile? The story had spread to the troupe and through them to all small-urban and provincial England. But they'd all loved him, handsome, jolly Ralph. Surely after eight years, even if he were recognized . . .

But now Max found not much to say. The girl dominated the conversation, and it was the kind of conversation Max had no knack for. Here were none of your post-mortems on the day past—vistas! tombs! curious beggars!—no bringing out of small prizes from the shops and bazaars, no speculation on tomorrow's itinerary; only a passing reference to a party tonight at the Austrian Consulate. Here instead was unilateral confession, and Mildred contemplating a rock with trilobite fossiles she'd found out near the site of the Pharos, and the other two men listening to Victoria but yet off somewhere else switching glances at each other, at the door, about the room. Dinner came, was eaten, went. But even with a filled belly Max could not cheer up. They were somehow depressing: Max felt disquieted. What had he walked into? It showed bad judgment, settling on this lot.

"My God," from Goodfellow. They looked up to see, materialized behind them, an emaciated figure in evening dress whose head appeared to be that of a nettled sparrow-hawk. The head guffawed, retaining its fierce expression. Victoria bubbled over in a laugh.

"It's Hugh!" she cried, delighted.

"Indeed," came a hollow voice from inside somewhere.

"Hugh Bongo-Shaftsbury," said Goodfellow, ungracious.

"Harmakhis." Bongo-Shaftsbury indicated the ceramic hawk's head. "God of Heliopolis and chief deity of Lower Egypt. Utterly genuine, this: a mask, you know, used in the ancient rituals." He seated himself next to Victoria. Goodfellow scowled. "Literally Horus on the horizon, also represented as a lion with the head of a man. Like the Sphinx."

"Oh," Victoria said (that languid "oh"), "the Sphinx."

"How far down the Nile do you intend to go," asked Porpentine. "Mr. Goodfellow has mentioned your interest in Luxor."

"I feel it is fresh territory, sir," Bongo-Shaftsbury replied. "No first-rate work around the area since Grébaut discovered the tomb of the Theban priests back in '91. Of course one should have a look round the pyramids at Gizeh, but that is

62

pretty much old hat since Mr. Flinders Petrie's painstaking inspection of sixteen or seventeen years ago."

Now what was this, Max wondered. An Egyptologist was he, or only reciting from the pages of his Baedeker? Victoria poised prettily between Goodfellow and Bongo-Shaftsbury, attempting to maintain a kind of flirtatious equilibrium.

On the face of it, all normal. Rivalry for the young lady's attentions between the two, Mildred a younger sister, Porpentine perhaps a personal secretary; for Goodfellow did have the affluent look. But beneath?

He came to the awareness reluctantly. In Baedeker land one doesn't often run across impostors. Duplicity is against the law, it is being a Bad Fellow.

But they were only posing as tourists. Playing a game different from Max's; and it frightened him.

Talk at the table stopped. The faces of the three men lost whatever marks of specific passion they had held. The cause was approaching their table: an unremarkable figure wearing a cape and blue eyeglasses.

"Hullo Lepsius," said Goodfellow. "Tire of the climate in Brindisi, did you?"

"Sudden business called me to Egypt."

So the party had already grown from four to seven. Max remembered his vision. What quaint manner of peregrine here: these two? He saw a flicker of communication between the newcomers, rapid and nearly coinciding with a similar glance between Porpentine and Goodfellow.

Was that how the sides were drawn up? Were there sides at all?

Goodfellow sniffed at his wine. "Your traveling companion," he said at last. "We'd rather hoped to see him again."

"Gone to a Switzerland," said Lepsius, "of clean winds, clean mountains. One can have enough, one day, of this soiled South."

"Unless you go far enough south. I imagine far enough down the Nile one gets back to a kind of primitive spotlessness."

Good timing, Max noted. And the gestures preceded the lines as they should. Whoever they were it was none of your amateur night.

Lepsius speculated: "Doesn't the law of the wild beast prevail down there? There are no property rights. There is

63

fighting. The victor wins all. Glory, life, power and property; all."

"Perhaps. But in Europe, you know, we are civilized. Fortunately jungle law is inadmissible."

Odd: neither Porpentine nor Bongo-Shaftsbury spoke. Each had bent a close eye on his own man, keeping expressionless.

"Shall we meet again in Cairo then," said Lepsius.

"Most certainly"; nodding.

Lepsius took his leave then.

"What a queer gentleman," Victoria smiled, restraining Mildred, who'd cocked an arm preparing to heave her rock at his retreating form.

Bongo-Shaftsbury turned to Porpentine. "Is it queer to favor the clean over the impure?"

"It may depend on one's employment," was Porpentine's rejoinder: "and employer."

Time had come for the Fink to close up. Bongo-Shaftsbury took the check with an alacrity which amused them all. Half the battle, thought Max. Out in the street he touched Porpentine's sleeve and began an apologetic denunciation of Cook's. Victoria skipped ahead across rue Chérif Pacha to the hotel. Behind them a closed carriage came rattling out of the drive beside the Austrian Consulate and dashed away hell-for-leather down rue de Rosette.

Porpentine turned to watch it. "Someone is in a hurry," Bongo-Shaftsbury noted.

"Indeed," said Goodfellow. The three watched a few lights in the upper windows of the consulate. "Quiet, though."

Bongo-Shaftsbury laughed quickly, perhaps a bit incredulous.

"Here. In the street . . ."

"A fiver would see me through," Max had continued, trying to regain Porpentine's attention.

"Oh," vague, "of course, I could spare it." Fumbling naively with his wallet.

Victoria watched them from the curb opposite. "Do come along," she called.

Goodfellow grinned. "Here, m'dear." And started across with Bongo-Shaftsbury.

She stamped her foot. "Mr. Porpentine." Porpentine, five quid between his fingertips, looked around. "Do finish with your cripple. Give him his shilling and come. It's late."

The white wine, a ghost of Alice, first doubts that Porpentine was genuine; all could contribute to a violation of code. The code being only: Max, take whatever they give you. Max had already turned away from the note which fluttered in the street's wind, moved off against the wind. Limping toward the next pool of light he sensed Porpentine still looked after him. Also knew what he must look like: a little halt, less sure of his own memories' safety and of how many more pools of light he could reasonably expect from the street at night.

IV

The Alexandria and Cairo morning express was late. It puffed into the Gare du Caire slow, noisy, venting black smoke and white steam to mingle among palms and acacias in the park across the tracks from the station house.

Of course the train was late. Waldetar the conductor snorted good-naturedly at those on the platform. Tourists and businessmen, porters from Cook's and Gaze's, poorer, third-class passengers with their impedimenta—like a bazaar—: what else did they expect? Seven years he'd made the same leisurely run, and the train had never been on time. Schedules were for the line's owners, for those who calculated profit and loss. The train itself ran on a different clock—its own, which no human could read.

Waldetar was not an Alexandrian. Born in Portugal, he now lived with a wife and three children near the railroad yards in Cairo. His life's progress had been inevitably east; having somehow escaped the hothouse of his fellow Sephardim he flew to the other extreme and developed an obsession with ancestral roots. Land of triumph, land of God. Land of suffering, also. Scenes of specific persecution upset him.

But Alexandria was a special case. In the Jewish year 3554 Ptolemy Philopator, having been refused entrance to the temple at Jerusalem, returned to Alexandria and imprisoned many of the Jewish colony there. Christians were not the first to be put on exhibition and mass-murdered for the amusement of a mob. Here Ptolemy, after ordering Alexandria's Jews confined in the Hippodrome, embarked on a two-day debauch. The king, his guests and a herd of killer elephants fed on wine and aphrodisiacs: when all had been worked up to the proper level of blood-lust, the elephants were turned loose into the arena and driven upon the prisoners. But turned (goes the tale) on the guards and spectators instead, trampling many to death. So impressed was Ptolemy that he released the condemned, restored their privileges, and gave them leave to kill their enemies.

Waldetar, a highly religious man, had heard the story from his father and was inclined to take the common-sense view. If there is no telling what a drunken human will do, so much less a herd of drunken elephants. Why put it down to God's intervention? There were enough instances of that in history, all regarded by Waldetar with terror and a sense of his own smallness: Noah's warning of the Flood, the parting of the Red Sea, Lot's escape from annihilated Sodom. Men, he felt, even perhaps Sephardim, are at the mercy of the earth and its seas. Whether a cataclysm is accident or design, they need a God to keep them from harm.

The storm and the earthquake have no mind. Soul cannot commend no-soul. Only God can.

But elephants have souls. Anything that can get drunk, he reasoned, must have some soul. Perhaps this is all "soul" means. Events between soul and soul are not God's direct province: they are under the influence either of Fortune, or of virtue. Fortune had saved the Jews in the Hippodrome.

Merely train's hardware for any casual onlooker, Waldetar in private life was exactly this mist of philosophy, imagination and continual worry over his several relationships—not only with God, but also with Nita, with their children, with his own history. There's no organized effort about it but there remains a grand joke on all visitors to Baedeker's world: the permanent residents are actually humans in disguise. This secret is as well kept as the others: that statues talk (though the vocal Memnon of Thebes, certain sunrises, had been indiscreet), that some government buildings go mad and mosques make love.

Passengers and baggage aboard, the train overcame its inertia and started off only a quarter of an hour behind schedule toward the climbing sun. The railway from Alexandria to Cairo describes a rough arc whose chord points southeast. But the train must first angle north to skirt Lake Mareotis. While Waldetar made his way among the first-class compartments to gather tickets, the train passed rich villages and gardens alive with palms and orange trees.

Abruptly these were left behind. Waldetar squeezed past a German with blue lenses for eyes and an Arab deep in conversation in time to enter a compartment and see from the window momentary death: desert. The site of the ancient Eleusis—a great mound, looking like the one spot on earth fertile Demeter had never seen, passed by to the south.

At Sidi Gaber the train swung at last toward the southeast, inching slow as the sun; zenith and Cairo would in fact be reached at the same time. Across the Mahmudiyeh Canal, into a slow bloom of green—the Delta—and clouds of ducks and pelicans rising from the shores of Mareotis, frightened by the noise. Beneath the lake were 150 villages, submerged by a man-made Flood in 1801, when the English cut through an isthmus of desert during the siege of Alexandria, to let the Mediterranean in. Waldetar liked to think that the waterfowl soaring thick in the air were ghosts of fellahin. What submarine wonders at the floor of Mareotis! Lost country: houses, hovels, farms, water wheels, all intact.

Did the narwhal pull their plows? Devilfish drive their water wheels?

Down the embankment a group of Arabs lazed about, evaporating water from the lake for salt. Far down the canal were barges, their sails brave white under this sun.

Under the same sun Nita would be moving now about their little yard growing heavy with what Waldetar hoped would be a boy. A boy could even it up, two and two. Women outnumber us now, he thought: why should I contribute further to the imbalance?

"Though I'm not against it," he'd once told her during their courtship (part way here—in Barcelona, when he was stevedoring at the docks); "God's will, is it not? Look at Solomon, at many great kings. One man, several wives."

"Great king," she yelled: "who?" They both started to laugh like children. "One peasant girl you can't even support." Which is no way to impress a young man you are bent on marrying. It was one of the reasons he fell in love with her shortly afterward and why they'd stayed in love for nearly seven years of monogamy.

Nita, Nita . . . The mind's picture was always of her seated behind their house at dusk, where the cries of children were drowned in the whistle of a night train for Suez; where cinders came to lodge in pores beginning to

67

widen under the stresses of some heart's geology ("Your complexion is going from bad to worse," he'd say: "I'll have to start paying more attention to the lovely young French girls who are always making eyes at me." "Fine," she'd retort, "I'll tell that to the baker when he comes to sleep with me tomorrow, it'll make him feel better"); where all the nostalgias of an Iberian littoral lost to them—the squid hung to dry, nets stretched across any skyglow morning or evening, singing or drunken cries of sailors and fishermen from behind only the next looming warehouse (find them, find them! voices whose misery is all the world's night)—came unreal, in a symbolic way, as a racketing over points, a chuff-chuff of inanimate breath, and had only pretended to gather among the pumpkins, purslane and cucumbers, lone date palm, roses and poinsettias of their garden.

Halfway to Damanhur he heard a child crying from a compartment nearby. Curious, Waldetar looked inside. The girl was English, eleven or so, nearsighted: her watering eyes swam distorted behind thick eyeglasses. Across from her a man, thirty or so, harangued. Another looked on, perhaps angry, his burning face at least giving the illusion. The girl held a rock to her flat bosom.

"But have you never played with a clockwork doll?" the man insisted, the voice muffled through the door. "A doll which does everything perfectly, because of the machinery inside. Walks, sings, jumps rope. Real little boys and girls, you know, cry: act sullen, won't behave." His hands lay perfectly still, long and starved-nervous, one on each knee.

"Bongo-Shaftsbury," the other began. Bongo-Shaftsbury waved him off, irritated.

"Come. May I show you a mechanical doll. An electromechanical doll."

"Have you one—" she was frightened, Waldetar thought with an onrush of sympathy, seeing his own girls. Damn some of these English—"have you one with you?"

"I am one," Bongo-Shaftsbury smiled. And pushed back the sleeve of his coat to remove a cufflink. He rolled up the shirt cuff and thrust the naked underside of his arm at the girl. Shiny and black, sewn into the flesh, was a miniature electric switch. Single-pole, double-throw. Waldetar recoiled and stood blinking. Thin silver wires ran from its terminals up the arm, disappearing under the sleeve.

"You see, Mildred. These wires run into my brain. When

the switch is closed like this I act the way I do now. When it is thrown the other—"

"Papa!" the girl cried.

"Everything works by electricity. Simple and clean."

"Stop it," said the other Englishman.

"Why, Porpentine." Vicious. "Why. For her? Touched by her fright, are you. Or is it for yourself."

Porpentine seemed to retreat bashfully. "One doesn't frighten a child, sir."

"Hurrah. General principles again." Corpse fingers jabbed in the air. "But someday, Porpentine, I, or another, will catch you off guard. Loving, hating, even showing some absent-minded sympathy. I'll watch you. The moment you forget yourself enough to admit another's humanity, see him as a person and not a symbol—then perhaps—"

"What is humanity."

"You ask the obvious, ha, ha. Humanity is something to destroy."

There was noise from the rear car, behind Waldetar. Porpentine came dashing out and they collided. Mildred had fled, clutching her rock, to the adjoining compartment.

The door to the rear platform was open: in front of it a fat florid Englishman wrestled with the Arab Waldetar had seen earlier talking to the German. The Arab had a pistol. Porpentine moved toward them, closing cautiously, choosing his point. Waldetar, recovering at last, hurried in to break up the fight. Before he could reach them Porpentine had let loose a kick at the Arab's throat, catching him across the windpipe. The Arab collapsed rattling.

"Now," Porpentine pondered. The fat Englishman had taken the pistol.

"What is the trouble," Waldetar demanded, in his best public-servant's voice.

"Nothing." Porpentine held out a sovereign. "Nothing that cannot be healed by this sovereign cure."

Waldetar shrugged. Between them they got the Arab to a third-class compartment, instructed the attendant there to look after him—he was sick—and to put him off at Damanhur. A blue mark was appearing on the Arab's throat. He tried to talk several times. He looked sick enough.

When the Englishmen had at last returned to their compartments Waldetar fell into reverie which continued on past Damanhur (where he saw the Arab and blue-lensed

German again conversing), through a narrowing Delta, as the sun rose toward noon and the train crawled toward Cairo's Principal Station; as dozens of small children ran alongside the train calling for baksheesh; as girls in blue cotton skirts, and veils, with breasts made sleek brown by the sun, traipsed down to the Nile to fill their water jars; as water wheels spun and irrigation canals glittered and interlaced away to the horizon; as fellahin lounged under the palms; as buffalo paced their every day's tracks round and round the sakiehs. The point of the green triangle is Cairo. It means that relatively speaking, assuming your train stands still and the land moves past, that the twin wastes of the Libyan and Arabian deserts to right and left creep in inexorably to narrow the fertile and quick part of your world until you are left with hardly more than a right-of-way, and before you a great city. So there crept in on the gentle Waldetar a suspicion cheerless as the desert.

If they are what I think: what sort of world is it when they must let children suffer?

Thinking, of course, of Manoel, Antonia and Maria: his own.

v

The desert creeps in on a man's land. Not a fellah, but he does own some land. Did own. From a boy, he has repaired the wall, mortared, carried stone heavy as he, lifted, set in place. Still the desert comes. Is the wall a traitor, letting it in? Is the boy possessed by a djinn who makes his hands do the work wrong? Is the desert's attack too powerful for any boy, or wall, or dead father and mother?

No. The desert moves in. It happens, nothing else. No djinn in the boy, no treachery in the wall, no hostility in the desert. Nothing.

Soon, nothing. Soon only the desert. The two goats must choke on sand, nuzzling down to find the white clover. He, never to taste their soured milk again. The melons die beneath the sand. Never more can you give comfort in the summer, cool abdelawi, shaped like the Angel's trumpet! The maize dies and there is no bread. The wife, the children grow sick and short-tempered. The man, he, runs one night out to where the wall was, begins to lift and toss imaginary rocks about, curses Allah, then begs forgiveness from the

70

Prophet, then urinates on the desert, hoping to insult what cannot be insulted.

They find him in the morning a mile from the house, skin blued, shivering in a sleep which is almost death, tears turned to frost on the sand.

And now the house begins to fill with desert, like the lower half of an hourglass which will never be inverted again.

What does a man do? Gebrail shot a quick look back at his fare. Even here, in the Ezbekiyeh Garden at high noon, these horse's hooves sounded hollow. You jolly damn right Inglizi; a man comes to the City and drives for you and every other Frank with land to return to. His family lives all together in a room no bigger than your W.C., out in Arabian Cairo where you never go because it's too dirty, and not "curious." Where the street is so narrow hardly a man's shadow can pass; a street, like many not on any guidebook's map. Where the houses pile up in steps; so high that the windows of two buildings may touch across the street; and hide the sun. Where goldsmiths live in filth and tend tiny flames to make adornment for your traveling English ladies.

Five years Gebrail had hated them. Hated the stone buildings and metaled roads, the iron bridges and glass windows of Shepheard's Hotel which it seemed were only different forms of the same dead sand that had taken his home. "The City," Gebrail often told his wife, just after admitting he'd come home drunk and just before beginning to yell at his children—the five of them curled blind in the windowless room above the barber like so many puppy-bodies—"the city is only the desert in disguise."

The Lord's angel, Gebrail, dictated the Koran to Mohammed the Lord's Prophet. What a joke if all that holy book were only twenty-three years of listening to the desert. A desert which has no voice. If the Koran were nothing, then Islam was nothing. Then Allah was a story, and his Paradise wishful thinking.

Stencil?

"Fine." The fare leaned over his shoulder, smelling of garlic, like an Italian. "Wait here." But dressed like an Inglizi. How horrible the face looked: dead skin peeling off the burned face in white rags. They were in front of Shepheard's Hotel.

Since noon they'd been all over the fashionable part of the

city. From Hotel Victoria (where, oddly, his fare had emerged from the servants' entrance) they had driven first to the Quarter Rossetti, then a few stops along the Muski; then uphill to the Rond-Point, where Gebrail waited while the Englishman disappeared for half an hour into the Bazaars' pungent labyrinth. Visiting, perhaps. Now he'd seen the girl before, surely. The girl in the Quarter Rossetti: Coptic, probably. Eyes made impossibly huge with mascara, nose slightly hooked and bowed, two vertical dimples on either side of the mouth, crocheted shawl covering hair and back, high cheekbones, warm-brown skin.

Of course she'd been a fare. He remembered the face. She was mistress to some clerk or other in the British Consulate. Gebrail had picked the boy up for her in front of the Hotel Victoria, across the street. Another time they'd gone to her rooms. It helped Gebrail to remember faces. Brought in more baksheesh if you bade them good-day any second time. How could you say they were people: they were money. What did he care about the love affairs of the English? Charity—selfless or erotic—was as much a lie as the Koran. Did not exist.

One merchant in the Muski too he had seen. A jewel merchant who had lent money to the Mahdists and was afraid his sympathies would become known now that the movement was crushed. What did the Englishman want there? He had brought no jewels away from the shop; though he'd remained inside for nearly an hour. Gebrail shrugged. They were both fools. The only Mahdi is the desert.

Mohammed Ahmed, the Mahdi of '83, was believed by some to be sleeping not dead in a cavern near Baghdad. And on the Last Day, when the prophet Christ re-establishes el-Islam as the religion of the world he will return to life to slay Dejal the antichrist at a church gate somewhere in Palestine. The Angel Asrafil will trumpet a blast to kill everything on earth, and another to awaken the dead.

But the desert's angel had hidden all the trumpets beneath the sand. The desert was prophecy enough of the Last Day.

Gebrail lounged exhausted against the seat of his pinto-colored phaeton. He watched the hindquarters of the poor horse. A poor horse's ass. He nearly laughed. Was this a revelation then from God? Haze hung over the city.

72

Tonight, he would get drunk with an acquaintance who sold sycamore figs, whose name Gebrail didn't know. The fig-hawker believed in the Last Day; saw it, in fact, close at hand.

"Rumors," he said darkly, smiling at the girl with the rotting teeth, who worked the Arabian cafés looking for love-needy Franks with her baby on one shoulder. "Political rumors."

"Politics is a lie."

Fashoda

"Far up the Bahr-el-Abyad, in the heathen jungle, is a place called Fashoda. The Franks—Inglizi, Feransawi—will fight a great battle there, which will spread in all directions to engulf the world."

"And Asrafil will sound the call to arms," snorted Gebrail. "He cannot. He is a lie, his trumpet is a lie. The only truth—"

"Is the desert, is the desert. Wahyat abuk! God forbid."

And the fig-hawker went off into the smoke to get more brandy.

Nothing was coming. Nothing was already here.

Back came the Englishman, with his gangrenous face. A fat friend followed him out of the hotel.

"Bide time," the fare called mirthfully.

"Ha, ho. I'm taking Victoria to the opera tomorrow night."

Back in the cab: "There is a chemist's shop near the Crédit Lyonnais." Weary Gebrail gathered the reins.

Night was coming rapidly. This haze would make the stars invisible. Brandy, too, would help. Gebrail enjoyed starless nights. As if a great lie were finally to be exposed . . .

VI

Three in the morning, hardly a sound in the streets, and time for Girgis the mountebank to be about his nighttime avocation, burglary.

Breeze in the acacias: that was all. Girgis huddled in bushes, near the back of Shepheard's Hotel. While the sun was up he and a crew of Syrian acrobats and a trio from Port Said (dulcimer, Nubian drum, reed pipe) performed in a cleared space by the Ismailiyeh Canal, out in the suburbs near the slaughterhouse of Abbasiyeh. A fair. There were swings and a fearsome steam-driven carousel for the children; serpent-charmers, and hawkers of all refreshment:

toasted seeds of abdelawi, limes, fried treacle, water flavored with licorice or orange blossom, meat puddings. His customers were the children of Cairo and those aged children of Europe, the tourists.

Take from them by day, take from them by night. If only his bones weren't beginning so much to feel it. Performing the tricks—with silk kerchiefs, folding boxes, a mysteriously pocketed cloak decorated outside with hieroglyphic ploughs, scepters, feeding ibis, lily and sun—sleight-of-hand and burglary needed light hands, bones of rubber. But the clowning—that took it out of him. Hardened the bones: bones that should be alive, not rock rods under the flesh. Falling off the top of a motley pyramid of Syrians, making the dive look as near-fatal as it actually was; or else engaging the bottom man in a slapstick routine so violent that the whole construction tottered and swayed; mock-horror appearing on the faces of the others. While the children laughed, shrieked, closed their eyes or enjoyed the suspense. That was the only real compensation, he supposed—God knew it wasn't the pay —a response from the children; buffoon's treasure.

Enough, enough. Best get this over, he decided, and to bed as soon as possible. One of these days he'd climb up on that pyramid so exhausted, reflexes off enough, that the neck-breaking routine would be no sham. Girgis shivered in the same wind that cooled the acacias. Up, he told his body: up. That window.

And was halfway erect before he saw his competition. Another comic acrobat, climbing out a window some ten feet above the bushes Girgis crouched in.

Patience, then. Study his technique. We can always learn. The other's face, turned in profile, seemed wrong: but it was only the streetlight. Feet now on a narrow ledge, the man began to inch along crablike, toward the corner of the building. After a few steps, stopped; began to pick at his face. Something white fluttered down, tissue-thin, into the bushes.

Skin? Girgis shivered again. He had a way of repressing thoughts of disease.

Apparently the ledge narrowed toward the corner. The thief was hugging the wall closer. He reached the corner. As he stood with each foot on a different side and the edge of the building bisecting him from eyebrows to abdomen he lost his balance and fell. On the way down he yelled out an obscenity in English. Then hit the shrubbery with a crash, rolled and lay still for a while. A match flared and went out, leaving only the pulsing coal of a cigarette.

Girgis was all sympathy. He could see it happening to himself one day, in front of the children, old and young. If he'd believed in signs he would have given it up for tonight and gone back to the tent they all shared near the slaughterhouse. But how could he stay alive on the few millièmes tossed his way during the day? "Mountebank is a dying profession," he'd reckon in his lighter moments. "All the good ones have moved into politics."

The Englishman put out his cigarette, rose and began to climb a tree nearby. Girgis lay muttering old curses. He could hear the Englishman wheezing and talking to himself as he ascended, crawled out on a limb, straddled it and peered in a window.

After a lag of fifteen seconds, Girgis distinctly heard the words, "A bit thick, you know," from the tree. Another cigarette-coal appeared, then abruptly swung in a quick arc downward and hung a few feet below the limb. The Englishman was swinging by one arm from the limb.

This is ridiculous, Girgis thought.

Crash. The Englishman fell into the bushes again. Girgis got cautiously to his feet and went over to him.

"Bongo-Shaftsbury?" the Englishman said, hearing Girgis approach. He lay looking up at a starless zenith, picking absently at flakes of dead skin on his face. Girgis stopped a few feet away. "Not yet," the other continued, "you haven't got me quite yet. They are up there, on my bed, Goodfellow and the girl. We've been together now for two years, and I can't begin, you know, to count all the girls he's done this to. As if every capital of Europe were Margate, and the promenade a continent long." He began to sing.

It isn't the girl I saw you wiv in Brighton,
Who, who, who's your lady friend?

Mad, thought Girgis, pitying. The sun hadn't stopped with this poor fellow's face, it had gone on into the brain.

"She will be in 'love' with him, whatever the word means. He will leave her. Do you think I care? One accepts his partner as one does any tool, with all its idiosyncrasies. I had read Goodfellow's dossier, I knew what I was getting. . . .

75

"But perhaps the sun, and what is happening down the Nile, and the knife-switch on your arm, which I did not expect; and the frightened child, and now—" he gestured up at the window he'd left—"have thrown me off. We all have a threshold. Put your revolver away, Bongo-Shaftsbury—there's a good fellow—and wait, only wait. She is still faceless, still expendable. God, who knows how many of us will have to be sacrificed this coming week? She is the least of my worries. She and Goodfellow."

What comfort could Girgis give him? His English wasn't good, he'd only understood half the words. The madman had not moved, had only continued to stare at the sky. Girgis opened his mouth to speak, thought better of it, and began to back away. He realized all at once how tired he was, how much the days of acrobatics took out of him. Would that alienated figure on the ground be Girgis someday?

I'm getting old, Girgis thought. I have seen my own ghost. But I'll have a look at the Hotel du Nil anyway. The tourists there aren't as rich. But we all do what we can.

VII

The bierhalle north of the Ezbekiyeh Garden had been created by north European tourists in their own image. One memory of home among the dark-skinned and tropical. But so German as to be ultimately a parody of home.

Hanne had held on to the job only because she was stout and blond. A smaller brunette from the south had stayed for a time but was finally let go because she didn't look German enough. A Bavarian peasant but not German enough! The whims of Boeblich the owner got only amusement from Hanne. Bred to patience—a barmaid since age thirteen—she had cultivated and perfected a vast cowlike calm which served her now in good stead among the drunkenness, sex for sale and general fatuousness of the bierhalle.

To the bovine of this world—this tourist world, at least —love comes, is undergone, and goes away unobtrusive as possible. So with Hanne and the itinerant Lepsius; a salesman—said he—of ladies' jewelry. Who was she to question? Having been through it (her phrase), Hanne, schooled in the ways of an unsentimental world, knew well enough that men were obsessed with politics almost as much as women with marriage. Knew the bierhalle to be more than a place only to get drunk or fixed up with a woman, just as its list of frequent customers did comprise individuals strange to Karl Baedeker's way of life.

How upset Boeblich would be could he see her lover. Hanne mooned about the kitchen now, in the slack period between dinner and serious drinking, up to her elbows in soapy water. Lepsius was certainly "not German enough." Half a head shorter than Hanne, eyes so delicate that he must wear tinted glasses even in the murk of Boeblich's, and such poor thin arms and legs.

"There is a competitor in town," he confided to her, pushing an inferior line, underselling us—it's unethical, don't you see?" She'd nodded.

Well if he came in . . . anything she happened to over-hear . . . a rotten business, nothing he'd ever want to subject a woman to . . . but . . .

For his poor weak eyes, his loud snoring, his boylike way of mounting her, taking too long to come to rest in the embrace of her fat legs . . . of course, she would go on watch for any "competitor." English he was, and somewhere had got a bad touch of the sun.

All day, through the slower morning hours, her hearing seemed to grow sharper. So that at noon when the kitchen erupted gently into disorder—nothing outright: a few delayed orders, a dropped plate which shattered like her tender eardrums—she'd heard perhaps more than she was intended to. Fashoda, Fashoda . . . the word washed about Boeblich's like a pestilent rain. Even the faces changed: Grüne the chef, Wernher the bartender, Musa the boy who swept floors, Lotte and Eva and the other girls, all seemed to've turned shifty, to've been hiding secrets all this time. There was even something sinister about the usual slap on the buttocks Boeblich gave Hanne as she passed by.

Imagination, she told herself. She'd always been a practical girl, not given to fancy. Could this be one of love's side-effects? To bring on visions, encourage voices which did not exist, to make the chewing and second digestion of any cud only more difficult? It worried Hanne, who thought she knew everything about love. How was Lepsius different: a little lower, a little weaker; certainly no high priest at the business, no more mysterious or remarkable than any other of a dozen strangers.

Damn men and their politics. Perhaps it was a kind of

77

sex for them. Didn't they even use the same word for what a man does to a woman and what a successful politician does to his unlucky opponent? What was Fashoda to her, or Marchand or Kitchener, or whatever their names were, the two who had "met"—met for what? Hanne laughed, shaking her head. She could imagine, for what.

Fashoda She pushed back a straggle of yellow hair with one soap-bleached hand. Odd how the skin died and grew soggy-white. It looked like leprosy. Since midday a certain leit-motif of disease had come jittering in, had half-revealed itself, latent in the music of Cairo's afternoon; Fashoda, Fashoda, a word to give pale, unspecific headaches, a word suggestive of jungle, and outlandish micro-organisms, and fevers which were not love's (the only she'd known, after all, being a healthy girl) or anything human's. Was it a change in the light, or were the skins of the others actually beginning to show the blotches of disease?

She rinsed and stacked the last plate. No. A stain. Back went the plate into the dishwater. Hanne scrubbed, then examined the plate again, tilting it toward the light. The stain was still there. Hardly visible. Roughly triangular, it extended from an apex near the center to a base an inch or so from the edge. A sort of brown color, outlines indistinct against the faded white of the plate's surface. She tilted the plate another few degrees toward the light and the stain disappeared. Puzzled, she moved her head to look at it from another angle. The stain flickered twice in and out of existence. Hanne found that if she focused her eyes a little behind and off the edge of the plate the stain would remain fairly constant, though its shape had begun to change out-line; now crescent, now trapezoid. Annoyed, she plunged the plate back into the water and searched among the kitchen gear under the sink for a stiffer brush.

Was the stain real? She didn't like its color. The color of her headache: pallid brown. It is a stain, she told herself. That's all it is. She scrubbed fiercely. Outside, the beer-drinkers were coming in from the street. "Hanne," called Boeblich.

O God, would it never go away? She gave it up at last and stacked the plate with the other dishes. But now it seemed the stain had fissioned, and transferred like an overlay to each of her retinae.

A quick look at her hair in the mirror-fragment over the

sink; then on went a smile and out went H[...]
her countrymen.

Of course the first face she saw was that o[...]
tor." It sickened her. Mottled red and white, a[...]
of skin hanging . . . He was conferring a[...]
Varkumian the pimp, whom she knew. She b[...]
passes.

" . . . Lord Cromer could keep it from avalanching . . ."

" . . . Sir, every whore and assassin in Cairo . . ."

In the corner someone vomited. Hanne rushed to clean
it up.

" . . . if they should assassinate Cromer . . ."

" . . . bad show, to have no Consul-General . . ."

" . . . it will degenerate . . ."

Amorous embrace from a customer. Boeblich approached
with a friendly scowl.

" . . . keep him safe at all costs . . ."

" . . . capable men in this sick world are at a . . ."

" . . . Bongo-Shaftsbury will try . . ."

" . . . the Opera . . ."

" . . . where? Not the Opera . . ."

" . . . Ezbekiyeh Garden . . ."

" . . . the Opera . . . *Manon Lescaut* . . ."

" . . . who did say? I know her . . . Zenobia the Copt . . ."

" . . . Kenneth Slime at the Embassy's girl . . ."

Love. She paid attention.

" . . . has it from Slime that Cromer is taking no precautions. My God: Goodfellow and I barged in this morning
as Irish tourists: he in a moldly morning hat with a shamrock, I in a red beard. They threw us bodily into the
street. . . ."

" . . . no precautions . . . O God . . ."

" . . . God, with a *shamrock* . . . Goodfellow wanted to lob
a bomb . . ."

" . . . as if nothing could wake him up . . . doesn't he read
the . . ."

A long wait by the bar while Wernher and Musa tapped
a new keg. The triangular stain swam somewhere over the
crowd, like a tongue on Pentecost.

" . . . now that they have met . . ."

" . . . they will stay, I imagine, round . . ."

" . . . the jungles round . . ."

" . . . will there be, do you think . . ."

...it begins it will be round . . ."

...ere?

Fashoda."

"Fashoda."

Hanne continued on her way, through the establishment's doors and into the street. Grüne the waiter found her ten minutes later leaning back against a shop front, gazing on the night-garden with mild eyes.

"Come."

"What is Fashoda, Grüne?"

Shrug. "A place. Like Munich, Weimar, Kiel. A town, but in the jungle."

"What does it have to do with women's jewelry?"

"Come in. The girls and I can't handle that herd."

"I see something. Do you? Floating over the park." From across the canal came the whistle of the night express for Alexandria.

"Bitte . . ." Some common nostalgia—for the cities of home; for the train or only its whistle?—may have held them for a moment. Then the girl shrugged and they returned to the bierhalle.

Vic Varkumian had been replaced by a young girl in a flowered dress. The leprous Englishman seemed upset. With ruminant resourcefulness Hanne rolled eyes, thrust bosoms at a middle-aged bank clerk seated with cronies at the table next to the couple. Received and accepted an invitation to join them.

"I followed you," the girl said. "Papa would die if he found out." Hanne could see her face, half in shadow. "About Mr. Goodfellow."

Pause. Then: "Your father was in a German church this afternoon. As we are now in a German beer hall. Sir Alastair was listening to someone play Bach. As if Bach were all that were left." Another pause. "So that he may know."

She hung her head, a mustache of beer foam on her upper lip. There came one of those queer lulls in the noise level of any room; in its center another whistle from the Alexandria express.

"You love Goodfellow," he said.

"Yes." Nearly a whisper.

"Whatever I may think," she said, "I have guessed. You can't believe me, but I must say it. It's true."

"What would you have me do, then?"

Twisting ringlets round her fingers: "Not[h]
[un]derstand."

"How can you—" exasperated—"men can ge[t]
you see, for 'understanding' someone. The way
Is your whole family daft? Will they be conte[nt]
[tak]ing less than the heart, lights and liver?"

It was not love. Hanne excused herself and left. It was
not man/woman. The stain was still with her. What could
she tell Lepsius tonight. She had only the desire to remove his spectacles, snap and crush them, and watch him
suffer. How delightful it would be.

This from gentle Hanne Echerze. Had the world gone mad
with Fashoda?

VIII

The corridor runs by the curtained entrances to four
boxes, located to audience right at the top level of the summer theatre in the Ezbekiyeh Garden.

A man wearing blue spectacles hurries into the second
box from the stage end of the corridor. The red curtains,
heavy velvet, swing to and fro, unsynchronized, after his
passage. The oscillation soon damps out because of the
weight. They hang still. Ten minutes pass.

Two men turn the corner by the allegorical statue of
Tragedy. Their feet crush unicorns and peacocks that repeat
diamond-fashion the entire length of the carpet. The face
of one is hardly to be distinguished beneath masses of
white tissue which have obscured the features, and changed
slightly the outlines of the face. The other is fat. They
enter the box next to the one the man with the blue spectacles is in. Light from outside, late summer light now falls
through a single window, turning the statue and the figured
carpet to a monochrome orange. Shadows become more
opaque. The air between seems to thicken with an indeterminate color, though it is probably orange. Then a girl in
a flowered dress comes down the hall and enters the box
occupied by the two men. Minutes later she emerges, tears
in her eyes and on her face. The fat man follows. They pass
out of the field of vision.

The silence is total. So there's no warning when the red-
and-white-faced man comes through his curtains holding a

81

...stol. The pistol smokes. He enters the next box. Soon the man with the blue spectacles, struggling, pitch ...ough the curtains and fall to the carpet. Their lower ...alves are still hidden by the curtains. The man with the white-blotched face removes the blue spectacles; snaps them in two and drops them to the floor. The other shuts his eyes tightly, tries to turn his head away from the light.

Another has been standing at the end of the corridor. From this vantage he appears only as a shadow; the window is behind him. The man who removed the spectacles now crouches, forcing the prostrate one's head toward the light. The man at the end of the corridor makes a small gesture with his right hand. The crouching man looks that way and half rises. A flame appears in the area of the other's right hand; another flame; another. The flames are colored a brighter orange than the sun.

Vision must be the last to go. There must also be a nearly imperceptible line between an eye that reflects and an eye that receives.

The half-crouched body collapses. The face and its masses of white skin loom ever closer. At rest the body is assumed exactly into the space of this vantage.

chapter four

*In which Esther
gets a nose
job*

V

Next evening, prim and nervous-thighed in a rear seat of
the crosstown bus, Esther divided her attention between
the delinquent wilderness outside and a paperback copy of
The Search for Bridey Murphy. This book had been written
by a Colorado businessman to tell people there was life after
death. In its course he touched upon metempsychosis, faith
healing, extrasensory perception and the rest of a weird
canon of twentieth-century metaphysics we've come now to
associate with the city of Los Angeles and similar regions.

The bus driver was of the normal or placid crosstown
type; having fewer traffic lights and stops to cope with than
the up-and-downtown drivers, he could afford to be genial.
A portable radio hung by his steering wheel, tuned to
WQXR. Tchaikovsky's Romeo and Juliet Overture flowed
syrupy around him and his passengers. As the bus crossed
Columbus Avenue, a faceless delinquent heaved a rock at
it. Cries in Spanish ascended to it out of the darkness. A
report which could have been either a backfire or a gunshot
sounded a few blocks downtown. Captured in the score's
black symbols, given life by vibrating air columns and strings,
having taken passage through transducers, coils, capacitors
and tubes to a shuddering paper cone, the eternal drama of
love and death continued to unfold entirely disconnected
from this evening and place.

The bus entered the sudden waste country of Central

Park. Out there, Esther knew, up and downtown, they would be going at it under bushes; mugging, raping, killing. She, her world, knew nothing of the square confines of the Park after sundown. It was reserved as if by convenant for cops, delinquents and all manner of deviates.

Suppose she were telepathic, and could tune in on what was going on out there. She preferred not to think about it. There would be power in telepathy, she thought, but much pain. And someone else might tap your own mind without your knowing. (Had Rachel been listening on the phone extension?)

She touched the tip of her new nose delicately, in secret: a mannerism she'd developed just recently. Not so much to point it out to whoever might be watching as to make sure it was still there. The bus came out of the park onto the safe, bright East Side, into the lights of Fifth Avenue. They reminded her to go shopping tomorrow for a dress she'd seen, $39.95 at Lord and Taylor, which he would like.

What a brave girl I am, she trilled to herself, coming through so much night and lawlessness to visit My Lover.

She got off at First Avenue and tap-tapped along the sidewalk, facing uptown and perhaps some dream. Soon she turned right, began to fish in her purse for a key. Found the door, opened, stepped inside. The front rooms were all deserted. Beneath the mirror, two golden imps in a clock danced the same unsyncopated tango they'd always danced. Esther felt home. Behind the operating room (a sentimental glance sideways through the open door toward the table on which her face had been altered) was a small chamber, in it a bed. He lay, head and shoulders circled by the intense halo of a paraboloid reading light. His eyes opened to her, her arms to him.

"You are early," he said.

"I am late," she answered. Already stepping out of her skirt.

I

Schoenmaker, being conservative, referred to his profession as the art of Tagliacozzi. His own methods, while not as primitive as those of the sixteenth-century Italian, were marked by a certain sentimental inertia, so that Shoenmaker was never quite up to date. He went out of his way to cultivate the Tagliacozzi look: showing his eyebrows thin and semicircular; wearing a bushy mustache, pointed beard, sometimes even a skullcap, his old schoolboy yarmulke.

He'd received his impetus—like the racket itself—from the World War. At seventeen, coeval with the century, he raised a mustache (which he never shaved off), falsified his age and name and wallowed off in a fetid troopship to fly, so he thought, high over the ruined châteaux and scarred fields of France, got up like an earless raccoon to scrimmage with the Hun; a brave Icarus.

Well, the kid never did get up in the air, but they made him a greasemonkey which was more than he'd expected anyway. It was enough. He got to know the guts not only of Breguets, Bristol Fighters and JN's, but also of the birdmen who did go up, and whom, of course, he adored. There was always a certain feudal-homosexual element in this division of labor. Schoenmaker felt like a page boy. Since those days as we know democracy has made its inroads and those crude flying-machines have evolved into "weapon systems" of a then undreamed-of complexity; so that the maintenance man today has to be as professional-noble as the flight crew he supports.

But then: it was a pure and abstract passion, directed for Schoenmaker, at least, toward the face. His own mustache may have been partly responsible; he was often mistaken for a pilot. On off hours, infrequently, he would sport a silk kerchief (obtained in Paris) at his throat, by way of imitation.

The war being what it was, certain of the faces—craggy or smooth, with slicked-down hair or bald—never came back. To this the young Schoenmaker responded with all adolescent love's flexibility: his free-floating affection sad and thwarted for a time till it managed to attach itself to a new face. But in each case, loss was as unspecified as the proposition "love dies." They flew off and were swallowed in the sky.

Until Evan Godolphin. A liaison officer in his middle thirties, TDY with the Americans for reconnaissance missions over the Argonne plateau, Godolphin carried the natural foppishness of the early aviators to extremes which in the time's hysterical context seemed perfectly normal. Here were no trenches, after all: the air up there was free of any taint of gas or comrades' decay. Combatants on both sides could afford to break champagne glasses in the majestic fireplaces of commandeered country seats; treat their captives with utmost courtesy, adhere to every point of the duello when it came to a dogfight; in short, practice with finicking care the entire rigmarole of nineteenth-century gentlemen at war. Evan Godolphin wore a Bond Street-tailored flying suit; would often, dashing clumsily across the scars of their makeshift airfield toward his French Spad, stop to pluck a lone poppy, survivor of strafing by autumn and the Germans (naturally aware of the Flanders Fields poem in Punch, three years ago when there'd still been an idealistic tinge to trench warfare), and insert it into one faultless lapel.

Godolphin became Schoenmaker's hero. Tokens tossed his way—an occasional salute, a "well done" for the preflights which came to be the boy-mechanic's responsibility, a tense smile—were hoarded fervently. Perhaps he saw an end also to this unrequited love; doesn't a latent sense of death always heighten the pleasure of such an "involvement"?

The end came soon enough. One rainy afternoon toward the end of the battle of Meuse-Argonne, Godolphin's crippled plane materialized suddenly out of all that gray, looped feebly, dipped on a wing toward the ground and slid like a kite in an air current toward the runway. It missed the runway by a hundred yards: by the time it impacted corpsmen and stretcher-bearers were already running out toward it. Schoenmaker happened to be nearby and tagged along, having no idea what had happened till he saw the heap of rags and splinters, already soggy in the rain, and from it, limping toward the medics, the worst possible travesty of a human face lolling atop an animate corpse. The top of the nose had been shot away; shrapnel had torn out part of one cheek and shattered half the chin. The eyes, intact, showed nothing.

Schoenmaker must have lost himself. The next he could remember he was back at an aid station, trying to convince the doctors there to take his own cartilage. Godolphin would live, they'd decided. But his face would have to be rebuilt. Life for the young officer would be, otherwise, unthinkable.

Now luckily for some a law of supply and demand had been at work in the field of plastic surgery. Godolphin's case, by 1918, was hardly unique. Methods had been in existence since the fifth century B.C. for rebuilding noses, Thiersch grafts had been around for forty or so years. During the war new techniques were developed by necessity and were practiced by GP's, eye-ear-nose-and-throat men, even a hastily recruited gynecologist or two. The techniques that worked were adopted and passed on quickly to the younger medics. Those that failed produced a generation of freaks and pariahs who along with those who'd received no restorative surgery at all became a secret and horrible postwar fraternity. No good at all in any of the usual rungs of society, where did they go?

(Profane would see some of them under the street. Others you could meet at any rural crossroads in America. As Profane had: come to a new road, right-angles to his progress, smelled the Diesel exhaust of a truck long gone—like walking through a ghost—and seen there like a milestone one of them. Whose limp might mean a brocade or bas-relief of scar tissue down one leg—how many women had looked and shied?—; whose cicatrix on the throat would be hidden modestly like a gaudy war decoration; whose tongue, protruding through a hole in the cheek, would never speak secret words with any extra mouth.)

Evan Godolphin proved to be one of them. The doctor was young, he had ideas of his own, which the AEF was no place for. His name was Halidom and he favored allografts: the introduction of inert substances into the living face. It was suspected at the time that the only safe transplants to use were cartilage or skin from the patient's own body. Schoenmaker, knowing nothing about medicine, offered his cartilage but the gift was rejected; allografting was plausible and Halidom saw no reason for two men being hospitalized when only one had to be.

Thus Godolphin received a nose bridge of ivory, a cheekbone of silver and a paraffin and celluloid chin. A month later Schoenmaker went to visit him in the hospital—the last time he ever saw Godolphin. The reconstruction had been perfect. He was being sent back to London, in some obscure staff position, and spoke with a grim flippancy.

"Take a long look. It won't be good for more than six months." Schoenmaker stammered: Godolphin continued: "See him, down the way?" Two cots over lay what would have been a similar casualty except that the skin of the face was whole, shiny. But the skull beneath was misshapen. "Foreign-body reaction, they call it. Sometimes infection, inflammation, sometimes only pain. The paraffin, for instance, doesn't hold shape. Before you know it, you're back where you started." He talked like a man under death sentence. "Perhaps I can pawn my cheekbone. It's worth a fortune. Before they melted it down it was one of a set of pastoral figurines, eighteenth century—nymphs, shepherdesses—looted from a château the Hun was using for a CP; Lord knows where they're originally from—"

"Couldn't—" Schoenmaker's throat was dry—"couldn't they fix it, somehow: start over . . ."

"Too rushed. I'm lucky to get what I got. I can't complain. Think of the devils who haven't even six months to bash around in."

"What will you do when—"

"I'm not thinking of that. But it will be a grand six months."

The young mechanic stayed in a kind of emotional limbo for weeks. He worked without the usual slacking off, believing himself no more animate than the spanners and screwdrivers he handled. When there were passes to be had he gave his to someone else. He slept on an average of four hours a night. This mineral period ended by an accidental meeting with a medical officer one evening in the barracks. Schoenmaker put it as primitively as he felt:

"How can I become a doctor."

Of course it was idealistic and uncomplex. He wanted only to do something for men like Godolphin, to help prevent a takeover of the profession by its unnatural and traitorous Halidoms. It took ten years of working at his first specialty—mechanic—as well as navvy in a score of markets and warehouses, bill-collector, once administrative assistant to a bootlegging syndicate operating out of Decatur, Illinois. These years of labor were interlarded with night courses and occasional day enrollments, though none more than three semesters in a row (after Decatur, when he could afford it); internship; finally, on the eve of the Great Depression, entrance to the medical freemasonry.

If alignment with the inanimate is the mark of a Bad Guy, Schoenmaker at least made a sympathetic beginning. But at some point along his way there occurred a shift in outlook so subtle that even Profane, who was unusually sensitive that way, probably couldn't have detected it. He was kept going by hatred for Halidom and perhaps a fading love for Godolphin. These had given rise to what is called a "sense of mission"—something so tenuous it has to be fed more solid fare than either hatred or love. So it came to be sustained, plausibly enough, by a number of bloodless theories about the "idea" of the plastic surgeon. Having heard his vocation on the embattled wind, Schoenmaker's dedication was toward repairing the havoc wrought by agencies outside his own sphere of responsibility. Others—politicians and machines—carried on wars; others—perhaps human machines—condemned his patients to the ravages of acquired syphilis; others—on the highways, in the factories—undid the work of nature with automobiles, milling machines, other instruments of civilian disfigurement. What could he do toward eliminating the causes? They existed, formed a body of things-as-they-are; he came to be afflicted with a conservative laziness. It was social awareness of a sort, but with boundaries and interfaces which made it less than the catholic rage filling him that night in the barracks with the M.O. It was in short a deterioration of purpose; a decay.

II

Esther met him, oddly enough, through Stencil, who at the time was only a newcomer to the Crew. Stencil, pursuing a different trail, happened for reasons of his own to be interested in Evan Godolphin's history. He'd followed it as far as Meuse-Argonne. Having finally got Schoenmaker's alias from the AEF records, it took Stencil months to trace him to Germantown and the Muzak-filled face hospital. The good doctor denied everything, after every variety of cajolement Stencil knew; it was another dead end.

As is usual after certain frustrations, we react with benevolence. Esther had been languishing ripe and hot-eyed about the Rusty Spoon, hating her figure-6 nose and proving as well as she could the unhappy undergraduate adage: "All the ugly ones fuck." The thwarted Stencil, casting about for somebody to take it all out on, glommed on to her despair hopefully—a taking which progressed to sad summer afternoons wandering among parched fountains, sunstruck shop fronts and streets bleeding tar, eventually to a father-daughter agreement casual enough to be canceled at any time should either of them desire, no post-mortems necessary. It struck him with a fine irony that the nicest sentimental trinket for her would be an introduction to Schoenmaker; accordingly, in September, the contact was made and Esther without ado went under his knives and kneading fingers.

Collected for her in the anteroom that day were a rogues' gallery of malformed. A bald woman without ears contemplated the gold imp-clock, skin flush and shiny from temples to occiput. Beside her sat a younger girl, whose skull was fissured such that three separate peaks, paraboloid in shape, protruded above the hair, which continued down either side of a densely acned face like a skipper's beard. Across the room, studying a copy of the Reader's Digest, sat an aged gentleman in a moss-green gabardine suit, who possessed three nostrils, no upper lip and an assortment of different-sized teeth which leaned and crowded together like the headstones of a boneyard in tornado country. And off in a corner, looking at nothing, was a sexless being with hereditary syphilis, whose bones had acquired lesions and had partially collapsed so that the gray face's profile was nearly a straight line, the nose hanging down like a loose flap of skin, nearly covering the mouth; the chin depressed at the side by a large sunken crater containing radial skin-wrinkles; the eyes squeezed shut by the same unnatural gravity that flattened the rest of the profile. Esther, who was still at an impressionable age, identified with them all. It was confirmation of this alien feeling which had driven her to bed with so many of the Whole Sick Crew.

This first day Schoenmaker spent in pre-operative reconnaissance of the terrain: photographing Esther's face and nose from various angles, checking for upper respiratory infections, running a Wassermann. Irving and Trench also assisted him in making two duplicate casts or death-masks. They gave her two paper straws to breathe through and in her childish way she thought of soda shops, cherry Cokes, True Confessions.

Next day she was back at the office. The two casts were there on his desk, side by side. "I'm twins," she giggled. Schoenmaker reached out and snapped the plaster nose from one of the masks.

"Now," he smiled; producing like a magician a lump of modeling clay with which he replaced the broken-off nose. "What sort of nose did you have in mind?"

What else: Irish, she wanted, turned up. Like they all wanted. To none of them did it occur that the retroussé nose too is an aesthetic misfit: a Jew nose in reverse, is all. Few had ever asked for a so-called "perfect" nose, where the roof is straight, the tip untilted and unhooked, the columella (separating the nostrils) meeting the upper lip at 90°. All of which went to support his private thesis that correction —along all dimensions: social, political, emotional—entails retreat to a diametric opposite rather than any reasonable search for a golden mean.

A few artistic finger-flourishes and wrist-twistings. "Would that be it?" Eyes aglow, she nodded. "It has to harmonize with the rest of your face, you see." It didn't, of course. All that could harmonize with a face, if you were going to be humanistic about it, was obviously what the face was born with.

"But," he'd been able to rationalize years before, "there is harmony and harmony." So, Esther's nose. Identical with an ideal of nasal beauty established by movies, advertisements, magazine illustrations. Cultural harmony, Schoenmaker called it.

"Try next week then." He gave her the time. Esther was thrilled. It was like waiting to be born, and talking over with God, calm and businesslike, exactly how you wanted to enter the world.

Next week she arrived, punctual: guts tight, skin sensitive. "Come." Schoenmaker took her gently by the hand. She felt passive, even (a little?) sexually aroused. She was seated in a dentist's chair, tilted back and prepared by Irving, who hovered about her like a handmaiden.

Esther's face was cleaned in the nasal region with green soap, iodine and alcohol. The hair inside her nostrils was clipped and the vestibules cleaned gently with antiseptics. She was then given Nembutal.

It was expected this would calm her down, but barbituric acid derivatives affect individuals differently. Perhaps her initial sexual arousal contributed; but by the time Esther was taken to the operating room she was near delirium. "Should have used Hyoscin," Trench said. "It gives them amnesia, man."

"Quiet, schlep," said the doctor, scrubbing. Irving set about arranging his armamentarium, while Trench strapped Esther to the operating table. Esther's eyes were wild; she sobbed quietly, obviously beginning to get second thoughts. "Too late now," Trench consoled her, grinning. "Lay quiet, hey."

91

All three wore surgical masks. The eyes looked suddenly malevolent to Esther. She tossed her head. "Trench, hold her head," came Schoenmaker's muffled voice, "and Irving can be the anaesthetist. You need practice, babe. Go get the Novocain bottle."

Sterile towels were placed under Esther's head and a drop of castor oil in each eye. Her face was again swabbed, this time with Metaphen and alcohol. Gauze packing was then jammed far up her nostrils to keep antiseptics and blood from flowing down her pharynx and throat.

Irving returned with the Novocain, a syringe, and a needle. First she put the anaesthetic into the tip of Esther's nose, one injection on each side. Next she made a number of injections radially around each nostril, to deaden the wings, or alae, her thumb going down on the plunger each time as the needle withdrew. "Switch to the big one," Schoenmaker said quietly. Irving fished a two-inch needle out of the autoclave. This time the needle was pushed, just under the skin, all the way up each side of the nose, from the nostril to where the nose joined forehead.

No one had told Esther that anything about the operation would hurt. But these injections hurt: nothing before in her experience had ever hurt quite so much. All she had free to move for the pain were her hips. Trench held her head and leered appreciatively as she squirmed, constrained, on the table.

Inside the nose again with another burden of anaesthetic, Irving's hypodermic was inserted between the upper and lower cartilage and pushed all the way up to the glabella—the bump between the eyebrows.

A series of internal injections to the septum—the wall of bone and cartilage which separates the two halves of the nose—and anaesthesia was complete. The sexual metaphor in all this wasn't lost on Trench, who kept chanting, "Stick it in . . . pull it out . . . stick it in . . . ooh that was good . . . pull it out . . ." and tittering softly above Esther's eyes. Irving would sigh each time, exasperated. "That boy," you expected her to say.

After a while Schoenmaker started pinching and twisting Esther's nose. "How does it feel? Hurt?" A whispered no: Schoenmaker twisted harder: "Hurt?" No. "Okay. Cover her eyes."

"Maybe she wants to look," Trench said.

"You want to look, Esther? See what we're going to do to you?"

"I don't know." Her voice was weak, teetering between here and hysteria.

"Watch, then," said Schoenmaker. "Get an education. First we'll cut out the hump. Let's see a scalpel."

It was a routine operation; Schoenmaker worked quickly, neither he nor his nurse wasting any motion. Caressing sponge-strokes made it nearly bloodless. Occasionally a trickle would elude him and get halfway to the towels before he caught it.

Schoenmaker first made two incisions, one on either side through the internal lining of the nose, near the septum at the lower border of the side cartilage. He then pushed a pair of long-handled, curved and pointed scissors through the nostril, up past the cartilage to the nasal bone. The scissors had been designed to cut both on opening and closing. Quickly, like a barber finishing up a high-tipping head, he separated the bone from the membrane and skin over it. "Undermining, we call this," he explained. He repeated the scissors work through the other nostril. "You see you have two nasal bones, they're separated by your septum. At the bottom they're each attached to a piece of lateral cartilage. I'm undermining you all the way from this attachment to where the nasal bones join the forehead."

Irving passed him a chisel-like instrument. "MacKenty's elevator, this is." With the elevator he probed around, completing the undermining.

"Now," gently, like a lover, "I'm going to saw off your hump." Esther watched his eyes as best she could, looking for something human there. Never had she felt so helpless. Later she would say, "It was almost a mystic experience. What religion is it—one of the Eastern ones—where the highest condition we can attain is that of an object—a rock. It was like that; I felt myself drifting down, this delicious loss of Estherhood, becoming more and more a blob, with no worries, traumas, nothing: only Being. . . ."

The mask with the clay nose lay on a small table nearby. Referring to it with quick side-glances, Schoenmaker inserted the saw blade through one of the incisions he'd made, and pushed it up to the bony part. Then lined it up with the line of the new nose-roof and carefully began to saw through the nasal bone on that side. "Bone saws easily," he remarked

93

to Esther. "We're all really quite frail." The blade reached soft septum; Schoenmaker withdrew the blade. "Now comes the tricky part. I got to saw off the other side exactly the same. Otherwise your nose will be lopsided." He inserted the saw in the same way on the other side, studied the mask for what seemed to Esther a quarter of an hour; made several minute adjustments. Then finally sawed off the bone there in a straight line.

"Your hump is now two loose pieces of bone, attached only to the septum. We have to cut that through, flush with the other two cuts." This he did with an angle-bladed pull-knife, cutting down swiftly, completing the phase with some graceful sponge-flourishing.

"And now the hump floats inside the nose." He pulled back one nostril with a retractor, inserted a pair of forceps and fished around for the hump. "Take that back," he smiled. "It doesn't want to come just yet." With scissors he snipped the hump loose from the lateral cartilage which had been holding it; then, with the bone-forceps, removed a dark-colored lump of gristle, which he waved triumphantly before Esther. "Twenty-two years of social unhappiness, nicht wahr? End of act one. We'll put it in formaldehyde, you can keep it for a souvenir if you wish." As he talked he smoothed the edges of the cuts with a small rasp file.

So much for the hump. But where the hump had been was now a flat area. The bridge of the nose had been too wide to begin with, and now had to be narrowed.

Again he undermined the nasal bones, this time around to where they met the cheekbones, and beyond. As he removed the scissors he inserted a right-angled saw in its place. "Your nasal bones are anchored firmly, you see; at the side to the cheekbone, at the top to the forehead. We must fracture them, so we can move your nose around. Just like that lump of clay."

He sawed through the nasal bones on each side, separating them from the cheekbones. He then took a chisel and inserted it through one nostril, pushing it as high as he could, until it touched bone.

"Let me know if you feel anything." He gave the chisel a few light taps with a mallet; stopped, puzzled, and then began to hammer harder. "It's a rough mother," he said, dropping his jocular tone. Tap, tap, tap. "Come on, you bastard." The chisel point edged its way, millimeter by

94

millimeter, between Esther's eyebrows. "Scheissel" With a loud snap, her nose was broken free of the forehead. By pushing in from either side with his thumbs, Schoenmaker completed the fracture.

"See? It's all wobbly now. That's act two. Now ve shorten das septum, ja."

With a scalpel he made an incision around the septum, between it and its two adjoining lateral cartilages. He then cut down around the front of the septum to the "spine," located just inside the nostrils at the back.

"Which should give you a free-floating septum. We use scissors to finish the job." With dissecting scissors he undermined the septum along its sides and up over the bones as far as the glabella, at the top of the nose.

He passed a scalpel next into one of the incisions just inside the nostril and out the other, and worked the cutting edge around until the septum was separated at the bottom. Then elevated one nostril with a retractor, reached in with Allis clamps and pulled out part of the loose septum. A quick transfer of calipers from mask to exposed septum; then with a pair of straight scissors Schoenmaker snipped off a triangular wedge of septum. "Now to put everything in place."

Keeping one eye on the mask, he brought together the nasal bones. This narrowed the bridge and eliminated the flat part where the hump had been cut off. He took some time making sure the two halves were lined up dead-center. The bones made a curious crackling sound as he moved them. "For your turned-up nose, we make two sutures."

The "seam" was between the recently-cut edge of the septum and the columella. With needle and needle-holder, two silk stitches were taken obliquely, through the entire widths of columella and septum.

The operation had taken, in all, less than an hour. They cleaned Esther up, removed the plain gauze packing and replaced it with sulfa ointment and more gauze. A strip of adhesive tape went on over her nostrils, another over the bridge of the new nose. On top of this went a Stent mold, a tin guard, and more adhesive plaster. Rubber tubes were put in each nostril so she could breathe.

Two days later the packing was removed. The adhesive plaster came off after five days. The sutures came out after seven. The uptilted end product looked ridiculous but

Schoenmaker assured her it would come down a little after a few months. It did.

III

That would have been all: except for Esther. Possibly her old humpnosed habits had continued on by virtue of momentum. But never before had she been so passive with any male. Passivity having only one meaning for her, she left the hospital Schoenmaker had sent her to after a day and a night, and roamed the East Side in fugue, scaring people with her white beak and a certain shock about the eyes. She was sexually turned on, was all: as if Schoenmaker had located and flipped a secret switch or clitoris somewhere inside her nasal cavity. A cavity is a cavity, after all: Trench's gift for metaphor might have been contagious.

Returning the following week to have the stitches removed, she crossed and uncrossed her legs, batted eyelashes, talked soft: everything crude she knew. Schoenmaker had spotted her at the outset as an easy make.

"Come back tomorrow," he told her. Irving was off. Esther arrived the next day garbed underneath as lacily and with as many fetishes as she could afford. There might even have been a dab of Shalimar on the gauze in the center of her face.

In the back room: "How do you feel."

She laughed, too loud. "It hurts. But."

"Yes, but. There are ways to forget the pain."

She seemed unable to get rid of a silly, half-apologetic smile. It stretched her face, adding to the pain in her nose.

"Do you know what we're going to do? No, what I am going to do to you? Of course."

She let him undress her. He commented only on a black garter belt.

"Oh. Oh God." An attack of conscience: Slab had given it to her. With love, presumably.

"Stop. Stop the peep-show routine. You're not a virgin."

Another self-deprecating laugh. "That's just it. Another boy. Gave it to me. Boy that I loved."

She's in shock, he thought, vaguely surprised.

"Come. We'll make believe it's your operation. You enjoyed your operation, didn't you."

96

Through a crack in the curtains opposite Trench looked on.

"Lie on the bed. That will be our operating table. You are to get an intermuscular injection."

"No," she cried.

"You have worked on many ways of saying no. No meaning yes. That no I don't like. Say it differently."

"No," with a little moan.

"Different. Again."

"No," this time a smile, eyelids at half-mast.

"Again."

"No."

"You're getting better." Unknotting his tie, trousers in a puddle about his feet, Schoenmaker serenaded her.

> Have I told you, fella
> She's got the sweetest columella
> And a septum that's swept 'em all on their ass;
> Each casual chondrectomy
> Meant only a big fat check to me
> Till I sawed this osteoclastible lass:

[Refrain]:

> Till you've cut into Esther
> You've cut nothing at all;
> She's one of the best, Thir,
> To her nose I'm in thrall.

> She never acts nasty
> But lies still as a rock;
> She loves my rhinoplasty
> But the others are schlock.

> Esther is passive,
> Her aplomb is massive,
> How could any poor ass've
> Ever passed her by?

> And let me to you say
> She puts Ireland to shame;
> For her nose is retroussé
> And Esther's her name. . . .

For the last eight bars she chanted "No" on one and three.

Such was the (as it were) Jacobean etiology of Esther's eventual trip to Cuba; which see.

chapter five

*In which Stencil nearly
goes West with
an alliga-
tor*

V

I

This alligator was pinto: pale white, seaweed black. It moved fast but clumsy. It could have been lazy, or old or stupid. Profane thought maybe it was tired of living.

The chase had been going on since nightfall. They were in a section of 48-inch pipe, his back was killing him. Profane hoped the alligator would not turn off into something smaller, somewhere he couldn't follow. Because then he would have to kneel in the sludge, aim half-blind and fire, all quickly, before the cocodrilo got out of range. Angel held the flashlight, but he had been drinking wine, and would crawl along behind Profane absent-mindedly, letting the beam waver all over the pipe. Profane could only see the coco in occasional flashes.

From time to time his quarry would half-turn, coy, enticing. A little sad. Up above it must have been raining. A continual thin drool sounded behind them at the last sewer opening. Ahead was darkness. The sewer tunnel here was tortuous, and built decades ago. Profane was hoping for a straightaway. He could make an easy kill there. If he fired anywhere in this stretch of short, crazy angles there'd be danger from ricochets.

It wouldn't be his first kill. He'd been on the job two

weeks now and bagged four alligators and one rat. Every morning and evening for each shift there was a shapeup in front of a candy store on Columbus Avenue. Zeitsuss the boss secretly wanted to be a union organizer. He wore sharkskin suits and horn rims. Normally, there weren't enough volunteers to cover even this Puerto Rican neighborhood, let alone the city of New York. Still Zeitsuss paced before them mornings at six, stubborn in his dream. His job was civil service but someday he would be Walter Reuther.

"Okay, there, Rodriguez, yeah. I guess we can take you." And here was the Department without enough volunteers to go round. Still, a few came, straggling and reluctant and not at all constant: most quit after the first day. A weird collection it was: bums . . . Mostly bums. Up from the winter sunlight of Union Square and a few gibbering pigeons for loneliness; up from the Chelsea district and down from the hills of Harlem or a little sea-level warmth sneaking glances from behind the concrete pillar of an overpass at the rusty Hudson and its tugs and stonebarges (what in this city pass, perhaps, for dryads: watch for them the next winter day you happen to be overpassed, gently growing out of the concrete, trying to be part of it or at least safe from the wind and the ugly feeling they—we?—have about where it is that persistent river is really flowing); bums from across both rivers (or just in from the Midwest, humped, cursed at, coupled and recoupled beyond all remembrance to the slow easy boys they used to be or the poor corpses they would make someday); one beggar—or the only one who talked about it—who owned a closetful of Hickey-Freeman and like-priced suits, who drove after working hours a shiny white Lincoln, who had three or four wives staggered back along the private Route 40 of his progress east; Mississippi, who came from Kielce in Poland and whose name nobody could pronounce, who had had a woman taken at the Oswiecim extermination camp, an eye taken by the bitter end of a hoist cable on the freighter Mikolaj Rej, and fingerprints taken by the San Diego cops when he tried to jump ship in '49; nomads from the end of a bean-picking season somewhere exotic, so exotic it might really have been last summer and east of Babylon, Long Island, but they with only the season to remember had to have it just ended, only just fading; wanderers uptown from the classic bums' keep of them all—the Bowery, lower Third Avenue, used shirt bins, barber schools, a curious loss of time.

They worked in teams of two. One held the flashlight, the other carried a 12-gauge repeating shotgun. Zeitsuss was aware that most hunters regard use of this weapon like anglers feel about dynamiting fish; but he was not looking for write-ups in Field and Stream. Repeaters were quick and sure. The department had developed a passion for honesty following the Great Sewer Scandal of 1955. They wanted dead alligators: rats, too, if any happened to get caught in the blast.

Each hunter got an armband—a Zeitsuss idea. ALLIGATOR PATROL, it said, in green lettering. At the beginning of the program, Zeitsuss had moved a big plexiglass plotting board, engraved with a map of the city and overlaid with a grid coordinate sheet, into his office. Zeitsuss would sit in front of this board, while a plotter—one V. A. ("Brushhook") Spugo, who claimed to be eighty-five and also to have slain 47 rats with a brushhook under the summer streets of Brownsville on 13 August 1922—would mark up with yellow grease pencil sightings, probables, hunts in progress, kills. All reports came back from roving anchor men, who would walk around a route of certain manholes and yell down and ask how it was going. Each anchor man had a walkie-talkie, tied in on a common network to Zeitsuss's office and a low-fidelity 15-inch speaker mounted on the ceiling. At the beginning it was pretty exciting business. Zeitsuss kept all the lights out except for those on the plotting board and a reading light over his desk. The place looked like a kind of combat center, and anybody walking in would immediately sense this tenseness, purpose, feeling of a great net spreading out all the way to the boondocks of the city, with this room its brains, its focus. That is, until they heard what was coming in over the radios.

"One good provolone, she says."

"I got her good provolone. Why can't she do shopping herself. She spends all day watching Mrs. Grosseria's TV."

"Did you see Ed Sullivan last night, hey Andy. He had this bunch of monkeys playing a piano with their—"

From another part of the city; "And Speedy Gonzales says, 'Señor, please get your hand off my ass.'"

"Ha, ha."

And: "You ought to be over here on the East Side. There is stuff all over the place."

"It all has a zipper on it, over on the East Side."

"That is how come yours is so short?"

"It is not how much you got, it's how you use it."

Naturally there was unpleasantness from the FCC, who ride around, it's said, in little monitor cars with direction-finding antennas just looking for people like this. First came warning letters, then phone calls, then finally somebody wearing a sharkskin suit glossier even than Zeitsuss's. So the walkie-talkies went. And soon after that Zeitsuss's supervisor called him in and told him, very paternal, that there wasn't enough budget to keep the Patrol going in the style it had been accustomed to. So Alligator Hunter-Killer Central was taken over by a minor branch of the payroll department, and old Brushhook Spugo went off to Astoria Queens, a pension, a flower garden where wild marijuana grew and an early grave.

Sometimes now when they mustered out in front of the candy store, Zeitsuss would give them pep talks. The day the Department put a limit on the shotgun shell allotment, he stood out hatless under a half-freezing February rain to tell them about it. It was hard to see if it was melted sleet running down his face, or tears.

"You guys," he said, "some of you been here since this Patrol started. I been seeing a couple of the same ugly faces out here every morning. A lot of you don't come back, and O.K. If it pays better someplace else more power to you, I say. This here is not a rich outfit. If it was union, I can tell you, a lot of them ugly faces would be back every day. You that do come back live in human shit and alligator blood eight hours a day and nobody complains and I'm proud of you. We seen a lot of cutbacks in our Patrol in just the short time it's been a Patrol, and you don't hear anybody go crying about that either, which is worse than shit.

"Well today, they chopped us down again. Each team will be issued five rounds a day instead of ten. Downtown they think you guys are wasting ammo. I know you don't, but how can you tell somebody like that, who has never been down-stairs because it might mess up their hundred-dollar suit. So all I'm saying is, only get the sure kills, don't waste your time on probables.

"Just keep going the way you have. I am proud of you guys. I am so proud!"

They all shuffled around, embarrassed. Zeitsuss didn't say anything else, just stood there half-turned watching an old Puerto Rican lady with a shopping basket limp her way uptown on the other side of Columbus Avenue. Zeitsuss was always saying how proud he was, and despite his loud mouth, his AF of L way of running things, his delusions of high purpose, they liked him. Because under the sharkskin and behind the tinted lenses, he was a bum too; only an accident of time and place kept them all from sharing a wine drunk together now. And because they liked him, his own pride in "our Patrol," which none of them doubted, made them uncomfortable—thinking of the shadows they had fired at (wine-shadows, loneliness-shadows); the snoozes taken during working hours against the sides of flushing tanks near the rivers; the bitching they had done, but in whispers so quiet their partner didn't even hear; the rats they had let get away because they felt sorry for them. They couldn't share the boss's pride but they could feel guilty about making what he felt a lie, having learned, through no very surprising or difficult schooling, that pride—in our Patrol, in yourself, even as a deadly sin—does not really exist in the same way that, say, three empty beer bottles exist to be cashed in for subway fare and warmth, someplace to sleep for awhile. Pride you could exchange for nothing at all. What was Zeitsuss, the poor innocent, getting for it? Chopped down, was what. But they liked him and nobody had the heart to wise him up.

So far as Profane knew Zeitsuss didn't know who he was, or care. Profane would have liked to think he was one of those recurring ugly faces, but what was he after all—only a latecomer. He had no right, he decided after the ammo speech, to think one way or the other about Zeitsuss. He didn't feel any group pride, God knew. It was a job, not a Patrol. He'd learned how to work a repeater—even how to fieldstrip and clean it—and now, two weeks on the job, he was almost beginning to feel less clumsy. Like he wouldn't accidentally shoot himself in the foot or someplace worse after all.

Angel was singing: "Mi corazón, está tan solo, mi corazón . . ." Profane watched his own hip boots move synched with the beat of Angel's song, watched the erratic gleam of the flashlight on the water, watched the gentle switching of the alligator's tail, ahead. They were coming up to a manhole. Rendezvous point. Look sharp, men of the Alligator Patrol. Angel wept as he sang.

"Knock it off," Profane said. "If Bung the foreman is up there, it's our ass. Act sober."

"I hate Bung the foreman," Angel said. He began to laugh.

"Shush," Profane said. Bung the foreman had carried a walkie-talkie before the FCC clamped down. Now he carried a clipboard and filed daily reports with Zeitsuss. He didn't talk much except to give orders. One phrase he used always: "I'm the foreman." Sometimes "I'm Bung, the foreman." Angel's theory was that he had to keep saying this to remind himself.

Ahead of them the alligator lumbered, forlorn. It was moving slower, as if to let them catch up and end it. They arrived at the manhole. Angel climbed up the ladder and hammered with a short crowbar on the underside of the cover. Profane held the flashlight and kept an eye on the coco. There were scraping sounds from above, and the cover was suddenly jacked to one side. A crescent of pink neon sky appeared. Rain came down splashing into Angel's eyes. Bung the foreman's head appeared in the crescent.

"Chinga tu madre," said Angel pleasantly.

"Report," said Bung.

"He's moving off," Profane called from below.

"We're after one now," Angel said.

"You're drunk," Bung said.

"No," said Angel.

"Yes," cried Bung. "I'm the foreman."

"Angel," Profane said. "Come on, we'll lose him."

"I'm sober," Angel said. It occurred to him how nice it might be to punch Bung in the mouth.

"I am going to write you up," said Bung, "I smell booze on your breath."

Angel started climbing out of the manhole. "I would like to discuss this with you."

"What are you guys doing," Profane said, "playing potsy?"

"Carry on," Bung called into the hole. "I am detaining your partner for disciplinary action." Angel, halfway out of the hole, sank his teeth into Bung's leg. Bung screamed. Profane saw Angel disappear, and the pink crescent replace him. Rain spattered down out of the sky and drooled along the old brick sides of the hole. Scuffling sounds were heard in the street.

"Now what the hell," Profane said. He swung the flashlight beam down the tunnel, saw the tip of the alligator's tail sashaying around the next bend. He shrugged. "Carry on, your ass," he said.

He moved away from the manhole, carrying the gun safetied under one arm, the flashlight in the other hand. It was the first time he'd hunted solo. He wasn't scared. When it came to the kill there would be something to prop the flashlight against.

Nearly as he could figure, he was on the East Side, uptown somewhere. He was out of his territory—God, had he chased this alligator all the way crosstown? He rounded the bend, the light from the pink sky was lost: now there moved only a sluggish ellipse with him and the alligator at foci, and a slender axis of light linking them.

They angled to the left, half uptown. The water began to get a little deeper. They were entering Fairing's Parish, named after a priest who'd lived topside years ago. During the Depression of the '30's, in an hour of apocalyptic well-being, he had decided that the rats were going to take over after New York died. Lasting eighteen hours a day, his beat had covered the breadlines and missions, where he gave comfort, stitched up raggedy souls. He foresaw nothing but a city of starved corpses, covering the sidewalks and the grass of the parks, lying belly up in the fountains, hanging wrynecked from the streetlamps. The city—maybe America, his horizons didn't extend that far—would belong to the rats before the year was out. This being the case, Father Fairing thought it best for the rats to be given a head start—which meant conversion to the Roman Church. One night early in Roosevelt's first term, he climbed downstairs through the nearest manhole, bringing a Baltimore Catechism, his breviary and, for reasons nobody found out, a copy of Knight's *Modern Seamanship*. The first thing he did, according to his journals (discovered months after he died) was to put an eternal blessing and a few exorcisms on all the water flowing through the sewers between Lexington and the East River and between 86th and 79th Streets. This was the area which became Fairing's Parish. These benisons made sure of an adequate supply of holy water; also eliminated the trouble of individual baptisms when he had finally converted all the rats in the parish. Too, he expected other rats to hear what was going on under the upper East Side, and come likewise to be converted. Before long he would be spiritual leader of the inheritors of the earth. He considered it small enough sacrifice on their part to provide three of their own per day for physical sustenance, in return for the spiritual nourishment he was giving them.

Accordingly, he built himself a small shelter on one bank of the sewer. His cassock for a bed, his breviary for a pillow. Each morning he'd make a small fire from driftwood collected and set out to dry the night before. Nearby was a depression in the concrete which sat beneath a downspout for rainwater. Here he drank and washed. After a breakfast of roast rat ("The livers," he wrote, "are particularly succulent") he set about his first task: learning to communicate with the rats. Presumably he succeeded. An entry for 23 November 1934 says:

Ignatius is proving a very difficult student indeed. He quarreled with me today over the nature of indulgences. Bartholomew and Teresa supported him. I read them from the catechism: "The Church by means of indulgences remits the temporal punishment due to sin by applying to us from her spiritual treasury part of the infinite satisfaction of Jesus Christ and of the superabundant satisfaction of the Blessed Virgin Mary and of the saints."

"And what," inquired Ignatius, "is this superabundant satisfaction?"

Again I read: "That which they gained during their lifetime but did not need, and which the Church applies to their fellow members of the communion of saints."

"Aha," crowed Ignatius, "then I cannot see how this differs from Marxist communism, which you told us is Godless. To each according to his needs, from each according to his abilities." I tried to explain that there were different sorts of communism: that the early Church, indeed, was based on a common charity and sharing of goods. Bartholomew chimed in at this point with the observation that perhaps this doctrine of a spiritual treasury arose from the economic and social conditions of the Church in her infancy. Teresa promptly accused Bartholomew of holding Marxist views himself, and a terrible fight broke out, in which poor Teresa had an eye scratched from the socket. To spare her further pain, I put her to sleep and made a delicious meal from her remains, shortly after sext. I have discovered the tails, if boiled long enough, are quite agreeable.

Evidently he converted at least one batch. There is no further mention in the journals of the skeptic Ignatius: perhaps he died in another fight, perhaps he left the community for the pagan reaches of Downtown. After the first conversion the entries begin to taper off: but all are optimistic, at times euphoric. They give a picture of the Parish as a little enclave of light in a howling Dark Age of ignorance and barbarity.

Rat meat didn't agree with the Father, in the long run. Perhaps there was infection. Perhaps, too, the Marxist tendencies of his flock reminded him too much of what he had seen and heard above ground, on the breadlines, by sick and maternity beds, even in the confessional; and thus the cheerful heart reflected by his late entries was really only a necessary delusion to protect himself from the bleak truth that his pale and sinuous parishioners might turn out no better than the animals whose estate they were succeeding to. His last entry gives a hint of some such feeling:

When Augustine is mayor of the city (for he is a splendid fellow, and the others are devoted to him) will he, or his council, remember an old priest? Not with any sinecure or fat pension, but with true charity in their hearts? For though devotion to God is rewarded in Heaven and just as surely is not rewarded on this earth, some spiritual satisfaction, I trust, will be found in the New City whose foundations we lay here, in this Iona beneath the old foundations. If it cannot be, I shall nevertheless go to peace, at one with God. Of course that is the best reward. I have been the classical Old Priest—never particularly robust, never affluent—most of my life. Perhaps

The journal ends here. It is still preserved in an inaccessible region of the Vatican library, and in the minds of the few old-timers in the New York Sewer Department who got to see it when it was discovered. It lay on top of a brick, stone and stick cairn large enough to cover a human corpse, assembled in a stretch of 36-inch pipe near a frontier of the Parish. Next to it lay the breviary. There was no trace of the catechism or Knight's *Modern Seamanship*.

"Maybe," said Zeitsuss's predecessor Manfred Katz after

reading the journal, "maybe they are studying the best way to leave a sinking ship."

The stories, by the time Profane heard them, were pretty much apocryphal and more fantasy than the record itself warranted. At no point in the twenty or so years the legend had been handed on did it occur to anyone to question the old priest's sanity. It is this way with sewer stories. They just are. Truth or falsity don't apply.

Profane had moved across the frontier, the alligator still in front of him. Scrawled on the walls were occasional quotes from the Gospels, Latin tags (Agnus Dei, qui tollis peccata mundi, dona nobis pacem—Lamb of God, who taketh away the sins of the world, grant us peace). Peace. Here had been peace, once in a depression season crushed slow, starving-nervous, into the street by the dead weight of its own sky. In spite of time-distortions in Father Fairing's tale, Profane had got the general idea. Excommunicated, most likely, by the very fact of his mission here, a skeleton in Rome's closet and in the priest-hole of his own cassock and bed, the old man sat preaching to a congregation of rats with saints' names, all to the intention of peace.

He swung the beam over the old inscriptions, saw a dark stain shaped like a crucifix and broke out in goose bumps. For the first time since leaving the manhole, Profane realized he was all alone. The alligator up there was no help, it'd be dead soon. To join other ghosts.

What had interested him most were the accounts of Veronica, the only female besides the luckless Teresa who is mentioned in the journal. Sewer hands being what they are (favorite rejoinder: "Your mind is in the sewer"), one of the apocrypha dealt with an unnatural relationship between the priest and this female rat, who was described as a kind of voluptuous Magdalen. From everything Profane had heard, Veronica was the only member of his flock Father Fairing felt to have a soul worth saving. She would come to him at night not as a succubus but seeking instruction, perhaps to carry back to her nest—wherever in the Parish it was—something of his desire to bring her to Christ: a scapular medal, a memorized verse from the New Testament, a partial indulgence, a penance. Something to keep. Veronica was none of your trader rats.

My little joke may have been in earnest. When they are

established firmly enough to begin thinking about canonization, I am sure Veronica will head the list. With some descendant of Ignatius no doubt acting as devil's advocate.

V. came to me tonight, upset. She and Paul have been at it again. The weight of guilt is so heavy on the child. She almost sees it: as a huge, white, lumbering beast, pursuing her, wanting to devour her. We discussed Satan and his wiles for several hours.

V. has expressed a desire to be a sister. I explained to her that to date there is no recognized order for which she would be eligible. She will talk to some of the other girls to see if there is interest widespread enough to require action on my part. It would mean a letter to the Bishop. And my Latin is so wretched . . .

Lamb of God, Profane thought. Did the priest teach them "rat of God"? How did he justify killing them off three a day? How would he feel about me or the Alligator Patrol? He checked the action of the shotgun. Here in the parish were twistings intricate as any early Christian catacomb. No use risking a shot, not here. Was it only that?

His back throbbed, he was getting tired. Beginning to wonder how much longer this would have to keep up. It was the longest he'd chased any alligator. He stopped for a minute, listened back along the tunnel. No sound except the dull wash of water. Angel wouldn't be coming. He sighed and started plodding again toward the river. The alligator was burbling in the sewage, blowing bubbles and growling gently. Is it saying anything, he wondered. To me? He wound on, feeling soon he'd start to think about collapsing and just letting the stream float him out with pornographic pictures, coffee grounds, contraceptives used and unused, shit, up through the flushing tank to the East River and across on the tide to the stone forests of Queens. And to hell with this alligator and this hunt, here between chalkwritten walls of legend. It was no place to kill. He felt the eyes of ghost-rats, kept his own eyes ahead for fear he might see the 36-inch pipe that was Father Fairing's sepulchre, tried to keep his ears closed to the sub-threshold squeakings of Veronica, the priest's old love.

Suddenly—so suddenly it scared him—there was light ahead, around a corner. Not the light of a rainy evening in the city, but paler, less certain. They rounded the corner. He noticed the flashlight bulb starting to flicker; lost the alligator momentarily. Then turned the corner and found a wide space like the nave of a church, an arched roof overhead, a phosphorescent light coming off walls whose exact arrangement was indistinct.

"Wha," he said out loud. Backwash from the river? Sea water shines in the dark sometimes; in the wake of a ship you see the same uncomfortable radiance. But not here. The alligator had turned to face him. It was a clear, easy shot.

He waited. He was waiting for something to happen. Something otherworldly, of course. He was sentimental and superstitious. Surely the alligator would receive the gift of tongues, the body of Father Fairing be resurrected, the sexy V. tempt him away from murder. He felt about to levitate and at a loss to say where, really, he was. In a bonecellar, a sepulchre.

"Ah, schlemihl," he whispered into the phosphorescence. Accident prone, schlimazzel. The gun would blow up in his hands. The alligator's heart would tick on, his own would burst, mainspring and escapement rust in this shindeep sewage, in this unholy light.

"Can I let you just go?" Bung the foreman knew he was after a sure thing. It was down on the clipboard. And then he saw the alligator couldn't go any further. Had settled down on its haunches to wait, knowing damn well it was going to be blasted.

In Independence Hall in Philly, when the floor was rebuilt, they left part of the original, a foot square, to show the tourists. "Maybe," the guide would tell you, "Benjamin Franklin stood right there, or even George Washington." Profane on an eighth-grade class trip had been suitably impressed. He got that feeling now. Here in this room an old man had killed and boiled a catechumen, had committed sodomy with a rat, had discussed a rodent nunhood with V., a future saint—depending which story you listened to.

"I'm sorry," he told the alligator. He was always saying he was sorry. It was a schlemihl's stock line. He raised the repeater to his shoulder, flicked off the safety. "Sorry," he said again. Father Fairing talked to rats. Profane talked to alligators. He fired. The alligator jerked, did a backflip, thrashed briefly, was still. Blood began to seep out amoeba-

110

like to form shifting patterns with the weak glow of the water. Abruptly, the flashlight went out.

II

Gouverneur ("Roony") Winsome sat on his grotesque espresso machine, smoking string and casting baleful looks at the girl in the next room. The apartment, perched high over Riverside Drive, ran to something like thirteen rooms, all decorated in Early Homosexual and arranged to present what the writers of the last century liked to call "vistas" when the connecting doors were open, as they were now.

Mafia his wife was in on the bed playing with Fang the cat. At the moment she was naked and dangling an inflatable brassiere before the frustrated claws of Fang who was Siamese, gray and neurotic. "Bouncy, bouncy," she was saying. "Is the dweat big kitties angwy cause he tant play wif the bwa? EEEE, he so cute and ickle."

Oh, man, thought Winsome, an intellectual. I had to pick an intellectual. They all revert.

The string was from Bloomingdale's, fine quality: procured by Charisma several months before on one of his sporadic work binges; he'd been a shipping clerk that time. Winsome made a mental note to see the pusher from Lord and Taylor's, a frail girl who hoped someday to sell pocketbooks in the accessories department. The stuff was highly valued by string smokers, on the same level as Chivas Regal Scotch or black Panamanian marijuana.

Roony was an executive for Outlandish Records (Volkswagens in Hi-Fi, The Leavenworth Glee Club Sings Old Favorites) and spent most of his time out prowling for new curiosities. He had once, for example, smuggled a tape recorder, disguised as a Kotex dispenser, into the ladies' room at Penn Station; could be seen, microphone in hand, lurking in false beard and levis in the Washington Square fountain, being thrown out of a whorehouse on 125th Street, sneaking along the bullpen at Yankee Stadium on opening day. Roony was everywhere and irrepressible. His closest scrape had come the morning two CIA agents, armed to the teeth, came storming into the office to destroy Winsome's great and secret dream: the version to end all versions of Tchaikovsky's 1812 Overture. What he planned to use for bells, brass band or orchestra God and Winsome only knew;

111

these were of no concern to the CIA. It was the cannon shots they had come to find out about. It seemed Winsome had been putting out feelers among higher-echelon personnel in the Strategic Air Command.

"Why," said the CIA man in the gray suit.

"Why not," said Winsome.

"Why," said the CIA man in the blue suit.

Winsome told them.

"My God," they said, blanching in unison.

"It would have to be the one dropped on Moscow, naturally," Roony said. "We want historical accuracy."

The cat let loose a nerve-jangling scream. Charisma came crawling in from one of the adjoining rooms, covered by a great green Hudson's Bay blanket. "Morning," Charisma said, his voice muffled by the blanket.

"No," said Winsome. "You guessed wrong again. It is midnight and Mafia my wife is playing with the cat. Go in and see. I'm thinking of selling tickets."

"Where is Fu," from under the blanket.

"Out rollicking," said Winsome, "downtown."

"Roon" the girl squealed, "come in and look at him." The cat was lying on its back with all four paws up in the air and a death grin on its face.

Winsome made no comment. The green mound in the middle of the room moved past the espresso machine; entered Mafia's room. Going past the bed it stopped briefly, a hand reached out and patted Mafia on the thigh, then it moved on again in the direction of the bathroom.

The Eskimos, Winsome reflected, consider it good hostmanship to offer a guest your wife for the night, along with food and lodging. I wonder if old Charisma is getting any there off of Mafia.

"Mukluk," he said aloud. He reckoned it was an Eskimo word. If it wasn't, too bad: he didn't know any others. Nobody heard him anyway.

The cat came flying through the air, into the espresso machine room. His wife was putting on a peignoir, kimono, housecoat, or negligee. He didn't know the difference, though periodically Mafia tried to explain to him. All Winsome knew was it was something you had to take off her. "I am going to work for a while," she said.

His wife was an authoress. Her novels—three to date—ran a thousand pages each and like sanitary napkins had gathered

112

in an immense and faithful sisterhood of consumers. There'd even evolved somehow a kind of sodality or fan club that sat around, read from her books and discussed her Theory.

If the two of them ever did get around to making a final split, it would be that Theory there that would do it. Unfortunately Mafia believed in it as fervently as any of her followers. It wasn't much of a Theory, more wishful thinking on Mafia's part than anything else. There being but the single proposition: the world can only be rescued from certain decay through Heroic Love.

In practice Heroic Love meant screwing five or six times a night, every night, with a great many athletic, half-sadistic wrestling holds thrown in. The one time Winsome had blown up he'd yelled, "You are turning our marriage into a trampoline act," which Mafia thought was a pretty good line. It appeared in her next novel, spoken by Schwartz, a weak, Jewish psychopath who was the major villain.

All her characters fell into this disturbingly predictable racial alignment. The sympathetic—those godlike, inexhaustible sex athletes she used for heroes and heroines (and heroin? he wondered) were all tall, strong, white though often robustly tanned (all over), Anglo-Saxon, Teutonic, and/or Scandinavian. Comic relief and villainy were invariably the lot of Negroes, Jews and South European immigrants. Winsome, being originally from North Carolina, resented her urban or Yankee way of hating Nigras. During their courtship he'd admired her vast repertoire of Negro jokes. Only after the marriage did he discover a truth horrible as the fact she wore falsies: she was in nearly total ignorance about the Southron feeling toward Negroes. She used "nigger" as a term of hatred, not apparently being capable herself of anything more demanding than sledgehammer emotions. Winsome was too upset to tell her it was not a matter of love, hate, like or not like so much as an inheritance you lived with. He'd let it slide, like everything else.

If she believed in Heroic Love, which is nothing really but a frequency, then obviously Winsome wasn't on the man end of half of what she was looking for. In five years of marriage all he knew was that both of them were whole selves, hardly fusing at all, with no more emotional osmosis than leakage of seed through the solid membranes of contraceptive or diaphragm that were sure to be there protecting them.

113

Now Winsome had been brought up on the white Protestant sentiments of magazines like The Family Circle. One of the frequent laws he encountered there was the one about how children sanctify a marriage. Mafia at one time had been daft to have kids. There may have been some intention of mothering a string of super-children, founding a new race, who knew. Winsome had apparently met her specifications, both genetic and eugenic. Sly, however, she waited, and the whole contraceptive rigmarole was gone through in the first year of Heroic Love. Things meanwhile having started to fall apart, Mafia became, naturally, more and more uncertain of how good a choice Winsome had been after all. Why she'd hung on this long Winsome didn't know. Literary reputation, maybe. Maybe she was holding off divorce till her public-relations sense told her go. He had a fair suspicion she'd describe him in court as near impotence as the limits of plausibility allowed. The Daily News and maybe even Confidential magazine would tell America he was a eunuch.

The only grounds for divorce in New York state is adultery. Roony, dreaming mildly of beating Mafia to the punch, had begun to look with more than routine interest at Paola Maijstral, Rachel's roommate. Pretty and sensitive; and unhappy, he'd heard, with her husband Pappy Hod, BM3, USN, from whom she was separated. But did that mean she'd think any better of Winsome?

Charisma was in the shower, splashing around. Was he wearing the green blanket in there? Winsome had the impression he lived in it.

"Hey," called Mafia from the writing desk. "How do you spell Prometheus, anybody." Winsome was about to say it started off like prophylactic when the phone rang. Winsome hopped down off the espresso machine and padded over to it. Let her publishers think she was illiterate.

"Roony, have you seen my roommate. The young one." He had not.

"Or Stencil."

"Stencil has not been here all week," Winsome said. "He is out tracking down leads, he says. All quite mysterious and Dashiell Hammettlike."

Rachel sounded upset: her breathing, something. "Would they be together?" Winsome spread his hands and shrugged, keeping the phone tucked between neck and shoulder. "Because she didn't come home last night."

"No telling what Stencil is doing," said Winsome, "but I will ask Charisma."

Charisma was standing in the bathroom, wrapped in the blanket, observing his teeth in the mirror. "Eigenvalue, Eigenvalue," he mumbled. "I could do a better root canal job. What is my buddy Winsome paying you for, anyway."

"Where is Stencil," said Winsome.

"He sent a note yesterday, by a vagrant in an old Army campaign hat, circa 1898. Something about he would be in the sewers, tracing down a lead, indefinitely."

"Don't slouch," Winsome's wife said as he chugged back to the phone emitting puffs of string smoke. "Stand up straight."

"Ei-gen-value!" moaned Charisma. The bathroom had a delayed echo.

"The what," Rachel said.

"None of us," Winsome told her, "have ever inquired into his business. If he wants to grouse around the sewer system, why let him. I doubt Paola is with him."

"Paola," Rachel said, "is a very sick girl." She hung up, angry but not at Winsome, and turned to see Esther sneaky-Peteing out the door wearing Rachel's white leather raincoat.

"You could have asked me," Rachel said. The girl was always swiping things and then getting all kittenish when she was caught.

"Where are you going at this hour," Rachel wanted to know.

"Oh, out." Vaguely. If she had any guts, Rachel thought, she would say: who the hell are you, I have to account to you for where I go? And Rachel would answer: I am who you owe a thousand-odd bucks to, is who. And Esther would get all hysterical and say: If that's the way it is, I'm leaving, I will go into prostitution or something and send you your money in the mail. And Rachel would watch her stomp out and then just as she was at the door, deliver the exit line: You'll go broke, you'll have to pay them. Go and be damned. The door would slam, high heels clatter away down the hall, a hiss-thump of elevator doors and hoorah: no more Esther. And next day she would read in the paper where Esther Harvitz, 22, honors graduate of CCNY, had taken a

Brody off some bridge, overpass or high building. And Rachel would be so shocked she wouldn't even be able to cry.

"Was that me?" out loud. Esther had left. "So," she continued in a Viennese dialect, "this is what we call repressed hostility. You secretly want to kill your roommate. Or something."

Somebody was banging on the door. She opened it to Fu and a Neanderthal wearing the uniform of a 3rd class boatswain's mate in the U. S. Navy.

"This is Pig Bodine," said Fu.

"Isn't it a small world," said Pig Bodine. "I'm looking for Pappy Hod's woman."

"So am I," said Rachel. "And what are you, playing Cupid for Pappy? Paola doesn't want to see him again."

Pig tossed his white hat at the desk lamp, scoring a ringer. "Beer in the icebox?" said Fu, all smiles. Rachel was used to being barged in on at all hours by members of the Crew and their random acquaintances. "MYSAH," she said, which is Crew talk for Make Yourself At Home.

"Pappy is over in the Med," said Pig, lying on the couch. He was short enough so that his feet didn't hang over the edge. He let one thick furry arm fall to the floor with a dull thump, which Rachel suspected would have been more like a splat if there hadn't been a rug there. "We are on the same ship."

"How come then you aren't over in the Med, wherever that is," said Rachel. She knew he meant Mediterranean but felt hostile.

"I am AWOL," said Pig. He closed his eyes. Fu came back with beer. "Oh boy, oh boy, yeah," said Pig. "I smell Ballantine."

"Pig has this remarkably acute nose," Fu said, putting an opened quart of Ballantine into Pig's fist, which looked like a badger with pituitary trouble. "I have never known him to guess wrong."

"How did you two get together," Rachel asked, seating herself on the floor. Pig, eyes still closed, was slobbering beer. It ran out of the corners of his mouth, formed brief pools in the bushy caverns of his ears and soaked on into the sofa.

"If you had been down the Spoon at all you would know," Fu said. He referred to the Rusty Spoon, a bar on the western fringes of Greenwich Village where, legend has it, a noted and colorful poet of the '20's drank himself to death. Ever since then it has had kind of a rep among groups like The Whole Sick Crew. "Pig has made a big hit there."

"I'll bet Pig is the darling of the Rusty Spoon," said Rachel, acid, "considering that sense of smell he has, and how he can tell what brand of beer it is, and all."

Pig removed the bottle from his mouth, where it had been somehow, miraculously, balanced. "Glug," he said. "Ahh."

Rachel smiled. "Perhaps your friend would like to hear some music," she said. She reached over and turned on the FM, full volume. She screwed the dial over to a hillbilly station. On came a heartbroken violin, guitar, banjo and vocalist:

> Last night I went and raced with the Highway Patrol
> But that Pontiac done had more guts than mine.
> And so I wrapped my tail around a telephone pole
> And now my baby she just sits a cryin'.
> I'm up in heaven, darlin', now don't you cry;
> Ain't no reason why you should be blue.
> Just go on out and race a cop in Daddy's old Ford
> And you can join me up in heaven, too.

Pig's right foot had begun to wobble, roughly in time with the music. Soon his stomach, where the beer bottle was now balanced, started to move up and down to the same rhythm. Fu watched Rachel, puzzled.

"There's nothing I love," said Pig and paused. Rachel did not doubt this. "Than good shitkicking music."

"Oh," she shouted, not wanting to get on the subject but too nosy, she was aware, to leave it: "I suppose you and Pappy Hod used to go out on liberty and have all sorts of fun kicking shit."

"We kicked a few jarheads," Pig bellowed over the music, "which is about the same thing. Where did you say Polly was?"

"I didn't. Your interest in her is purely Platonic, is that it."

"Wha," said Pig.

"No screwing," Fu explained.

"I wouldn't do that to anybody but an officer," Pig said. "I have a code. All I want to see her for is Pappy told me before they got under way I should look her up if I was ever in New York."

"Well, I don't know where she is," Rachel yelled. "I wish I did," she said, quieter. For a minute or so they heard about a soldier who was overseas in Korea fighting for the red, white and blue and one day his sweetheart Belinda Sue (to rhyme with blue) up and run off with an itinerant propeller salesman. Said for that lonely GI. Abruptly Pig swung his head toward Rachel, opened his eyes and said, "What do you think of Sartre's thesis that we are all impersonating an identity?"

Which did not surprise her: after all he had been hanging around the Spoon. For the next hour they talked proper nouns. The hillbilly station continued full blast. Rachel opened a quart of beer for herself and things soon grew convivial. Fu even became gleeful enough to tell one of a bottomless repertoire of Chinese jokes, which went:

"The vagrant minstrel Ling, having insinuated himself into the confidence of a great and influential mandarin, made off one night with a thousand gold yuan and a priceless jade lion, a theft which so unhinged his former employer that in one night the old man's hair turned snow white, and to the end of his life he did little more than sit on the dusty floor of his chamber, plucking listlessly at a p'ip'a and chanting, 'Was that not a curious minstrel?' "

At half past one the phone rang. It was Stencil.

"Stencil's just been shot at," he said.

Private eye, indeed. "Are you all right, where are you." He gave her the address, in the east 80's. "Sit down and wait," she said. "We'll come get you."

"He can't sit down, you know." He hung up.

"Come," she said, grabbing her coat. "Fun, excitement, thrills. Stencil has just been wounded, tracking down a lead."

Fu whistled, giggled. "Those leads are beginning to fight back."

Stencil had called from a Hungarian coffee shop on York Avenue known as Hungarian Coffee Shop. At this hour, the only customers were two elderly ladies and a cop off duty. The woman behind the pastry counter was all tomato cheeks and smiles, looking like the type who gave extra portions to poor growing boys and mothered bums with free refills on coffee, though it was a neighborhood of rich kids and bums who were only accidental there and knew it and so "moved on" quickly.

Stencil was in an embarrassing and possibly dangerous

position. A few pellets from the first shotgun blast (he'd dodged the second by an adroit flop in the sewage) had ricocheted into his left buttock. He wasn't especially anxious to sit down. He'd stowed the waterproof suit and mask near a walkway abutment on East River Drive; combed his hair and straightened his clothing by mercury light in a nearby rain-puddle. He wondered how presentable he looked. Not a good job, this policeman being here.

Stencil left the phone booth and edged his right buttock gingerly onto a stool at the counter, trying not to wince, hoping his middle-aged appearance would account for any creakiness he showed. He asked for a cup of coffee, lit a cigarette and noticed that his hand wasn't shaking. The match flame burned pure, conical, unwavering. Stencil, you're a cool one, he told himself, but God: how did they get on to you?

That was the worst part of it. He and Zeitsuss had met only by accident. Stencil had been on the way over to Rachel's place. As he crossed Columbus Avenue he noticed a few ragged files of workmen lined up on the sidewalk opposite and being harangued by Zeitsuss. Any organized body fascinated him, especially irregulars. These looked like revolutionaries.

He crossed the street. The group broke up and wandered away. Zeitsuss stood watching them for a moment, then turned and caught sight of Stencil. The light in the east turned the lenses of Zeitsuss's glasses pale and blank. "You're late," Zeitsuss called. So he was, Stencil thought. Years. "See Bung the foreman, that fella there in the plaid shirt." Stencil realized then that he had a three-day stubble and had been sleeping in his clothes for the same length of time. Curious about anything even suggesting overthrow, he approached Zeitsuss, smiling his father's Foreign Service smile. "Not looking for employment," he said.

"You're a Limey," Zeitsuss said. "Last Limey we had wrestled his alligators to death. You boys are all right. Why don't you try it for a day."

Naturally Stencil asked try what, and so the contact was made. Soon they were back in the office Zeitsuss shared with some vaguely-defined estimates group, talking sewers. Somewhere in the Paris dossier, Stencil knew, was recorded an interview with one of the Collecteurs Généraux who worked the main sewer line which ran under Boulevard St. Michel.

119

The fellow, old at the time of the interview but with an amazing memory, recalled seeing a woman who might have been V. on one of the semimonthly Wednesday tours shortly before the outbreak of the Great War. Having been lucky with sewers once, Stencil saw nothing wrong with trying again. They went out to lunch. In the early afternoon it rained, and the conversation got around to sewer stories. A few old-timers drifted in with their own memories. It was only a matter of an hour or so before Veronica was mentioned: a priest's mistress who wanted to become a nun, referred to by her initial in the journal.

Persuasive and charming even in a wrinkled suit, nascent beard, trying not to betray any excitement, Stencil talked his way downstairs. But had found them waiting. And where to go from here? He'd seen all he wanted to see of Fairing's Parish.

Two cups of coffee later the cop left and five minutes after that Rachel, Fu and Pig Bodine showed up. They piled into Fu's Plymouth. Fu suggested they go to the Spoon. Pig was all for it. Rachel, bless her heart, didn't make a scene or ask questions. They got off two blocks from her apartment. Fu peeled out down the Drive. It had started to rain again. All Rachel said on the way back was, "I'll bet your ass is sore." She said it through long eyelashes and a little-girl grin and for ten seconds or so Stencil felt like the alter kocker Rachel may have thought he was.

chapter six

*In which Profane returns
to street
level*

V

Women had always happened to Profane the schlemihl like accidents: broken shoelaces, dropped dishes, pins in new shirts. Fina was no exception. Profane had figured at first that he was only the disembodied object of a corporal work of mercy. That, in the company of innumerable small and wounded animals, bums on the street, near-dying and lost to God, he was only another means to grace or indulgence for Fina.

But as usual he was wrong. His first indication came with the cheerless celebration Angel and Geronimo staged following his first eight hours of alligator hunting. They had all been on a night shift, and got back to the Mendozas around 5 A.M. "Put on a suit," said Angel.

"I don't have a suit," Profane said.

They gave him one of Angel's. It was too small and he felt ridiculous. "All I want to do," he said, "really, is sleep."

"Sleep in the daytime," Geronimo said, "ho-ho. You crazy, man. We are going out after some coño."

Fina came in all warm and sleepy-eyed; heard they were holding a party, wanted to tag along. She worked 8 to 4:30 as a secretary but she had sick leave coming. Angel got all embarrassed. This sort of put his sister in the class of coño. Geronimo suggested calling up Dolores and Pilar,

121

two girls they knew. Girls are different from coño. Angel brightened.

The six of them started at an after-hours club up near 125th Street, drinking Gallo wine with ice in it. A small group, vibes and rhythm, played listlessly in one corner. These musicians had been to high school with Angel, Fina and Geronimo. During the breaks they came over and sat at the table. They were drunk and threw pieces of ice at each other. Everybody talked in Spanish and Profane responded in what Italo-American he'd heard around the house as a kid. There was about 10 per cent communication but nobody cared: Profane was only guest of honor.

Soon Fina's eyes changed from sleepy to shiny from wine, and she talked less and spent more of her time smiling at Profane. This made him uncomfortable. It turned out Delgado the vibes player was going to be married the next day and having second thoughts. A violent and pointless argument developed about marriage, pro and con. While everybody else was screaming, Fina leaned toward Profane till their foreheads touched and whispered, "Benito," her breath light and acid with wine.

"Josephine," he nodded, pleasant. He was getting a headache. She continued to lean against his head until the next set, when Geronimo grabbed her and they went off to dance. Dolores, fat and amiable, asked Profane to dance. "Non posso ballare," he said. "No puedo bailar," she corrected him and yanked him to his feet. The world became filled with the sounds of inanimate calluses slapping inanimate goatskin, felt hitting metal, sticks knocking together. Of course, he couldn't dance. His shoes kept getting in the way. Dolores, halfway across the room, didn't notice. Commotion broke out at the door and half a dozen teenagers wearing Playboy jackets invaded. The music bonged and clattered on. Profane kicked off his shoes—old black loafers of Geronimo's —and concentrated on dancing in his socks. After awhile Dolores was there again and five seconds later a spike heel came down square in the middle of his foot. He was too tired to yell. He limped off to a table in the corner, crawled under it and went to sleep. The next thing he knew there was sunlight in his eyes. They were carrying him down Amsterdam Avenue like pallbearers, all chanting, "Mierda. Mierda. Mierda . . ."

He lost count of all the bars they visited. He became

drunk. His worst memory was of being alone with Fina somewhere in a telephone booth. They were discussing love. He couldn't remember what he'd said. The only other thing he remembered between then and the time he woke up—in Union Square at sundown, blindfolded by a raging hangover and covered by a comforter of chilly pigeons who looked like vultures—was some sort of unpleasantness with the police after Angel and Geronimo had tried to smuggle parts of a toilet under their coats out of the men's room in a bar on Second Avenue.

In the next few days Profane came to tally his time in reverse or schlemihl's light: time on the job as escape, time exposed to any possibility of getting involved with Fina as assbreaking, wageless labor.

What had he said in that phone booth? The question met him at the end of every shift, day, night or swing, like an evil fog that hovered over whatever manhole he happened to climb out of. Nearly that whole day of slewfooting drunk under February's sun was a blank. He was not about to ask Fina what had happened. There grew a mutual embarrassment between them, as if they'd been to bed after all.

"Benito," she said one night, "how come we never talk."

"Wha," said Profane, who was watching a Randolph Scott movie on television. "Wha. I talk to you."

"Sure. Nice dress. How about more coffee. I got me another cocodrilo today. You know what I mean."

He knew what she meant. Now here was Randolph Scott: cool, imperturbable, keeping his trap shut and only talking when he had to—and then saying the right things and not running off haphazard and inefficient at the mouth—and here on the other side of the phosphor screen was Profane, who knew that one wrong word would put him closer than he cared to be to street level, and whose vocabulary it seemed was made up of nothing but wrong words.

"Why don't we go to a movie or something," she said.

"This here," he answered, "is a good movie. Randolph Scott is this U.S. marshal and that sheriff, there he goes now, is getting paid off by the gang and all he does all day long is play fan-tan with a widow who lives up the hill."

She withdrew after a while, sad and pouting.

Why? Why did she have to behave like he was a human being. Why couldn't he be just an object of mercy. What did Fina have to go pushing it for? What did she want—

123

which was a stupid question. She was a restless girl, this Josephine: warm and viscous-moving, ready to come in a flying machine or anyplace else.

But curious, he decided to ask Angel.

"How do I know," Angel said. "It's her business. She don't like anybody in the office. They are all maricón, she says. Except for Mr. Winsome the boss, but he's married so he's out."

"What does she want to be," Profane said, "a career girl? What does your mother think?"

"My mother thinks everybody should get married: me, Fina, Geronimo. She'll be after your ass soon. Fina doesn't want anybody. You, Geronimo, the Playboys. She doesn't want. Nobody knows what she wants."

"Playboys," Profane said. "Wha."

It came out then that Fina was spiritual leader or Den Mother of this youth gang. She had learned in school about a saint, called Joan of Arc, who went around doing the same thing for armies who were more or less chicken and no good in a rumble. The Playboys, Angel felt, were pretty much the same way.

Profane knew better than to ask whether she was giving them sexual comfort too. He didn't have to ask. He knew this was another work of mercy. The mother to the troops bit, he guessed—not knowing anything about women—was a harmless way to be what maybe every girl wants to be, a camp follower. With the advantage that here she was not a follower but a leader. How many in the Playboys? Nobody knew, Angel said. Maybe hundreds. They all were crazy for Fina, in a spiritual way. In return she had to put out nothing but charity and comfort, which she was only too glad to do, punchy with grace already.

The Playboys were a strangely exhausted group. Mercenaries, many of them lived in Fina's neighborhood; but unlike other gangs they had no turf of their own. They were spread out all over the city; having no common geographical or cultural ground, they put their arsenal and street-fighting prowess at the disposal of any interested party who might be considering a rumble. The Youth Board had never taken a count on them: they were everywhere, but as Angel had mentioned, chicken. The main advantage in having them on your side was psychological. They cultivated a carefully sinister image: coal-black velvet jackets with the

124

clan name discreetly lettered small and bloody on the back; faces pale and soulless as the other side of the night (and you felt that was where they lived: for they would appear suddenly across the street from you and keep pace for a while, and then vanish again as if back behind some invisible curtain); all of them affecting prowling walks, hungry eyes, feral mouths.

Profane didn't meet them in any social way until the Feast of San' Ercole dei Rinoceronti, which comes on the Ides of March, and is celebrated downtown in the neighborhood called Little Italy. High over all Mulberry Street that night soared arches of light bulbs, arranged in receding sets of whorls, each spanning the street, shining clear to the horizon because the air was so windless. Under the lights were jury-rigged stalls for penny-toss, bingo, pick up the plastic duck and win a prize. Every few steps were stands for zeppole, beer, sausage-pepper sandwiches. Behind it all was music from two bandstands, one at the downtown end of the street and one halfway along. Popular songs, operas. Not too loud in the cold night: as if confined only to the area below the lights. Chinese and Italian residents sat out on the stoops as if it were summer, watching the crowds, the lights, the smoke from the zeppole stands which rose lazy and unturbulent up toward the lights but disappeared before it reached them.

Profane, Angel and Geronimo were out prowling for coño. It was Thursday night, tomorrow—according to the nimble calculations of Geronimo—they were working not for Zeitsuss but for the U. S. Government, since Friday is one-fifth of the week and the government takes one-fifth of your check for withholding tax. The beauty of Geronimo's scheme was that it didn't have to be Friday but could be any day—or days—in the week depressing enough to make you feel it would be a breach of loyalty if the time were dedicated to good old Zeitsuss. Profane had got into this way of thinking, and along with parties in the daytime and a rotating shift system devised by Bung the foreman whereby you didn't know till the day before which hours you would be working the next, it put him on a weird calendar which was not ruled off into neat squares at all but more into a mosaic of tilted street-surfaces that changed position according to sunlight, streetlight, moonlight, nightlight. . . .

He wasn't comfortable in this street. The people mobbing the pavement between the stalls seemed no more logical than the objects in his dream. "They don't have faces," he said to Angel.

"A lot of nice asses, though," Angel said.

"Look, look," said Geronimo. Three jailbait, all lipstick and shiny-machined breast- and buttock-surfaces, stood in front of the wheel of Fortune, twitching and hollow-eyed.

"Benito, you speak guinea. Go tell them how about a little."

Behind them the band was playing *Madame Butterfly.* Non-professional, non-rehearsed.

"It isn't like it was a foreign country," Profane said.

"Geronimo is a tourist," Angel said. "He wants to go down to San Juan and live in the Caribe Hilton and ride around the city looking at puertorriqueños."

They'd been moseying slow, casing the jailbait at the wheel. Profane's foot came down on an empty beer can. He started to roll. Angel and Geronimo, flanking him, caught him by the arms about halfway down. The girls had turned around and were giggling, the eyes mirthless, ringed in shadow.

Angel waved. "He goes weak in the knees," Geronimo purred, "when he sees beautiful girls."

The giggling got louder. Someplace else the American ensign and the geisha would be singing in Italian to the music behind them; and how was that for a tourist's confusion of tongues? The girls moved away and the three fell into step beside them. They bought beer and took over an unoccupied stoop.

"Benny here talks guinea," said Angel. "Say something in guinea, hey."

"Sfacim," Profane said. The girls got all shocked.

"Your friend is a nasty mouth," one of them said.

"I don't want to sit with any nasty mouth," said the girl sitting next to Profane. She got up, flipped her butt and moved down into the street, where she stood hipshot and stared at Profane out of her dark eyeholes.

"That's his name," Geronimo said, "is all. And I am Peter O'Leary and this here is Chain Ferguson." Peter O'Leary being an old school chum who was now at a seminary upstate studying to be a priest. He'd been so clean-living in high school that Geronimo and his friends always used him for an alias whenever there might be any trouble. God knew how many had been deflowered, hustled off of for beer or slugged in his name. Chain Ferguson was the hero of a western they'd been watching on the Mendoza TV the night before.

"Benny Sfacim is really your name?" said the one in the street.

"Sfacimento." In Italian it meant destruction or decay. "You didn't let me finish."

"That's all right then," she said. "That isn't bad at all." Bet your shiny, twitching ass, he thought, all unhappy. The other could knock her up higher than those arches of light. She couldn't be more than fourteen but she knew already that men are drifters. Good for her. Bedmates and all the sfacim they have yet to get rid of drift on, and if some stays with her and swells into a little drifter who'll go someday too, why she wouldn't like that too much, he reckoned. He wasn't angry with her. He looked that thought at her, but who knew what went on in those eyes? They seemed to absorb all the light in the street: from flames beneath sausage grills, from the bridges of light bulbs, windows of neighborhood apartments, glowing ends of De Nobili cigars, flashing gold and silver of instruments on the bandstand, even light from the eyes of what innocent there were among the tourists:

The eyes of a New York woman [he started to sing]
Are the twilit side of the moon,
Nobody knows what goes on back there
Where it's always late afternoon.

Under the lights of Broadway,
Far from the lights of home,
With a smile as sweet as a candy cane
And a heart all plated with chrome.

Do they ever see the wandering bums
And the boys with no place to go,
And the drifter who cried for an ugly girl
That he left in Buffalo?

Dead as the leaves in Union Square,
Dead as the graveyard sea,
The eyes of a New York woman
Are never going to cry for me.
Are never going to cry for me.

The girl on the sidewalk twitched. "It doesn't have any beat." It was a song of the Great Depression. They were singing it in 1932, the year Profane was born. He didn't know where he'd heard it. If it had a beat it was the beat of beans thumping into an old bucket someplace down in Jersey. Some WPA pick against the pavement, some bum-laden freight car on a downgrade hitting the gaps between the rails every 39 feet. She'd have been born in 1942. Wars don't have my beat. They're all noise.

Zeppole man across the street began to sing. Angel and Geronimo started to sing. The band across the street acquired an Italian tenor from the neighborhood:

> Non dimenticar, che t'i'ho voluto tanto bene,
> Ho saputo amar; non dimenticar . . .

And the cold street seemed all at once to've bloomed into singing. He wanted to take the girl by the fingers, lead her to someplace out of the wind, anyplace warm, pivot her back on those poor ballbearing heels and show her his name was Sfacim after all. It was a desire he got, off and on, to be cruel and feel at the same time sorrow so big it filled him, leaked out his eyes and the holes in his shoes to make one big pool of human sorrow on the street, which had everything spilled on it from beer to blood, but very little compassion. "I'm Lucille," the girl said to Profane. The other two introduced themselves, Lucille came back up the stoop to sit next to Profane, Geronimo went off for more beer. Angel continued to sing. "What do you guys do," Lucille said.

I tell tall stories to girls I want to screw, Profane thought. He scratched his armpit. "Kill alligators," he said.

"Wha."

He told her about the alligators; Angel, who had a fertile imagination too, added detail, color. Together on the stoop they hammered together a myth. Because it wasn't born from fear of thunder, dreams, astonishment at how the crops kept dying after harvest and coming up again every spring, or anything else very permanent, only a temporary interest, a spur-of-the-moment tumescence, it was a myth rickety and transient as the bandstands and the sausage-pepper of Mulberry Street.

Geronimo came back with beer. They sat and drank beer

and watched people and told sewer stories. Every once in a while the girls would want to sing. Soon enough they became kittenish. Lucille jumped up and pranced away. "Catch me," she said.

"Oh God," said Profane.

"You have to chase her," said one of her friends. Angel and Geronimo were laughing.

"I have to wha," said Profane. The other two girls, annoyed that Angel and Geronimo were laughing, arose and went running off after Lucille.

"Chase them?" Geronimo said.

Angel belched. "Sweat out some of this beer." They got off the stoop unsteadily and fell, side by side, into a little jog-trot. "Where'd they go," Profane said.

"Over there." It seemed after a while they were knocking people over. Somebody swung a punch at Geronimo and missed. They dived under an empty stand, single file, and found themselves out on the sidewalk. The girls were loping along, up ahead. Geronimo was breathing hard. They followed the girls, who cut off on a side street. By the time they got around the corner there wasn't girl one to be seen. There followed a confused quarter-hour of wandering along the streets bordering Mulberry, looking under parked cars, behind telephone poles, in back of stoops.

"Nobody here," said Angel.

There was music on Mott Street. Coming out of a basement. They investigated. A sign outside said SOCIAL CLUB. BEER. DANCING. They went down, opened a door and there sure enough was a small beer bar set up in one corner, a jukebox in another and fifteen or twenty curious-looking juvenile delinquents. The boys wore Ivy League suits, the girls wore cocktail dresses. There was rock 'n' roll on the jukebox. The greasy heads and cantilever brassieres were still there, but the atmosphere was refined, like a country club dance.

The three of them just stood. Profane saw Lucille after a while bopping in the middle of the floor with somebody who looked like a chairman of the board of some delinquent's corporation. Over his shoulder she stuck out her tongue at Profane, who looked away. "I don't like it," he heard somebody say, "fuzzwise. Why don't we send it through Central Park and see if anybody rapes it."

He happened to glance off to the left. There was a coat

129

room. Hanging on a row of hooks, neat and uniform, padded shoulders falling symmetrical either side of the hooks, were two dozen black velvet jackets with red lettering on the back. Ding dang, thought Profane: Playboy country.

Angel and Geronimo had been looking the same way. "Do you think we should maybe," Angel wondered. Lucille was beckoning to Profane from a doorway across the dance floor.

"Wait a minute," he said. He weaved between the couples on the floor. Nobody noticed him.

"What took you so long?" She had him by the hand. It was dark in the room. He walked into a pool table. "Here," she whispered. She was lying spread on the green felt. Corner pockets, side pockets, and Lucille. "There are some funny things I could say," he began.

"They've all been said," she whispered. In the dim light from the doorway, her fringed eyes seemed part of the felt. It was as if he were looking through her face to the surface of the table. Skirt raised, mouth open, teeth all white, sharp, ready to sink into whatever soft part of him got that close, oh she would surely haunt him. He unzipped his fly and started to climb up on the pool table.

There was a sudden scream from the next room, somebody knocked over the jukebox, the lights went out. "Wha," she said, sitting up.

"Rumble?" Profane said. She came flying off the table, knocked him over. He lay on the floor, his head against a cue rack. Her sudden movement dislodged an avalanche of pool balls on his stomach. "Dear God," he said, covering his head. Her high heels tapped away, fading with distance, over the empty dance floor. He opened his eyes. A pool ball lay even with his eyes. All he could see was a white circle, and this black 8 inside it. He started to laugh. Outside somewhere he thought he heard Angel yelling for help. Profane creaked to his feet, zipped his fly up again, blundered out through the darkness. He got out to the street after tripping over two folding chairs and the cord to the jukebox.

Crouched behind the brownstone balusters of the front stoop he saw a great mob of Playboys milling around in the street. Girls were sitting on the stoop and lining the sidewalk, cheering. In the middle of the street Lucille's late partner the board chairman was going round and round with a huge Negro in a jacket that read BOP KINGS. A few other Bop Kings were mixing it up with the Playboys at the fringes of the crowd. Jurisdictional dispute, Profane figured. He couldn't see either Angel or Geronimo. "Somebody is going to get burned," said a girl who sat almost directly above him on the steps.

Like tinsel suddenly tossed on a Christmas tree, the merry twinkling of switchblades, tire irons and filed-down garrison belt buckles appeared among the crowd in the street. The girls on the stoop drew breath in concert through bared teeth. They watched eagerly, as if each had kicked in on a pool for who'd draw first blood.

It never happened, whatever they were waiting for: not tonight. Out of nowhere Fina, St. Fina of the Playboys, came walking her sexy walk, in among fangs, talons, tusks. The air turned summer-mild, a boys' choir on a brilliant mauve cloud came floating over from the direction of Canal Street singing O Salutaris Hostia; the board chairman and the Bop King clasped arms in token of friendship as their followers stacked arms and embraced; and Fina was borne up by a swarm of pneumatically fat, darling cherubs, to hover over the sudden peace she'd created, beaming, serene.

Profane gaped, snuffled, and slunk away. For the next week or so he pondered on Fina and the Playboys and presently began to worry in earnest. There was nothing so special about the gang, punks are punks. He was sure any love between her and the Playboys was for the moment Christian, unworldly and proper. But how long was that going to go on? How long could Fina herself hold out? The minute her horny boys caught a glimpse of the wanton behind the saint, the black lace slip beneath the surplice, Fina could find herself on the receiving end of a gang bang, having in a way asked for it. She was overdue now.

One evening he came into the bathroom, mattress slung over his back. He'd been watching an ancient Tom Mix movie on television. Fina was lying in the bathtub, seductive. No water, no clothes—just Fina.

"Now look," he said.

"Benny, I'm cherry. I want it to be you." She said it defiantly. For a minute it seemed plausible. After all, if it

wasn't him it might be that whole godforsaken wolf pack.
He glanced at himself in the mirror. Fat. Pig-pouches
around the eyes. Why did she want it to be him?

"Why me," he said. "You save it for the guy you marry."

"Who wants to get married," she said.

"Look, what is Sister Maria Annunziata going to think.
Here you been doing all these nice things for me, for those
unfortunate delinquents down the street. You want to get
that all scratched off the books?" Who'd have thought
Profane would ever be arguing like this? Her eyes burned,
she twisted slow and sexy, all those tawny surfaces quivering
like quicksand.

"No," said Profane. "Now hop out of there, I want to
go to sleep. And don't go yelling rape to your brother. He
believes in his sister shouldn't do any jazzing around but
he knows you better."

She climbed out of the bathtub and put a robe around
her. "I'm sorry," she said. He threw the mattress in the tub,
threw himself on top of it and lit a cigarette. She turned
off the light and shut the door behind her.

II

Profane's worries about Fina turned real and ugly, soon
enough. Spring came: quiet, unspectacular and after many
false starts: hailstorms and high winds dovetailed with days
of unwintry peace. The alligators living in the sewers had
dwindled to a handful. Zeitsuss found himself with more
hunters than he needed, so Profane, Angel and Geronimo
started working part-time.

More and more Profane was coming to feel a stranger to
the world downstairs. It had probably happened as imperceptibly as the fall-off in the alligator population; but
somehow it began to look like he was losing contact with a
circle of friends. What am I, he yelled at himself, a St.
Francis for alligators? I don't talk to them, I don't even
like them. I shoot them.

Your ass, answered his devil's advocate. How many times
have they come waddling up to you out of the darkness,
like friends, looking for you. Did it ever occur to you they
want to be shot?

He thought back to the one he'd chased solo almost to
the East River, through Fairing's Parish. It had lagged, let

him catch up. Had been looking for it. It occurred to him that somewhere—when he was drunk, too horny to think straight, tired—he'd signed a contract above the paw-prints of what were now alligator ghosts. Almost as if there had been this agreement, a covenant, Profane giving death, the alligators giving him employment: tit for tat. He needed them and if they needed him at all it was because in some prehistoric circuit of the alligator brain they knew that as babies they'd been only another consumer—object, along with the wallets and pocketbooks of what might have been parents or kin, and all the junk of the world's Macy's. And the soul's passage down the toilet and into the underworld was only a temporary peace-in-tension, borrowed time till they would have to return to being falsely animated kids' toys. Of course they wouldn't like it. Would want to go back to what they'd been; and the most perfect shape of that was dead—what else?—to be gnawed into exquisite rococo by rat-artisans, eroded to an antique bone-finish by the holy water of the Parish, tinted to phosphorescence by whatever had made that one alligator's sepulchre so bright that night.

When he went down for his now four hours a day he talked to them sometimes. It annoyed his partners. He had a close call one night when a gator turned and attacked. The tail caught the flashlight man a glancing blow off his left leg. Profane yelled at him to get out of the way and pumped all five rounds in a cascade of re-echoing blasts, square in the alligator's teeth. "It's all right," his partner said. "I can walk on it." Profane wasn't listening. He was standing by the headless corpse, watching a steady stream of sewage wash its life blood out to one of the rivers—he'd lost sense of direction. "Baby," he told the corpse, "you didn't play it right. You don't fight back. That's not in the contract." Bung the foreman lectured him once or twice about this talking to alligators, how it set a bad example for the Patrol. Profane said sure, OK, and remembered after that to say what he was coming to believe he had to say under his breath.

Finally, one night in mid-April, he admitted to himself what he'd been trying for a week not to think about: that he and the Patrol as functioning units of the Sewer Department had about had it.

Fina had been aware that there weren't many alligators

133

left and the three of them would soon be jobless. She came upon Profane one evening by the TV set. He was watching a rerun of *The Great Train Robbery*.

"Benito," she said, "you ought to start looking around for another job."

Profane agreed. She told him her boss, Winsome of Outlandish Records, was looking for a clerk and she could get him an interview.

"Me," Profane said, "I'm not a clerk. I'm not smart enough and I don't go for that inside work too much." She told him people stupider than he worked as clerks. She said he'd have a chance to move up, make something of himself.

A schlemihl is a schlemihl. What can you "make" out of one? What can one "make" out of himself? You reach a point, and Profane knew he'd reached it, where you know how much you can and cannot do. But every now and again he got attacks of acute optimism. "I will give it a try," he told her, "and thanks." She was grace-happy—here he had kicked her out of the bathtub and now she was turning the other cheek. He began to get lewd thoughts.

Next day she called up. Angel and Geronimo were on day shift, Profane was off till Friday. He lay on the floor playing pinochle with Kook, who was on the hook from school.

"Find a suit," she said. "One o'clock is your interview."

"Wha," said Profane. He'd grown fatter after these weeks of Mrs. Mendoza's cooking. Angel's suit didn't fit him any more. "Borrow one of my father's," she said, and hung up.

Old Mendoza didn't mind. The biggest suit in the closet was a George Raft model, circa mid-'30's, double-breasted, dark blue serge, padded shoulders. He put it on and borrowed a pair of shoes from Angel. On the way downtown on the subway he decided that we suffer from great temporal homesickness for the decade we were born in. Because he felt now as if he were living in some private depression days: the suit, the job with the city that would not exist after two weeks more at the most. All around him people in new suits, millions of inanimate objects being produced brand-new every week, new cars in the streets, houses going up by the thousands all over the suburbs he had left months ago. Where was the depression? In the sphere of Benny Profane's guts and in the sphere of his skull, concealed optimistically by a tight blue serge coat and a schlemihl's hopeful face.

134

The Outlandish office was in the Grand Central area, seventeen floors up. He sat in an anteroom full of tropical hothouse growths while the wind streamed bleak and heat-sucking past the windows. The receptionist gave him an application to fill out. He didn't see Fina.

As he handed the completed form to the girl at the desk, a messenger came through: a Negro wearing an old suede jacket. He dropped a stack of interoffice mail envelopes on the desk and for a second his eyes and Profane's met.

Maybe Profane had seen him under the street or at one of the shapeups. But there was a little half-smile and a kind of half-telepathy and it was as if this messenger had brought a message to Profane too, sheathed to everybody but the two of them in an envelope of eyebeams touching, that said: Who are you trying to kid? Listen to the wind.

He listened to the wind. The messenger left. "Mr. Winsome will see you in a moment," said the receptionist. Profane wandered over to the window and looked down at 42nd Street. It was as if he could see the wind, too. The suit felt wrong on him. Maybe it was doing nothing after all to conceal this curious depression which showed up in no stock market or year-end report. "Hey, where are you going," said the receptionist. "Changed my mind," Profane told her. Out in the hall and going down in the elevator, in the lobby and in the street he looked for the messenger, but couldn't find him. He unbuttoned the jacket of old Mendoza's suit and shuffled along 42nd Street, head down, straight into the wind.

Friday at the shapeup Zeitsuss, almost crying, gave them the word. From now on, only two days a week operation, only five teams for some mopping up out in Brooklyn. On the way home that evening Profane, Angel and Geronimo stopped off at a neighborhood bar on Broadway.

They stayed till near 9:30 or 10, when a few of the girls wandered in. This was on Broadway in the 80's, which is not the Broadway of Show Biz, or even a broken heart for every light on it. Uptown was a bleak district with no identity, where a heart never does anything so violent or final as break: merely gets increased tensile, compressive, shear loads piled on it bit by bit every day till eventually these and its own shudderings fatigue it.

The first wave of girls came in to get change for the evening's clients. They weren't pretty and the bartender always had a word for them. Some would be back in again near closing time to have a nightcap, whether there'd been any business or not. If they did have a customer along—usually one of the small gangsters around the neighborhood—the bartender would be as attentive and cordial as if they were young lovers, which in a way they were. And if a girl came in without having found any business all night the bartender would give her coffee with a big shot of brandy and say something about how it was raining or too cold, and not much good, he supposed, for customers. She'd usually have a last try at whoever was in the place.

Profane, Angel and Geronimo left after talking with the girls and having a few rounds at the bowling machine. Coming out they met Mrs. Mendoza.

"You seen your sister?" she asked Angel. "She was going to come help me shop right after work. She never did anything like this before, Angelito, I'm worried."

Kook came running up. "Dolores says she's out with the Playboys but she doesn't know where. Fina just called up and Dolores says she sounded funny." Mrs. Mendoza grabbed him by the head and asked where from this phone call, and Kook said he'd told her already, nobody knew. Profane looked toward Angel and caught Angel looking at him. When Mrs. Mendoza was gone, Angel said, "I don't like to think about it, my own sister, but if one of those little pingas tries anything, man . . ."

Profane didn't say he'd been thinking the same thing. Angel was upset enough already. But he knew Profane was thinking about a gang bang too. They both knew Fina. "We ought to find her," he said.

"They're all over the city," Geronimo said. "I know a couple of their hangouts." They decided to start at the Mott Street clubhouse. Till midnight they took subways all over the city, finding only empty clubhouses or locked doors. But as they were wandering along Amsterdam in the 60's, they heard noise around the corner.

"Jesus Christ," Geronimo said. A full-scale rumble was on. A few guns in evidence but mostly knives, lengths of pipe, garrison belts. The three skirted along the side of the street where cars were parked, and found somebody in a tweed suit hiding behind a new Lincoln and fiddling with the controls of a tape recorder. A sound man was up in a nearby tree, dangling microphones. The night had become cold and windy.

"Howdy," said the tweed suit. "My name is Winsome."

"My sister's boss," Angel whispered. Profane heard a scream up the street which might have been Fina. He started running. There was shooting and a lot of yelling. Five Bop Kings came running out of an alley ten feet ahead, into the street. Angel and Geronimo were right behind Profane. Somebody had parked a car in the middle of the street with WLIB on the radio, turned up to top volume. Close at hand they heard a belt whiz through the air and a scream of pain: but a big tree's black shadow hid whatever was happening.

They cased the street for a clubhouse. Soon they found PB and an arrow chalked on the sidewalk, the arrow pointing in toward a brownstone. They ran up the steps and saw PB chalked on the door. The door wouldn't open. Angel kicked at it a couple of times and the lock broke. Behind them the street was chaos. A few bodies lay prostrate near the sidewalk. Angel ran down the hall, Profane and Geronimo behind him. Police sirens from uptown and crosstown started to converge on the rumble.

Angel opened a door at the end of the hall and for half a second Profane saw Fina through it lying on an old army cot, naked, hair in disarray, smiling. Her eyes had become hollowed as Lucille's, that night on the pool table. Angel turned and showed all his teeth. "Don't come in," he said, "wait." The door closed behind him and soon they heard him hitting her.

Angel might have been satisfied only with her life, Profane didn't know how deep the code ran. He couldn't go in and stop it; didn't know if he wanted to. The police sirens had grown to a crescendo and suddenly cut off. Rumble was over. More than that, he suspected, was over. He said good night to Geronimo and left the brownstone, didn't turn his head to see what was happening behind him in the street.

He wouldn't go back to Mendozas', he figured. There was no more work under the street. What peace there had been was over. He had to come back to the surface, the dream-street. Soon he found a subway station, twenty minutes later he was downtown looking for a cheap mattress.

chapter seven

*She hangs on the
western
wall*

V

Dudley Eigenvalue, D.D.S., browsed among treasures in his Park Avenue office/residence. Mounted on black velvet in a locked mahogany case, showpiece of the office, was a set of false dentures, each tooth a different precious metal. The upper right canine was pure titanium and for Eigenvalue the focal point of the set. He had seen the original sponge at a foundry near Colorado Springs a year ago, having flown there in the private plane of one Clayton ("Bloody") Chiclitz. Chiclitz of Yoyodyne, one of the biggest defense contractors on the east coast, with subsidiaries all over the country. He and Eigenvalue were part of the same Circle. That was what the enthusiast, Stencil, said. And believed.

For those who keep an eye on such things, bright little flags had begun to appear toward the end of Eisenhower's first term, fluttering bravely in history's gray turbulence, signaling that a new and unlikely profession was gaining moral ascendancy. Back around the turn of the century, psychoanalysis had usurped from the priesthood the role of father-confessor. Now, it seemed, the analyst in his turn was about to be deposed by, of all people, the dentist.

It appeared actually to have been little more than a change in nomenclature. Appointments became sessions, profound statements about oneself came to be prefaced by "My dentist says . . ." Psychodontia, like its predecessors, developed a jargon: you called neurosis "malocclusion," oral, anal and genital stages "deciduous dentition," id "pulp" and superego "enamel."

The pulp is soft and laced with little blood vessels and nerves. The enamel, mostly calcium, is inanimate. These were the it and I psychodontia had to deal with. The hard, lifeless I covered up the warm, pulsing it; protecting and sheltering.

Eigenvalue, enchanted by the titanium's dull spark, brooded on Stencil's fantasy (thinking of it with conscious effort as a distal amalgam: an alloy of the illusory flow and gleam of mercury with the pure truth of gold or silver, filling a breach in the protective enamel, far from the root). *conspiracy*

Cavities in the teeth occur for good reason, Eigenvalue reflected. But even if there are several per tooth, there's no conscious organization there against the life of the pulp, no conspiracy. Yet we have men like Stencil, who must go about grouping the world's random caries into cabals.

Intercom blinked gently. "Mr. Stencil," it said. So. What pretext this time. He'd spent three appointments getting his teeth cleaned. Gracious and flowing, Dr. Eigenvalue entered the private waiting room. Stencil rose to meet him, stammering. "Toothache?" the doctor suggested, solicitous.

"Nothing wrong with the teeth," Stencil got out. "You must talk. You must both drop pretense."

From behind his desk, in the office, Eigenvalue said, "You're a bad detective and a worse spy."

"It isn't espionage," Stencil protested, "but the Situation is intolerable." A term he'd learned from his father. "They're abandoning the Alligator Patrol. Slowly, so as not to attract attention."

"You think you've frightened them?"

"Please." The man was ashen. He produced a pipe and pouch and set about scattering tobacco on the wall-to-wall carpeting.

"You presented the Alligator Patrol to me," said Eigenvalue, "in a humorous light. An interesting conversation piece, while my hygienist was in your mouth. Were you waiting for her hands to tremble? For me to go all pale? Had it been myself and a drill, such a guilt reaction might have been very, very uncomfortable." Stencil had filled the pipe and was lighting it. "You've conceived somewhere the notion that I am intimate with the details of a conspiracy.

139

In a world such as you inhabit, Mr. Stencil, any cluster of phenomena can be a conspiracy. So no doubt your suspicion is correct. But why consult me? Why not the Encyclopaedia Britannica? It knows more than I about any phenomena you should ever have interest in. Unless, of course, you're curious about dentistry." How weak he looked, sitting there. How old was he—fifty-five—and he looked seventy. Whereas Eigenvalue at roughly the same age looked thirty-five. Young as he felt. "Which field?" he asked playfully. "Peridontia, oral surgery, orthodontia? Prosthetics?"

"Suppose it was prosthetics," taking Eigenvalue by surprise. Stencil was building a protective curtain of aromatic pipe smoke, to be inscrutable behind. But his voice had somehow regained a measure of self-possession.

"Come," said Eigenvalue. They entered a rear office, where the museum was. Here were a pair of forceps once handled by Fauchard; a first edition of *The Surgeon Dentist*, Paris, 1728; a chair sat in by patients of Chapin Aaron Harris; a brick from one of the first buildings of the Baltimore College of Dental Surgery. Eigenvalue led Stencil to the mahogany case.

"Whose," said Stencil, looking at the dentures.

"Like Cinderella's prince," Eigenvalue smiled, "I'm still looking for the jaw to fit these."

"And Stencil, possibly. It would be something she'd wear."

"I made them," said Eigenvalue. "Anybody you'd be looking for would never have seen them. Only you, I and a few other privileged have seen them."

"How does Stencil know."

"That I'm telling the truth? Tut, Mr. Stencil."

The false teeth in the case smiled too, twinkling as if in reproach.

Back in the office, Eigenvalue, to see what he could see, inquired: "Who then is V.?"

But the conversational tone didn't take Stencil aback, he didn't look surprised that the dentist knew of his obsession. "Psychodontia has its secrets and so does Stencil," Stencil answered. "But most important, so does V. She's yielded him only the poor skeleton of a dossier. Most of what he has is inference. He doesn't know who she is, nor what she is. He's trying to find out. As a legacy from his father."

The afternoon curled outside, with only a little wind to stir it. Stencil's words seemed to fall insubstantial inside a cube

140

no wider than Eigenvalue's desk. The dentist kept quiet as
Stencil told how his father had come to hear of the girl
V. When he'd finished, Eigenvalue said, "You followed up, of
course. On-the-spot investigation."

"Yes. But found out hardly more than Stencil has told
you." Which was the case. Florence only a few summers ago
had seemed crowded with the same tourists as at the turn
of the century. But V., whoever she was, might have been
swallowed in the airy Renaissance spaces of that city, assumed
into the fabric of any of a thousand Great Paintings, for all
Stencil was able to determine. He had discovered, however,
what was pertinent to his purpose: that she'd been connected, though perhaps only tangentially, with one of those grand
conspiracies or foretastes of Armageddon which seemed
to have captivated all diplomatic sensibilities in the years
preceding the Great War. V. and a conspiracy. Its particular
shape governed only by the surface accidents of history at
the time.

Perhaps history this century, thought Eigenvalue, is rip-
pled with gathers in its fabric such that if we are situated,
as Stencil seemed to be, at the bottom of a fold, it's impossible to determine warp, woof or pattern anywhere else.
By virtue, however, of existing in one gather it is assumed
there are others, compartmented off into sinuous cycles each
of which come to assume greater importance than the weave
itself and destroy any continuity. Thus it is that we are
charmed by the funny-looking automobiles of the '30's, the
curious fashions of the '20's, the peculiar moral habits of
our grandparents. We produce and attend musical comedies
about them and are conned into a false memory, a phony
nostalgia about what they were. We are accordingly lost to
any sense of a continuous tradition. Perhaps if we lived on a
crest, things would be different. We could at least see.

I

In April of 1899 young Evan Godolphin, daft with the spring
and sporting a costume too Esthetic for such a fat boy,
pranced into Florence. Camouflaged by a gorgeous sun-
shower which had burst over the city at three in the afternoon, his face was the color of a freshly-baked pork pie and
as noncommittal. Alighting at the Stazione Centrale he
flagged down an open cab with his umbrella of cerise silk,

141

roared the address of his hotel to a Cook's luggage agent and, with a clumsy entrechat deux and a jolly-ho to no one in particular, leaped in and was driven caroling away down Via dei Panzani. He had come to meet his old father, Captain Hugh, F.R.G.S. and explorer of the Antarctic—at least such was the ostensible reason. He was, however, the sort of ne'er-do-well who needs no reason for anything, ostensible or otherwise. The family called him Evan the Oaf. In return, in his more playful moments, he referred to all other Godolphins as The Establishment. But like his other utterances, there was no rancor here: in his early youth he had looked aghast at Dickens's Fat Boy as a challenge to his faith in all fat boys as innately Nice Fellows, and subsequently worked as hard at contradicting that insult to the breed as he did at being a ne'er-do-well. For despite protests from the Establishment to the contrary, shiftlessness did not come easily to Evan. He was not, though fond of his father, much of a conservative; for as long as he could remember he had labored beneath the shadow of Captain Hugh, a hero of the Empire, resisting any compulsion to glory which the name Godolphin might have implied for himself. But this was a characteristic acquired from the age, and Evan was too nice a fellow not to turn with the century. He had dallied for a while with the idea of getting a commission and going to sea; not to follow in his old father's wake but simply to get away from the Establishment. His adolescent mutterings in times of family stress were all prayerful, exotic syllables: Bahrein, Dar es Salaam, Samarang. But in his second year at Dartmouth, he was expelled for leading a Nihilist group called the League of the Red Sunrise, whose method of hastening the revolution was to hold mad and drunken parties beneath the Commodore's window. Flinging up their collective arms at last in despair, the family exiled him to the Continent, hoping, possibly, that he would stage some prank harmful enough to society to have him put away in a foreign prison.

At Deauville, recuperating after two months of good-natured lechery in Paris, he'd returned to his hotel one evening 17,000 francs to the good and grateful to a bay named Cher Ballon, to find a telegram from Captain Hugh which said: "Hear you were sacked. If you need someone to talk to I am at Piazza della Signoria 5 eighth floor. I should like

142

Vheissu

very much to see you son. Unwise to say too much in telegram. Vheissu. You understand. FATHER."

Vheissu, of course. A summons he couldn't ignore, Vheissu. He understood. Hadn't it been their only nexus for longer than Evan could remember; had it not stood preëminent in his catalogue of outlandish regions where the Establishment held no sway? It was something which, to his knowledge, Evan alone shared with his father, though he himself had stopped believing in the place around the age of sixteen. His first impression on reading the wire—that Captain Hugh was senile at last, or raving, or both—was soon replaced by a more charitable opinion. Perhaps, Evan reasoned, his recent expedition to the South had been too much for the old boy. But on route to Pisa, Evan had finally begun to feel disquieted at the tone of the thing. He'd taken of late to examining everything in print—menus, railway timetables, posted advertisements—for literary merit; he belonged to a generation of young men who no longer called their fathers pater because of an understandable confusion with the author of *The Renaissance*, and was sensitive to things like tone. And this had a je ne sais quoi de sinistre about it which sent pleasurable chills racing along his spinal column. His imagination ran riot. Unwise to say too much in telegram: intimations of a plot, a cabal grand and mysterious: combined with that appeal to their only common possession. Either by itself would have made Evan ashamed: ashamed at hallucinations belonging in a spy thriller, even more painfully ashamed for an attempt at something which should have existed but did not, based only on the sharing long ago of a bedside story. But both, together, were like a parlay of horses, capable of a whole arrived at by some operation more alien than simple addition of parts.

He would see his father. In spite of the heart's vagrancy, the cerise umbrella, the madcap clothes. Was rebellion in his blood? He'd never been troubled enough to wonder. Certainly the League of the Red Sunrise had been no more than a jolly lark; he couldn't yet become serious over politics. But he had a mighty impatience with the older generation, which is almost as good as open rebellion. He became more bored with talk of Empire the further he lumbered upward out of the slough of adolescence; shunned every hint of glory like the sound of a leper's rattle. China, the Sudan, the East Indies, Vheissu had served their purpose: given him a sphere

143

of influence roughly congruent with that of his skull, private colonies of the imagination whose borders were solidly defended against the Establishment's incursions or depredations. He wanted to be left alone, never to "do well" in his own way, and would defend that oaf's integrity to the last lazy heartbeat.

The cab swung left, crossing the tram tracks with two bone-rattling jolts, and then right again into Via dei Vecchietti. Evan shook four fingers in the air and swore at the driver, who smiled absently. A tram came blithering up behind them; drew abreast. Evan turned his head and saw a young girl in dimity blinking huge eyes at him.

"Signorina," he cried, "ah, brava fanciulla, sei tu inglesa?"

She blushed and began to study the embroidery on her parasol. Evan stood up on the cab's seat, postured, winked, began to sing Deh, vieni alla finestra from *Don Giovanni*. Whether or not she understood Italian, the song had a negative effect: she withdrew from the window and hid among a mob of Italians standing in the center aisle. Evan's driver chose this moment to lash the horses into a gallop and swerve across the tracks again, in front of the tram. Evan, still singing, lost his balance and fell halfway over the back of the carriage. He managed to catch hold of the boot's top with one flailing arm and after a deal of graceless floundering to haul himself back in. By this time they were in Via Pecori. He looked back and saw the girl getting out of the tram. He sighed as his cab bounced on past Giotto's Campanile, still wondering if she were English.

II

In front of a wine shop on the Ponte Vecchio sat Signor Mantissa and his accomplice in crime, a seedy-looking Calabrese named Cesare. Both were drinking Broglio wine and feeling unhappy. It had occurred to Cesare sometime during the rain that he was a steamboat. Now that the rain was only a slight drizzle the English tourists were beginning to emerge once more from the shops lining the bridge, and Cesare was announcing his discovery to those who came within earshot. He would emit short blasts across the mouth of the wine bottle to encourage the illusion. "Toot," he would go, "toot. Vaporetto, io."

Signor Mantissa was not paying attention. His five feet

guide book

three rested angular on the folding chair, a body small, well-wrought and somehow precious, as if it were the forgotten creation of any goldsmith—even Cellini—shrouded now in dark serge and waiting to be put up for auction. His eyes were streaked and rimmed with the pinkness of what seemed to be years of lamenting. Sunlight, bouncing off the Arno, off the fronts of shops, fractured into spectra by the falling rain, seemed to tangle or lodge in his blond hair, eyebrows, mustache, turning that face to a mask of inaccessible ecstasy; contradicting the sorrowing and weary eyeholes. You would be drawn inevitably again to these eyes, linger as you might have on the rest of the face: any Visitors' Guide to Signor Mantissa must accord them an asterisk denoting especial interest. Though offering no clue to their enigma; for they reflected a free-floating sadness, unfocused, indeterminate: a woman, the casual tourist might think at first, be almost convinced until some more catholic light moving in and out of a web of capillaries would make him not so sure. What then? Politics, perhaps. Thinking of gentle-eyed Mazzini with his lambent dreams, the observer would sense frailness, a poet-liberal. But if he kept watching long enough the plasma behind those eyes would soon run through every fashionable permutation of grief—financial trouble, declining health, destroyed faith, betrayal, impotence, loss—until eventually it would dawn on our tourist that he had been attending no wake after all: rather a street-long festival of sorrow with no booth the same, no exhibit offering anything solid enough to merit lingering at.

The reason was obvious and disappointing: simply that Signor Mantissa himself had been through them all, each booth was a permanent exhibit in memory of some time in his life when there had been a blond seamstress in Lyons, or an abortive plot to smuggle tobacco over the Pyrenees, or a minor assassination attempt in Belgrade. All his reversals had occurred, had been registered: he had assigned each one equal weight, had learned nothing from any of them except that they would happen again. Like Machiavelli he was in exile, and visited by shadows of rhythm and decay. He mused inviolate by the serene river of Italian pessimism, and all men were corrupt: history would continue to recapitulate the same patterns. There was hardly ever a dossier on him, wherever in the world his tiny, nimble feet should happen to walk. No one in authority seemed to care. He belonged to that inner circle of deracinated seers whose eyesight was clouded over only by occasional tears, whose outer rim was tangent to rims enclosing the Decadents of England and France, the Generation of '98 in Spain, for whom the continent of Europe was like a gallery one is familiar with but long weary of, useful now only as shelter from the rain, or some obscure pestilence.

Cesare drank from the wine bottle. He sang:

Il piove, dolor mia
Ed anch'io piango . . .

"No," said Signor Mantissa, waving away the bottle. "No more for me till he arrives."

"There are two English ladies," Cesare cried. "I will sing to them."

"For God's sake—"

Vedi, donna vezzosa, questo poveretto,
Sempre cantante d'amore come—

"Be quiet, can't you."

"—un vaporetto." Triumphantly he boomed a hundred-cycle note across the Ponte Vecchio. The English ladies cringed and passed on.

After a while Signor Mantissa reached under his chair, coming up with a new fiasco of wine.

"Here is the Gaucho," he said. A tall, lumbering person in a wideawake hat loomed over them, blinking curiously.

Biting his thumb irritably at Cesare, Signor Mantissa found a corkscrew; gripped the bottle between his knees, drew the cork. The Gaucho straddled a chair backwards and took a long swallow from the wine bottle.

"Broglio," Signor Mantissa said, "the finest."

The Gaucho fiddled absently with his hatbrim. Then burst out: "I'm a man of action, signor, I'd rather not waste time. Allora. To business. I have considered your plan. I asked for no details last night. I dislike details. As it was, the few you gave me were superfluous. I'm sorry, I have many objections. It is much too subtle. There are too many things that can go wrong. How many people are in it now? You, myself and this lout." Cesare beamed. "Two too many. You should have done it all alone. You mentioned wanting

146

to bribe one of the attendants. It would make four. How many more will have to be paid off, consciences set at ease. Chances arise that someone can betray us to the guardie before this wretched business is done?"

Signor Mantissa drank, wiped his mustaches, smiled painfully. "Cesare is able to make the necessary contacts," he protested, "he's below suspicion, no one notices him. The river barge to Pisa, the boat from there to Nice, who should have arranged these if not—"

"You, my friend," the Gaucho said menacingly, prodding Signor Mantissa in the ribs with the corkscrew. "You, alone. Is it necessary to bargain with the captains of barges and boats? No: it is necessary only to get on board, to stow away. From there on in, assert yourself. Be a man. If the person in authority objects—" He twisted the corkscrew savagely, furling several square inches of Signor Mantissa's white linen shirt around it. "Capisci?"

Signor Mantissa, skewered like a butterfly, flapped his arms, grimaced, tossed his golden head.

"Certo io," he finally managed to say, "of course, signor commendatore, to the military mind . . . direct action, of course . . . but in such a delicate matter . . ."

"Pah!" The Gaucho disengaged the corkscrew, sat glaring at Signor Mantissa. The rain had stopped, the sun was setting. The bridge was thronged with tourists, returning to their hotels on the Lungarno. Cesare gazed benignly at them. The three sat in silence until the Gaucho began to talk, calmly but with an undercurrent of passion.

"Last year in Venezuela it was not like this. Nowhere in America was it like this. There were no twistings, no elaborate maneuverings. The conflict was simple: we wanted liberty, they didn't want us to have it. Liberty or slavery, my Jesuit friend, two words only. It needed none of your extra phrases, your tracts, none of your moralizing, no essays on political justice. We knew where we stood, and where one day we would stand. And when it came to the fighting we were equally as direct. You think you are being Machiavellian with all these artful tactics. You once heard him speak of the lion and the fox and now your devious brain can see only the fox. What has happened to the strength, the aggressiveness, the natural nobility of the lion? What sort of an age is this where a man becomes one's enemy only when his back is turned?"

Signor Mantissa had regained some of his composure. "It is necessary to have both, of course," he said placatingly. "Which is why I chose you as a collaborator, commendatore. You are the lion, I—" humbly—"a very small fox."

"And he is the pig," the Gaucho roared, clapping Cesare on the shoulder. "Bravo! A fine cadre."

"Pig," said Cesare happily, making a grab for the wine bottle.

"No more," the Gaucho said. "The signor here has taken the trouble to build us all a house of cards. Much as I dislike living in it, I won't permit your totally drunken breath to blow it over in indiscreet talk." He turned back to Signor Mantissa. "No," he continued, "you are not a true Machiavellian. He was an apostle of freedom for all men. Who can read the last chapter of *Il Principe* and doubt his desire for a republican and united Italy? Right over there—" he gestured toward the left bank, the sunset—"he lived, suffered under the Medici. They were the foxes, and he hated them. His final exhortation is for a lion, an embodiment of power, to arise in Italy and run all foxes to earth forever. His morality was as simple and honest as my own and my comrades' in South America. And now, under his banner, you wish to perpetuate the detestable cunning of the Medici, who suppressed freedom in this very city for so long. I am dishonored irrevocably, merely having associated with you."

"If—" again the pained smile—"if the commendatore has perhaps some alternative plan, we should be happy . . ."

"Of course there's another plan," the Gaucho retorted, "the only plan. Here, you have a map?" Eagerly Signor Mantissa produced from an inside pocket a folded diagram, hand-sketched in pencil. The Gaucho peered at it distastefully. "So that is the Uffizi," he said. "I've never been inside the place. I suppose I shall have to, to get the feel of the terrain. And where is the objective?"

Signor Mantissa pointed to the lower left-hand corner. "The Sala di Lorenzo Monaco," he said. "Here, you see. I have already had a key made for the main entrance. Three main corridors: east, west, and a short one on the south connecting them. From the west corridor, number three, we enter a smaller one here, marked 'Ritratti diversi.' At the end, on the right, is a single entrance to the gallery. She hangs on the western wall."

"A single entrance which is also the single exit," the Gaucho said. "Not good. A dead end. And to leave the building itself one must go all the way back up the eastern corridor to the steps leading to Piazza della Signoria."

"There is a lift," said Signor Mantissa, "leading to a passage which lets one out in the Palazzo Vecchio."

"A lift," the Gaucho sneered. "About what I'd expect from you." He leaned forward, baring his teeth. "You already propose to commit an act of supreme idiocy by walking all the way down one corridor, along another, halfway up a third, down one more into a cul-de-sac and then out again the same way you came in. A distance of—" he measured rapidly—"some six hundred meters, with guards ready to jump out at you every time you pass a gallery or turn a corner. But even this isn't confining enough for you. You must take a lift."

"Besides which," Cesare put in, "she's so big."

The Gaucho clenched one fist. "How big."

"175 by 279 centimeters," admitted Signor Mantissa.

"Capo di minghe!" The Gaucho sat back, shaking his head. With an obvious effort at controlling his temper, he addressed Signor Mantissa. "I'm not a small man," he explained patiently. "In fact I am rather a large man. And broad. I am built like a lion. Perhaps it's a racial trait. I come from the north, and there may be some tedesco blood in these veins. The tedeschi are taller than the Latin races. Taller and broader. Perhaps someday this body will run to fat, but now it is all muscle. So, I am big, non è vero? Good. Then let me inform you—" his voice rising in violent crescendo—"that there would be room enough under your damnable Botticelli for me and the fattest whore in Florence, with plenty left over for her elephant of a mother to act as chaperone! How in God's name do you intend to walk 300 meters with that? Will it be hidden in your pocket?"

"Calm, commendatore," Signor Mantissa pleaded. "Anyone might be listening. It is a detail, I assure you. Provided for. The florist Cesare visited last night—"

"Florist. Florist: you've let a florist into your confidence. Wouldn't it make you happier to publish your intentions in the evening newspapers?"

"But he is safe. He is only providing the tree."

"The tree."

149

"The Judas tree. Small: some four meters, no taller. Cesare has been at work all morning, hollowing out the trunk. So we shall have to execute our plans soon, before the purple flowers die."

"Forgive what may be my appalling stupidity," the Gaucho said, "but as I understand it, you intend to roll up the Birth of Venus, hide it in the hollow trunk of a Judas tree, and carry it some 300 meters, past an army of guards who will soon be aware of its theft, and out into Piazza della Signoria, where presumably you will then lose yourself in the crowds?"

"Precisely. Early evening would be the best time—"

"A rivederci."

Signor Mantissa leaped to his feet. "I beg you, commendatore," he cried. "Aspetti. Cesare and I will be disguised as workmen, you see. The Uffizi is being redecorated, there will be nothing unusual—"

"Forgive me," the Gaucho said, "you are both lunatics."

"But your cooperation is essential. We need a lion, someone skilled in military tactics, in strategy . . ."

"Very well." The Gaucho retraced his steps and stood towering over Signor Mantissa. "I suggest this: the Sala di Lorenzo Monaco has windows, does it not?"

"Heavily barred."

"No matter. A bomb, a small bomb, which I'll provide. Anyone who tries to interfere will be disposed of by force. The window should let us out next to the Posta Centrale. Your rendezvous with the barge?"

"Under the Ponte San Trinitá."

"Some four or five hundred yards up the Lungarno. We can commandeer a carriage. Have your barge waiting at midnight tonight. That's my proposal. Take it or leave it. I shall be at the Uffizi till supper time, reconnoitering. From then till nine, at home making the bomb. After that, at Scheissvogel's, the birriere. Let me know by ten."

"But the tree, commendatore. It cost close to 200 lire."

"Damn your tree." With a smart about-face the Gaucho turned and strode away in the direction of the right bank.

The sun hovered over the Arno. Its declining rays tinged the liquid gathering in Signor Mantissa's eyes to a pale red, as if the wine he'd drunk were overflowing, watered down with tears.

Cesare let a consoling arm fall round Signor Mantissa's

thin shoulders. "It will go well," he said. "The Gaucho is a barbarian. He's been in the jungles too long. He doesn't understand."

"She is so beautiful," Signor Mantissa whispered.

"Davvero. And I love her too. We are comrades in love." Signor Mantissa did not answer. After a little while he reached for the wine.

III

Miss Victoria Wren, late of Lardwick-in-the-Fen, Yorks., recently self-proclaimed a citizen of the world, knelt devoutly in the front pew of a church just off Via dello Studio. She was saying an act of contrition. An hour before, in the Via dei Vecchietti, she'd had impure thoughts while watching a fat English boy cavort in a cab; she was now being heartily sorry for them. At nineteen she'd already recorded a serious affair: having the autumn before in Cairo seduced one Goodfellow, an agent of the British Foreign Office. Such is the resilience of the young that his face was already forgotten. Afterward they'd both been quick to blame the violent emotions which arise during any tense international situation (this was at the time of the Fashoda crisis) for her deflowering. Now, six or seven months later, she found it difficult to determine how much she had in fact planned, how much had been out of her control. The liaison had in due course been discovered by her widowed father Sir Alastair, with whom she and her sister Mildred were traveling. There were words, sobbings, threats, insults, late one afternoon under the trees in the Ezbekiyeh Garden, with little Mildred gazing struck and tearful at it all, while God knew what scars were carved into her. At length Victoria had ended it with a glacial good-bye and a vow never to return to England; Sir Alastair had nodded and taken Mildred by the hand. Neither had looked back.

Support after that was readily available. By prudent saving Victoria had amassed some £400 from a wine merchant in Antibes, a Polish cavalry lieutenant in Athens, an art dealer in Rome; she was in Florence now to negotiate the purchase of a small couturière's establishment on the left bank. A young lady of enterprise, she found herself acquiring political convictions, beginning to detest anarchists, the Fabian Society, even the Earl of Rosebery. Since her

The comb of the 5 crucified

eighteenth birthday she had been carrying a certain innocence like a penny candle, sheltering the flame under a
ringless hand still soft with baby fat, redeemed from all
stain by her candid eyes and small mouth and a girl's body
entirely honest as any act of contrition. So she knelt,
unadorned save for an ivory comb, gleaming among all
the plausibly English quantities of brown hair. An ivory
comb, five-toothed: whose shape was that of five crucified,
all sharing at least one common arm. None of them was a
religious figure: they were soldiers of the British Army.
She had found the comb in one of the Cairo bazaars. It
had apparently been hand-carved by a Fuzzy-Wuzzy, an
artisan among the Mahdists, in commemoration of the cru-
cifixions of '83, in the country east of invested Khartoum.
Her motives in buying it may have been as instinctive and
uncomplex as those by which any young girl chooses a
dress or gewgaw of a particular hue and shape.

Now she did not regard her time with Goodfellow or with
the three since him as sinful: she only remembered Goodfellow at all because he had been the first. It was not that
her private, outré brand of Roman Catholicism merely
condoned what the Church as a whole regarded as sin:
this was more than simple sanction, it was implicit acceptance of the four episodes as outward and visible signs
of an inward and spiritual grace belonging to Victoria alone.
Perhaps it was a few weeks she had spent as a girl in the
novitiate, preparing to become a sister, perhaps some malady
of the generation; but somehow at age nineteen she had
crystallized into a nunlike temperament pushed to its most
dangerous extreme. Whether she had taken the veil or not,
it was as if she felt Christ were her husband and that the
marriage's physical consummation must be achieved
through imperfect, mortal versions of himself—of which
there had been, to date, four. And he would continue to
perform his husband's duties through as many more such
agents as he deemed fit. It is easy enough to see where
such an attitude might lead: in Paris similarly-minded
ladies were attending Black Masses, in Italy they lived in
Pre-Raphaelite splendor as the mistresses of archbishops or
cardinals. It happened that Victoria was not so exclusive.

She arose and walked down the center aisle to the rear
of the church. She'd dipped her fingers in holy water and
was about to genuflect when someone collided with her from

152

behind. She turned, startled, to see an elderly man a head shorter than herself, his hands held in front of him, his eyes frightened.

"You are English," he said.

"I am."

"You must help me. I am in trouble. I can't go to the Consul-General."

He didn't look like a beggar or a hard-up tourist. She was reminded somehow of Goodfellow. "Are you a spy, then?"

The old man laughed mirthlessly. "Yes. In a way I am engaged in espionage. But against my will, you know. I didn't want it this way."

Distraught: "I want to confess, don't you see? I'm in a church, a church is where one confesses . . ."

"Come," she whispered.

"Not outside," he said. "The cafés are being watched."

She took his arm. "There is a garden in the back, I think. This way. Through the sacristy."

He let her guide him, docile. A priest was kneeling in the sacristy, reading his breviary. She handed him ten soldi as they passed. He didn't look up. A short groined arcade led into a miniature garden surrounded by mossy stone walls and containing a stunted pine, some grass and a carp pool. She led him to a stone bench by the pool. Rain came over the walls in occasional gusts. He carried a morning news-paper under his arm: now he spread sheets of it over the bench. They sat. Victoria opened her parasol and the old man took a minute lighting a Cavour. He sent a few puffs of smoke out into the rain, and began:

"I don't expect you've ever heard of a place called Vheissu."

She had not.

He started telling her about Vheissu. How it was reached, on camel-back over a vast tundra, past the dolmens and temples of dead cities; finally to the banks of a broad river which never sees the sun, so thickly roofed is it with foliage. The river is traveled in long teak boats which are carved like dragons and paddled by brown men whose language is unknown to all but themselves. In eight days' time there is a portage over a neck of treacherous swampland to a green lake, and across the lake rise the first foothills of the mountains which ring Vheissu. Native guides will only go a short distance into these mountains. Soon they will turn

153

back, pointing out the way. Depending on the weather, it is
• one to two more weeks over moraine, sheer granite and hard
blue ice before the borders of Vheissu are reached.

"Then you have been there," she said.

He had been there. Fifteen years ago. And been fury-rid-
den since. Even in the Antarctic, huddling in hasty shelter
from a winter storm, striking camp high on the shoulder of
some as yet unnamed glacier, there would come to him
hints of the perfume those people distill from the wings of
black moths. Sometimes sentimental scraps of their music
would seem to lace the wind; memories of their faded mur-
als, depicting old battles and older love affairs among the
gods, would appear without warning in the aurora.

"You are Godolphin," she said, as if she had always
known.

He nodded, smiled vaguely. "I hope you are not connected with the press." She shook her head, scattering droplets
of rain. "This isn't for general dissemination," he said, "and
it may be wrong. Who am I to know my own motives. But
I did foolhardy things."

"Brave things," she protested. "I've read about them. In
newspapers, in books."

"But things which did not have to be done. The trek along
the Barrier. The try for the Pole in June. June down there
is midwinter. It was madness."

"It was grand." Another minute, he thought hopelessly,
and she'd begin talking about a Union Jack flying over the
Pole. Somehow this church towering Gothic and solid over
their heads, the quietness, her impassivity, his confessional
humor; he was talking too much, must stop. But could not.

"We can always so easily give the wrong reasons," he
cried; "can say: the Chinese campaigns, they were for the
Queen, and India for some gorgeous notion of Empire. I
know. I have said these things to my men, the public, to
myself. There are Englishmen dying in South Africa today
and about to die tomorrow who believe these words as—I
dare say as you believe in God."

She smiled secretly. "And you did not?" she asked gently.
She was gazing at the rim of her parasol.

"I did. Until . . ."

"Yes."

"But why? Have you never harrowed yourself halfway to
—disorder—with that single word? Why." His cigar had gone

out. He paused to relight it. "It's not," he continued, "as if it were unusual in any supernatural way. No high priests with secrets lost to the rest of the world, jealously guarded since the dawn of time, generation to generation. No universal cures, nor even panaceas for human suffering. Vheissu is hardly a restful place. There's barbarity, insurrection, internecine feud. It's no different from any other godforsakenly remote region. The English have been jaunting in and out of places like Vheissu for centuries. Except . . ."

She had been gazing at him. The parasol leaned against the bench, its handle hidden in the wet grass.

"The colors. So many colors." His eyes were tightly closed, his forehead resting on the bowed edge of one hand. "The trees outside the head shaman's house have spider monkeys which are iridescent. They change color in the sunlight. Everything changes. The mountains, the lowlands are never the same color from one hour to the next. No sequence of colors is the same from day to day. As if you lived inside a madman's kaleidoscope. Even your dreams become flooded with colors, with shapes no Occidental ever saw. Not real shapes, not meaningful ones. Simply random, the way clouds change over a Yorkshire landscape."

She was taken by surprise: her laugh was high and brittle. He hadn't heard. "They stay with you," he went on, "they aren't fleecy lambs or jagged profiles. They are, they are Vheissu, its raiment, perhaps its skin."

"And beneath?"

"You mean soul don't you. Of course you do. I wondered about the soul of that place. If it had a soul. Because their music, poetry, laws and ceremonies come no closer. They are skin too. Like the skin of a tattooed savage. I often put it that way to myself—like a woman. I hope I don't offend."

"It's all right."

"Civilians have curious ideas about the military, but I expect in this case there's some justice to what they think about us. This idea of the randy young subaltern somewhere out in the back of beyond, collecting himself a harem of dusky native women. I dare say a lot of us have this dream, though I've yet to run across anyone who's realized it. And I won't deny I get to thinking this way myself. I got to thinking that way in Vheissu. Somehow, there—" his forehead furrowed—"dreams are not, not closer to the waking

155

world, but somehow, I think, they do seem more real. Am I making sense to you?"

"Go on." She was watching him, rapt.

"But as if the place were, were a woman you had found somewhere out there, a dark woman tattooed from head to toes. And somehow you had got separated from the garrison and found yourself unable to get back, so that you had to be with her, close to her, day in and day out . . ."

"And you would be in love with her."

"At first. But soon that skin, the gaudy godawful riot of pattern and color, would begin to get between you and whatever it was in her that you thought you loved. And soon, in perhaps only a matter of days, it would get so bad that you would begin praying to whatever god you knew of to send some leprosy to her. To flay that tattooing to a heap of red, purple and green debris, leave the veins and ligaments raw and quivering and open at last to your eyes and your touch. I'm sorry." He wouldn't look at her. The wind blew rain over the wall. "Fifteen years. It was directly after we'd entered Khartoum. I'd seen some beastliness in my Oriental campaigning, but nothing to match that. We were to relieve General Gordon—oh you were, I suppose, a chit of a girl then, but you've read about it, surely. What the Mahdi had done to that city. To General Gordon, to his men. I was having trouble with fever then and no doubt it was seeing all the carrion and the waste on top of that. I wanted to get away, suddenly; it was as if a world of neat hollow squares and snappy counter-marching had deteriorated into rout or mindlessness. I'd always had friends on the staffs at Cairo, Bombay, Singapore. And in two weeks this surveying business came up, and I was in. I was always weaseling in, you know, on some show where you wouldn't expect to find naval personnel. This time it was escorting a crew of civilian engineers into some of the worst country on earth. Oh, wild, romantic. Contour lines and fathom-markings, crosshatchings and colors where before there were only blank spaces on the map. All for the Empire. This sort of thing might have been lurking at the back of my head. But then I only knew I wanted to get away. All very good to be crying St. George and no quarter about the Orient, but then the Mahdist army had been gibbering the same thing, really, in Arabic, and had certainly meant it at Khartoum."

Mercifully, he did not catch sight of her comb.

"Did you get maps of Vheissu?"

He hesitated. "No," he said. "No data ever got back, either to F.O. or to the Geographic Society. Only a report of failure. Bear in mind: It was bad country. Thirteen of us went in and three came out. Myself, my second-in-command, and a civilian whose name I have forgotten and who so far as I know has vanished from the earth without a trace."

"And your second-in-command?"

"He is, he is in hospital. Retired now." There was a silence. "There was never a second expedition," old Godolphin went on. "Political reasons, who could say? No one cared. I got out of it scotfree. Not my fault, they told me. I even received a personal commendation from the Queen, though it was all hushed up."

Victoria was tapping her foot absently. "And all this has some bearing on your, oh, espionage activities at present?"

Suddenly he looked older. The cigar had gone out again. He flung it into the grass; his hand shook. "Yes." He gestured helplessly at the church, the gray walls. "For all I know you might be—I may have been indiscreet."

Realizing that he was afraid of her, she leaned forward, intent. "Those who watch the cafés. Are they from Vheissu? Emissaries?"

The old man began to bite at his nails; slowly and methodically, using the top central and lower lateral incisors to make minute cuts along a perfect arc-segment. "You have discovered something about them," she pleaded, "something you cannot tell." Her voice, compassionate and exasperated, rang out in the little garden. "You must let me help you." Snip, snip. The rain fell off, stopped. "What sort of world is it where there isn't at least one person you can turn to if you're in danger?" Snip, snip. No answer. "How do you know the Consul-General can't help. Please, let me do something." The wind came in, lorn now of rain, over the wall. Something splashed lazily in the pool. The girl continued to harangue old Godolphin as he completed his right hand and switched to his left. Overhead the sky began to darken.

IV

The eighth floor at Piazza della Signoria 5 was murky and smelled of fried octopus. Evan, puffing from the last three flights of stairs, had to light four matches before he found his father's door. Tacked to it, instead of the card he'd expected to find, was a note on ragged-edged paper, which read simply "Evan." He squinted at it curiously. Except for the rain and the house's creakings the hallway was silent. He shrugged and tried the door. It opened. He groped his way inside, found the gas, lit it. The room was sparsely furnished. A pair of trousers had been tossed haphazard over the back of a chair; a white shirt, arms outstretched, lay on the bed. There were no other signs that anyone lived there: no trunks, no papers. Puzzled, he sat on the bed and tried to think. He pulled the telegram out of his pocket and read it again. Vheissu. The only clue he had to go on. Had old Godolphin really, after all, believed such a place existed?

∨

Evan—even the boy—had never pressed his father for details. He had been aware that the expedition was a failure, caught perhaps some sense of personal guilt or agency in the droning, kindly voice which recited those stories. But that was all: he'd asked no questions, had simply sat and listened, as if anticipating that someday he would have to renounce Vheissu and that such renunciation would be simpler if he formed no commitment now. Very well: his father had been undisturbed a year ago, when Evan had last seen him; something must therefore have happened in the Antarctic. Or on the way back. Perhaps here in Florence. Why should the old man have left a note with only his son's name on it? Two possibilities: (a) if it were no note but rather a name-card and Evan the first alias to occur to Captain Hugh, or (b) if he had wished Evan to enter the room. Perhaps both. On a sudden hunch Evan picked up the pair of trousers, began rummaging through the pockets. He came up with three soldi and a cigarette case. Opening the case, he found four cigarettes, all hand-rolled. He scratched his stomach. Words came back to him: unwise to say too much in telegram. He sighed.

"All right then, young Evan," he muttered to himself, "we shall play this thing to the hilt. Enter Godolphin, the veteran spy." Carefully he examined the case for hidden springs: felt along the lining for anything which might have been put underneath. Nothing. He began to search the room, prodding the mattress and scrutinizing it for recently-stitched seams. He combed the armoire, lit matches in dark corners, looked to see if anything was taped to the bottoms of chair seats. After twenty minutes he'd still found nothing and was beginning to feel inadequate as a spy. He threw himself disconsolate into a chair, picked up one of his father's cigarettes, struck a match. "Wait," he said. Shook out the match, pulled a table over, produced a penknife from his pocket and carefully slit each cigarette down the side, brushing the tobacco off onto the floor. On the third try he was successful. Written in pencil on the inside of the cigarette paper was: "Discovered here. Scheissvogel's 10 P.M. Be careful. FATHER."

Evan looked at his watch. Now what in the devil was all this about? Why so elaborate? Had the old man been fooling with politics or was it a second childhood? He could do nothing for a few hours at least. He hoped something was afoot, if only to relieve the grayness of his exile, but was ready to be disappointed. Turning off the gas, he stepped into the hall, closed the door behind him, began to descend the stairs. He was wondering where Scheissvogel's could be when the stairs suddenly gave under his weight and he crashed through, clutching frantically in the air. He caught hold of the banister; it splintered at the lower end and swung him out over the stairwell, seven flights up. He hung there, listening to the nails edge slowly out of the railing's upper end. I, he thought, am the most uncoordinated oaf in the world. That thing is going to give any second now. He looked around, wondering what he should do. His feet hung two yards away from and several inches above the next banister. The ruined stairway he'd just left was a foot away from his right shoulder. The railing he hung on swayed dangerously. What can I lose, he thought. Only hope my timing isn't too off. Carefully he bent his right forearm up until his hand rested flat against the side of the stairway: then gave himself a violent shove. He swung out over the gaping well, heard the nails shriek free of the wood above him as he reached the extreme point of his swing, flung the railing away, dropped neatly astride the next banister and slid down it backwards, arriving at the seventh floor just as the railing crashed to earth far below. He climbed off the banister, shaking, and sat on the steps. Neat, he thought. Bravo, lad. Do well as an acrobat or something. But a moment later, after he had nearly been sick between his knees, he thought: how accidental was it, really? Those stairs were all right when I came up. He smiled nervously. He was getting almost as loony as his father. By the time he reached the street his shakiness had almost gone. He stood in front of the house for a minute, getting his bearings.

Before he knew it he'd been flanked by two policemen. "Your papers," one of them said.

Evan came aware, protesting automatically.

"Those are our orders, cavaliere." Evan caught a slight note of contempt in the "cavaliere." He produced his passport; the guardie nodded together on seeing his name.

"Would you mind telling me—" Evan began.

They were sorry, they could give him no information. He would have to accompany them.

"I demand to see the English Consul-General."

"But cavaliere, how do we know you are English? This passport could be forged. You may be from any country in the world. Even one we have never heard of."

Flesh began to crawl on the back of his neck. He had suddenly got the insane notion they were talking about Vheissu. "If your superiors can give a satisfactory explanation," he said, "I am at your service."

"Certainly, cavaliere." They walked across the square and around a corner to a waiting carriage. One of the policemen courteously relieved him of his umbrella and began to examine it closely. "Avanti," cried the other, and away they galloped down the Borgo di Greci.

v

Earlier that day, the Venezuelan Consulate had been in an uproar. A coded message had come through from Rome at noon in the daily bag, warning of an upswing in revolutionary activities around Florence. Various of the local contacts had already reported a tall, mysterious figure in a wideawake hat lurking in the vicinity of the Consulate during the past few days.

"Be reasonable," urged Salazar, the Vice-Consul. "The worst we have to expect is a demonstration or two. What can they do? Break a few windows, trample the shrubbery."

"Bombs," screamed Ratón, his chief. "Destruction, pillage, rape, chaos. They can take us over, stage a coup, set up a junta. What better place? They remember Garibaldi in this country. Look at Uruguay. They will have many allies.

160

What do we have? You, myself, one cretin of a clerk and the charwoman."

The Vice-Consul opened his desk drawer and produced a bottle of Rufina. "My dear Ratón," he said, "calm yourself. This ogre in the flapping hat may be one of our own men, sent over from Caracas to keep an eye on us." He poured the wine into two tumblers, handed one to Ratón. "Besides which the communiqué from Rome said nothing definite. It did not even mention this enigmatic person."

"He is in on it," Ratón said, slurping wine. "I have inquired. I know his name and that his activities are shady and illegal. Do you know what he is called?" He hesitated dramatically. "The Gaucho."

"Gauchos are in Argentina," Salazar observed soothingly. "And the name might also be a corruption of the French gauche. Perhaps he is left-handed."

"It is all we have to go on," Ratón said obstinately. "It is the same continent, is it not?"

Salazar sighed. "What is it you want to do?"

"Enlist help from the government police here. What other course is there?"

Salazar refilled the tumblers. "First," he said, "international complications. There may be a question of jurisdiction. The grounds of this consulate are legally Venezuelan soil."

"We can have them place a cordon of guardie around us, outside the property," Ratón said craftily. "That way they would be suppressing riot in Italian territory."

"Es posibile," the Vice-Consul shrugged. "But secondly, it might mean a loss of prestige with the higher echelons in Rome, in Caracas. We could easily make fools of ourselves, acting with such elaborate precautions on mere suspicion, mere whimsy."

"Whimsy!" shouted Ratón. "Have I not seen this sinister figure with my own eyes?" One side of his mustache was soaked with wine. He wrung it out irritably. "There is something afoot," he went on, "something bigger than simple insurrection, bigger than a single country. The Foreign Office of this country has its eye on us. I cannot, of course, speak too indiscreetly, but I have been in this business longer than you, Salazar, and I tell you: we shall have much more to worry about than trampled bushes before this business is done."

161

"Of course," Salazar said peevishly, "if I am no longer party to your confidences . . ."

"You would not know. Perhaps they do not know at Rome. You will discover everything in due time. Soon enough," he added darkly.

"If it were only your job, I would say, fine: call in the Italians. Call in the English and the Germans too, for all I care. But if your glorious coup doesn't materialize, I come out of it just as badly."

"And then," Ratón chuckled, "that idiot clerk can take over both our jobs."

Salazar was not mollified. "I wonder," he said thoughtfully, "what sort of Consul-General he would make."

Ratón glowered. "I am still your superior."

"Very well then, your excellency—" spreading his hands hopelessly—"I await your orders."

"Contact the government police at once. Outline the situation, stress its urgency. Ask for a conference at their earliest possible convenience. Before sundown, that means."

"That is all?"

"You might request that this Gaucho be put under apprehension." Salazar did not answer. After a moment of glaring at the Rufina bottle, Ratón turned and left the office. Salazar chewed on the end of his pen meditatively. It was midday. He gazed out the window, across the street at the Uffizi Gallery. He noticed clouds massing over the Arno. Perhaps there would be rain.

They caught up with the Gaucho finally in the Uffizi. He'd been lounging against one wall of the Sala di Lorenzo Monaco, leering at the Birth of Venus. She was standing in half of what looked like a scungille shell; fat and blond, and the Gaucho, being a tedesco in spirit, appreciated this. But he didn't understand what was going on in the rest of the picture. There seemed to be some dispute over whether or not she should be nude or draped: on the right a glassy-eyed lady built like a pear tried to cover her up with a blanket and on the left an irritated young man with wings tried to blow the blanket away while a girl wearing hardly anything twined around him, probably trying to coax him back to bed. While this curious crew wrangled, Venus stood gazing off into God knew where, covering up with her long tresses. No one seemed to be looking at anyone else. A confusing picture. The Gaucho had no idea why Signor Mantissa should want it, but it was none of the Gaucho's affair. He scratched his head under the wideawake hat and turned with a still-tolerant smile to see four guardie heading into the gallery toward him. His first impulse was to run, his second to leap out a window. But he'd familiarized himself with the terrain and both impulses were checked almost immediately. "It is he," one of the guardie announced; "avanti!" The Gaucho stood his ground, cocking the hat aslant and putting his fists on his hips.

They surrounded him and a tenente with a beard informed him that he must be placed under apprehension. It was regrettable, true, but doubtless he would be released within a few days. The tenente advised him to make no disturbance.

"I could take all four of you," the Gaucho said. His mind was racing, planning tactics, calculating angles of enfilade. Had il gran signore Mantissa blundered so extravagantly as to be arrested? Had there been a complaint from the Venezuelan Consulate? He must be calm and admit nothing until he saw how things lay. He was escorted along the "Ritratti diversi"; then two short rights into a long passageway. He didn't remember it from Mantissa's map. "Where does this lead?"

"Over the Ponte Vecchio to the Pitti Gallery," the tenente said. "It is for tourists. We are not going that far." A perfect escape route. The idiot Mantissa! But halfway across the bridge they came out into the back room of a tobacconist's. The police seemed familiar with this exit; not so good then, after all. Yet why all this secrecy? No city government was ever this cautious. It must therefore be the Venezuelan business. In the street was a closed landau, painted black. They hustled him in and started toward the right bank. He knew they wouldn't head directly for their destination. They did not: once over the bridge the driver began to zigzag, run in circles, retrace his way. The Gaucho settled back, cadged a cigarette from the tenente, and surveyed the situation. If it were the Venezuelans, he was in trouble. He had come to Florence specifically to organize the Venezuelan colony, who were centered in the northeast part of the city, near Via Cavour. There were only a few hundred of them: they kept to themselves and worked either in the tobacco factory or at the Mercato Centrale, or as sutlers to the Fourth Army

163

Corps, whose installations were nearby. In two months the Gaucho had squared them away into ranks and uniforms, under the collective title Figli di Machiavelli. Not that they had any particular fondness for authority; nor that they were, politically speaking, especially liberal or nationalistic; it was simply that they enjoyed a good riot now and again, and if martial organization and the aegis of Machiavelli could expedite things, so much the better. The Gaucho had been promising them a riot for two months now, but the time was not yet favorable: things were quiet in Caracas, with only a few small skirmishes going on in the jungles. He was waiting for a major incident, a stimulus to which he could provide a thunderous antiphonal response back across the Atlantic's nave. It had been, after all, only two years since settlement of the boundary dispute with British Guiana, over which England and the United States nearly came to blows. His agents in Caracas kept reassuring him: the scene was being set, men were being armed, bribes given, it was only a matter of time. Apparently something had happened, or why should they be pulling him in? He had to figure out some way of getting a message to his lieutenant, Cuernacabrón. Their usual rendezvous was at Scheissvogel's beer garden, in Piazza Vittorio Emmanuele. And there was still Mantissa and his Botticelli. Regrettable about that. It would have to wait till another night. . . .

Imbecile!

Wasn't the Venezuelan Consulate located only some fifty meters from the Uffizi? If there were a demonstration in progress, the guardie would have their hands full; might not even hear the bomb go off. A diversionary feint! Mantissa, Cesare and the fat blonde would all get away cleanly. He might even escort them to their rendezvous under the bridge: as instigator it wouldn't be prudent to remain at the scene of the riot for very long.

This was all assuming, of course, that he could talk his way out of whatever charges the police would try to press, or, failing that, escape. But the essential thing right now was to get word to Cuernacabrón. He felt the carriage begin to slacken speed. One of the guardie produced a silk handkerchief, doubled and redoubled it, and bound it over the Gaucho's eyes. The landau bounced to a halt. The tenente took his arm and led him through a courtyard, in a doorway, around a few corners, down a flight of stairs. "In here," ordered the tenente.

"May I ask a favor," the Gaucho said, feigning embarrassment. "With all the wine I have drunk today, I have not had the chance— That is, if I am to answer your questions honestly and amiably, I should feel more at ease if—"

"All right," the tenente growled. "Angelo, you keep an eye on him." The Gaucho smiled his thanks. He trailed down the hall after Angelo, who opened the door for him. "May I remove this?" he asked. "After all, un gabinetto è un gabinetto."

"Quite true," the guardia said. "And the windows are opaque. Go ahead."

"Mille grazie." The Gaucho removed his blindfold and was surprised to find himself in an elaborate W. C. There were even stalls. Only the Americans and the English could be so fastidious about plumbing. And the hallway outside, he remembered, had smelled of ink, paper and sealing wax; a consulate, surely. Both the American and the British consuls had their headquarters in Via Tornabuoni, so he knew that he was roughly three blocks west of Piazza Vittorio Emmanuele. Scheissvogel's was almost within calling distance.

"Hurry up," Angelo said.

"Are you going to watch?" the Gaucho asked, indignant. "Can't I have a little privacy? I am still a citizen of Florence. This was a republic once." Without waiting for a reply he entered a stall and shut the door behind him. "How do you expect me to escape?" he called jovially from inside. "Flush myself and swim away down the Arno?" While urinating he removed his collar and tie, scribbled a note to Cuernacabrón on the back of the collar, reflected that occasionally the fox had his uses as well as the lion, replaced collar, tie and blindfold and stepped out.

"You decided to wear it after all," Angelo said.

"Testing my marksmanship." They both laughed. The tenente had stationed the other two guardie outside the door. "The man lacks charity," mused the Gaucho as they steered him back down the hall.

Soon he was in a private office, seated on a hard wooden chair. "Take the blindfold off," ordered a voice with an English accent. A wizened man, going bald, blinked at him across a desk.

"You are the Gaucho," he said.

"We can speak English if you like," the Gaucho said. Three of the guardie had withdrawn. The tenente and three plainclothesmen who looked to the Gaucho like state police stood ranged about the walls.

"You are perceptive," the balding man said.

The Gaucho decided to give at least the appearance of honesty. All the inglesi he knew seemed to have a fetish about playing cricket. "I am," he admitted. "Enough to know what this place is, your excellency."

The balding man smiled wistfully. "I am not the Consul-General," he said. "That is Major Percy Chapman, and he is occupied with other matters."

"Then I would guess," the Gaucho guessed, "that you are from the English Foreign Office. Cooperating with Italian police."

"Possibly. Since you seem to be of the inner circle in this matter, I presume you know why you have been brought here."

The possibility of a private arrangement with this man suddenly seemed plausible. He nodded.

"And we can talk honestly."

The Gaucho nodded again, grinning.

"Then let us start," the balding man said, "by your telling me all you know about Vheissu."

The Gaucho tugged perplexedly at one ear. Perhaps he had miscalculated, after all. "Venezuela, you mean?"

"I thought we had agreed not to fence. I said Vheissu."

All at once the Gaucho, for the first time since the jungles, felt afraid. When he answered it was with an insolence that rang hollow even to himself. "I know nothing about Vheissu," he said.

The balding man sighed. "Very well." He shuffled papers around on the desk for a moment. "Let us get down to the loathsome business of interrogation." He signaled to the three policemen, who closed swiftly in a triangle around the Gaucho.

VI

When old Godolphin awoke it was to a wash of red sunset through the window. It was a minute or two till he remembered where he was. His eyes flickered from the darkening

166

ceiling to a flowered bouffant dress hanging on the door of the armoire, to a confusion of brushes, vials and jars on the dressing table, and then he remembered that this was the girl, Victoria's, room. She had brought him here to rest for a while. He sat up on the bed, peering about the room nervously. He knew he was in the Savoy, on the eastern side of the Piazza Vittorio Emmanuele. But where had she gone? She had said she would stay, keep watch over him, see that no harm came. Now she had disappeared. He looked at his watch, twisting the dial to catch the failing sunlight. He'd been asleep only an hour or so. She had wasted little time in leaving. He arose, walked to the window, stood gazing out over the square, watching the sun go down. The thought struck him that she might after all be one of the enemy. He turned furiously, dashed across the room, twisted the doorknob. The door was locked. Damn the weakness, this compulsion to beg shrift of any random passer-by! He felt betrayal welling up around him, eager to drown, to destroy. He had stepped into the confessional and found himself instead in an oubliette. He crossed swiftly to the dressing table, looking for something to force the door, and discovered a message, neatly indited on scented note paper, for him:

If you value your well-being as much as I do, please do not try to leave. Understand that I believe you and want to help you in your terrible need. I have gone to inform the British Consulate of what you have told me. I have had personal experience with them before; I know the Foreign Office to be highly capable and discreet. I shall return shortly after dark.

He balled the paper up in his fist, flung it across the room. Even taking a Christian view of the situation, even assuming her intentions were well-meant and that she was not leagued with those who watched the cafés, informing Chapman was a fatal error. He could not afford to have the F.O. in on this. He sank down on the bed, head hung, hands clasped tightly between his knees. Remorse and a numb impotence: they had been jolly chums, riding arrogant on his epaulets like guardian angels for fifteen years. "It was not my fault," he protested aloud to the empty room, as if the mother-of-pearl brushes, the lace and dimity, the delicate vessels of scent would somehow find tongue and rally round him. "I was not meant to leave those mountains alive. That poor civilian engineer, dropped out of human sight; Pike-Leeming, incurable and insensate in a home in Wales; and Hugh Godolphin . . ." He arose, walked to the dressing table, stood staring at his face in the mirror. "He will only be a matter of time." A few yards of calico lay on the table, near them a pair of pinking shears. The girl seemed to be serious about her dressmaking scheme (she'd been quite honest with him about her past, not moved by his own confessional spirit so much as wanting to give him some token to prepare the way toward a mutual trustfulness. He hadn't been shocked by her disclosure of the affair with Goodfellow in Cairo. He thought it unfortunate: it seemed to have given her some quaint and romantic views about espionage.) He picked up the shears, turned them over in his hands. They were long and glittering. The ripple edges would make a nasty wound. He raised his eyes to those of his reflection with an inquiring look. The reflection smiled dolefully. "No," he said aloud. "Not yet."

Forcing the door with the shears took only half a minute. Two flights down the back stairs and out a service entrance, and he found himself in Via Tosinghi, a block north of the Piazza. He headed east, away from the center of town. He had to find a way out of Florence. However he came out of this, he would have to resign his commission and live from here on in a fugitive, a temporary occupant of pension rooms, a dweller in the demimonde. Marching through the dusk, he saw his fate complete, pre-assembled, inescapable. No matter how he tacked, yawed or dodged about he'd only be standing still while that treacherous reef loomed closer with every shift in course.

He turned right and headed toward the Duomo. Tourists sauntered by, cabs clattered in the street. He felt isolated from a human community—even a common humanity—which he had regarded until recently as little more than a cant concept which liberals were apt to use in making speeches. He watched the tourists gaping at the Campanile; he watched dispassionately without effort, curiously without commitment. He wondered at this phenomenon of tourism: what was it drove them to Thomas Cook & Son in ever-increasing flocks every year to let themselves in for the Campagna's fevers, the Levant's squalor, the septic foods of Greece? To return to Ludgate Circus at the desolate end of every season having caressed the skin of each alien place, a peregrine or Don

168

Juan of cities but no more able to talk of any mistress's heart than to cease keeping that interminable Catalogue, that non picciol' libro. Did he owe it to them, the lovers of skins, not to tell about Vheissu, not even to let them suspect the suicidal fact that below the glittering integument of every foreign land there is a hard dead-point of truth and that in all cases—even England's—it is the same kind of truth, can be phrased in identical words? He had lived with his knowledge since June and that headlong drive for the Pole; was able now to control or repress it almost at will. But the humans—those from whom, prodigal, he had strayed and could expect no future blessing—those four fat schoolmistresses whinnying softly to one another by the south portals of the Duomo, that fop in tweeds and clipped mustaches who came hastening by in fumes of lavender toward God knew what assignation; had they any notion of what inner magnitudes such control must draw on? His own, he knew, were nearly played out. He wandered down Via dell' Orivolo, counting the dark spaces between street lamps as he had once counted the number of puffs it took him to extinguish all his birthday candles. This year, next year, sometime, never. There were more candles at this point perhaps than even he could dream; but nearly all had been blown to twisted black wicks and the party needed very little to modulate to the most gently radiant of wakes. He turned left toward the hospital and surgeons' school, tiny and grayhaired and casting a shadow, he felt, much too large.

Footsteps behind him. On passing the next street lamp he saw the elongated shadows of helmeted heads bobbing about his quickening feet. Guardie? He nearly panicked: he'd been followed. He turned to face them, arms spread like the drooping wings of a condor at bay. He couldn't see them. "You are wanted for questioning," a voice purred in Italian, out of the darkness.

For no good reason he could see, life returned to him all at once, things were as they had always been, no different from leading a renegade squad against the Mahdi, invading Borneo in a whaleboat, attempting the Pole in midwinter. "Go to hell," he said cheerfully. Skipped out of the pool of light they'd trapped him in and went dashing off down a narrow, twisting side street. He heard footsteps, curses, cries of "Avanti!" behind him: would have laughed but couldn't waste the breath. Fifty meters on he turned abruptly down an alley. At the end was a trellis: he grasped it, swung himself up, began to climb. Young rose-thorns pricked his hands, the enemy howled closer. He came to a balcony, vaulted over, kicked in a set of French windows and entered a bedroom where a single candle burned. A man and a woman cringed nude and dumbfounded on the bed, their caresses frozen to immobility. "Madonna!" the woman screamed. "È il mio marito!" The man swore and tried to dive under the bed. Old Godolphin, blundering through the room, guffawed. My God, he was thinking irrelevantly, I have seen them before. I have seen this all twenty years ago in a music hall. He opened a door, found a stairway, hesitated briefly, then started up. No doubt about it, he was in a romantic mood. He'd be let down if there weren't a dash over the rooftops. By the time he gained the roof the voices of his pursuers were roaring in confusion far to his left. Disappointed, he made his way over the tops of two or three more buildings anyway, found an outside stairway and descended to another alley. For ten minutes he jogged along, taking in great breaths, steering sinuous course. A brilliantly lighted back window finally attracted his attention. He catfooted up to it, peered in. Inside, three men conferred anxiously amid a jungle of hothouse flowers, shrubs and trees. One of them he recognized, and chuckled in amazement. It is a small planet indeed, he thought, whose nether end I have seen. He tapped on the window. "Raf," he called softly.

Signor Mantissa glanced up, startled. "Minghe," he said, seeing Godolphin's grinning face. "The old inglese. Let him in, someone." The florist, red-faced and disapproving, opened the rear door. Godolphin stepped in quickly, the two men embraced, Cesare scratched his head. The florist retreated behind a fan palm after resecuring the door.

"A long way from Port Said," Signor Mantissa said.

"Not so far," Godolphin said, "nor so long."

Here was the sort of friendship which doesn't decay, however gapped it may be over the years with arid stretches of isolation from one another; more significant a renewal of that instant, motiveless acknowledgment of kinship one autumn morning four years back on the coaling piers at the head of the Suez Canal. Godolphin, impeccable in full dress uniform, preparing to inspect his man-o'-war, Rafael Mantissa the entrepreneur, overseeing the embarkation of a fleet of bumboats he'd acquired in a drunken baccarat game in

170

Cannes the month before, had each touched glances and seen immediately in the other an identical uprootedness, a similarly catholic despair. Before they spoke they were friends. Soon they had gone out and got drunk together, told each other their lives; were in fights, found, it seemed, a temporary home in the half-world behind Port Said's Europeanized boulevards. No rot about eternal friendship or blood brotherhood ever needed to be spoken.

"What is it, my friend," Signor Mantissa said now.

"Do you remember, once," Godolphin said, "a place, I told you: Vheissu." It hadn't been the same as telling his son, or the Board of Inquiry, or Victoria a few hours before. Telling Raf had been like comparing notes with a fellow sea dog on a liberty port both had visited.

Signor Mantissa made a sympathetic moue. "That again," he said.

"You have business now. I'll tell you later."

"No, nothing. This matter of a Judas tree."

"I have no more," Gadrulfi the florist muttered. "I've been telling him this for half an hour."

"He's holding out," Cesare said ominously. "Two hundred and fifty lire he wants, this time."

Godolphin smiled. "What chicanery with the law requires a Judas tree?"

Without hesitation Signor Mantissa explained. "And now," he concluded, "we need a duplicate, which we will let the police find."

Godolphin whistled. "You leave Florence tonight then."

"One way or the other, on the river barge at midnight, si."

"And there would be room for one more?"

"My friend." Signor Mantissa gripped him by the biceps. "For you," he said. Godolphin nodded. "You are in trouble. Of course. You need not even have asked. If you had come along even without a word I would have slain the barge captain at his first protest." The old man grinned. He was beginning to feel at least halfway secure for the first time in weeks.

"Let me make up the extra fifty lire," he said.

"I could not allow—"

"Nonsense. Get the Judas tree." Sullenly the florist pocketed the money, shambled to the corner and dragged a Judas tree, growing in a wine vat, from behind a thick tangle of ferns.

171

"The three of us can handle it," Cesare said. "Where to?"

"The Ponte Vecchio," Signor Mantissa said. "And then to Scheissvogel's. Remember, Cesare, a firm and united front. We must not let the Gaucho intimidate us. We may have to use his bomb, but we shall also have the Judas trees. The lion *and* the fox."

They formed a triangle around the tree and lifted. The florist held the back door open for them. They carried the tree twenty meters down an alley to a waiting carriage.

"Andiam'," Signor Mantissa cried. The horses moved off at a trot.

"I am to meet my son at Scheissvogel's in a few hours," Godolphin said. He had almost forgotten that Evan was probably now in the city. "I thought a beer hall would be safer than a café. But perhaps it is dangerous after all. The guardie are after me. They and others may have the place under surveillance."

Signor Mantissa took a sharp right expertly. "Ridiculous," he said. "Trust me. You are safe with Mantissa, I will defend your life as long as I have my own." Godolphin did not answer for a moment, then only shook his head in acceptance. For now he found himself wanting to see Evan; almost desperately. "You will see your son. It will be a jolly family reunion."

Cesare was uncorking a bottle of wine and singing an old revolutionary song. A wind had risen off the Arno. It blew Signor Mantissa's hair into a pale flutter. They headed toward the center of town, rattling along at a hollow clip. Cesare's mournful singing soon dissipated in the seeming vastness of that street.

VII

The Englishman who had questioned the Gaucho was named Stencil. A little after sundown he was in Major Chapman's study, sitting bemused in a deep leather chair, his scarred Algerian briar gone out unnoticed in the ashtray beside him. In his left hand he held a dozen wooden penholders, recently fitted with shiny new nibs. With his right hand he was hurling the pens methodically, like darts, at a large photograph of the current Foreign Minister which hung on the wall opposite. So far he had scored only a single hit, in the center of the Minister's forehead. This had made his chief resemble a benevolent unicorn, which was amusing but hardly rectified The Situation. The Situation at the moment was frankly appalling. More than that, it seemed to be irreparably bitched up.

The door suddenly burst open and a rangy man, prematurely gray, came roaring in. "They've found him," he said, not too elated.

Stencil glanced up quizzically, a pen poised in his hand. "The old man?"

"At the Savoy. A girl, a young English girl. Has him locked in. She just told us. Walked in and announced, calmly enough—"

"Go check it out, then," Stencil interrupted. "Though he's probably bolted by now."

"Don't you want to see her?"

"Pretty?"

"Rather."

"No, then. Things are bad enough as it is, if you see my point. I'll leave her to you, Demivolt."

"Bravo, Sidney. Dedicated to duty, aren't you. St. George and no quarter. I say. Well. I'm off, then. Don't say I didn't give you first chance."

Stencil smiled. "You're acting like a chorus boy. Perhaps I will see her. Later, when you're done."

Demivolt smiled woefully. "It makes The Situation halfway tolerable, you know." And bounded sadly back out through the door.

Stencil gritted his teeth. Oh, The Situation. The bloody Situation. In his more philosophical moments he would wonder about this abstract entity The Situation, its idea, the details of its mechanism. He remembered times when whole embassiesful of personnel had simply run amok and gibbering in the streets when confronted with a Situation which refused to make sense no matter who looked at it, or from what angle. He had once had a school chum named Covess. They had entered the diplomatic service together, worked their way up neck and neck. Until last year along came the Fashoda crisis and quite early one morning Covess was discovered in spats and a pith helmet, working his way around Piccadilly trying to recruit volunteers to invade France. There had been some idea of commandeering a Cunard liner. By the time they caught him he'd sworn in several costermongers, two streetwalkers and a music-hall comedian. Sten-

cil remembered painfully that they had all been singing On-
ward, Christian Soldiers in various keys and tempi.

He had decided long ago that no Situation had any objective reality: it only existed in the minds of those who
happened to be in on it at any specific moment. Since these
several minds tended to form a sum total or complex more
mongrel than homogeneous, The Situation must necessarily
appear to a single observer much like a diagram in four dimensions to an eye conditioned to seeing its world in only
three. Hence the success or failure of any diplomatic issue
must vary directly with the degree of rapport achieved by
the team confronting it. This had led to the near-obsession
with teamwork which had inspired his colleagues to dub him
Soft-shoe Sidney, on the assumption that he was at his best
working in front of a chorus line.

But it was a neat theory, and he was in love with it. The
only consolation he drew from the present chaos was that
his theory managed to explain it. Brought up by a pair of
bleak Nonconformist aunts, he had acquired the Anglo-
Saxon tendency to group northern/Protestant/intellectual
against Mediterranean/Roman Catholic/irrational. He had
thus arrived in Florence with a deep-rooted and chiefly sub-
liminal ill will toward all things Italian, and the subsequent
conduct of his running mates from the secret police confirmed
it. What sort of Situation could one expect from such a
scurvy and heterogeneous crew?

The matter of this English lad, for example: Godolphin,
alias Gadrulfi. The Italians claimed they had been unable
after an hour of interrogation to extract anything about his
father, the naval officer. Yet the first thing the boy had done
when they'd finally brought him round to the British Consulate was to ask for Stencil's help in locating old Godolphin.
He had been quite ready to answer all inquiries about
Vheissu (although he'd done little more than recapitulate information already in F.O.'s possession); he had gratuitously
made mention of the rendezvous at Scheissvogel's at ten
tonight; in general he'd exhibited the honest concern and
bewilderment of any English tourist confronted with a happening outside the ken of his Baedeker or the power of Cook's
to deal with it. And this simply did not fit in with the picture
Stencil had formed of father and son as cunning arch-pro-
fessionals. Their employers, whoever they might be (Scheissvogel's was a German beer hall, which might be significant,
174

especially so with Italy a member of the Dreibund), could not tolerate such simplicity. This show was too big, too serious, to be carried out by any but the top men in the field.

The Department had been keeping a dossier on old Godolphin since '84, when the surveying expedition had been all but wiped out. The name Vheissu occurred in it only once, in a secret F.O. memorandum to the Secretary of State for War, a memo condensed from Godolphin's personal testimony. But a week ago the Italian Embassy in London sent round a copy of a telegram which the censor at Florence, after informing the state police, had let go through. The Embassy had included no explanation except for a scribbled note on the copy: "This may be of interest to you. Cooperation to our mutual advantage." It was initialed by the Italian Ambassador. On seeing Vheissu a live file again, Stencil's chief had alerted operatives in Deauville and Florence to keep a close eye on father and son. Inquiries began to be made around the Geographical Society. Since the original had been somehow lost, junior researchers started piecing together the text of Godolphin's testimony at the time of the incident by interviewing all available members of the original Board of Inquiry. The chief had been puzzled that no code was used in the telegram; but it had only strengthened Stencil's conviction that the Department was up against a pair of veterans. Such arrogance, he felt, such cocksureness was exasperating and one hated them for it, but at the same time one was overcome with admiration. Not bothering to use a code was the devil-may-care gesture of the true sportsman.

The door opened hesitantly. "I say, Mr. Stencil."

"Yes, Moffit. Do what I told you?"

"They're together. Mine not to reason why, you know."

"Bravo. Give them an hour or so together. After that we let young Gadrulfi out. Tell him we have nothing really to hold him on, sorry for the inconvenience, pip-pip, a rivederci. You know."

"And then follow him, eh. Game is afoot, ha, ha."

"Oh, he'll go to Scheissvogel's. We've advised him to keep the rendezvous, and whether he's straight or not he'll meet the old man. At least if he's playing his game the way we think he is."

"And the Gaucho?"

"Give him another hour. Then if he wants to escape, let him."

"Chancy, Mr. Stencil."

"Enough, Moffit. Back in the chorus line."

"Ta-ra-ra-boom-de-ay," said Moffit, soft-shoeing out the door. Stencil heaved a sigh, leaned forward in the chair and recommenced his dart game. Soon a second hit, two inches from the first, had transfigured the Minister into a lopsided goat. Stencil gritted his teeth. "Pluck, lad," he muttered. "Before the girl arrives the old bastard should look like a blooming hedgehog."

Two cells away there was a loud morra game in progress. Outside the window, somewhere, a girl sang about her love, killed defending his homeland in a faraway war.

"She's singing for the tourists," the Gaucho complained bitterly, "she must be. No one ever sings in Florence. No one ever used to. Except now and again the Venezuelan friends I told you about. But they sing marching songs, which are useful for morale."

Evan stood by the cell door, leaning his forehead against the bars. "You may no longer have any Venezuelan friends," he said. "They've probably all been rounded up and pushed into the sea."

The Gaucho came over and gripped Evan's shoulder sympathetically. "You are still young," he said; "I know how it must have been. That's the way they work. They attack a man's spirit. You will see your father again. I will see my friends. Tonight. We're going to stage the most wonderful festa this city has seen since Savonarola was burned."

Evan looked around hopelessly at the small cell, the heavy bars. "They told me I might be released soon. But you stand a fat chance of doing anything tonight. Except lose sleep."

The Gaucho laughed. "I think they will release me too. I told them nothing. I'm used to their ways. They are stupid, and easily gotten round."

Evan clenched the bars furiously. "Stupid! Not only stupid. Deranged. Illiterate. Some bungling clerk misspelled my name Gadrulfi, and they refused to call me anything else. It was an alias, they said. Did it not say Gadrulfi in my dossier? Was it not down in black and white?"

"Ideas are so novel to them. Once they get hold of one,

having the vague idea it is somehow precious, they wish to keep possession of it."

"If that were all. But someone in the higher echelons had got the idea Vheissu was a code name for Venezuela. Either that or it was the same bloody clerk, or his brother, who never learned to spell."

"They asked me about Vheissu," the Gaucho mused. "What could I say? This time I really knew nothing. The English consider it important."

"But they don't tell you why. All they give you are mysterious hints. The Germans are apparently in on it. The Antarctic is concerned in some way. Perhaps in a matter of weeks, they say, the whole world will be plunged into apocalypse. And they think I am in on it. And you. Why else, if they are going to release us anyway, did they throw us into the same cell? We'll be followed wherever we go. Here we are, in the thick of a grand cabal, and we haven't the slightest notion of what's going on."

"I hope you didn't believe them. Diplomatic people always talk that way. They are living always on the verge of some precipice or other. Without a crisis they wouldn't be able to sleep nights."

Evan turned slowly to face his companion. "But I do believe them," he said calmly. "Let me tell you. About my father. He would sit in my room, before I went to sleep, and spin yarns about this Vheissu. About the spider-monkeys, and the time he saw a human sacrifice, and the rivers whose fish are sometimes opalescent and sometimes the color of fire. They circle round you when you go in to bathe and dance a kind of elaborate ritual all about, to protect you from evil. And there are volcanoes with cities inside them which once every hundred years erupt into flaming hell but people go to live in them anyway. And men in the hills with blue faces and women in the valleys who give birth to nothing but sets of triplets, and beggars who belong to guilds and hold jolly festivals and entertainments all summer long.

"You know how a boy is. There comes a time for departure, a point where he sees confirmed the suspicion he'd had for some time that his father is not a god, not even an oracle. He sees that he no longer has any right to any such faith. So Vheissu becomes a bedtime story or fairy tale after all, and the boy a superior version of his merely human father.

177

"I thought Captain Hugh was mad; I would have signed the commitment papers myself. But at Piazza della Signoria 5 I was nearly killed in something that could not have been an accident, a caprice of the inanimate world; and from then till now I have seen two governments hagridden to alienation over this fairy tale or obsession I thought was my father's own. As if this condition of being just human, which had made Vheissu and my boy's love for him a lie, were now vindicating them both for me, showing them to have been truth all along and after all. Because the Italians and the English in those consulates and even that illiterate clerk are all men. Their anxiety is the same as my father's, what is coming to be my own, and perhaps in a few weeks what will be the anxiety of everyone living in a world none of us wants to see lit into holocaust. Call it a kind of communion, surviving somehow on a mucked-up planet which God knows none of us like very much. But it is our planet and we live on it anyway."

The Gaucho did not answer. He walked to the window, stood gazing out. The girl was singing now about a sailor, halfway round the world from home and his betrothed. From down the corridor floated cries: "Cinque, tre, otto, brrrr!" Soon the Gaucho put his hands to his neck, removed his collar. He came back to Evan.

"If they let you out," he said, "in time to see your father, there is also at Scheissvogel's a friend of mine. His name is Cuernacabrón. Everyone knows him there. I would esteem it a favor if you would take him this, a message." Evan took the collar and pocketed it absently. A thought occurred to him.

"But they will see your collar missing."

The Gaucho grinned, stripped off his shirt and tossed it under a bunk. "It is warm, I will tell them. Thank you for reminding me. It's not easy for me to think like a fox."

"How do you propose to get out?"

"Simply. When the turnkey comes to let you out, we beat him unconscious, take his keys, fight our way to freedom."

"If both of us get away, should I still take the message?"

"Si. I must first go to Via Cavour. I will be at Scheissvogel's later, to see some associates on another matter. Un gran colpo, if things work right."

Soon footsteps, jangling keys approached down the cor-

178

ridor. "He reads our minds," the Gaucho chuckled. Evan
turned to him quickly, clasped his hand.

"Good luck."

"Put down your bludgeon, Gaucho," the turnkey called
in a cheerful voice. "You are to be released, both of you."

"Ah, che fortuna," said the Gaucho mournfully. He went
back to the window. It seemed that the girl's voice could
be heard all over April. The Gaucho stood on tiptoe. "Un'
gazz'l" he screamed.

VIII

Around Italian spy circles the latest joke was about an Englishman who cuckolded his Italian friend. The husband
came home one night to find the faithless pair in flagrante
delicto on the bed. Enraged, he pulled out a pistol and
was about to take revenge when the Englishman held up a
restraining hand. "I say old chap," he said loftily, "we're not
going to have any dissension in the ranks, are we? Think
what this might do to the Quadruple Alliance."

The author of this parable was one Ferrante, a drinker of
absinthe and destroyer of virginity. He was trying to grow a
beard. He hated politics. Like a few thousand other young
men in Florence he fancied himself a neo-Machiavellian.
He took the long view, having only two articles of faith:
(a) the Foreign Service in Italy was irreparably corrupt
and nitwit, and (b) someone should assassinate Umberto I.
Ferrante had been assigned to the Venezuelan problem for
half a year and was beginning to see no way out of it except
suicide.

That evening he was wandering around secret police
headquarters with a small squid in one hand, looking for
someplace to cook it. He'd just bought it at the market, it
was for supper. The hub of spy activities in Florence was
the second floor of a factory which made musical instruments for devotees of the Renaissance and Middle Ages. It
was run nominally by an Austrian named Vogt, who worked
painstakingly during the daylight hours putting together re-
becs, shawms and theorbos, and spied at night. In the legal
or everyday segment of his life he employed as helpers a
Negro named Gascoigne who would bring in his friends
from time to time to test out the instruments, and Vogt's
mother, an incredibly aged butterball of a woman who was

179

under the curious illusion that she'd had an affair with Palestrina in her girlhood. She would be constantly haranguing visitors with fond reminiscences about "Giovannino," these being mostly colorful allegations of sexual eccentricity in the composer. If these two were in on Vogt's espionage activities, no one was aware of it, not even Ferrante, who made it his business to spy on his colleagues as well as any more appropriate quarry. Vogt, however, being Austrian, could probably be given credit for discretion. Ferrante had no faith in covenants, he regarded them as temporary and more often than not farcical. But he reasoned that as long as you'd made an alliance in the first place you might as well comply with its rules as long as was expedient. Since 1882, then, Germans and Austrians had been temporarily acceptable. But English most assuredly not. Which had given rise to his joke about the cuckolded husband. He saw no reason for cooperating with London on this matter. It was a plot, he suspected, on Britain's part, to force a wedge into the Triple Alliance, to divide the enemies of England so that England could deal with them separately and at her leisure.

He descended into the kitchen. Horrible screeching noises were coming from inside. Naturally leery of anything deviating from his private norm, Ferrante dropped quietly to hands and knees, crawled cautiously up behind the stove and peered around it. It was the old woman, playing some sort of air on a viola da gamba. She did not play very well. When she saw Ferrante she put the bow down and glared at him.

"A thousand pardons, signora," Ferrante said, getting to his feet. "I did not mean to interrupt the music. I was wondering if I might borrow a skillet and some oil. My supper. Which will take no more than a few minutes." He waved the squid at her placatingly.

"Ferrante," she croaked abruptly, "this is no time for subtlety. Much is at stake."

Ferrante was taken aback. Had she been snooping? Or merely in her son's confidence? "I do not understand," he replied cautiously.

"That is nonsense," she retorted. "The English know something you did not. It all began with this silly Venezuelan business, but by accident, unaware, your colleagues have stumbled on something so vast and terrifying that they are afraid even to speak its name aloud."

"Perhaps."

"Is it not true, then, that the young Gadrulfi has testified to Herr Stencil that his father believes there to be agents of Vheissu present in this city?"

"Gadrulfi is a florist," said Ferrante impassively, "whom we have under surveillance. He is associated with partners of the Gaucho, an agitator against the legally constituted government of Venezuela. We have followed them to this florist's establishment. You have got your facts confused."

"More likely you and your fellow spies have got your names confused. I suppose you are maintaining as well this ridiculous fiction that Vheissu is a code name for Venezuela."

"That is the way it appears in our files."

"You are clever, Ferrante. You trust no one."

He shrugged. "Can I afford to?"

"I suppose not. Not when a barbaric and unknown race, employed by God knows whom, are even now blasting the Antarctic ice with dynamite, preparing to enter a subterranean network of natural tunnels, a network whose existence is known only to the inhabitants of Vheissu, the Royal Geographic Society in London, Herr Godolphin, and the spies of Florence."

Ferrante stood suddenly breathless. She was paraphrasing the secret memorandum Stencil had sent back to London not an hour ago.

"Having explored the volcanoes of their own region," she went on, "certain natives of the Vheissu district were the first to become aware of these tunnels, which lace the earth's interior at depths varying—"

"Aspetti!" Ferrante cried. "You are raving."

"Tell the truth," she said sharply. "Tell me what Vheissu is really the code name for. Tell me, you idiot, what I already know: that it stands for Vesuvius." She cackled horribly.

He was breathing with difficulty. She had guessed or spied it out or been told. She was probably safe. But how could he say: I detest politics, no matter if they are international or only within a single department. And the politics which have led to this worked the same way and are equally as detestable. Everyone had assumed that the code word referred to Venezuela, a routine matter, until the English informed them that Vheissu actually existed. There was testimony from young Gadrulfi, corroborating data already obtained from the Geographic Society and the Board of Inquiry fifteen years ago, about the volcanoes. And from then on fact had been added to meager fact and the censorship of that single telegram had avalanched into a harrowing afternoon-long session of give-and-take, of logrolling, bullying, factions and secret votes until Ferrante and his chief had to face the sickening truth of the matter: that they must league with the English in view of a highly probable common peril. That they could hardly afford not to.

"It could stand for Venus, for all I know," he said. "Please, I cannot discuss the matter." The old woman laughed again and began to saw away once more on her viola da gamba. She watched Ferrante contemptuously as he took down a skillet from a hook in the wall above the stove, poured olive oil into it and poked the embers into flame. When the oil began to sizzle, he placed his squid carefully in it, like an offering. He suddenly found himself sweating, though the stove gave off no great heat. Ancient music whined in the room, echoed off its walls. Ferrante let himself wonder, for no good reason, if it had been composed by Palestrina.

IX

Adjoining the prison which Evan had recently vacated, and not far from the British Consulate, are two narrow streets, Via del Purgatorio and Via dell'Inferno, which intersect in a T whose long side parallels the Arno. Victoria stood in this intersection, the night gloomy about her, a tiny erect figure in white dimity. She was trembling as if she waited for some lover. They had been considerate at the Consulate; more than that, she had seen the dull pounding of some knowledge heavy behind their eyes, and known all at once that old Godolphin had indeed been wrung by a "terrible need," and that her intuition had once more been correct. Her pride in this faculty was an athlete's pride in his strength or skill; it had once told her, for example, that Goodfellow was a spy and not a casual tourist; more, had revealed to her all at once a latent talent of her own for espionage. Her decision to help Godolphin came not out of any romantic illusion about spying—in that business she saw mostly ugliness, little glamour—but rather because she felt that skill or any virtú was a desirable and lovely thing purely for its own sake; and it became more effective the further divorced it was from moral intention. Though she would have denied it, she was one with Ferrante, with the Gaucho, with Signor Mantissa; like them she would act, when occasion arose, on the strength of a unique and private gloss on *The Prince*. She overrated virtú, individual agency, in much the same way Signor Mantissa overrated the fox. Perhaps one day one of them might ask: what was the tag-end of an age if not that sort of imbalance, that tilt toward the more devious, the less forceful?

She wondered, standing stone-still at the crossroads, whether the old man had trusted her, had waited after all. She prayed that he had, less perhaps from concern for him than from some obvoluted breed of self-aggrandizement which read the conforming of events to the channels she'd set out for them as glorious testimony to her own skill. One thing she had avoided—probably because of the supernatural tinge men acquired in her perception—was the schoolgirlish tendency to describe every male over the age of fifty as "sweet," "dear," or "nice." Dormant in every aged man she saw rather his image regressed twenty or thirty years, like a wraith which nearly merged outlines with its counterpart: young, potent, possessing mighty sinews and sensitive hands. So that in Captain Hugh it had been the young version she wished to help and make a part of the vast system of channels, locks and basins she had dug for the rampant river Fortune.

If there were, as some doctors of the mind were beginning to suspect, an ancestral memory, an inherited reservoir of primordial knowledge which shapes certain of our actions and casual desires, then not only her presence here and now between purgatory and hell, but also her entire commitment to Roman Catholicism as needful and plausible stemmed from and depended on an article of the primitive faith which glimmered shiny and supreme in that reservoir like a crucial valve-handle: the notion of the wraith or spiritual double, happening on rare occasions by multiplication but more often by fission, and the natural corollary which says the son is doppelgänger to the father. Having once accepted duality Victoria had found it only a single step to Trinity. And having seen the halo of a second and more virile self flickering about old Godolphin, she waited now outside the prison while somewhere to her right a girl sang lonely, telling a tale of hesitation, between a rich man who was old and a young man who was fair.

At length she heard the prison door open, heard his footsteps begin to approach down a narrow alleyway, heard the door slam to again. She dug the point of her parasol into the ground beside one tiny foot and gazed down at it. He was upon her before she realized it, nearly colliding with her. "I say," he exclaimed.

She looked up. His face was indistinct. He peered closer at her. "I saw you this afternoon," he said. "The girl in the tram, isn't it."

She murmured assent. "And you sang Mozart to me." He did not look at all like his father.

"A bit of a lark," Evan bumbled. "Didn't mean to embarrass you."

"You did."

Evan hung his head, sheepish. "But what are you doing out here, at this time of night?" He forced a laugh. "Not waiting for me, surely."

"Yes," she said quietly. "Waiting for you."

"That's terribly flattering. But if I may say so, you aren't the sort of young lady who . . . I mean, are you? I mean, dash it, why should you be waiting for me? Not because you liked my singing voice."

"Because you are his son," she said.

He did not, he realized, have to ask for explanation: wouldn't have to stammer, how did you meet my father, how did you know I was here, that I would be released? It was as if what he'd said to the Gaucho, back in their cell, had been like confession; an acknowledgment of weakness; as if the Gaucho's silence in turn had served as absolution, redeeming the weakness, propelling him suddenly into the trembling planes of a new kind of manhood. He felt that belief in Vheissu gave him no right any more to doubt as arrogantly as he had before, that perhaps wherever he went from now on he would perform like penance a ready acceptance of miracles or visions such as this meeting at the crossroads seemed to him to be. They began to walk. She tucked her hands around his bicep.

From his slight elevation he noted an ornate ivory comb, sunk to the armpits in her hair. Faces, helmets, arms linked: crucified? He blinked closer at the faces. All looked drawn-down by the weight of the bodies beneath: but seemed to

184

grimace more by convention—with an Eastern idea of patience—than with any more explicit or Caucasian pain. What a curious girl it was beside him. He was about to use the comb for a conversational opening when she spoke.

"How strange tonight, this city. As if something trembled below its surface, waiting to burst through."

"Oh I've felt it. I think to myself: we are not, any of us, in the Renaissance at all. Despite the Fra Angelicos, the Titians, Botticellis; Brunelleschi church, ghosts of the Medici. It is another time. Like radium, I expect: they say radium changes, bit by bit, over unimaginable spaces of time, to lead. A glow about old Firenze seems to be missing, seems more a leaden gray."

"Perhaps the only radiance left is in Vheissu."

He looked down at her. "How odd you are," he said. "I almost feel you know more than I about the place."

She pursed her lips. "Do you know how I felt when I spoke with him? As if he'd told me the same stories he told you when you were a boy, and I had forgotten them, but needed only to see him, hear his voice, for all the memories to come rushing back undecayed."

He smiled. "That would make us brother and sister."

She didn't answer. They turned into Via Porta Rossa. Tourists were thick in the streets. Three rambling musicians, guitar, violin and kazoo, stood on a corner, playing sentimental airs.

"Perhaps we are in limbo," he said. "Or like the place we met: some still point between hell and purgatory. Strange there's no Via del Paradiso anywhere in Florence."

"Perhaps nowhere in the world."

For that moment at least they seemed to give up external plans, theories and codes, even the inescapable romantic curiosity about one another, to indulge in being simply and purely young, to share that sense of the world's affliction, that outgoing sorrow at the spectacle of Our Human Condition which anyone this age regards as reward or gratuity for having survived adolescence. For them the music was sweet and painful, the strolling chains of tourists like a Dance of Death. They stood on the curb, gazing at one another, jostled against by hawkers and sightseers, lost as much perhaps in that bond of youth as in the depths of the eyes each contemplated.

He broke it first. "You haven't told me your name."

She told him.

"Victoria," he said. She felt a kind of triumph. It was the way he'd said it.

He patted her hand. "Come," he said feeling protective, almost fatherly. "I am to meet him, at Scheissvogel's."

"Of course," she said. They turned left, away from the Arno, toward Piazza Vittorio Emmanuele.

The Figli di Machiavelli had taken over for their garrison an abandoned tobacco warehouse off Via Cavour. It was deserted at the moment except for an aristocratic-looking man named Borracho, who was performing his nightly duty of checking the rifles. There was a sudden pounding at the door. "Digame," yelled Borracho.

"The lion and the fox," came the answer. Borracho unlatched the door and was nearly bowled over by a thick-set mestizo called Tito, who earned his living selling obscene photographs to the Fourth Army Corps. He appeared highly excited.

"They're marching," he began to babble, "tonight, half a battalion, they have rifles, and fixed bayonets—"

"What in God's name is this," Borracho growled, "has Italy declared war? Qué pasa?"

"The Consulate. The Consulate of Venezuela. They are to guard it. They expect us. Someone has betrayed the Figli di Machiavelli."

"Calm down," Borracho said. "Perhaps the moment which the Gaucho promised us has arrived at last. We must expect him, then. Quickly. Alert the others. Put them on standby. Send a messenger into town to find Cuernacabrón. He will likely be at the beer garden."

Tito saluted, wheeled, ran to the door on the double, unlocked it. A thought occurred to him. "Perhaps," he said, "perhaps the Gaucho himself is the traitor." He opened the door. The Gaucho stood there, glowering. Tito gaped. Without a word the Gaucho brought his closed fist down on the mestizo's head. Tito toppled and crashed to the floor.

"Idiot," the Gaucho said. "What's happened? Is everyone insane?"

Borracho told him about the army.

The Gaucho rubbed his hands. "Bravissimo. A major action. And yet we've not heard from Caracas. No matter. We

186

move tonight. Alert the troops. We must be there at midnight."

"Not much time, commendatore."

"We will be there at midnight. Vada."

"Si, commendatore." Borracho saluted and left, stepping carefully over Tito on his way out.

The Gaucho took a deep breath, crossed his arms, flung them wide, crossed them again. "So," he cried to the empty warehouse. "The night of the lion has come again to Florence!"

X

Scheissvogel's Biergarten und Rathskeller was a nighttime favorite not only with the German travelers in Florence but also, it seemed, with those of the other touring nations. An Italian caffé (it was conceded) being fine for the afternoon, when the city lazed in contemplation of its art treasures. But the hours after sundown demanded a conviviality, a boisterousness which the easygoing—perhaps even a bit cliquish —caffés did not supply. English, American, Dutch, Spanish, they seemed to seek some Hofbrauhaus of the spirit like a grail, hold a krug of Munich beer like a chalice. Here at Scheissvogel's were all the desired elements: blond barmaids, with thick braids wound round the back of the head, who could carry eight foaming kruger at a time, a pavilion with a small brass band out in the garden, an accordionist inside, confidences roared across a table, much smoke, group singing.

Old Godolphin and Rafael Mantissa sat out in back in the garden, at a small table, while the wind from the river played chilly about their mouths and the wheeze of the band frolicked about their ears, more absolutely alone, it seemed to them, than anyone else in the city.

"Am I not your friend?" Signor Mantissa pleaded. "You must tell me. Perhaps, as you say, you have wandered outside the world's communion. But haven't I as well? Have I not been ripped up by the roots, screaming like the mandrake, transplanted from country to country only to find the soil arid, or the sun unfriendly, the air tainted? Whom should you tell this terrible secret to if not to your brother?"

"Perhaps to my son," said Godolphin.

"I never had a son. But isn't it true that we spend our

187

son

lives seeking for something valuable, some truth to tell to a son, to give to him with love? Most of us aren't as lucky as you, perhaps we have to be torn away from the rest of men before we can have such words to give to a son. But it has been all these years. You can wait a few minutes more. He will take your gift and use it for himself, for his own life. I do not malign him. It is the way a younger generation acts: that, simply. You, as a boy, probably bore away some such gift from your own father, not realizing that it was still as valuable to him as it would be to you. But when the English speak of 'passing down' something from one generation to another, it is only that. A son passes nothing back up. Perhaps this is a sad thing, and not Christian, but it has been that way since time out of mind, and will never change. Giving, and giving back, can be only between you and one of your own generation. Between you and Mantissa, your dear friend."

The old man shook his head, half-smiling; "It isn't so much, Raf, I've grown used to it. Perhaps you will find it not so much."

"Perhaps. It is difficult to understand how an English explorer thinks. Was it the Antarctic? What sends the English into these terrible places?"

Godolphin stared at nothing. "I think it is the opposite of what sends English reeling all over the globe in the mad dances called Cook's tours. They want only the skin of a place, the explorer wants its heart. It is perhaps a little like being in love. I had never penetrated to the heart of any of those wild places, Raf. Until Vheissu. It was not till the Southern Expedition last year that I saw what was beneath her skin."

"What did you see?" asked Signor Mantissa, leaning forward.

"Nothing," Godolphin whispered. "It was Nothing I saw." Signor Mantissa reached out a hand to the old man's shoulder. "Understand," Godolphin said, bowed and motionless, "I had been tortured by Vheissu for fifteen years. I dreamed of it, half the time I lived in it. It wouldn't leave me. Colors, music, fragrances. No matter where I got assigned, I was pursued by memories. Now I am pursued by agents. That feral and lunatic dominion cannot afford to let me escape.

"Raf, you will be ridden by it longer than I. I haven't
188

much time left. You must never tell anyone, I won't ask for your promise; I take that for granted. I have done what no man has done. I have been at the Pole."

"The Pole. My friend. Then why have we not—"

"Seen it in the press. Because I made it that way. They found me, you remember, at the last depot, half dead and snowed in by a blizzard. Everyone assumed I had tried for the Pole and failed. But I was on my way back. I let them tell it their way. Do you see? I had thrown away a sure knighthood, rejected glory for the first time in my career, something my son has been doing since he was born. Evan is rebellious, his was no sudden decision. But mine was, sudden and necessary, because of what I found waiting for me at the Pole."

Two carabinieri and their girls arose from a table and weaved arm-in-arm out of the garden. The band began to play a sad waltz. Sounds of carousing in the beer hall floated out to the two men. The wind blew steady, there was no moon. The leaves of trees whipped to and fro like tiny automata.

"It was a foolish thing," Godolphin said, "what I did. There was nearly a mutiny. After all, one man, trying for the Pole, in the dead of winter. They thought I was insane. Possibly I was, by that time. But I had to reach it. I had begun to think that there, at one of the only two motionless places on this gyrating world, I might have peace to solve Vheissu's riddle. Do you understand? I wanted to stand in the dead center of the carousel, if only for a moment; try to catch my bearings. And sure enough: waiting for me was my answer. I'd begun to dig a cache nearby, after planting the flag. The barrenness of that place howled around me, like a country the demiurge had forgotten. There could have been no more entirely lifeless and empty place anywhere on earth. Two or three feet down I struck clear ice. A strange light, which seemed to move inside it, caught my attention. I cleared a space away. Staring up at me through the ice, perfectly preserved, its fur still rainbow-colored, was the corpse of one of their spider monkeys. It was quite real; not like the vague hints they had given me before. I say 'they had given.' I think they left it there for me. Why? Perhaps for some alien, not-quite-human reason that I can never comprehend. Perhaps only to see what I would do. A mockery, you see: a mockery of life, planted where everything

189

but Hugh Godolphin was inanimate. With of course the implication . . . It did tell me the truth about them. If Eden was the creation of God, God only knows what evil created Vheissu. The skin which had wrinkled through my nightmares was all there had ever been. Vheissu itself, a gaudy dream. Of what the Antarctic in this world is closest to: a dream of annihilation."

Signor Mantissa looked disappointed. "Are you sure, Hugh? I have heard that in the polar regions men, after long exposure, see things which—"

"Does it make any difference?" Godolphin said. "If it were only a hallucination, it was not what I saw or believed I saw that in the end is important. It is what I thought. What truth I came to."

Signor Mantissa shrugged helplessly. "And now? Those who are after you?"

"Think I will tell. Know I have guessed the meaning of their clue, and fear I will try to publish it. But dear Christ, how could I? Am I mistaken, Raf? I think it must send the world mad. Your eyes are puzzled. I know. You can't see it yet. But you will. You are strong. It will hurt you no more—" he laughed—"than it has hurt me." He looked up, over Signor Mantissa's shoulder. "Here is my son. The girl is with him."

Evan stood over them. "Father," he said.

"Son." They shook hands. Signor Mantissa yelled for Cesare and drew up a chair for Victoria.

"Could you all excuse me for a moment. I must deliver a message. For a Señor Cuernacabrón."

"He is a friend of the Gaucho," Cesare said, coming up behind them.

"You have seen the Gaucho?" asked Signor Mantissa.

"Half an hour ago."

"Where is he?"

"Out at Via Cavour. He is coming here later, he said he had to meet friends on another matter."

"Aha!" Signor Mantissa glanced at his watch. "We haven't much time. Cesare, go and inform the barge of our rendezvous. Then to the Ponte Vecchio for the trees. The cabman can help. Hurry." Cesare ambled off. Signor Mantissa waylaid a waitress, who set down four liters of beer on the table. "To our enterprise," he said.

Three tables away Moffit watched, smiling.

That march from Via Cavour was the most splendid the
Gaucho could remember. Somehow, miraculously, Borracho,
Tito and a few friends had managed in a surprise raid to
make off with a hundred horses from the cavalry. The theft
was discovered quickly, but not before Figli di Machiavelli,
hollering and singing, were mounted and galloping toward
the center of town. The Gaucho rode in front, wearing a
red shirt and a wide grin. "Avanti, i miei fratelli," they sang,
"Figli di Machiavelli, avanti alla donna Libertá!" Close
behind came the army, pursuing in ragged, furious files, half
of them on foot, a few in carriages. Halfway into town the
renegades met Cuernacabrón in a gig: the Gaucho wheeled,
swooped, gathered him up bodily, turned again to rejoin the
Figli. "My comrade," he roared to his bewildered second-in-
command, "isn't it a glorious evening."

They reached the Consulate at a few minutes to midnight
and dismounted, still singing and yelling. Those who worked
at the Mercato Centrale had provided enough rotten fruit
and vegetables to set up a heavy and sustained barrage
against the Consulate. The army arrived. Salazar and Ratón
watched cringing from the second-floor window. Fistfights
broke out. So far no shots had been fired. The square had
erupted suddenly into a great whirling confusion. Passers-by
fled bawling to what shelter they could find.

The Gaucho caught sight of Cesare and Signor Mantissa,
with two Judas trees, shuffling impatiently near the Posta
Centrale. "Good God," he said. "Two trees? Cuernacabrón,
I have to leave for a while. You are now commendatore.
Take charge." Cuernacabrón saluted and dived into the
melee. The Gaucho, making his way over to Signor Mantissa,
saw Evan, the father, and the girl waiting nearby. "Buona
sera once again, Gadrulfi," he called, flipping a salute in
Evan's direction. "Mantissa, are we ready?" He unclipped a
large grenade from one of the ammunition belts crisscrossing
his chest. Signor Mantissa and Cesare picked up the hollow
tree.

"Guard the other one," Signor Mantissa called back to
Godolphin. "Don't let anyone know it's there until we return."

191

"Evan," the girl whispered, moving closer to him. "Will there be shooting?"

He did not hear her eagerness, only her fear. "Don't be afraid," he said, aching to shelter her.

Old Godolphin had been looking at them, shuffling his feet, embarrassed. "Son," he finally began, conscious of being a fool, "I suppose this is hardly the time to mention it. But I must leave Florence. Tonight. I would—I wish you would come with me." He couldn't look at his son. The boy smiled wistfully, his arm round Victoria's shoulders.

"But Papa," he said, "I would be leaving my only true love behind."

Victoria stood on tiptoe to kiss his neck. "We will meet again," she whispered sadly, playing the game.

The old man turned away from them, trembling, not understanding, feeling betrayed once again. "I am terribly sorry," he said.

Evan released Victoria, moved to Godolphin. "Father," he said, "Father, it's our way only. It's my fault, the joke. A trivial oaf's joke. You know I'll come with you."

"My fault," the father said. "My oversight, I dare say, for not keeping up with the younger people. Imagine, something so simple as a way of speaking . . ."

Evan let his hand rest splayed on Godolphin's back. Neither moved for a moment. "On the barge," Evan said, "there we'll be able to talk."

The old man turned at last. "Time we got round to it."

"We will," Evan said, trying to smile. "After all, here we've been, so many years, biffing about at opposite ends of the world."

The old man did not answer, but burrowed his face against Evan's shoulder. Both felt slightly embarrassed. Victoria watched them for a moment, then turned away to gaze, placid, at the rioting. Shots began to ring out. Blood began to stain the pavements, screams to punctuate the singing of the Figli di Machiavelli. She saw a rioter in a shirt of motley, sprawled over the limb of a tree, being bayoneted again and again by two soldiers. She stood as still as she had at the crossroads waiting for Evan; her face betrayed no emotion. It was as if she saw herself embodying a feminine principle, acting as complement to all this bursting, explosive male energy. Inviolate and calm, she watched the spasms of wounded bodies, the fair of violent death, framed and staged, it seemed, for her alone in that tiny square. From her hair the heads of five crucified also looked on, no more expressive than she.

Lugging the tree, Signor Mantissa and Cesare staggered through the "Ritratti diversi," while the Gaucho guarded their rear. He'd already had to fire at two guards. "Hurry," he said. "We must be out of here soon. They won't be diverted for long."

Inside the Sala di Lorenzo Monaco Cesare unsheathed a razor-edged dagger and prepared to slice the Botticelli from its frame. Signor Mantissa gazed at her, at the asymmetric eyes, tilt of the frail head, streaming gold hair. He could not move; as if he were any gentle libertine before a lady he had writhed for years to possess, and now that the dream was about to be consummated he had been struck suddenly impotent. Cesare dug the knife into the canvas, began to saw downward. Light, shining in from the street, reflected from the blade, flickering from the lantern they had brought, danced over the painting's gorgeous surface. Signor Mantissa watched its movement, a slow horror growing in him. In that instant he was reminded of Hugh Godolphin's spider-monkey, still shimmering through crystal ice at the bottom of the world. The whole surface of the painting now seemed to move, to be flooded with color and motion. He thought, for the first time in years, of the blond seamstress in Lyons. She would drink absinthe at night and torture herself for it in the afternoon. God hated her, she said. At the same time she was finding it more difficult to believe in him. She wanted to go to Paris, she had a pleasant voice, did she not? She would go on the stage, it had been her dream since girlhood. Countless mornings, in the hours when passion's inertia of motion had carried them along faster than sleep could overtake them, she had poured out to him schemes, despairs, all tiny, relevant loves.

What sort of mistress, then, would Venus be? What outlying worlds would he conquer in their headlong, three-in-the-morning excursions away from the cities of sleep? What of her God, her voice, her dreams? She was already a goddess. She had no voice he could ever hear. And she herself (perhaps even her native demesne?) was only . . .

A gaudy dream, a dream of annihilation. Was that what

193

Godolphin had meant? Yet she was no less Rafael Mantissa's entire love.

"Aspetti," he shouted, leaping forward to grab Cesare's hand.

"Sei pazzo?" Cesare snarled.

"Guards coming this way," the Gaucho announced from the entrance to the gallery. "An army of them. For God's sake, hurry."

"You have come all this way," Cesare protested, "and now you will leave her?"

"Yes."

The Gaucho raised his head, suddenly alert. The rattle of gunfire came to him, faintly. With an angry motion he flung the grenade down the corridor; the approaching guards scattered and it went off with a roar in the "Ritratti diversi." Signor Mantissa and Cesare, empty-handed, were at his back. "We must run for our lives," the Gaucho said. "Have you got your lady with you?"

"No," Cesare said, disgusted. "Not even the damned tree."

They dashed down a corridor smelling of burnt cordite. Signor Mantissa noticed that paintings in the "Ritratti diversi" had all been taken down for the redecorating. The grenade had harmed nothing except the walls and a few guards. It was a mad, all-out sprint, with the Gaucho taking pot-shots at guards, Cesare waving his knife, Signor Mantissa flapping his arms wildly. Miraculously they reached the entrance and half-ran, half tumbled down 126 steps to the Piazza della Signoria. Evan and Godolphin joined them.

"I must return to the battle," the Gaucho said, breathless. He stood for a moment watching the carnage. "But don't they look like apes, now, fighting over a female? Even if the female is named Liberty." He drew a long pistol, checked the action. "There are nights," he mused, "nights, alone, when I think we are apes in a circus, mocking the ways of men. Perhaps it is all a mockery, and the only condition we can ever bring to men a mockery of liberty, of dignity. But that cannot be. Or else I have lived . . ."

Signor Mantissa grasped his hand. "Thank you," he said.

The Gaucho shook his head. "Per niente," he muttered, then abruptly turned and made his way toward the riot in the square. Signor Mantissa watched him briefly. "Come," he said at last.

Evan looked over to where Victoria was standing en-

great plans come to nothing

chanted. He seemed about to move, or call to her. Then he shrugged and turned away to follow the others. Perhaps he didn't want to disturb her.

Moffit, knocked sprawling by a not-so-rotten turnip, saw them. "They're getting away," he said. He got to his feet and began clawing his way through the rioters, expecting to be shot at any minute. "In the name of the Queen," he cried. "Halt." Someone careened into him.

"I say," said Moffit, "it's Sidney."

"I've been looking all over for you," Stencil said.

"Not a mo too soon. They're getting away."

"Forget it."

"Down that alley. Hurry." He tugged at Stencil's sleeve.

"Forget it, Moffit. It's off. The whole show."

"Why?"

"Don't ask why. It's over."

"But."

"There was just a communiqué from London. From the Chief. He knows more than I do. He called it off. How should I know? No one ever tells me anything."

"Oh, my God."

They edged into a doorway. Stencil pulled out his pipe and lit it. The sounds of firing rose in a crescendo which it seemed would never stop. "Moffit," Stencil said after a while, puffing meditatively, "if there is ever a plot to assassinate the Foreign Minister, I pray I never get assigned to the job of preventing it. Conflict of interest, you know."

They scurried down a narrow street to the Lungarno. There, after Cesare had removed two middle-aged ladies and a cab driver, they took possession of a fiacre and clattered off pell-mell for the Ponte San Trinitá. The barge was waiting for them, dim amid the river's shadows. The captain jumped to the quay. "Three of you," he bellowed. "Our bargain included only one." Signor Mantissa flew into a rage, leaped from the carriage, picked up the captain bodily and before anyone had time to register amazement, flung him into the Arno. "On board!" he cried. Evan and Godolphin jumped onto a cargo of crated Chianti flasks. Cesare moaned, thinking of how that trip would be.

"Can anyone pilot a barge," Signor Mantissa wondered.

"It is like a man-o'-war," Godolphin smiled, "only smaller and no sails. Son, would you cast off."

195

"Aye, aye, sir." In a moment they were free of the quay. Soon the barge was drifting off into the current which flows strong and steady toward Pisa and the sea. "Cesare," they called, in what were already ghosts' voices, "addio. A rivederla."

Cesare waved. "A rivederci." Soon they had disappeared, dissolved in the darkness. Cesare put his hands in his pockets and started to stroll. He found a stone in the street and began to kick it aimlessly along the Lungarno. Soon, he thought, I will go and buy a liter fiasco of Chianti. As he passed the Palazzo Corsini, towering nebulous and fair above him, he thought: what an amusing world it still is, where things and people can be found in places where they do not belong. For example, out there on the river now with a thousand liters of wine are a man in love with Venus, and a sea captain, and his fat son. And back in the Uffizi . . . He roared aloud. In the room of Lorenzo Monaco, he remembered amazed, before Botticelli's Birth of Venus, still blooming purple and gay, there is a hollow Judas tree.

chapter eight

*In which Rachel gets her yo-yo
back, Roony sings a song,
and Stencil calls
on Bloody
Chiclitz*

V

Profane, sweating in April's heat, sat on a bench in the little park behind the Public Library, swatting at flies with rolled-up pages of the Times classified. From mental cross-plotting he'd decided where he sat now was the geographical center of the midtown employment agency belt.

A weird area it was. For a week now he'd sat patient in a dozen offices, filling out forms, having interviews and watching other people, especially girls. He had an interesting daydream all built up, which went: You're jobless, I'm jobless, here we both are out of work, let's screw. He was horny. What little money he'd saved from the sewer job had almost run out and here he was considering seduction. It kept the time moving right along.

So far no agency he'd been to had sent him anywhere for a job interview. He had to agree with them. To amuse himself he'd looked in Help Wanted under S. Nobody wanted a schlemihl. Laborers were for out of the city: Profane wanted to stay in Manhattan, he'd had enough of wandering out in the suburbs. He wanted a single point, a base of operations, someplace to screw in private. It was difficult when you brought a girl to a flophouse. A young kid with

197

a beard and old dungarees had tried that a few nights ago down where Profane was staying. The audience, winos and bums, had decided to serenade them after a few minutes of just watching. "Let me call you sweetheart," they sang, all somehow on key. A few had fine voices, some sang harmony. It may have been like the bartender on upper Broadway who was nice to the girls and their customers. There is a way we behave around young people excited with each other, even if we haven't been getting any for a while and aren't likely to very soon. It is a little cynical, a little self-pitying, a little withdrawn; but at the same time a genuine desire to see young people get together. Though it springs from a self-centered concern, it is often as much as a young man like Profane ever does go out of himself and take an interest in human strangers. Which is better, one would suppose, than nothing at all.

Profane sighed. The eyes of New York women do not see the wandering bums or the boys with no place to go. Material wealth and getting laid strolled arm-in-arm the midway of Profane's mind. If he'd been the type who evolves theories of history for his own amusement, he might have said all political events: wars, governments and uprisings, have the desire to get laid as their roots; because history unfolds according to economic forces and the only reason anybody wants to get rich is so he can get laid steadily, with whomever he chooses. All he believed at this point, on the bench behind the Library, was that anybody who worked for inanimate money so he could buy more inanimate objects was out of his head. Inanimate money was to get animate warmth, dead fingernails in the living shoulderblades, quick cries against the pillow, tangled hair, lidded eyes, twisting loins. . . .

He'd thought himself into an erection. He covered it with the Times classified and waited for it to subside. A few pigeons watched him, curious. It was shortly after noon and the sun was hot. I ought to keep looking, he thought, the day isn't over. What was he going to do? He was, they told him, unspecialized. Everybody else was at peace with some machine or other. Not even a pick and shovel had been safe for Profane.

He happened to look down. His erection had produced in the newspaper a crosswise fold, which moved line by line down the page as the swelling gradually diminished. It was a list of employment agencies. O.K, thought Profane, just for the heck of it I will close my eyes, count three and open them and whatever agency listing that fold is on I will go to them. It will be like flipping a coin: inanimate schmuck, inanimate paper, pure chance.

He opened his eyes on Space/Time Employment Agency, down on lower Broadway, near Fulton Street. Bad choice, he thought. It meant 15 cents for the subway. But a deal was a deal. On the Lexington Avenue downtown he saw a bum lying across the aisle, diagonal on the seat, Nobody would sit near him. He was king of the subway. He must have been there all night, yo-yoing out to Brooklyn and back, tons of water swirling over his head and he perhaps dreaming his own submarine country, peopled by mermaids and deep-sea creatures all at peace among the rocks and sunken galleons; must have slept through rush hour, with all sorts of suit-wearers and high-heel dolls glaring at him because he was taking up three sitting spaces but none of them daring to wake him. If under the street and under the sea are the same then he was king of both. Profane remembered himself on the shuttle back in February, wondered how he'd looked to Kook, to Fina. Not like a king, he figured: more like a schlemihl, a follower.

Having sunk into self-pity he nearly missed the Fulton Street stop. Got the bottom edge of his suede jacket caught in the doors when they closed; was nearly carried that way out to Brooklyn. He found Space/Time Employment down the street and ten floors up. The waiting area was crowded when he got there. A quick check revealed no girls worth looking at, nobody in fact but a family who might have stepped through time's hanging arras directly out of the Great Depression; journeyed to this city in an old Plymouth pickup from their land of dust: husband, wife and one mother-in-law, all yelling at each other, none but the old lady really caring about a job, so that she stood, legs braced, in the middle of the waiting area, telling them both how to make out their applications, a cigarette dangling from and about to burn her lipstick.

Profane made out his application, dropped it on the receptionist's desk and sat down to wait. Soon there came the hurried and sexy tap of high heels in the corridor outside. As if magnetized his head swiveled around and he saw coming in the door a tiny girl, lifted up to all of 5′1″ by her heels. Oboy, oboy, he thought: good stuff. She was not, however, an applicant: she belonged on the other side of the rail. Smiling and waving hello to everyone in her country, she clickety-clacked gracefully over to her desk. He could hear the quiet brush of her thighs, kissing each other in their nylon. Oh, oh, he thought, look at what I seem to be getting again. Go down, you bastard.

Obstinate, it would not. The back of his neck began to grow heated and rosy. The receptionist, a slim girl who seemed to be all tight—tight underwear, stockings, ligaments, tendons, mouth, a true windup woman—moved precisely among the decks, depositing applications like an automatic card-dealing machine. Six interviewers, he counted. Six to one odds she drew me. Like Russian roulette. Why like that? Would she destroy him, she so frail-looking, such gentle, well-bred legs? She had her head down, studying the application in her hand. She looked up, he saw the eyes, both slanted the same way.

"Profane," she called. Looking at him with a little frown.

Oh God, he thought, the loaded chamber. The luck of a schlemihl, who by common sense should lose at the game. Russian roulette is only one of its names, he groaned inside, and look: me with this hard on. She called his name again. He stumbled up from the chair, and proceeded with the Times over his groin and he bent at a 120° angle behind the rail and in to her own desk. The sign said RACHEL OWLGLASS.

He sat down quickly. She lit a cigarette and cased the upper half of his body. "It's about time," she said.

He fumbled for a cigarette, nervous. She flicked over a pack of matches with a fingernail he could feel already gliding across his back, poised to dig in frenzied when she should come.

And would she ever. Already they were in bed; he could see nothing but a new extemporized daydream in which no other face but this sad one with its brimming slash-slash of eyes tightened slowly in his own shadow, pale under him. God, she had him.

Strangely then the tumescence began to subside, the flesh at his neck to pale. Any sovereign or broken yo-yo must feel like this after a short time of lying inert, rolling, falling: suddenly to have its own umbilical string reconnected, and know the other end is in hands it cannot escape. Hands it doesn't want to escape. Know that the simple clockwork of itself has no more need for symptoms of inutility, lonesomeness, directionlessness, because now it has a path marked out for it over which it has no control. That's what the feeling would be, if there were such things as animate yo-yos. Pending any such warp in the world Profane felt like the closest thing to one and above her eyes began to doubt his own animateness.

"How about a night watchman," she said at last. Over you? he wondered.

"Where," he said. She mentioned an address nearby in Maiden Lane. "Anthroresearch Associates." He knew he couldn't say it as fast. On the back of a card she scribbled the address and a name—Oley Bergomask. "He hires." Handed it to him, a quick touch of fingernails. "Come back as soon as you find out. Bergomask will tell you right away; he doesn't waste time. If it doesn't work out we'll see what else we have."

At the door he looked back. Was she blowing a kiss or yawning?

II

Winsome had left work early. When he got back to the apartment he found his wife, Mafia, sitting on the floor with Pig Bodine. They were drinking beer and discussing her Theory. Mafia was sitting crosslegged and wearing very tight Bermuda shorts. Pig stared captivated at her crotch. That fella irritates me, Winsome thought. He got beer and sat down next to them. He wondered idly if Pig were getting any off of his wife. But it was hard to say who was getting what off Mafia.

There is a curious sea story about Pig Bodine, which Winsome had heard from Pig himself. Winsome was aware that Pig wanted to make a career someday of playing male leads in pornographic movies. He'd get this evil smile on his face, as if he were viewing or possibly committing reel on reel of depravities. The bilges of the radio shack of U.S.S. Scaffold—Pig's ship—were jammed solid with Pig's lending library, amassed during the ship's Mediterranean travels and rented out to the crew at 10 cents per book. The collection was foul enough to make Pig Bodine a byword of decadence throughout the squadron. But no one suspected that Pig might have creative as well as custodial talents.

One night Task Force 60, made up of two carriers, some other heavies and a circular screen of twelve destroyers, including the Scaffold, was steaming a few hundred miles east of Gibraltar. It was maybe two in the morning, visibility unlimited, stars blooming fat and sultry over a tar-colored Mediterranean. No closing contacts on the radars, everybody on after steering watch asleep, forward lookouts telling themselves sea stories to keep awake. That sort of night. All at once every teletype machine in the task force started clanging away, ding, ding, ding, ding, ding. Five bells, or FLASH, initial contact with enemy forces. It being '55 and more or less peacetime, captains were routed out of bed, general quarters called, dispersal plans executed. Nobody knew what was happening. By the time the teletypes started up again the formation was scattered out over a few hundred square miles of ocean and most radio shacks were crowded to capacity. The machines started to type.

"Message follows." Teletype operators, com officers leaned forward tense, thinking of Russian torpedoes, evil and barracudalike.

"Flash." Yes, yes, they thought: five bells, Flash. Go ahead.

Pause. Finally the keys started clattering again.

"THE GREEN DOOR. One night Dolores, Veronica, Justine, Sharon, Cindy Lou, Geraldine and Irving decided to hold an orgy. . . ." Followed, on four and a half feet of teletype paper, the functional implications of their decision, told from Irving's point of view.

For some reason Pig never got caught. Possibly because half the Scaffold's radio gang, also the communications officer, an Annapolis graduate named Knoop, were in on it and had locked the door to Radio as soon as GQ was called.

It caught on as a sort of fad. The next night, precedence Operational Immediate, came A DOG STORY, involving a St. Bernard named Fido and two WAVES. Pig was on watch when it came over and admitted to his henchman Knoop that it showed a certain flair. It was followed by other high-priority efforts: THE FIRST TIME I GOT LAID, WHY OUR X.O. IS QUEER, LUCKY PIERRE RUNS AMOK. By the time the Scaffold reached Naples, its first port of call, there were an even dozen, all carefully filed away by Pig under F.

But initial sin entails eventual retribution. Later, somewhere between Barcelona and Cannes, evil days fell on Pig. One night, routing the message board, he went to sleep in the doorway of the executive officer's stateroom. The ship chose that moment to roll ten degrees to port. Pig toppled onto the terrified lieutenant commander like a corpse. "Bodine," the X.O. shouted, aghast. "Were you sleeping?" Pig snored away among a litter of special-request chits. He was sent down on mess cooking. The first day he fell asleep in the serving line, rendering inedible a gunboat full of mashed potatoes. So the next meal he was stationed in front of the soup, which was made by Potamós the cook and which nobody ate anyway. Apparently Pig's knees had developed this odd way of locking, which if the Scaffold were on an even keel would enable him to sleep standing up. He was a medical curiosity. When the ship got back to the States he went under observation at Portsmouth Naval Hospital. When he returned to the Scaffold he was put on the deck force of one Pappy Hod, a boatswain's mate. In two days Pappy had driven him, for the first of what were to be many occasions, over the hill.

Now on the radio at the moment was a song about Davy Crockett, which upset Winsome considerably. This was '56, height of the coonskin hat craze. Millions of kids everywhere you looked were running around with these bushy Freudian hermaphrodite symbols on their heads. Nonsensical legends were being propagated about Crockett, all in direct contradiction to what Winsome had heard as a boy, across the mountains from Tennessee. This man, a foul-mouthed louse-ridden boozehound, a corrupt legislator and an indifferent pioneer, was being set up for the nation's youth as a towering and cleanlimbed example of Anglo-Saxon superiority. He had swelled into a hero such as Mafia might have created after waking from a particularly loony and erotic dream. The song invited parody. Winsome had even cast his own autobiography into aaaa rhyme and that simpleminded combination of three—count them—chord changes:

Born in Durham in '23,
By a pappy who was absentee,
Was took to a lynching at the neighborhood tree,
Whopped him a nigger when he was only three.

    Roony, Roony Winsome, king of the decky-dance.

    Pretty soon he started to grow,
    Everyone knew he'd be a loving beau,
    Cause down by the tracks he would frequently go
    To change his luck at a dollar a throw.

    Well he hit Winston-Salem with a rebel yell,
    Found his self a pretty Southron belle
    Was doing fine till her pappy raised hell
    When he noticed her belly was beginning to swell.

    Luckily the war up and came along,
    He joined the army feeling brave and strong,
    His patriotism didn't last for long,
    They put him in a foxhole where he didn't belong.

    He worked him a hustle with his first C.O.,
    Got transferred back to a PIO,
    Sat out the war in a fancy château,
    Egging on the troops toward Tokyo.

    When the war was over, his fighting done,
    He hung up his khakis and his Garand gun
    Came along to Noo York to have some fun,
    But couldn't find a job till '51.

    Started writing copy for MCA
    It wasn't any fun but it was steady pay,
    Sneaking out of work one lovely day
    He met him a dolly called Mafi-yay.

    Mafia thought he had a future ahead,
    And looked like she knew how to bounce a bed
    Old Roony must've been sick in the head
    Cause pretty soon, they up and they wed.

    Now he's got a record company,
    A third of the profits plus salary,
    A beautiful wife who wants to be free
    So she can practice her Theory.

[Refrain]:
    Roony, Roony Winsome, king of the decky-dance.

  Pig Bodine had fallen asleep. Mafia was in the next room,
    204

watching herself undress in the mirror. And Paola, Roony thought, where are you? She'd taken to disappearing, sometimes for two- or three-day stretches, and nobody ever knew where she went.

Maybe Rachel would put in a word for him with Paola. He had, he knew, certain nineteenth-century ideas of what was proper. The girl herself was an enigma. She hardly spoke, she went to the Rusty Spoon now only rarely when she knew Pig would be somewhere else. Pig coveted her. Concealing himself behind a code which only did officers dirty (and executives? Winsome wondered), Pig he was sure envisioned Paola playing opposite him in each frame of his stag-movie fantasies. It was natural, he supposed; the girl had the passive look of an object of sadism, something to be attired in various inanimate costumes and fetishes, tortured, subjected to the weird indignities of Pig's catalogue, have her smooth and of course virginal-looking limbs twisted into attitudes to inflame a decadent taste. Rachel was right, Pig—and even perhaps Paola—could only be products of a decky-dance. Winsome, self-proclaimed king of it, felt only sorry it should ever have happened. How it had happened, how anybody, himself included, had contributed to it he didn't know.

He entered the room as Mafia was bent, stripping off a knee sock. College girl attire, he thought. He slapped her hard on the nearest buttock; she straightened, turned, and he slapped her across the face. "Wha," she said.

"Something new," said Winsome. "For variety's sake." One hand at her crotch, one twisted in her hair, he lifted her like the victim she wasn't, half-carried, half-tossed her to the bed where she lay in a sprawl of white skin, black pubic hair and socks, all confused. He unzipped his fly. "Aren't you forgetting something," she said, coy and half-scared, flipping her hair toward the dresser drawer.

"No," said Winsome, "not that I can think of."

III

Profane returned to the Space/Time agency convinced that if nothing else Rachel was luck. Bergomask had given him the job.

"Wonderful," she said. "He's paying the fee, you don't owe us anything."

It was near quitting time. She started straightening things on her desk. "Come home with me," she said quietly. "Wait out by the elevator."

But he remembered, leaning against the wall out in the corridor: with Fina it had been like that too. She'd taken him home like a rosary found in the street and convinced herself he was magic. Fina had been devoutly R.C. like his father. Rachel was Jewish, he recalled, like his mother. Maybe all she wanted to do was to feed him, be a Jewish mother.

They rode down in the elevator crowded together and quiet, she wrapped serenely in a gray raincoat. At the turnstile in the subway she put in two tokens for them.

"Hey," said Profane.

"You're broke," she told him.

"I feel like a gigolo." He did. There'd always be some 15 cents, maybe half a salami in the refrigerator—whatever she'd feed him.

Rachel decided to lodge Profane at Winsome's place and feed him at her own. Winsome's was known to the Crew as the West Side flophouse. There was floor space there for all of them at once, and Winsome didn't mind who slept on it.

The next night Pig Bodine showed up at Rachel's at supper time drunk and in search of Paola, who was away God knew where.

"Hey," Pig addressed Profane.

"Buddy," Profane said. They opened beer.

Soon Pig had dragged them down to the V-Note to hear McClintic Sphere. Rachel sat and concentrated on the music while Pig and Profane remembered sea stories at each other. During one of the breaks she drifted over to Sphere's table and found out he'd picked up a contract with Winsome to do two LP's for Outlandish.

They talked for a while. Break ended. The quartet drifted back to the stand, fiddled around, started off with a Sphere composition called Fugue Your Buddy. Rachel returned to Pig and Profane. They were discussing Pappy Hod and Paola. Damn, damn, to herself, what have I brought him to? What have I brought him back to?

She woke up the next morning, Sunday, mildly hung over. Winsome was outside, pounding at the door.

"It is a day of rest," she growled. "What the hell."

"Dear father-confessor," he said, looking as if he'd not slept all night, "don't be angry."

"Tell it to Eigenvalue." She stomped to the kitchen, put coffee on. "Now," she said. "What is your problem?"

What else: Mafia. Now this was all deliberate. He had put on the day before yesterday's shirt and neglected to comb his hair that morning to put Rachel in the mood. If you wanted a girl to go pimping for her roommate you didn't come right out and say so. There were subtleties to be gone through. Wanting to talk about Mafia was only an excuse.

Rachel wanted to know naturally enough if he'd spoken to the dentist at all and Winsome said no. Eigenvalue had been busy lately holding bull sessions with Stencil. Roony wanted a woman's point of view. She poured coffee and told him the two roommates were gone. He closed his eyes and jumped in:

"I think she's been slipping around, Rachel."

"So. Find out and divorce her."

They drained the coffeepot twice. Roony drained himself. At three Paola came in, smiled at them briefly, disappeared into her room. Did he blush a little? His heartbeat had speeded up. Dingy damn, he was acting like a young blood. He rose. "Can we keep talking about this?" he said. "Even small-talk."

"If it helps," she smiled, not believing it for a minute. "And what's this about a contract with McClintic? Don't tell me Outlandish is putting out normal records now. What are you getting, religion?"

"If I am," Roony told her, "it's all I'm getting."

He walked back to his apartment through Riverside Park, wondering if he'd done right. Maybe, it occurred to him, Rachel might think it was herself he wanted, not her roommate.

Back at the apartment he found Profane talking with Mafia. Dear God, he thought, all I want to do is sleep. He went in to the bed, assumed the foetal position and soon, oddly enough, did drift off.

"You tell me you are half-Jewish and half-Italian," Mafia was saying in the other room. "What a terribly amusing role. Like Shylock, non è vero, ha, ha. There is a young actor down at the Rusty Spoon who claims to be an Irish Armenian Jew. You two must meet."

Profane decided not to argue. So all he said was: "It is probably a nice place, that Rusty Spoon. But out of my class."

"Rot," she said, "class. Aristocracy is in the soul. You may be a descendant of kings. Who knows."

I know, Profane thought. I am a descendant of schlemihls, Job founded my line. Mafia wore a knit dress of some fabric that could be seen through. She sat with her chin on her knees so that the lower part of the skirt fell away. Profane rolled over on his stomach. Now this would be interesting, he thought. Yesterday Rachel had led him in by the hand to find Charisma, Fu and Mafia playing Australian tag-teams minus one on the living room floor.

Mafia had squirmed to a prone position parallel to Profane. Apparently she had some idea of touching noses. Boy I'll bet she thinks that's cute, he thought. But Fang the cat came tearing in and jumped between them. Mafia lay on her back and started scratching and dandling the cat. Profane padded to the icebox for more beer. In came Pig Bodine and Charisma, singing a drinking song:

> There are sick bars in every town in America,
> Where sick people can pass the time o' day.
> You can screw on the floor in Baltimore,
> Make Freudian scenes in New Orleans,
> Talk Zen and Beckett in Keokuk, Ioway.
> There's espresso machines in Terre Haute, Indiana
> Which is a cultural void if ever a void there be,
> But though I've dragged my ass from Boston, Mass.
> To the wide Pacific sea,
> The Rusty Spoon is still the bar for me,
> The Rusty Spoon is the only place for me.

It was like bringing a little bit of that gathering-place in among the proper façades of Riverside Drive. Soon without anyone realizing it there was a party. Fu wandered in, got on the phone and started calling people. Girls appeared miraculously at the front door, which had been left open. Someone turned on the FM, someone else went out for beer. Cigarette smoke began to hang from the low ceiling in murky strata. Two or three members got Profane off in a corner and began to indoctrinate him in the ways of the Crew. He let them lecture, and drank beer. Soon he was drunk and it was night. He remembered to set the alarm clock, found an unoccupied corner of a room and went to sleep.

That night, April 15, David Ben-Gurion warned his country in an Independence Day speech that Egypt planned to slaughter Israel. A Mideast crisis had been growing since winter. April 19, a cease-fire between the two countries went into effect. Grace Kelly married Prince Rainier III of Monaco the same day. The spring thus wore on, large currents and small eddies alike resulting in headlines. People read what news they wanted to and each accordingly built his own rathouse of history's rags and straws. In the city of New York alone there were at a rough estimate five million different rathouses. God knew what was going on in the minds of cabinet ministers, heads of state and civil servants in the capitals of the world. Doubtless their private versions of history showed up in action. If a normal distribution of types prevailed they did.

Stencil fell outside the pattern. Civil servant without rating, architect-by-necessity of intrigues and breathings-together, he should have been, like his father, inclined toward action. But spent his days instead at a certain vegetation, talking with Eigenvalue, waiting for Paola to reveal how she fitted into this grand Gothic pile of inferences he was hard at work creating. Of course too there were his "leads" which he hunted down now lackadaisical and only half-interested, as if there were after all something more important he ought to be doing. What this mission was, however, came no clearer to him than the ultimate shape of his V-structure—no clearer, indeed, than why he should have begun pursuit of V. in the first place. He only felt (he said "by instinct") when a bit of information was useful, when not: when a lead ought to be abandoned, when hounded to the inevitable looped trail. Naturally about drives as intellectualized as Stencil's there can be no question of instinct: the obsession was acquired, surely, but where along the line, how in the world? Unless he was as he insisted purely the century's man, something which does not exist in nature. It would be simple in Rusty Spoon-talk to call him contemporary man in search of an identity. Many of them had already decided this was his Problem. The only trouble was that Stencil had all the identities he could cope with conveniently right at the moment: he was quite purely He Who Looks for V. (and whatever impersonations that might involve), and she was no more his own identity than Eigenvalue the soul-dentist or any other member of the Crew.

It did bring up, however, an interesting note of sexual ambiguity. What a joke if at the end of this hunt he came face to face with himself afflicted by a kind of soul-transvestism. How the Crew would laugh and laugh. Truthfully he didn't know what sex V. might be, nor even what genus and species. To go along assuming that Victoria the girl tourist and Veronica the sewer rat were one and the same V. was not at all to bring up any metempsychosis: only to affirm that his quarry fitted in with The Big One, the century's master cabal, in the same way Victoria had with the Vheissu plot and Veronica with the new rat-order. If she was a historical fact then she continued active today and at the moment, because the ultimate Plot Which Has No Name was as yet unrealized, though V. might be no more a she than a sailing vessel or a nation.

Early in May Eigenvalue introduced Stencil to Bloody Chiclitz, president of Yoyodyne, Inc., a company with factories scattered careless about the country and more government contracts than it really knew what to do with. In the late 1940's Yoyodyne had been breezing along comfortably as the Chiclitz Toy Company, with one tiny independent-making shop on the outskirts of Nutley, New Jersey. For some reason the children of America conceived around this time a simultaneous and psychopathic craving for simple gyroscopes, the kind which are set in motion by a string wound around the rotating shaft, something like a top. Chiclitz, recognizing a market potential there, decided to expand. He was well on the way to cornering the toy gyroscope market when along came a group of school kids on tour to point out that these toys worked on the same principle as a gyrocompass. "As wha," said Chiclitz. They explained gyrocompasses to him, also rate and free gyros. Chiclitz remembered vaguely from a trade magazine that the government was always in the market for these. They used them on ships, airplanes, more lately, missiles. "Well," figured Chiclitz, "why not." Small-business opportunities in the field at the time were being described as abundant. Chiclitz started making gyros for the government. Before he knew it he was also in telemeter instrumentation, test-set components, small communications equipment. He kept expanding, buying, merging. Now less than ten years later he had built up an interlocking kingdom responsible for systems management, airframes, propulsion, command systems, ground support equipment. Dyne, one newly hired engineer had told him, was a unit of force. So to symbolize the humble beginnings of the Chiclitz empire and to get the idea of force, enterprise, engineering skill and rugged individualism in there too, Chiclitz christened the company Yoyodyne.

Stencil toured one plant out on Long Island. Among instruments of war, he reasoned, some clue to the cabal might show up. It did. He'd wandered into a region of offices, drafting boards, blueprint files. Soon Stencil discovered, sitting half hidden in a forest of file cabinets, and sipping occasionally at the coffee in a paper cup which for today's engineer is practically uniform-of-the-day, a balding and porcine gentleman in a suit of European cut. The engineer's name was Kurt Mondaugen, he had worked, yes, at Peenemunde, developing Vergeltungswaffe Eins and Zwei. The magic initiall Soon the afternoon had gone and Stencil had made an appointment to renew the conversation.

A week or so later, in one of the secluded side rooms of the Rusty Spoon, Mondaugen yarned, over an abominable imitation of Munich beer, about youthful days in South-West Africa.

Stencil listened attentively. The tale proper and the questioning after took no more than thirty minutes. Yet the next Wednesday afternoon at Eigenvalue's office, when Stencil retold it, the yarn had undergone considerable change: had become, as Eigenvalue put it, Stencilized.

chapter nine

*Mondaugen's
story*

V

[handwritten margin notes: sounds / who narrates? / humanity/inhumanity / blood / time — in/outside of Foppl's / 1904 / decadence / inanimate]

I

One May morning in 1922 (meaning nearly winter here in the Warmbad district) a young engineering student named Kurt Mondaugen, late of the Technical University in Munich, arrived at a white outpost near the village of Kalkfontein South. More voluptuous than fat, with fair hair, long eyelashes and a shy smile that enchanted older women, Mondaugen sat in an aged Cape cart idly picking his nose, waiting for the sun to come up and contemplating the pontok or grass hut of Willem van Wijk, a minor extremity of the Administration in Windhoek. His horse drowsed and collected dew while Mondaugen squirmed on the seat, trying to control anger, confusion, petulance; and below the farthest verge of the Kalahari, that vast death, the tardy sun mocked him.

Originally a native of Leipzig, Mondaugen exhibited at least two aberrations peculiar to the region. One (minor), he had the Saxon habit of attaching diminutive endings to nouns, animate or inanimate, at apparent random. Two (major), he shared with his fellow-citizen Karl Baedeker a basic distrust of the South, however relative a region that might be. Imagine then the irony with which he viewed his present condition, and the horrid perversity he fancied had driven him first to Munich for advanced study, then (as if, like melancholy, this southsickness were progressive and in-

212

curable) finally to leave depression-time in Munich, journey into this other hemisphere, and enter mirror-time in the South-West Protectorate.

Mondaugen was here as part of a program having to do with atmospheric radio disturbances: sferics for short. During the Great War one H. Barkhausen, listening in on telephone messages among the Allied forces, heard a series of falling tones, much like a slide whistle descending in pitch. Each of these "whistlers" (as Barkhausen named them) lasted only about a second and seemed to be in the low or audio-frequency range. As it turned out, the whistler was only the first of a family of sferics whose taxonomy was to include clicks, hooks, risers, nose-whistlers and one like a warbling of birds called the dawn chorus. No one knew exactly what caused any of them. Some said sunspots, others lightning bursts; but everyone agreed that in there someplace was the earth's magnetic field, so a plan evolved to keep a record of sferics received at different latitudes. Mondaugen, near the bottom of the list, drew South-West Africa, and was ordered to set up his equipment as close to 28° S. as he conveniently could.

It had disturbed him at first, having to live in what had once been a German colony. Like most violent young men—and not a few stuffy old ones—he found the idea of defeat hateful. But he soon discovered that many Germans who'd been landowners before the war had simply continued on, allowed by the government of the Cape to keep their citizenship, property and native workers. A kind of expatriate social life had indeed developed at the farm of one Foppl, in the northern part of the district, between the Karas range and the marches of the Kalahari, and within a day's journey of Mondaugen's recovery station. Boisterous were the parties, lively the music, jolly the girls that had filled Foppl's baroque plantation house nearly every night since Mondaugen's arrival, in a seemingly eternal Fasching. But now what well-being he'd found in this godforsaken region seemed about to evaporate.

The sun rose and van Wijk appeared in his doorway like a two-dimensional figure jerked suddenly onstage by hidden pulleys. A vulture lit in front of the hut and stared at van Wijk. Mondaugen himself acquired motion; jumped down off the cart, moved toward the hut.

Van Wijk waved a bottle of homemade beer at him. "I

know," he shouted across the parched earth between them, "I know. I've been up all night with it. You think I don't have more to worry about?"

"My antennas," Mondaugen cried.

"Your antennas, my Warmbad district," the Boer said. He was half drunk. "Do you know what happened yesterday? Get worried. Abraham Morris has crossed the Orange."

Which, as had been intended, shook Mondaugen. He managed, "Only Morris?"

"Six men, some women and children, rifles, stock. It isn't that. Morris isn't a man. He's a Messiah."

Mondaugen's annoyance had given way all at once to fear; fear began to bud from his intestinal walls.

"They threatened to rip down your antennas, didn't they." But he'd done nothing. . . .

Van Wijk snorted. "You contributed. You told me you'd listen for disturbances and record certain data. You didn't say you'd blast them out all over my bush country and become a disturbance yourself. The Bondelswaartz believe in ghosts, the sferics frighten them. Frightened, they're dangerous."

Mondaugen admitted he'd been using an audio amplifier and loudspeaker. "I fall asleep," he explained. "Different sorts come in at different times of day. I'm a one-man research team, I have to sleep sometime. The little loudspeaker is set up at the head of my cot, I've conditioned myself to awake instantaneously, so no more than the first few of any group are lost. . . ."

"When you return to your station," van Wijk cut in, "those antennas will be down, and your equipment smashed. A moment—" as the young man turned, redfaced and snuffling—"before you dash off screaming revenge, one word. Just one. An unpleasant word: rebellion."

"Every time a Bondel talks back to you people, it's rebellion." Mondaugen looked as if he might cry.

"Abraham Morris has joined forces by now with Jacobus Christian and Tim Beukes. They're trekking north. You saw for yourself that they'd heard about it already in your own neighborhood. It wouldn't surprise me if every Bondelswaartz in the district were under arms within the week. Not to mention a number of homicidally-disposed Veldschoendragers and Witboois from up north. Witboois are always looking for a fight." Inside the hut a telephone began to

214

ring. Van Wijk saw the look on Mondaugen's face. "Yes," he said. "Wait here, it may be interesting news." He vanished inside. From a nearby hut came the sound of a Bondelswaartz pennywhistle, insubstantial as wind, monotonous as sunlight in a dry season. Mondaugen listened as if it had something to say to him. It didn't.

Van Wijk appeared in the doorway. "Now listen to me, younker, if I were you I would go to Warmbad and stay there until this blows over."

"What's happened."

"That was the location superintendent at Guruchas. Apparently they caught up with Morris, and a Sergeant van Niekerk tried an hour ago to get him to come in to Warmbad peacefully. Morris refused, van Niekerk placed his hand on Morris's shoulder in token of arrest. According to the Bondel version—which you may be sure has already spread to the Portuguese frontier—the Sergeant then proclaimed 'Die lood van die Goevernement sal nou op julle smelt.' The lead of the Government shall now melt upon you. Poetic, wouldn't you say?

"The Bondels with Morris took it as a declaration of war. So the balloon's gone up, Mondaugen. Go to Warmbad, better yet keep going and get safely across the Orange. That's my best advice."

"No, no," Mondaugen said, "I am something of a coward, you know that. But tell me your second-best advice, because you see there are my antennas."

"You worry about your antennas as if they sprouted from your forehead. Go ahead. Return—if you have the courage, which I certainly don't—return up-country and tell them at Foppl's what you've heard here. Hole up in that fortress of his. If you want my own opinion it will be a blood bath. You weren't here in 1904. But ask Foppl. He remembers. Tell him the days of von Trotha are back again."

"You could have prevented this," Mondaugen cried. "Isn't that what you're all here for, to keep them happy? To remove any need for rebellion?"

Van Wijk exploded in a bitter fit of laughing. "You seem," he finally drawled, "to be under certain delusions about the civil service. History, the proverb says, is made at night. The European civil servant normally sleeps at night. What waits in his IN basket to confront him at nine in the morning is history. He doesn't fight it, he tries to coexist with it.

215

"Die lood van die Goevernement indeed. We are, perhaps, the lead weights of a fantastic clock, necessary to keep it in motion, to keep an ordered sense of history and time prevailing against chaos. Very well! Let a few of them melt. Let the clock tell false time for a while. But the weights will be reforged, and rehung, and if there doesn't happen to be one there in the shape or name of Willem van Wijk to make it run right again, so much the worse for me."

To this curious soliloquy Kurt Mondaugen flipped a desperate farewell salute, climbed into his Cape cart, and headed back up-country. The trip was uneventful. Once in a great while an oxcart would materialize out of the scrubland; or a jet-black kite would come to hang in the sky, studying something small and quick among the cactus and thorn trees. The sun was hot. Mondaugen leaked at every orifice; fell asleep, was jolted awake; once dreamed gunshots and human screams. He arrived at the recovery station in the afternoon, found the Bondel village nearby quiet and his equipment undisturbed. Working as quickly as he could, he dismantled the antennas and packed them and the receiving equipment in the Cape cart. Half a dozen Bondelswaartz stood around watching. By the time he was ready to leave the sun was nearly down. From time to time, at the edges of his field of vision, Mondaugen would see small scurrying bands of Bondels, seeming almost to merge with the twilight, moving in and out of the small settlement in every direction. Somewhere to the west a dogfight had started. As he tightened the last half-hitch a pennywhistle began to play nearby, and it took him only a moment to realize that the player was imitating sferics. Bondels who were watching started to giggle. The laughter swelled, until it sounded like a jungleful of small exotic animals, fleeing some basic danger. But Mondaugen knew well enough who was fleeing what. The sun set, he climbed on the cart. No one said anything in farewell: all he heard at his back were the whistle and the laughter.

It was several more hours to Foppl's. The only incident on route was a flurry of gunfire—real, this time—off to his left, behind a hill. At last, quite early in the morning, the lights of Foppl's burst on him suddenly out of the scrubland's absolute blackness. He crossed a small ravine on a plank bridge and drew up before the door.

As usual a party was in progress, a hundred windows

blazed, the gargoyles, arabesques, pargeting and fretwork of Foppl's "villa" vibrated in the African night. A cluster of girls and Foppl himself stood at the door while the farm's Bondels offloaded the Cape cart and Mondaugen reported the situation.

The news alarmed certain of Foppl's neighbors who owned farms and stock nearby. "But it would be best," Foppl announced to the party, "if we all stayed here. If there's to be burning and destruction, it will happen whether or not you're there to defend your own. If we disperse our strength they can destroy us as well as our farms. This house is the best fortress in the region: strong, easily defended. House and grounds are protected on all sides by deep ravines. There is more than enough food, good wine, music and—" winking lewdly—"beautiful women.

"To hell with them out there. Let them have their war. In here we shall hold Fasching. Bolt the doors, seal the windows, tear down the plank bridges and distribute arms. Tonight we enter a state of siege."

II

Thus began Foppl's Siege Party. Mondaugen left after two and a half months. In that time no one had ventured outside, or received any news from the rest of the district. By the time Mondaugen departed, a dozen bottles of wine still lay cobwebbed in the cellar, a dozen cattle remained to be slaughtered. The vegetable garden behind the house was still abundant with tomatoes, yams, chard, herbs. So affluent was the farmer Foppl.

The day after Mondaugen's arrival, the house and grounds were sealed off from the outside world. Up went an inner palisade of strong logs, pointed at the top, and down went the bridges. A watch list was made up, a General Staff appointed, all in the spirit of a new party game.

A curious crew were thus thrown together. Many, of course, were German: rich neighbors, visitors from Windhoek and Swakopmund. But there were also Dutch and English from the Union; Italians, Austrians, Belgians from the diamond fields near the coast; French, Russian, Spanish and one Pole from various corners of the earth; all creating the appearance of a tiny European Conclave or League of Nations, assembled here while political chaos howled outside.

Early on the morning after his arrival, Mondaugen was up on the roof, stringing his antennas along the iron fanci-work that topped the villa's highest gable. He had an uninspiring view of ravines, grass, dry pans, dust, scrub; all repeating, undulating east to the eventual wastes of the Kalahari; north to a distant yellow exhalation that rose from far under the horizon and seemed to hang eternally over the Tropic of Capricorn.

Back here Mondaugen could also see down into a kind of inner courtyard. Sunlight, filtered through a great sandstorm far away in the desert, bounced off an open bay window and down, too bright, as if amplified, into the courtyard to illuminate a patch or pool of deep red. Twin tendrils of it extended to a nearby doorway. Mondaugen shivered and stared. The reflected sunlight vanished up a wall and into the sky. He looked up, saw the window opposite complete its swing open and a woman of indeterminate age in a negli-gee of peacock blues and greens squint into the sun. Her left hand rose to her left eye, fumbled there as if positioning a monocle. Mondaugen crouched behind curlicues of wrought iron, astonished not so much at anything in her appearance as at his own latent desire to see and not be seen. He waited for the sun or her chance movement to show him nipples, navel, pubic hair.

But she had seen him. "Come out, come out, gargoyle," she called playfully. Mondaugen lurched vertical, lost his balance, nearly fell off the roof, grabbed hold of a lightning rod, slid to a 45° angle and began to laugh.

"My little antennas," he gurgled.

"Come to the roof garden," she invited, and disappeared then back into a white room turned to blinding enigma by a sun finally free of its Kalahari.

He completed his job of setting up the antennas, then made his way round cupolas and chimney pots, up and down slopes and slates till at length he vaulted clumsily over a low wall and it seemed some tropic as well, for the life there he found too lavish, spectral, probably carnivorous; not in good taste.

"How pretty he is." The woman, dressed now in jodhpurs and an army shirt, leaned against the wall, smoking a cigarette. All at once, as he'd been half-expecting, cries of pain lanced a morning quiet that had known only visiting kites and wind, and the dry rustling of the exterior veld.

218

Mondaugen knew, without having to run to see, that the cries had come from the courtyard where he'd seen the crimson stain. Neither he nor the woman moved. It somehow having become part of a mutual constraint that neither of them show curiosity. Voilà: conspiracy already, without a dozen words having passed between them.

Her name proved to be Vera Meroving, her companion a Lieutenant Weissmann, her city Munich.

"Perhaps we even met one Fasching," she said, "masked and strangers."

Mondaugen doubted, but had they met: were there any least basis for that "conspiracy" a moment ago: it would surely have been somewhere like Munich, a city dying of abandon, venality, a mark swollen with fiscal cancer.

As the distance between them gradually diminished Mondaugen saw that her left eye was artificial: she, noticing his curiosity, obligingly removed the eye and held it out to him in the hollow of her hand. A bubble blown translucent, its "white" would show up when in the socket as a half-lit sea green. A fine network of nearly microscopic fractures covered its surface. Inside were the delicately-wrought wheels, springs, ratchets of a watch, wound by a gold key which Fräulein Meroving wore on a slender chain round her neck. Darker green and flecks of gold had been fused into twelve vaguely zodiacal shapes, placed annular on the surface of the bubble to represent the iris and also the face of the watch.

"What was it like outside?"

He told her the little he knew. Her hands had begun to tremble: he noticed it when she went to replace the eye. He could scarcely hear her when she said:

"It could be 1904 again."

Curious: van Wijk had said that. What was 1904 to these people? He was about to ask her when Lieutenant Weissmann appeared in mufti from behind an unwholesome-looking palm and pulled her by the hand, back into the depths of the house.

Two things made Foppl's a fortunate place to be carrying on sferic research. First, the farmer had given Mondaugen a room to himself in a turret at one corner of the house; a little enclave of scientific endeavor, buffered by a number of empty storage rooms and with access to the roof through a stained-glass window portraying an early Christian martyr being devoured by wild beasts.

Second, modest though their demands were, there was an auxiliary source of electric power for his receivers in the small generator Foppl kept to light the giant chandelier in the dining hall. Rather than rely, as he had been doing, on a number of bulky batteries, Mondaugen was sure it wouldn't be too difficult simply to tap off and devise circuitry to modify what power he needed, either to operate the equipment directly or to recharge the batteries. Accordingly, that afternoon, after arranging his effects, equipment and the attendant paper work into an imitation of professional disorder, Mondaugen set off into the house and down, in search of this generator.

Soon, padding down a narrow, sloping corridor, he was brought to attention by a mirror hung some twenty feet ahead, angled to reflect the interior of a room around the next corner. Framed for him there were Vera Meroving and her lieutenant in profile, she striking at his chest with what appeared to be a small riding crop, he twisting a gloved hand into her hair and talking to her all the while, so precisely that the voyeur Mondaugen could lip-read each obscenity. The geometry of the corridors somehow baffled all sound: Mondaugen, with the queer excitement he'd felt watching her at her window that morning, expected captions explaining it all to flash on to the mirror. But she finally released Weissmann; he reached out with the curiously gloved hand and closed the door, and it was as if Mondaugen had dreamed them.

Presently he began to hear music, which grew louder the deeper he descended into this house. Accordion, fiddle and guitar were playing a tango full of minor chords and an eerie flatting of certain notes which to German ears should have remained natural. A young girl's voice was singing sweetly:

Love's a lash,
Kisses gall the tongue, harrow the heart;
Caresses tease
Cankered tissue apart.

Liebchen, come
Be my Hottentot bondsman tonight,
The sjambok's kiss

220

Is unending delight.

Love, my little slave,
Is color-blind;
For white and black
Are only states of mind.

So at my feet
Nod and genuflect, whimper for me:
Though tears are dried
Their pain is yet to be.

Enchanted, Mondaugen peered round the door jamb and found the singer to be a child of not more than sixteen, with white-blond, hip-length hair and breasts perhaps too large for her slender frame.

"I am Hedwig Vogelsang," she informed him, "and my purpose on earth is to tantalize and send raving the race of man." Whereupon the musicians, hidden from them in an alcove behind a hanging arras, struck up a kind of schottische; Mondaugen, overcome by the sudden scent of musk, brought in a puff to his nostrils by interior winds which could not have arisen by accident, seized her round the waist and wheeled with her across the room, and out, and through a bedroom lined with mirrors, round a canopied four-poster and into a long gallery, stabbed at ten-yard intervals down its length by yellow daggers of African sun, hung with nostalgic landscapes of a Rhine valley that never existed, portraits of Prussian officers who'd died long before Caprivi (some even before Bismarck) and their blond, untender ladies who'd nothing now but dust to bloom in; past rhythmic gusts of blond sun that crazed the eyeballs with vein-images; out of the gallery and into a tiny unfurnished room hung all in black velvet, high as the house, narrowing into a chimney and open at the top, so that one could see the stars in the daytime; finally down three or four steps to Foppl's own planetarium, a circular room with a great wooden sun, overlaid with gold leaf, burning cold in the very center and round it the nine planets and their moons, suspended from tracks in the ceiling, actuated by a coarse cobweb of chains, pulleys, belts, racks, pinions and worms, all receiving their prime impulse from a treadmill in the corner, usually operated for the amusement of the guests by a Bondelswaartz, now unoccupied. Having long fled all vestiges of music Mondaugen released her here, skipped to the tread-mill and began a jog-trot that set the solar system in motion, creaking and whining in a way that raised a prickling in the teeth. Rattling, shuddering, the wooden planets began to ro-tate and spin, Saturn's rings to whirl, moons their precessions, our own Earth its nutational wobble, all picking up speed; as the girl continued to dance, having chosen the planet Venus for her partner; as Mondaugen dashed along his own geodesic, following in the footsteps of a generation of slaves.

When at length he tired, slowed and stopped she'd gone, vanished into the wooden reaches of what remained after all a parody of space. Mondaugen, breathing heavily, stag-gered off the treadmill to carry on his descent and search for the generator.

Soon he stumbled into a basement room where gardening implements were stored. As if the entire day had come into being only to prepare him for this, he discovered a Bondel male, face down and naked, the back and buttocks showing scar tissue from old sjambokings as well as more recent wounds, laid open across the flesh like so many toothless smiles. Hardening himself the weakling Mondaugen ap-proached the man and stooped to listen for breathing or a heartbeat, trying not to see the white vertebra that winked at him from one long opening.

"Don't touch him." Foppl stood holding a sjambok or cat-tle whip of giraffe hide, tapping the handle against his leg in a steady, syncopated figure. "He doesn't want you to help. Even to sympathize. He doesn't want anything but the sjambok." Raising his voice till it found the hysterical-bitch level Foppl always affected with Bondels: "You like the sjambok, don't you, Andreas."

Andreas moved his head feebly and whispered; "Baas . . ."

"Your people have defied the Government," Foppl con-tinued, "they've rebelled, they have sinned. General von Trotha will have to come back to punish you all. He'll have to bring his soldiers with the beards and the bright eyes, and his artillery that speaks with a loud voice. How you will enjoy it, Andreas. Like Jesus returning to earth, von Trotha is coming to deliver you. Be joyful; sing hymns of thanks. And until then love me as your parent, because I am von Trotha's arm, and the agent of his will."

As van Wijk had bade him do, Mondaugen remembered to ask Foppl about 1904 and the "days of von Trotha." If

Foppl's response was sick, it was sick of more than simple enthusiasm; not only did he yarn about the past—first there in the cellar as both stood watching a Bondelswaartz whose face Mondaugen was never to see continue to die; later at riotous feasting, on watch or patrol, to ragtime accompaniment in the grand ballroom; even up in the turret, as deliberate interruption to the experiment—but he also seemed under compulsion somehow to recreate the Deutsch-Südwestafrika of nearly twenty years ago, in word and perhaps in deed. "Perhaps" because as the siege party progressed it became more and more difficult to make the distinction.

One midnight Mondaugen stood on a small balcony just under the eaves, officially on watch, though little could be seen in the uncertain illumination. The moon, or half of it, had risen above the house: his antennas cut like rigging dead-black across its face. As he swung his rifle idly by its shoulder strap, gazing out across the ravine at nothing in particular, someone stepped on to the balcony beside him: it was an old Englishman named Godolphin, tiny in the moonlight. Small scrubland noises now and again rose to them from the outside.

"I hope I don't disturb you," Godolphin said. Mondaugen shrugged, keeping his eyes in a constant sweep over what he guessed to be the horizon. "I enjoy it on watch," the Englishman continued, "it's the only peace there is to this eternal celebration." He was a retired sea captain; in his seventies, Mondaugen would guess. "I was in Cape Town, trying to raise a crew for the Pole."

Mondaugen's eyebrows went up. Embarrassed, he began to pick at his nose. "The South Pole?"

"Of course. Rather awkward if it were the other, haw-haw. "And I'd heard of a stout boat in Swakopmund. But of course she was too small. Hardly do for the pack ice. Foppl was in town, and invited me out for a weekend. I imagine I needed the rest."

"You sound cheerful. In the face of what must be frequent disappointment."

"They leave the sting out. Treat the doddering old fool with sympathy. He's living in the past. Of course I'm living in the past. I was there."

"At the Pole."

"Certainly. Now I have to go back, it's that simple. I'm

223

beginning to think that if I get through our siege party I shall be quite ready for anything the Antarctic has for me."

Mondaugen was inclined to agree. "Though I don't plan on any little Antarctic."

The old sea dog chuckled. "Oh there will be. You wait. Everyone has an Antarctic."

Which, it occurred to Mondaugen, was as far South as one could get. At first he'd plunged eagerly into the social life that jittered all over the sprawling plantation house, usually leaving his scientific duties until the early afternoon, when everyone but the watch was asleep. He had even begun a dogged pursuit of Hedwig Vogelsang, but somehow kept running into Vera Meroving instead. Southsickness in its tertiary stage, whispered that adenoidal Saxon youth who was Mondaugen's doubleganger: beware, beware.

The woman, twice as old as he, exerted a sexual fascination he found impossible to explain away. He'd meet her head-on in corridors, or rounding some salient of cabinetwork, or on the roof, or simply in the night, always unlooked for. He would make no advances, she no response; but despite all efforts to hold it in check, their conspiracy grew.

As if it were a real affair, Lieutenant Weissmann cornered him in the billiard room. Mondaugen quivered and prepared to flee: but it proved to be something else entirely.

"You're from Munich," Weissmann established. "Ever been around the Schwabing quarter?" On occasion. "The Brennessel cabaret?" Never. "Ever heard of D'Annunzio?" Then: Mussolini? Fiume? Italia irredenta? Fascisti? National Socialist German Workers' Party? Adolf Hitler? Kautsky's Independents?

"So many capital letters," Mondaugen protested.

"From Munich, and never heard of Hitler," said Weissmann, as if "Hitler" were the name of an avant-garde play. "What the hell's wrong with young people." Light from the green overhead lamp turned his spectacles to twin, tender leaves, giving him a gentle look.

"I'm an engineer, you see. Politics isn't my line."

"Someday we'll need you," Weissmann told him, "for something or other, I'm sure. Specialized and limited as you are, you fellows will be valuable. I didn't mean to get angry."

"Politics is a kind of engineering, isn't it. With people as your raw material."

"I don't know," Weissmann said. "Tell me, how long are you staying in this part of the world."

"No longer than I have to. Six months? it's indefinite."

"If I could put you in the way of something, oh, with a little authority to it, not really involving much of your time . . ."

"Organizing, you'd call it?"

"Yes, you're sharp. You knew right away, didn't you. Yes. You are my man. The young people especially, Mondaugen, because you see—I know this won't be repeated—we could be getting it back."

"The Protectorate? But it's under the League of Nations."

Weissmann threw back his head and began to laugh, and would say no more. Mondaugen shrugged, took down a cue, dumped the three balls from their velvet bag and practiced draw shots till well into the morning.

He emerged from the billiard room to hot jazz from somewhere overhead. Blinking, he made his way up marble steps to the grand ballroom and found the dance floor empty. Clothing of both sexes was littered about; the music, which came from a Gramophone in the corner, roared gay and hollow under the electric chandelier. But no one was there, no one at all. He plodded up to his turret room with its ludicrous circular bed and found that a typhoon of sferics had been bombarding the earth. He fell asleep and dreamed, for the first time since he'd left it, of Munich.

In the dream it was Fasching, the mad German Carnival or Mardi Gras that ends the day before Lent begins. The season in Munich, under the Weimar Republic and the inflation, had followed since the war a constantly rising curve, taking human depravity as ordinate. Chief reason being that no one in the city knew if he'd be alive or well come next Fasching. Any windfall—food, firewood, coal—was consumed as quickly as possible. Why hoard, why ration? Depression hung in the gray strata of clouds, looked at you out of faces waiting in bread queues and dehumanized by the bitter cold. Depression stalked the Liebigstrasse, where Mondaugen had had an attic room in a mansarde: a figure with an old woman's face, bent against the wind off the Isar and wrapped tightly in a frayed black coat; who might, like some angel of death, mark in pink spittle the doorsteps of those who'd starve tomorrow.

225

It was dark. He was in an old cloth jacket, a stocking cap tugged down over his ears, arms linked with a number of young people he didn't know but suspected were students, all singing a death-song and weaving side to side in a chain, broadside to the street's centerline. He could hear bands of other rollickers, drunk and singing lustily in other streets. Beneath a tree, near one of the infrequent street lights, he came upon a boy and girl, coupled, one of the girl's fat and aging thighs exposed to the still-winter wind. He stooped and covered them with his old jacket, his tears fell and froze in mid-air, and rattled like sleet on the couple, who'd turned to stone.

He was in a beer hall. Young, old, students, workmen, grandfathers, adolescent girls drank, sang, cried, fondled blindly after same and different-sexed alike. Someone had set a blaze in the fireplace and was roasting a cat he'd found in the street. The black oak clock above the fireplace ticked terribly loud in strange waves of silence that swept regularly over the company. Girls appeared out of the confusion of moving faces, sat on his lap while he squeezed breasts and thighs and tweaked noses; beer spilled at the far end of the table and swept the table's length in a great foam cascade. The fire that had been roasting the cat spread to a number of tables and had to be doused with more beer; fat and charred-black, the cat itself was snatched from the hands of its unfortunate cook and tossed about the room like a football, blistering the hands that passed it on, till it disintegrated among roars of laughter. Smoke hung like winter fog in the beer hall, changing the massed weaving of bodies to more a writhing perhaps of damned in some underworld. Faces all had the same curious whiteness: concave cheeks, highlighted temples, bone of the starved corpse there just under the skin.

Vera Meroving appeared (why Vera? her black mask covered the entire head) in black sweater and black dancer's tights. "Come," she whispered; led him by the hand through narrow streets, hardly lit but thronged with celebrants who sang and cheered in tubercular voices. White faces, like diseased blooms, bobbed along in the dark as if moved by other forces toward some graveyard, to pay homage at an important burial.

At dawn she came in through the stained-glass window to tell him that another Bondel had been executed, this time by hanging.

"Come and see," she urged him. "In the
"No, no." It had been a popular form of
the Great Rebellion of 1904-07, when the He
tentots, who usually fought one another, s
taneous but uncoordinated rising against a
German administration. General Lothar von Trotha, having
demonstrated to Berlin during his Chinese and East African
campaigns a certain expertise at suppressing pigmented pop-
ulations, was brought in to deal with the Hereros. In August
1904, von Trotha issued his "Vernichtungs Befehl," whereby
the German forces were ordered to exterminate systematically
every Herero man, woman and child they could find. He
was about 80 per cent successful. Out of the estimated
80,000 Hereros living in the territory in 1904, an official
German census taken seven years later set the Herero population at only 15,130, this being a decrease of 64,870.
Similarly the Hottentots were reduced in the same period by
about 10,000, the Berg-Damaras by 17,000. Allowing for
natural causes during those unnatural years, von Trotha,
who stayed for only one of them, is reckoned to have done
away with about 60,000 people. This is only 1 per cent of
six million, but still pretty good.

Foppl had first come to Südwestafrika as a young Army
recruit. It didn't take him long to find out how much he enjoyed it all. He'd ridden out with von Trotha that August,
that inverted spring. "You'd find them wounded, or sick, by
the side of the road," he told Mondaugen, "but you didn't
want to waste the ammunition. Logistics at the time were
sluggish. Some you bayoneted, others you hanged. Procedure
was simple: one led the fellow or woman to the nearest tree,
stood him on an ammunition box, fashioned a noose of rope
(failing that, telegraph or fencing wire), slipped it round
his neck, ran the rope through a fork in the tree and secured
it to the trunk, kicked the box away. It was slow strangula-
tion, but then these were summary courts-martial. Field
expedients had to be used when you couldn't put up a
scaffold each time."

"Of course not," said Mondaugen in his nit-picking engineer's way, "but with so much telegraph wire and so many
ammunition boxes lying around, logistics couldn't have been
all that sluggish."

"Oh," Foppl said. "Well. You're busy."

As it happened, Mondaugen was. Though it may have

only because of bodily exhaustion from too much party-, he'd begun to notice something unusual in the sferic signals. Having dexterously scavenged a motor from one of Foppl's phonographs, a pen and rollers and several long sheets of paper, the resourceful Mondaugen had fashioned a crude sort of oscillograph to record signals in his absence. The project hadn't seen fit to provide him with one and he'd had nowhere to go at his former station, making one up till now unnecessary. As he looked now at the cryptic pen-scrawls, he detected a regularity or patterning which might almost have been a kind of code. But it took him weeks even to decide that the only way to see if it were a code was to try to break it. His room became littered with tables, equations, graphs; he appeared to labor to the accompaniment of twitterings, hisses, clicks and carolings but in reality he dawdled. Something kept him off. Events intimidated him: one night during another "typhoon" the oscillograph broke, chattering and scratching away madly. The difficulty was minor and Mondaugen was able to fix it. But he wondered if the malfunction had been quite an accident.

He took to roaming the house at odd hours, at loose ends. Like the "eye" in his dream of Fasching he now found he had a gift of visual serendipity: a sense of timing, a perverse certainty about not whether but when to play the voyeur. A taming, possibly, of the original heat with which he'd watched Vera Meroving in the earlier days of the siege party. For example, leaning in bleak winter sunlight against a Corinthian column, Mondaugen could hear her voice not far away.

"No. Non-military it may be, but a false siege it is not."

Mondaugen lit a cigarette and peered around the column. She was sitting in the rockery with old Godolphin, beside a goldfish pool.

"Do you remember," she began. But then noticed perhaps the pain of a return home choking him more than any noose of memory she could provide, because she let him interrupt:

"I have done believing in siege as anything more than military technic. That was well over with twenty years ago, before even your beloved 1904."

Condescending, she explained that she'd been off in another country in 1904, and that a year and place don't have to include the physical person for there to be a certain ownership.

It was beyond Godolphin. "I was advising the Russian Fleet in 1904," he remembered. "They didn't take my advice, the Japanese you'll remember bottled us up in Port Arthur. Good God. It was a siege in the great tradition, it lasted a year. I remember frozen hillsides, and the ghastly nagging of those field-mortars, coughing away day in and day out. And white spotlights, moving over the positions at night. Blinding you. A devout junior officer with an arm gone and the empty sleeve pinned across like a sash said they looked like the fingers of God, seeking soft throats to strangle."

"Lieutenant Weissmann and Herr Foppl have given me my 1904," she told him, like a schoolgirl enumerating birthday gifts. "Just as you were given your Vheissu."

Hardly any time at all passed before he cried, "No! No, I was there." Then, his head moving with difficulty to face her, "I didn't tell you about Vheissu. Did I?"

"Of course you did."

"I hardly remember Vheissu myself."

"I do. I have remembered for us."

" 'Have remembered,' " with a sudden canny tilt to one eye. But it relaxed, and he rambled off:

"If anything gave me my Vheissu it was the time, the Pole, the service. . . . But it's all been taken away, I mean the leisure and the sympathy. It's fashionable to say the War did it. Whatever you choose. But Vheissu is gone and impossible to bring back, along with so many other old jokes, songs, 'rages.' And the sort of beauty one had in Cléo de Mérode, or Eleonora Duse. The way those eyes turned down at the corners; the incredible expanse of eyelid above, like old vellum . . . But you're too young, you wouldn't remember."

"I'm past forty," smiled Vera Meroving, "and of course I remember. I was given the Duse too, by the man in fact who gave her to Europe, over twenty years ago, in *Il Fuoco*. We were in Fiume. Another siege. The Christmas before last, he called it the Christmas of blood. He gave her to me as memories, in his palace, while the Andrea Doria dropped shells on us."

"They'd go to the Adriatic on holiday," Godolphin said with a foolish smile, as if the memory were his own; "he, naked, rode his sorrel into the sea while she waited on the strand. . . ."

229

"No," suddenly and only for the moment vicious, "nor selling her jewels to suppress the novel about her, nor using a virgin's skull for a loving cup, none of that's true. She was past forty and in love, and he hurt her. Went out of his way to hurt her. That's all there was to it."

"Weren't we both in Florence then? While he was writing the novel about their affair; how could we have avoided them! Yet it seemed always that I was just missing him. First in Florence, then in Paris just before the war, as if I'd been condemned to wait until he reached his supreme moment, his peak of virtù: Fiume!"

"In Florence . . . we . . ." quizzical, weak.

She leaned forward, as if hinting she'd like to be kissed. "Don't you see? This siege. It's Vheissu. It's finally happened."

Abruptly then occurred one of those ironic reversals in which the weakling for a short while gains the upper hand, and the attacker is forced, at best, into a holding operation. Mondaugen, watching, credited this less to any internal logic in their discussion than to a latent virility in the old man, hidden against contingencies like this from the cormorant graspings of age.

Godolphin laughed at her. "There's been a war, Fräulein. Vheissu was a luxury, an indulgence. We can no longer afford the likes of Vheissu."

"But the need," she protested, "its void. What can fill that?"

He cocked his head and grinned at her. "What is already filling it. The real thing. Unfortunately. Take your friend D'Annunzio. Whether we like it or not that war destroyed a kind of privacy, perhaps the privacy of dream. Committed us like him to work out three-o'clock anxieties, excesses of character, political hallucinations on a live mass, a real human population. The discretion, the sense of comedy about the Vheissu affair are with us no more, our Vheissus are no longer our own, or even confined to a circle of friends; they're public property. God knows how much of it the world will see, or what lengths it will be taken to. It's a pity; and I'm only glad I don't have to live in it too much longer."

"You're remarkable," was all she'd say; and after braining an inquisitive goldfish with a rock, she left Godolphin.

Alone, he said: "We simply grow up. In Florence, at age fifty-four, I was a brash youth. Had I known the Duse was there her poet chap might have found dangerous competition, ha-ha. The only trouble is that now, nearing eighty, I keep discovering that damned war has made the world older than I. The world frowns now on youth in a vacuum, it insists youth be turned-to, utilized, exploited. No time for pranks. No more Vheissus. Ah, well." And to a catchy, rather syncopated fox-trot tune, he sang:

> Once we could flirt and spoon,
> Down by the summertime sea.
> Your aunt Iphigenia found it terribly odd
> To see us stealing a kiss there on the Promenade, oh
> You weren't past seventeen,
> Parasol-pretty for me;
> Ah, could we but return to that season of light,
> With our puppy-love soaring like a gay summer kite,
> When it wasn't yet time to think of autumn, or night;
> Down by the summertime sea.

(Here Eigenvalue made his single interruption: "They spoke in German? English? Did Mondaugen know English then?" Forestalling a nervous outburst by Stencil: "I only think it strange that he should remember an unremarkable conversation, let alone in that much detail, thirty-four years later. A conversation meaning nothing to Mondaugen but everything to Stencil."

Stencil, silenced, puffed his pipe and watched the psychodontist, a quirk to one side of his mouth revealed now and again, enigmatic, through the white fumes. Finally: "Stencil called it serendipity, not he. Do you understand? Of course you do. But you want to hear him say it."

"I understand only," Eigenvalue drawled, "that your attitude toward V. must have more sides to it than you're ready to admit. It's what the psychoanalysts used to call ambivalence, what we now call simply a heterodont configuration."

Stencil made no answer; Eigenvalue shrugged and let him continue.)

In the evening a roasted veal was set out on a long table in the dining hall. Guests fell upon it drunkenly, tearing away choice pieces of flesh with their hands, staining what clothes they wore with gravy and grease. Mondaugen was feeling his usual reluctance to return to work. He padded along crimson-carpeted passageways, mirrored, unpopulated, ill-lit, without echoes. He was, tonight, a bit upset and depressed without being able to say exactly why. Perhaps because he'd begun to detect the same desperation in Foppl's siege party as there'd been in Munich during Fasching; but without any clear reason, for here after all was abundance not depression, luxury not a daily struggle for life; above all, possibly, breasts and buttocks that could be pinched.

Somehow he'd wandered by Hedwig's room. Her door was open. She sat before her vanity mirror making up her eyes. "Come in," she called, "don't stand there leering."

"Your little eyes look so antiquated."

"Herr Foppl has ordered all the ladies to dress and make up as they would have done in 1904." She giggled. "I wasn't even born in 1904, so I really shouldn't be wearing anything." She sighed. "But after all the trouble I'd gone to to pluck my eyebrows to look like Dietrich's. Now I must draw them in again like great dark wings, and point them at either end; and so much mascara!" She pouted, "Pray no one breaks my heart, Kurt, for tears would ruin these old-fashioned eyes."

"Oh, you have a heart then."

"Please, Kurt, I said don't make me cry. Come: you may help me arrange my hair."

When he lifted the heavy, pale locks from her nape he saw two parallel rings of recently chafed skin running round the neck, about two inches apart. If surprise was communicated through her hair by any movement his hands may have made, Hedwig gave no sign. Together they put up her hair in an elaborate curly bun, securing it with a black satin band. Round her neck, to cover each abrasion, she wound a thin string of little onyx beads, letting three more loops or so drop progressively looser down between her breasts.

He bent to kiss one shoulder. "No," she moaned, then went berserk; picked up a flacon of Cologne water, inverted it on his head, arose from her vanity, hitting Mondaugen in the jaw with the shoulder he'd been trying to kiss. He, felled, lost consciousness for a fraction of a minute, woke to see her cakewalking out the door, singing Auf dem Zippel-Zappel-Zeppelin, a tune popular at the turn of the century.

He staggered to the corridor: she'd vanished. Feeling rather a sexual failure, Mondaugen set out for his turret and oscillograph, and the comforts of Science, which are glacial and few.

He got as far as a decorative grotto, located in the very guts of the house. There Weissmann, in full uniform, lunged at him from behind a stalagmite. "Upington!" he screamed.

"Ah?" inquired Mondaugen, blinking.

"You're a cool one. Professional traitors are always so cool." His mouth remaining open, Weissmann sniffed the air. "Oh, my. Don't we smell nice." His eyeglasses blazed.

Mondaugen, still groggy and enveloped in a miasma of cologne, wanted only to sleep. He tried to push past the piqued lieutenant, who barred his path with the butt end of a sjambok.

"Whom have you been in contact with at Upington?"

"Upington."

"It has to be, it's the nearest large town in the Union. You can't expect English operatives to give up the comforts of civilization."

"I don't know anyone in the Union."

"Careful how you answer, Mondaugen."

It finally came to him that Weissmann was talking about the sferic experiment. "It can't transmit," he yelled. "If you knew anything at all you'd see that immediately. It's for receiving only, stupid."

Weissmann favored him with a smile. "You just convicted yourself. They send you instructions. I may not know electronics, but I can recognize the scrawlings of a bad cryptanalyst."

"If you can do any better you're welcome," Mondaugen sighed. He told Weissmann about his whim, the "code."

"You mean that?" abruptly almost childlike. "You'll let me see what you've received?"

"You've obviously seen everything. But it'll put us that much closer to a solution."

Quite soon he had Weissmann laughing shyly. "Oh. Oh, I see. You're ingenious. Amazing. Ja. Stupid of me, you see. I do apologize."

Struck by an inspiration, Mondaugen whispered, "I'm monitoring their little broadcasts."

Weissmann frowned. "That's what I just said."

Mondaugen shrugged. The lieutenant lit a whale-oil lamp and they set out for the turret. As they ascended a sloping hallway, the great villa was filled with a single, deafening pulse of laughter. Mondaugen became numb, the lantern went smash behind him. He turned to see Weissmann standing among little blue flames and shiny fragments of glass.

"The strand wolf," was all Weissmann could manage.

233

In his room Mondaugen had brandy, but Weissmann's face remained the color of cigar smoke. He wouldn't talk. He got drunk and presently feel asleep in a chair.

Mondaugen worked on the code into the early morning, getting, as usual, nowhere. He kept dozing off and being brought awake by brief chuckling sounds from the loudspeaker. They sounded to Mondaugen, half in dream, like that other chilling laugh, and made him reluctant to go back to sleep. But he continued to, fitfully.

Somewhere out in the house (though he may have dreamed that too) a chorus had begun singing a Dies Irae in plainsong. It got so loud it woke Mondaugen. Irritated, he lurched to the door and went out to tell them to keep quiet.

Once past the storage rooms, he found the adjoining corridors brilliantly lit. On the whitewashed floor he saw a trail of blood-spatters, still wet. Intrigued, he followed. The blood led him perhaps fifty yards through drapes and around corners to what may have been a human form, lying covered with a piece of old canvas sail, blocking further passage. Beyond it the floor of the corridor gleamed white and bloodless.

Mondaugen broke into a sprint, jumped neatly over whatever it was and continued on at a jogging pace. Eventually he found himself at the head of a portrait gallery he and Hedwig Vogelsang had once danced down. His head still reeled with her cologne. Halfway along, illuminated by a nearby sconce, he saw Foppl, dressed in his old private-soldier's uniform and standing on tiptoe to kiss one of the portraits. When he'd gone, Mondaugen looked at the brass plate on the frame to verify his suspicion. It was indeed von Trotha.

"I loved the man," he'd said. "He taught us not to fear. It's impossible to describe the sudden release; the comfort, the luxury; when you knew you could safely forget all the rote-lessons you'd had to learn about the value and dignity of human life. I had the same feeling once in the Realgymnasium when they told us we wouldn't be responsible in the examination for all the historical dates we'd spent weeks memorizing. . . .

"Till we've done it, we're taught that it's evil. Having done it, then's the struggle: to admit to yourself that it's not really evil at all. That like forbidden sex it's enjoyable."

Shuffling sounds behind him. Mondaugen turned; it was Godolphin. "Evan," the old man whispered.

"I beg your pardon."

"It's I, son. Captain Hugh."

Mondaugen came closer, thinking possibly Godolphin's eyes were troubling him. But worse troubled him and there was nothing remarkable about the eyes save tears.

"Good morning, Captain."

"You don't have to hide any more, son. She told me; I know; it's all right. You can be Evan again. Father's here." The old man gripped his arm above the elbow and smiled bravely. "Son. It's time we went home. God, we've been so long away. Come."

Trying to be gentle, Mondaugen let the sea captain steer him along the corridor. "Who told you? You said 'she.'"

Godolphin had gone vague. "The girl. Your girl. What's-her-name."

A minute passed before Mondaugen remembered enough of Godolphin to ask, with a certain sense of shock: "What has she done to you."

Godolphin's little head nodded, brushed Mondaugen's arm. "I'm so tired."

Mondaugen stooped and picked up the old man, who seemed to weigh less than a child, and bore him along the white ramps, between mirrors and past tapestries, among scores of separate lives brought to ripeness by this siege and hidden each behind its heavy door; up through the enormous house to his own turret. Weissmann still snored in the chair. Mondaugen laid the old man on the circular bed, covered him with a black satin comforter. And stood over him, and sang:

Dream tonight of peacock tails,
Diamond fields and spouter whales.
Ills are many, blessings few,
But dreams tonight will shelter you.

Let the vampire's creaking wing
Hide the stars while banshees sing;
Let the ghouls gorge all night long;
Dreams will keep you safe and strong.

Skeletons with poison teeth,
Risen from the world beneath,

Ogre, troll, and loup-garou,
Bloody wraith who looks like you,

Shadow on the window shade,
Harpies in a midnight raid,
Goblins seeking tender prey,
Dreams will chase them all away.

Dreams are like a magic cloak
Woven by the fairy folk,
Covering from top to toe,
Keeping you from winds and woe.

And should the Angel come this night
To fetch your soul away from light,
Cross yourself, and face the wall:
Dreams will help you not at all.

Outside the strand wolf screamed again. Mondaugen
pounded a bag of dirty laundry into a pillow, doused the
light, and lay down trembling on the rug to sleep.

III

But his own musical commentary on dreams had not included the obvious and perhaps for him indispensable: that
if dreams are only waking sensation first stored and later
operated on, then the dreams of a voyeur can never be his
own. This soon showed up, not too surprisingly, as an in-
creasing inability to distinguish Godolphin from Foppl: it
may or may not have been helped along by Vera Meroving,
and some of it could have been dreamed. There, precisely,
was the difficulty. He'd no idea, for instance, where this
had come from:
   . . . so much rot spoken about their inferior kultur-position
and our herrenschaft—but that was for the Kaiser and the
businessmen at home; no one, not even our gay Lothario
(as we called the General), believed it out here. They may
have been as civilized as we, I'm not an anthropologist, you
can't compare anyway—they were an agricultural, pastoral
people. They loved their cattle as we perhaps love toys
from childhood. Under Leutwein's administration the cattle
were taken away and given to white settlers. Of course the
Hereros revolted, though the Bondelswaartz Hottentots actually started it because their chief Abraham Christian had

236

been shot in Warmbad. No one is sure who fired first. It's an old dispute: who knows, who cares? The flint had been struck, and we were needed, and we came.

Foppl. Perhaps.

Except that the shape of Mondaugen's "conspiracy" with Vera Meroving was finally beginning to come clear to him. She apparently wanted Godolphin, for reasons he could only guess at, though her desire seemed to arise out of a nostalgic sensuality whose appetites knew nothing at all of nerves, or heat, but instead belonged entirely to the barren touchlessness of memory. She had obviously needed Mondaugen only to be called (he might assume cruelly) a long-ago son, to weaken her prey.

Not unreasonably then she would also have used Foppl, perhaps to replace the father as she thought she'd replaced the son, Foppl the siege party's demon, who was in fact coming more and more to define his guests assembled, to prescribe their common dream. Possibly Mondaugen alone among them was escaping it, because of his peculiar habits of observation. So in a passage (memory, nightmare, yarn, maundering, anything) ostensibly his host's Mondaugen could at least note that though the events were Foppl's, the humanity could easily have been Godolphin's.

Again one night he heard the Dies Irae, or some organized foreign chant, approach to the verge of his buffer zone of empty rooms. Feeling invisible he glided out to look and not be seen. His neighbor, an elderly merchant from Milan, had in recent days it seemed collapsed from a heart attack, lingered, died. The others, roisterers, had organized a wake. With ceremony they wrapped his body in silk sheets stripped from his bed: but before the last brightness of dead flesh had been covered Mondaugen saw in a quick sly look its decoration of furrows and poor young scar tissue cut down in its prime. Sjambok, makoss, donkey whip . . . something long that could cut.

They took the cadaver off to a ravine to toss it in. One stayed behind.

"He remains in your room, then," she began.

"By choice."

"He has no choice. You'll make him go."

"You'll have to make him go, Fräulein."

"Then bring me to him?" almost importunate. Her eyes, rimmed in black after Foppl's 1904, needed something less hermetic than this empty corridor to frame them: palazzo's façade, provincial square, esplanade in the winter—yet more human, perhaps only more humorous than, say, the Kalahari. It was her inability to come to rest anywhere inside plausible extremes, her nervous, endless motion, like the counter-crepitating of the ball along its roulette spokes, seeking a random compartment but finally making, having made, sense only as precisely the dynamic uncertainty she was, this that upset Mondaugen enough to scowl quietly and say with a certain dignity no, turn, leave her there and return to his sferics. They both knew he'd done nothing decisive.

Having found the sad imitation of a strayed son, Godolphin wouldn't think of returning to his own room. One of them had taken the other in. The old officer slept, drowsed, talked. Because he'd "found" Mondaugen only after she'd well begun some program of indoctrination on him that Mondaugen would rather not guess at, there was no way to say for certain, later, whether Foppl himself might not have come in to tell tales of when he'd been a trooper, eighteen years ago.

Eighteen years ago everyone was in better condition. You were shown how his upper arms and thighs had become flabby; and the roll of fat around his middle. His hair was beginning to fall out. He was developing breasts; even they reminded him of when he first arrived in Africa. They'd all had their inoculations on route: for bubonic plague the ship's medic jabbed you with a tremendous needle in the muscle by the left breast, and for a week or so it puffed up. In the way troops have when there's not much else to do, they amused themselves by unbuttoning the tops of their shirts and coyly exposing these new female acquisitions.

Later, when it had got into deep winter, the sun bleached their hair white and browned their skins. The standing joke was "Don't walk up on me unless you're in uniform, I might mistake you for a nigger." The "mistake" was made more than once. Around Waterberg especially, he remembered, when they were chasing Hereros into the bush and the desert, there were a few unpopular soldiers—reluctant? humanitarian. Their bitching got so bad you found yourself hoping. . . . How much of a "mistake" it was was open to question, that's all he meant. By him bleeding hearts like that weren't much better than the natives.

238

Most of the time, thank God, you were with your own kind: comrades who all felt the same way, who weren't going to give you any nonsense no matter what you did. When a man wants to appear politically moral he speaks of human brotherhood. In the field you actually found it. You weren't ashamed. For the first time in twenty years of continuous education-to-guilt, a guilt that had never really had meaning, that the Church and the secular entrenched had made out of whole cloth; after twenty years, simply not to be ashamed. Before you disemboweled or whatever you did with her to be able to take a Herero girl before the eyes of your superior officer, and stay potent. And talk with them before you killed them without the sheep's eye, the shuffling, the prickly-heat of embarrassment. . . .

His efforts at the code, such as they were, didn't succeed in keeping back the nightfall of ambiguity that filled his room progressively as time—such as it was—went by. When Weissmann came in and asked if he could help, Mondaugen turned surly. "Out," he snarled.

"But we were to collaborate."

"I know what your interest is," Mondaugen said mysteriously. "I know what 'code' you're after."

"It's part of my job." Putting on his sincere farm-lad face, removing the eyeglasses and cleaning them mock-distracted on his necktie.

"Tell her it won't, it didn't work," Mondaugen said.

The lieutenant ground his teeth solicitously. "I can't indulge your whims much longer," he tried to explain; "Berlin is impatient, I'm not going to make excuses forever."

"I am working for you?" Mondaugen screamed. "Scheisse." But this woke up Godolphin, who began to sing splinters of sentimental ballads and to call for his Evan. Weissmann regarded the old man with wide eyes and only his two front teeth showing.

"My God," he said finally, tonelessly; about-faced and left.

But when Mondaugen found the first oscillograph roll missing he was charitable enough to ask, "Lost or taken?" out loud to his inert equipment and a faraway old skipper, before putting the blame on Weissmann.

"He must have come in when I was asleep." Not even Mondaugen knew when that was. And was the roll all he'd taken? Shaking Godolphin: "Do you know who I am, where we are," and other elementary questions that we shouldn't ask, that only prove how afraid we are to a hypothetical anybody.

Afraid he was and as it turned out with good reason. For, half an hour later, the old man still sat on the edge of the bed, making friends with Mondaugen, whom he was seeing for the first time. With the Weimar Republic's bitter breed of humor (but none of his own) Mondaugen stood at his stained-glass window and asked that evening's veld: was I being that successful a voyeur? As his days at the siege party became less current and more numbered (though not by him) he was to wonder with exponential frequency who in fact had seen him. Anyone at all? Being cowardly and thus a gourmet of fear, Mondaugen prepared himself for an unprecedented, exquisite treat. This unglimpsed item on his menu of anxieties took the form of a very German question: if no one has seen me then am I really here at all; and as a sort of savory, if I am not here then where are all these dreams coming from, if dreams is what they are.

He was given a lovely mare named Firelily: how he adored that animal! You couldn't keep her from prancing and posturing; she was a typical woman. How her deep sorrel flanks and hindquarters would flash in the sun! He was careful to have his Bastard servant keep her always curried and clean. He believed the first time the General ever addressed him directly was to compliment him on Firelily.

He rode her all over the territory. From the coastal desert to the Kalahari, from Warmbad to the Portuguese frontier, Firelily and he, and his good comrades Schwach and Fleische, they dashed madcap over sand, rock, bush; forded streams that could go from a trickle to a mile-wide flood in half an hour. Always, no matter which region it was, through those ever-dwindling herds of blacks. What were they chasing? What youthful dream?

For it was hard to avoid a feeling of impracticality about their adventure. Idealism, fatedness. As if first the missionaries, then the merchants and miners, and lately the settlers and bourgeoisie had all had their chance at something and had failed, and now it was the army's turn. To go in and chase about that silly wedge of German earth two tropics away for no other reason, apparently, than to give the warrior class equal time with God, Mammon, Freyr. Certainly not for the usual soldatesque reasons—young as they were they could see that. Next to nothing to plunder; and as for glory, what was there to hanging, clubbing, bayoneting something that did not resist? It had been a terribly unequal show from the start: Hereros were simply not the adversaries a young warrior expects. He felt cheated out of the army life the posters had shown. Only a pitiful minority of the niggers were even armed, and then only a fraction of those had rifles that worked, or ammunition. The army had Maxim and Krupp guns, and little howitzers. Often they never even saw the natives before they killed them; merely stood off on a kopje and bombarded the village, then went in afterward to finish any they'd missed.

His gums ached, he felt tired and possibly slept more than normal, whatever normal was. But this had modulated at some point into yellow skin, high thirst, flat purple spots on his legs; and his own breath sickened him. Godolphin in one of his lucid moments diagnosed this as scurvy, the cause being simply bad (in fact hardly any) diet: he'd lost twenty pounds since the beginning of the siege.

"You want fresh vegetables," the sea dog informed him, fretting. "There must be something in the larder."

"No. For God's sake," Mondaugen raved, "don't leave the room. Hyenas and jackals are padding up and down those little corridors."

"Try to lie quietly," Godolphin told him. "I can handle myself. I won't be a moment."

Mondaugen lunged off the bed, but flaccid muscles betrayed him. Nimble Godolphin vanished, the door swung to. For the first time since hearing about the Treaty of Versailles in detail, Mondaugen found himself crying.

They'll drain his juices, he thought; caress his bones with their paw-pads, gag on his fine white hair.

Mondaugen's own father had died not so many years ago, somehow involved in the Kiel revolt. That the son should think of him at this point indicated perhaps that Godolphin hadn't been the only one in that room to be "visited." As the partying rushed in phantasmagoria at and around their supposedly insulated turret, into blur, there had grown increasingly more visible one unwavering projection on the wall of night: Evan Godolphin, whom Mondaugen had never seen save by the dubious fluorescence of nostalgia he didn't want, nostalgia forced on him by something he was coming to look on as a coalition.

Presently, heavy footsteps approached through the outer

241

regions of his Versuchsstelle. Too heavy, he decided, to be Godolphin's returning: so craftily Mondaugen wiped his gums once more on the bedsheets and allowed himself to fall off the bed and roll back under an arras of satin comforter, into that cool, dusty world of old burlesque jokes and so many unhappy-go-accident-prone lovers in this real life. He made a little peephole in the coverlet and looked out: his view was directly into a high mirror that commanded, say, a third of the circular room. The knob turned, the door opened and Weissmann, draped in an ankle-length white dress with ruffled neck, bodice and sleeves, circa 1904, tiptoed into the room, crossing between the mirror's frontiers and vanishing again near the sferic equipment. All at once a dawn chorus burst from the loudspeaker, chaotic at first but resolving eventually into a deep-space madrigal for three or four voices. To which the intruder Weissmann, out of sight, added still another, in falsetto, to a minor-keyed Charleston:

Now that the twilight's just beginning,
World, stop
Spinning;
Cuckoo's in his clock with laryngitis,
So he can't tell us what night tonight is.

No one among the other dancers has
Any
Answers, just
You, I, the night
And a little black sjambok . . .

When Weissmann came back into the mirror he was carrying another oscillograph roll. Mondaugen lay among dust babies, feeling too impotent to yell stop, thief. The transvestite lieutenant had parted his hair in the middle and larded his eyelashes with mascara; these, batting against his lenses, left dark parallel streaks so that each eye looked out from its own prison window. As he passed the imprint on the coverlet of the scurvified body which had lately occupied it, Weissmann gave it (so Mondaugen fancied) a coy, sidewise smile. Then he vanished. Not too long after that Mondaugen's retinae withdrew, for a time, from light. Or it is presumed they did; either that or Under-the-Bed is even stranger country than neurasthenic children have dreamt it to be.

One could as well have been a stonemason. It dawned on you slowly, but the conclusion was irresistible: you were in no sense killing. The voluptuous feeling of safety, the delicious lassitude you went into the extermination with was sooner or later replaced by a very curious—not emotion because part of it was obviously a lack of what we commonly call "feeling"—"functional agreement" would come closer to it; operational sympathy.

The first clear instance of it he could remember came one day during a trek from Warmbad to Keetmanshoop. His outfit were moving consignments of Hottentot prisoners for some reason which doubtless made sense to the upper echelons. It was 140 miles and took generally a week or ten days to do, and none of them liked the detail much. A lot of prisoners died on route, and that meant stopping the whole trek, finding the sergeant with the keys, who it seemed was always miles back under a kameeldoorn tree, dead drunk or well on the way, then riding back, unlocking the neck-ring of the fellow who'd died; sometimes rearranging the line so the weight of the extra chain would be more evenly distributed. Not to make it easier on them, exactly, but so one wouldn't wear out any more blacks than one had to.

It was a glorious day, December and hot, a bird somewhere gone mad with the season. Firelily, under him, seemed sexually aroused, she curveted and frolicked so about the line of march, covering five miles to the prisoners' one. From the side it always looked medieval, the way the chain hung down in bights between their neck-rings, the way the weight pulled them constantly toward earth, the force only just overcome as long as they managed to keep their legs moving. Behind them came army oxcarts, driven by loyal Rehoboth Bastards. How many can understand the resemblance he saw? In his village church in the Palatinate was a mural of the Dance of Death, led by a rather sinuous, effeminate Death in his black cloak, carrying his scythe and followed by all ranks of society from prince to peasant. Their own African progress was hardly so elegant: they could only boast a homogeneous string of suffering Negroes and a drunken sergeant in a wideawake hat who carried a Mauser. Yet that association, which most of them shared, was enough to give the unpopular chore an atmosphere of ceremony.

The trek hadn't been under way more than an hour before one of the blacks began to complain about his feet. They were bleeding, he said. His overseer brought Firelily close in and looked: so they were. Hardly would the blood soak into the sand than the prisoner behind would kick it invisible. Not long after that the same prisoner complained that the sand was working its way into the cuts on his feet and the pain was making it difficult for him to walk. No doubt this was also true. He was told either to be quiet or forfeit his share of water when they outspanned for the noon rest. The soldiers had learned on previous treks that if one native was allowed to complain the others soon enough took it up and this for some reason slowed everyone. They wouldn't sing or chant; that perhaps could have been borne. But the wailing, self-indulgent babel that would go up— God, it was awful. Silence, for practical reasons, was the rule and was enforced.

But this Hottentot would not keep silent. He was only limping slightly, he didn't stumble. But he bitched more than the most malcontent of infantry. The young trooper edged Firelily toward him in her sensual strut and flicked him once or twice with a sjambok. From the height of a man on horseback a good rhinoceros sjambok used properly can quiet a nigger in less time and with less trouble than it takes to shoot him. But it had no effect on this one. Fleische saw what was happening and brought his black gelding up from the other side. Together the troopers sjamboked the Hottentot on the buttocks and thighs, forcing him into a queer little dance. It took a certain talent to make a prisoner dance that way without slowing down the rest of the trek because of the way they were all chained together. They were doing quite well until through some stupid misjudgment, Fleische's sjambok caught in the chain and he was pulled from his horse and under the feet of the prisoners.

Their reflexes are fast, they're like animals. Before the other trooper had really taken it in the fellow they'd been sjamboking leaped on Fleische, trying to get his bight of chain around Fleische's neck. The rest of the line, realizing through some extra sense what had happened—anticipating murder—had come to a halt.

Fleische managed to roll away. The two of them got the key from the sergeant, unlocked and removed their Hottentot from the trek, and brought him off to the side. After

Fleische, with the tip of his sjambok, had had the obligatory sport with the black's genitals, they clubbed him to death with the butts of their rifles and tossed what was left behind a rock for the vultures and flies.

But as they did this thing—and Fleische said later that he'd felt something like it too—there came over him for the first time an odd sort of peace, perhaps like what the black was feeling as he gave up the ghost. Usually the most you felt was annoyance; the kind of annoyance you have for an insect that's buzzed around you for too long. You have to obliterate its life, and the physical effort, the obviousness of the act, the knowledge that this is only one unit in a seemingly infinite series, that killing this one won't end it, won't relieve you from having to kill more tomorrow, and the day after, and on, and on . . . the futility of it irritates you and so to each individual act you bring something of the savagery of military boredom, which as any trooper knows is mighty indeed.

This time it wasn't like that. Things seemed all at once to fall into a pattern: a great cosmic fluttering in the blank, bright sky and each grain of sand, each cactus spine, each feather of the circling vulture above them and invisible molecule of heated air seemed to shift imperceptibly so that this black and he, and he and every other black he would henceforth have to kill slid into alignment, assumed a set symmetry, a dancelike poise. It finally meant something different: different from the recruiting poster, the mural in the church and the natives already exterminated—sleeping and lame burned en masse in their pontoks, babies tossed in the air and caught on bayonets, girls approached with organ at the ready, their eyes filming over in anticipated pleasure or possibly only an anticipated five more minutes of life, only to be shot through the head first and then ravished, after of course being made aware at the last moment that this would happen to them—different from the official language of von Trotha's orders and directives, different from the sense of function and the delightful, powerless languor that are both part of following a military order that's filtered like spring rain down countless levels before reaching you; different from colonial policy, international finagling, hope of advancement within the army or enrichment out of it.

It had only to do with the destroyer and the destroyed, and the act which united them, and it had never been that way before. Returning from the Waterberg with von Trotha and his staff, they came upon an old woman digging wild onions at the side of the road. A trooper named König jumped down off his horse and shot her dead: but before he pulled the trigger he put the muzzle against her forehead and said, "I am going to kill you." She looked up and said, "I thank you." Later, toward dusk, there was one Herero girl, sixteen or seventeen years old, for the platoon; and Firelily's rider was last. After he'd had her he must have hesitated a moment between sidearm and bayonet. She actually smiled then; pointed to both, and began to shift her hips lazily in the dust. He used both.

When through some levitation he again found himself on top of the bed, Hedwig Vogelsang was just entering the room astride a male Bondel who crawled on all fours. She wore only a pair of black tights and had let her long hair down.

"Good evening, poor Kurt." She rode the Bondel as far as the bed and dismounted. "You may go, Firelily. I call it Firelily," she smiled at Mondaugen, "because of its sorrel skin."

Mondaugen attempted a greeting, found himself too weak to talk. Hedwig was slithering out of the tights. "I made up only my eyes," she told him in a decadent whisper: "my lips can redden with your blood as we kiss." She began making love to him. He tried to respond but the scurvy had weakened him. How long it went on he didn't know. It seemed to go on for days. The light in the room kept changing, Hedwig seemed to be everywhere at once in this black satin circle the world had shrunk to: either she was inexhaustible or Mondaugen had lost all sense of duration. They seemed wound into a cocoon of blond hair and ubiquitous, dry kisses: once or twice she may have brought in a Bondel girl to assist.

"Where is Godolphin," he cried.

"She has him."

"O God . . ."

Sometimes impotent, sometimes aroused despite his lassitude, Mondaugen stayed neutral, neither enjoying her attentions nor worrying about her opinion of his virility. At length she grew frustrated. He knew what she was looking for.

"You hate me," her lip quivering unnaturally as a forced vibrato.

246

"But I have to recuperate."

In through the window came Weissmann with his hair combed in bangs, wearing white silk lounging pajamas, rhinestone pumps, and black eyeholes and lips, to steal another oscillograph roll. The loudspeaker blithered at him as if it were angry.

Later Foppl appeared in the door with Vera Meroving, held her hand, and sang to a sprightly waltz melody:

> I know what you want,
> Princess of coquettes:
> Deviations, fantasies and secret amulets.
>
> Only try to go
> Further than you've gone
> If you never want to live to see another dawn.
>
> Seventeen is cruel,
> Yet at forty-two,
> Purgatory fires burn no livelier than you.
>
> So, come away from him,
> Take my hand instead,
> Let the dead get to the task of burying their dead;
> Through that hidden door again,
> Bravo for '04 again; I'm a
> Deutschesüdwestafrikaner in love . . .

Once mustered out, those who stayed either drifted west to work at mines like the Khan or homesteaded their own land where the farming was good. He was restless. After doing what he'd been doing for three years a man doesn't settle down, at least not too quickly. So he went to the coast.

Just as its own loose sand was licked away by the cold tongue of a current from the Antarctic south, that coast began to devour time the moment you arrived. It offered life nothing: its soil was arid; salt-bearing winds, chilled by the great Benguela, swept in off the sea to blight anything that tried to grow. There was constant battle between the fog, which wanted to freeze your marrow, and the sun: which, once having burned off the fog, sought you. Over Swakopmund the sun often seemed to fill the entire sky, so diffracted was it by the sea fog. A luminous gray tending to yellow, that hurt the eyes. You learned soon enough to wear tinted glasses for the sky. If you stayed long enough you came to feel it was almost an affront for humans to be living there at all. The sky was too large, the coastal settlements under it too mean. The harbor at Swakopmund was slowly, continuously filling with sand, men were felled mysteriously by the afternoon's sun, horses went mad and were lost in the tenacious ooze down along the beaches. It was a brute coast, and survival for white and black less a matter of choice than anywhere else in the Territory.

He'd been deceived, that was his first thought: it wasn't to be like the army. Something had changed. The blacks mattered even less. You didn't recognize their being there in the same way you once had. Objectives were different, that may simply have been all. The harbor needed dredging; railroads had to be built inland from the seaports, which couldn't thrive by themselves any more than the interior could survive without them. Having legitimized their presence in the Territory the colonists were now obliged to improve what they had taken.

There were compensations, but they were not the luxuries army life had offered. As Schachtmeister you got a house to yourself and first look at girls who came in from the bush to surrender. Lindequist, who'd succeeded von Trotha, had canceled the extermination order, asking all the natives who'd fled to return, promising that no one would be hurt. It was cheaper than sending out search expeditions and rounding them up. Because they were starving out in the bush, promises of mercy included promises of food. After being fed they were taken into custody and sent out to the mines, or the coast, or the Cameroons. Their laagers, under military escort, arrived from the interior almost daily. Mornings he'd go down to the staging area and assist in the sorting-out. The Hottentots were mostly women. Among the few Hereros they got, the proportion was of course more nearly equal.

After three years of ripe, Southern indulgence to come upon this ash plain impregnated with a killer sea may have needed a strength not really found in nature: sustained necessarily by illusion. Not even whales could skirt that strand with impunity: walking along what served for an esplanade you might see one of the rotting creatures, beached, covered by feeding gulls who with the coming of night would be relieved at the giant carrion by a pack of strand wolves. And in a matter of days there would be left only the

248

portals of great jaws and a picked, architectural web of bone, mellowing eventually to false ivory in the sun and fog.

The barren islets off Lüderitzbucht were natural concentration camps. Walking among huddled forms in the evening, distributing blankets, food and occasional kisses from the sjambok, you felt like the father colonial policy wanted you to be when it spoke of Väterliche Züchtigung; fatherly chastisement, an inalienable right. Their bodies, so terribly thin and slick with cloud, lay drawn together to pool what marginal warmth was left to them. Here and there a torch of bound reeds soaked in whale oil hissed bravely in the fog. A swaddled silence would be over the island, nights like that: if they complained, or had to cry for some lesion or cramp, it was baffled by the thick mists and all you heard was the tide, slapping ever sideways along the strand, viscous, reverberating; then seltzering back to sea, violently salt, leaving a white skin on the sand it hadn't taken. And only occasionally above the mindless rhythm, from across the narrow strait, over on the great African continent itself, a sound would arise to make the fog colder, the night darker, the Atlantic more menacing: if it were human it could have been called laughter, but it was not human. It was a product of alien secretions, boiling over into blood already choked and heady; causing ganglia to twitch, the field of night-vision to be grayed into shapes that threatened, putting an itch into every fiber, an unbalance, a general sensation of error that could only be nulled by those hideous paroxysms, those fat, spindle-shaped bursts of air up the pharynx, counter-irritating the top of the mouth cavity, filling the nostrils, easing the prickliness under the jaw and down the center-line of the skull: it was the cry of the brown hyena called the strand wolf, who prowled the beach singly or with companions in search of shellfish, dead gulls, anything flesh and unmoving.

And so, as you moved among them, you were forced to look at them as a collection: knowing from statistics that twelve to fifteen of them died per day, but eventually unable even to wonder which twelve to fifteen: in the dark they differed only in size, and that made it easier not to care as you once had. But every time the strand wolf howled across the water, as, perhaps, you were stooping down to examine a prospective concubine missed in the first winnowing, it was only by suppressing memories of the three years just passed that you kept from wondering if it was this particular girl the beast waited for.

As a civilian Schachtmeister drawing government pay this was one among many luxuries he'd had to abandon: the luxury of being able to see them as individuals. This extended even to one's concubines; one had several, some purely for housework, others for pleasure, domesticity too having become a massed affair. They were the exclusive possession of no one save the high-ranking officers. Subalterns, enlisted men and gangers like himself shared them out of a common pool, housed in a barbed-wire compound near the B.O.Q.

It was problematical who among the females had the better time of it in the way of creature comfort; the courtesans who lived inside the barbed wire or the workers who were housed in a great thorn enclosure nearer the beach. They had to rely on primarily female labor, there simply being, for obvious reasons, a severe shortage of males. They found the distaff side useful for a number of functions. Women could be inspanned to the heavy-duty carts to pull loads of silt dredged from the floor of the harbor; or to carry the rails for the road of iron being driven across the Namib toward Keetmanshoop. That destination naturally enough reminded him of the old days when he'd helped march blacks there. Often, under the hazed-out sun, he'd daydream; remembering water holes filled to the brim with black corpses, their ears, nostrils and mouths bejeweled green, white, black, iridescent with flies and their offspring; human pyres whose flames seemed to leap high as the Southern Cross; the frangibility of bone, the splitting-open of body sacs, the sudden heaviness of even a frail child. But here there could be none of that: they were organized, made to perform en masse—you'd have to supervise not a chained trek but a long double line of women, carrying rails with iron ties attached; if one woman fell it meant only a fractional increase in the force required per carrier, not the confusion and paralysis resulting from a single failure in one of the old treks. Only once could he remember anything like that happening, and it may have been because the fog and cold the previous week had been worse than usual, so that their sockets and joints may have become inflamed—that day his own neck ached and he had trouble turning it to see what had happened—but a sudden wail went up and he saw that one of the women had stumbled and fallen and brought the whole line down. His heart rose, the wind off the ocean turned balmy; here was a fragment of the old past, revealed as if by a parting in the fog. He went back to her, ascertained that the falling rail had broken her leg; dragged her out from under it without bothering to lift it, rolled her down the embankment and left her to die. It did him good, he thought; it took him temporarily away from nostalgia, which on that coast was a kind of despondency.

But if physical labor exhausted those who lived inside thorns, sexual labor could as easily fatigue those who lived inside steel. Some of the military had brought with them curious ideas. One sergeant, too far down the chain of command to rate a young boy (young boys being rare), did the best he could with pre-adolescent, breastless girls whose heads he shaved and whom he kept naked except for shrunken army leggings. Another made his partners lie still, like corpses; any sexual responses, sudden breaths or involuntary jerks were reprimanded with an elegant jeweled sjambok he'd had designed for him in Berlin. So if the women thought about any of this at all there couldn't have been much to choose between thorns and steel.

Himself, he could have been happy in that new corporative life; could have made a career out of construction work, except for one of his concubines, a Herero child named Sarah. She brought his discontent to a focus; perhaps even became one reason finally why he quit it all and headed inland to try to regain a little of the luxury and abundance that had vanished (he feared) with von Trotha.

He found her first a mile out in the Atlantic, on a breakwater they were building of sleek dark rocks that the women carried out by hand, deep-sixed and slowly, painfully stacked into a tentacle crawling along the sea. That day gray sheets were tacked to the sky, and a black cloud remained all day at the western horizon. It was her eyes he saw first, whites reflecting something of the sea's slow turbulence; then her back, beaded with old sjambok scars. He supposed it was simple lust that made him go over and motion to her to put down the rock she'd begun to lift: scribble and give her a note for her compound supervisor. "Give it to him," he warned her, "or—" and he made the sjambok whistle in the salt wind. In earlier days you hadn't had to warn them: somehow, because of that "operational sympathy," they

251

always delivered notes, even when they knew the note might well be a death warrant.

She looked at the chit, then at him. Clouds moved across those eyes; whether reflected or transmitted he'd never know. Brine slapped at their feet, carrion birds wheeled in the sky. The breakwater stretched behind them back to land and safety; but it could take only a word; any, the most inconsequential, to implant in each of them the perverse notion that their own path lay the other way, on the invisible mole not yet built; as if the sea were pavement for them, as for our Redeemer.

Here was another like the woman pinned under the rail, another piece of those soldiering days. He knew he didn't want to share this girl; he was feeling again the pleasure of making a choice whose consequences, even the most terrible, he could ignore.

He asked her name, she answered Sarah, eyes never having left him. A squall, cold as Antarctica, came rushing across the water, drenched them, continued on toward the north, though it would die without ever seeing the Congo's mouth or the Bight of Benin. She shivered, his hand in apparent reflex went to touch her but she avoided it and stooped to pick up the rock. He tapped her lightly on the rear with his sjambok and the moment, whatever it had meant, was over.

That night she didn't come. Next morning he caught her on the breakwater, made her kneel, placed his boot on her nape and pushed her head under the sea until his sense of timing told him to let her up for air. He noticed then how long and snakelike her thighs were; how clearly the musculature of her hips stood under the skin, skin with a certain glow, but finely striated because of her long fast in the bush. That day he'd sjambok her on any least pretense. At dusk he wrote out another chit and handed it to her. "You have an hour." She watched him, nothing about her at all of the animal he'd seen in other nigger women. Only eyes giving back the red sun, and the white stalks of fog that had already begun to rise off the water.

He didn't eat supper. He waited alone in his house near the barbed-wire compound, listening to the drunks selecting their mates for the night. He couldn't stay off his feet and perhaps he'd caught a chill. The hour passed; she didn't come. He walked out without a coat into low clouds and

made his way to her thorn compound. It was pitch-b
out. Wet gusts slapped his cheeks, he stumbled. Once
the enclosure he took up a torch and went looking for her.
Perhaps they thought he was mad, perhaps he was. He
didn't know how long he looked. He couldn't find her. They
all looked alike.

The next morning she appeared as usual. He chose two
strong women, bent her back over a rock and while they
held her he first sjamboked, then took her. She lay in a cold
rigor; and when it was over he was astonished to find that at
some point during it the women had, like good-natured
duennas, released her and gone about their morning's
labor.

And that night, long after he'd turned in, she came to his
house and slid into the bed next to him. Woman's perversity!
She was his.

Yet how long could he have had her to himself? During
the day he manacled her to the bed, and he continued to
use the woman-pool at night so he wouldn't arouse suspicion.
Sarah might have cooked, cleaned, comforted, been the
closest thing to a wife he'd ever had. But on that foggy,
sweating, sterile coast there were no owners, nothing owned.
Community may have been the only solution possible against
such an assertion of the Inanimate. Soon enough his neighbor
the pederast had discovered her and become enchanted. He
requested Sarah; this was answered by the lie that she'd
come from the pool and the pederast could wait his turn. But
it could only get them a reprieve. The neighbor visited his
house during the day, found her manacled and helpless, took
her his own way and then decided, like a thoughtful sergeant, to share this good fortune with his platoon. Between
noon and suppertime, as the fog's glare shifted in the sky,
they took out an abnormal distribution of sexual preferences on her, poor Sarah, "his" Sarah only in a way that
poisonous strand could never support.

He came home to find her drooling, her eyes drained for
good of all weather. Not thinking, probably not having
taken it all in, he unlocked her shackles and it was as if
like a spring she'd been storing the additive force that convivial platoon had expended in amusing themselves; for with
an incredible strength she broke out of his embrace and fled,
and that was how he saw her, alive, for the last time.

The next day her body was washed up on the beach. She

n a sea they would perhaps never succeed in
rt of. Jackals had eaten her breasts. It seemed
thing had at last been brought to consumma-
arrival centuries ago on the troop ship
had only as obviousness and immediacy to do
with the sergeant-pederast's preference as to women or that
old bubonic plague injection. If it were parable (which he
doubted) it probably went to illustrate the progress of ap-
petite or evolution of indulgence, both in a direction he
found unpleasant to contemplate. If a season like the Great
Rebellion ever came to him again, he feared, it could never
be in that same personal, random array of picaresque acts
he was to recall and celebrate in later years at best furious
and nostalgic; but rather with a logic that chilled the comfortable perversity of the heart, that substituted capability
for character, deliberate scheme for political epiphany (so
incomparably African); and for Sarah, the sjambok, the
dances of death between Warmbad and Keetmanshoop, the
taut haunches of his Firelily, the black corpse impaled on a
thorn tree in a river swollen with sudden rain, for these
the dearest canvases in his soul's gallery, it was to substitute
the bleak, abstracted and for him rather meaningless hanging on which he now turned his back, but which was to back-
drop his retreat until he reached the Other Wall, the engineering design for a world he knew with numb leeriness
nothing could now keep from becoming reality, a world
whose full despair he, at the vantage of eighteen years
later, couldn't even find adequate parables for, but a design
whose first fumbling sketches he thought must have been
done the year after Jacob Marengo died, on that terrible
coast, where the beach between Lüderitzbucht and the
cemetery was actually littered each morning with a score
of identical female corpses, an agglomeration no more sub-
stantial-looking than seaweed against the unhealthy yellow
sand; where the soul's passage was more a mass migration
across that choppy fetch of Atlantic the wind never left alone,
from an island of low cloud, like an anchored prison ship,
to simple integration with the unimaginable mass of their
continent; where the single line of track still edged toward
a Keetmanshoop that could in no conceivable iconology be
any part of the Kingdom of Death; where, finally, humanity
was reduced, out of a necessity which in his loonier moments
he could almost believe was only Deutsch-Südwestafrika's

(actually he knew better), out of a confrontation the young of one's contemporaries, God help them, had yet to make, humanity was reduced to a nervous, disquieted, forever inadequate but indissoluble Popular Front against deceptively unpolitical and apparently minor enemies, enemies that would be with him to the grave: a sun with no shape, a beach alien as the moon's antarctic, restless concubines in barbed wire, salt mists, alkaline earth, the Benguela Current that would never cease bringing sand to raise the harbor floor, the inertia of rock, the frailty of flesh, the structural unreliability of thorns; the unheard whimper of a dying woman; the frightening but necessary cry of the strand wolf in the fog.

IV

"Kurt, why do you never kiss me any more?"

"How long have I been sleeping," he wanted to know. Heavy blue drapes had at some point been drawn across the window.

"It's night."

He grew aware of an absence in the room: located this eventually as an absence of background noise from the loudspeaker, and was off the bed and tottering toward his receivers before realizing he'd recovered enough to be walking at all. His mouth tasted vile but his joints no longer ached, gums no longer felt as sore or spongy. The purple spots on his legs had gone.

Hedwig giggled. "They made you look like a hyena."

The mirror had nothing encouraging to show him. He batted his eyes at himself and the lashes of the left one promptly stuck together.

"Don't squint, darling." She had a toe pointed toward the ceiling and was adjusting a stocking. Mondaugen leered at her crookedly and began trouble-shooting his equipment. Behind him he heard someone enter the room and Hedwig begin to moan. Chains tinkled in the heavy sickroom air, something whistled and impacted with a loud report against what might have been flesh. Satin tore, silk hissed, French heels beat a tattoo against the parquetry. Had the scurvy changed him from voyeur to écouteur, or was it deeper and part of a general change of heart? The trouble was a burned-out tube in the power amplifier. He replaced it with

255

a spare and turned and saw that Hedwig had vanished.

Mondaugen stayed alone in the turret for a few dozen visitations from the sferics, this being the only link remaining with the kind of time that continued to pass outside Foppl's. He was awakened from a light sleep by the sound of explosions to the east. When he finally decided to climb out the stained-glass window to investigate, he found that everyone had rushed to the roof. A battle, a real one, was in progress across the ravine. Such was their elevation that they could see everything spread out in panorama, as if for their amusement. A small group of Bondels huddled among some rocks: men, women, children and a few starved-looking goats. Hedwig inched her way across the roof's shallow slope to Mondaugen and held his hand. "How exciting," she whispered, eyes huger than he'd ever seen them, blood crusted on her wrists and ankles. Declining sunlight stained the bodies of the Bondels to a certain orange. Thin wisps of cirrus floated diaphanous in a late afternoon sky. But soon the sun had turned them blinding white.

Surrounding the besieged Bondels, in a ragged noose, were whites, closing, mostly volunteer except for a cadre of Union officers and non-coms. They exchanged occasional gunfire with the natives, who seemed to have only half-a-dozen rifles among them. Doubtless there were human voices down there, uttering cries of command, triumph, pain; but at this distance only the tiny pop-pop of gunshots could be heard. To one side was a singed area, streaked with the gray of pulverized rock and littered with bodies and parts of bodies which had once belonged to Bondels.

"Bombs," Foppl commented. "That's what woke us up." Someone had come up from below with wine and glasses, and cigars. The accordionist had brought his instrument, but after a few bars was silenced: no one on the roof wanted to miss any sound of death that should reach them. They leaned toward the battle: cords of the neck drawn tense, eyes sleep-puffed, hair in disarray and dotted with dandruff, fingers with dirty nails clutching like talons the sunreddened stems of their wine goblets; lips blackened with yesterday's wine, nicotine, blood and drawn back from the tartared teeth so that the original hue only showed in cracks. Aging women shifted their legs frequently, makeup they'd not cleaned away clinging in blotches to pore-riddled cheeks. Over the horizon from the direction of the Union came two biplanes, flying low and lazy, like birds wandered away from a flock. "That's where the bombs came from," announced Foppl to his company. So excited now that he slopped wine on the roof. Mondaugen watched it flow in twin streams all the way to the eaves. It reminded him somehow of his first morning at Foppl's, and the two streaks of blood (when had he began to call it blood?) in the courtyard. A kite lit lower down on the roof and began to peck at the wine. Soon it took wing again. When had he begun to call it blood?

The planes looked as if they would come no nearer, only hang forever in the sky. The sun was going down. The clouds had been blown terribly thin, and begun to glow red, and seemed to ribbon the sky its entire length, filmy and splendid, as if it were they that held it all together. One of the Bondels suddenly appeared to run amok: stood upright, waving a spear, and began to run toward the nearest part of the advancing cordon. The whites there bunched together and fired at him in a flurry of pops, echoed by the pop of corks on Foppl's roof. He had almost reached them before he fell.

Now the planes could be heard: a snarling, intermittent sound. They swooped clumsy in a dive toward the Bondel-swaartz position: the sun caught suddenly the three canisters dropped from each, turned them to six drops of orange fire. They seemed to take a century to fall. But soon, two bracketing the rocks, two among the Bondels and two in the area where the corpses lay, there bloomed at last six explosions, sending earth, stone and flesh cascading toward the nearly black sky with its scarlet overlay of cloud. Seconds later the loud, coughing blasts, overlapping, reached the roof. How the watchers cheered. The cordon moved rapidly then, through what was now a pall of thin smoke, killing the still-active and wounded, sending bullets into corpses, into women and children, even into the one goat that had survived. Then abruptly the crescendo of cork-pops ceased and night fell. And after a few minutes someone lit a campfire out on the battlefield. The watchers on the roof retired inside for a night of more than usually riotous celebration.

Had a new phase of the siege party begun with that dusk's intrusion from the present year, 1922, or was the change internal and Mondaugen's: a shift in the configuration of sights and sounds he was now filtering out, choosing not to notice? No way to tell; no one to say. Whatever it arose from, health returning or simple impatience with the hermetic, he was starting to feel those first tentative glandular pressures that one day develop into moral outrage. At least he was to experience a for him rare Achphenomenon: the discovery that his voyeurism had been determined purely by events seen, and not by any deliberate choice, or preexisting set of personal psychic needs.

No one saw any more battles. From time to time a body of horse-soldiers might be noted in the distance, tearing desperate across the plateau, raising a little dust; there would be explosions, miles away in the direction of the Karas mountains. And they heard a Bondel one night, lost in the dark, scream the name of Abraham Morris as he stumbled and fell into a ravine. In the last weeks of Mondaugen's stay everyone remained in the house, getting only a few hours' sleep per twenty-four-hour period. Easily a third of their number were bedridden: several, besides Foppl's Bondels, had died. It had become an amusement to visit an invalid each night to feed him wine and arouse him sexually.

Mondaugen remained up in his turret, working diligently at his code, taking occasional breaks to stand out alone on the roof and wonder if he would ever escape a curse that seemed to have been put on him one Fasching: to become surrounded by decadence no matter what exotic region, north or south, he wandered into. It couldn't be only Munich, he decided at some point: nor even the fact of economic depression. This was a soul-depression which must surely infest Europe as it infested this house.

One night he was awakened by a disheveled Weissmann, who could scarcely stand still for excitement. "Look, look," he cried, waving a sheet of paper under Mondaugen's slowly blinking eyes. Mondaugen read:

DIGEWOELDTIMSTEALALENSWTASNDEURFUALRLIKST

"So," he yawned.

"It's your code. I've broken it. See: I remove every third letter and obtain: GODMEANTNUURK. This rearranged spells Kurt Mondaugen."

"Well, then," Mondaugen snarled. "And who the hell told you you could read my mail."

"The remainder of the message," Weissmann continued, "now reads: DIEWELTISTALLESWASDERFALLIST."

"The world is all that the case is," Mondaugen said. "I've heard that somewhere before." A smile began to spread. "Weissmann, for shame. Resign your commission, you're in the wrong line of work. You'd make a fine engineer: you've been finagling."

"I swear," Weissmann protested, hurt.

Later on, finding the turret oppressive, Mondaugen exited through the window and wandered the gables, corridors and stairways of the villa till the moon was down. Early in the morning, with only the nacreous beginnings of a dawn visible out over the Kalahari, he came around a brick wall and entered a small hopyard. Hanging over the rows, each wrist attached to a different stringing-wire, feet dangling over young hops already sick with downy mildew, was another Bondel, perhaps Foppl's last. Below, dancing about the body and flicking its buttocks with a sjambok, was old Godolphin. Vera Meroving stood by his side and they appeared to have exchanged clothing. Godolphin, keeping time with the sjambok, launched quaveringly into a reprise of Down by the Summertime Sea.

Mondaugen this time withdrew, preferring at last neither to watch nor to listen. Instead he returned to the turret and gathered up his log books, oscillograms and a small knapsack of clothing and toilet articles. He sneaked downstairs and went out by a French window; located a long plank at the rear of the house and dragged it to the ravine. Foppl and guests had been somehow alerted to his departure. They crowded the windows; some sat out on the balconies and roof, some came to the veranda to watch. With a final grunt Mondaugen dropped the plank across a narrow part of the ravine. As he was working his way gingerly across, trying not to look down at the tiny stream two hundred feet below, the accordion began a slow sad tango, as if piping him ashore. This soon modulated into a rousing valediction, which they all sang in chorus:

Why are you leaving the party so early,
Just when it was getting good?
Were the crowds and the laughter just a little too tame,
Did the girl you had your eye on go and forfeit the game?
    O tell me
Where is there music any gayer than ours, and tell me
Where are wine and ladies in such ample supply?
If you know a better party in the Southwest Protectorate,

inanimate landscape

Tell us and we'll drop on by
(Right after this one)
Tell us and we'll drop on by.

He reached the other side, adjusted the knapsack and began to trudge toward a distant clump of trees. After a few hundred yards he decided to look back after all. They still watched him and their hush now was a part of the same that hung over all the scrubland. The morning's sun bleached their faces a Fasching-white he remembered seeing in another place. They gazed across the ravine dehumanized and aloof, as if they were the last gods on earth.

Two miles further on at a fork in the road he met a Bondel riding on a donkey. The Bondel had lost his right arm. "All over," he said. "Many Bondels dead, baases dead, van Wijk dead. My woman, younkers dead." He let Mondaugen ride behind him. At that point Mondaugen didn't know where they were going. As the sun climbed he dozed on and off, his cheek against the Bondel's scarred back. They seemed the only three animate objects on the yellow road which led, he knew, sooner or later, to the Atlantic. The sunlight was immense, the plateau country wide, and Mondaugen felt little and lost in the dun-colored waste. Soon as they trotted along the Bondel began to sing, in a small voice which was lost before it reached the nearest Ganna bush. The song was in Hottentot dialect, and Mondaugen couldn't understand it.

chapter ten

*In which various
sets of young
people get
together*

V

I

McClintic Sphere, whose horn man was soloing, stood by the empty piano, looking off at nothing in particular. He was half listening to the music (touching the keys of his alto now and again, as if by sympathetic magic to make that natural horn develop the idea differently, some way Sphere thought could be better) and half watching the customers at the tables.

This was last set and it'd been a bad week for Sphere. Some of the colleges were let out and the place had been crowded with these types who liked to talk to each other a lot. Every now and again, they'd invite him over to a table between sets and ask him what he thought about other altos. Some of them would go through the old Northern liberal routine: look at me, I'll sit with anybody. Either that or they would say: "Hey fella, how about Night Train?" Yes, bwana. Yazzuh, boss. Dis darkey, ol' Uncle McClintic, he play you de finest Night Train you evah did hear. An' aftah de set he gwine take dis ol' alto an' shove it up yo' white Ivy League ass.

The horn wanted to finish off: he'd been tired all week as Sphere. They took fours with the drummer, stated the main theme in unison and left the stand.

The bums stood outside like a receiving line. Spring had hit New York all warm and aphrodisiac. Sphere found his

Triumph in the lot, got in and took off uptown. He needed to relax.

Half an hour later he was in Harlem, in a friendly rooming (and in a sense cat) house run by one Matilda Winthrop, who was little and wizened and looked like any elderly little lady you might see in the street, going along with gentle steps in the waning afternoon to look for spleens and greens at the market.

"She's up there," Matilda said, with a smile for everybody, even musicians with a headful of righteous moss who were making money and drove sports cars. Sphere shadowboxed with her for a few minutes. She had better reflexes than he did.

The girl was sitting on the bed, smoking and reading a western. Sphere tossed his coat on a chair. She moved over to make room for him, dog-eared a page, put the book on the floor. Soon he was telling her about the week, about the kids with money who used him for background music and the musicians from other bigger groups, also with money, who were cautious and had mixed reactions and the few who couldn't really afford dollar beers at the V-Note but did or wanted to understand except that the space they might have occupied was already taken up by the rich kids and musicians. He told it all into the pillow and she rubbed his back with amazingly gentle hands. Her name, she said, was Ruby but he didn't believe that. Soon:

"Do you ever dig what I'm trying to say," he wondered.

"On the horn I don't," she answered, honest enough, "a girl doesn't understand. All she does is feel. I feel what you play, like I feel what you need when you're inside me. Maybe they're the same thing. McClintic, I don't know. You're kind to me, what is it you want?"

"Sorry," he said. After a while, "This is a good way to relax."

"Stay tonight?"

"Sure."

Slab and Esther, uncomfortable with each other, stood in front of an easel in his place, looking at Cheese Danish # 35. The cheese Danish was a recent obsession of Slab's. He had taken, some time ago, to painting in a frenzy these morning-pastries in every conceivable style, light and setting. The room was already littered with Cubist, Fauve and Surrealist cheese Danishes. "Monet spent his declining years at his home in Giverny, painting the water lilies in the garden pool," reasoned Slab. "He painted all kinds of water lilies. He liked water lilies. These are my declining years. I like cheese Danishes, they have kept me alive now for longer than I can remember. Why not."

The subject of Cheese Danish # 35 occupied only a small area, to the lower left of center, where it was pictured impaled on one of the metal steps of a telephone pole. The landscape was an empty street, drastically foreshortened, the only living things in it a tree in the middle distance, on which perched an ornate bird, busily textured with a great many swirls, flourishes and bright-colored patches.

"This," explained Slab in answer to her question, "is my revolt against Catatonic Expressionism: the universal symbol I have decided will replace the Cross in western civilization. It is the Partridge in the Pear Tree. You remember the old Christmas song, which is a linguistic joke. Perdrix, pear tree. The beauty is that it works like a machine yet is animate. The partridge eats pears off the tree, and his droppings in turn nourish the tree which grows higher and higher, every day lifting the partridge up and at the same time assuring him of a continuous supply of good. It is perpetual motion, except for one thing." He pointed out a gargoyle with sharp fangs near the top of the picture. The point of the largest fang lay on an imaginary line projected parallel to the axis of the tree and drawn through the head of the bird. "It could as well have been a low-flying airplane or high-tension wire," Slab said. "But someday that bird will be impaled on the gargoyle's teeth, just like the poor cheese Danish is already on the phone pole."

"Why can't he fly away?" Esther said.

"He is too stupid. He used to know how to fly once, but he's forgotten."

"I detect allegory in all this," she said.

"No," said Slab. "That is on the same intellectual level as doing the Times crossword puzzle on Sunday. Phony. Unworthy of you."

She'd wandered to the bed. "No," he almost yelled.

"Slab, it's so bad. It's a physical pain, here." She drew her fingers across her abdomen.

"I'm not getting any either," said Slab. "I can't help it that Schoenmaker cut you off."

"Aren't I your friend?"

"No," said Slab.

"What can I do to show you—"

"Go," said Slab, "is what you can do. And let me sleep. In my chaste army cot. Alone." He crawled to the bed and lay face down. Soon Esther left, forgetting to close the door. Not being the type to slam doors on being rejected.

Roony and Rachel sat at the bar of a neighborhood tavern on Second Avenue. Over in the corner an Irishman and a Hungarian were yelling at each other over the bowling game.

"Where does she go at night," Roony wondered.

"Paola is a strange girl," said Rachel. "You learn after a while not to ask her questions she doesn't want to answer."

"Maybe seeing Pig."

"No. Pig Bodine lives at the V-Note and the Rusty Spoon. He has a letch for Paola a mile long but he reminds her too much, I think, of Pappy Hod. The Navy has a certain way of endearing itself. She stays away from him and it's killing him and I for one am glad to see it."

It's killing me, Winsome wanted to say. He didn't. Lately he'd been running for comfort to Rachel. He'd come in a way to depend on it. Her sanity and aloofness from the Crew, her own self-sufficiency drew him. But he was no nearer to arranging any assignation with Paola. Perhaps he was afraid of Rachel's reaction. He was beginning to suspect she was not the sort who approved of pimping for one's roommate. He ordered another boilermaker.

"Roony, you drink too much," she said. "I worry about you."

"Nag, nag, nag." He smiled.

II

Next evening, Profane was sitting in the guardroom at Anthroresearch Associates, feet propped on a gas stove, reading an avant-garde western called *Existentialist Sheriff*, which Pig Bodine had recommended. Across one of the laboratory spaces, features lit Frankenstein's-monsterlike by a night light, facing Profane, sat SHROUD: synthetic human, radiation output determined.

Its skin was cellulose acetate butyrate, a plastic transparent not only to light but also to X-rays, gamma rays and neutrons. Its skeleton had once been that of a living human;

now the bones were decontaminated and the long ones and spinal column hollowed inside to receive radiation dosimeters. SHROUD was five feet nine inches tall—the fiftieth percentile of Air Force standards. The lungs, sex organs, kidneys, thyroid, liver, spleen and other internal organs were hollow and made of the same clear plastic as the body shell. These could be filled with aqueous solutions which absorbed the same amount of radiation as the tissue they represented.

Anthroresearch Associates was a subsidiary of Yoyodyne. It did research for the government on the effects of high-altitude and space flight; for the National Safety Council on automobile accidents; and for Civil Defense on radiation absorption, which was where SHROUD came in. In the eighteenth century it was often convenient to regard man as a clockwork automaton. In the nineteenth century, with Newtonian physics pretty well assimilated and a lot of work in thermodynamics going on, man was looked on more as a heat-engine, about 40 per cent efficient. Now in the twentieth century, with nuclear and subatomic physics a going thing, man had become something which absorbs X-rays, gamma rays and neutrons. Such at least was Oley Bergomask's notion of progress. It was the subject of his welcome-aboard lecture on Profane's first day of employment, at five in the afternoon as Profane was going on and Bergomask off. There were two eight-hour night shifts, early and late (though Profane, whose time scale was skewed toward the past, preferred to call them late and early) and Profane to date had worked them both.

Three times a night he had to make the rounds of the lab areas, windows and heavy equipment. If an all-night routine experiment was in progress he'd have to take readings and if they were out of tolerance wake up the technician on duty, who'd usually be sleeping on a cot in one of the offices. At first there'd been a certain interest in visiting the accident research area, which was jokingly referred to as the chamber of horrors. Here weights were dropped on aged automobiles, inside which would be sitting a manikin. The study now under way had to do with first-aid training, and various versions of SHOCK—synthetic human object, casualty kinematics—got to sit in the driver's, death, or back seat of the test cars. Profane still felt a certain kinship with SHOCK, which was the first inanimate schlemihl he'd ever encountered. But in there too was a certain wariness because the manikin was still only a "human object"; plus a feeling of disdain as if SHOCK had decided to sell out to humans; so that now what had been its inanimate own were taking revenge.

SHOCK was a marvelous manikin. It had the same build as SHROUD but its flesh was molded of foam vinyl, its skin vinyl plastisol, its hair a wig, its eyes cosmetic-plastic, its teeth (for which, in fact, Eigenvalue had acted as subcontractor) the same kind of dentures worn today by 19 per cent of the American population, most of them respectable. Inside were a blood reservoir in the thorax, a blood pump in the midsection and a nickel-cadmium battery power supply in the abdomen. The control panel, at the side of the chest, had toggles and rheostat controls for venous and arterial bleeding, pulse rate, and even respiration rate, when a sucking chest wound was involved. In the latter case plastic lungs provided the necessary suction and bubbling. They were controlled by an air pump in the abdomen, with the motor's cooling vent located in the crotch. An injury of the sexual organs could still be simulated by an attachable moulage, but then this blocked the cooling vent. SHOCK could not therefore have a sucking chest wound and mutilated sexual organs simultaneously. A new retrofit, however, eliminated this difficulty, which was felt to be a basic design deficiency.

SHOCK was thus entirely lifelike in every way. It scared the hell out of Profane the first time he saw it, lying half out the smashed windshield of an old Plymouth, fitted with moulages for depressed-skull and jaw injuries and compound arm and leg fractures. But now he'd got used to it. The only thing at Anthroresearch that still fazed him a little was SHROUD, whose face was a human skull that looked at you through a more-or-less abstracted butyrate head.

It was time to make another round. The building was empty except for Profane. No experiments tonight. On the way back to the guardroom he stopped in front of SHROUD.

"What's it like," he said.

Better than you have it.

"Wha."

Wha yourself. Me and SHOCK are what you and everybody will be someday. (The skull seemed to be grinning at Profane.)

266

"There are other ways besides fallout and road accidents."

But those are most likely. If somebody else doesn't do it to you, you'll do it to yourselves.

"You don't even have a soul. How can you talk."

Since when did you ever have one? What are you doing, getting religion? All I am is a dry run. They take readings off my dosimeters. Who is to say whether I'm here so the people can read the meters or whether the radiation in me is because they have to measure. Which way does it go?

"It's one way," said Profane. "All one way."

Mazel tov. (Maybe the hint of a smile?)

Somehow Profane had difficulty getting back in the plot of *Existentialist Sheriff*. After a while he got up and went over to SHROUD. "What do you mean, we'll be like you and SHOCK someday? You mean dead?"

Am I dead? If I am then that's what I mean.

"If you aren't then what are you?"

Nearly what you are. None of you have very far to go.

"I don't understand."

So I see. But you're not alone. That's a comfort, isn't it?

To hell with it. Profane went back to the guardroom and busied himself making coffee.

III

The next weekend there was a party at Raoul, Slab and Melvin's. The Whole Sick Crew was there.

At one in the morning Roony and Pig started a fight.

"Son of a bitch," Roony yelled. "You keep your hands off her."

"His wife," Esther informed Slab. The Crew had withdrawn to the walls, leaving Pig and Roony most of the floor space. Both were drunk and sweating. They wrestled around, stumbling and inexpert, trying to fight like a western movie. It is incredible how many amateur brawlers believe the movie saloon fight is the only acceptable model to follow. At last Pig dropped Roony with a fist to the abdomen. Roony just lay there, eyes closed, trying to hold down his breathing because it hurt. Pig wandered out to the kitchen. The fight had been over a girl but both of them knew her name was Paola, not Mafia.

"I don't hate the Jewish people," Mafia was explaining,

"only the things they do." She and Profane were alone in her apartment. Roony was out drinking. Perhaps seeing Eigenvalue. It was the day after the fight. She didn't seem to care where her husband was.

All at once Profane got a marvelous idea. She wanted to keep Jews out? Maybe half a Jew could get in.

She beat him to it: her hand reached for his belt buckle and started to unfasten it.

"No," he said, having changed his mind. Needing a zipper to undo, her hands slid away, around her hips to the back of her skirt. "Now look."

"I need a man," already half out of the skirt, "fashioned for Heroic Love. I've wanted you ever since we met."

"Heroic Love's ass," said Profane. "You're married."

Charisma was having nightmares in the next room. He started thumping around under the green blanket, flailing out at the elusive shadow of his own Persecutor.

"Here," she said, lower half denuded, "here on the rug." Profane got up and rooted around in the icebox for beer. Mafia lay on the floor, screaming at him.

"Here yourself." He set a can of beer on her soft abdomen. She yelped, knocking it over. The beer made a soggy spot on the rug between them, like a bundling board or Tristan's blade. "Drink your beer and tell me about Heroic Love." She was making no move to get dressed.

"A woman wants to feel like a woman," breathing hard, "is all. She wants to be taken, penetrated, ravished. But more than that she wants to enclose the man."

With spiderwebs woven of yo-yo string: a net or trap. Profane could think of nothing but Rachel.

"Nothing heroic about a schlemihl," Profane told her. What was a hero? Randolph Scott, who could handle a six-gun, horse's reins, lariat. Master of the inanimate. But a schlemihl, that was hardly a man: somebody who lies back and takes it from objects, like any passive woman.

"Why," he wondered, "does something like sex have to be so confused. Mafia, why do you have to have names for it." Here he was arguing again. Like with Fina in the bathtub.

"What are you," she snarled, "a latent homosexual? You afraid of women?"

"No, I'm not queer." How could you say: sometimes wom-

268

en remind me of inanimate objects. Young Rachel, even: half an MG.

Charisma came in, two beady eyes peering through burnholes in the blanket. He spotted Mafia, moved toward her. The green wool mound began to sing:

> It is something less than heaven
> To be quoted Thesis 1.7
> Every time I make an advance;
> If the world is all that the case is
> That's a pretty discouraging basis
> On which to pursue
> Any sort of romance.
> I've got a proposition for you;
> Logical, positive and brief.
> And at least it could serve as a kind of comic relief:

[Refrain]

> Let P equal me,
> With my heart in command;
> Let Q equal you
> With *Tractatus* in hand;
> And R could stand for a lifetime of love,
> Filled with music to fondle and purr to.
> We'll define love as anything lovely you'd care to infer to.
> On the right, put that bright,
> Hypothetical case;
> On the left, our uncleft,
> Parenthetical chase.
> And that horseshoe there in the middle
> Could be lucky; we've nothing to lose,
> If in these parentheses
> We just mind our little P's
> And Q's.

> If P [Mafia sang in reply] thinks of me
> As a girl hard to make,
> Then Q wishes you
> Would go jump in the lake.
> For R is a meaningless concept,
> Having nothing to do with pleasure:
> I prefer the hard and tangible things I can measure.
> Man, you chase in the face
> Of impossible odds;
> I'm a lass in the class
> Of unbossable broads.

If you'll promise no more sticky phrases,
Half a mo while I kick off my shoes.
There are birds, there are bees,
And to hell with all your P's
And Q's.

By the time Profane finished his beer, the blanket covered them both.

Twenty days before the Dog Star moved into conjunction with the sun, the dog days began. The world started to run more and more afoul of the inanimate. Fifteen were killed in a train wreck near Oaxaca, Mexico, on 1 July. The next day fifteen people died when an apartment house collapsed in Madrid. July 4 a bus fell into a river near Karachi and thirty-one passengers drowned. Thirty-nine more were drowned two days later in a tropical storm in the central Philippines. 9 July the Aegean Islands were hit by an earthquake and tidal waves, which killed forty-three. 14 July a MATS plane crashed after takeoff from McGuire Air Force Base in New Jersey, killing forty-five. An earthquake at Anjar, India, 21 July, killed 117. From 22 to 24 July floods rampaged in central and southern Iran, killing three hundred. 28 July a bus ran off a ferryboat at Kuopio, Finland, and fifteen were killed. Four petroleum tanks blew up near Dumas, Texas, 29 July, killing nineteen. 1 August, seventeen died in a train wreck near Rio de Janeiro. Fifteen more died the 4th and 5th, in floods in southwest Pennsylvania. 2161 people died the same week in a typhoon which hit Chekiang, Honan and Hopeh Provinces. 7 August six dynamite trucks blew up in Cali, Colombia, killing about 1100. The same day there was a train wreck at Přerov, Czechoslovakia, killing nine. The next day 262 miners, trapped by fire, died in a coal mine under Marcinelle, in Belgium. Ice avalanches on Mont Blanc swept fifteen mountain climbers into the kingdom of death in the week 12 to 18 August. The same week a gas explosion in Monticello, Utah, killed fifteen and a typhoon through Japan and Okinawa killed thirty. Twenty-nine more coal miners died of gas poisoning in a mine in Upper Silesia on 27 August. Also on the 27th a Navy bomber crashed among houses in Sanford, Florida, and killed four. Next day a gas explosion in Montreal killed seven and flash floods in Turkey killed 138.

These were the mass deaths. There were also the attendant maimed, malfunctioning, homeless, lorn. It happens every month in a succession of encounters between groups of living and a congruent world which simply doesn't care. Look in any yearly Almanac, under "Disasters"—which is where the figures above come from. The business is transacted month after month after month.

IV

McClintic Sphere had been reading fakebooks all afternoon. "If you ever want to get depressed," he told Ruby, "read through a fakebook. I don't mean the music, I mean the words."

The girl didn't answer. She'd been nervous the past couple of weeks. "What is wrong, baby," he'd say; but she'd shrug it off. One night she told him it was her father who was bugging her. She missed him. Maybe he was sick.

"You been seeing him? A little girl should do that. You don't know how lucky you are to have your father."

"He lives in another city," and she wouldn't say any more.

Tonight he said, "Look, you need the fare? You go see him. That's what you ought to do."

"McClintic," she said, "what business does a whore have going anywhere? A whore isn't human."

"You are. You are with me, Ruby. You know it; we aren't playing any games here," patting the bed.

"Whore lives in one place and stays there. Like some little virgin girl in a fairy tale. She doesn't do any traveling, unless she works the streets."

"You haven't been thinking about that."

"Maybe." She wouldn't look at him.

"Matilda likes you. You crazy?"

"What else is there? Either the street or all cooped up. If I do go see him I won't come back."

"Where does he live. South Africa?"

"Maybe."

"Oh Christ."

Now, McClintic Sphere told himself, nobody goes and falls in love with a prostitute. Not unless he's fourteen or so and she's the first piece of tail he's ever had. But this Ruby, whatever she might be in bed, was a good friend outside it too. He worried about her. It was (for a change) that good kind of worry; not, say, like Roony Winsome's, which

271

seemed to bug the man worse every time McClintic saw him.

It had been going on now for at least a couple of weeks. McClintic, who'd never gone along all the way with the "cool" outlook that developed in the postwar years, didn't mind as much as some other musicians might have when Roony got juiced and started talking about his personal problems. A few times Rachel had been along with him, and McClintic knew Rachel was straight, and there wasn't any jazzing going on there, so Roony must have genuinely had problems with this Mafia woman.

It was moving into deep summer time in Nueva York, the worst time of the year. Time for rumbles in the park and a lot of kids getting killed; time for tempers to get frayed, marriages to break up, all homicidal and chaotic impulses, frozen inside for the winter, to thaw now and come to the surface, and glitter out the pores of your face. McClintic was heading up for Lenox, Mass., for that jazz festival. He knew he couldn't stand it here. But what about Roony? What he was getting at home (most likely) was edging him toward something. McClintic noticed that last night, between sets at the V-Note. He'd seen the look before: a bass player he'd known in Fort Worth who never changed expression, who was always telling you "I have this problem with narcotics," who'd flipped one night and they took him away to the hospital at Lexington or someplace. McClintic would never know. But Roony had the same look: too cool. Too unemotional when he said "I have a problem with my woman." What was there inside for deep summer in Nueva York to melt? What would happen when it did?

This word flip was weird. Every recording date of McClintic's he'd got into the habit of talking electricity with the audio men and technicians in the studio. McClintic once couldn't have cared less about electricity, but now it seemed if that was helping him reach a bigger audience, some digging, some who would never dig, but all paying and those royalties keeping the Triumph in gas and McClintic in J. Press suits, then McClintic ought to be grateful to electricity, ought maybe to learn a little more about it. So he'd picked up some here and there, and one day last summer he got around to talking stochastic music and digital computers with one technician. Out of the conversation had come Set/Reset, which was getting to be a signature for the

272

group. He had found out from this sound man about a two-triode circuit called a flip-flop, which when it was turned on could be one of two ways, depending on which tube was conducting and which was cut off: set or reset, flip or flop.

"And that," the man said, "can be yes or no, or one or zero. And that is what you might call one of the basic units, or specialized 'cells' in a big 'electronic brain.'"

"Crazy," said McClintic, having lost him back there someplace. But one thing that did occur to him was if a computer's brain could go flip and flop, why so could a musician's. As long as you were flop, everything was cool. But where did the trigger-pulse come from to make you flip?

McClintic, no lyricist, had made up nonsense words to go along with Set/Reset. He sang them to himself sometimes on the stand, while the natural horn was soloing:

Gwine cross de Jordan
Ecclesiastically:
Flop, flip, once I was hip,
Flip, flop, now you're on top,
Set-REset, why are we BEset
With crazy and cool in the same molecule . . .

"What are you thinking about," said the girl Ruby.

"Flipping," said McClintic.

"You'll never flip."

"Not me," McClintic said, "whole lot of people."

After a while he said, not really to her, "Ruby, what happened after the war? That war, the world flipped. But come '45, and they flopped. Here in Harlem they flopped. Everything got cool—no love, no hate, no worries, no excitement. Every once in a while, though, somebody flips back. Back to where he can love . . ."

"Maybe that's it," the girl said, after a while. "Maybe you have to be crazy to love somebody."

"But you take a whole bunch of people flip at the same time and you've got a war. Now war is not loving, is it?"

"Flip, flop," she said, "get the mop."

"You're just like a little kid."

"McClintic," she said. "I am. I worry about you. I worry about my father. Maybe he's flipped."

"Why don't you go see him." The same argument again. Tonight they were in for a long spell of arguing.

"You are beautiful," Schoenmaker was saying.

"Shale, am I."

"Perhaps not as you are. But as I see you."

She sat up. "It can't keep going the way it's been."

"Come back."

"No, Shale, my nerves can't take this—"

"Come back."

"It's getting so I can't look at Rachel, or Slab—"

"Come back." At last she lay again beside him. "Pelvic bones," he said, touching there, "should protrude more. That would be very sexy. I could do that for you."

"Please."

"Esther, I want to give. I want to do things for you. If I can bring out the beautiful girl inside you, the idea of Esther, as I have done already with your face . . ."

She became aware of a clock ticking on the table next to them. She lay stiff, ready to run to the street, naked if need be.

"Come," he said, "half an hour in the next room. So simple I can do it alone. Nothing but a local anaesthetic."

She began to cry.

"What would it be next?" she said a few moments later. "Larger breasts, you'd want. Then my ears might be a shade too big for you: Shale, why can't it be just me?"

He rolled over, exasperated. "How do you tell a woman," he asked the floor. "What is loving if not—"

"You don't love me." She was up, struggling clumsy into a brassiere. "You've never said it and if you did you wouldn't mean it."

"You'll be back," he said, still watching the floor.

"I won't," through the light wool of her sweater. But of course she would be.

After she left, there was only the ticking of the clock, until Schoenmaker yawned, sudden and explosive; rolled over to confront the ceiling and begin swearing at it softly.

While at Anthroresearch Profane listened with half an ear to the coffee percolating; and carried on another imaginary conversation with SHROUD. By now that had become a tradition.

Remember, Profane, how it is on Route 14, south, outside Elmira, New York? You walk on an overpass and look west and see the sun setting on a junkpile. Acres of old cars, piled up ten high in rusting tiers. A graveyard for cars. If I could die, that's what my graveyard would look like.

"I wish you would. Look at you, masquerading like a human being. You ought to be junked. Not burned or cremated."

Of course. Like a human being. Now remember, right after the war, the Nuremberg war trials? Remember the photographs of Auschwitz? Thousands of Jewish corpses, stacked up like those poor car-bodies. Schlemihl: It's already started.

"Hitler did that. He was crazy."

Hitler, Eichmann, Mengele. Fifteen years ago. Has it occurred to you there may be no more standards for crazy or sane, now that it's started?

"What, for Christ sake?"

While Slab lounged meticulous about his canvas, Cheese Danish # 41, making quick little stabs with a fine old kolinsky brush at the surface of the painting. Two brown slugs—snails without shells—lay crosswise and copulating on a polygonal slab of marble, a translucent white bubble rising between them. No impasto here: "long" paint, everything put there more than real could ever be. Weird illumination, shadows all wrong, surfaces of marble, slugs and a half-eaten cheese Danish in the upper right textured painstakingly fine. So that their slimy trails, converging straight and inevitable from bottom and side to the X of their union, did shine like moonlight.

And Charisma, Fu and Pig Bodine came rollicking out of a grocery store up on the West Side, yelling football signals and tossing a poor-looking eggplant about under the lights of Broadway.

And Rachel and Roony sat on a bench in Sheridan Square, talking about Mafia and Paola. It was one in the morning, a wind had risen and something curious too had happened; as if everyone in the city, simultaneously, had become sick of news of any kind; for thousands of newspaper pages blew through the small park on the way crosstown, blundered like pale bats against the trees, tangled themselves around the feet of Roony and Rachel, and of a bum sleeping across the way. Millions of unread and useless words had come to a kind of life in Sheridan Square; while the two on the bench wove cross-talk of their own, oblivious, among them.

And Stencil sat dour and undrunk, in the Rusty Spoon, while Slab's friend, another Catatonic Expressionist, harangued him with the Great Betrayal, told of the Dance of Death. While around them something of the sort was in fact going on: for here was the Whole Sick Crew, was it not, linked maybe by a spectral chain and rollicking along over some moor or other. Stencil thought of Mondaugen's story, The Crew at Foppl's, saw here the same leprous pointillism of orris root, weak jaws and bloodshot eyes, tongues and backs of teeth stained purple by this morning's home-made wine, lipstick which it seemed could be peeled off intact, tossed to the earth to join a trail of similar jetsam —the disembodied smiles or pouts which might serve, perhaps, as spoor for next generation's Crew . . . God.

"Wha," said the Catatonic Expressionist.

"Melancholy," said Stencil.

And Mafia Winsome, mateless, stood undressed before the mirror, contemplating herself and little else. And the cat yowled in the courtyard.

And who knew where Paola was?

In the past few days Esther had become more and more impossible for Schoenmaker to get along with. He began to think about breaking it off again, only this time permanently.

"It isn't me you love," she kept saying. "You want to change me into something I'm not."

In return he could only argue a kind of Platonism at her. Did she want him so shallow he should only love her body? It was her soul he loved. What was the matter with her, didn't every girl want a man to love the soul, the true them? Sure, they did. Well, what is the soul. It is the idea of the body, the abstraction behind the reality: what Esther really was, shown to the senses with certain imperfections there in the bone and tissue. Schoenmaker could bring out the true, perfect Esther which dwelled inside the imperfect one. Her soul would be there on the outside, radiant, unutterably beautiful.

"Who are you," she yelled back, "to say what my soul looks like. You know what you're in love with? Yourself. Your own skill in plastic surgery, is what."

In answer to which Schoenmaker rolled over and stared at the floor; and wondered aloud if he would ever understand women.

Eigenvalue the soul-dentist had even given Schoenmaker counsel. Schoenmaker was not a colleague, but as if Stencil's notion of an inner circle were correct after all, things got around. "Dudley, fella," he told himself, "you've got no business with any of these people."

But then, he did. He gave cut rates on cleaning, drilling and root-canal jobs for members of the Crew. Why? If they were all bums but still providing society with valuable art and thought, why that would be fine. If that were the case then someday, possibly in the next rising period of history, when this Decadence was past and the planets were being colonized and the world at peace, a dental historian would mention Eigenvalue in a footnote as Patron of the Arts, discreet physician to the neo-Jacobean school.

But they produced nothing but talk and at that not very good talk. A few like Slab actually did what they professed; turned out a tangible product. But again, what? Cheese Danishes. Or this technique for the sake of technique—Catatonic Expressionism. Or parodies on what someone else had already done.

So much for Art. What of Thought? The Crew had developed a kind of shorthand whereby they could set forth any visions that might come their way. Conversations at the Spoon had become little more than proper nouns, literary allusions, critical or philosophical terms linked in certain ways. Depending on how you arranged the building blocks at your disposal, you were smart or stupid. Depending on how others reacted they were In or Out. The number of blocks, however, was finite.

"Mathematically, boy," he told himself, "if nobody else original comes along, they're bound to run out of arrangements someday. What then?" What indeed. This sort of arranging and rearranging was Decadence, but the exhaustion of all possible permutations and combinations was death. It scared Eigenvalue, sometimes. He would go in back and look at the set of dentures. Teeth and metals endure.

v

McClintic, back for a weekend from Lenox, found August in Nueva York bad as he'd expected. Buzzing close to sundown through Central Park in the Triumph he saw all manner of symptoms: girls on the grass, sweating all over

277

in thin (vulnerable) summer dresses; groups of boys prowling off on the horizon, twitchless, sure, waiting for night; cops and solid citizens, all nervous (maybe only in a business way; but the cops' business had to do with these boys and the coming of night).

He'd come back to see Ruby. Faithful, he'd sent her post-cards showing different views of Tanglewood and the Berkshires once a week; cards she never answered. But he'd called long-distance once or twice and she was still there close to home.

For some reason one night he'd dashed lengthwise across the state (a tiny state considering the Triumph's speed), McClintic and the bass player; nearly missed Cape Cod and driven into the sea. But sheer momentum carried them up that croissant of land and out to a settlement called French Town, a resort.

Out in front of a seafood place on the main and only drag, they found two more musicians playing mumbledy-peg with clam knives. They were on route to a party. "O yes," they cried in unison. One climbed in the Triumph's trunk, the other, who had a bottle—rum, 150 proof—and a pineapple, sat on the hood. At 80 mph over roads which are ill-lit and near-unusable by the end of the Season, this happy hood-ornament cut open the fruit with a clam knife and built rum-and-pineapple-juices in paper cups which McClintic's bass handed him over the windscreen.

At the party McClintic's eye was taken by a little girl in dungarees, who sat in the kitchen entertaining a progress of summer types.

"Give me back my eye," said McClintic.

"I haven't got your eye."

"Later." He was one of those who can be infected by the drunkenness of others. He was juiced five minutes after they climbed in the window to the party.

Bass was outside, in the tree, with a girl. "You got eyes for the kitchen," he called down, waggish. McClintic went out and sat down under the tree. The two above him were singing:

Have you heard, baby did you know:
There ain't no dope in Lenox. . . .

Fireflies surrounded McClintic, inquisitive. Somewhere you

could hear waves crashing. The party inside was quiet, though the house was crowded. The girl appeared at a kitchen window. McClintic closed his eyes, rolled over and pushed his face into the grass.

Along came Harvey Fazzo, a piano player. "Eunice wants to know," he told McClintic, "if possibly she could see you alone." Eunice was the girl in the kitchen.

"No," McClintic said. There was movement in the tree over him.

"You got a wife in New York?" Harvey asked, sympathetic.

"Something like that."

Not long after along came Eunice. "I have a bottle of gin," she coaxed him.

"You will have to do better," said McClintic.

He hadn't brought any horn. He let them have their inevitable session inside. He couldn't ever see that kind of session: his own kind of session didn't belong here, wasn't so frantic, was in fact one of the only good results of the cool scene after the war: this easy knowledge on both ends of the instrument of what exactly is there, this quiet feeling-together. Like kissing a girl's ear: mouth is one person's, ear is another, but both of you know. He stayed out under the tree. When the bass and his girl descended McClintic got a soft stocking-foot in the small of the back, which woke him up. Leaving (nearly dawn) Eunice, entirely plastered, scowled at him horribly, mouthing curses.

Time was McClintic wouldn't have thought twice. Wife in New York? Ha, ho.

She was there when he reached Matilda's; but only just. Packing a good-size suitcase; quarter of an hour the wrong way and he'd have missed.

Ruby started bawling the minute he showed in the doorway. She threw a slip at him which gave up halfway across the room and floated to the bare floor, peach-colored and sad. It passed through the slant-rays of the sun almost down. They both watched it settle.

"Don't worry," she finally said. "I made a bet with myself."

Started unpacking the suitcase then, tears still falling promiscuous on her silk, rayon, cotton; linen sheets.

"Stupid," McClintic yelled. "God, that's stupid." He had to yell at something. It wasn't that he didn't believe in telepathic flashes.

"What is there to talk about," she said a little later, the

suitcase like a ticking time-bomb shoved back, empty, under the bed.

When had it become a matter of having her or losing her?

Charisma and Fu crashed into the room, drunk and singing English vaudeville songs. With them was a Saint Bernard they had found in the street drooling and sick. Evenings were hot, this August.

"Oh God," Profane said into the phone: "the roaring boys are back."

Through an open door, on a bed there, an itinerant race-driver named Murray Sable sweated and snored. The girl with him rolled away. On her back began half a dream-dialogue. Down on the Drive sat somebody atop a '56 Lincoln's hood, singing to himself:

> Oh man,
> I want some young blood,
> Drink it, gargle it, use it for a moufwash.
> Hey, young blood, what's happening tonight. . . .

Werewolf season: August.

Rachel kissed the mouthpiece on her end. How could you kiss an object?

The dog staggered away into the kitchen and fell with a crash among two hundred or so of Charisma's empty beer bottles. Charisma sang on.

"I find one," Fu screamed from the kitchen. "One bucket, hey."

"Fill it wiv beer," from Charisma, still a Cockney.

"He look pretty sick."

"Beer is the best thing for him. Hair of the dog." Charisma began to laugh. Fu after a moment joined in bubbling, hysterical, a hundred geishas all set going at once.

"It's hot," Rachel said.

"It will be cool. Rachel—" But their timing was off: his "I want—" and her "Please—" collided somewhere underground in midcircuit, came out mostly noise. Neither spoke. The room was dark: out the window across the Hudson, heat lightning walked sneaky-Pete over Jersey.

Soon Murray Sable stopped snoring, the girl fell quiet: everything a sudden hush for the moment except the dog's beer sloshing into its bucket and an almost inaudible hiss.

280

The air mattress Profane slept on had a slow leak. He reinflated it once a week with a bicycle pump Winsome kept in the closet.

"Have you been talking," he said.

"No . . ."

"All right. But what goes on underground. Do we I wonder come out the same people at the other end?"

"There are things under the city," she admitted.

Alligators, daft priests, bums in subways. He thought of the night she'd called him at the Norfolk bus station. Who'd monitored then? Did she really want him back then or was it all maybe a troll's idea of fun?

"I have to sleep. I have the second shift. Call me at midnight?"

"Of course."

"I mean I broke the electric alarm clock here."

"Schlemihl. They hate you."

"They've declared war on me," said Profane.

Wars begin in August. In the temperate zone and twentieth century we have this tradition. Not only seasonal Augusts; nor only public wars.

Hung up the phone now looked evil, as if it schemed in secret. Profane flopped on the air mattress. In the kitchen the Saint Bernard began to lap beer.

"Hey, he going to puke?"

The dog puked, loud and horrible. Winsome came charging in from a remote room.

"I broke your alarm clock," Profane said into the mattress.

"What, what," Winsome was saying. Next to Murray Sable a girl-voice began talking drowsy in no language known to a waking world. "Where have you guys been." Winsome ran straight at the espresso machine; broke stride at the last moment, jumped on top of it and sat manipulating the taps with his toes. He had a direct view into the kitchen. "Oh, ha, ho," he said, sounding as if he'd been stabbed. "Oh, mi casa, su casa, you guys. Where is it you've been."

Charisma, head hanging, shuffled around in a greenish pool of vomit. The Saint Bernard was sleeping among the beer bottles. "Where else," he said.

"Out rollicking," said Fu. The dog began to scream at humid nightmare-shapes.

Back in August 1956, rollicking was the Whole Sick Crew's favorite pastime, in- or outdoor. One of the frequent forms

281

it took was yo-yoing. Though probably not inspired by Profane's peregrinations along the east coast, the Crew did undertake something similar on a city-scale. Rule: you had to be genuinely drunk. Certain of the theater crowd inhabiting the Spoon had had fantastic yo-yo records invalidated because it was discovered later they'd been sober all along: "Quarterdeck drunkards," Pig called them scornfully. Rule: you had to wake up at least once on each transit. Otherwise there'd only be a time gap, and that you could have spent on a bench in the subway station. Rule: it had to be a subway line running up and downtown, because this is the way a yo-yo goes. In the early days of yo-yoing certain false "champions" had admitted shamefaced to racking up scores on the 42nd Street shuttle, which was looked now on as something of a scandal in yo-yo circles.

Slab was king; after a memorable party a year ago at Raoul, he and Melvin's, a night he and Esther broke up, he'd spent a weekend on the West Side express, making sixty-nine complete cycles. At the end of it, starved, he stumbled out near Fulton Street on the way uptown again and ate a dozen cheese Danishes; got sick and was taken in for vagrancy and puking in the street.

Stencil thought it all nonsense.

"Get in there at rush hour," said Slab. "There are nine million yo-yos in this town."

Stencil took this advice one evening after five, came out with one rib to his umbrella broken and a vow never to do it again. Vertical corpses, eyes with no life, crowded loins, buttocks and hip-points together. Little sound except for the racketing of the subway, echoes in the tunnels. Violence (seeking exit): some of them carried out two stops before their time and unable to go upstream, get back in. All wordless. Was it the Dance of Death brought up to date?

Trauma: possibly only remembering his last shock under ground, he headed for Rachel's, found her out to dinner with Profane (Profane?) but Paola, whom he had been trying to avoid, pinned him between the black fireplace and a print of di Chirico's street.

"You ought to see this." Handing him a small packet of typewritten pages.

Confessions, the title. Confessions of Fausto Maijstral.

"I ought to go back," she said.

"Stencil has stayed off Malta." As if she'd asked him to go.

"Read," she said, "and see."

"His father died in Valletta."

"Is that all?"

Was that all? Did she really intend to go? Oh, God. Did he?

Phone rang, mercifully. It was Slab, who was holding a party over the weekend. "Of course," she said; and Stencil echoed of course, silent.

chapter eleven

Confessions of Fausto
Maijstral

V

siege
the Bad Priest
(dis)continuity of history
confessional
where?

It takes, unhappily, no more than a desk and writing sup-
plies to turn any room into a confessional. This may have
nothing to do with the acts we have committed, or the
humours we do go in and out of. It may be only the room—
a cube—having no persuasive powers of its own. The room
simply is. To occupy it, and find a metaphor there for memory, is our own fault.

Let me describe the room. The room measures 17 by 11½
by 7 feet. The walls are lath and plaster, and painted the
same shade of grey as were the decks of His Majesty's corvettes during the war. The room is oriented so that its diago-
nals fall NNE/SSW, and NW/SE. Thus any observer
may see, from the window and balcony on the NNW side
(a short side), the city Valletta.

One enters from the WSW, by a door midway in a long
wall of the room. Standing just inside the door and turning
clockwise one sees a portable wood stove in the NNE
corner, surrounded by boxes, bowls, sacks containing food;
the mattress, located halfway along the long ENE wall; a
slop bucket in the SE corner; a washbasin in the SSW
corner; a window facing the Dockyard; the door one has just
entered; and finally in the NW corner, a small writing table
and chair. The chair faces the WSW wall; so that the head
must be turned 135° to the rear in order to have a line-of-
sight with the city. The walls are unadorned, the floor is

inanimate

carpetless. A dark grey stain is located on the ceiling directly over the stove.

That is the room. To say the mattress was begged from the Navy B.O.Q. here in Valletta shortly after the war, the stove and food supplied by CARE, or the table from a house now rubble and covered by earth; <u>what have these to do with the room? The facts</u> are history, and only <del>men have</del> histories. <u>The facts call up emotional responses,</u> <del>which no</del> <u>inert room has ever showed us.</u>

The room is in a building which had nine such rooms before the war. Now there are three. The building is on an escarpment above the Dockyard. The room is stacked atop two others—the other two-thirds of the building were removed by the bombing, sometime during the winter of 1942–43.

Fausto himself may be defined in only three ways. As a relationship: your father. As a given name. Most important, as an occupant. Since shortly after you left, an occupant of the room.

Why? Why use the room as introduction to an apologia? Because the room, though windowless and cold at night, is a hothouse. Because the room is the past, though it has no history of its own. Because, as the physical being-there of a bed or horizontal plane determines what we call love; as a high place must exist before God's word can come to a flock and any sort of religion begin; so must there be a room, sealed against the present, before we can make any attempt to deal with the past.

In the University, before the war, before I had married your poor mother, I felt as do many young men a sure wind of Greatness flowing over my shoulders like an invisible cape. Maratt, Dnubietna and I were to be the cadre for a grand School of Anglo-Maltese Poetry—the Generation of '37. This undergraduate certainty of success gives rise to anxieties, foremost being the autobiography or apologia pro vita sua the poet someday has to write. How, the reasoning goes: how can a man write his life unless he is virtually certain of the hour of his death? A harrowing question. Who knows what Herculean poetic feats might be left to him in perhaps the score of years between a premature apologia and death? Achievements so great as to cancel out the effect of the apologia itself. And if on the other hand nothing at all is accomplished in twenty or thirty stagnant years—how distasteful is anticlimax to the young!

Time of course has showed the question up in all its young illogic. We can justify any apologia simply by calling life a successive rejection of personalities. No apologia is any more than a romance—half a fiction—in which all the successive identities taken on and rejected by the writer as a function of linear time are treated as separate characters. The writing itself even constitutes another rejection, another "character" added to the past. So we do sell our souls: paying them away to history in little installments. It isn't so much to pay for eyes clear enough to see past the fiction of continuity, the fiction of cause and effect, the fiction of a humanized history endowed with "reason."

Before 1938, then, came Fausto Maijstral the First. A young sovereign, dithering between Caesar and God. Maratt was going into politics; Dnubietna would be an engineer; I was slated to be the priest. Thus among us all major areas of human struggle would come under the scrutiny of the Generation of '37.

Maijstral the Second arrived with you, child, and with the war. You were unplanned for and in a way resented. Though if Fausto I had ever had a serious vocation, Elena Xemxi your mother—and you—would never have come into his life at all. The plans of our Movement were disturbed. We still wrote—but there was other work to do. Our poetic "destiny" was replaced by the discovery of an aristocracy deeper and older. We were builders.

Fausto Maijstral III was born on the Day of the 13 Raids. Generated: out of Elena's death, out of a horrible encounter with one we only knew as the Bad Priest. An encounter I am only now attempting to put in English. The journal for weeks after has nothing but gibberish to describe that "birth trauma." Fausto III is the closest any of the characters comes to non-humanity. Not "inhumanity," which means bestiality; beasts are still animate. Fausto III had taken on much of the non-humanity of the debris, crushed stone, broken masonry, destroyed churches and auberges of his city.

His successor, Fausto IV, inherited a physically and spiritually broken world. No single event produced him. Fausto III had merely passed a certain level in his slow return to consciousness or humanity. That curve is still rising. Somehow there had accumulated a number of poems (at least

286

one sonnet-cycle the present Fausto is still happy with);
monographs on religion, language, history; critical essays
(Hopkins, T. S. Eliot, di Chirico's novel *Hebdomeros*).
Fausto IV was the "man of letters" and only survivor of the
Generation of '37, for Dnubietna is building roads in America, and Maratt is somewhere south of Mount Ruwenzori,
organizing riots among our linguistic brothers the Bantu.

We have now reached an interregnum. Stagnant; the only
throne a wooden chair in the NW corner of this room.
Hermetic: for who can hear the Dockyard whistle, rivet
guns, vehicles in the street when one is occupied with the
past?

Now memory is a traitor: gilding, altering. The word is,
in sad fact, meaningless, based as it is on the false assumption that identity is single, soul continuous. A man has no
more right to set forth any self-memory as truth than to say
"Maratt is a sour-mouthed University cynic" or "Dnubietna
is a liberal and madman."

Already you see: the "is"—unconsciously we've drifted into
the past. You must now be subjected, dear Paola, to a
barrage of undergraduate sentiment. The journals, I mean,
of Fausto I and II. What other way can there be to regain
him, as we must? Here, for example:

> How wondrous is this St. Giles Fair called history! Her
> rhythms pulse regular and sinusoidal—a freak show in cara-
> van, travelling over thousands of little hills. A serpent hyp-
> notic and undulant, bearing on her back like infinitesimal fleas
> such hunchbacks, dwarves, prodigies, centaurs, poltergeists!
> Two-headed, three-eyed, hopelessly in love; satyrs with the
> skin of werewolves, werewolves with the eyes of young girls
> and perhaps even an old man with a navel of glass, through
> which can be seen goldfish nuzzling the coral country of
> his guts.

The date is of course 3 September 1939: the mixing of
metaphors, crowding of detail, rhetoric-for-its-own-sake only
a way of saying the balloon had gone up, illustrating
again and certainly not for the last time the colorful whimsy
of history.

Could we have been so much in the midst of life? With
such a sense of grand adventure about it all? "Oh, God is
here, you know, in the crimson carpets of sulla each spring,
in the blood-orange groves, in the sweet pods of my carob

287

tree, the St.-John's-bread of this dear island. His fingers raked the ravines; His breath keeps the rain clouds from over us, His voice once guided the shipwrecked St. Paul to bless our Malta." And Maratt wrote:

> Britain and Crown, we join thy swelling guard
> To drive the brute invader from our strand.
> For God His own shall rout the evil-starred
> And God light peace's lamps with His dear hand. . . .

"God His own"; that brings a smile. Shakespeare. Shakespeare and T. S. Eliot ruined us all. On Ash Wednesday of '42, for example, Dnubietna wrote a "satire" on Eliot's poem:

> Because I do
> Because I do not hope
> Because I do not hope to survive
> Injustice from the Palace, death from the air.
> Because I do,
> Only do,
> I continue. . . .

We were most fond, I believe, of "The Hollow Men." And we did like to use Elizabethan phrases even in our speech. There is a description, sometime in 1937, of a farewell celebration for Maratt on the eve of his marriage. All of us drunk, arguing politics: it was in a café in Kingsway—scusi, Strada Reale then. Before the Italians starting bombing us. Dnubietna had called our Constitution "hypocritical camouflage for a slave state." Maratt objected. Dnubietna leapt up on the table, upsetting glasses, knocking the bottle to the floor, screaming "Go to, caitiff!" It became the cant phrase for our "set": go to. The entry was written, I suppose, next morning: but even in the misery of a headache the dehydrated Fausto I was still able to talk of the pretty girls, the hot-jazz band, the gallant conversation. The prewar University years were probably as happy as he described, and the conversation as "good." They must have argued everything under the sun, and in Malta then was a good deal of sun.

But Fausto I was as bastardised as the others. In the midst of the bombing in '42, his successor commented:

> Our poets write of nothing now but the rain of bombs

from what was once Heaven. We builders practice, as we must, patience and strength but—the curse of knowing English and its emotional nuances!—with it a desperate-nervous hatred of this war, an impatience for it to be over.

I think our education in the English school and University alloyed what was pure in us. Younger, we talked of love, fear, motherhood; speaking in Maltese as Elena and I do now. But what a language! Have it, or today's Builders, advanced at all since the half-men who built the sanctuaries of Hagiar Kim? We talk as animals might.

Can I explain "love"? Tell her my love for her is the same and part of my love for the Bofors crews, the Spitfire pilots, our Governor? That it is love which embraces this island, love for everything on it that moves! There are no words in Maltese for this. Nor finer shades; nor words for intellectual states of mind. She cannot read my poetry, I cannot translate it for her.

Are we only animals then. Still one with the troglodytes who lived here 400 centuries before dear Christ's birth. We do live as they did in the bowels of the earth. Copulate, spawn, die without uttering any but the grossest words. Do any of us even understand the words of God, teachings of His Church? Perhaps Maijstral, Maltese, one with his people, was meant only to live at the threshold of consciousness, only exist as a hardly animate lump of flesh, an automaton.

But we are torn, our grand "Generation of '37." To be merely Maltese: endure almost mindless, without sense of time? Or to think—continuously—in English, to be too aware of war, of time, of all the greys and shadows of love?

Perhaps British colonialism has produced a new sort of being, a dual man, aimed two ways at once: towards peace and simplicity on the one hand, towards an exhausted intellectual searching on the other. Perhaps Maratt, Dnubietna and Maijstral are the first of a new race. What monsters shall rise in our wake. . . .

These thoughts are from the darker side of my mind— mohh, brain. Not even a word for mind. We must use the hateful Italian, menti.

What monsters. You, child, what sort of monster are you? Perhaps not at all of course what Fausto meant: he may have been talking of a spiritual heritage. Perhaps of Fausto III and IV, et seq. But the excerpt shows clearly a charming quality of youth: to begin with optimism; and once the inadequacy of optimism is borne in on him by an inevitably hostile world, to retreat into abstractions. Abstractions even in the midst of the bombing. For a year and a half Malta averaged ten raids per day. How he sustained that hermetic retreat, God alone knows. There's no indication in the journals. Perhaps it too sprang from the Anglicized half of Fausto II: for he wrote poetry. Even in the journals we get sudden shifts from reality to something less:

> I write this during a night raid, down in the abandoned sewer. It is raining outside. The only light is from phosphorous flares above the city, a few candles in here, bombs. Elena is beside me, holding the child who sleeps drooling against her shoulder. Packed close round us are other Maltese, English civil servants, a few Indian tradesmen. There's little talk. Children listen, all wide eyes, to bombs above in the streets. For them it is only an amusement. At first they cried on being wakened in the middle of the night. But they've grown used to it. Some even stand now near the entrance to our shelter, watching the flares and bombs, chattering, nudging, pointing. It will be a strange generation. What of our own? She sleeps.

And then, for no apparent reason, this:

> O Malta of the Knights of St. John! History's serpent is one; what matter where on her body we lie. Here in this wretched tunnel we are the Knights and the Giaours; we are L'Isle-Adam and his ermine arm, and his maniple on a field of blue sea and gold sun, we are M. Parisot, lonely in his wind-haunted grave high above the Harbour; battling on the ramparts during the Great Siege—both! My Grandmaster, both: death and life, ermine and old cloth, noble and common, in feast and combat and mourning we are Malta, one, pure and a motley of races at once; no time has passed since we lived in caves, grappled with fish at the reedy shore, buried our dead with a song, with red-ochre and pulled up our dolmens, temples and menhirs and standing stones to the glory of some indeterminate god or gods, rose toward the light in andanti of singing, lived our lives through circling centuries of rape, looting, invasion, still one; one in the dark ravines, one in this God-favoured plot of sweet Mediterranean earth, one in whatever temple or sewer or catacomb's darkness is ours, by fate or historical writhings or still by the will of God.

He must have written the latter part at home, after the raid; but the "shift" is still there. Fausto II was a young man in retreat. It's seen not only in his fascination for the conceptual—even in the midst of that ongoing, vast—but somehow boring—destruction of an island; but also in his relationship with your mother.

First mention of Elena Xemxi comes from Fausto I, shortly after Maratt's marriage. Perhaps, a breach having been made in the bachelorhood of the Generation of '37—though from all indications the movement was anything but celibate—Fausto now felt safe enough to follow suit. And of course at the same time taking these fidgeting and inconclusive steps towards Church celibacy.

Oh, he was "in love": no doubt. But his own ideas on the matter always in a state of flux, never I think getting quite in line with the Maltese version: Church-approved copulation for the purpose, and glorification, of motherhood. We already know for example how Fausto in the worst part of the Siege of '40-'43 had arrived at a notion and practice of love wide, high and deep as Malta itself.

> The dog days have ended, the maijstral has ceased to blow. Soon the other wind called gregale will bring the gentle rains to solemnize the sowing of our red wheat.
>
> Myself: what am I if not a wind, my very name a hissing of queer zephyrs through the carob trees? I stand in time between the two winds, my will no more than a puff of air. But air too are the clever, cynical arguments of Dnubietna. His views on marriage—even Maratt's marriage—blow by my poor flapping ears unnoticed.
>
> For Elena—tonight! O Elena Xemxi: small as the she-goat, sweet your milk and your love-cry. Dark-eyed as the space between stars over Ghaudex where we have gazed so often in our childish summers. Tonight will I go to your little house in Vittoriosa, and before your black eyes break open this small pod of a heart and offer in communion the St.-John's-bread I have cherished like a Eucharist these nineteen years.

He did not propose marriage; but confessed his love. There was still, you see, the vague "program"—the vocation to priesthood he was never quite sure of. Elena hesitated. When young Fausto questioned, she became evasive. He promptly began to display symptoms of intense jealousy:

> Has she lost her faith? I've heard she has been out with Dnubietna—Dnubietna! Under his hands. Our Lord, is there

291

no recourse? Must I go out and find them together: follow through the old farce of challenge, combat, murder . . . How he must be gloating: It was all planned. Must have been. Our discussions of marriage. He even told me one evening—hypothetically, of course, oh yes!—precisely how he would find a virgin someday and "educate" her to sin. Told me knowing all the time that someday it would be Elena Xemxi. My friend. Comrade-in-arms. One third of our Generation. I could never take her back. One touch from him and eighteen years of purity—gone!

Etc., etc. Dnubietna, as Fausto must have known even in the worst depths of suspicion, had nothing at all to do with her reluctance. Suspicion softened to a nostalgic brooding:

Sunday there was rain, leaving me with memories. Rain seems to make them swell like bothersome flowers whose perfume is bittersweet. A night I remember: we were children, embracing in a garden above the Harbour. The rustling of azaleas, smell of oranges, a black frock she wore that absorbed all the stars and moon; reflecting nothing back. As she had taken from me, all my light. She has the carob-softness of my heart.

Ultimately their quarrel took in a third party. In typically Maltese fashion, a priest, one Father Avalanche, came in as the intermediary. He appears infrequently in these journals, always faceless, serving more as foil to his opposite number the Bad Priest. But he did finally persuade Elena to return to Fausto.

She came to me today, out of smoke, rain, silence. Wearing black, nearly invisible. Sobbing plausibly enough in my too-welcoming arms.

She's to have a child. Dnubietna's, came my first thought (of course it did—for all of half a second—fool). The Father said mine. She had been to A. for confession. God knows what passed there. This good priest cannot break the secrecy of the confessional. Only let slip what the three of us know—that it is my child—so that we should be two souls united before God.

So much for our plan. Maratt and Dnubietna will be disappointed.

So much for their plan. We will return to this matter of vocation.

From a distraught Elena then, Fausto learned of his "rival": the Bad Priest.

> No one knows his name or his parish. There is only superstitious rumour; excommunicated, confederates with the Dark One. He lives in an old villa past Sliema, near the sea. Found E. one night alone in the street. Perhaps he'd been out prowling for souls. A sinister figure, she said, but with the mouth of a Christ. The eyes were shadowed by a wide-brimmed hat; all she could see were soft cheeks, even teeth.

Now it was none of your mysterious "corruption." Priests here are second only to mothers in order of prestige. A young girl is naturally enough deferent to and awed by the mere glimpse of any fluttering soutane in the street. Under subsequent questioning, it came out:

> "It was near the church—our church. By a long low wall in the street, after sunset, but still light. He asked if I was going to the church. I hadn't thought to go. Confessions were over. I don't know why I agreed to walk there with him. It was not a command—though I would have obeyed if it had been—but we went up the hill, and into the church, up the side aisle to the confessional.
>
> " 'Have you confessed?' he asked.
>
> "I looked at his eyes. I thought at first he was drunk, or marid b'mohhu. I was afraid.
>
> " 'Come then.' We entered the confessional. At the time I thought: don't priests have the right? But I did tell him things I have never told Father Avalanche. I didn't know then who this priest was, you see."

Now sin for Elena Xemxi had been heretofore as natural a function as breathing, eating, or gossiping. Under the agile instruction of the Bad Priest, however, it began to take on the shape of an evil spirit: alien, parasitic, attached like a black slug to her soul.

> How could she marry anyone? She was fit, said the Bad Priest, not for the world but for the convent. Christ was her proper husband. No human male could coexist with the sin which fed on her girl-soul. Only Christ was mighty enough, loving enough, forgiving enough. Had He not cured the lepers and exorcised malignant fevers? Only He could welcome disease, clasp it to His bosom, rub against it, kiss it. It had been His mission on earth as now, a spiritual husband in

heaven, to know sickness intimately, love it, cure it. This was parable, the Bad Priest told her, metaphor for spirit's cancer. But the Maltese mind, conditioned by its language, is unreceptive to such talk. All my Elena saw was the disease, the literal sickness. Afraid I, or our children, would reap its ravages.

She stayed away from me and from Father A.'s confessional. Stayed in her own house, searched her body each morning and examined her conscience each night for progressive symptoms of the metastasis she feared was in her. Another vocation: whose words were garbled and somehow sinister, as Fausto's own had been.

These, poor child, are the sad events surrounding your given name. It is a different name now that you've been carried off by the U. S. Navy. But beneath that accident you are still Maijstral-Xemxi—a terrible misalliance. May you survive it. I fear not so much a reappearance in you of Elena's mythical "disease" as a fracturing of personality such as your father has undergone. May you be only Paola, one girl: a single given heart, a whole mind at peace. That is a prayer, if you wish.

Later, after the marriage, after your birth, well into the reign of Fausto II when the bombs were falling, the relationship with Elena must have come under some kind of moratorium. There being, perhaps, enough else to do. Fausto enlisted in the home defence; Elena had taken to nursing: feeding and keeping sheltered the bombed-out, comforting the wounded, bandaging, burying. At this time—assuming his theory of the "dual man" to be so—Fausto II was becoming more Maltese and less British.

> German bombers over today: ME-109's. No more need to look. We have grown used to the sound. Five times. Concentrated, as luck would have it, on Ta Kali. These grand chaps in the "Hurries" and Spitfires! What would we not do for them!

Moving towards that island-wide sense of communion. And at the same time towards the lowest form of consciousness. His work at the Ta Kali airfield was a sapper's drudgery; keeping the runways in condition for the British fighter planes; repairing the barracks, mess hall and hangars. At first he was able to look on it all over his shoulder, as it were: in retreat.

Not a night since Italy declared war have we known raid-less. How was it in the years of peace? Somewhere—what centuries ago?—one could sleep a night through. That's all gone. Routed out by sirens at three in the morning—at 3:30 out to the airfield past the Bofors emplacements, the wardens, the fire-fighting crews. With death—its smell, slow after-trickling of powdered plaster, stubborn smoke and flame, still fresh in the air. The R.A.F. are magnificent, all magnificent: ground artillery, the few merchant seamen who do get through, my own comrades-in-arms. I speak of them that way: our home defence though little more than common labourers are military in the highest sense. Surely if war has any nobility it is in the rebuilding not the destruction. A few portable searchlights (they are at a premium) for us to see by. So with pick, shovel and rake we reshape our Maltese earth for those game little Spitfires.

But isn't it a way of glorifying God? Hard-labour surely. But as if somewhere once without our knowledge we'd been condemned for a term to prison. With the next raid all our filling and levelling is blasted away into pits and rubble piles which must then be refilled and relevelled only to be de-stroyed again. Day and night it never eases off. I have let pass my nightly prayers on more than one occasion. I say them now on my feet, on the job, often in rhythm to the shovelling. To kneel is a luxury these days.

No sleep, little food; but no complaints. Are we not, Mal-tese, English and the few Americans, one? There is, we are taught, a communion of saints in heaven. So perhaps on earth, also in this Purgatory, a communion: not of gods or heroes, merely men expiating sins they are unaware of, caught somehow all at once within the reaches of a sea un-crossable and guarded by instruments of death. Here on our dear tiny prison plot, our Malta.

Retreat, then, into religious abstraction. Retreat also into poetry, which somehow he found time to write down. Fausto IV has commented elsewhere on the poetry which came out of Malta's second Great Siege. Fausto II's had fallen into the same patterns. Certain images recurred, major among them Valletta of the Knights. Fausto IV was tempted to put this down to simple "escape" and leave it there. It was cer-tainly wish-fulfillment. Maratt had a vision of La Vallette patrolling the streets during blackout; Dnubietna wrote a sonnet about a dogfight (Spitfire v. ME-109) taking a knights' duel for the sustained image. Retreat into a time when personal combat was more equal, when warfare could at least be gilded with an illusion of honour. But beyond this; could it not be a true absence of time? Fausto II even noticed this:

> Here towards midnight in a lull between raids, watching Elena and Paola sleep, I seem to have come inside time again. Midnight does mark the hairline between days, as was our Lord's design. But when the bombs fall, or at work, then it's as if time were suspended. As if we all laboured and sheltered in timeless Purgatory. Perhaps it comes only from living on an island. With another kind of nerves possibly one has a dimension, a vector pointing sternly to some land's-end or other, the tip of a peninsula. But here with nowhere to go in space but into the sea it can be only the barb-and-shaft of one's own arrogance that insists there is somewhere to go in time as well.

Or in a more poignant vein:

> Spring has come. Perhaps there are sulla blossoms in the country. Here in the city is sun, and more rain than is really necessary. It cannot matter, can it? Even I suspect the growth of our child has nothing to do with time. Her name-wind will be here again; to soothe her face which is always dirty. Is it a world anyone could have brought a child into?

None of us has the right to ask that any more, Paola. Only you.

The other great image is of something I can only call slow apocalypse. Even the radical Dnubietna, whose tastes assuredly ran to apocalypse at full gallop, eventually created a world in which the truth had precedence over his engineer's politics. He was probably the best of our poets. First, at least, to come to a halt, about-face and toil back along his own retreat's path; back towards the real world the bombs were leaving us. The Ash Wednesday poem marked his lowest point: after that he gave up abstraction and a political rage which he later admitted was "all posturing" to be concerned increasingly with what was, not what ought to have been or what could be under the right form of government.

We all came back eventually. Maratt in a way which in any other context would be labelled absurdly theatrical. He was working as mechanic out at Ta Kali and had grown fond of several pilots. One by one they were shot from the sky. On the night the last one died he went calmly into the

296

officers' club, stole a bottle of wine—scarce then like everything else because no convoys were getting through—and got
belligerently drunk. The next anyone knew he was on the
edge of town at one of the Bofors emplacements, being shown
how to operate the guns. They taught him in time for the
next raid. He divided his time after that between airfield and
artillery, getting, I believe, two to three hours' sleep out
of every twenty-four. He had an excellent record of kills.
And his poetry began to show the same "retreat from retreat."

Fausto II's return was most violent of all. He dropped
away from abstraction and into Fausto III: a non-humanity
which was the most real state of affairs. Probably. One
would rather not think so.

But all shared this sensitivity to decadence, of a slow
falling, as if the island were being hammered inch by inch
into the sea. "I remember," that other Fausto wrote,

> I remember
> A sad tango on the last night of the old world
> A girl who peeped from between the palms
> At the Phoenicia Hotel
> Maria, alma de mi corazón,
> Before the crucible
> And the slag heap,
> Before the sudden craters
> And the cancerous blooming of displaced earth.
> Before the carrion birds came sweeping from the sky;
> Before that cicada,
> These locusts,
> This empty street.

Oh we were full of lyrical lines like "At the Phoenicia
Hotel." Free verse: why not? There was simply not the
time to cast it into rhyme or metre, to take care with as-
sonance and ambiguity. Poetry had to be as hasty and rough
as eating, sleep or sex. Jury-rigged and not as graceful as
it might have been. But it did the job; put the truth on
record.

"Truth" I mean, in the sense of attainable accuracy.
No metaphysics. Poetry is not communication with angels or
with the "subconscious." It is communication with the guts,
genitals and five portals of sense. Nothing more.

Now there is your grandmother, child, who also comes

297

into this briefly. Carla Maijstral: she died as you know last March, outliving my father by three years. An event which might have been enough to produce a new Fausto, had it been in an earlier "reign." Fausto II, for instance, was that sort of confused Maltese youth who finds island-love and mother-love impossible to separate. Had Fausto IV been more of a nationalist when Carla died, we might now have a Fausto V.

Early in the war we get passages like this:

> Malta is a noun feminine and proper. Italians have indeed been attempting her defloration since the 8th of June. She lies on her back in the sea, sullen; an immemorial woman. Spread to the explosive orgasms of Mussolini bombs. But her soul hasn't been touched; cannot be. Her soul is the Maltese people, who wait—only wait—down in her clefts and catacombs alive and with a numb strength, filled with faith in God His Church. How can her flesh matter? It is vulnerable, a victim. But as the Ark was to Noah so is the inviolable womb of our Maltese rock to her children. Something given us in return for being filial and constant, children also of God.

Womb of rock. What subterranean confessions we wandered into! Carla must have told him at some point of the circumstances surrounding his birth. It had been near the time of the June Disturbances, in which old Maijstral was involved. Precisely how never came clear. But deeply enough to alienate Carla both from him and from herself. Enough so that one night we both nearly took a doomed acrobat's way down the steps at the Harbour end of Str. San Giovanni; I to limbo, she to a suicide's hell. What had kept her? The boy Fausto could only gather from listening in to her evening prayers that it was an Englishman; a mysterious being named Stencil.

Did he feel trapped? Having escaped lucky from one womb, now forced into the oubliette of another not so happily starred?

Again the classic response: retreat. Again into his damnable "communion." When Elena's mother died from a stray bomb dropped on Vittoriosa:

> Oh, we've become accustomed to these things. My own mother is alive and well. God willing will continue so. But if she is to be taken from me (or me from her) ikun li trid

298

Int: Thy will be done. I refuse to dwell on death because I know well enough that a young man, even here, dotes along in an illusion of immortality.

But perhaps more on this island because we've become, after all, one another. Parts of a unity. Some die, others continue. If a hair falls or a fingernail is torn away, am I any less alive and determined?

Seven raids today; so far. One "plot" of nearly a hundred Messerschmitts. They have levelled the churches, the Knights' auberges, the old monuments. They have left us a Sodom. Nine raids yesterday. Work harder than I've known it. My body would grow but there's little enough food. Few ships get through; convoys are sunk. Some of my comrades have dropped out. Weak from hunger. A miracle I was not the first to fall. Imagine. Maijstral, the frail University-poet, a labourer, a builder! And one who will survive. I must.

It's the rock they come back to. Fausto II managed to work himself into superstition:

Don't touch them, these walls. They carry the explosions for miles. The rock hears everything, and brings it to bone, up the fingers and arm, down through the bone-cage and bone-sticks and out again through the bone-webs. Its little passage through you is accident, merely in the nature of rock and bone: but it's as if you were given a reminder.

The vibration is impossible to talk about. Felt sound. Buzzing. The teeth buzz: Pain, a numb prickling along the jawbone, stifling concussion at the eardrums. Over and over. Mallet-blows as long as the raid, raids as long as the day. You never get used to it. You'd think we'd all have gone mad by now. What keeps me standing erect and away from the walls? And silent. A brute clinging to awareness, nothing else. Pure Maltese. Perhaps it is meant to go on forever. If "forever" still has any meaning.

Stand free, Maijstral. . . .

The passage above comes towards the Siege's end. The phrase "womb of rock" now had emphasis for Dnubietna, Maratt and Fausto at the end not the beginning. It is part of time's chiromancy to reduce those days to simple passage through a grammatical sequence. Dnubietna wrote:

Motes of rock's dust
Caught among corpses of carob trees;
Atoms of iron
Swirl above the dead forge

On that cormorant side of the moon.

Maratt wrote:

> We knew they were only puppets
> And the music from a gramophone:
> Knew the gathered silk would fade,
> Ball-fringe fray,
> Plush contract the mange;
> Knew, or suspected, that children do grow up;
> Would begin to shuffle after the first hundred years
> Of the performance; yawn toward afternoon,
> Begin to see the peeling paint on Judy's cheek,
> Detect implausibility in the palsied stick
> And self-deception in the villain's laugh.
> But dear Christ, whose slim jewelled hand was it
> Flicked from the wings so unexpected,
> Holding the lighted wax taper
> To send up all our poor but precious tinder
> In flame of terrible colours?
> Who was she who gently laughed, "Good night,"
> Among the hoarse screaming of aged children?

From the quick to the inanimate. The great "movement" of the Siege poetry. As went Fausto II's already dual soul. All the while only in the process of learning life's single lesson: that there is more accident to it than a man can ever admit to in a lifetime and stay sane.

Seeing his mother after a period of months away:

> Time has touched her. I found myself wondering: did she know that in this infant she brought forth, to whom she gave the name for happy (ironic?) was a soul which would become torn and unhappy? Does any mother anticipate the future; acknowledge when the time comes that a son is now a man and must leave her to make whatever peace he can alone on a treacherous earth. No, it's the same Maltese timelessness. They don't feel the fingers of years jittering age, fallibility, blindness into face, heart and eyes. A son is a son, fixed always in the red and wrinkled image as they first see it. There are always elephants to be made drunk.

This last from an old folk tale. The king wants a palace made of elephant tusks. The boy had inherited physical strength from his father, a military hero. But it was for the mother to teach the son cunning. Make friends with them, feed them wine, kill them, steal their ivory. The boy is successful of course. But no mention of a sea voyage.

"There must have been," Fausto explains, "millennia ago, a land-bridge. They called Africa the Land of the Axe. There were elephants south of Mount Ruwenzori. Since then the sea has steadily crept in. German bombs may finish it."

Decadence, decadence. What is it? Only a clear movement toward death or, preferably, non-humanity. As Fausto II and III, like their island, became more inanimate, they moved closer to the time when like any dead leaf or fragment of metal they'd be finally subject to the laws of physics. All the time pretending it was a great struggle between the laws of man and the laws of God.

Is it only because Malta is a matriarchal island that Fausto felt so strongly that connection between mother-rule and decadence?

"Mothers are closer than anyone to accident. They are most painfully conscious of the fertilized egg; as Mary knew the moment of conception. But the zygote has no soul. Is matter." Further along these lines he would not go. But;

> Their babies always seem to come by happenstance; a random conjunction of events. Mothers close ranks, and perpetrate a fictional mystery about motherhood. It's only a way of compensating for an inability to live with the truth. Truth being that they do not understand what is going on inside them; that it is a mechanical and alien growth which at some point acquires a soul. They are possessed. Or: the same forces which dictate the bomb's trajectory, the deaths of stars, the wind and the waterspout have focussed somewhere inside the pelvic frontiers without their consent, to generate one more mighty accident. It frightens them to death. It would frighten anyone.

So it moves us on toward the question of Fausto's "understanding" with God. Apparently his problem was never as simple as God v. Caesar, especially Caesar inanimate— the one we see in old medals and statues, the "force" we read of in history texts. Caesar for one thing was animate once, and had his own difficulties with a world of things as well as a degenerate crew of gods. It would be easier, since drama arises out of conflict, to call it simply human law v. divine, all within the arena in quarantine that had been Fausto's home. I mean his soul and I also mean the island. But this isn't drama. Only an apologia for the Day of the 13 Raids. Even what happened then had no clear lines drawn.

I know of machines that are more complex than people. If this is apostasy, hekk ikun. To have humanism we must first be convinced of our humanity. As we move further into decadence this becomes more difficult.

More and more alien from himself, Fausto II began to detect signs of lovely inanimateness in the world around him.

Now the winter's gregale brings in bombers from the north; as Euroclydon it brought in St. Paul. Blessings, curses. But is the wind any part of us? Has it anything at all to do with us?

Somewhere perhaps behind a hill—some shelter—farmers are sowing wheat for a June harvest. Bombing is concentrated around Valletta, the Three Cities, the Harbour. Pastoral life has become enormously attractive. But there are strays: one killed Elena's mother. We cannot expect more of the bombs than of the wind. We should not expect. If I am not to become marid b'mohhu, I can only go on as sapper, as gravedigger, I must refuse to think of any other condition, past or future. Better to say: "This has always been. We've always lived in Purgatory and our term here is at best indefinite."

Apparently he took at this time to shambling about in the streets, during raids. Hours away from Ta Kali, when he should have been sleeping. Not out of any bravery, or for any reason connected with his job. Nor, at first, for very long.

Pile of brick, grave-shaped. Green beret lying nearby. Royal Commandoes? Star-shells from the Bofors over Marsamuscetto. Red light, long shadows from behind the shop at the corner which move in the unsteady light about a hidden pivot-point. Impossible to tell shadows of what.

Early sun still low on the sea. Blinding. Long blinding track, white road in from the sun to point of view. Sound of Messerschmitts. Invisible. Sound which grows louder. Spitfires scramble aloft, high angle of climb. Small, black in such bright sun. Course toward sun. Dirty marks appear on the sky. Orange-brown-yellow. Colour of excrement. Black.

302

Sun turns the edges gold. And the edges trail like jellyfish toward the horizon. Marks spread, new ones bloom in the centres of old. Air up there is often so still. Other times a wind, up high, must streak them into nothing in seconds. Wind, machines, dirty smoke. Sometimes the sun. When there's rain nothing can be seen. But the wind sweeps in and down and everything can be heard.

For a matter of months, little more than "impressions." And was it not Valletta? During the raids everything civilian and with a soul was underground. Others were too busy to "observe." The city was left to itself; except for stragglers like Fausto, who felt nothing more than an unvoiced affinity and were enough like the city not to change the truth of the "impressions" by the act of receiving them. A city uninhabited is different. Different from what a "normal" observer, straggling in the dark—the occasional dark—would see. It is a universal sin among the false-animate or unimaginative to refuse to let well enough alone. Their compulsion to gather together, their pathological fear of loneliness extends on past the threshold of sleep; so that when they turn the corner, as we all must, as we all have done and do—some more often than others—to find ourselves on the street . . . You know the street I mean, child. The street of the 20th Century, at whose far end or turning—we hope—is some sense of home or safety. But no guarantees. A street we are put at the wrong end of, for reasons best known to the agents who put us there. If there are agents. But a street we must walk.

It is the acid test. To populate, or not to populate. Ghosts, monsters, criminals, deviates represent melodrama and weakness. The only horror about them is the dreamer's own horror of isolation. But the desert, or a row of false shop fronts; a slag pile, a forge where the fires are banked, these and the street and the dreamer, only an inconsequential shadow himself in the landscape, partaking of the soullessness of these other masses and shadows; this is 20th Century nightmare.

It was not hostility, Paola, this leaving you and Elena alone during the raids. Nor was it the usual selfish irresponsibility of youth. His youth, Maratt's, Dnubietna's, the youth of a "generation" (both in a literary and in a literal sense) had vanished abruptly with the first bomb of 8 June 1940. The old Chinese artificers and their successors Schultze and

Nobel had devised a philtre far more potent than they knew. One does and the "Generation" were immune for life; immune to the fear of death, hunger, hard labour, immune to the trivial seductions which pull a man away from a wife and child and the need to care. Immune to everything but what happened to Fausto one afternoon during the seventh of thirteen raids. In a lucid moment during his fugue, Fausto wrote:

How beautiful is blackout in Valletta. Before tonight's "plot" comes in from the north. Night fills the street like a black fluid; flows along the gutters, its current tugging at your ankles. As if the city were underwater; an Atlantis, under the night sea.

Is it night only that wraps Valletta? Or is it a human emotion; "an air of expectancy"? Not the expectancy of dreams, where our awaited is unclear and unnameable. Valletta knows well enough what she waits for. There is no tension or malaise to this silence; it's cool, secure; the silence of boredom or well-accustomed ritual. A gang of artillerymen in the next street make hastily for their emplacement. But their vulgar song fades away, leaving one embarrassed voice which finally runs out in mid-word.

Thank God you're safe, Elena, in our other, subterranean home. You and the child. If old Saturno Aghtina and his wife have now moved permanently to the old sewer, then there is care for Paola when you must go out to do your work. How many other families have cared for her? All our babies have had only one father, the war; one mother, Malta her women. Bad lookout for the Family, and for mother-rule. Clans and matriarchy are incompatible with this Communion war has brought to Malta.

I go from you love not because I must. We men are not a race of freebooters or giaours; not when our argosies are prey and food to the evil fish-of-metal whose lair is a German U-boat. There is no more world but the island; and it's only a day to any sea's verge. There is no leaving you, Elena; not in truth.

But in dream there are two worlds: the street and under the street. One is the kingdom of death and one of life. And how can a poet live without exploring the other kingdom, even if only as a kind of tourist? A poet feeds on dream. If no convoys come what else is there to feed on?

Poor Fausto. The "vulgar song" was sung to a march called Colonel Bogie:

Hitler
Has only one left ball,
Goering
Has two but they are small;
Himmler
Has something similar,
But Goebbels
Has no balls
At all. . . .

Proving perhaps that virility on Malta did not depend on mobility. They were all, as Fausto was first to admit, labourers not adventurers. Malta, and her inhabitants, stood like an immovable rock in the river Fortune, now at war's flood. The same motives which cause us to populate a dreamstreet also cause us to apply to a rock human qualities like "invincibility," "tenacity," "perseverance," etc. More than metaphor, it is delusion. But on the strength of this delusion Malta survived.

Manhood on Malta thus became increasingly defined in terms of rockhood. This had its dangers for Fausto. Living as he does much of the time in a world of metaphor, the poet is always acutely conscious that metaphor has no value apart from its function; that it is a device, an artifice. So that while others may look on the laws of physics as legislation and God as a human form with beard measured in light-years and nebulae for sandals, Fausto's kind are alone with the task of living in a universe of things which simply are, and cloaking that innate mindlessness with comfortable and pious metaphor so that the "practical" half of humanity may continue in the Great Lie, confident that their machines, dwellings, streets and weather share the same human motives, personal traits and fits of contrariness as they.

Poets have been at this for centuries. It is the only useful purpose they do serve in society: and if every poet were to vanish tomorrow, society would live no longer than the quick memories and dead books of their poetry.

It is the "role" of the poet, this 20th Century. To lie. Dnubietna wrote:

If I told the truth
You would not believe me.
If I said: no fellow soul

Drops death from the air, no conscious plot
Drove us underground, you would laugh
As if I had twitched the wax mouth
Of my tragic mask into a smile—
A smile to you; to me the truth behind
The catenary: locus of the transcendental:
$$y = a/2 \; (e^{x/a} + e^{-x/a}).$$

Fausto ran across the engineer-poet one afternoon in the street. Dnubietna had been drunk, and now that it was wearing off was returning to the scene of his bat. An unscrupulous merchant named Tifkira had a hoard of wine. It was Sunday and raining. Weather had been foul, raids fewer. The two young men met next to the ruin of a small church. The one confessional had been sheared in two but which half was left, priest's or parishioner's, Fausto could not tell. Sun behind the rain clouds appeared as a patch of luminous grey, a dozen times its normal size, halfway down from the zenith. Almost brilliant enough to cast shadows. But falling from behind Dnubietna so that the engineer's features were indistinct. He wore khakis stained with grease, and a blue fatigue cap; large drops of rain fell on the two.

Dnubietna indicated the church with his head. "Have you been, priest?"

"To Mass: no." They hadn't met for a month. But no need to bring each other up to date.

"Come on. We'll get drunk. How are Elena and your kid?"

"Well."

"Maratt's is pregnant again. Don't you miss the bachelor life?" They were walking down a narrow cobbled street made slick by the rain. To either side were rubble heaps, a few standing walls or porch steps. Streaks of stone-dust, matte against the shiny cobblestones, interrupted at random the pavement's patterning. The sun had almost achieved reality. Their attenuated shadows strung out behind. Rain still fell. "Or having married when you did," Dnubietna went on, "perhaps you equate singleness with peace."

"Peace," said Fausto. "Quaint word." They skipped around and over stray chunks of masonry.

"Sylvana," Dnubietna sang, "in your red petticoat/ Come back, come back/ You may keep my heart/ But bring back my money. . . ."

"You should get married," Fausto said, mournful: "It's not fair otherwise."

"Poetry and engineering have nothing to do with domesticity."

"We haven't," Fausto remembered, "had a good argument for months."

"In here." They went down a flight of steps which led under a building still reasonably intact. Clouds of powdered plaster rose as they descended. Sirens began. Inside the room Tifkira lay on a table, asleep. Two girls played cards listlessly in a corner. Dnubietna vanished for a moment behind the bar, reappearing with a small bottle of wine. A bomb fell in the next street, rattling the beams of the ceiling, starting an oil lamp hung there to swinging.

"I ought to be asleep," Fausto said. "I work tonight."

"Remorse of a uxorious half-man," Dnubietna snarled, pouring wine. The girls looked up. "It's the uniform," he confided, which was so ridiculous that Fausto had to laugh. Soon they had moved to the girls' table. Talk was irregular, there being an artillery emplacement almost directly above them. The girls were professional and tried for a while to proposition Fausto and Dnubietna.

"No use," Dnubietna said. "I've never had to pay for mine and this one is married and a priest." Three laughed: Fausto, getting drunk, was not amused.

"That is long gone," he said quietly.

"Once a priest always a priest," Dnubietna retorted. "Come. Bless this wine. Consecrate it. It's Sunday and you haven't been to Mass."

Overhead, the Bofors began an intermittent and deafening hack: two explosions every second. The four concentrated on drinking wine. Another bomb fell. "Bracketed," Dnubietna shouted above the a/a barrage. A word which no longer meant anything in Valletta. Tifkira woke up.

"Stealing my wine," the owner cried. He stumbled to the wall and leaned his forehead against it. Thoroughly he began to scratch his hairy stomach and back under their singlet. "You might give me a drink."

"It isn't consecrated. Maijstral the apostate is at fault."

"Now God and I have an agreement," Fausto began as if to correct a misapprehension. "He will forget about my not answering His call if I cease to question. Simply survive, you see."

When had that come to him? In what street: at what point in these months of impressions? Perhaps he'd thought it up on the spot. He was drunk. So tired it had only taken four glasses of wine.

"How," one of the girls asked seriously, "how can there be faith if you don't ask questions? The priest said it's right for us to ask questions."

Dnubietna looked at his friend's face, saw no answer forthcoming: so turned and patted the girl's shoulder.

"That's the hell of it, love. Drink your wine."

"No," screamed Tifkira, propped against the other wall, watching them. "You'll waste it all." The gun began its racket again.

"Waste," Dnubietna laughed above the noise. "Don't talk of waste, you idiot." Belligerent, he started across the room. Fausto put his head down on the table to rest for a moment. The girls resumed their card game, using his back for a table. Dnubietna had taken the owner by the shoulders. He began a lengthy denunciation of Tifkira, punctuating it with shakes which sent the fat torso into cyclic shudders.

Above, the all-clear sounded. Soon after there was noise at the door. Dnubietna opened and in rollicked the artillery crew, dirty, exhausted and in search of wine. Fausto awoke and jumped to his feet saluting, scattering the cards in a shower of hearts and spades.

"Away, away!" shouted Dnubietna. Tifkira, giving up his dream of a great wine-hoard, slumped down to a sitting position against the wall and closed his eyes. "We must get Maijstral to work!"

"Go to, caitiff," Fausto cried, saluted again and fell over backwards. With much giggling and unsteadiness Dnubietna and one of the girls helped him to his feet. It was apparently Dnubietna's intention to bring Fausto to Ta Kali on foot (usual method was to hitch a ride from a lorry) to sober him up. As they reached the darkening street the sirens began again. Members of the Bofors crew, each holding a glass of wine, came clattering up the steps and collided with them. Dnubietna, irritated, abruptly ducked out from under Fausto's arm and came up with a fist to the stomach of the nearest artilleryman. A brawl developed. Bombs were falling over by the Grand Harbour. The explosions began to approach slow and steady, like the footsteps of a child's ogre. Fausto lay on the ground feeling no particular desire to come to the aid of his friend who was outnumbered and being worked over thoroughly. They finally dropped Dnubietna and headed towards the Bofors. Not so far overhead, an ME-109, pinned by searchlights, suddenly broke out of the cloud-cover and swooped in. Orange tracers followed. "Get the bugger," someone at the gun emplacement screamed. The Bofors opened up. Fausto looked on with mild interest. Shadows of the gun crew, lit from above by the exploding projectiles and "scatter" from the searchlights, flickered in and out of the night. In one flash Fausto saw the red glow of Tifkira's wine in a glass held to an ammo-handler's lips and slowly diminishing. Somewhere over the Harbour a/a shells caught up with the Messerschmitt; its fuel tanks ignited in a great yellow flowering and down it went, slow as a balloon, the black smoke of its passage billowing through the searchlight beams, which lingered a moment at the point of intercept before going on to other business.

Dnubietna hung over him, haggard, one eye beginning to swell. "Away, away," he croaked. Fausto got to his feet reluctant and off they went. There is no indication in the journal of how they did it, but the two reached Ta Kali just as the all-clear sounded. They went perhaps a mile on foot. Presumably they dove for cover whenever the bombing got too close. Finally they clambered on the back of a passing lorry.

"It was hardly heroic," Fausto wrote. "We were both drunk. But I've not been able to get it out of my mind that we were given a dispensation that night. That God had suspended the laws of chance, by which we should rightly have been killed. Somehow the street—the kingdom of death—was friendly. Perhaps it was because I observed our agreement and did not bless the wine."

Post hoc. And only part of the over-all "relationship." This is what I meant about Fausto's simplicity. He did nothing so complex as drift away from God or reject his church. Losing faith is a complicated business and takes time. There are no epiphanies, no "moments of truth." It takes much thought and concentration in the later phases. which themselves come about through an accumulation of small accidents: examples of general injustice, misfortune falling upon the godly, prayers of one's own unanswered. Fausto and his "Generation" simply hadn't the time for this leisurely intellectual hanky-panky. They'd got out of the habit, had lost a certain sense of themselves, had come further from the University-at-peace and closer to the beleaguered city than any were ready to admit, were more Maltese, i.e., than English.

All else in his life having gone underground; having acquired a trajectory in which the sirens figured as only one parameter, Fausto realized that the old covenants, the old agreements with God would have to change too. For at least a working relevancy to God therefore, Fausto did exactly what he'd been doing for a home, food, marital love: he jury-rigged—"made do." But the English part of him was still there, keeping up the journal.

The child—you—grew healthier, more active. By '42 you had fallen in with a roistering crew of children whose chief amusement was a game called R.A.F. Between raids a dozen or so of you would go out in the streets, spread your arms like aeroplanes and run screaming and buzzing in and out of the ruined walls, rubble heaps and holes of the city. The stronger and taller boys were, of course, Spitfires. Others—unpopular boys, girls, and younger children—went to make up the planes of the enemy. You were usually, I believe, an Italian dirigible. The most buoyant balloon-girl in the stretch of sewer we occupied that season. Harassed, chased, dodging the rocks and sticks tossed your way, you managed each time with the "Italian" agility your role demanded, to escape subjugation. But always, having outwitted your opponents, you would finally do your patriotic duty by surrendering. And only when you were ready.

Your mother and Fausto were away from you most of the time: nurse and sapper. You were left to the two extremes of our underground society: the old, for whom the distinction between sudden and gradual affliction hardly existed, and the young—your true own—who unconsciously were creating a discrete world, a prototype of the world Fausto III, already outdated, would inherit. Did the two forces neutralize and leave you on the lonely promontory between two worlds? Can you still look both ways, child? If so you stand at an enviable vantage: you're still that four-year-old belligerent with history in defilade. The present Fausto can look nowhere but back on the separate stages of his own history. No continuity. No logic. "History," Dnubietna wrote, "is a step-function."

Was Fausto believing too much: was the Communion all sham to compensate for some failure as a father and husband? By peacetime standards a failure he certainly was.

The normal, pre-war course would have been a slow growing into love for Elena and Paola as the young man, thrown into marriage and fatherhood prematurely, learned to take on the burden which is every man's portion in the adult world.

But the Siege created different burdens and it was impossible to say whose world was more real: the children's or the parents'. For all their dirt, noise and roughnecking the kids of Malta served a poetic function. The R.A.F. game was only one metaphor they devised to veil the world that was. For whose benefit? The adults were at work, the old did not care, the kids themselves were all "in" the secret. It must have been for lack of anything better: until their muscles and brains developed to where they could take on part of the work-load in the ruin their island was becoming. It was biding time: it was poetry in a vacuum. *human and non-h*

Paola: my child, Elena's child but most of all Malta's, you were one of them. These children knew what was happening: knew that bombs killed. But what's a human, after all? No different from a church, obelisk, statue. Only one thing matters: it's the bomb that wins. Their view of death was non-human. One wonders if our grown-up attitudes, hopelessly tangled as they were with love, social forms and metaphysics, worked any better. Certainly there was more common sense about the children's way.

The children got about Valletta by their private routes, mostly underground. Fausto II records their separate world, superimposed on a blasted city: ragged tribes scattered about Xaghriet Mewwija, indulging now and again in internecine skirmishes. Reconnaissance and foraging parties were always there, always at the edges of the field of vision.

> The tide must be turning. Only one raid today, that in the early morning. We slept last night in the sewer, near Aghtina and his wife. Little Paola went off soon after the all-clear to explore the Dockyard country with Maratt's boy and some others. Even the weather seemed to signal a kind of intermission. Last night's rain had laid the plaster and stone-dust, cleaned the leaves of trees and caused a merry waterfall to enter our quarters, not ten steps from the mattress of clean laundry. Accordingly we made our ablutions in this well-disposed rivulet, retiring soon thereafter to the domicile of Mrs. Aghtina, where we broke our fast on a hearty porridge the good woman had but recently devised against just such a

contingency. What abundant graciousness and dignity have been our lot since this Siege began!

Above in the street the sun was shining. We ascended to the street, Elena took my hand, and once on level ground did not let it go. We began to walk. Her face, fresh from sleep, was so pure in that sun. Malta's old sun, Elena's young face. It seemed I had only now met her for the first time; or that, children again, we'd strayed into the same orange grove, walked into a breathing of azaleas unaware. She began to talk, adolescent girl talk, Maltese: how brave the soldiers and sailors looked ("You mean how sober," I commented: she laughed, mock-annoyed); how amusing was a lone flush-toilet located in the upper right-hand room of an English club building whose side wall had been blown away: feeling young I became angry and political at this toilet. "What fine democracy in war," I ranted. "Before, they locked us out of their grand clubs. Anglo-Maltese intercourse was a farce. Pro bono; ha-ha. Keep the natives in their place. But now even the most sacrosanct room of that temple is open to the public gaze." So we nearly roistered along the sunlit street, rain having brought a kind of spring. On days like that, we felt, Valletta had recalled her own pastoral history. As if vineyards would suddenly bloom along the sea-bastions, olive and pomegranate trees spring up from the pale wounds of Kingsway. The Harbour sparkled: we waved, spoke or smiled to every passer-by; Elena's hair caught the sun in its viscous net, sun-freckles danced along her cheeks.

How we came to that garden or park I can never tell. All morning we walked by the sea. Fishing boats were out. A few wives gossiped among the seaweed and chunks of yellow bastion the bombs had left on the strand. They mended nets, watched the sea, shouted at their children. There were children everywhere in Valletta today, swinging down from the trees, jumping off the ruined ends of jetties into the sea: heard but not seen in the empty shells of bombed-out houses. They sang: chanted, chaffed or merely screeched. Weren't they really our own voices caught for years in any house and only now come to embarrass us at our passing-by?

We found a café, there was wine from the last convoy—rare vintage!—wine and a poor chicken we heard the proprietor killing in the other room. We sat, drank the wine, watched the Harbour. Birds were heading out into the Mediterranean. High barometer. Perhaps they had a portal of sense for the Germans too. Hair blew in her eyes. For the first time in a year we could talk. I'd given her some lessons in English conversation before '39. Today she wanted to continue them: who knew, she said, when there would be another chance? Serious child. How I loved her.

312

In the early afternoon the proprietor came out to sit with us: one hand still sticky with blood and a few feathers caught there. "I am pleased to make your acquaintance, sir," Elena greeted him. Gleeful. The old man cackled.

"English," he said. "Yes I knew the moment I saw you. English tourists." It became our private joke. While she kept touching me under the table, mischievous Elena, the owner continued a foolish discourse about the English. Wind off the Harbour was cool, and the water which for some reason I only remembered as yellow-green or brown now was blue— a carnival blue and stippled with whitecaps. Jolly Harbour.

Half a dozen children came running round the corner: boys in singlets, brown arms, two little girls in shifts tagging behind but ours was not one. They went by without seeing us, running downhill towards the Harbour. From somewhere a cloud had appeared, a solid-looking puff hung stock-still between the sun's invisible trolleys. Sun was on collision-course. Elena and I rose at last and wandered down the street. Soon from an alley burst another crowd of children, twenty yards ahead of us: cutting across in front, angling up the street to disappear single-file into the basement of what had been a house. Sunlight came to us broken by walls, window frames, roof beams: skeletal. Our street was pocked by thousands of little holes like the Harbour in noon's unbroken sun. We stumbled, unsprightly, each using the other now and again for balance.

Forenoon for sea, afternoon for the city. Poor shattered city. Tilted toward Marsamuscetto; no stone shell—roofless, walless, windowless—could hide from the sun, which threw all their shadows uphill and out to sea. Children, it seemed, dogged our footsteps. We'd hear them behind a broken wall: or only a whispering of bare feet and the small wind of a passage. And they'd call, now and again, somewhere over in the next street. Name indistinct for the wind off the Harbour. Sun inched downhill closer to the cloud that blocked its way.

Fausto, were they calling? Elena? And was our child one of their own or off on some private tracing-of-steps? We did trace our own about the city's grid, aimless, in fugue: a fugue of love or memory or some abstract sentiment which always comes after the fact and had nothing to do that afternoon with the quality of the light or the pressure of five fingers on my arm which awoke my five senses and more. . . .

Sad is a foolish word. Light is not sad: or should not be. Afraid even to look behind at our shadows lest they move differently, slip away into the gutter or one of the earth's cracks, we combed Valletta till late afternoon as if it were something finite we sought.

Until at length—late afternoon—we arrived at a tiny park

313

in the heart of the city. At one end a band pavilion creaked in the wind, its roof supported miraculously by only a few upright beams. The structure sagged and birds of some sort had abandoned their nests all round the edge: all but one whose head was visible, looking out at God knew what, unfrightened at our approach. It looked stuffed.

It was there we awoke, there the children closed in on us. Had it been hare-and-hounds all day? Had all residual music gone with the quick birds, or was there a waltz we'd only now dreamed? We stood in sawdust and wood chips from an unlucky tree. Azalea bushes waited for us across from the pavilion but the wind was the wrong way: from the future, driving all scent back to its past. Above, tall palms leaned over us, false-solicitous, casting blade-shadows.

Cold. And then the sun met its cloud, and other clouds we'd not noticed at all began it seemed to move in radially towards the suncloud. As if winds were blowing today from all thirty-two points of the rose at once to meet at the centre in a great windspout to bear up the fire-balloon like an offering—set alight the undershorings of Heaven. Blade-shadows disappeared, all light and shadow were passing into a great acid-green. The fire-balloon continued its creep downhill. Leaves of all trees in the park began to scrape at one another like the legs of locusts. Music enough.

She shivered, held to me for a moment, then abruptly seated herself on the littered grass. I sat beside her. We must have been a queer-looking pair: shoulders hunched for the wind, facing the pavilion silent, as if waiting for a performance to begin. In the trees, at the edges of eyes, we saw children. White flashes which could have been faces, or only the other sides of leaves, signalling storm. Sky was clouding: the green light deepened, drowning the island of Malta and the island of Fausto and Elena hopelessly deeper in its oneiric chill.

O God, it was the same stupidity to be gone through again: the sudden fall in the barometer which we did not expect; the bad faith of dreams that send surprise skirmish-parties across a frontier which ought to be stable; the terror at the unfamiliar stair-step in the dark on what we thought was a level street. We'd traced nostalgic steps indeed this afternoon. Where had they brought us?

To a park we'd never find again.

We had been using, it seemed, nothing but Valletta to fill up the hollows of ourselves. Stone and metal cannot nourish. We sat hungry-eyed, listening to the nervous leaves. What could there be to feed on? Only one another.

"I am cold." In Maltese: and she did not move closer. There could be no more question of English today. I wanted to ask: Elena what do we wait for—for the weather to break, the trees or dead buildings to speak to us? I asked: "What is wrong?" She shook her head. Let her eyes wander between the ground and the creaking pavilion.

The more I studied her face—dark hair blowing, foreshortened eyes, freckles fading into the general green of that afternoon—the more anxious I became. I wanted to protest, but there was no one to protest to. Perhaps I wanted to cry, but the salt Harbour we had left to gulls and fishing boats; had not taken it in as we had the city.

Were there in her the same memories of azaleas, or any sense that this city was a mockery, a promise always unfulfilled? Did we share anything? The deeper we all sank into twilight the less I knew. I did—so I argued—love this woman with all there was in me to expedite or make secure any love: but here it was love in a growing dark: giving out, with no clear knowledge of how much was being lost, how much would ever be returned. Was she even seeing the same pavilion, hearing the same children at the frontiers of our park: was she here in fact or like Paola—dear God, not even our child but Valletta's—out alone, vibrating like a shadow in some street where the light is too clear, the horizon too sharp to be anything but a street created out of sickness for the past, for the Malta that was but can never be again!

Palm leaves abraded together, shredding one another to green fibres of light; tree limbs scraped, leaves of the carob, dry as leather, throbbed and shook. As if there were a gathering behind the trees, a gathering in the sky. The quiverings about us, mounting, panicked, grew louder than the children or ghosts of children. Afraid to look, we could stare only at the pavilion though God knew what might appear there.

Her nails, broken from burying the dead, had been digging into the bare part of my arm where the shirt was rolled up. Pressure and pain increased, our heads lolled slowly like the heads of puppets toward a meeting of eyes. In the dusk her eyes had grown huge and filmed. I tried to look at the whites as we look at the margins of a page, trying to avoid what was written in iris-black. Was it only night "gathering" outside? Something nightlike had found its way here, distilled and pre-shaped in eyes that only this morning had reflected sun, whitecaps, real children.

My own nails fastened in reply and we became twinned, symmetric, sharing pain, perhaps all we could ever share: her face began to go distorted, half with the strength it took to hurt me, half with what I was doing to her. The pain mounted, palms and carob trees went mad: her irises rolled towards the sky.

"Missierna li-inti fis-smewwiet, jitqaddes ismek. . . ." She

315

was praying. In retreat. Having reached a threshold, slipped
back to what was most sure. Raids, the death of a parent, the
daily handling of corpses had not been able to do it. It took
a park, a siege of children, trees astir, night coming in.

"Elena."

Her eyes returned to me. "I love you," moving on the
grass, "love you, Fausto." Pain, nostalgia, want mixed in her
eyes: so it seemed. But how could I know: with the same
positive comfort in knowing the sun grows colder, the Hagiar
Kim ruins progress towards dust, as do we, as does my little
Hillman Minx which was sent to a garage for old age in
1939 and is now disintegrating quietly under tons of ga-
rage-rubble. How could I infer: the only ghost of an excuse
being to reason by analogy that the nerves chafed and
stabbed by my fingernails were the same as my own, that
her pain was mine and by extension that of the jittering
leaves all round us.

Looking past her eyes I saw all white leaves. They had
turned their pale sides out and the clouds were storm clouds
after all. "The children," I heard her say. "We have lost
them."

Lost them. Or they had lost us.

"O," she breathed, "O look," releasing me as I released
her and we both stood and watched the gulls filling half the
visible sky, gulls that were all in our island now catching the
sunlight. Coming in all together, because of a storm somewhere out at sea—terribly silent—drifting slow, up and down
and inexorably landward, a thousand drops of fire.

There had been nothing. Whether children, maddened
leaves or dream-meteorology were or were not real, there are
no epiphanies on Malta this season, no moments of truth.
We had used our dead fingernails only to swage quick flesh;
to gouge or destroy, not to probe the wards of either soul.

I will limit the inevitable annotating to this request. Observe the predominance of human attributes applied to the
inanimate. The entire "day"—if it was a single day, rather
than the projection of a mood lasting perhaps longer—reads
like a resurgence of humanity in the automaton, health
in the decadent.

The passage is important not so much for this apparent
contradiction as for the children, who were quite real, whatever their function in Fausto's iconology. They seemed to
be the only ones conscious at the time that history had not
been suspended after all. That troops were relocated, Spitfires delivered, convoys lying to off St. Elmo. This was,

to be sure, in 1943, at the "turn of the tide" when bombers based here had begun to return part of the war to Italy and when the quality of anti-submarine warfare in the Mediterranean had developed to where we could see more than Dr. Johnson's "three meals ahead." But earlier—after the kids had recovered from the first shock—we "adults" looked on them with a kind of superstitious leeriness, as if they were recording angels, keeping the rolls of quick, dead, malingering; noting what Governor Dobbie wore, what churches had been destroyed, what was the volume of turnover at the hospitals.

They also knew about the Bad Priest. There is a certain fondness for the Manichaean common to all children. Here the combination of a siege, a Roman Catholic upbringing and an unconscious identification of one's own mother with the Virgin all sent simple dualism into strange patterns indeed. Preached to they might be about some abstract struggle between good and evil; but even the dogfights were too high above them to be real. They'd brought the Spitfires and ME's down to earth with their R.A.F. game, but it was only simple metaphor, as noted. The Germans to be sure were pure evil and the Allies pure good. The children weren't alone in that feeling. But if their idea of the struggle could be described graphically it would not be as two equal-sized vectors head-to-head—their heads making an X of unknown quantity; rather as a point, dimensionless—good—surrounded by any number of radial arrows—vectors of evil—pointing inward. Good, i.e., at bay. The Virgin assailed. The wingéd mother protective. The woman passive. Malta in siege.

A wheel, this diagram: Fortune's wheel. Spin as it might the basic arrangement was constant. Stroboscopic effects could change the apparent number of spokes; direction could change; but the hub still held the spokes in place and the meeting-place of the spokes still defined the hub. The old cyclic idea of history had taught only the rim, to which princes and serfs alike were lashed; that wheel was oriented vertical; one rose and fell. But the children's wheel was dead-level, its own rim only that of the sea's horizon—so sensuous, so "visual" a race are we Maltese.

Thus they assigned the Bad Priest no opposite number: neither Dobbie nor Archbishop Gonzi nor Father Avalanche. The Bad Priest was ubiquitous as night and the children, to sustain their observations, had to be at least as mobile.

317

It wasn't an organized affair. These recording angels never wrote anything down. It was more, if you will, a "group awareness." They merely watched, passive: you'd see them like sentinels at the top of a rubble pile any sunset; or peering round the corner of the street, squatting on the steps, loping in pairs, arms flung round each other's shoulders, across a vacant lot, going apparently nowhere. But always somewhere in their line-of-sight would be the flicker of a soutane or a shadow darker than the rest.

What was there about this priest to put him Outside; a radius along with leather-winged Lucifer, Hitler, Mussolini? Only part, I think, of what makes us suspect the wolf in the dog, the traitor in the ally. There was little wishful thinking about those children. Priests, like mothers, were to be venerated: but look at Italy, look at the sky. Here had been betrayal and hypocrisy: why not even among the priests? Once the sky had been our most constant and safe friend: a medium or plasma for the sun. A sun which the government is now trying to exploit for reasons of tourism: but formerly—in the days of Fausto I—the watchful eye of God and the sky his clear cheek. Since 3 September 1939 there had appeared pustules, blemishes and marks of pestilence: Messerschmitts. God's face had gone sick and his eye begun to wander, close (wink, insisted the rampant atheist, Dnubietna). But such is the devotion of the people and the sure strength of the Church that the betrayal was not looked on as God's; rather as the sky's—knavery of the skin which could harbour such germs and thus turn so against its divine owner.

The children, being poets in a vacuum, adept at metaphor, had no trouble in transferring a similar infection to any of God's representatives the priests. Not all priests; but one, parishless, an alien—Sliema was like another country—and having already a bad reputation, was fit vehicle for their scepticism.

Reports of him were confused. Fausto would hear—through the children or Father Avalanche—that the Bad Priest "was converting by the shores of Marsamuscetto" or "had been active in Xaghriet Mewwija." Sinister uncertainty surrounded the priest. Elena showed no concern: did not feel that she herself had encountered any evil that day in the street, was not worried about Paola coming under any evil influence, though the Bad Priest had been known to gather about him a small knot of children in the street and give them sermons. He taught no consistent philosophy that anyone could piece together from the fragments borne back to us by the children. The girls he advised to become nuns, avoid the sensual extremes—pleasure of intercourse, pain of childbirth. The boys he told to find strength in—and be like—the rock of their island. He returned, curiously like the Generation of '37, often to the rock: preaching that the object of male existence was to be like a crystal: beautiful and soulless. "God is soulless?" speculated Father Avalanche. "Having created souls, He Himself has none? So that to be like God we must allow to be eroded the soul in ourselves. Seek mineral symmetry, for here is eternal life: the immortality of rock. Plausible. But apostasy."

The children were not, of course, having any. Knowing full well that if every girl became a sister there would be no more Maltese: and that rock, however fine as an object of contemplation, does no work: labours not and thus displeases God, who is favourably disposed towards human labour. So they stayed passive, letting him talk, hanging like shadows at his heels, keeping a watchful eye. Surveillance in various forms continued for three years. With an apparent abating of the Siege—begun perhaps the day of Fausto and Elena's walk—the stalking only intensified because there was more time for it.

Intensified too—beginning, one suspects, the same day—was a friction between Fausto and Elena—the same unceasing, wearying friction of the leaves in the park that afternoon. The smaller arguments were centred, unhappily, around you, Paola. As if the pair had both rediscovered a parental duty. With more time on their hands they belatedly took up providing for their child moral guidance, mother love, comfort in moments of fear. Both were inept at it and each time their energies inevitably turned away from the child and on one another. During such times the child would more often than not slip away quietly to trail the Bad Priest.

Until one evening Elena told the rest of her meeting with the Bad Priest. The argument itself isn't recorded in any detail; only:

> Our words became more and more agitated, higher in pitch, more bitter until finally she cried, "Oh the child. I should have done what he told me . . ." Then realizing what she'd said, silence. She moved away, I caught her.

319

"Told you." I shook her until she spoke. I would have killed her, I think.

"The Bad Priest," finally, "told me not to have the child. Told me he knew of a way. I would have. But I met Father Avalanche. By accident."

And as she had begun to pray in the park, had then apparently let the old habits reassert themselves. By accident.

I would never be telling you this had you been brought up under any illusion you were "wanted." But having been abandoned so early to a common underworld, questions of want or possession never occurred to you. So at least I assume; not, I hope, falsely.

The day after Elena's revelation the Luftwaffe came in thirteen times. Elena was killed early in the morning, the ambulance in which she was riding having apparently suffered a direct hit.

Word got to me at Ta Kali in the afternoon, during a lull. I don't remember the messenger's face. I do remember sliding the shovel into a pile of dirt and walking away. And then a blank space.

The next I knew I was in the street, in a part of the city I did not recognise. The all-clear had sounded so I must have walked through a raid. I stood at the top of a slope of debris. I heard cries: hostile shouting. Children. A hundred yards away they swarmed among the ruins, closing in on a broken structure I recognized as the cellar of a house. Curious, I lurched down the slope after them. For some reason, I felt like a spy. Circling the ruin I went up another small bank to the roof. There were holes: I could look through. The children inside were clustered round a figure in black. The Bad Priest. Wedged under a fallen beam. Face—what could be seen—impassive.

"Is he dead," one asked. Others were picking already at the black rags.

"Speak to us, Father," they called, mocking. "What is your sermon for today?"

"Funny hat," giggled a little girl. She reached out and tugged off the hat. A long coil of white hair came loose and fell into the plaster-dust. One beam of sunlight cut across the space and the dust now turned it white.

"It's a lady," said the girl.

"Ladies can't be priests," replied a boy scornfully. He

began to examine the hair. Soon he had pulled out an ivory comb and handed it to the little girl. She smiled. Other girls gathered round her to look at the prize. "It's not real hair," the boy announced. "See." He removed the long white wig from the priest's head.

"That's Jesus," cried a tall boy. Tattooed on the bare scalp was a two-colour Crucifixion. It was to be only the first of many surprises.

Two children had been busy at the victim's feet, unlacing the shoes. Shoes were a welcome windfall in Malta at this time.

"Please," the priest said suddenly.

"He's alive."

"*She's* alive, stupid."

"Please what, Father."

"*Sister*. May sisters dress up as priests, sister?"

"Please lift this beam," said the sister/priest.

"Look, look," came cries at the woman's feet. They held up one of the black shoes. It was high-topped and impossible to wear. The cavity of the shoe was the exact imprint of a woman's high-heeled slipper. I could now see one of the slippers, dull gold, protruding from under the black robes. Girls whispered excitedly about how pretty the slippers were. One began to undo the buckles.

"If you can't lift the beam," the woman said (with perhaps a hint of panic), "please get help."

"Ah." From the other end. Up came one of the slippers and a foot—an artificial foot—the two sliding out as a unit, lug-and-slot.

"She comes apart."

The woman did not seem to notice. Perhaps she could no longer feel. But when they brought the feet to her head to show her, I saw two tears grow and slip from the outside corners of her eyes. She remained quiet while the children removed her robes and the shirt; and the gold cufflinks in the shape of a claw, and the black trousers which fit close to her skin. One of the boys had stolen a Commando's bayonet. There were rust-spots. They had to use it twice to get the trousers off.

The nude body was surprisingly young. The skin healthy-looking. Somehow we'd all thought of the Bad Priest as an older person. At her navel was a star sapphire. The boy with the knife picked at the stone. It would not come

321

away. He dug in with the point of the bayonet, working for a few minutes before he was able to bring out the sapphire. Blood had begun to well in its place.

Other children crowded round her head. One pried her jaws apart while another removed a set of false teeth. She did not struggle: only closed her eyes and waited.

But she could not even keep them closed. For the children peeled back one eyelid to reveal a glass eye with the iris in the shape of a clock. This, too, they removed.

I wondered if the disassembly of the Bad Priest might not go on, and on, into evening. Surely her arms and breasts could be detached; the skin of her legs be peeled away to reveal some intricate understructure of silver openwork. Perhaps the trunk itself contained other wonders: intestines of parti-coloured silk, gay balloon-lungs, a rococo heart. But the sirens started up then. The children dispersed bearing away their new-found treasures, and the abdominal wound made by the bayonet was doing its work. I lay prone under a hostile sky looking down for moments more at what the children had left; suffering Christ foreshortened on the bare skull, one eye and one socket, staring up at me: a dark hole for the mouth, stumps at the bottoms of the legs. And the blood which had formed a black sash across the waist, flowing down both sides from the navel.

I went down into the cellar to kneel by her.

"Are you alive."

At the first bomb-bursts, she moaned.

"I will pray for you." Night was coming in.

She began to cry. Tearless, half-nasal; more a curious succession of drawn-out wails, originating far back in the mouth cavity. All through the raid she cried.

I gave her what I remembered of the sacrament of Extreme Unction. I could not hear her confession: her teeth were gone and she must have been past speech. But in those cries—so unlike human or even animal sound that they might have been only the wind blowing past any dead reed—I detected a sincere hatred for all her sins which must have been countless; a profound sorrow at having hurt God by sinning; a fear of losing Him which was worse than the fear of death. The interior darkness was lit by flares over Valletta, incendiary bombs in the Dockyard. Often both our voices were drowned in the explosions or the chattering of the ground artillery.

322

I did not hear only what I wanted to hear in the sounds that issued unceasing from the poor woman. I have been over it, Paola, and over it. I have since attacked myself more scathingly than any of your doubts could. You will say I had forgotten my understanding with God in administering a sacrament only a priest can give. That after losing Elena I'd "regressed" to the priesthood I would have joined had I not married her.

At the time I only knew that a dying human must be prepared. I had no oil to anoint her organs of sense—so mutilated now—and so used her own blood, dipping it from the navel as from a chalice. Her lips were cold. Though I saw and handled many corpses in the course of the siege, to this day I cannot live with that cold. Often, when I fall asleep at my desk, the blood supply to an arm is cut off. I wake and touch it and am no further from nightmare, for it is night's cold, object's cold, nothing human, nothing of me about it at all.

Now touching her lips my fingers recoiled and I returned from wherever I'd been. The all-clear sounded. She cried once or twice more and fell silent. I knelt by her and began to pray for myself. For her I'd done all I could. How long did I pray? No way of knowing.

But soon the cold of the wind—shared now with what had been a quick body—began to chill me. Kneeling grew uncomfortable. Only saints and lunatics can remain "devoted" for extended periods of time. I did feel for a pulse or heartbeat. None. I arose, limped about the cellar aimlessly, and finally emerged into Valletta without looking back.

I returned to Ta Kali, on foot. My shovel was still where I had left it.

Of Fausto III's return to life, little can be said. It happened. What inner resources were there to give it nourishment are still unknown to the present Fausto. This is a confession and in that return from the rock was nothing to confess. There are no records of Fausto III except for indecipherable entries.

And sketches of an azalea blossom, a carob tree.

There remained two unanswered questions. If he had truly broken his covenant with God in administering the sacrament why did he survive the raid?

And why did he not stop the children: or lift the beam?

323

o the first one can only suggest that he was
I, with no further need for God.

has caused his successor to write this con-
to Maijstral is guilty of murder: a sin of omis-
ill. He will answer to no tribunal but God. And
moment is far away.

May He be closer to you.

Valletta: 27 August 1956

Stencil let the last thin scribbled sheet flutter to bare
linoleum. Had his coincidence, the accident to shatter the
surface of this stagnant pool and send all the mosquitoes of
hope zinging away to the exterior night; had it happened?

"An Englishman; a mysterious being named Stencil."

Valletta. As if Paola's silence since—God, eight months.
Had she, by her refusal to tell him anything, been all this
time forcing him closer to the day when he'd have to admit
Valletta as a possibility? Why?

Stencil would have liked to go on believing the death and
V. had been separate for his father. This he still could choose
to do (couldn't he?), and continue on in calm weather.
He could go to Malta and possibly end it. He had stayed
off Malta. He was afraid of ending it; but, damn it all,
staying here would end it too. Funking out; finding V.; he
didn't know which he was most afraid of, V. or sleep.
Or whether they were two versions of the same thing.

Was there nothing for it but Valletta?

chapter twelve

In which things are not
so amusing

V

I

The party had begun late, with a core of only a dozen Sick. Evening was hot and not likely to get any cooler. They all sweated. The loft itself was part of an old warehouse and not a legal residence; buildings in this area of the city had been condemned years ago. Someday there would be cranes, dump trucks, payloaders, bulldozers to come and level the neighborhood; but in the meantime, nobody—city or land-lords—saw any objection in turning a minor profit.

There hung therefore about Raoul, Slab and Melvin's pad a climate of impermanence, as if the sand-sculptures, un-finished canvases, thousands of paperback books suspended in tiers of cement blocks and warped planks, even the great marble toilet stolen from a mansion in the east 70's (since replaced by a glass and aluminum apartment building) were all part of the set to an experimental play which its cabal of faceless angels could cause to be struck at any moment without having to give their reasons.

People would arrive, come the late hours. Raoul, Slab and Melvin's refrigerator was already half filled with a ruby con-struction of wine bottles; gallon of Vino Paisano slightly above center, left, off-balancing two 25-cent bottles of Gallo Grenache Rosé, and one of Chilean Riesling, lower right, and so on. The icebox door was left open so people could admire, could dig. Why not? Accidental art had great vogue that year.

Winsome wasn't there when the party began and didn't show up at all that night. Nor any night after that. He'd had another fight with Mafia in the afternoon, over playing tapes of McClintic Sphere's group in the parlor while she was trying to create in the bedroom.

"If you ever tried to create," she yelled, "instead of live off what other people create, you'd understand."

"Who creates," Winsome said. "Your editor, publisher? Without them, girl, you would be nowhere."

"Anywhere you are, old sweet, is nowhere." Winsome gave it up and left her to scream at Fang. He had to step over three sleeping bodies on the way out. Which one was Pig Bodine? They were all covered by blankets. Like the old pea-and-nutshell dodge. Did it make any difference? She'd have company.

He headed downtown and after a while had wandered by the V-Note. Inside were stacked tables and the bartender watching a ball game on TV. Two fat Siamese kittens played on the piano, one outside chasing up and down the keyboard, one inside, clawing at the strings. It didn't sound like much.

"Roon."

"Man, I need a change of luck, no racial slur intended."

"Get a divorce." McClintic appeared in a foul mood. "Roon, let's go to Lenox. I can't last the weekend. Don't tell me any woman trouble. I got enough for both of us."

"Why not. Out to the boondocks. Green hills. Well people."

"Come on. There is a little girl I have to get out of this town before she flips from the heat. Or whatever it is."

It took them a while. They drank beer till sunset and then headed up to Winsome's where they swapped the Triumph for a black Buick. "It looks like a staff car for the Mafia," said McClintic. "Whoops."

"Ha, ha," replied Winsome. They continued uptown along the nighttime Hudson, veering finally right into Harlem. And there began working their way in to Matilda Winthrop's, bar by bar.

Not long after they were arguing like undergraduates over who was the most juiced, gathering hostile stares which had less to do with color than with an inherent quality of con-

servatism which neighborhood bars possess and bars where
how much you can drink is a test of manhood do not.

They arrived at Matilda's well past midnight. The old
lady, hearing Winsome's rebel accent, talked only to Mc-
Clintic. Ruby came downstairs and McClintic introduced them.

Crash, shrieks, deep-chested laughter from topside. Matilda ran out of the room screaming.

"Sylvia, Ruby's friend, is busy tonight," McClintic said.

Winsome was charming. "You young folks just take it
easy," he said. "Old Uncle Roony will drive you anywhere you want, won't look in the rear view mirror, won't
be anything but the kindly old chauffeur he is."

Which cheered McClintic up. There being a certain
strained politeness in the way Ruby held his arm. Winsome
could see how McClintic was daft to get out in the country.

More noise from upstairs, louder this time. "McClintic,"
Matilda yelled.

"I must go play bouncer," he told Roony. "Back in five."

Which left only Roony and Ruby in the parlor.

"I know a girl I can take along," said he, "I suppose,
her name is Rachel Owlglass, who lives on 112th."

Ruby fiddled with the catches on her overnight bag. "Your
wife wouldn't like that too much. Why don't McClintic and
I just go up in the Triumph. You shouldn't go to that
trouble."

"My wife," angry all at once, "is a fucking Fascist, I think
you should know that."

"But if you brought along—"

"All I want to do is go now somewhere out of town, away
from New York, away to where things you expect to happen do happen. Didn't they ever use to? You're still
young enough. It's still that way for kids, isn't it?"

"I'm not that young," she whispered. "Please Roony, be
easy."

"Girl, if it isn't Lenox it will be someplace. Further east,
Walden Pond, ha ha. No. No, that's public beach now where
slobs from Boston who'd be at Revere Beach except for too
many other slobs like themselves already there crowding
them out, these slobs sit on the rocks around Walden Pond
belching, drinking beer they've cleverly smuggled in past the
guards, checking the young stuff, hating their wives, their
evil-smelling kids who urinate in the water on the sly . . .
Where? Where in Massachusetts. Where in the country."

me."

nly to see how bad Lenox is."

baby," she sang soft, absent: "Have you heard,/ Did you know/There ain't no dope in Lenox."

"How did you do it."

"Burnt cork," she told him. "Like a minstrel show."

"No," he started across the room away from her. "You didn't use anything. Didn't have to. No makeup. Mafia, you know, thinks you're German. I thought you were Puerto Rican before Rachel told me. Is that what you are, something we can look at and see whatever we want? Protective coloration?"

"I have read books," said Paola, "and listen, Roony, nobody knows what a Maltese is. The Maltese think they're a pure race and the Europeans think they're Semitic, Hamitic, crossbred with North Africans, Turks and God knows what all. But for McClintic, for anybody else round here I am a Negro girl named Ruby—" he snorted—"and don't tell them, him, please man."

"I'll never tell, Paola." Then McClintic was back. "You two wait till I find a friend."

"Rach," beamed McClintic. "Good show." Paola looked upset.

"I think us four, out in the country—" his words were for Paola, he was drunk, he was messing it up—"we could make it, it would be a fresh thing, clean, a beginning."

"Maybe I should drive," McClintic said. It would give him something to concentrate on till things got easier, out of the city. And Roony looked drunk. More than that, maybe.

"You drive," Winsome agreed, weary. God, let her be there. All the way down to 112th (and McClintic gunned it) he wondered what he'd do if she wasn't there.

She wasn't there. The door was open, noteless. She usually left some word. She usually locked doors. Winsome went inside. Two or three lights were on. Nobody was there.

Only her slip tossed awry on the bed. He picked it up, black and slippery. Slippery slip, he thought and kissed it by the left breast. The phone rang. He let it ring. Finally:

"Where is Esther?" She sounded out of breath.

"You wear nice lingerie," Winsome said.

"Thank you. She hasn't come in?"

"Beware of girls with black underwear."

"Roony, not now. She has really gone and got her ass in a sling. Could you look and see if there's a note."

"Come with me to Lenox, Massachusetts."

Patient sigh.

"There's no note. No nothing."

"Would you look anyway. I'm in the subway."

Come with me to Lenox [Roony sang],
It's August in Nueva York Ciudad;
You've told so many good men nix;
Please don't put me down with a dark, "See you Dad" . . .

Refrain [beguine tempo]:

Come out where the wind is cool and the streets are colonial
    lanes.
Though the ghosts of a million Puritans pace in our phony
    old brains,
I still get an erection when I hear the reed section of the
    Boston Pops,
Come and leave this Bohemia, life's really dreamy away
    from the JDs and cops.
Lenox is grand, are you digging me, Rachel,
Broadening a's by the width of an h'll
Be something we've never tried . . .
Up in the country of Alden and Walden,
Country to grow sentimental and bald in
With you by my side,
How can it go wrong?
Hey, Rachel [snap, snap—on one and three]: you coming
    along . . .

She'd hung up halfway through. Winsome sat by the phone, holding the slip. Just sat.

II

Esther had indeed got her ass in a sling. Her emotional ass, anyway. Rachel had found her earlier that afternoon crying down in the laundry room.

"Wha," Rachel said. Esther only bawled louder.

"Girl," gently. "Tell Rach."

"Get off my back." So they chased each other around the washers and centrifuges and in and out of the flapping sheets, rag rugs and brassieres of the drying room.

"Look, I want to help you, is all." Esther had got tangled in a sheet. Rachel stood helpless in the dark laundry room, yelling at her. Washing machine in the next room ran all at once amok; a cascade of soapy water came funneling through the doorway, bearing down on them. Rachel with a foul expression kicked off her Capezios, hiked her skirt up and headed for a mop.

She hadn't been swabbing five minutes when Pig Bodine stuck his head around the door. "You are doing that wrong. Where did you ever learn to handle a swab."

"Here," she said. "You want a swab? I got your swab." She ran at him, spinning the mop. Pig retreated.

"What's wrong with Esther. I wrapped into her on the way down." Rachel wished she knew. By the time she'd dried the floor and run up the fire escape and in the window to their apartment Esther was, of course, gone.

"Slab," Rachel figured. Slab was on the phone after half a ring.

"I'll let you know if she shows."

"But Slab—"

"Wha," said Slab.

Wha. Oh, well. She hung up.

Pig was sitting in the transom. Automatically she turned on the radio for him. Little Willie John came on singing Fever.

"What's wrong with Esther," she said, for something to say.

"I asked you that," said Pig. "I bet she's knocked up."

"You would." Rachel had a headache. She headed for the bathroom to meditate.

Fever was touching them all.

Pig, evil-minded Pig, inferred right for once. Esther showed up at Slab's looking like any traditional mill hand, seamstress or shop girl Done Wrong: dull hair, puffy face, looking heavier already in the breasts and abdomen.

Five minutes and she had Slab railing. He stood before Cheese Danish #56, a cockeyed specimen covering an entire wall, dwarfing him in his shadowy clothes as he waved arms, tossed his forelock.

"Don't tell me. Schoenmaker won't give you a dime. I know that already. You want to put a small bet on this? I say it'll come out with a big hook nose."

That shut her up. Kindly Slab was of the shock-treatment school.

"Look," he grabbed a pencil. "It is no time of year to go

to Cuba. Hotter than Nueva York, no doubt, off season. But for all his Fascist tendencies, Battista has one golden virtue: abortion he maintains is legal. Which means you get an M.D. who knows what he's about, not some fumbling amateur. It's clean, it's safe, it's legal, above all, it's cheap."

"It's murder."

"You've turned R. C. Good show. For some reason it always becomes fashionable during a Decadence."

"You know what I am," she whispered.

"We'll leave that go. I wish I did." He stopped a minute because he felt himself going sentimental. He finagled around with figures on a scrap of vellum. "For 300," he said, "we can get you there and back. Including meals if you feel like eating."

"We."

"The Whole Sick Crew. You can do it inside a week, down to Havana and back. You'll be yo-yo champion."

"No."

So they talked metaphysics while the afternoon waned. Neither felt he was defending or trying to prove anything important. It was like playing one-up at a party, or Botticelli. They quoted to each other from Liguorian tracts, Galen, Aristotle, David Riesman, T. S. Eliot.

"How can you say there's a soul there. How can you tell when the soul enters the flesh. Or whether you even have a soul?"

"It's murdering your own child, is what it is."

"Child, schmild. A complex protein molecule, is all."

"I guess on the rare occasions you bathe you wouldn't mind using Nazi soap made from one of those six million Jews."

"All right—" he was mad—"show me the difference."

After that it ceased being logical and phony and became emotional and phony. They were like a drunk with dry heaves: having brought up and expelled all manner of old words which had always, somehow, sat wrong, they then proceeded to fill the loft with futile yelling, trying to heave up their own living tissue, organs which had no business anywhere but where they were.

As the sun went down she broke out of a point-by-point condemnation of Slab's moral code to assault Cheese Danish #56, charging at it with windmilling nails.

"Go ahead," Slab said, "it will help the texture." He was

on the phone. "Winsome's not home." He jittered the receiver, dialed information. "Where can I get 300 bills," he said. "No, the banks are closed. . . . I am against usury." He quoted to the phone operator from Ezra Pound's Cantos.

"How come," he wondered, "all you phone operators talk through your nose." Laughter. "Fine, we'll try it sometime." Esther yelped, having just broken a fingernail. Slab hung up. "It fights back," he said. "Baby, we need 300. Somebody must have it." He decided to call all his friends who had savings accounts. A minute later this list was exhausted and he was no closer to financing Esther's trip south. Esther was tramping around looking for a bandage. She finally had to settle for a wad of toilet paper and a rubber band.

"I'll think of something," he said. "Stick by Slab, babe. Who is a humanitarian." They both knew she would. To whom else? She was the sticking sort.

So Slab sat thinking and Esther waved the paper ball at the end of her finger to a private tune, maybe an old love song. Though neither would admit it they also waited for Raoul and Melvin and the Crew to arrive for the party; while all the time the colors in the wall-size painting were shifting, reflecting new wavelengths to compensate for the wasting sun.

Rachel, out looking for Esther, didn't arrive at the party till late. Coming up the seven flights to the loft she passed at each landing, like frontier guards, nuzzling couples, hopelessly drunken boys, brooding types who read out of and scrawled cryptic notes in paper books stolen from Raoul, Slab and Melvin's library; all of whom informed her how she had missed all the fun. What this fun was she found out before she'd fairly wedged her way into the kitchen where all the Good People were.

Melvin was holding forth on his guitar, in an improvised folk song, about how humanitarian a cove his roommate Slab was; crediting him with being (a) a neo-Wobbly and reincarnation of Joe Hill, (b) the world's leading pacifist, (c) a rebel with taproots in the American Tradition, (d) in militant opposition to Fascism, private capital, the Republican administration and Westbrook Pegler.

While Melvin sang Raoul provided Rachel with a kind of marginal gloss on the sources of Melvin's present adulation.

It seemed earlier Slab had waited till the room was jammed to capacity, then mounted the marble toilet and called for silence.

"Esther here is pregnant," he announced, "and needs 300 bucks to go to Cuba and have an abortion." Cheering, warm-hearted, grinning ear to ear, juiced, the Whole Sick Crew dug deep into their pockets and the wellsprings of a common humanity to come up with loose change, worn bills, and a few subway tokens, all of which Slab collected in an old pith helmet with Greek letters on it, left over from somebody's fraternity weekend years ago.

Surprisingly it came to $295 and some change. Slab with a flourish produced a ten he'd borrowed fifteen minutes before his speech from Fergus Mixolydian, who had just received a Ford Foundation grant and was having more than wistful thoughts about Buenos Aires, from which there is no extradition.

If Esther objected verbally to the proceedings, no record of it exists, there being too much noise in the room, for one thing. After the collection Slab handed her the pith helmet and she was helped up on the toilet, where she made a brief but moving acceptance speech. Amid the ensuing applause Slab roared "Off to Idlewild," or something, and they were both lifted bodily and carried out of the loft and down the stairs. The only gauche note to the evening was struck by one of their bearers, an undergraduate and recent arrival on the Sick Scene, who suggested they could save all the trouble of a trip to Cuba and use the money for another party if they induced a miscarriage by dropping Esther down the stairwell. He was quickly silenced.

"Dear God," said Rachel. She had never seen so many red faces, the linoleum wet with so much spilled alcohol, vomit, wine.

"I need a car," she told Raoul.

"Wheels," Raoul screamed. "Four wheels for Rach." But the Crew's generosity had been exhausted. Nobody listened. Maybe from her lack of enthusiasm they'd deduced she was about to roar off to Idlewild and try to stop Esther. They weren't having any.

It was only at that point, early in the morning, that Rachel thought of Profane. He would be off shift now. Dear Profane. An adjective which hung unvoiced in the party's shivaree, hung in her most secret cortex to bloom—she helpless against it—only far enough to surround her 4′ 10″ with an envelope of peace. Knowing all the time Profane too was wheelless.

"So," she said. All it was was no wheels on Profane, the boy a born pedestrian. Under his own power which was also power over her. Then what was she doing: declaring herself a dependent? As if here were the heart's authentic income-tax form, tortuous enough, mucked up with enough polysyllabic words to take her all of twenty-two years to figure out. At least that long: for surely it was complicated, being a duty you could rightfully avoid with none of fancy's Feds ever to worry about tracking you down on it, but. That "but." If you did take the trouble, even any first step, it meant stacking income against output; and who knew what embarrassments, exposés of self that might drag you into?

Strange the places these things can happen in. Stranger that they ever do happen. She headed for the phone. It was in use. But she could wait.

III

Profane arrived at Winsome's to find Mafia wearing only the inflatable brassiere and playing a game of her own invention called Musical Blankets with three beaux who were new to Profane. The record being stopped at random was Hank Snow singing It Don't Hurt Any More. Profane went to the icebox and got beer; was thinking of calling Paola when the phone rang.

"Idlewild?" he said. "Maybe we can borrow Roony's car. The Buick. Only I can't drive."

"I can," Rachel said, "stand by."

Profane with a rueful look back at the buoyant Mafia and her friends, moseyed down the fire stairs to the garage. No Buick. Only McClintic Sphere's Triumph, locked, keys gone. Profane sat on the Triumph's hood, surrounded by his inanimate buddies from Detroit. Rachel was there in fifteen minutes.

"No car," he said, "we're screwed."

"Oh dear." She told him why they had to get to Idlewild. "I don't see why you're so excited. She wants to get her uterus scraped, let her."

What Rachel should have said then was "You callous son of a bitch," slugged him and sought transportation elsewhere.

334

But having come to him with a certain fondness—perhaps only satisfied with this new, maybe temporary, definition of peace—she tried to reason.

"I don't know if it's murder or not," she said. "Nor care. How close is close? I'm against it because of what it does to the abortionee. Ask the girl who's had one."

For a second Profane thought she was talking about herself. There came this impulse to get away. She was acting weird tonight.

"Because Esther is weak, Esther is a victim. She will come out of the ether hating men, believing they're all liars and still knowing she'll take what she can get whether he's careful or not. She'll get to where she can take on anybody: neighborhood racketeers, college boys, arty types, daft and delinquent, because it's something she can't get along without."

"Don't, Rachel. Esther, wha. Are you in love with her, you sweat it so much."

"I am."

"Close your mouth," she told him. "What is your name, Pig Bodine? You know what I'm saying. How many times have you told me about under the street, and on the street, and in the subway."

"Them," chopfallen. "Sure, but."

"I mean I love Esther like you love the dispossessed, the wayward. What else can I feel? For somebody who guilt's such an aphrodisiac for. Up to now she's been selective. But when she's felt it, feeling always this own breed of half-assed love for Slab, and the pig Schoenmaker. Going for these exhausted, ulcerous, lonely rejects."

"Slab and you were—" kicking a tire—"horizontal once."

"OK." Quiet. "It is myself, what I could slide back into, maybe a girl-victim underneath this red mop—" she had one little hand pushed up from under into her hair and was slowly lifting the thick mane of it, while Profane watched and began to grow erect—"part of me that I can see in her. Just as it is Profane the Depression Kid, that lump that wasn't aborted, that became an awareness on the floor of one old Hooverville shack in '32, it's him you see in every no-name drifter, mooch, square's tenant, him you love."

Who was she talking about? Profane'd had all night to rehearse but never expected this. He hung his head and kicked inanimate tires, knowing they'd take revenge when he was looking for it least. He was afraid now to say anything.

She held her hair up, eyes gone all rainy; came off the fender she'd been leaning back on and stood spraddle-legged, hips poised in a bow, his direction.

"Slab and I rotated our 90° because we were incompatible. The Crew lost all glamour for me, I grew up, I don't know what happened. But he will never leave it, though his eyes are open and he sees as much as I do. I didn't want to be sucked in, was all. But then you . . ."

Thus the maverick daughter of Stuyvesant Owlglass perched like any pinup beauty. Ready at the slightest pressure surge in the blood lines, endocrine imbalance, quickening of nerves at the lovebreeding zones to pivot into some covenant with Profane the schlemihl. Her breasts seemed to expand toward him, but he stood fast; unwilling to retreat from pleasure, unwilling to convict himself of love for bums, himself, her, unwilling to see her proved inanimate as the rest.

Why that last? Only a general desire to find somebody for once on the right or real side of the TV screen? What made her hold any promise of being any more human?

You ask too many questions, he told himself. Stop asking, take. Give. Whatever she wants to call it. Whether the bulge is in your skivvies or your brain do something. She doesn't know, you don't know.

Only that the nipples which came to make a warm diamond with his navel and the padded cusp of his ribcage, the girl's ass one hand moved to automatic, the recently fluffed hairs tickling his nostrils had nothing, for once, at all to do with this black garage or the car-shadows which did accidentally include the two of them.

Rachel now only wanted to hold him, feel the top of his beer belly flattening her bra-less breasts, already evolving schemes to make him lose weight, exercise more.

McClintic came in and found them like that, holding together until now and again one or the other lost balance and made tiny staggers to compensate. Underground garage for a dancing-floor. So they dance all over the cities.

Rachel grasped Everything outside as Paola climbed from the Buick. The two girls confronted, smiled, passed; their histories would go different from here on, said the shy twin looks they swapped. All McClintic said was, "Roony is asleep on your bed. Somebody ought to look after him."

"Profane, Profane," she laughed while the Buic to her touch, "dear; we've got so many of them to of now."

IV

Winsome came awake from a dream of defenestration, wondering why he hadn't thought of it before. From Rachel's bedroom window it was seven stories to a courtyard used for mean purposes only: drunk's evacuation, a dump for old beer cans and mop-dust, the pleasures of nighttime cats. How his cadaver could glorify that!

He moved to the window, opened, straddled, listened. Girls being tailed somewhere along Broadway, giggling. Musician out of work practicing trombone. Rock 'n' roll across the way:

Little teen-age goddess
Don't tell me no,
Into the park tonight
We're going to go,
Let me be
Your teen-age Romeo. . . .

Dedicated to the duck's-ass heads and bursting straight skirts of the Street. That gave cops ulcers and the Youth Board gainful employment.

Why not go down there? Heat rises. On the areaway's jagged floor there'd be no August.

"Listen friends," Winsome said, "there is a word for all our crew and it is sick. Some of us cannot keep our flies zipped, others remain faithful to one mate till menopause or the Grand Climacteric steps in. But randy or monogamous, on one side of the night or the other, on or off the Street, there is no one of us you can point to and call well.

"Fergus Mixolydian the Irish Armenian Jew takes money from a Foundation named after a man who spent millions trying to prove thirteen rabbis rule the world. Fergus sees nothing wrong there.

"Esther Harvitz pays to get the body she was born with altered and then falls deeply in love with the man who mutilated her. Esther sees nothing wrong either.

"Raoul the television writer can produce drama devious enough to slip by any sponsor's roadblock and still tell the staring fans what's wrong with them and what they're tching. But he's happy with westerns and detective stories.

"Slab the painter, whose eyes are open, has technical skill and if you will 'soul.' But is committed to cheese Danishes.

"Melvin the folk-singer has no talent. Ironically he does more social commenting than the rest of the Crew put together. He accomplishes nothing.

"Mafia Winsome is smart enough to create a world but too stupid not to live in it. Finding the real world never jibing with her fancy she spends all kinds of energy—sexual, emotional—trying to make it conform, never succeeding.

"And on it goes. Anybody who continues to live in a subculture so demonstrably sick has no right to call himself well. The only well thing to do is what I am going to do now, namely, jump out this window."

So speaking Winsome straightened his tie and prepared to defenestrate.

"I say," said Pig Bodine, who'd been out in the kitchen listening. "Don't you know life is the most precious possession you have?"

"I have heard that one before," said Winsome, and jumped. He had forgotten about the fire escape three feet below the window. By the time he'd picked himself up and swung a leg over, Pig was out the window. Pig grabbed Winsome's belt just as he went over the second time.

"Now look," said Pig. A drunk, urinating below in the courtyard, glanced up and started yelling for everybody to come watch the suicide. Lights came on, windows opened and pretty soon Pig and Winsome had an audience. Winsome hung jackknifed, looking placidly down at the drunk and calling him obscene names.

"How about letting go," Winsome said after a while. "Aren't your arms getting tired?"

Pig admitted they were. "Did I ever tell you," Pig said, "the story about the coke sacker, the cork soaker and the sock tucker."

Winsome started to laugh and with a mighty heave, Pig brought him back over the low rail of the fire escape.

"No fair," said Winsome who had knocked the wind out of Pig. He tore away and went running down the steps. Pig, sounding like an espresso machine with faulty valves, joined the pursuit a second later. He caught Winsome two stories down, standing on the rail holding his nose. This

338

time he slung Winsome over a shoulder and started grimly up the fire escape. Winsome slithered away and ran down another floor. "Ah, good," he said. "Still four stories. High enough."

The rock 'n' roll enthusiast across the court had turned his radio up. Elvis Presley, singing Don't Be Cruel, gave them background music. Pig could hear cop sirens arriving out in front.

So they chased each other up, down and around the fire escapes. After a while they got dizzy and started to giggle. The audience cheered them on. So little happens in New York. Police came charging into the areaway with nets, spotlights, ladders.

Finally Pig had chased Winsome down to the first landing, half a story above the ground. By this time the cops had spread out a net.

"You still want to jump," Pig said.

"Yes," said Winsome.

"Go ahead," said Pig.

Winsome went down in a swan dive, trying to land on his head. The net, of course, was there. He bounced once and lay all flabby while they wrapped him in a strait jacket and carted him off to Bellevue.

Pig, suddenly realizing that he had been AWOL for eight months today, and that "cop" may be defined as "civilian Shore Patrolman," turned and raced fleetly up the fire escape for Rachel's window, leaving the solid citizens to turn their lights off and go back to Elvis Presley. Once inside, he reckoned he could put on an old dress of Esther's and a babushka and talk in falsetto, should the cops decide to come up and inquire. They were so stupid they'd never know the difference.

V

At Idlewild was a fat three-year-old who waited to bounce over the tarmac to a waiting plane—Miami, Havana, San Juan—looking blasé and heavy-lidded over the dandruffed shoulder of her father's black suit at the claque of relatives assembled to see her off. "Cucarachita," they cried, "adios, adios."

For such wee hours the airport was mobbed. After having

Esther paged, Rachel went weaving in and out of the crowd in a random search-pattern for her strayed roommate. At last she joined Profane at the rail.

"Some guardian angels we are."

"I checked on Pan American and all of them," Profane said. "The big ones. They were full up days ago. This Anglo Airlines here is the only one going out this morning."

Loudspeaker announced the flight, DC-3 waited across the strip, dilapidated and hardly gleaming under the lights. The gate opened, waiting passengers began to move. The Puerto Rican baby's friends had come armed with maracas, claves, timbales. They all moved in like a bodyguard to escort her out to the plane. A few cops tried to break it up. Somebody started to sing, pretty soon everybody was singing.

"There she is," Rachel yelled. Esther came scooting around from behind a row of lockers, with Slab running interference. Eyes and mouth bawling, overnight case leaking a trail of cologne which would dry quickly on the pavement, she charged in among the Puerto Ricans. Rachel, running after her, sidestepped a cop only to run head on into Slab.

"Oof," said Slab.

"What the hell's the idea, lout." He had hold of one arm.

"Let her go," Slab said. "She wants to."

"You've slammed her around," yelled Rachel. "You trying to total her? It didn't work with me so you had to pick on somebody as weak as you are. Why couldn't you confine your mistakes to paint and canvas."

One way or another the Whole Sick Crew was giving the cops a busy night. Whistles started blowing. The area between the rail and the DC-3 was swelling into a small-scale riot.

Why not? It was August and cops do not like Puerto Ricans. The multimetronome clatter from Cucarachita's rhythm section turned angry like a swarm of locusts turning for the approach on some rich field. Slab began shouting unkind reminiscences of the days he and Rachel had been horizontal.

Profane meanwhile was trying to keep from being clobbered. He'd lost Esther who was naturally using the riot for a screen. Somebody started blinking all the lights in that part of Idlewild which made things even worse.

He finally broke clear of a small knot of wellwishers and spotted Esther running across the airstrip. She'd lost one shoe. He was about to go after her when a body fell across his path. He tripped, went down, opened his eyes to a pair of girl's legs he knew.

"Benito." The sad pout, sexy as ever.

"God, what else."

She was going back to San Juan. Of the months between the gang bang and now she'd say nothing.

"Fina, Fina, don't go." Like photographs in your wallet, what good is an old love—however ill-defined—down in San Juan?

"Angel and Geronimo are here." She looked around vaguely.

"They want me to go," she told him, on her way again. He followed, haranguing. He'd forgotten about Esther. Cucarachita and father came running past. Profane and Fina passed Esther's shoe, lying on its side with a broken heel.

Finally Fina turned, dry-eyed. "Remember the night in the bathtub?" spat, spun, dashed off for the plane.

"Your ass," he said, "they would have got you sooner or later." But stood there anyway, still as any object.

"I did it," he said after a while. "It was me." Schlemihls being, as he believed, passive, he could not remember ever having admitted anything like this. "Oh, man." Plus letting Esther get away, plus having Rachel now for a dependent, plus whatever would happen with Paola. For a boy not getting any he had more woman problems than anybody he knew.

He started back for Rachel. The riot was breaking up. Behind him propellers spun; the plane taxied, slewed, became airborne, was gone. He didn't turn to watch it.

VI

Patrolman Joneš and Officer Ten Eyck, disdaining the elevator, marched in perfect unison up two flights of palatial stairway, down the hall toward Winsome's apartment. A few tabloid reporters who had taken the elevator intercepted them halfway there. Noise from Winsome's apartment could be heard down on Riverside Drive.

"Never know what Bellevue is going to turn up," said Joneš.

He and his sidekick were faithful viewers of the TV program Dragnet. They'd cultivated deadpan expressions, unsyncopated speech rhythms, monotone voices. One was tall and skinny, the other was short and fat. They walked in step.

"Talked to a doctor there," said Ten Eyck. "Young fella named Gottschalk. Winsome had a lot to say."

"We'll see, Al."

Before the door, Joneš and Ten Eyck waited politely for the one cameraman in the group to check his flash attachment. A girl was heard to shriek happily inside.

"Oboy, oboy," said a reporter.

The cops knocked. "Come in, come in," called many juiced voices.

"It's the police, ma'am."

"I hate fuzz," somebody snarled. Ten Eyck kicked in the door, which had been open. Bodies inside fell back to provide the cameraman a line-of-sight to Mafia, Charisma, Fu and friends, playing Musical Blankets. Zap, went the camera.

"Too bad," the photographer said, "we can't print that one." Ten Eyck shouldered his way over to Mafia.

"All right, ma'am."

"Would you like to play," hysterical.

The cop smiled, tolerantly. "We've talked to your husband."

"We'd better go," said the other cop.

"Guess Al is right, ma'am." Flash attachment lit up the room from time to time, like a spell of heat lightning.

Ten Eyck flapped a warrant. "All you folks are under arrest," he said. To Joneš: "Call the Lieutenant, Steve."

"What charge," people started yelling.

Ten Eyck's timing was good. He waited a few heartbeats. "Disturbing the peace will do," he said.

Maybe the only peace undisturbed that night was Mc-Clintic's and Paola's. The little Triumph forged along up the Hudson, their own wind was cool, taking away whatever of Nueva York had clogged ears, nostrils, mouths.

She talked to him straight and McClintic kept cool. While she told him about who she was, about Stencil and Fausto—even a homesick travelogue of Malta—there came to Mc-Clintic something it was time he got around to seeing: that the only way clear of the cool/crazy flipflop was obviously slow, frustrating and hard work. Love with your mouth shut, help without breaking your ass or publicizing it: keep cool,

342

but care. He might have known, if he'd used any common sense. It didn't come as a revelation, only something he'd as soon not've admitted.

"Sure," he said later, as they headed into the Berkshires. "Paola, did you know I have been blowing a silly line all this time. Mister Flab the original, is me. Lazy and taking for granted some wonder drug someplace to cure that town, to cure me. Now there isn't and never will be. Nobody is going to step down from heaven and square away Roony and his woman, or Alabama, or South Africa or us and Russia. There's no magic words. Not even I love you is magic enough. Can you see Eisenhower telling Malenkov or Khrushchev that? Ho-ho."

"Keep cool but care," he said. Somebody had run over a skunk a ways back. The smell had followed them for miles. "If my mother was alive I would have her make a sampler with that on it."

"You know, don't you," she began, "that I have to—"

"Go back home, sure. But the week's not over yet. Be easy, girl."

"I can't. Can I ever?"

"We'll stay away from musicians," was all he said. Did he know of anything she could be, ever?

"Flop, flip," he sang to the trees of Massachusetts. "Once I was hip . . ."

chapter thirteen

*In which the yo-yo string
is revealed as
a state of
mind*

V

I

The passage to Malta took place in late September, over an
Atlantic whose sky never showed a sun. The ship was Susanna Squaducci, which had figured once before in Profane's
long-interrupted guardianship of Paola. He came back to the
ship that morning in the fog knowing that Fortune's yo-yo
had also returned to some reference-point, not unwilling, not
anticipating, not anything; merely prepared to float, acquire
a set and drift wherever Fortune willed. If Fortune could
will.

A few of the Crew had come to give Profane, Paola and
Stencil bon voyage; those who weren't in jail, out of the
country or in the hospital. Rachel had stayed away. It was a
weekday, she had a job. Profane supposed so.

He was here by accident. While weeks back, off on the
fringes of the field-of-two Rachel and Profane had set up,
Stencil roamed the city exerting "pull," seeing about tickets,
passports, visas, inoculations for Paola and him, Profane
felt that at last he'd come to dead center in Nueva York;
had found his Girl, his vocation as watchman against the
night and straight man for SHROUD, his home in a three-
girl apartment with one gone to Cuba, one about to go to
Malta, and one, his own, remaining.

He'd forgotten about the inanimate world and any law of retribution. Forgotten that the field-of-two, the twin envelope of peace had come to birth only a few minutes after he'd been kicking tires, which for a schlemihl is pure wising-off.

It didn't take Them long. Only a few nights later Profane sacked in at four, figuring to get in a good eight hours of Z's before he had to get up and go to work. When his eyes finally did come open he knew from the quality of light in the room and the state of his bladder that he'd overslept. Rachel's electric clock whined merrily beside him, hands pointing to 1:30. Rachel was off somewhere. He turned on the light, saw that the alarm was set for midnight, the button on the back switched to ON. Malfunction. "You little bastard"; he picked the clock up and heaved it across the room. On hitting the bathroom door the alarm went off, a loud and arrogant BZZZ.

Well, he got his feet in the wrong shoes, cut himself shaving, token he had wouldn't fit into the turnstile, subway took off about ten seconds ahead of him. When he arrived downtown it was not much south of three and Anthroresearch Associates was in an uproar. Bergomask met him at the door, livid. "Guess what," the boss yelled. It seemed an all-night, routine test was on. Around 1:15, one of the larger heaps of electronic gear had run amok; half the circuitry fused, alarm bells went off, the sprinkler system and a couple of CO_2 cylinders kicked in, all of which the attendant technician had slept through peacefully.

"Technicians," Bergomask snorted, "are not paid to wake up. This is why we have night watchmen." SHROUD sat over against the wall, hooting quietly.

Soon as it had all come through to Profane he shrugged. "It's stupid, but it's something I say all the time. A bad habit. So. Anyway. I'm sorry." Getting no response, turned and shuffled off. They'd send him severance pay, he reckoned, in the mail. Unless they intended to make him cover the cost of the damaged gear. SHROUD called after him:

Bon voyage.

"What is that supposed to mean."

We'll see.

"So long, old buddy."

Keep cool. Keep cool but care. It's a watchword, Profane, for your side of the morning. There, I've told you too much as it is.

"I'll bet under that cynical butyrate hide is a slob. A sentimentalist."

There's nothing under here. Who are we kidding?

The last words he ever had with SHROUD. Back at 112th Street he woke up Rachel.

"Back to pounding the pavements, lad." She was trying to be cheerful. He gave her that much but was mad with himself for going flabby enough to forget his schlemihl birthright. She being all he had to take it out on,

"Fine for you," he said. "You've been solvent all your life."

"Solvent enough to keep us going till me and Space/Time Employment find something good for you. Really good."

Fina had tried to shove him along the same path. Had it been her that night at Idlewild? Or only another SHROUD, another guilty conscience bugging him over a baión rhythm?

"Maybe I don't want to get a job. Maybe I'd rather be a bum. Remember? I'm the one that loves bums."

She edged over to make room for him, having now those inevitable second thoughts. "I don't want to talk about loving anything," she told the wall. "It's always dangerous. You have to con each other a little, Profane. Why don't we go to sleep."

No: he couldn't let it go. "Let me warn you, is all. That I don't love anything, not even you. Whenever I say that —and I will—it will be a lie. Even what I'm saying now is half a play for sympathy."

She made believe she was snoring.

"All right, you know I am a schlemihl. You talk two-way. Rachel O., are you that stupid? All a schlemihl can do is take. From the pigeons in the park, from a girl picked up on any street, bad and good, a schlemihl like me takes and gives nothing back."

"Can't there be a time for that later," she asked meekly. "Can't it wait on tears sometime, a lovers' crisis. Not now, dear Profane. Only sleep."

"No," he leaned over her, "babe I am not showing you anything of me, anything hidden. I can say what I've said and be safe because it's no secret, it's there for anybody to see. It's got nothing to do with me, all schlemihls are like that."

She turned to him, moving her legs apart: "Hush . . ."

"Can't you see," growing excited though it was now the last thing he wanted, "that whenever I, any schlemihl lets a

346

girl think there is a past, or a secret dream that can't be talked about, why Rachel that's a con job. Is all it is." As if SHROUD were prompting him: "There's nothing inside. Only the scungille shell. Dear girl—" saying it as phony as he knew how—"schlemihls know this and use it, because they know most girls need mystery, something romantic there. Because a girl knows her man would be only a bore if she found out everything there was to know. I know you're thinking now: the poor boy, why does he put himself down like that. And I'm using this love that you still, poor stupe, think is two-way to come like this between your legs, like this, and take, never thinking how you feel, caring about whether you come only so I can think of myself as good enough to make you come . . ." So he talked, all the way through, till both had done and he rolled on his back to feel traditionally sad.

"You have to grow up," she finally said. "That's all: my own unlucky boy, didn't you ever think maybe ours is an act too? We're older than you, we lived inside you once: the fifth rib, closest to the heart. We learned all about it then. After that it had to become our game to nourish a heart you all believe is hollow though we know different. Now you all live inside us, for nine months, and when ever you decide to come back after that."

He was snoring, for real.

"Dear, how pompous I'm getting. Good night . . ." And she fell asleep to have cheerful, brightly colored, explicit dreams about sexual intercourse.

Next day, rolling out of bed to get dressed, she continued. "I'll see what we've got. Stand by. I'll call you." Which of course kept him from going back to sleep. He stumbled around the apartment for a while swearing at things. "Subway," he said, like the hunchback of Notre Dame yelling sanctuary. After a day of yo-yoing he came up to the street at nightfall, sat in a neighborhood bar and got juiced. Rachel met him at home (home?) smiling and playing the game.

"How would you like to be a salesman. Electric shavers for French poodles."

"Nothing inanimate," he managed to say. "Slave girls, maybe." She followed him to the bedroom and took off his shoes when he passed out on the bed. Even tucked him in.

Next day, hung over, he yo-yoed on the Staten Island

ferry, watching juveniles-in-love neck, grab, miss, connect.

Day after that he got up before her and journeyed down to the Fulton Fish Market to watch the early-morning activity. Pig Bodine tagged along. "I got a fish," said Pig, "I would like to give Paola, hyeugh, hyeugh." Which Profane resented. They moseyed by Wall Street and watched the boards of a few brokers. They walked uptown as far as Central Park. This took them till mid-afternoon. They dug a traffic light for an hour. They went into a bar and watched a soap opera on TV.

They came rollicking in late. Rachel was gone.

Out came Paola though, sleepy-eyed, benightgowned. Pig began to shuffle furrows in the rug. "Oh," seeing Pig. "You can put coffee on," she yawned. "I'm going back to bed."

"Right," Pig muttered, "right you are." And glaring at the small of her back, followed zombielike to the bedroom and closed the door behind them. Soon Profane, making coffee, heard screams.

"Wha." He looked into the bedroom. Pig had managed to get atop Paola and seemed linked to her pillow by a long string of drool which glittered in the fluorescent light from the kitchen.

"Help?" Profane puzzled. "Rape?"

"Get this pig off of me," Paola yelled.

"Pig, hey. Get off."

"I want to get laid," protested Pig.

"Off," said Profane.

"Up thine," snarled Pig, "with turpentine."

"Nope." So saying, Profane grabbed the big collar on Pig's jumper and pulled.

"You are strangling me, hey," said Pig after a while.

"True," said Profane. "But I saved your life once, remember."

Which was the case. Back in the Scaffold days, Pig had long announced, to anybody in ship's company who'd listen, his refusal ever to don a contraceptive unless it was a French tickler. This device being your common rubber ornamented in bas-relief (often with a figurehead on the end) to stimulate female nerve ends not stimulated by the usual means. From Kingston Jamaica last cruise Pig had brought back 50 Jumbo the Elephant and 50 Mickey Mouse French ticklers. The night finally came when Pig ran out, his last having been expended in the memorable battle with his one-time colleague Knoop, LtJG, a week before on the Scaffold's bridge.

Pig and his friend Hiroshima the electronics technician had a going thing on the beach with radio tubes. ET's on a destroyer like the Scaffold keep their own inventory of electronic components. Hiroshima could therefore finagle, which as soon as he'd found a discreet outlet in downtown Norfolk he proceeded to do. Every so often Hiroshima would heist a few tubes and Pig would stow them in an AWOL bag and run them ashore.

One night Knoop had OOD watch. All an OOD usually does is stand on the quarterdeck and salute people going on and off. He is also a sort of monitor, making sure that everybody leaves with their neckerchief straight, fly zipped and wearing their own uniform; also that nobody is swiping anything from the ship or bringing anything on board they shouldn't. Lately old Knoop had been getting hawkeyed. Howie Surd the drunken yeoman, who had two grooves worn bare in the hair of his leg from adhesive-taping pints of various booze under one bellbottom by way of providing the crew with something tastier than torpedo juice, had almost made it the two steps from quarterdeck to ship's office when Knoop like a Siamese boxer fetched him an agile kick in the calf. And there stood Howie with Schenley Reserve and blood running over his best liberty shoes. Knoop of course crowed in triumph. He'd also caught Profane trying to take over 5 pounds of hamburger swiped from the galley. Profane escaped legal action by splitting the loot with Knoop who was having marital difficulties and had somehow come up with the notion that 2½ pounds of hamburger might serve as a peace-offering.

So only a few nights after that Pig was understandably nervous, trying simultaneously to salute, produce ID and liberty cards, and keep one eye on Knoop and another on the tube-laden AWOL bag.

"Request permission to go ashore, sir, hey," said Pig.

"Permission granted. What is in the AWOL bag."

"In the AWOL bag."

"That one, yes."

"What is in it." Pig pondered.

"Change of skivvies," suggested Knoop, "douche kit, magazine to read, dirty laundry for Mom to wash—"

"Now that you mention it, Mr. Knoop—"

"Radio tubes, also."

"Wha."

"Open the bag."

"I would like, I think," said Pig, "maybe to just dash in ship's office there for a minute to read the Naval Regulations, sir, and see if maybe what you are ordering me to do might not be a little, how would you say it, illegal. . . ."

Grinning horribly, Knoop made a sudden leap in the air and came down square on the AWOL bag, which went crunch, tinkle in a sickening way.

"Aha," said Knoop.

Pig came up for captain's mast a week later and got restricted. Hiroshima was never mentioned. Normally larceny of this sort is rewarded with a court-martial, the brig, a dishonorable discharge, all of which strengthen morale. It seemed however that the Scaffold's old man, one C. Osric Lych, commander, had gathered round him an inner circle of enlisted men, all of whom you could call habitual offenders. This troupe included Baby Face Falange, the machinist mate striker, who periodically would put on a babushka and let the members of the A gang line up in the compartment to pinch his cheek; Lazar the deck ape who wrote foul sayings on the Confederate monument downtown and was usually brought back off liberty in a strait jacket; Teledu his friend who one time avoiding a work detail had gone to hide in a refrigerator, decided he liked it and lived there for two weeks on raw eggs and frozen hamburger until the master-at-arms and a posse dragged him away; and Groomsman the quartermaster, whose second home was sick bay, being as how he was constantly infested by a breed of crabs which unhappily only thrived on the chief corpsman's super-formula crab-killer.

The captain, having seen this element of the crew at every mast, came to look on them fondly as His Boys. He pulled strings and indulged in all manner of extra-legal procedure to keep them in the Navy and on board the Scaffold. Pig, being a charter member of the Captain's (so to speak) Own Men, got off with no liberty for a month. Time soon hung heavy. So it was of course toward the crab-ridden Groomsman that Pig gravitated.

Groomsman was the agent in Pig's near-fatal involvement with the airline stewardesses Hanky and Panky, who along

350

with half a dozen more of their kind, shared a large pad out near Virginia Beach. The night after Pig's restriction ended, Groomsman took him out there after stopping by a state liquor store for booze.

Well, it was Panky Pig went for, Hanky being Groomsman's girl. Pig after all had a code. He never did find out their real names, though did it make any difference? They were virtually interchangeable; both unnatural blondes, both between twenty-one and twenty-seven, between 5' 2" and 5' 7" (weights in proportion), clear complexions, no eyeglasses or contact lenses. They read the same magazines, shared the same toothpaste, soap and deodorant; swapped civilian clothes when off duty. One night Pig did in fact end up in bed with Hanky. Next morning he pretended to've been drunk out of his mind. Groomsman was apologized to easily enough, having it turned out hit the sack with Panky under the same misapprehension.

Things cruised along all idyllic; spring and summer brought hordes to the beach and Shore Patrolman (now and again) to chez Hanky Panky to quell riots and stay for coffee. It came out under incessant questioning by Groomsman that there was something Panky "did" during the act of love which turned Pig, as Pig put it, on. What this was nobody ever found out. Pig, not normally reticent in these matters, now acted like a mystic after a vision; unable, maybe unwilling, to put in words this ineffable or supernal talent of Panky's. Whatever it was it drew Pig out to Virginia Beach all his liberty and a few duty nights. One duty night, Scaffold bound, he wandered down to C&O compartment after the movie to find the quartermaster swinging from the overhead whooping like an ape. "After-shave lotion," Groomsman yelled down to Pig, "is the only thing that gets to the little bastards." Pig winced. "They get drunk on it and fall asleep." He descended to tell Pig about his crabs, having lately developed the theory that they held barn dances among the forest of his pubic hair on Saturday nights.

"Enough," said Pig. "What about our Club." This was the Prisoners-at-Large and Restricted Men's Club, formed recently for the purpose of hatching plots against Knoop, who was also Groomsman's division officer.

"One thing," Groomsman said, "that Knoop cannot stand is water. He can't swim, he owns three umbrellas."

They discussed ways of exposing Knoop to water, short of

throwing him over the side. A few hours after lights out Lazar and Teledu joined the plot after a blackjack game (payday stakes) in the mess hall. Both had been losers. As were all the Captain's Men. They had a fifth of Old Stag conned from Howie Surd.

Saturday Knoop had the duty. At sundown the Navy has this tradition called Evening Colors, which around the Convoy Escort Piers in Norfolk is impressive. Looking at it from any destroyer's bridge you would see all motion—afoot and vehicular—stop; everyone come to attention, turn and salute the American flags going down on dozens of fantails.

Knoop had the first dog watch, 4 to 6 P.M., as OOD. Groomsman was to pass the word "Now on deck attention to colors." The destroyer tender U.S.S. Mammoth Cave, alongside which the Scaffold and its division were moored, had recently acquired a trumpet player from shore duty in Washington, D. C., so tonight there was even a bugle to play retreat.

Meanwhile Pig was lying on top of the pilot house, a pile of curious objects beside him. Teledu was down at the water tap aft of the pilot house, filling up rubbers—among them Pig's French ticklers—and passing them to Lazar who was putting them next to Pig.

"Now on deck," said Groomsman. From over the way came the first note of Taps. A few tin cans down the line, jumping the gun, started lowering their own flags. Out on the bridge came Knoop to supervise. "Attention to colors." Splat, went a rubber, two inches from Knoop's foot. "Oh, oh," said Pig. "Get him while he's still saluting," Lazar whispered, frantic. The second rubber landed on Knoop's hat, intact. From out of the corner of one eye Pig saw that great nightly immobility, dyed orange by the sun, grip the entire C.E. Piers area. The bugle knew what he was doing, and played Taps clear and strong.

The third rubber missed completely, going over the side. Pig had the shakes. "I can't hit him," he kept saying. Lazar, exasperated, had picked up two and fled. "Traitor," Pig snarled and threw one after him. "Aha," said Lazar from down among the 3-inch mounts, and lobbed one back at Pig. Bugle blew a riff. "Carry on," said Groomsman. Knoop brought his right hand smartly to his side and with his left removed the water-filled rubber from his hat. He started calmly up the ladder on the pilot house after Pig. The first person he saw was Teledu, crouching by the water tap, still filling rubbers. Down on the torpedo deck Pig and Lazar were having a water fight, chasing each other among the gray tubes now highlighted vermilion by the sunset. Arming himself with the stockpile Pig had abandoned, Knoop joined the struggle.

They ended up drenched, exhausted and swearing mutual fealty. Groomsman even named Knoop to honorary membership in the PAL and Restricted Men's Club.

The reconciliation came as a surprise to Pig, who'd expected to get the book thrown at him. He felt let down and saw no other way to improve his outlook but to get laid. Unfortunately he was now afflicted by contraceptivelessness. He tried to borrow a few. It was that horrible and cheerless time just before payday when everybody is out of everything: money, cigarettes, soap, and especially rubbers, much less French ticklers. "Gawd," moaned Pig, "what do I do?" To his rescue came Hiroshima, ET3.

"Didn't anybody ever tell you," said this worthy, "about the biological effects of r-f energy?"

"Wha," said Pig.

"Stand in front of the radar antenna," said Hiroshima, "while it is radiating, and what it will do is, it will make you temporarily sterile."

"Indeed," said Pig. Indeed. Hiroshima showed him a book which said so.

"I am scared of heights?" said Pig.

"It is the only way out," Hiroshima told him. "What you do is, you climb up the mast and I will go light off the old SPA 4 Able."

Already tottering, Pig made his way topside and prepared to climb the mast. Howie Surd had come along and solicitously offered a shot of something murky in an unlabeled bottle. On the way up, Pig passed Profane swinging like a bird in a boatswain's chair hooked to the spar. Profane was painting the mast. "Dum de dum, de dum," sang Profane. "Good afternoon, Pig." My old buddy, thought Pig. His are probably the last words I will ever hear.

Hiroshima appeared below. "Yo, Pig," he yelled. Pig made the mistake of looking down. Hiroshima gave him the thumb-and-index-finger-in-a-circle sign. Pig felt like vomiting.

"What are you doing in this neck of the woods," Profane said.

"Oh, just out for a stroll," said Pig. "I see you are painting the mast, there."

"Right," said Profane, "deck gray." They examined at length the subject of the Scaffold's color scheme, as well as the long-standing jurisdictional dispute which had Profane, a deck ape, painting the mast when it was really the radar gang's responsibility.

Hiroshima and Surd, impatient, started yelling. "Well," said Pig, "good-bye old buddy."

"Be careful walking around on that platform," Profane said. "I robbed some more hamburger out of the galley and stowed it up there. I figure on sneaking it off over the 01 deck." Pig, nodding, creaked slowly up the ladder.

At the top he latched his nose over the platform like Kilroy and cased the situation. There was Profane's hamburger all right. Pig started to climb on the platform when his ultra-sensitive nose detected something. He lifted it off the deck.

"How remarkable," said Pig out loud, "it smells like hamburger frying." He looked a little closer at Profane's cache. "Guess what," he said, and started backing quickly down the ladder. When he got level with Profane he yelled over: "Buddy, you just saved my life. You got a piece of line?"

"What are you going to do," said Profane, tossing him a piece of line: "hang yourself?"

Pig made a noose on one end and headed up the ladder again. After a couple-three tries he managed to snare the hamburger, pulled it over, dragged off his white hat and dumped the hamburger in it, being careful all the time to stay as much as he could out of any line-of-sight with the radar antenna. Down at Profane again he showed him the hamburger.

"Amazing," Profane said. "How did you do it?"

"Someday," Pig said, "I will have to tell you about the biological effects of r-f energy." And so saying inverted the white hat in the direction of Hiroshima and Howie Surd, showering them both with cooked hamburger.

"Anything you want," Pig said then, "just ask, buddy. I have a code and I don't forget."

"OK," Profane said a few years later, standing by Paola's bed in an apartment on Nueva York's 112th Street and twisting Pig's collar a little, "I'm collecting that one now."

"A code is a code," Pig choked. Off he got, and fled sadly.

When he was gone, Paola reached out for Pro [...] him down and in against her.

"No," said Profane, "I'm always saying no, b[...]

"You have been gone so long. So long since ou[...]

"Who says I'm back."

"Rachel?" She held his head, nothing but maternal.

"There is her, yes, but . . ."

She waited.

"Anyway I say it is nasty. But I'm not looking for any dependents, is all."

"You have them," she whispered.

No, he thought, she's out of her head. Not me. Not a schlemihl.

"Then why did you make Pig go away?"

He thought about that one for a few weeks.

II

All things gathered to farewell.

One afternoon, close to the time Profane was to embark for Malta, he happened to be down around Houston Street, his old neighborhood. It was cooler, fall: dark came earlier and little kids out playing stoop ball were about to call it a day. For no special reason, Profane decided to look in on his parents.

Around two corners and up the stairs, past apartments of Basilisco the cop whose wife left garbage in the hallway, past Miss Angevine who was in business in a small way, past the Venusbergs whose fat daughter had always tried to lure young Profane into the bathroom, past Maxixe the drunk and Flake the sculptor and his girl, and old Min De Costa who kept orphan mice and was a practicing witch; past his past though who knew it? Not Profane.

Standing before his old door he knocked, though knowing from the sound of it (like we can tell from the buzz in the phone receiver whether or not she's home) that inside was empty. So soon, of course, he tried the knob; having come this far. They never locked doors: on the other side of this one he wandered automatic into the kitchen to check the table. A ham, a turkey, a roast beef. Fruit: grapes, oranges, a pineapple, plums. Plate of knishes, bowl of almonds and Brazil nuts. String of garlic tossed like a rich lady's necklace across fresh bunches of fennel, rosemary, tarragon. A brace baccale, dead eyes directed at a huge provolone, a pale yellow parmigian and God knew how many fish-cousins, gefülte, in an ice bucket.

No his mother wasn't telepathic, she wasn't expecting Profane. Wasn't expecting her husband Gino, rain, poverty, anything. Only that she had this compulsion to feed. Profane was sure that the world would be worse off without mothers like that in it.

He stayed in the kitchen an hour, while night came along, wandering through this field of inanimate food, making bits and pieces of it animate, his own. Soon it was dark and the baked outsides of meats, the skins of fruits only highlighted all shiny by light from the apartment across the courtyard. Rain started falling. He left.

They would know he'd been by.

Profane, whose nights were now free, decided he could afford to frequent the Rusty Spoon and the Forked Yew without serious compromise.

"Ben," Rachel yelled, "this is putting me down." Since the night he was fired from Anthroresearch Associates, it seemed he'd been trying every way he knew to put her down. "Why won't you let me get you a job? It is September, college kids are fleeing the city, the labor market was never better."

"Call it a vacation," said Profane. But how do you swing a vacation from two dependents?

Before anyone knew it there was Profane, full-fledged Crew member. Under the tutelage of Charisma and Fu, he learned how to use proper nouns; how not to get too drunk, keep a straight face, use marijuana.

"Rachel," running in a week later, "I smoked pot."

"Get out of here."

"Wha."

"You are turning into a phony," said Rachel.

"You're not interested in what it's like?"

"I have smoked pot. It is a stupid business, like masturbation. If you get kicks that way, fine. But not around me."

"It was only once. Only for the experience."

"Once I will say it, is all: that Crew does not live, it experiences. It does not create, it talks about people who do. Varèse, Ionesco, de Kooning, Wittgenstein, I could puke.

356

It satirizes itself and doesn't mean it. Time magazine takes it seriously and does mean it."

"It's fun."

"And you are becoming less of a man."

He was still high, too high to argue. Off he rollicked, in train with Charisma and Fu.

Rachel locked herself in the bathroom with a portable radio and bawled for a while. Somebody was singing the old standard about how you always hurt the one you love, the one you shouldn't hurt at all. Indeed, thought Rachel, but does Benny even love me? I love him. I think. There's no reason why I should. She kept crying.

So near one in the morning she was at the Spoon with her hair hanging straight, dressed in black, no makeup except for mascara in sad raccoon-rings round her eyes, looking like all those other women and girls: camp followers.

"Benny," she said, "I'm sorry." And later:

"You don't have to try not to hurt me. Only come home, with me, to bed. . . ." And much later, at her apartment, facing the wall, "You don't even have to be a man. Only pretend to love me."

None of which made Profane feel any better. But it didn't stop him going to the Spoon.

One night at the Forked Yew, he and Stencil got juiced. "Stencil is leaving the country," Stencil said. He apparently wanted to talk.

"I wish I was leaving the country."

Young Stencil, old Machiavel. Soon he had Profane talking about his women problems.

"I don't know what Paola wants. You know her better. Do you know what she wants?"

An embarrassing question for Stencil. He dodged:

"Aren't you two—how shall one say."

"No," Profane said. "No, no."

But Stencil was there again, next evening. "Truth of it is," he admitted, "Stencil can't handle her. But you can."

"Don't talk," said Profane. "Drink."

Hours later they were both out of their heads. "You wouldn't consider coming along with them," Stencil wondered.

"I have been there once. Why should I want to go back."

"But didn't Valletta—somehow—get to you? Make you feel anything?"

"I went down to the Gut and got drunk like everybody else. I was too drunk to feel anything."

Which eased Stencil. He was scared to death of Valletta. He'd feel better with Profane, anybody else, along on this jaunt (a) to take care of Paola, (b) so he wouldn't be alone.

Shame, said his conscience. Old Sidney went in there with the cards stacked against him. Alone.

And look what he got, thought Stencil, a little wry, a little shaky.

On the offensive: "Where do you belong, Profane?"

"Wherever I am."

"Deracinated. Which of them is not. Which of this Crew couldn't pick up tomorrow and go off to Malta, go off to the moon. Ask them why and they'll answer why not."

"I could not care less about Valletta." But hadn't there been something after all about the bombed-out buildings, buff-colored rubble, excitement of Kingsway? What had Paola called the island: a cradle of life.

"I have always wanted to be buried at sea," said Profane.

Had Stencil seen the coupling in that associative train he would have gathered heart of grace, surely. But Paola and he had never spoken of Profane. Who, after all, was Profane?

Until now. They decided to rollick off to a party on Jefferson Street.

Next day was Saturday. Early morning found Stencil rushing around to his contacts, informing them all of a third tentative passage.

The third passage, meanwhile, was horribly hung over. His Girl was having more than second thoughts.

"Why do you go to the Spoon, Benny."

"Why not?"

She edged up on one elbow. "That's the first time you've said that."

"You break your cherry on something every day."

Without thinking: "What about love? When are you going to end your virgin status there, Ben?"

In reply Profane fell out of bed, crawled to the bathroom and hung over the toilet, thinking about barfing. Rachel clasped hands in front of one breast, like a concert soprano. "My man." Profane decided instead to make noises at himself in the mirror.

She came up behind him, hair all down and [in] the night, and set her cheek against his back, a[s] on the Newport News ferry last winter. Profan[e] his teeth.

"Get off my back," he said.

Still holding on: "So. Only smoked pot once and already he's hooked. Is that your monkey talking?"

"It's me talking. Off."

She moved away. "How off is off, Ben." Things were quiet then. Soft, penitent, "If I am hooked on anything it's you, Rachel O." Watching her shifty in the mirror.

"On women," she said, "on what you think love is: take, take. Not on me."

He started brushing his teeth fiercely. In the mirror as she watched there bloomed a great flower of leprous-colored foam, out of his mouth and down both sides of his chin.

"You want to go," she yelled, "go then."

He said something but around the toothbrush and through the foam neither could understand the words.

"You are scared of love and all that means is somebody else," she said. "As long as you don't have to give anything, be held to anything, sure: you can talk about love. Anything you have to talk about isn't real. It's only a way of putting yourself up. And anybody who tries to get through to you —me—down."

Profane made gurgling noises in the sink: drinking out of the tap, flushing out his mouth. "Look," coming up for air, "what did I tell you? Didn't I warn you?"

"People can change. Couldn't you make the effort?" She was damned if she'd cry.

"I don't change. Schlemihls don't change."

"Oh that makes me sick. Can't you stop feeling sorry for yourself? You've taken your own flabby, clumsy soul and amplified it into a Universal Principle."

"What about you and that MG."

"What does that have to do with any—" _humans in a_ _·_

"You know what I always thought? That you were an accessory. That you, flesh, you'd fall apart sooner than the car. That the car would go on, in a junkyard even it would look like it always had, and it would have to be a thousand years before that thing could rust so you wouldn't recognize it. But old Rachel, she'd be long gone. A part, a cheesy part, like a radio, heater, windshield-wiper blade."

359

She looked upset. He pushed it.

"I only started to think about being a schlemihl, about a world of things that had to be watched out for, after I saw you alone with the MG. I didn't even stop to think it might be perverted, what I was watching. All I was was scared."

"Showing how much you know about girls."

He started scratching his head, sending wide flakes of dandruff showering about the bathroom.

"Slab was my first. None of those tweed jockstraps at Schlozhauer's got any more than bare hand. Don't you know, poor Ben, that a young girl has to take out her virginity on something, a pet parakeet, a car—though most of the time on herself."

"No," he said, his hair all in clumps, fingernails gone yellow with dead scalp. "There's more. Don't try to get out of it that way."

"You're not a schlemihl. You're nobody special. Everybody is some kind of a schlemihl. Only come out of that scungille shell and you'd see."

He stood, pear-shaped, bags under the eyes, all forlorn. "What do you want? How much are you out to get? Isn't this—" he waved at her an inanimate schmuck—"enough?"

"It can't be. Not for me, nor Paola."

"Where does she—"

"Anywhere you go there'll always be a woman for Benny. Let it be a comfort. Always a hole to let yourself come in without fear of losing any of that precious schlemihlhood." She stomped around the room. "All right. We're all hookers. Our price is fixed and single for everything: straight, French, round-the-world. Can you pay it, honey? Bare brain, bare heart?"

"If you think me and Paola—"

"You and anybody. Until that thing doesn't work any more. A whole line of them, some better than me, but all just as stupid. We can all be conned because we've all got one of these," touching her crotch, "and when it talks we listen."

She was on the bed. "Come on baby," she said, too close to crying, "this one's for free. For love. Climb on. Good stuff, no charge."

Absurdly he thought of Hiroshima the electronics technician, reciting a mnemonic guide for resistor color-coding.

Bad boys rape our young girls behind victory garden

360

walls (or "but Violet gives willingly"). Good stuff, no charge.

Could any of their resistances be measured in ohms? Someday, please God, there would be an all-electronic woman. Maybe her name would be Violet. Any problems with her, you could look it up in the maintenance manual. Module concept: fingers' weight, heart's temperature, mouth's size out of tolerance? Remove and replace, was all.

He climbed on anyway.

That night at the Spoon, things were louder than usual, despite Mafia's being in stir and a few of the Crew out on bail and their best behavior. Saturday night toward the end of the dog days; after all.

Near closing time, Stencil approached Profane, who'd been drinking all night but for some reason was still sober.

"Stencil heard you and Rachel are having difficulties."

"Don't start."

"Paola told him."

"Rachel told her. Fine. Buy me a beer."

"Paola loves you, Profane."

"You think that impresses me? What is your act, ace?" Young Stencil sighed. Along came a bartender's rinkydink, yelling "Time, gentlemen, please." Anything properly English like that went over well with the Whole Sick Crew.

"Time for what," Stencil mused. "More words, more beer. Another party, another girl. In short, no time for anything of importance. Profane. Stencil has a problem. A woman."

"Indeed," said Profane. "That's unusual. I never heard of anything like that before."

"Come. Walk."

"I can't help you."

"Be an ear. It's all he needs."

Outside, walking up Hudson Street: "Stencil doesn't want to go to Malta. He is quite simply afraid. Since 1945, you see, he's been on a private manhunt. Or womanhunt, no one is sure."

"Why?" said Profane.

"Why not?" said Stencil. "His giving you any clear reason would mean he'd already found her. Why does one decide to pick up one girl in a bar over another. If one knew why, she would never be a problem. Why do wars start: if

361

one knew why there would be eternal peace. So in this search the motive is part of the quarry.

"Stencil's father mentioned her in his journals: this was near the turn of the century. Stencil became curious in 1945. Was it boredom, was it that old Sidney had never said anything of use to his son; or was it something buried in the son that needed a mystery, any sense of pursuit to keep active a borderline metabolism? Perhaps he feeds on mystery.

"But he stayed off Malta. He had pieces of thread: clues. Young Stencil has been in all her cities, chased her down till faulty memories or vanished buildings defeated him. All her cities but Valletta. His father died in Valletta. He tried to tell himself meeting V. and dying were separate and unconnected for Sidney.

"Not so. Because: all along the first thread, from a young, crude Mata Hari act in Egypt—as always, in no one's employ but her own—while Fashoda tossed sparks in search of a fuse; until 1913 when she knew she'd done all she could and so took time out for love—all that while, something monstrous had been building. Not the War, nor the socialist tide which brought us Soviet Russia. Those were symptoms, that's all."

They'd turned into 14th Street and were walking east. More bums came roving by the closer they got to Third Avenue. Some nights 14th Street can be the widest street with the tallest wind in the earth.

"Not even as if she were any cause, any agent. She was only there. But being there was enough, even as a symptom. Of course Stencil could have chosen the War, or Russia to investigate. But he doesn't have that much time.

"He is a hunter."

"You are expecting to find this chick in Malta?" Profane said. "Or how your father died? Or something? Wha."

"How does Stencil know," Stencil yelled. "How does he know what he'll do once he finds her. Does he want to find her? They're all stupid questions. He must go to Malta. Preferably with somebody along. You."

"That again."

"He is afraid. Because if she went there to wait out one war, a war she'd not started but whose etiology was also her own, a war which came least as a surprise to her, then perhaps too she was there during the first. There to meet

362

old Sidney at its end. Paris for love, Malta for war. If so then now, of all times . . ."

"You think there'll be a war."

"Perhaps. You've been reading the newspapers." Profane's newspaper reading was in fact confined to glancing at the front page of the New York Times. If there was no banner headline on that paper then the world was in good enough shape. "The Middle East, cradle of civilization, may yet be its grave.

"If he must go to Malta, it can't be only with Paola. He can't trust her. He needs someone to—occupy her, to serve as buffer zone, if you will."

"That could be anybody. You said the Crew was at home anywhere. Why not Raoul, Slab, Melvin."

"It's you she loves. Why not you."

"Why not."

"You are not of the Crew, Profane. You have stayed out of that machine. All August."

"No. No, there was Rachel."

"You stayed out of it." And a sly smile. Profane looked away.

So they went up Third Avenue, drowned in the Street's great wind: all flapping and Irish pennants. Stencil yarned. Told Profane of a whorehouse in Nice with mirrors on the ceiling where he thought, once, he'd found his V. Told of his mystical experience before a plaster death-cast of Chopin's hand in the Celda Museo in Mallorca.

"There was no difference," he caroled, causing two strolling bums to laugh along with him: "that was all. Chopin had a plaster hand!" Profane shrugged. The bums tagged along.

"She stole an airplane: an old Spad, the kind young Godolphin crashed in. God, what a flight it must have been: from Le Havre over the Bay of Biscay to somewhere in the back country of Spain. The officer on duty only remembered a fierce—what did he call her—'hussar,' who came rushing by in a red field-cape, glaring out of a glass eye in the shape of a clock: 'as if I'd been fixed by the evil eye of time itself.'

"Disguise is one of her attributes. In Mallorca she spent at least a year as an old fisherman who, evenings, would smoke dried seaweed in a pipe and tell the children stories of gun-running in the Red Sea."

363

V — "a remarkably scattered concept"

"Rimbaud," suggested one of the bums.

"Did she know Rimbaud as a child? Drift up-country at age three or four through that district and its trees festooned gray and scarlet with crucified English corpses? Act as lucky mascot to the Mahdists? Live in Cairo and take Sir Alastair Wren for a lover when she came of age?

"Who knows. Stencil would rather depend on the imperfect vision of humans for his history. Somehow government reports, bar graphs, mass movements are too treacherous."

"Stencil," Profane announced, "you are juiced."

True. Autumn, coming on, was cold enough to've sobered Profane. But Stencil appeared drunk on something else.

V. in Spain, V. on Crete: V. crippled in Corfu, a partisan in Asia Minor. Giving tango lessons in Rotterdam she had commanded the rain to stop; it had. Dressed in tights adorned with two Chinese dragons she handed swords, balloons and colored handkerchiefs to Ugo Medichevole, a minor magician, for one lustless summer in the Roman Campagna. And, learning quickly, found time to perform a certain magic of her own; for one morning Medichevole was found out in a field, discussing the shadows of clouds with a sheep. His hair had become white, his mental age roughly five. V. had fled.

It went on like this, all the way up into the 70's, this progress-of-four; Stencil caught up in a compulsive yarning, the others listening with interest. It wasn't that Third Avenue was any kind of drunk's confessional. Did Stencil like his father suffer some private leeriness about Valletta—foresee some submersion, against his will, in a history too old for him, or at least of a different order from what he'd known? Probably not; only that he was on the verge of a major farewell. If it hadn't been Profane and the two bums it would have been somebody: cop, barkeep, girl. Stencil that way had left pieces of himself—and V.—all over the western world.

V. by this time was a remarkably scattered concept.

"Stencil's going to Malta like a nervous groom to matrimony. It is a marriage of convenience, arranged by Fortune, father and mother to everyone. Perhaps Fortune even cares about the success of these things: wants one to look after it in its old age." Which struck Profane as outright foolish. Somehow they had wandered over by Park Avenue. The two bums, sensing unfamiliar territory, veered away toward the west and the Park. Toward what assignation? Stencil said: "Should one bring a peace-offering?"

"Wha. Box of candy, flowers, ha, ha."

"Stencil knows just the thing," said Stencil. They were before Eigenvalue's office building. Intention or accident?

"Stay here in the street," Stencil said. "He won't be but a minute." And vanished into the lobby of the building. Simultaneously a prowl car appeared a few blocks uptown, turned and headed downtown on Park Avenue. Profane started walking. Car passed him and didn't stop. Profane got to the corner and turned west. By the time he'd walked all around the block, Stencil was at a top floor window, yelling down.

"Come on up. You have to help."

"I have to— You are out of your head."

Impatient: "Come up. Before the police get back."

Profane stood outside for a minute, counting floors. Nine. Shrugged, went inside the lobby and took the self-service elevator up.

"Can you pick a lock," Stencil asked. Profane laughed.

"Fine. You will have to go in a window, then."

Stencil rummaged in the broom closet and came up with a length of line.

"Me," said Profane. They started up to the roof.

"This is important." Stencil was pleading. "Suppose you were enemies with someone. But had to see him, her. Wouldn't you try to make it as painless as you could?"

They reached a point on the roof directly above Eigenvalue's office.

Profane looked down into the street. "You," with exaggerated gestures, "are going to put me, over that wall, with no fire escape there, to open, that window, right?" Stencil nodded. So. Back to the boatswain's chair for Profane. Though this time no Pig to save, no good will to cash in on. There'd be no reward from Stencil because there's no honor among second- (or ninth-) story men. Because Stencil was more a bum than he.

They looped the line round Profane's middle. He being so shapeless, it was difficult to locate any center of gravity. Stencil gave the line a few turns round a TV antenna. Profane climbed over the edge and they began to lower away.

"How is it," Stencil said after a while.

"Except for those three cops down there, who are looking at me sort of fishy—"

The line jerked.

"Ha, ha," said Profane. "Made you look." Not that his mood tonight was suicidal. But with the inanimate line, antenna, building and street nine floors below, what common sense could he have?

The center of gravity calculation, it turned out, was way off. As Profane inched down toward Eigenvalue's window, his body's attitude slowly tilted from nearly vertical to face down and parallel with the street. Hanging thus in the air, it occurred to him to practice an Australian crawl.

"Dear God," muttered Stencil. He tugged at the line, impatient. Soon Profane, a dim figure looking like a quadruply-amputated octopus, stopped flailing around. Then he hung still in the air, pondering.

"Hey," he called after a while.

Stencil said what.

"Pull me back up. Hurry." Wheezing, feeling his middle age acutely, Stencil began hauling in line. It took him ten minutes. Profane appeared and hung his nose over the edge of the roof.

"What's wrong."

"You forgot to tell me what it was I was supposed to do when I got in the window." Stencil only looked at him. "Oh. Oh you mean I open the door for you—"

"—and you lock it when you go out," they recited together.

Profane flipped a salute. "Carry on." Stencil began lowering again. Down at the window, Profane called up:

"Stencil, hey. The window won't open."

Stencil took a few half-hitches round the antenna.

"Break it," he gritted. All at once another police car, sirens screaming, lights flashing round and round, came tearing down Park. Stencil ducked behind the roof's low wall. The car kept going. Stencil waited till it was way downtown, out of earshot. And a minute or so more. Then arose cautiously and looked after Profane.

Profane was horizontal again. He'd covered his head with his suede jacket and showed no signs of moving.

"What are you doing," said Stencil.

"Hiding," said Profane. "How about a little torque." Stencil turned the rope: Profane's head slowly began to rotate away from the building. When he came around to where he was facing straight out, like a gargoyle, Profane kicked in the window, a crash horrible and deafening in that night.

"Now the other way."

He got the window open, climbed inside and unlocked for Stencil. Wasting no time, Stencil proceeded through a train of rooms to the museum, forced open the case, slipped that set of false teeth wrought from all precious metals into a coat pocket. From another room he heard more glass breaking.

"What the hell."

Profane looked around. "One pane broken is crude," he explained, "because that looks like a burglary. So I am breaking a few more, is all, so it won't be too suspicious."

Back on the street, scot-free, they followed the bums' way into Central Park. It was two in the morning.

In the wilds of that skinny rectangle they found a rock near a stream. Stencil sat down and produced the teeth.

"The booty," he announced.

"It's yours. What do I need with more teeth." Especially these, more dead than the half-alive hardware in his mouth now.

"Decent of you, Profane. Helping Stencil like that."

"Yeah," Profane agreed.

Part of a moon was out. The teeth, lying on the sloping rock, beamed at their reflection in the water.

All manner of life moved in the dying shrubbery around them.

"Is your name Neil?" inquired a male voice.

"Yes."

"I saw your note. In the men's room of the Port Authority terminal, third stall in the . . ."

Oho, thought Profane. That had cop written all over it.

"With the picture of your sexual organ. Actual size."

"There is one thing," said Neil, "that I like better than having homosexual intercourse. And that is knocking the shit out of a wise cop."

There was then a soft clobbering sound followed by the plainclothesman's crash into the underbrush.

"What day is it," somebody asked. "Say, what day is it?"

Out there something had happened, probably atmospheric. But the moon shone brighter. The number of objects

367

and shadows in the park seemed to multiply: warm white, warm black.

A band of juvenile delinquents marched by, singing.

"Look at the moon," one of them called.

A used contraceptive came floating along the stream. A girl, built like a garbage-truck driver and holding in one hand a sodden brassiere which trailed behind her, trudged after the rubber, head down.

Somewhere else a traveling clock chimed seven. "It is Tuesday," said an old man's voice, half-asleep. It was Saturday.

But about the night-park, near-deserted and cold, was somehow a sense of population and warmth, and high noon. The stream made a curious half cracking, half ringing sound: like the glass of a chandelier, in a wintry drawing room when all the heat is turned off suddenly and forever. The moon shivered, impossibly bright.

"How quiet," said Stencil.

"Quiet. It's like the shuttle at 5 P.M."

"No. Nothing at all is happening in here."

"So what year is it."

"It is 1913," said Stencil.

"Why not," said Profane.

chapter fourteen

V. *in love*

V

I

The clock inside the Gare du Nord read 11:17: Paris time minus five minutes, Belgian railway time plus four minutes, mid-Europe time minus 56 minutes. To Mélanie, who had forgotten her traveling clock—who had forgotten everything —the hands might have stood anywhere. She hurried through the station behind an Algerian-looking facteur who carried her one embroidered bag lightly on his shoulder, who smiled and joked with customs officials being driven slowly to frenzy by a beseeching mob of English tourists.

By the cover of Le Soleil, the Orleanist morning paper, it was 24 July 1913. Louis Philippe Robert, duc d'Orleans, was the current Pretender. Certain quarters of Paris raved under the heat of Sirius, were touched by its halo of plague, which is nine light-years from rim to center. Among the upper rooms of a new middle-class home in the 17th ar-rondissement, Black Mass was held every Sunday.

Mélanie l'Heuremaudit was driven away down the rue La Fayette in a noisy auto-taxi. She sat in the exact center of the seat, while behind her the three massive arcades and seven allegorical statues of the Gare slowly receded into a lowering, pre-autumn sky. Her eyes were dead, her nose French: the strength there and about the chin and lips made her resemble the classical rendering of Liberty. In all, the face was quite beautiful except for the eyes, which were the color of freezing rain. Mélanie was fifteen.

Had fled from school in Belgium as soon as she received the letter from her mother, with 1500 francs and the announcement that her support would continue, though all Papa's possessions had been attached by the court. The mother had gone off to tour Austria-Hungary. She did not expect to see Mélanie in the foreseeable future.

Mélanie's head ached, but she didn't care. Or did, but not where she was, here present as a face and a ballerina's figure on the bouncing back seat of a taxi. The driver's neck was soft, white: wisps of white hair straggled from under the blue stocking cap. On reaching the intersection with the Boulevard Haussmann, the car turned right up rue de la Chaussée d'Antin. To her left rose the dome of the Opéra, and tiny Apollo, with his golden lyre . . .

"Papa!" she screamed.

The driver winced, tapped the brake reflexively. "I am not your father," he muttered.

Up into the heights of Montmartre, aimed for the most diseased part of the sky. Would it rain? The clouds hung like leprous tissue. Under that light the color of her hair reduced to neutral browns, buffs. Let down the hair reached halfway over her buttocks. But she wore it high with two large curls covering her ears, tickling the sides of her neck.

Papa had a strong bald skull and a brave mustache. Evenings she would come softly into the room, the mysterious place walled in silk where he and her mother slept. And while Madeleine combed the hair of Maman in the other room, Mélanie lay on the wide bed beside him, while he touched her in many places, and she squirmed and fought not to make a sound. It was their game. One night there had been heat lightning outside, and a small night bird had lit on the windowsill and watched them. How long ago it seemed! Late summer, like today.

This had been at Serre Chaude, their estate in Normandy, once the ancestral home of a family whose blood had long since turned to a pale ichor and vaporized away into the frosty skies over Amiens. The house, which dated from the reign of Henri IV, was large but unimpressive, like most architecture of the period. She had always wanted to slide down the great mansard roof: begin at the top and skid down the first gentle slope. Her skirt would fly above her hips, her black-stockinged legs would writhe matte against a wilderness of chimneys, under the Norman sunlight. High over the elms and the hidden carp pools, up where Maman could only be a tiny blotch under a parasol, gazing at her. She imagined the sensation often: the feeling of roof-tiles rapidly sliding beneath the hard curve of her rump, the wind trapped under her blouse teasing the new breasts. And then the break: where the lower, steeper slope of the roof began, the point of no return, where the friction against her body would lessen and she would accelerate, flip over to twist the skirt—perhaps rip it off, be done with it, see it flutter away, like a dark kite!—to let the dovetailed tiles tense her nipple-points to an angry red, see a pigeon clinging to the eaves just before flight, taste the long hair caught against her teeth and tongue, cry out . . .

The taxi stopped in front of a cabaret in the rue Germaine Pilon, near Boulevard Clichy. Mélanie paid the fare and was handed her bag from the top of the cab. She felt something which might be the beginning of the rain against her cheek. The cab drove away, she stood before Le Nerf in an empty street, the flowered bag without gaiety under the clouds.

"You believed us after all." M. Itague stood, half-stooping, holding the handle of the traveling bag. "Come, fétiche, inside. There's news."

On the small stage, which faced a dining room filled only with stacked tables and chairs, and lit by uncertain August daylight, came the confrontation with Satin.

"Mlle. Jarretière"; using her stage name. He was short and heavily built: the hair stuck out in tufts from each side of his head. He wore tights and a dress shirt, and directed his eyes parallel to a line connecting her hip-points. The skirt was two years old, she was growing. She felt embarrassed.

"I have nowhere to stay," she murmured.

"Here," announced Itague, "there's a back room. Here, until we move."

"Move?" She gazed at the raving flesh of tropical blossoms decorating her bag.

"We have the Théâtre de Vincent Castor," cried Satin. He spun, leaped, landed atop a small stepladder.

Itague grew excited, describing L'Enlèvement des Vierges Chinoises—Rape of the Chinese Virgins. It was to be Satin's finest ballet, the greatest music of Vladimir Porcépic, everything formidable. Rehearsals began tomorrow, she'd saved the day, they would have waited until the last minute because it could only be Mélanie, La Jarretière, to play Su Feng, the virgin who is tortured to death defending her purity against the invading Mongolians.

She had wandered away, to the edge of stage right. Itague stood in the center, gesturing, declaiming; while enigmatic on the stepladder, stage left, perched Satin, humming a music-hall song.

A remarkable innovation would be the use of automata, to play Su Feng's handmaidens. "A German engineer is building them," said Itague. "They're lovely creatures: one will even unfasten your robes. Another will play a zither—although the music itself comes from the pit. But they move so gracefully! Not like machines at all."

Was she listening? Of course: part of her. She stood awkwardly on one leg, reached down and scratched her calf, hot under its black stocking. Satin watched hungrily. She felt the twin curls moving restless against her neck. What was he saying? Automata . . .

She gazed up at the sky, through one of the room's side windows. God, would it ever rain?

Her room was hot and airless. Asprawl in one corner was an artist's lay figure, without a head. Old theater posters were scattered on the floor and bed, tacked to the wall. She thought once she heard thunder rumbling from outside.

"Rehearsals will be here," Itague told her. "Two weeks before the performance we move into the Théâtre de Vincent Castor, to get the feel of the boards." He used much theater talk. Not long ago he'd been a bartender near Place Pigalle.

Alone, she lay on the bed, wishing she could pray for rain. She was glad she couldn't see the sky. Perhaps certain of its tentacles already touched the roof of the cabaret. Someone rattled the door. She had thought to lock it. It was Satin, she knew. Soon she heard the Russian and Itague leave together by the back door.

She may not have slept: her eyes opened to the same dim ceiling. A mirror hung on the ceiling directly over the bed. She hadn't noticed it before. Deliberately she moved her legs, leaving her arms limp at her sides, till the hem of the blue skirt had worked high above the tops of the stockings. And lay gazing at the black and tender white. Papa had said, "How pretty your legs are: the legs of a dancer." She could not wait for the rain.

She rose, in a near-frenzy, removed blouse, skirt and undergarments and moved swiftly to the door, wearing only the black stockings and white buck tennis shoes. Somewhere on the way she managed to let down her hair. In the next room she found the costumes for L'Enlèvement des Vierges Chinoises. She felt her hair, heavy and almost viscous along the length of her back and tickling the tops of her buttocks as she knelt beside the large box and searched for the costume of Su Feng.

Back in the hot room she quickly removed shoes and stockings, keeping her eyes closed tight until she had fastened her hair in back with the spangled amber comb. She was not pretty unless she wore something. The sight of her nude body repelled her. Until she had drawn on the blond silk tights, embroidered up each leg with a long, slender dragon; stepped into the slippers with the cut steel buckles, and intricate straps which writhed up halfway to her knees. Nothing to restrain her breasts: she wrapped the underskirt tightly around her hips. It fastened with thirty hooks and eyes from waist to thigh-top, leaving a fur-trimmed slit so that she could dance. And finally, the kimono, translucent and dyed rainbowlike with sunbursts and concentric rings of cerise, amethyst, gold and jungly green.

She lay back once more, hair spread above her on the pillowless mattress, breath taken by her own beauty. If Papa could see her.

The lay figure in the corner was light and carried easily to the bed. She raised her knees high and—interested—saw her calves in the mirror crisscross over the small of its plaster back. Felt the coolness of the figure's flanks against the nude-colored silk, high on her thighs, hugged it tight. The neck top, jagged and flaking off, came to her breasts. She pointed her toes, began to dance horizontal, thinking of how her handmaidens would be.

Tonight there would be a magic-lantern show. Itague sat outside L'Ouganda, drinking absinthe and water. The stuff was supposed to be aphrodisiac but it affected Itague the opposite. He watched a Negro girl, one of the dancers, adjusting her stocking. He thought of francs and centimes.

There weren't many. The scheme might succeed. Porcépic had a name among the avant-garde in French music. Opinion in the city was violently divided: once the composer had been loudly insulted in the street by one of the most venerable of the Post-Romantics. Certainly the man's personal life wasn't one to endear many prospective patrons, either. Itague suspected him of smoking hashish. And there was the Black Mass.

"The poor child," Satin was saying. The table in front of him was nearly covered with empty wine glasses. The Russian moved them from time to time, blocking out the choreography to l'Enlèvement. Satin drank wine like a Frenchman, Itague thought: never outright falling-down drunk. But growing more unstable, more nervous, as his chorus of hollow glass dancers grew. "Does she know where her father's gone?" Satin wondered aloud, looking off into the street. The night was windless, hot. Darker than Itague could ever remember it. Behind them the small orchestra began to play a tango. The Negro girl arose and went inside. To the south, the lights along the Champs Élysées picked out the underbelly of a nauseous-yellow cloud.

"With the father deserted," said Itague, "she's free. The mother doesn't care."

The Russian looked up, sudden. A glass fell over on his table.

"—or nearly free."

"Fled to the jungles, I understand," Satin said. A waiter brought more wine.

"A gift. What had he ever given before? Have you seen the child's furs, her silks, the way she watches her own body? Heard the noblesse in the way she speaks? He gave her all that. Or was he giving it all to himself, by way of her?"

"Itague, she certainly could be the most giving—"

"No. No, it is merely being reflected. The girl functions as a mirror. You, that waiter, the chiffonnier in the next empty street she turns into: whoever happens to be standing in front of the mirror in the place of that wretched man. You will see the reflection of a ghost."

"M. Itague, your late readings may have convinced you—"

"I said ghost," Itague answered softly. "Its name is not l'Heuremaudit, or l'Heuremaudit is only one of its names. That ghost fills the walls of this café and the streets of this district, perhaps every one of the world's arrondissements breathes its substance. Cast in the image of what? Not God. Whatever potent spirit can mesmerize the gift of ir-

374

reversible flight into a grown man and the gift of self-arousal into the eyes of a young girl, his name is unknown. Or if known then he is Yahweh and we are all Jews, for no one will ever speak it." Which was strong talk for M. Itague. He read La Libre Parole, had stood among the crowds to spit at Captain Dreyfus.

The woman stood at their table, not waiting for them to rise, merely standing and looking as if she'd never waited for anything.

"Will you join us," said Satin eagerly. Itague looked far to the south, at the hanging yellow cloud which hadn't changed its shape.

She owned a dress shop in the rue du Quatre-Septembre. Wore tonight a Poiret-inspired evening dress of crepe Georgette the color of a Negro's head, beaded all over, covered with a cerise tunic which was drawn in under her breasts, Empire style. A harem veil covered the lower part of her face and fastened behind to a tiny hat riotous with the plumage of equatorial birds. Fan with amber stick, ostrich feathers, silk tassel. Sand-colored stockings, clocked exquisitely on the calf. Two brilliant-studded tortoise-shell pins through her hair; silver mesh bag, high-buttoned kid shoes with patent leather at the toe and French heel.

Who knew her "soul," Itague wondered, glancing sideways at the Russian. It was her clothes, her accessories, which determined her, fixed her among the mobs of tourist ladies and putains that filled the street.

"Our prima ballerina has arrived today," said Itague. He was always nervous around patrons. As bartender he'd seen no need to be diplomatic.

"Mélanie l'Heuremaudit," his patroness smiled. "When shall I meet her?"

"Any time," Satin muttered, shifting glasses, keeping his eyes on the table.

"Was there objection from the mother?" she asked.

The mother did not care, the girl herself, he suspected, did not care. The father's flight had affected her in some curious way. Last year she'd been eager to learn, inventive, creative. Satin would have his hands full this year. They would end up screaming at each other. No: the girl wouldn't scream.

The woman sat, lost in watching the night, which enveloped them like a velvet teaser-curtain. Itague, for all his time in Montmartre, had never seen behind it to the bare wall of the night. But had this one? He scrutinized her, looking for some such betrayal. He'd observed the face some dozen times. It had always gone through conventional grimaces, smiles, expressions of what passed for emotion. The German could build another, Itague thought, and no one could tell them apart.

The tango still played: or perhaps a different one, he hadn't been listening. A new dance, and popular. The head and body had to be kept erect, the steps had to be precise, sweeping, graceful. It wasn't like the waltz. In that dance was room for an indiscreet billow of crinolines, a naughty word whispered through mustaches into an ear all ready to blush. But here no words, no deviating: simply the wide spiral, turning about the dancing floor, gradually narrowing, tighter, until there was no motion except for the steps, which led nowhere. A dance for automata.

The curtain hung in total stillness. If Itague could have found its pulleys or linkage, he might make it stir. Might penetrate to the wall of the night's theater. Feeling suddenly alone in the wheeling, mechanical darkness of la Ville-Lumière, he wanted to cry, Strike! Strike the set of night and let us all see. . . .

The woman had been watching him, expressionless, poised like one of her own mannequins. Blank eyes, something to hang a Poiret dress on. Porcépic, drunk and singing, approached their table.

The song was in Latin. He'd just composed it for a Black Mass to be held tonight at his home in Les Batignolles. The woman wanted to come. Itague saw this immediately: a film seemed to drop from her eyes. He sat forlorn, feeling as if that most feared enemy of sleep had entered silently on a busy night, the one person whom you must come face to face with someday, who asks you, in the earshot of your oldest customers, to mix a cocktail whose name you have never heard.

They left Satin shuffling empty wine-glasses, looking as if tonight, in some tenantless street, he would murder.

Mélanie dreamed. The lay figure hung half off the bed, its arms stretched out, crucified, one stump touching her breast. It was the sort of dream in which, possibly, the eyes are open: or the last vision of the room is so reproduced in memory that all details are perfect, and the dreamer is unclear whether he is asleep or awake. The German stood over the bed watching her. He was Papa, but also a German.

"You must turn over," he repeated insistently. She was too embarrassed to ask why. Her eyes—which somehow she was able to see, as if she were disembodied and floating above the bed, perhaps somewhere behind the quicksilver of the mirror—her eyes were slanted Oriental: long lashes, spangled on the upper lids with tiny fragments of gold leaf. She glanced sideways at the lay figure. It had grown a head, she thought. The face was turned away. "To reach between your shoulderblades," said the German. What does he look for there, she wondered.

"Between my thighs," she whispered, moving on the bed. The silk there was dotted with the same gold, like sequins. He placed his hand under her shoulder, turned her. The skirt twisted on her thighs: she saw their two inner edges blond and set off by the muskrat skin on the slit of the skirt. The Mélanie in the mirror watched sure fingers move to the center of her back, search, find a small key, which he began to wind.

"I got you in time," he breathed. "You would have stopped, had I not . . ."

The face of the lay figure had been turned toward her, all the time. There was no face.

She woke up, not screaming, but moaning as if sexually aroused.

Itague was bored. This Black Mass had attracted the usual complement of nervous and blasé. Porcépic's music was striking, as usual; highly dissonant. Lately he had been experimenting with African polyrhythms. Afterward Gerfaut the writer sat by a window, discoursing on how for some reason the young girl—adolescent or younger—had again become the mode in erotic fiction. Gerfaut had two or three chins, sat erect and spoke pedantically, though he had only Itague for an audience.

Itague didn't really want to talk with Gerfaut. He wanted to watch the woman who had come with them. She sat now in a side pew with one of the acolytes, a little sculptress from Vaugirard. The woman's hand, gloveless, and decorated only with a ring, stroked the girl's temple as they spoke. From the ring there sprouted a slender female arm, fashioned in silver. The hand was cupped, and held the lady's

377

cigarette. As Itague watched she lit another: black paper, gold crest. A small pile of stubs lay scattered beneath her shoes.

Gerfaut had been describing the plot of his latest novel. The heroine was one Doucette, thirteen and struggled within by passions she could not name.

"A child, and yet a woman," Gerfaut said. "And a quality of something eternal about her. I even confess to a certain leaning of my own that way. La Jarretière . . ."

The old satyr.

Gerfaut at length moved away. It was nearly morning. Itague's head ached. He needed sleep, needed a woman. The lady still smoked her black cigarettes. The little sculptress lay, legs curled up on the seat, head pillowed against her companion's breasts. The black hair seemed to float like a drowned corpse's hair against the cerise tunic. The entire room and the bodies inside it—some twisted, some coupled, some awake—the scattered Hosts, the black furniture, were all bathed in an exhausted yellow light, filtered through rain clouds which refused to burst.

The lady was absorbed in burning tiny holes with the tip of her cigarette, through the skirt of the young girl. Itague watched as the pattern grew. She was writing ma fétiche, in black-rimmed holes. The sculptress wore no lingerie. So that when the lady finished the words would be spelled out by the young sheen of the girl's thighs. Defenseless? Itague wondered briefly.

II

The next day the same clouds were over the city, but it did not rain. Mélanie had awakened in the Su Feng costume, excited as soon as her eyes recognized the image in the mirror, knowing it hadn't rained. Porcépic showed up early with a guitar. He sat on the stage and sang sentimental Russian ballads about willow trees, students getting drunk and going off on sleigh-rides, the body of his love floating belly up in the Don. (A dozen young gathered round the samovar to read novels aloud: where had youth gone?) Porcépic, nostalgic, snuffled over his guitar.

Mélanie, looking newly scrubbed and wearing the dress she'd arrived in, stood behind him, hands over his eyes, and caroled harmony. Itague found them that way. In the yellow light, framed by the stage, they seemed like a picture he'd seen somewhere once. Or perhaps it was only the melancholy notes of the guitar, the subdued looks of precarious joy on their faces. Two young people conditionally at peace in the dog days. He went into the bar and began chipping away at a large block of ice; put the chips into an empty champagne bottle and filled the bottle with water.

By noon the dancers had arrived, most of the girls seemingly deep in a love affair with Isadora Duncan. They moved over the stage like languid moths, gauzy tunics fluttering limp. Itague guessed half the men were homosexual. The other half dressed that way: foppish. He sat at the bar and watched as Satin began the blocking.

"Which one is she?" The woman again. In Montmartre, 1913, people materialized.

"Over there with Porcépic."

She hurried over to be introduced. Vulgar, thought Itague, and then amended it at once to "uncontrollable." Perhaps? A little. La Jarretière stood there only gazing. Porcépic looked upset, as if they'd had an argument. Poor, young, pursued, fatherless. What would Gerfaut make of her? A wanton. In body if he could; in the pages of a manuscript most certainly. Writers had no moral sense.

Porcépic sat at the piano, playing Adoration of the Sun. It was a tango with cross-rhythms. Satin had devised some near-impossible movements to go with it. "It cannot be danced," screamed a young man, leaping from the stage to land, belligerent, in front of Satin.

Mélanie had hurried off to change to her Su Feng costume. Lacing on her slippers she looked up and saw the woman, leaning in the doorway.

"You are not real."

"I . . ." Hands resting dead on her thighs.

"Do you know what a fetish is? Something of a woman which gives pleasure but is not a woman. A shoe, a locket . . . une jarretière. You are the same, not real but an object of pleasure."

Mélanie could not speak.

"What are you like unclothed? A chaos of flesh. But as Su Feng, lit by hydrogen, oxygen, a cylinder of lime, moving doll-like in the confines of your costume . . . You will drive Paris mad. Women and men alike."

The eyes would not respond. Not with fear, desire, anticipation. Only the Mélanie in the mirror could make them do that. The woman had moved to the foot of the bed, ring hand resting on the lay figure. Mélanie darted past her, continued on toes and in twirls to the wings; appeared on stage, improvising to Porcépic's lackadaisical attack on the piano. Outside thunder could be heard, punctuating the music at random.

It was never going to rain.

The Russian influence in Porcépic's music was usually traced to his mother, who'd been a milliner in St. Petersburg. Porcépic now, between his hashish dreams, his furious attacks on the grand piano out in Les Batignolles, fraternized with a strange collection of Russian expatriates led by a certain Kholsky, a huge and homicidal tailor. They were all engaged in clandestine political activity, they spoke volubly and at length of Bakunin, Marx, Ulyanov.

Kholsky entered as the sun fell, hidden by yellow clouds. He drew Porcépic into an argument. The dancers dispersed, the stage emptied until only Mélanie and the woman remained. Satin produced his guitar; Porcépic sat on the piano, and they sang revolutionary songs. "Porcépic," grinned the tailor, "you'll be surprised one day. At what we will do."

"Nothing surprises me," answered Porcépic. "If history were cyclical, we'd now be in a decadence, would we not, and your projected Revolution only another symptom of it."

"A decadence is a falling-away," said Kholsky. "We rise."

"A decadence," Itague put in, "is a falling-away from what is human, and the further we fall the less human we become. Because we are less human, we foist off the humanity we have lost on inanimate objects and abstract theories."

The girl and the woman had moved away from the stage's one overhead light. They could hardly be seen. No sound came from up there. Itague finished the last of the ice water.

"Your beliefs are non-human," he said. "You talk of people as if they were point-clusters or curves on a graph."

"So they are," mused Kholsky, dreamy-eyed. "I, Satin, Porcépic may fall by the wayside. No matter. The Socialist Awareness grows, the tide is irresistible and irreversible. It is a bleak world we live in, M. Itague; atoms collide, brain cells fatigue, economies collapse and others rise to succeed them, all in accord with the basic rhythms of History. Perhaps she is a woman; women are a mystery to me. But her ways are at least measurable."

"Rhythm," snorted Itague, "as if you listened to the jitterings and squeaks of a metaphysical bedspring." The tailor laughed, delighted, like a great fierce child. Acoustics of the room gave his mirthfulness a sepulchral ring. The stage was empty.

"Come," said Porcépic. "To L'Ouganda," Satin on a table danced absently to himself.

Outside they passed the woman, holding Mélanie by the arm. They were headed toward the Métro station; neither spoke. Itague stopped at a kiosk to buy a copy of La Patrie, the closest one could get to an anti-Semitic newspaper in the evening. Soon they had vanished down the Boulevard Clichy.

As they descended the moving stairs, the woman said, "You are afraid." The girl didn't answer. She still wore the costume, covered now with a dolman wrap which looked expensive and was, and which the woman approved of. She bought them first-class tickets. Closeted in the suddenly-materialized train, the woman asked: "Do you only lie passive then, like an object? Of course you do. It is what you are. Une fétiche." She pronounced the silent e's, as if she were singing. Air in the Métro was close. The same as outside. Mélanie studied the tail of the dragon on her calf.

After some time had passed the train climbed to ground level. Mélanie may have noticed they were crossing the river. To her left she saw the Eiffel Tower, quite near. They were crossing the Pont de Passy. At the first stop on the Left Bank the woman arose. She'd not left off clutching Mélanie's arm. Out on the street they began to walk, bearing southwest, into the district of Grenelle: a landscape of factories, chemical works, iron foundries. They were alone in the street. Mélanie wondered if the woman indeed lived among factories.

They walked for what seemed a mile: arrived, finally, at a loft building, in which only the third floor was occupied, by a manufacturer of belts. They climbed narrow stairs, flight after flight. The woman lived on the top floor. Mélanie, though a dancer and strong-legged, now showed signs of exhaustion. When they arrived at the woman's rooms, the girl lay down without invitation on a large pouf in the cen-

381

ter of the room. The place was decorated African and oriental: black pieces of primitive sculpture, lamp in the shape of a dragon, silks, Chinese red. The bed was a great four-poster. Mélanie's wrap had fallen away: her legs, blond and bedragoned, lay unmoving half on the pouf, half on the oriental rug. The woman sat down beside the girl, resting her hand lightly on Mélanie's shoulder, and began to talk.

If we've not already guessed, "the woman" is, again, the lady V. of Stencil's mad time-search. No one knew her name in Paris.

Not only was she V., however, but also V. in love. Herbert Stencil was willing to let the key to his conspiracy have a few of the human passions. Lesbianism, we are prone to think in this Freudian period of history, stems from self-love projected on to some other human object. If a girl gets to feeling narcissist, she will also sooner or later come upon the idea that women, the class she belongs to, are not so bad either. Such may have been the case with Mélanie, though who could say: perhaps the spell of incest at Serre Chaude was an indication that her preferences merely lay outside the usual, exogamous-heterosexual pattern which prevailed in 1913.

But as for V.—V. in love—the hidden motives, if there were any, remained a mystery to all observers. Everyone connected with the production knew what was going on; but because intelligence of the affair remained inside a circle inclined toward sadism, sacrilege, endogamy and homosexuality anyway, there was little concern, and the two were let alone, like young lovers. Mélanie showed up faithfully at all rehearsals and as long as the woman wasn't enticing her away from the production—which, apparently, she had no intention of doing, being a patroness—Itague for one couldn't have cared less.

One day the girl arrived at Le Nerf accompanied by the woman and wearing schoolboys' clothing: tight black trousers, a white shirt, a short black jacket. Moreover, her head —all her thick buttock-length hair—had been shorn. She was nearly bald; and but for the dancer's body no clothes could conceal, she might have been a young lad playing hooky. There was, fortunately, a long black wig in the costume box. Satin greeted the idea with enthusiasm. Su Feng would appear in the first act with hair, in the second without: having been tortured anyway by Mongolians. It would shock the audience, whose tastes, he felt, were jaded.

At every rehearsal, the woman sat at a rear table, watching, silent. All her attention was concentrated on the girl. Itague tried at first to engage her in conversation; but failed and went back to La Vie Heureuse, Le Rire, Le Charivari. When the company moved to the Théâtre de Vincent Castor, she followed like a faithful lover. Mélanie continued dressing transvestite for the street. Speculation among the company was that a peculiar inversion had taken place: since an affair of this sort generally involves one dominant and one submissive, and it was clear which one was which, the woman should have appeared in the clothing of an aggressive male. Porcépic, to the amusement of all, produced at L'Ouganda one evening a chart of the possible combinations the two could be practicing. It came out to 64 different sets of roles, using the subheadings "dressed as," "social role," "sexual role." They could both for example be dressed as males, both have dominant social roles and strive for dominance sexually. They could be dressed different-sexed and both be entirely passive, the game then being to trick the other into making an aggressive move. Or any of 62 other combinations. Perhaps, Satin suggested, there were also inanimate mechanical aids. This, it was agreed, would confuse the picture. At one point someone suggested that the woman might actually be a transvestite to begin with, which made things even more amusing.

But what actually was going on at the loft in Grenelle? Each mind at L'Ouganda and among the troupe at the Théâtre Vincent Castor had conjured up a different scene; machines of exquisite torture, bizarre costuming, grotesque movements of muscle under flesh.

How disappointed they all would have been. Had they seen the skirt of the little sculptress-acolyte from Vaugirard, heard the pet-name the woman had for Mélanie, or read—as had Itague—in the new science of the mind, they would have known that certain fetishes never have to be touched or handled at all; only seen, for there to be complete fulfillment. As for Mélanie, her lover had provided her with mirrors, dozens of them. Mirrors with handles, with ornate frames, full-length and pocket mirrors came to adorn the loft wherever one turned to look.

Baedeker

V. at the age of thirty-three (Stencil's calculation) had found love at last in her peregrinations through (let us be honest) a world if not created then at least described to its fullest by Karl Baedeker of Leipzig. This is a curious country, populated only by a breed called "tourists." Its landscape is one of <u>inanimate monuments and buildings</u>; near-inanimate barmen, taxi-drivers, bellhops, guides: there to do any bidding, to various degrees of efficiency, on receipt of the recommended baksheesh, pourboire, mancia, tip. More than this it is two-dimensional, as is the Street, as are the pages and maps of those little red handbooks. As long as the Cook's, Travellers' Clubs and banks are open, the Distribution of Time section followed scrupulously, the plumbing at the hotel in order ("No hotel," writes Karl Baedeker, "can be recommended as first-class that is not satisfactory in its sanitary arrangements, which should include an abundant flush of water and a supply of proper toilette paper"), the tourist may wander anywhere in this coordinate system without fear. War never becomes more serious than a scuffle with a pickpocket, one of "the huge army . . . who are quick to recognize the stranger and skilful in taking advantage of his ignorance"; depression and prosperity are reflected only in the rate of exchange; politics are of course never discussed with the native population. Tourism thus is supranational, like the Catholic Church, and perhaps the most absolute communion we know on earth: for be its members American, German, Italian, whatever, the Tour Eiffel, Pyramids, and Campanile all evoke identical responses from them; their Bible is clearly written and does not admit of private interpretation; they share the same landscapes, suffer the same inconveniences; live by the same pellucid time-scale. They are the Street's own.

The lady V., one of them for so long, now suddenly found herself excommunicated; bounced unceremoniously into the null-time of human love, without having recognized the exact moment as any but when Mélanie entered a side door to Le Nerf on Porcépic's arm and time—for a while—ceased. Stencil's dossier has it on the authority of Porcépic himself, to whom V. told much of their affair. He repeated none of it then, neither at L'Ouganda nor anywhere else: only to Stencil, years later. Perhaps he felt guilty about his chart of permutations and combinations, but to this extent

384

at least he acted like a gentleman. His description of them is a well-composed and ageless still-life of love at one of its many extremes: V. on the pouf, watching Mélanie on the bed; Mélanie watching herself in the mirror; the mirror-image perhaps contemplating V. from time to time. No movement but a minimum friction. And yet one solution to a most ancient paradox of love: simultaneous sovereignty yet a fusing-together. Dominance and submissiveness didn't apply; the pattern of three was symbiotic and mutual. V. needed her fetish, Mélanie a mirror, temporary peace, another to watch her have pleasure. For such is the self-love of the young that a social aspect enters in: an adolescent girl whose existence is so visual observes in a mirror her double; the double becomes a voyeur. Frustration at not being able to fragment herself into an audience of enough only adds to her sexual excitement. She needs, it seems, a real voyeur to complete the illusion that her reflections are, in fact, this audience. With the addition of this other—multiplied also, perhaps, by mirrors—comes consummation: for the other is also her own double. She is like a woman who dresses only to be looked at and talked about by other women: their jealousy, whispered remarks, reluctant admiration are her own. They are she.

As for V., she recognized—perhaps aware of her own progression toward inanimateness—the fetish of Mélanie and the fetish of herself to be one. As all inanimate objects, to one victimized by them, are alike. It was a variation on the Porpentine theme, the Tristan-and-Iseult theme, indeed, according to some, the single melody, banal and exasperating, of all Romanticism since the Middle Ages: "the act of love and the act of death are one." Dead at last, they would be one with the inanimate universe and with each other. Love-play until then thus becomes an impersonation of the inanimate, a transvestism not between sexes but between quick and dead; human and fetish. The clothing each wore was incidental. The hair shorn from Mélanie's head was incidental: only an obscure bit of private symbolism for the lady V.: perhaps, if she were in fact Victoria Wren, having to do with her time in the novitiate.

If she were Victoria Wren, even Stencil couldn't remain all unstirred by the ironic failure her life was moving toward, too rapidly by that prewar August ever to be reversed. The Florentine spring, the young entrepreneuse with all

385

spring's hope in her virtù, with her girl's faith that Fortune (if only her skill, her timing held true) could be brought under control; that Victoria was being gradually replaced by V.; something entirely different, for which the young century had as yet no name. We all get involved to an extent in the politics of slow dying, but poor Victoria had become intimate also with the Things in the Back Room.

If V. suspected her fetishism at all to be part of any conspiracy leveled against the animate world, any sudden establishment here of a colony of the Kingdom of Death, then this might justify the opinion held in the Rusty Spoon that Stencil was seeking in her his own identity. But such was her rapture at Mélanie's having sought and found her own identity in her and in the mirror's soulless gleam that she continued unaware, off-balanced by love; forgetting even that although the Distribution of Time here on pouf, bed and mirrors had been abandoned, their love was in its way only another version of tourism; for as tourists bring into the world as it has evolved part of another, and eventually create a parallel society of their own in every city, so the Kingdom of Death is served by fetish-constructions like V.'s, which represent a kind of infiltration.

What would have been her reaction, had she known? Again, an ambiguity. It would have meant, ultimately, V.'s death: in a sudden establishment here, of the inanimate Kingdom, despite all efforts to prevent it. The smallest realization—at any step: Cairo, Florence, Paris—that she fitted into a larger scheme leading eventually to her personal destruction and she might have shied off, come to establish eventually so many controls over herself that she became—to Freudian, behaviorist, man of religion, no matter—a purely determined organism, an automaton, constructed, only quaintly, of human flesh. Or by contrast, might have reacted against the above, which we have come to call Puritan, by journeying even deeper into a fetish-country until she became entirely and in reality—not merely as a love-game with any Mélanie—an inanimate object of desire. Stencil even departed from his usual ploddings to daydream a vision of her now, at age seventy-six: skin radiant with the bloom of some new plastic; both eyes glass but now containing photoelectric cells, connected by silver electrode to optic nerves of purest copper wire and leading to a brain exquisitely wrought as a diode matrix could ever be. Sole
386

noid relays would be her ganglia, servo-actuators move her flawless nylon limbs, hydraulic fluid be sent by a platinum heart-pump through butyrate veins and arteries. Perhaps—Stencil on occasion could have as vile a mind as any of the Crew—even a complex system of pressure transducers located in a marvelous vagina of polyethylene; the variable arms of their Wheatstone bridges all leading to a single silver cable which fed pleasure-voltages direct to the correct register of the digital machine in her skull. And whenever she smiled or grinned in ecstasy there would gleam her crowning feature: Eigenvalue's precious dentures.

Why did she tell so much to Porcépic? She was afraid, she said, that it wouldn't last; that Mélanie might leave her. Glittering world of the stage, fame, foul-mind's darling of a male audience: the woe of many a lover. Porcépic gave her what comfort he could. He was under no delusions about love as anything but transitory, he left all such dreaming to his compatriot Satin, who was an idiot anyway. Sad-eyed, he commiserated with her: what else should he've done? Pass moral judgment? Love is love. It shows up in strange displacements. This poor woman was racked by it. Stencil however only shrugged. Let her be a lesbian, let her turn to a fetish, let her die: she was a beast of venery and he had no tears for her.

The night of the performance arrived. What happened then was available to Stencil in police records, and still told, perhaps, by old people around the Butte. Even as the pit orchestra tuned up there was loud argument in the audience. Somehow the performance had taken on a political cast. Orientalism—at this period showing up all over Paris in fashions, music, theater—had been connected along with Russia to an international movement seeking to overthrow Western civilization. Only six years before a newspaper had been able to sponsor an auto-race from Peking to Paris, and enlist the willing assistance of all the countries between. The political situation these days was somewhat darker. Hence, the turmoil which erupted that night in the Théâtre Vincent Castor.

Before the first act was barely under way, there came catcalls and uncouth gestures from the anti-Porcépic faction. Friends, already calling themselves Porcépiquistes, sought to suppress them. Also present in the audience was a third force who merely wanted quiet enough to enjoy the performance and naturally enough tried to silence, prevent or mediate all disputes. A three-way wrangle developed. By intermission it had degenerated into near-chaos.

Itague and Satin screamed at each other in the wings, neither able to hear the other for the noise out in the audience. Porcépic sat by himself in a corner, drinking coffee, expressionless. A young ballerina, returning from the dressing room, stopped to talk.

"Can you hear the music?" Not too well, she admitted. "Dommage. How does La Jarretière feel?" Mélanie knew the dance by heart, she had perfect rhythm, she inspired the whole troupe. The dancer was ecstatic in her praise: another Isadora Duncan! Porcépic shrugged, made a moue. "If I ever have money again," more to himself than to her, "I'll hire an orchestra and dance company for my own amusement and have them perform L'Enlèvement. Only to see what the work is like. Perhaps I will catcall too." They laughed sadly with one another, and the girl passed on.

The second act was even noisier. Only toward the end were the attentions of the few serious onlookers taken entirely by La Jarretière. As the orchestra, sweating and nervous, moved baton-driven into the last portion, Sacrifice of the Virgin, a powerful, slow-building seven-minute crescendo which seemed at its end to've explored the furthest possible reaches of dissonance, tonal color and (as Le Figaro's critic put it next morning) "orchestral barbarity," light seemed all at once to be reborn behind Mélanie's rainy eyes and she became again the Norman dervish Porcépic remembered. He moved closer to the stage, watching her with a kind of love. An apocryphal story relates that he vowed at that moment never to touch drugs again, never to attend another Black Mass.

Two of the male dancers, whom Itague had never left off calling Mongolized fairies, produced a long pole, pointed wickedly at one end. The music, near triple-forte, could be heard now above the roaring of the audience. Gendarmes had moved in at the rear entrances, and were trying ineffectually to restore order. Satin, next to Porcépic, one hand on the composer's shoulder, leaned forward, shaking. It was a tricky bit of choreography, Satin's own. He'd got the idea from reading an account of an Indian massacre in America. While two of the other Mongolians held her, struggling and head shaven, Su Feng was impaled at the crotch on the point of the pole and slowly raised by the entire male part of the company, while the females lamented below. Suddenly one of the automaton handmaidens seemed to run amok, tossing itself about the stage. Satin moaned, gritted his teeth. "Damn the German," he said, "it will distract." The conception depended on Su Feng continuing her dance while impaled, all movement restricted to one point in space, an elevated point, a focus, a climax.

The pole was now erect, the music four bars from the end. A terrible hush fell over the audience, gendarmes and combatants all turned as if magnetized to watch the stage. La Jarretière's movements became more spastic, agonized: the expression on the normally dead face was one which would disturb for years the dreams of those in the front rows. Porcépic's music was now almost deafening: all tonal location had been lost, notes screamed out simultaneous and random like fragments of a bomb: winds, strings, brass and percussion were indistinguishable as blood ran down the pole, the impaled girl went limp, the last chord blasted out, filled the theater, echoed, hung, subsided. Someone cut all the stage lights, someone else ran to close the curtain.

It never opened. Mélanie was supposed to have worn a protective metal device, a species of chastity belt, into which the point of the pole fit. She had left it off. A physician in the audience had been summoned at once by Itague as soon as he saw the blood. Shirt torn, one eye blackened, the doctor knelt over the girl and pronounced her dead.

Of the woman, her lover, nothing further was seen. Some versions tell of her gone hysterical backstage, having to be detached forcibly from Mélanie's corpse; of her screaming vendetta at Satin and Itague for plotting to kill the girl. The coroner's verdict, charitably, was death by accident. Perhaps Mélanie, exhausted by love, excited as at any première, had forgotten. Adorned with so many combs, bracelets, sequins, she might have become confused in this fetish-world and neglected to add to herself the one inanimate object that would have saved her. Itague thought it was suicide, Satin refused to talk about it, Porcépic suspended judgment. But they lived with it for many years.

Rumor had it that a week or so later the lady V. ran off

with one Sgherraccio, a mad Irredentist. At least they both disappeared from Paris at the same time; from Paris and as far as anyone on the Butte could say, from the face of the earth.

chapter fifteen

Sahha

V

Sunday morning around nine the Rollicking Boys arrived at Rachel's after their night of burglary and lounging in the park. Neither had slept. On the wall was a sign:

I am heading for the Whitney. Kisch mein tokus, Profane.

"Mene, mene, tekel, upharsin," said Stencil.

"Ho, hum," said Profane, preparing to sack out on the floor. In came Paola with a babushka over her head and a brown paper bag which clinked in her arms.

"Eigenvalue got robbed last night," she said. "It made the front page of the Times." They all attacked the brown bag at once, coming up with the Times in sections and four quarts of beer.

"How about that," Profane said, scrutinizing the front page. "Police are expecting to make an arrest any time now. Daring early morning burglary."

"Paola," said Stencil, behind him. Profane flinched. Paola, holding the church key, turned to gaze past Profane's left ear at what glittered in Stencil's hand. She kept quiet, eyes motionless.

"Three are in it. Now."

At last she looked back at Profane: "You're coming to Malta, Ben?"

"No," but weak.

"Why?" he said. "Malta never showed me anything. Any-

391

where you care to go in the Med there is a Strait Street, a Gut."

"Benny, if the cops—"

"Who are the cops to me? Stencil's got the teeth." He was terrified. It had only now occurred to him that he'd broken the law.

"Stencil, buddy, what do you say to one of us going back there with a toothache and figuring out a way . . ." He tapered off. Stencil kept quiet.

"Was all that rigmarole with the rope just a way to get me to come along? What's so special about me?"

Nobody said anything. Paola looked about ready to burst from her tracks, bawling and looking to be held by Profane.

All of a sudden there was noise in the hallway. Somebody began banging on the door. "Police," a voice said.

Stencil, jamming the teeth into one pocket, dashed away for the fire escape. "Now, what the hell," Profane said. By the time Paola did open up Stencil was long gone. The same Ten Eyck who had broken up the orgy at Mafia's stood there with one arm slung under a sodden Roony Winsome.

"Is this here Rachel Owlglass at home," he said. Explained he'd found Roony drunk on the stoop of St. Patrick's Cathedral, fly open, face awry, scaring little kids and offending the solid citizens. "Here was all he wanted to come," Ten Eyck almost pleaded, "he wouldn't go home. They released him from Bellevue last night."

"Rachel will be back soon," said Paola gravely. "We'll take him till then."

"I got his feet," Profane said. They hauled Roony into Rachel's room and dumped him on the bed.

"Thank you, officer." Cool as any old-movie's international jewel thief, Profane wished he had a mustache.

Ten Eyck left, deadpan.

"Benito, things are falling apart. The sooner I get home—"

"Good luck."

"Why won't you come?"

"We're not in love."

"No."

"No debts outstanding, either way, not even an old romance to flare up again."

Shook her head: real tears now.

"Why then."

"Because we left Teflon's place in Norfolk."

"No, no."

"Poor Ben." They all called him poor. But to save his feelings never explained, let it stand as an endearment.

"You are only eighteen," he said, "and have this crush on me. You will see by the time you get to be my age—" She interrupted him by rushing at him as you would rush at a tackling dummy, surrounding him, beginning to soak the suede jacket with all those overdue tears. He thumped her back, bewildered.

So it was of course then that Rachel walked in. Being a girl who recovered fast, first thing she said was:

"Oho. So this is what happens behind my back. While I was at church, praying for you, Profane. And the children."

He had the common sense to go along with her. "Believe me, it was all perfectly innocent." Rachel shrugged, meaning the two-line act was over, she'd had a few seconds to think. "You didn't go to St. Patrick's, did you? You should of." Waggling a thumb at what was now snoring in the next room: "Dig."

And we know who it was Rachel spent the rest of the day with, and the night. Holding his head, tucking him in, touching the beard-stubble and dirt on his face; watching him sleep and the frown lines there relax slowly.

After a while Profane went off to the Spoon. Once there he announced to the Crew that he was going to Malta. Of course they held a going-away party. Profane ended up with two adoring camp followers working him over, eyes shining with a kind of love. You got the idea they were like prisoners in stir, vicariously happy to see any of their number reach the outside again.

Profane saw no street ahead but the Gut; thought that it would have to go some to be worse than East Main.

There was also the sea's highway. But that was a different kind entirely.

II

Stencil, Profane and Pig Bodine made a flying visit to Washington, D. C., one weekend: the world-adventurer to expedite their coming passage, the schlemihl to spend a last liberty; Pig to help him. They chose for pied-à-terre a flophouse in Chinatown and Stencil nipped over to the State Department to see what he could see.

"I don't believe any of it," said Pig. "Stencil is a fake."

"Stand by," was all Profane said.

"I suppose we ought to go out and get drunk," Pig said. So they did. Either Profane was growing old and losing his capacity, or it was the worst drunk he had ever thrown. There were blank spaces, which are always, of course, frightening. As near as Profane could remember afterward they had headed first for the National Gallery, Pig having decided they ought to have company. Sure enough, in front of Dali's Last Supper they found two government girls.

"I'm Flip," said the blonde, "and this is Flop."

Pig groaned, momentarily nostalgic for Hanky and Panky. "Fine," he said, "That is Benny and I am—hyeugh, hyeugh—Pig."

"Obviously," said Flop. But the girl/boy ratio in Washington has been estimated as high as 8 to 1. She grabbed Pig's arm, looking around the room as if those other spectral sisters were lurking somewhere among the statuary.

Their place was near P Street, and they had amassed every Pat Boone record in existence. Before Pig had even set down the large paper bag containing the fruits of their afternoon's sortie among the booze outlets of the nation's capital—legal and otherwise—25 watts of that worthy, singing Be Bop A Lula, burst on them unaware.

After this overture, the weekend proceeded in flashes: Pig going to sleep halfway up the Washington Monument and falling half a flight into a considerate troop of Boy Scouts; the four of them in Flip's Mercury, riding round and round Dupont Circle at three in the morning and being joined eventually by six Negroes in an Oldsmobile who wanted to race; the two cars then proceeding to an apartment on New York Avenue occupied only by one inanimate audio system, fifty jazz enthusiasts and God knows how many bottles of circulating and communal wine; being awakened, wrapped with Flip in a Hudson Bay blanket on the steps of a Masonic Temple somewhere in Northwest Washington, by an insurance executive named Iago Saperstein, who wanted them to come to another party.

"Where is Pig," Profane wondered.

"He stole my Mercury and he and Flop are on the way to Miami," said Flip.

"Oh."

"To get married."

"It's a hobby of mine," continued Iago Saperstein, "to find young people like this, who would be interesting to bring along to a party."

"Benny is a schlemihl," said Flip.

"Schlemihls are very interesting," said Iago.

The party was out near the Maryland line; in attendance Profane found an escapee from Devil's Island, who was on route to Vassar under the alias of Maynard Basilisk to teach beekeeping; an inventor celebrating his seventy-second rejection by the U. S. Patent Office, this time on a coin-operated whorehouse for bus and railway stations which he was explaining with blueprints and gestures to a small group of Tyrosemiophiles (collectors of labels on French cheese boxes) kidnaped by Iago from their annual convention; a gentle lady plant pathologist, originally from the Isle of Man, who had the distinction of being the only Manx monoglot in the world and consequently spoke to no one; an unemployed musicologist named Petard who had dedicated his life to finding the lost Vivaldi Kazoo Concerto, first brought to his attention by one Squasimodeo, formerly a civil servant under Mussolini and now lying drunk under the piano, who had heard not only of its theft from a monastery by certain Fascist music-lovers but also about twenty bars from the slow movement, which Petard would from time to time wander round the party blowing on a plastic kazoo; and other "interesting" people. Profane, who only wanted to sleep, talked to none of them. He woke up in Iago's bathtub around dawn to the gigglings of a blonde clad only in an enlisted man's white hat, who was pouring bourbon on Profane out of a gallon coffee pot. Profane was about to open his mouth and try to put it in the way of the descending stream when who should come in but Pig Bodine.

"Give me back my white hat," said Pig.

"I thought you were in Florida," said Profane.

"Ha, ha," said the blonde, "you will have to catch me." And away they went, satyr and nymph.

The next Profane knew they were all back in Flip and Flop's apartment, his head in Flip's lap and Pat Boone on the turntable. "You have the same initials," Flop cooed from across the room. "Pat Boone, Pig Bodine." Profane arose, stumbled to the kitchen and vomited in the sink.

"Out," screamed Flip.

"Indeed," said Profane. At the bottom of the stairs were two bicycles, which the girls rode to work to save bus fare. Profane grabbed one and carried it down the stoop to the street. A mess—fly unzipped, crew cut matted down both sides of his head, beard let go for two days, holed skivvy shirt pushed by his beer belly through a few open buttons on his shirt—he pedaled away wobbly for the flophouse.

He hadn't gone two blocks when there were yells behind him. It was Pig on the other bike, chasing him with Flop on the handlebars. Far behind was Flip, on foot.

"Oh-oh," said Profane. He fiddled with the gears, and promptly dropped into low.

"Thief," yelled Pig, laughing his obscene laugh. "Thief." A prowl car materialized out of nowhere and moved in to intercept Profane. Profane finally got the bike in high and whizzed round a corner. Thus they chased about the city, in fall's cold, in a Sunday street deserted except for them. The cops and Pig finally caught up.

"It's all right officer," said Pig. "He's a friend, I won't press charges."

"Fine," said the cop. "I will." They were hauled down to the precinct and put in the drunk tank. Pig fell asleep and two of the occupants of the tank set to work removing his shoes. Profane was too tired to interrupt.

"Hey," said a cheerful wino from across the room, "you want to play hits and cuts?"

Under the blue stamp on a pack of Camels is either an H or a C, followed by a number. You take turns guessing which it is. If you guess wrong the other gets to Hit (with the fist) or Cut (with the edge of the hand) you across the bicep, for the number of times indicated by the number. The wino's hands looked like small boulders. "I don't smoke," said Profane.

"Oh," said the wino. "What about rock, scissors and paper?"

Just about then a detail of Shore Patrolmen and civilian police entered, dragging a boatswain's mate about seven feet tall who had run amok, under the impression he was King Kong, the well-known ape.

"Aiyee!" he screamed. "Me King Kong. Don't screw with me."

"There, there," an SP said, "King Kong doesn't talk. He growls."

So the boatswain's mate growled, and made a leap for an old electric fan overhead. Round and round he went, uttering ape yells and pounding his chest. SP's and cops milled around down below, bewildered, some of the braver making grabs for his feet.

"Now what?" said one cop. This was answered by the fan, which gave way, dumping the boatswain's mate in their midst. They jumped on and managed to secure him with three or four guard belts. A cop brought in a small dolly from the garage next door, loaded the boatswain's mate on and rolled him off.

"Hey," said one of the SP's. "Lookit there in the drunk tank. That is Pig Bodine that's wanted down in Norfolk for desertion."

Pig opened an eye at them. "Oh well," he said, closed the eye and went back to sleep.

The cops came around to tell Profane he could go. "So long, Pig," said Profane.

"Give Paola six for me," Pig grunted, shoeless, half asleep.

Back at the flophouse Stencil had a poker game going which was about to break up because of the next shift coming on. "Just as well," Stencil said, "they've about cleaned Stencil out."

"You're soft," Profane said, "you let them win on purpose."

"No," Stencil said. "Money will be needed for the trip."

"It's set?"

"All set."

Somehow, it seemed to Profane, things never should have come this far.

III

Now there was a private going-away party, just Profane and Rachel, about two weeks later. After the passport photos and the booster shots and the rest Stencil acted like his valet, removing all official roadblocks by some magic of his own.

Eigenvalue kept cool. Stencil even went to see him—perhaps as a test of the guts he'd need to confront whatever of V. was still on Malta. They discussed the concept of property and agreed that a true owner need not have physical possession. If the soul-dentist knew (as Stencil was nearly sure he did), then "owner," Eigenvalue-defined, was Eigenvalue; Stencil-defined, V. It was a complete failure of communication. They parted friends.

Sunday night Profane spent in Rachel's room with one sentimental magnum of champagne. Roony slept in Esther's room. For two weeks he'd done little else but sleep.

Later Profane lay with his head in her lap, her long hair falling over to cover him and keep him warm. It being September the landlord was still reluctant about heat. They were both naked. Profane rested his ear near her labia majora, as if it were a mouth there, which could speak to him. Rachel was absently listening to the champagne bottle.

"Listen," she whispered, holding the mouth of the bottle near his free ear. He heard carbon dioxide coming out of solution, magnified in a false-bottomed echo chamber.

"It's a happy sound."

"Yes." What percentage was there in telling her what it really sounded like? At Anthroresearch Associates there'd been radiation counters—and radiation—enough to make the place sound like a locust-season gone mad.

Next day they sailed. Fulbright types crowded them at the rail of the Susanna Squaducci. Coils of crepe, showers of confetti and a band, all rented, made things look festive. "Ciao," the Crew called. "Ciao."

"Sahha," said Paola.

"Sahha," echoed Profane.

chapter sixteen

Valletta

V

I

Now there was a sun-shower over Valletta, and even a rainbow. Howie Surd the drunken yeoman lay on his stomach under mount 52, head propped on arms, staring at a British landing craft that chugged its way through the rainy Harbour. Fat Clyde from Chi, who was 6′ 1″/ 142 pounds, came from Winnetka and had been christened Harvey, stood by the lifelines spitting dreamily down into the drydock.

"Fat Clyde," bellowed Howie.

"No," said Fat Clyde. "Whatever it is."

He must have been upset. Nobody ever says things like that to a yeoman. "I'm going over tonight," Howie said gently, "and I need a raincoat because it is raining out, as you may have noticed."

Fat Clyde took a white hat out of his back pocket and tugged it down over his head like a cloche. "I also got liberty," he said.

Bitch box came on. "Now turn in all paint and paint brushes to the paint locker," it said.

"About that time," said Howie. He crawled out from under the gun mount and squatted on the 01 deck. The rain came down and ran into his ears and down his neck and he watched the sun smearing the sky red over Valletta. "What is wrong, hey, Fat Clyde."

"Oh," said Fat Clyde and spat over the side. His eyes followed the white drop of spit all the way down. Howie gave up after about five minutes of silence. He went around the starboard side and down the ladder to bother Tiger Youngblood the spud coxswain who sat at the bottom of the ladder right outside the galley slicing cucumbers.

Fat Clyde yawned. It rained in his mouth, but he didn't seem to notice. He had a problem. Being an ectomorph he was inclined to brood. He was a gunner's mate third and normally it would be none of his business except that his rack was directly over Pappy Hod's and since arrival in Valletta, Malta, Pappy had commenced talking to himself. Not loud; not loud enough to be heard by anyone but Fat Clyde.

Now scuttlebutt being what it is, and sailors being, under frequently sentimental and swinish exteriors, sentimental swine, Clyde knew well enough what it was about being in Malta that upset Pappy Hod. Pappy hadn't been eating anything. Normally a liberty hound, he hadn't even been over yet. Because it was usually Fat Clyde who Pappy went out and got drunk with, this was lousing up Fat Clyde's liberty.

Lazar the deck ape, who had been trying the radar gang now for two weeks, came out with a broom and started sweeping water into the drain on the port side. "I don't know why I should be doing this," he bitched conversationally. "I don't have the duty."

"You should of stayed down in first division," Fat Clyde ventured, glum. Lazar began sweeping water at Fat Clyde, who jumped out of the way and continued on down the starboard ladder. To the spud coxswain: "Give me a cucumber, hey Tiger."

"You want a cucumber," said Tiger, who was chopping up onions. "Here. I got a cucumber for you." His eyes were watering so bad he looked like a sullen boy which is what he was.

"Slice it and put it on a plate," said Fat Clyde, "and maybe I will—"

"Here." From the galley porthole. Pappy Hod was hanging out, waving a crescent of watermelon. He spat a seed at Tiger.

That's the old Pappy Hod, thought Clyde. And he is wearing dress blues and a neckerchief.

"Get your ass in gear, Clyde," said Pappy Hod. "Liberty call any minute now."

So of course Clyde was off like a streak for the fo'c's'le

and back inside of five minutes, squared away as he ever got for liberty.

"832 days," Tiger Youngblood snarled as Pappy and Clyde headed for the quarterdeck. "And I'll never make it."

The Scaffold, resting on keel blocks, was propped up on each side by a dozen wood beams a foot square which extended from the sides of the ship to the sides of the dry-dock. From above, the Scaffold must have looked like a great squid with wood-colored tentacles. Pappy and Clyde crossed the long brow and stood in the rain for a moment, looking at the ship. The sonar dome was shrouded in a secret tarpaulin. At the top of the mast flew the biggest American flag Captain Lych had been able to find. It would not be lowered come Evening Colors; and come true nightfall portable spotlights would be turned on and focused on it. This was for the benefit of any Egyptian bomber pilots who might be coming in, Scaffold being the only American ship in Valletta at the moment.

On the starboard side rose a school or seminary with a clock tower, growing out of a bastion high as the surface-search radar antenna.

"High and dry," said Clyde.

"They say the Limeys are going to kidnap us," said Pappy. "And leave our ass high and dry till this is over."

"It may take longer than that anyway. Give me a cigarette. There's the generator and the screw—"

"And the barnacles." Pappy Hod was disgusted. "They will probably want to sandblast, long as she's in the yards. Even though there's a yard period in Philly coming up as soon as we get back. They'll find something for us to do, Fat Clyde."

They made their way through the Dockyard. Around them straggled most of the Scaffold's liberty section in files and bunches. Submarines too were under wraps: perhaps for secrecy, perhaps for the rain. The quitting time whistle blew and Pappy and Clyde were caught all at once in a torrent of yardbirds: disgorged from earth, vessels and pissoirs, all heading for the gate.

"Yardbirds are the same all over," Pappy said. He and Clyde took their time. The dock workers fled by, jostling them: ragged, gray. By the time Pappy and Clyde reached the stone gateway they'd all gone. Waiting for them were only two old nuns who sat to either side of the gate, holding little straw collection baskets in their laps and black umbrellas over their heads. Bottoms of the baskets were barely covered with sixpences and a shilling or two. Clyde came up with a crown; Pappy, who hadn't been over to exchange any currency, dropped a dollar in the other basket. The nuns smiled briefly and resumed their vigil.

"What was that," Pappy smiled to nobody. "Admission charge?"

Towered over by ruins, they walked up a hill, around a great curve in the road and through a tunnel. At the other end of the tunnel was a bus stop: threepence into Valletta, as far as the Phoenicia Hotel. When the bus arrived they got on with a few straggling yardbirds and many Scaffold sailors, who sat in the back and sang. "Pappy," Fat Clyde began, "I know it's no business of mine, but—"

"Driver," came a yell from in back. "Hey driver. Stop the bus. I got to take a leak."

Pappy slumped lower in his seat; tilted the white hat down over his eyes. "Teledu," he muttered. "That will be Teledu."

"Driver," said Teledu of the A gang. "If you don't stop the bus I will have to piss out the window." Despite himself Pappy turned around to watch. A number of snipes were endeavoring to pull Teledu away from the window. The driver drove on grimly. The yardbirds weren't talking, but watched closely. Scaffold sailors were singing:

Let's all go down and piss on the Forrestal
Till the damn thing floats away,

which went to the tune of The Old Gray Mare and had started at Gitmo Bay in the winter of '55.

"Once he has got an idea in his head," said Pappy, "he won't let go. So if they don't let him piss out the window, he will probably—"

"Look, look," said Fat Clyde. A yellow river of urine was advancing up the center aisle. Teledu was just zipping up.

"A fun-loving good will ambassador," somebody remarked, "is all Teledu is." As the river crept forward sailors and yardbirds hurriedly covered it with the leaves of a few morning newspapers, left lying on the seats. Teledu's comrades applauded.

"Pappy," Fat Clyde said, "you intending to go out and get juiced tonight?"

"I was thinking about it," said Pappy.

"That's what I was afraid of. Look, I know I'm out of line—"

He was interrupted by a burst of merriment from the back of the bus. Teledu's friend Lazar, whom Fat Clyde had last seen sweeping water off the 01 deck, had succeeded now in setting fire to the newspapers on the floor of the bus. Smoke billowed up and with a most horrible smell. Yardbirds began to mutter among themselves. "I should of saved some," crowed Teledu, "to put it out with."

"Oh God," said Pappy. A couple-three of Teledu's fellow snipes were stomping around trying to put out the fire. The bus driver was cursing audibly.

They pulled up to the Phoenicia Hotel at last: smoke still leaking from the windows. Night had fallen. Raucous with song, the men of the Scaffold boat descended on Valletta.

Clyde and Pappy were last to get out. They apologized to the driver. Palm leaves in front of the hotel chattered in the wind. It seemed Pappy was hanging back.

"Why don't we go to a movie," Clyde said, a little desperate. Pappy wasn't listening. They walked under an arch and into Kingsway.

"Tomorrow is Hallowe'en," said Pappy, "and they better put those idiots in a strait jacket."

"They never made one to hold old Lazar. Hot damn, it's crowded in here."

Kingsway seethed. There was this sense of containment, like a sound stage. As an indication of the military buildup in Malta since the beginning of the Suez crisis, there overflowed into the street a choppy sea of green Commando berets, laced with the white and blue of naval uniforms. The Ark Royal was in, and corvettes, and troop carriers to take the Marines to Egypt to occupy and hold.

"Now I was on an AKA during the war," observed Pappy as they elbowed their way along Kingsway, "and just before D-day it was like this."

"Oh they was getting drunk in Yoko too, back during Korea," said Clyde, defensive.

"Not like that was, or like this either. The Limeys have a way of getting drunk just before they have to go off and fight. Not like we get drunk. All we do is puke, or break furniture. But the Limeys show imagination. Listen."

All it was was an English ruddy-faced jarhead and his

Maltese girl, standing in the entrance to a men's clothing store and looking at silk scarves. But they were singing People Will Say We're In Love, from *Oklahoma*.

Overhead bombers screamed away toward Egypt. On some street corners trinket-stalls were set up, and doing a peak trade in good-luck charms and Maltese lace.

"Lace," said Fat Clyde. "What is it about lace."

"To make you think about a girl. Even if you don't have a girl, it's better somehow if you . . ." He trailed off. Fat Clyde didn't try to keep the subject alive.

From a Phillips Radio store to their left, news broadcasts were going full blast. Little tense knots of civilians stood around, just listening. Nearby at a newspaper kiosk, red scare headlines proclaimed BRITISH INTEND TO MOVE INTO SUEZ! "Parliament," said the newscaster, "after an emergency session, issued a resolution late this afternoon calling for the engagement of airborne troops in the Suez crisis. The paratroopers, based on Cyprus and Malta, are on one-hour alert."

"Oboy, oboy," said Fat Clyde wearily.

"High and dry," said Pappy Hod, "and the only ship in the Sixth Fleet getting liberty." All the others were off in the Eastern Mediterranean evacuating American nationals from the Egyptian mainland. Abruptly Pappy cut round a corner to the left. He'd gone about ten steps down the hill when he noticed Fat Clyde wasn't there.

"Where are you going," Fat Clyde yelled from the corner.

"The Gut," said Pappy, "where else."

"Oh." Clyde came stumbling downhill. "I figured maybe we could wander around the main drag a little."

Pappy grinned: reached out and patted Clyde's beer belly. "Easy there, mother Clyde," he said. "Old Hod is doing all right."

I'm just trying to be helpful, Clyde thought. But: "Yes," he agreed, "I am pregnant with a baby elephant. You want to see its trunk?"

Pappy guffawed and they roistered away down the hill. There is nothing like old jokes. It's a kind of stability about them: familiar ground.

Strait Street—the Gut—was crowded as Kingsway but more poorly lit. First familiar face they saw was Leman the red-headed water-king, who came reeling out the swinging doors of a pub called the Four Aces, minus a white hat. Leman was a bad drunk, so Pappy and Clyde ducked down behind a potted palm in front to watch. Sure enough, Leman started searching in the gutter, bent over at a 90° angle. "Rocks," whispered Clyde. "He always looks for rocks." The water-king found a rock and prepared to heave it through the front window of the Four Aces. The U. S. Cavalry, in the form of one Tourneur, the ship's barber, arrived also by way of the swinging doors and grabbed Leman's arm. The two fell to the street and began wrestling around in the dust. A passing band of British Marines looked at them curiously for a moment, then went by, laughing, a little embarrassed.

"See," said Pappy, getting philosophical. "Richest country in the world and we never learned how to throw a good-bye drunk like the Limeys."

"But it's not good-bye for us," said Clyde.

"Who knows. There's revolutions in Hungary and Poland, fighting in Egypt." Pause. "And Jayne Mansfield is getting married."

"She can't, she can't. She said she'd wait for me."

They entered the Four Aces. It was early yet and no one but a few low-tolerance drunks like Leman were causing any commotion. They sat at a table. "Guinness stout," said Pappy and the words fell on Clyde like a nostalgic sandbag. He wanted to say, Pappy it is not the old days and why didn't you stay on board the Scaffold boat because a boring liberty is better for me than one that hurts, and this hurts more all the time.

The barmaid who brought their drinks was new: at least Clyde didn't remember her from last cruise. But one across the room, jitterbugging with one of Pappy's strikers, she'd been around. And though Paola's bar had been the Metro, further on down the street, this girl—Elisa?—knew through the barmaids' grapevine that Pappy had married one of her own. If only Clyde could keep him away from the Metropole. If only Elisa didn't spot them.

But the music stopped, she saw them, headed over. Clyde concentrated on his beer. Pappy smiled at Elisa.

"How's your wife?" she asked, of course.

"I hope she's well."

Elisa, bless her heart, dropped it. "You want to dance?

405

Nobody broke your record yet. Twenty-two straight."

Nimble Pappy was on his feet. "Let's set a new one."

Good, thought Clyde: good. After a while who should come over but LtJG Johnny Contango, the Scaffold's damage-control assistant, in civvies.

"When we going to get the screw fixed, Johnny?"

Johnny because this officer had been a white hat sent to OCS, and having been then faced with the usual two alternatives—to persecute those of his former estate or to keep fraternizing and to hell with the wardroom—had chosen the latter. He had gone possibly overboard on this, at least running afoul of the Book at every turn: stealing a motorcycle in Barcelona, inciting an impromptu mass midnight swim at Fleet Landing in the Piraeus. Somehow—maybe because of Captain Lych's fondness for incorrigibles—he'd escaped court-martial.

"I am feeling more and more guilty about the screw," said Johnny Contango. "I have just slipped off from a stuffy do over at the British Officers' Club. You know what the big joke is? 'Let's have another drink, old boy, before we have to go to war with each other.'"

"I don't get it," said Fat Clyde.

"We voted in the Security Council with Russia and against England and France on this Suez business."

"Pappy says the Limeys are going to kidnap us."

"I don't know."

"What about the screw?"

"Drink your beer, Fat Clyde." Johnny Contango felt guilty about the mangled ship's propeller not so much in a world-political way. It was personal guilt which, Fat Clyde suspected, upset him more than he showed. He'd been OOD. the midwatch old Scaffold boat had hit whatever it was—submerged wreck, oil drum—going through the Straits of Messina. Radar gang had been too busy keeping tabs on a fleet of night fishing boats who'd chosen the same route to notice the object—if it had protruded above the surface at all. Set, and drift, and pure accident had brought them here to get a screw fixed. God knew what the Med had brought into Johnny Contango's path. The report had called it "hostile marine life," and there'd been much raillery since about the mysterious screw-chewing fish, but Johnny still felt it was his fault. The Navy would rather blame something alive

406

preferably human and with a service number—than pure accident. Fish? Mermaid? Scylla, Charybdis, wha. Who knew how many female monsters this Med harbored?

"Bwaagghh."

"Pinguez, I'll bet," Johnny said without looking around.

"Yup. All over his blues." The owner had materialized and stood now truculent over Pinguez, steward's mate striker, hollering "SP, SP," with no results. Pinguez sat on the floor afflicted with the dry heaves.

"Poor Pinguez," Johnny said. "He's an early one."

Out on the floor Pappy was up to about a dozen and showed no signs of stopping.

"We ought to get him into a cab," Fat Clyde said.

"Where is Baby Face." Falange the snipe, and Pinguez's buddy. Pinguez now lay sprawled among the legs of a table, and had begun talking to himself in Filipino. A bartender approached with something dark in a glass that fizzed. Baby Face Falange, wearing as was his wont a babushka, joined the group around Pinguez. A number of British sailors looked on with interest.

"Here, you drink it," the bartender said. Pinguez lifted his head and moved it, mouth open, toward the bartender's hand. Bartender got the message and jerked his hand away: Pinguez's shiny teeth closed on the air with a loud snap. Johnny Contango knelt by the steward.

"Andale, man," he said gently, raising Pinguez's head. Pinguez bit him on the arm. "Let go," just as quiet. "It's a Hathaway shirt, I don't want no cabrón puking on it."

"Falange!" Pinguez screamed, drawing out the *a*'s.

"You hear that," said Baby Face. "That's all he has to say on the quarterdeck and my ass has had it."

Johnny took Pinguez under the arms; Fat Clyde, more nervous, lifted his feet. They bore him to the street, found a cab, and got him off in it.

"Back to the great gray mother," said Johnny. "Come on. You want to try the Union Jack?"

"I should keep an eye on Pappy. You know."

"I know. But he'll be busy dancing."

"As long as he doesn't get to the Metro," said Fat Clyde. They strolled down half a block to the Union Jack. Inside Antoine Zippo, captain of the second division head, and Nasty Chobb the baker, who periodically used salt in place of sugar in the early morning's pies to discourage thieves, had taken over not only the bandstand in back but also a trumpet and guitar respectively; and were now making Route 66, respectfully.

"Sort of quiet," said Johnny Contango. But this was premature because sly young Sam Mannaro, the corpsman striker, was even now sneaking alum into Antoine's beer which sat uneyed by Antoine on the piano.

"SP's will be busy tonight," said Johnny. "How come Pappy came over at all?"

"I never had that happen to me, that way," Clyde said, a little brusque.

"Sorry. I was thinking today in the rain how it was I could light a king-sized cigarette without getting it wet."

"Oh I think he should have stayed on board," said Clyde, "but all we can do is keep an eye out that window."

"Right ho," said Johnny Contango, slurping beer.

A scream from the street. "That's tonight's," said Johnny. "Or one of tonight's."

"Bad street."

"Back during the beginning of all this in July the Gut ran one killing a night. Average. God knows what it is now."

In came two Commandos, looking around for somewhere to sit. They picked Clyde and Johnny's table.

David and Maurice their names were, and heading off for Egypt tomorrow.

"We shall be there," said Maurice, "to wave hello when you people come steaming in."

"If ever," said Johnny.

"World's going to hell," said David. They'd been drinking heavily but held it well.

"Don't expect to hear from us till the election is over," said Johnny.

"Oh is that it then."

"Why America is sitting on its ass," brooded Johnny, "is the same reason our ship is sitting on its ass. Crosscurrents, seismic movements, unknown things in the night. But you can't help thinking it's somebody's fault."

"The jolly, jolly balloon," said Maurice. "Going up."

"Did you hear a bloke got murdered just as we came in." David leaned forward, melodramatic.

"More blokes than that will get murdered in Egypt," said

408

Maurice, "and don't I wish they would truss up a few M.P.'s now, in those jumping rigs and chutes. Send them out the door. They're the ones who want it. Not us."

"But my brother is on Cyprus and I shall never live it down if he gets there first."

The Commandos outdrank them two-for-one. Johnny, never having talked to anyone who might be dead inside a week, was curious in a macabre way. Clyde, who had, only felt unhappy.

The group on the stand had moved from Route 66 to Every Day I Have the Blues. Antoine Zippo, who had wrecked one jugular vein last year with a shore-based Navy band in Norfolk and was now trying for two, took a break, shook the spit out of his horn and reached for the beer on the piano. He looked hot and sweaty, as a suicidal work-horse trumpet should. Alum however being what it is, the predictable occurred.

"Ech," said Antoine Zippo, slamming the beer down on the piano. He looked around, belligerent. His lip had just been attacked. "Sam the werewolf," said Antoine, "is the only sumbitch here who could get alum." He couldn't talk too well.

"There goes Pappy," said Clyde, grabbing for his hat. Antoine Zippo leaped like a puma from the stand, landing feet first on Sam Mannaro's table.

David turned to Maurice. "I wish the Yanks would save their energy for Nasser."

"Still," said Maurice, "it would be good practice."

"I heartily agree," pip-pipped David in a toff's voice: "Shall we, old man?"

"Bung ho." The two Commandos waded into the growing melee about Sam.

Clyde and Johnny were the only two heading for the door. Everybody else wanted to get in on the fight. It took them five minutes to reach the street. Behind them they heard glass breaking and chairs being knocked over. Pappy Hod was nowhere in sight.

Clyde hung his head. "I suppose we ought to go to the Metro." They took their time, neither savoring the night's work ahead. Pappy was a loud and merciless drunk. He demanded that his keepers sympathize and of course they always did, so much that it was always worse for them.

They passed an alley. Facing them on the blank wall, in chalk, was a Kilroy, thus:

flanked by two of the most common British sentiments in time of crisis: WOT NO PETROL and END CALL-UP.

"No petrol, indeed," said Johnny Contango. "They're blowing up oil refineries all over the Middle East." Nasser it seems having gone on the radio, urging a sort of economic jihad.

Kilroy was possibly the only objective onlooker in Valletta that night. Common legend had it he'd been born in the U.S. right before the war, on a fence or latrine wall. Later he showed up everywhere the American armies moved: farmhouses in France, pillboxes in North Africa, bulkheads of troop ships in the Pacific. Somehow he'd acquired the reputation of a schlemihl or sad sack. The foolish nose hanging over the wall was vulnerable to all manner of indignities: fist, shrapnel, machete. Hinting perhaps at a precarious virility, a flirting with castration, though ideas like this are inevitable in a latrine-oriented (as well as Freudian) psychology.

But it was all deception. Kilroy by 1940 was already bald, middle-aged. His true origins forgotten, he was able to ingratiate himself with a human world, keeping schlemihl-silence about what he'd been as a curly-haired youth. It was a masterful disguise: a metaphor. For Kilroy had sprung into life, in truth, as part of a band-pass filter, thus:

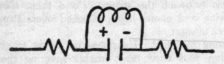

Inanimate. But Grandmaster of Valletta tonight.

"The Bobbsey Twins," said Clyde. Running around the corner in a jog trot came Dahoud (who'd discouraged little Ploy from taking a Brody) and Leroy Tongue the midget storekeeper, both of them with night sticks and SP armbands. It looked like a vaudeville act, Dahoud being one and a half times as high as Leroy. Clyde had a general idea of their technique for keeping the peace. Leroy would hop up on Dahoud's shoulders piggyback and rain pacification about the heads and shoulders of boisterous bluejackets, while Dahoud exerted his calming influence down below.

"Look," yelled Dahoud approaching. "We can do it running." Leroy slowed down and cut in behind his running mate. "Hup-hup-hup," said Dahoud. "YO." Sure enough: neither of them breaking stride, up hopped Leroy, clinging to Dahoud's big collar to ride his shoulders like a jockey.

"Giddap there, hoss," Leroy screamed, and away they dashed for the Union Jack. A small detachment of Marines, all in step, came marching out of a side street. One farm lad, blond and candid-faced, counted cadence unintelligibly. Passing Clyde and Johnny, he broke off for a moment to ask:

"Wot's all that noise we hear?"

"Fight," said Johnny. "Union Jack."

"Right ho." Back in formation, the boy ordered a column left and his charges set course dutifully for the Union Jack.

"We're missing all the fun," whined Clyde.

"There is Pappy."

They entered the Metro. Pappy sat at a table with a barmaid who looked like Paola but fatter and older. It was pitiful to watch. He was doing his "Chicago" bit. They waited till it was over. The barmaid, indignant, arose and waddled off. Pappy used the handkerchief to swab off his face which was sweating.

"Twenty-five dances," he said as they approached. "I broke my own record."

"There is a nice fight on at the Union Jack," suggested Clyde. "Wouldn't you like to go to it, Pappy?"

"Or how about that whorehouse the chief off the Hank that we met in Barcelona told us about," said Johnny. "Why don't we try to find it."

Pappy shook his head. "You guys ought to know this was the only place I wanted to come."

So they begin: these vigils. Having put up their token resistance, Clyde and Johnny straddled chairs to either side of Pappy and settled down to drinking as much as Pappy but staying soberer.

411

The Metro looked like a nobleman's pied-à-terre applied to mean purposes. The dancing floor and bar lay up a wide curving flight of marble steps lined with statues in niches: statues of Knights, ladies and Turks. Such was a quality of suspended animation about them that you felt come the owl-hours, the departure of the last sailor and the extinguishment of the last electric light, these statues must unfreeze, step down from their pedestals, and ascend stately to the dance floor bringing with them their own light: the sea's phosphorescence. There to form sets and dance till sunup, utterly silent; no music; their stone feet only just kissing the wood planks.

Along the sides of the room were great stone urns, with palms and poincianas. On the red-carpeted dais sat a small hot-jazz band: violin, trombone, saxophone, trumpet, guitar, piano, drums. It was a plump middle-aged lady, playing the violin. At the moment they were playing C'est Magnifique tailgate fashion, while a Commando six and a half feet tall jitterbugged with two barmaids at once and three or four friends stood around, clapping hands, cheering them on. It was not so much a matter of Dick Powell, the American Singing Marine, caroling Sally and Sue, Don't Be Blue: more a taking-on of traditional attitudes which (one suspects) must be latent in all English germ plasm: another loony chromosome along with afternoon tea and respect for the Crown; where the Yanks saw novelty and an excuse for musical comedy, the English saw history, and Sally and Sue were only incidental.

Early tomorrow deck hands would come out in the bleaching glare of the pier's lights and single up all lines for some of these green berets. The night before, then, was for sentiment, larking in shadows with jolly barmaids, another pint and another smoke in this manufactured farewell-hall; this enlisted men's version of that great ball, the Saturday night before Waterloo. One way you could tell which ones were going tomorrow: they left without looking back.

Pappy got drunk, stinking drunk: and drew his two keepers into a personal past neither wanted to investigate. They endured a step-by-step account of the brief marriage: the presents he'd given her, the places they'd gone, the cooking, the kindnesses. Toward the end, half of it was noise: maundering. But they didn't ask for clarity. Didn't ask anything, not so much from booze-tangled tongues as from a stuffi-ness-by-induction in the nasal cavities. So susceptible were Fat Clyde and Johnny Contango.

But it was Cinderella liberty in Malta and though the drunk's clock slows down it doesn't stop. "Come on," said Clyde finally, floundering afoot. "It is about that time." Pappy smiled sadly and fell out of his chair.

"We'll go get a taxi," said John. "Carry him home in a taxi."

"Jeez, it's late." They were the last Americans in the Metro. The English were quietly absorbed in saying good-bye to at least this part of Valletta. With the departure of the Scaffold boat's men all things had grown more matter-of-fact.

Clyde and Johnny draped Pappy around them and got him down the stairs, past the Knights' reproachful eyes and into the street. "Taxi, hey," Clyde screamed.

"No taxis," said Johnny Contango. "All gone. God how big the stars are."

Clyde wanted to argue. "You just let me take him," he said. "You're an officer, you can stay out all night."

"Who said I was an officer. I'm a white hat. Your brother, Pappy's brother. Brother's keeper."

"Taxi, taxi, taxi."

"Limey's brother, everybody's brother. Who says I'm an officer. Congress. Officer and gentlemen by act of Congress. Congress won't even go into the Suez to help the Limeys. They're wrong about that, they're wrong about me."

"Paola," Pappy moaned and pitched forward. They grabbed him. His white hat was long gone. His head hung and hair had fallen over his eyes.

"Pappy is going bald," said Clyde. "I never noticed."

"You never do till you're drunk."

They made their way slow and unsteady down the Gut, yelling occasionally for a taxi. None came. The street had a silent look but was not so; not so far away, on the hill as-cending to Kingsway, they heard sharp little explosions. And the voice of a great crowd around the next corner.

"What is it," said Johnny, "revolution?"

Better than that: it was a free-for-all among 200 Royal Commandos and maybe 30 Scaffold sailors.

Clyde and Johnny dragged Pappy round the corner and into the fringes of it.

413

"Oh-oh," said Johnny. The noise woke Pappy, who called for his wife. A few dangling belts were in evidence, but no broken beer bottles or boatswain's knives. Or none anybody could see. Or not yet. Dahoud stood against a wall, facing 20 Commandos. By his left bicep another Kilroy looked on, with nothing to say but WOT NO AMERICANS. Leroy Tongue must have been off underfoot somewhere, clubbing at shins with his night stick. Something red and sputtering came arcing through the air, landed by Johnny Contango's foot and blew up. "Firecrackers," said Johnny, landing three feet away. Clyde had also fled, and Pappy, unsupported, fell to the street. "Let's get him out of here," said Johnny. But they found their way blocked by Marines, who'd come up from behind.

"Hey Billy Eckstine," yelled the Commandos in front of Dahoud. "Billy Eckstine! sing us a song!" A volley of firecrackers went off somewhere to the right. Most of the fist-fighting was still concentrated in the center of the mob. Only shoving, elbowing and curiosity at the edges. Dahoud removed his hat, drew himself up and began to sing I Only Have Eyes for You. Commandos were struck dumb. Somewhere down the street a police whistle blew. Glass broke in the middle of the crowd. It sent human waves back, concentric. A couple-three Marines staggered back and fell over Pappy, who was still on the ground. Johnny and Clyde moved in to rescue him. A few sailors moved in to help the fallen Marines. Unobtrusive as possible, Clyde and Johnny lifted their charge by an arm each and sneaky-Peted away. Behind them the Marines and sailors began scuffling with one another.

"Cops," somebody yelled. Half a dozen cherry bombs went off. Dahoud finished his song. A number of Commandos applauded. "Now sing I Apologize."

"You mean that," Dahoud scratched his head, "that if I told a lie, if I made you cry, forgive me?"

"Hoorah Billy Eckstine!" they cried.

"O no man," Dahoud said. "I don't apologize to nobody." Commandos squared off. Dahoud surveyed the situation, then abruptly lifted a gigantic arm, straight up. "All right there troopers, get in ranks now. Square away."

For some reason they shuffled into a kind of formation.

"Yeah," Dahoud grinned. "Right, FACE." So they did.

"Awright men. Let's gooool" Down came the arm, and

414

away they marched. In step. Kilroy looked on deadpan. From nowhere Leroy Tongue emerged to bring up the rear.

Clyde, Johnny and Pappy Hod struggled free of the brawl, dodged round a corner and began the struggle up the hill to Kingsway. Halfway along, Dahoud's detachment passed them, Dahoud counting cadence, singing it like a blues. For all anyone knew he was marching them back to the troop carriers.

A taxi pulled up next to the three. "Follow that platoon," Johnny said and they piled in. The cab had a skylight, so of course before it reached Kingsway three heads had appeared through the roof. As they crawled behind the Commandos, they sang:

> Who's the little rodent
> That's getting more than me?
> F-U-C-K-E-Y Y-O-U-S-E.

A legacy from Pig Bodine, who'd watched this particular kid's program religiously on the mess hall TV every night in port; had furnished black clip-on ears to all the mess cooks at his own expense and composed on the show's theme song an obscene parody of which this variation in spelling was the most palatable part. Commandos in the rear ranks asked Johnny to teach them the words. He did, receiving in exchange a fifth of Irish whisky when its owner insisted he could not possibly finish it before they got under way next morning. (To this day the bottle has remained in Johnny Contango's possession, unopened. No one knows what he's keeping it for.)

This weird procession crept along Kingsway until intercepted by a British cattle car or lorry. The Commandos climbed on, thanked everyone for a jolly evening and snarled away forever. Dahoud and Leroy climbed wearily into the cab.

"Billy Eckstine," Dahoud grinned. "Jeez."

"We got to go back," Leroy said. The driver made a U-turn and they circled back to the scene of the free-for-all. No more than fifteen minutes had passed; but the street was deserted. Quiet: no more firecrackers, shouts; nothing.

"I'll be damned," said Dahoud.

"You'd think it never happened," said Leroy.

"Dockyard," Clyde instructed the driver, yawning. "Drydock two. American tin can with the teeth marks of a screw-chewing fish."

All the way out to the Dockyard Pappy snored.

Liberty had been expired an hour when they arrived. The two SP's bounded past the rows of latrines and across the gangplank. Clyde and Johnny, with Pappy in the middle, lagged.

"Now none of that was worth it," Johnny said bitterly. Two figures, fat and slim, stood by the latrine wall.

"Come on," Clyde urged Pappy. "Few more steps."

Nasty Chobb came running by, wearing an English sailor hat with H.M.S. Ceylon printed on the band. The shadow-figures detached themselves from the latrine wall and approached. Pappy tripped.

"Robert," she said. Not a question.

"Hello Pappy," said the other.

"Who zat," said Clyde.

Johnny stopped dead and Clyde's momentum carried Pappy round to face her directly. "I'll be dipped in mess-hall coffee," said Johnny.

"Poor Robert." But she said it gently, and was smiling, and had either Johnny or Clyde been less drunk they would have bawled like children.

Pappy waggled his arms. "Go ahead," he told them, "I can stand. I'll be along."

From over on the quarterdeck Nasty Chobb was heard arguing with the OOD. "What you mean go away," yelled Nasty.

"Your hat says H.M.S. Ceylon, Chobb."

"So."

"So what can I say? You're on the wrong ship."

"Profane," said Pappy. "You came back. I thought you would."

"I didn't," Profane said. "But she did." He went off to wait. Leaned against a latrine wall out of earshot, looking at the Scaffold.

"Hello Paola," said Pappy. "Sahha." It means both.

"You—"

"You—" at the same time. He motioned her to talk.

"Tomorrow," she said, "you'll be hung over and probably will think this didn't happen. That the Metro's booze sends visions as well as a big head. But I'm real, and here, and if they restrict you—"

"I can put in a chit."

"Or send you off to Egypt or anywhere else, it should make no difference. Because I will be back in Norfolk before you, and be there on the pier. Like any other wife. But wait till then to kiss or even touch you."

"If I can get off?"

"I'll be gone. Let it be this way, Robert." How tired her face looked, in the white scatter from the brow lights. "It will be better, and more the way it should have been. You sailed a week after I left you. So a week is all we've lost. All that's gone on since then is only a sea-story. I will sit home in Norfolk, faithful, and spin. Spin a yarn for your coming-home present." *Helen?*

"I love you," was all he could find to say. He'd been saying it every night to a steel bulkhead and the earthwide sea on the other side. *Nory comb*

White hands flickered up, behind her face. "Here. In case you think tomorrow it was a dream." Her hair fell loose. She handed him an ivory comb. Five crucified Limeys —five Kilroys—stared briefly at Valletta's sky till he pocketed it. "Don't lose it in a poker game. I've had it a long time."

He nodded. "We ought to be back early December."

"You'll get your good-night kiss then." She smiled, withdrew, turned, was gone.

Pappy ambled on past the latrine without looking back. The American flag, skewered by spotlights, fluttered limp, high over them all. Pappy began his walk to the quarterdeck, across the long brow, hoping he'd be soberer when he reached the other end.

II

Of their dash across the Continent in a stolen Renault; Profane's one-night sojourn in a jail near Genoa, when the police mistook him for an American gangster; the drunk they all threw which began in Liguria and lasted well past Naples; the dropped transmission at the outskirts of that city and the week they spent waiting its repair in a ruined villa on Ischia, inhabited by friends of Stencil—a monk long defrocked named Fenice who spent his time breeding giant scorpions in marble cages once used by the Roman blood to punish their young boy and girl concubines, and the poet

417

Cinoglossa who had the misfortune to be both homosexual and epileptic—wandering listlessly in an unseasonable heat among vistas of marble fractured by earthquake, pines blasted by lightning, sea wrinkled by a dying mistral; of their arrival in Sicily and the difficulty with local bandits on a mountain road (from which Stencil extricated them by telling foul Sicilian jokes and giving them whisky); of the day-long trip from Syracuse to Valletta on the Laferla steamer Star of Malta, during which Stencil lost $100 and a pair of cufflinks at stud poker to a mild-faced clergyman who called himself Robin Petitpoint; and of Paola's steadfast silence through it all, there was little for any of them to remember. Malta alone drew them, a clenched fist around a yo-yo string.

They came in to Valletta, cold, yawning, in the rain. They rode to Maijstral's room neither anticipating nor remembering—outwardly, at least, apathetic and low-keyed as the rain. Maijstral greeted them calmly. Paola would stay with him. Stencil and Profane had planned to doss at the Phoenicia Hotel, but at 2/8 per day the agile Robin Petitpoint had had his effect. They settled for a lodging-house near the Harbour. "What now," said Profane, tossing his ditty bag in a corner.

Stencil thought a long time.

"I like," Profane continued, "living off of your money. But you and Paola conned me into coming here."

"First things first," said Stencil. The rain had stopped; he was nervous. "See Maijstral. See Maijstral."

See Maijstral he did: but only next day, and after a morning-long argument with the whisky bottle which the bottle lost. He walked to the room in the ruined building through a brilliant gray afternoon. Light seemed to cling to his shoulders like fine rain. His knees shook.

But it wasn't hard to talk to Maijstral.

"Stencil has seen your confession to Paola."

"Then you know," Maijstral said, "I only made it into this world through the good offices of one Stencil."

Stencil hung his head. "It may have been his father."

"Making us brothers."

There was wine, which helped. Stencil yarned far into the night but with a voice always threatening to break, as if now at last he were pleading for his life. Maijstral kept a

418

decorous silence, waiting patiently whenever Stencil faltered.

Stencil sketched the entire history of V. that night and strengthened a long suspicion. That it did add up only to the recurrence of an initial and a few dead objects. At one point in Mondaugen's story:

"Ah," Maijstral said. "The glass eye."

"And you." Stencil mopped his forehead. "You listen like a priest."

"I have wondered." Smiling.

At the end of it:

"But Paola showed you my apologia. Who is the priest? We have heard one another's confessions."

"Not Stencil's," Stencil insisted. "Hers."

Maijstral shrugged. "Why have you come? She is dead."

"He must know."

"I could never find that cellar again. If I could: it must be rebuilt now. Your confirmation would lie deep."

"Too deep already," Stencil whispered. "Stencil's long over his head, you know."

"I was lost."

"But not apt to have visions."

"Oh, real enough. You always look inside first, don't you, to find what's missing. What gap a 'vision' could possibly fill. I was all gap then, and there was too wide a field to choose from."

"Yet you'd just come from—"

"I did think of Elena. Yes. Latins warp everything to the sexual anyway. Death becomes an adulterer or rival, need arises to see one rival at least done in. . . . But I was bastardized enough, you see, before that. Too much so to feel hatred or triumph, watching."

"Only pity. Is that what you mean? At least in what Stencil read. Read into. How can he—"

"More a passiveness. The characteristic stillness, perhaps, of the rock. Inertia. I'd come back—no, in—come in to the rock as far as I would."

Stencil brightened after a while and changed course. "A token. Comb, shoe, glass eye. The children."

"I wasn't watching the children. I was watching your V. What I did see of the children—I recognized none of the faces. No. They may have died before the war ended or emigrated after it. Try Australia. Try the pawnbrokers and

419

curio shops. But as for placing a notice in the agony column: 'Anyone participating in the disassembly of a priest—'"

"Please."

Next day, and for days after, he investigated the inventories of curio merchants, pawnbrokers, ragmen. He returned one morning to find Paola brewing tea on the ring for Profane, who lay bundled up in bed.

"Fever," she said. "Too much booze, too much everything back in New York. He hasn't been eating much since we arrived. God knows where he does eat. What the water there is like."

"I'll recover," Profane croaked. "Tough shit, Stencil."

"He says you're down on him."

"O God," said Stencil.

The next day brought momentary encouragement to Stencil. A shopowner named Cassar did know of an eye such as Stencil described. The girl lived in Valletta, her husband was an auto mechanic at the garage which cared for Cassar's Morris. He had tried every device he knew to purchase the eye, but the foolish girl would not part with it. A keepsake, she said.

She lived in a tenement. Stucco walls, a row of balconies on the top floor. Light that afternoon produced a "burn" between whites and blacks: fuzzy edges, blurrings. White was too white, black too black. Stencil's eyes hurt. Colors were nearly absent, leaning either to white or black.

"I threw it into the sea." Hands on hips, defiant. He smiled uncertainly. Where had Sidney's charm fled? Under the same sea, back to its owner. Light angling through the window fell across a bowl of fruit—oranges, limes—bleaching them and throwing the bowl's interior to black shadow. Something was wrong with the light. Stencil felt tired, unable to pursue it further—not just now—wanting only to leave. He left.

Profane sat in a worn flowered robe of Fausto Maijstral's, looking ghastly, chewing on the stump of an old cigar. He glared at Stencil. Stencil ignored him: threw himself on the bed and slept soundly for twelve hours.

He awoke at four in the morning and walked through a sea-phosphorescence to Maijstral's. Dawn leaked in, turning the illumination conventional. Along a mudway and up twenty steps. A light burned.

Maijstral was asleep at his table. "Don't haunt me, Stencil," he mumbled, still dreamy and belligerent.

"Stencil is passing on the discomfort of being haunted," Stencil shivered.

They huddled over tea in chipped cups.

"She cannot be dead," Stencil said.

"One feels her in the city," he cried.

"In the city."

"In the light. It has to do with the light."

"If the soul," Maijstral ventured, "is light. Is it a presence?"

"Damn the word. Stencil's father, had he possessed imagination, might have used it." Stencil's eyebrows puckered, as if he would cry. He weaved irritably in his seat, blinked, fumbled for his pipe. He'd left it at the lodging-house. Maijstral tapped across a pack of Players.

Lighting up: "Maijstral. Stencil expresses himself like an idiot."

"But your search fascinates me."

"Did you know, he's devised a prayer. Walking about this city, to be said in rhythm to his footsteps. Fortune, may Stencil be steady enough not to fasten on one of these poor ruins at his own random or at any least hint from Maijstral. Let him not roam out all Gothic some night with lantern and shovel to exhume an hallucination, and be found by the authorities mud-streaked and mad, and tossing meaningless clay about."

"Come, come," muttered Maijstral. "I feel uncomfortable enough, being in this position."

Stencil drew in his breath too loudly.

"No I am not beginning to requestion. That is long done."

Beginning then Maijstral took up the study of Stencil more closely. Though suspending judgment. He'd aged enough to know the written apologia would only be a first step in exorcising the sense of sin that had hung with him since '43. But this $V.$ was surely more than a sense of sin?

Mounting crisis in the Suez, Hungary and Poland hardly touched them. Maijstral, leery like any Maltese of the Balloon's least bobbing, was grateful for something else—Stencil—to take his mind off the headlines. But Stencil himself, who seemed more unaware each day (under questioning) of what was happening in the rest of the world, reinforced Maijstral's growing theory that V. was an obsession

421

after all, and that such an obsession is a hothouse: constant temperature, windless, too crowded with particolored sports, unnatural blooms.

Stencil, returning to the lodging-house, walked into a loud argument between Paola and Profane.

"So go," he was yelling. Something crashed against the door.

"Don't try to make up my mind for me," she yelled back. Stencil opened the door warily, peered around and was hit in the face with a pillow. Shades were drawn and Stencil saw only blurred figures: Profane still ducking out of the way, Paola's arm in follow-through.

"What the hell."

Profane, crouching like a toad, flapped a newspaper at him. "My old ship is in." All Stencil could see were the whites of his eyes. Paola was crying.

"Ah." Stencil dived for the bed. Profane had been sleeping on the floor. Let them use that, thought spiteful Stencil; snuffled, and drifted off to sleep.

At length it occurred to him to talk with the old priest, Father Avalanche, who according to Maijstral had been here since 1919.

The moment he entered the church he knew he'd lost again. The old priest knelt at the communion rail: white hair above a black cassock. Too old.

Later, in the priest's house:

"God lets some of us wait, in queer backwaters," said Father Avalanche. "Do you know how long it's been since I have shriven a murderer? At the time of the Challis Tower murder last year I had hopes . . ." He maundered thus, taking Stencil by an unwilling hand, and began to charge aimless about thickets of memory. Stencil tried to point them toward the June Disturbances.

"Oh I was only a young lad then, full of myth. The Knights, you know. One cannot come to Valletta without knowing about the Knights. I still believe—" chuckling— "as I believed then, that they roam the streets after sunset. Somewhere. And I had only served as padre—in the actual fighting—long enough to have illusions left about Avalanche as crusading Knight. But then to compare the Malta that was, in 1919, to their Malta. . . . You'd have to talk, I suppose, to my predecessor here, Father Fairing. He went to

America. Though the poor old man, wherever he is, must be dead by now."

Politely as he could Stencil took leave of the old priest, plunged into the sunlight and began to walk. There was too much adrenalin, contracting the smooth muscle, deepening his breathing, quickening his pulse. "Stencil must walk," he said to the street: "walk."

Foolish Stencil: he was out of condition. He returned to his pied-à-terre long after midnight, hardly able to stand. The room was empty.

"Clinches it," he muttered. If it were the same Fairing. Even if it were not, could it matter? A phrase (it often happened when he was exhausted) kept cycling round and round, preconsciously, just under the threshold of lip and tongue movement: "Events seem to be ordered into an ominous logic." It repeated itself automatically and Stencil improved on it each time, placing emphasis on different words—"events *seem*"; "seem to be *ordered*"; "*ominous* logic" —pronouncing them differently, changing the "tone of voice" from sepulchral to jaunty: round and round and round. Events seem to be ordered into an ominous logic. He found paper and pencil and began to write the sentence in varying hands and type faces. Profane lurched in on him thus.

"Paola's back with her husband," said Profane and collapsed on the bed. "She'll go back to the States."

"Someone," Stencil muttered, "is out of it, then." Profane groaned and pulled blankets around him. "Look here," said Stencil. "Now, you're sick." He crossed to Profane, felt his forehead. "High fever. Stencil must get a doctor. What the hell were you doing out at this hour anyway."

"No." Profane flopped over, fished under the bed in his ditty bag. "APC's. I'll sweat it out."

Neither spoke for a while but Stencil was too distraught to hold anything in. "Profane," he said.

"Tell Paola's father. I'm only along for the ride."

Stencil began to pace. Laughed: "Stencil doesn't think he believes him any longer." Profane rolled over laboriously and blinked at him.

"V.'s is a country of coincidence, ruled by a ministry of myth. Whose emissaries haunt this century's streets. Porcépic, Mondaugen, Stencil père, this Maijstral, Stencil fils. Could any of them create a coincidence? Only Providence creates. If the coincidences are real then Stencil has

423

never encountered history at all, but something far more appalling.

"Stencil came on Father Fairing's name once, apparently by accident. Today he came on it again, by what only could have been design."

"I wonder," said Profane, "if that was the same Father Fairing . . ."

Stencil froze, the booze jittering in his glass. While Profane, dreamy, went on to tell of his nights with the Alligator Patrol, and how he'd hunted one pinto beast through Fairing's Parish; cornered and killed it in a chamber lit by some frightening radiance.

Carefully Stencil finished the whisky, cleaned out the glass with a handkerchief, set the glass on the table. He put on his overcoat.

"You going out for a doctor," Profane said into the pillow.

"Of sorts," Stencil said.

An hour later he was at Maijstral's.

"Don't wake her," Maijstral said. "Poor child. I'd never seen her cry."

"Nor have you seen Stencil cry," said Stencil, "but you may. Ex-priest. He has a soul possessed by the devil sleeping in his bed."

"Profane?" In an attempt at good humor: "We must get to Father A., he's a frustrated exorcist, always complaining about the lack of excitement."

"Aren't you a frustrated exorcist?"

Maijstral frowned. "That's another Maijstral."

"She possesses him," Stencil whispered. "V."

"You are as sick."

"Please."

Maijstral opened the window and stepped out on the balcony. Valletta by nightlight looked totally uninhabited. "No," Maijstral said, "you wouldn't get what you wanted. What —if it were your world—would be necessary. One would have to exorcise the city, the island, every ship's crew on that Mediterranean. The continents, the world. Or the western part," as an afterthought. "We are western men."

Stencil shrank at the cold air moving in through the window.

"I'm not a priest. Don't try appealing to someone you've only known in a written confession. We do not walk ganged,

424

Stencil, all our separate selves, like Siamese quintuplets or more. God knows (how many Stencils) have chased V. about the world."

"Fairing," Stencil croaked, "in whose Parish Stencil was shot, preceded your Father Avalanche."

"I could have told you. Told you the name."

"But."

"Saw no advantage in making things worse."

Stencil's eyes narrowed. Maijstral turned, caught him looking cagy.

"Yes, yes. Thirteen of us rule the world in secret."

"Stencil went out of his way to bring Profane here. He should have been more careful; he wasn't. Is it really his own extermination he's after?"

Maijstral turned smiling to him. Gestured behind his back at the ramparts of Valletta. "Ask her," he whispered. "Ask the rock."

III

Two days later Maijstral arrived at the lodging-house to find Profane lying dead drunk and slaunchwise on the bed. Afternoon sun illuminated a swathe of face in which every hair of a week's growth showed up separate and distinct. Profane's mouth was open, he was snoring and drooling and apparently enjoying himself.

Maijstral gave Profane's forehead the back of his hand: fine. The fever had broken. But where was Stencil? No sooner asked than Maijstral saw the note. A cubist moth, alit forever on the gross heap of Profane's beer belly.

> A shipfitter named Aquilina has intelligence of one Mme. Viola, oneiromancer and hypnotist, who passed through Valletta in 1944. The glass eye went with her. Cassar's girl lied. V. used it for an hypnotic aid. Her destination, Stockholm. As is Stencil's. It will do for the frayed end of another clue. Dispose as you will of Profane. Stencil has no further need for any of you. Sahha.

Maijstral looked around for booze. Profane had finished everything in the house.

"Swine."

Profane woke. "Wha."

Maijstral read him the note. Profane rolled out of bed and crawled to the window.

"What day is it." After a while: "Paola's gone too?"

"Last night."

"Leaving me. Well. How do you dispose of me."

"Lend you a fiver, to begin with."

"Lend," roared Profane. "You ought to know better."

"I'll be back," said Maijstral.

That night Profane shaved, bathed, donned suede jacket, levis and big cowboy hat and went a-roving down Kingsway, looking for amusement. He found it in the form of one Brenda Wigglesworth, an American WASP who attended Beaver College and owned, she said, 72 pairs of Bermuda shorts, half of which she had brought over to Europe back around June at the beginning of a Grand Tour which had then held high promise. High she had remained all the way across the Atlantic; high as the boat deck and mostly on sloe gin fizzes. The various lifeboats of this most underelict passage east were shared by a purser (summer job) from the academic flatlands of Jersey who gave her an orange and black toy tiger, a pregnancy scare (hers only) and a promise to meet her in Amsterdam, somewhere behind the Five Flies. He'd not come: she came to herself—or at least to the inviolable Puritan she'd show up as come marriage and the Good Life, someday soon now—in a bar's parking lot near a canal, filled with a hundred black bicycles: her junkyard, her own locust season. Skeletons, carapaces, no matter: her inside too was her outside and on she went, streak-blond, far-from-frail Brenda, along the Rhine, up and down the soft slopes of the wine districts, into the Tyrol and out into Tuscany, all in a rented Morris whose fuel pump clicked random and loud in times of stress; as did her camera, as did her heart.

Valletta was the end of another season and all her friends were long sailed back to the States. She was nearly out of money. Profane couldn't help her. She found him fascinating.

So over sloe gin fizzes for her which took tiny sweet bites out of Maijstral's five-pound note, and beer for Benny, they talked of how it was they had come this far and where they would go after Valletta, and it seemed there were Beaver and the Street for them separately to return to; and both agreed this was nowhere, but some of us do go nowhere and can con ourselves into believing it to be somewhere: it is a kind of talent and objections to it are rare but even at that captious.

That night between them they established at least that the world was screwed up. English Marines, Commandos and sailors who came by—going nowhere also—helped them believe it. Profane saw no Scaffold sailors and decided that since some of them must be clean-living enough to stay away from the Gut, the Scaffold too had left. It made him sadder: as if all his homes were temporary and even they, inanimate, still wandering as he: for motion is relative, and hadn't he, now, really stood there still on the sea like a schlemihl Redeemer while that enormous malingering city and its one livable inner space and one unconnable (therefore hi-valu) girl had all slid away from him over a great horizon's curve comprising, from this vantage, at once, at least one century's worth of wavelets?

"Don't be sad."

"Brenda, we're all sad."

"Benny, we are." She laughed, raucous, having a low tolerance for sloe gin.

They went back to his place and she must have left him sometime during the night, in the dark. Profane was a heavy sleeper. He awoke alone in bed to the sound of forenoon traffic. Maijstral sat on the table, observing a plaid knee sock, the kind worn with Bermuda shorts, which was draped over the electric lamp hanging from the center of the ceiling.

"I have brought wine," said Maijstral.

"Good enough."

They went out to a café for breakfast, about two. "I have no intention of supporting you indefinitely," Maijstral said.

"I should get a job. Any road work in Malta?"

"They are building a grade intersection—an underground tunnel—at Porte-des-Bombes. They also need men to plant trees along the roads."

"Road work and sewer work is all I know."

"Sewers? There's a new pumping station going up at Marsa."

"They hire aliens?"

"Possibly."

"Possibly, then."

That evening Brenda wore paisley shorts and black socks. "I write poetry," she announced. They were at her place, a modest hotel near the great lift.

"Oh," said Profane.

"I am the twentieth century," she read. Profane rolled away and stared at the pattern in the rug.

"I am the ragtime and the tango; sans-serif, clean geometry. I am the virgin's-hair whip and the cunningly detailed shackles of decadent passion. I am every lonely railway station in every capital of Europe. I am the Street, the fanciless buildings of government; the café-dansant, the clockwork figure, the jazz saxophone; the tourist-lady's hairpiece, the fairy's rubber breasts, the traveling clock which always tells the wrong time and chimes in different keys. I am the dead palm tree, the Negro's dancing pumps, the dried fountain after tourist season. I am all the appurtenances of night."

"That sounds about right," said Profane.

"I don't know." She made a paper airplane out of the poem and sailed it across the room on strata of her own exhaled smoke. "It's a phony college-girl poem. Things I've read for courses. Does it sound right?"

"Yes."

"You've done so much more. Boys do."

"What?"

"You've had all these fabulous experiences. I wish mine would show me something."

"Why."

"The experience, the experience. Haven't you learned?"

Profane didn't have to think long. "No," he said, "offhand I'd say I haven't learned a goddamn thing."

They were quiet for a while. She said: "Let's take a walk."

Later, out in the street, near the sea steps she inexplicably took his hand and began to run. The buildings in this part of Valletta, eleven years after war's end, had not been rebuilt. The street, however, was level and clear. Hand in hand with Brenda whom he'd met yesterday, Profane ran down the street. Presently, sudden and in silence, all illumination in Valletta, houselight and streetlight, was extinguished. Profane and Brenda continued to run through the abruptly absolute night, momentum alone carrying them toward the edge of Malta, and the Mediterranean beyond.

Epilogue
1919
V

Winter. The green xebec whose figurehead was Astarte, goddess of sexual love, tacked slowly into the Grand Harbour. Yellow bastions, Moorish-looking city, rainy sky. What more on first glance? In his youth no one of those score or so other cities had ever shown old Stencil much in the way of Romance. But now as if making up for lost time his mind seemed to've gone rainy as the sky.

He kept near the stern, rained on, bird-frame wrapped in oilskin, sheltering his pipe's match from the wind. Overhead for a while hung Fort St. Angelo, dirty yellow and wrapped in a quiet not of this earth. Abeam gradually came H.M.S. Egmont, a few seamen on her decks like blue-and-white dolls shivering for the Harbour wind, holy stoning to work off this morning's chill. His cheeks hollowed and flattened as the xebec seemed to describe a complete circle and Grand-master La Vallette's dream whirled away for Fort St. Elmo and the Mediterranean, which in their turn spun past into Ricasoli, Vittoriosa, the Dockyard. Mehemet the master swore at his helmsman, Astarte now leaned from the xebec's bowsprit toward the city as if it were male and asleep and she, inanimate figurehead, a succubus preparing to ravish. Mehemet approached him. "Mara lives in a strange house," said Stencil. Wind flapped one whitening forelock, rooted halfway back on his scalp. He said it for the city, not for Mehemet; but the master understood.

"Whenever we came to Malta," he said in some Levantine

429

tongue, "I got the feeling. As if a great hush were on this sea and the island its heart. As if I'd come back to something my own heart needs as deeply as a heart can." He lit a cigarette from Stencil's pipe. "But it is a deception. She's an inconstant city. Be wary of her."

One hulking boy stood on the quay to receive their lines. He and Mehemet exchanged salaam aleikums. A pillar of cloud stood to the north behind Marsamuscetto, looking solid and about to topple, to crush the city. Mehemet wandered about kicking the crew. One by one they drifted below decks and began hauling the cargo topside: a few live goats, some sacks of sugar, dried tarragon from Sicily, salted pilchards in barrels, from Greece.

Stencil had his gear collected. The rain descended more quickly. He opened a great umbrella and stood under it watching the Dockyard country. Well, what am I waiting for, he wondered. The crew had retired below decks all sullen. Mehemet came squishing across the deck. "Fortune," he said.

"An inconstant goddess." The pier hand who'd taken their lines now sat on a piling, facing the water, hunched up like a bedraggled sea bird. "Island of sunshine?" Stencil laughed. His pipe was still lit. Among white fumes then he and Mehemet made farewell. He teetered across a single plank to shore, balancing a ditty bag on one shoulder, the umbrella looking like a tightrope-walker's parasol. Indeed, he thought. What safety, after all, on this shore. Ashore anywhere?

From the window of a cab, proceeding in the rain along Strada Reale, Stencil could detect none of the holiday one saw in other capitals of Europe. Perhaps it was only the rain. But welcome relief surely. Stencil was fed to surfeit on songs, bunting, parades, promiscuous loves, uncouth noisemakings; all the normal responses of noncombatants-in-the-mass to Armistice or peace. Even in the normally sober offices in Whitehall, it had been impossible. Armistice, ha!

"I cannot understand your attitude," from Carruthers-Pillow, then Stencil's superior. "Armistice, ha, indeed."

Stencil muttered something about things not being stabilized. How could he tell Carruthers-Pillow of all people, who felt in the presence of the most inconsequential chit initialed by the Foreign Secretary much as Moses must have toward the Decalogue God blasted out for him on stone.

Wasn't the Armistice signed by legally-constituted heads of government? How could there not be peace? It would never be worth the trouble arguing. So they'd stood that November morning, watching the lamplighter extinguish the lights in St. James's Park, as if having long ago passed through some quicksilver surface from when Viscount Grey had stood perhaps at the same window and made his famous remark about the lamps going out all over Europe. Stencil of course didn't see the difference between event and image, but saw no advantage in disturbing his chief's euphoria. Let the poor innocent sleep. Stencil had merely been dour, which in him passed for high celebration.

Lieutenant Mungo Sheaves, aide to the Officer Administrating Government on Malta, had set before Whitehall an architecture of discontent: among the police force, the University students, the civil service, the Dockyard workers. Behind it all lurked "the Doctor"; organizer, civil engineer: E. Mizzi. A bogeyman to Major General Hunter-Blair, the OAG, Stencil guessed; but found it took him an effort to see Mizzi as anything but a busy man-of-policy, agile, Machiavellian, a trifle old-fashioned, who'd managed to last as far as 1919. For a survival like that Stencil could only feel a wistful pride. His good friend Porpentine—twenty years ago in Egypt—hadn't he been the same sort? Belonged to a time where which side a man was on didn't matter: only the state of opposition itself, the tests of virtue, the cricket game? Stencil may have come in on the tail end.

It must be shock, fine: even Stencil could feel shock. Ten million dead and twice that wounded if nothing else. "But we reach a point," he'd thought of telling Carruthers-Pillow, "we old campaigners, when the habits of the past become too strong. Where we can say, and believe, that this abattoir, but lately bankrupt, was fundamentally no different from the Franco-Prussian conflict, the Sudanese wars, even the Crimea. It is perhaps a delusion—say a convenience—necessary to our line of work. But more honorable surely than this loathsome weakness of retreat into dreams: pastel visions of disarmament, a League, a universal law. Ten million dead. Gas. Passchendaele. Let that be now a large figure, now a chemical formula, now an historical account. But dear lord, not the Nameless Horror, the sudden prodigy sprung on a world unaware. We all saw it. There was no innovation, no

431

special breach of nature, or suspension of familiar principles. If it came as any surprise to the public then their own blindness is the Great Tragedy, hardly the war itself."

On route to Valletta—the steamer to Syracuse, the week of lying doggo in a waterfront tavern till Mehemet's xebec arrived; all the way across a Mediterranean whose teeming history and full depth he could not feel, nor try, nor afford to try to feel, old Stencil had had it out with himself. Mehemet had helped.

"You're old," the skipper mused over his nightly hashish. "I am old, the world is old; but the world changes always; we, only so far. It's no secret, what sort of change this is. Both the world and we, M. Stencil, began to die from the moment of birth. Your game is politics which I don't pretend to understand. But it seems that these—" he shrugged—"noisy attempts to devise political happiness: new forms of government, new ways to arrange the fields and workshops; aren't they like the sailor I saw off Bizerte in 1324." Stencil chuckled. Mehemet's recurring lament was for a world taken from him. He belonged to the trade routes of the Middle Ages. According to the yarn he had in fact sailed the xebec through a rift in time's fabric, pursued then among the Aegean Islands by a Tuscan corsair which mysteriously dropped from sight. But it was the same sea and not until docking at Rhodes did Mehemet learn of his displacement. And since had forsaken land for a Mediterranean which thank Allah would never change. Whatever his true nostalgia he reckoned by the Moslem calendar not only in conversation but also in logs and account books; though the religion and perhaps the birthright he'd let pass years ago.

"Slung on a stage over the gunwale of an old felucca, the Peri. A storm had just passed, rushing away toward the land in a great slope of clouds; already turning yellowish from the desert. The sea there is the color of Damascus plums; and how quiet. Sun was going down; not a beautiful sunset, more a gradual darkening of the air and that storm's mountainside. The Peri had been damaged, we hove to alongside and hailed her master. No reply. Only the sailor—I never saw his face—one of your fellahin who abandon the land like a restless husband and then grumble for the rest of their term afloat. It's the strongest marriage in the world. This one wore a kind of loincloth and a rag round his head for the sun which was almost gone. After we'd shouted in every

432

dialect we had among us, he replied in Tuareg: 'The master is gone, the crew is gone, I am here and I am painting the ship.' It was true: he was painting the ship. She'd been damaged, not a load line in sight, and a bad list. 'Come aboard,' we told him, 'night is nearly on us and you cannot swim to land.' He never answered, merely continued dipping the brush in his earthen jar and slapping it smoothly on the Peri's creaking sides. What color? It looked gray but the air was dark. This felucca would never again see the sun. Finally I told the helmsman to swing our ship round and continue on course. I watched the fellah until it was too dark: becoming smaller, inching closer to the sea with every swell but never slackening his pace. A peasant with all his uptorn roots showing, alone on the sea at nightfall, painting the side of a sinking ship."

"Am I only getting old?" Stencil wondered. "Perhaps past the time I can change with the world."

"The only change is toward death," repeated Mehemet cheerfully. "Early and late we are in decay." The helmsman began to sing a monotonous, Levantine lanterloo. There were no stars and the sea was hushed. Stencil refused hashish and filled his pipe with a respectable English blend; lit up, puffed, began:

"Which way does it go? As a youth I believed in social progress because I saw chances for personal progress of my own. Today, at age sixty, having gone as far as I'm about to go, I see nothing but a dead end for myself, and if you're right, for my society as well. But then: suppose Sidney Stencil has remained constant after all—suppose instead sometime between 1859 and 1919, the world contracted a disease which no one ever took the trouble to diagnose because the symptoms were too subtle—blending in with the events of history, no different one by one but altogether—fatal. This is how the public, you know, see the late war. As a new and rare disease which has now been cured and conquered for ever."

"Is old age a disease?" Mehemet asked. "The body slows down, machines wear out, planets falter and loop, sun and stars gutter and smoke. Why say a disease? Only to bring it down to a size you can look at and feel comfortable?"

"Because we do paint the side of some Peri or other, don't we. We call it society. A new coat of paint; don't you see? She can't change her own color."

"No more than the pustules of smallpox have anything to do with death. A new complexion, a new coat of paint."

"Of course," said Stencil, thinking of something else, "of course we would all prefer to die of old age. . . ."

The Armageddon had swept past, the professionals who'd survived had received no blessing, no gift of tongues. Despite all attempts to cut its career short the tough old earth would take its own time in dying and would die of old age. Then Mehemet told him of Mara.

"Another of your women."

"Ha, ha. Indeed. Maltese for woman."

"Of course."

"She is—if you care for the word—a spirit, constrained to live in Xaghriet Mewwija. The inhabited plain; the peninsula whose tip is Valletta, her domain. She nursed the shipwrecked St. Paul—as Nausicaä and Odysseus—taught love to every invader from Phoenician to French. Perhaps even to the English, though the legend loses respectability after Napoleon. She was from all evidence a perfectly historical personage, like St. Agatha, another of the island's minor saints.

"Now the Great Siege was after my time, but legend—one of them—says that she once had access to the entire island and the waters as far as the fishing banks off Lampedusa. The fishing fleets would always lie to there in the shape of a carob pod, her proper symbol. Early in your 1565, at any rate, two privateers, Giou and Romegas, captured a Turkish galleon belonging to the chief eunuch of the Imperial Seraglio. In retaliation Mara was taken prisoner on one of her jaunts to Lampedusa by the corsair Dragut, and brought back to Constantinople. Soon as the ship had passed the invisible circle centered at Xaghriet Mewwija with Lampedusa on the rim, she fell into a strange trance, from which neither caresses nor tortures could rouse her. At length, having lost their own figurehead in a collision with a Sicilian ragusy the week before, the Turks lashed Mara to the bowsprit and that was how she entered Constantinople: a living figurehead. On drawing near to that city, blinding yellow and dun under a clear sky, she was heard to awake and cry: "Lejl, hekk ikun." Night, so be it. The Turks thought she was raving. Or blind.

"They brought her to the serail, into the presence of the Sultan. Now she never was pictured as a raving beauty. She shows up as a number of goddesses, minor deities. Disguise

434

eternal feminine

is one of her attributes. But one curious thing about those images: jar ornaments, friezes, sculptures, no matter: she's always tall, slim, small-breasted and bellied. No matter what the prevalent fashion in females, she remains constant. In her face is always a slight bow to the nose, a wide spacing of the eyes, which are small. No one you'd turn to watch on the street. But she was a teacher of love after all. Only pupils of love need be beautiful.

"She pleased the Sultan. Perhaps she made the effort. But was installed somehow as a concubine about the time La Vallette back on her island was blocking the creek between Senglea and St. Angelo with an iron chain and poisoning the springs in the Marsa plain with hemp and arsenic. Once in the seraglio she proceeded to raise hell. She'd always been attributed magical talents. Perhaps the carob pod—she's often depicted holding one—had something to do with it. Wand, scepter. Perhaps too, some kind of fertility goddess—do I embarrass your Anglo-Saxon nerves?—though it is a quaint, hermaphrodite sort of deity.

"Soon—a matter of weeks—the Sultan noticed a certain coldness infecting each of his nightly companions; a reluctance, a lack of talent. Also a change in attitude among the eunuchs. Almost—how to say it—smug and keeping a bad secret of it. Nothing he could establish definitely; and so like most unreasonable men with suspicions he had certain girls and eunuchs tortured horribly. All protested innocence, showed honest fear to the last twist of the neck, the last upward thrust of the iron spike. And yet it progressed. Spies reported that shy concubines who had once paced with ladylike steps—limited by a slim chain between the ankles—and downcast eyes now smiled and flirted promiscuously with the eunuchs, and the eunuchs—horror!—flirted back. Girls left to themselves would suddenly leap on one another with fierce caresses; on occasion make loud abandoned love before the scandalized eyes of the Sultan's agents.

"At length it occurred to His Ghostly Magnificence, nearly out of his mind with jealousy, to call in the sorceress Mara. Standing before him in a shift fashioned of tigermoth wings she faced the Imperial dais with a wicked smile. The Imperial retainers were charmed.

"'Woman,' began the Sultan.

"She raised a hand. 'I have done it all,' she recited sweet-

435

ly: 'taught your wives to love their own bodies, showed them the luxury of a woman's love; restored potency to your eunuchs so that they may enjoy one another as well as the three hundred perfumed, female beasts of your harem.'

"Bewildered at such ready confession, his tender Moslem sensibilities outraged by the epidemic of perversion she'd unleashed upon his domestic repose, the Sultan made what is a fatal mistake with any woman: he decided to argue. Jolted into a rare sarcasm he explained to her, as to an idiot, why eunuchs cannot have sexual intercourse.

"Her smile never fading, her voice placid as before, Mara replied: 'I have provided them with the means.'

"So confidently did she speak that the Sultan began to feel the first groundswell of an atavistic terror. Oh, at last he knew: he was in the presence of a witch.

"Back home the Turks, led by Dragut and the pashas Piali and Mustafa, had laid siege to Malta. You know generally how it went. They occupied Xaghriet Mewwija, took Fort St. Elmo, and began their assault on Notabile, Borgo —today that's Vittoriosa—and Senglea, where La Vallette and the Knights were making their final stand.

"Now after St. Elmo had fallen, Mustafa (possibly in sorrow for Dragut, killed in that encounter by a stone cannonball) had also launched a grisly offensive on the morale of the Knights. He beheaded their slaughtered brethren, tied the corpses to planks and floated them into the Grand Harbour. Imagine being on sunrise watch and seeing the dawn touch those ex-comrades-in-arms, belly up and crowding the water: death's flotilla.

"One of the great mysteries about the Siege is why, when the Turks outnumbered the invested Knights, when the days of the besieged were numbered on a single hand, when Borgo and thus Malta were almost in the same hand —Mustafa's—why should they suddenly pull up and retreat, hoist anchor and leave the island?

"History says because of a rumor. Don Garcia de Toledo, viceroy of Sicily, was on route with forty-eight galleys. Pompeo Colonna and twelve hundred men, sent by the Pope to relieve La Vallette, eventually reached Gozo. But somehow the Turks got hold of intelligence that twenty thousand troops had landed at Melleha Bay and were on route to Notabile. General retreat was ordered; church bells all over Xaghriet Mewwija began to ring; the people thronged the streets, cheering. The Turks fled, embarked and sailed away to the southeast forever. History attributes it all to bad reconnaissance.

"But the truth is this: the words were spoken directly to Mustafa by the head of the Sultan himself. The witch Mara had sent him into a kind of mesmeric trance; detached his head and put it into the Dardanelles, where some miraculous set and drift—who knows all the currents, all the things which happen in this sea?—sent it on a collision course with Malta. There is a song written by a latter-day jongleur named Falconière. No Renaissance had ever touched him; he resided at the Auberge of Aragon, Catalonia and Navarre at the time of the Siege. You know the sort of poet who can fall into belief in any fashionable cult, current philosophy, new-found foreign superstition. This one fell into belief and possibly love for Mara. Even distinguished himself on the ramparts of Borgo, braining four Janissaries with his lute before someone handed him a sword. She was, you see, his Lady."

Mehemet recited:

Fleeing the mistral, fleeing the sun's hot lash,
Serene in scalloped waves, and sculptured sky
The head feels no rain, fears no pitchy night,
As o'er this ancient sea it races stars,
Empty but for a dozen fatal words,
Charmed by Mara, Mara my only love . . .

There follows an apostrophe to Mara."

Stencil nodded sagely, trying to fill in with Spanish cognates.

"Apparently," Mehemet concluded, "the head returned to Constantinople and its owner, the sly Mara meanwhile having slipped aboard a friendly galiot, disguised as a cabin boy. Back in Valletta at last she appeared in a vision to La Vallette, greeting him with the words "Shalom aleikum."

The joke being that shalom is Hebrew for peace and also the root for the Greek Salome, who beheaded St. John.

"Beware of Mara," the old sailor said then. "Guardian spirit of Xaghriet Mewwija. Whoever or whatever sees to such things condemned her to haunt the inhabited plain, as punishment for her show at Constantinople. About as useful as clapping any faithless wife in a chastity belt.

437

"She's restless. She will find ways to reach out from Valletta, a city named after a man, but of feminine gender, a peninsula shaped like the mons Veneris—you see? It is a chastity belt. But there are more ways than one to consummation, as she proved to the Sultan."

Now sprinting from the taxi through the rain to his hotel, Stencil did indeed feel a tug. Not so much at his loins—there had been company enough in Syracuse to anaesthetize that for a while—as at the wizened adolescent he was always apt to turn into. A little later, scrunched up in an undersize tub, Stencil sang. It was a tune, in fact, from his "music-hall" days before the war, and primarily a way to relax:

> Every night to the Dog and Bell
> Young Stencil loved to go
> To dance on the tables and shout and sing
> And give 'is pals a show.
> His little wife would stay to home
> 'Er 'eart all filled wiv pain
> But the next night sharp at a quarter to six
> 'E'd be down to the pub again. Until
> That one fine evening in the monf of May
> He announced to all as came wivin 'is sight
> You must get along wivout me boys
> I'm through wiv rowdiness and noise.
> Cause Stencil's going 'ome tonight.

[In palmier days a chorus of junior F.O. operatives would enter here singing]:

> 'Ere, wot's this? Wot's the matter wiv Stencil?
> Wot's the reason for such a change of 'eart?

[To which Stencil would answer]:

> Gather round me closely lads
> And I the most forlorn of cads
> Will tell you all ere I depart:

[Refrain]:

> I've just become the father to a bouncing baby boy
> And Herbert blithering Stencil is 'is name.
> 'E's a card

438

And treats me wiv regard
Though I 'ave to change 'is nappies all the same.
I don't know where we got the time to make 'im,
Cause I've been coming 'ome drunk most every night,
But 'e's cute and fat as a kidney pie
And looks like 'is ma and that is why
Stencil's going 'ome tonight
(Just ask the milkman)
Stencil's going 'ome tonight.

Out of the tub, dry, back in tweeds, Stencil stood at the window, looking out idly at the night.

At length came a knock at the door. It would be Maijstral. A quick twitch of eyeballs about the room to check for loose papers, anything compromising. Then to the door to admit the shipfitter who'd been described to him as looking like a stunted oak. Maijstral stood there neither aggressive nor humble, merely existing: whitening hair, unkempt mustaches. A nervous tic in the man's upper lip made the food particles trapped there vibrate disturbingly.

"He comes of noble family," Mehemet had revealed sadly. Stencil fell into the trap, asking which family. "Della Torre," Mehemet replied. Delatore, informer.

"What of the Dockyard people," Stencil asked.

"They will attack the Chronicle." (A grievance stemming from the strike of 1917; the newspaper had published a letter condemning the strike, but had given no equal time for a reply.) "There was a meeting a few minutes ago." Maijstral gave him a brief digest. Stencil knew all the objections. Workers from England got a colonial allowance: local yardbirds received only normal wages. Most would like to emigrate, after hearing glowing reports from the Maltese Labour Corps and other crews from abroad of higher pay outside Malta. But the rumor had started, somehow, that the government was refusing passports to keep workers on the island, against any future requirement. "What else can they do but emigrate?" Maijstral digressed: "With the war the number of Dockyard workers swelled to three times what it was before. Now, with Armistice, they're already laying off. There are only so many jobs here outside the Dockyard. Not enough to keep everyone eating."

Stencil wanted to ask: if you sympathize, why inform? He had used informers as a journeyman his tools and had never tried to understand their motives. Usually he supposed it was no more than a personal grudge, a desire for revenge. But he'd seen them before, torn: committed to some program or other, and still helping along its defeat. Would Maijstral be there in the van of the mob storming the Daily Malta Chronicle? Stencil did want to ask why, but could hardly. It being none of his affair.

Maijstral told him all he knew and left, expressionless as before. Stencil lit a pipe, consulted a map of Valletta, and five minutes later was strolling sprightly down Strada Reale, trailing Maijstral.

This was normal precaution. Of course, a certain double standard was at work; the feeling being "If he will inform for me he will also inform against me."

Ahead Maijstral now turned left, away from the lights of the main thoroughfare; down the hill toward Strada Stretta. Here were the borders of this city's Disreputable Quarter; Stencil looked around without much curiosity. It was all the same. What a warped idea of cities one got in this occupation! If no record of this century should survive except the personal logs of F.O. operatives, the historians of the future must reconstruct a curious landscape indeed.

Massive public buildings with characterless façades; networks of streets from which the civilian populace seems mysteriously absent. An aseptic administrative world, surrounded by an outlying vandal-country of twisting lanes, houses of prostitution, taverns; ill-lit except for rendezvous points, which stand out like sequins on an old and misused ball-gown.

"If there is any political moral to be found in this world," Stencil once wrote in his journal, "it is that we carry on the business of this century with an intolerable double vision. Right and Left; the hothouse and the street. The Right can only live and work hermetically, in the hothouse of the past, while outside the Left prosecute their affairs in the streets by manipulated mob violence. And cannot live but in the dreamscape of the future.

"What of the real present, the men-of-no-politics, the once-respectable Golden Mean? Obsolete; in any case, lost sight of. In a West of such extremes we can expect, at the very least, a highly 'alienated' populace within not many more years."

Strada Stretta; Strait Street. A passage meant, one felt, to be choked with mobs. Such was nearly the case: early evening had brought to it sailors ashore from H.M.S. Egmont and smaller men-o-war; seamen from Greek, Italian and North African merchantmen; and a supporting cast of shoeshine boys, pimps, hawkers of trinkets, confections, dirty pictures. Such were the topological deformities of this street that one seemed to walk through a succession of musichall stages, each demarcated by a curve or slope, each with a different set and acting company but all for the same low entertainment. Stencil, old soft-shoe artist, felt quite at home.

But he increased his pace through the thickening crowds; noticing with some anxiety that Maijstral had begun to disappear more and more frequently in the surgings of white and blue ahead.

To his right he became aware of a persistent image, flickering in and out of his field of vision. Tall, black, somehow conical. He risked a sidewise glance. What seemed to be a Greek pope or parish priest had been keeping abreast of him for some time. What was a man of God doing in this territory? Seeking perhaps to reclaim souls; but their glances touched and Stencil saw no merciful intention there.

"Chaire," muttered the priest.

"Chaire, Papá," said Stencil out of the side of his mouth, and tried to push ahead. He was restrained by the pope's ringed hand.

"One moment, Sidney," said the voice. "Come over here, out of this mob."

That voice was damned familiar. "Maijstral is going to the John Bull," said the pope. "We can catch up with him later." They proceeded down an alley to a small courtyard. In the center was a cistern, its rim adorned with a dark sunburst of sewage.

"Presto change-ho," and off came the holy man's black beard and calotte.

"Demivolt, you've grown crude in your old age. What sort of low comedy is this? What's the matter with Whitehall?"

"They're all right," sang Demivolt, hopping clumsily about the courtyard. "You're as much a surprise to me, you know."

"What about Moffit," Stencil said. "As long as they're staging a reunion of the Florence crew."

"Moffit caught it in Belgrade. I thought you'd heard." Demivolt removed the soutane and rolled his paraphernalia in it. Underneath he wore a suit of English tweed. After quickly recombing his hair and twirling his mustache, he looked no different from the Demivolt Stencil had last seen in '99. Except for more gray in the hair, a few more lines in the face.

"God knows who all they've sent to Valletta," said Demivolt cheerfully, as they returned to the street. "I suspect it's only another fad—F.O. gets these fits, you know. Like a spa or watering place. The Fashionable Place To Go seems to be different every season."

"Don't look at me. I have only a hint what's up. The natives here are, as we say, restless. This chap Fairing—R.C. priest, Jesuit I suspect—thinks there will be a blood bath before very long."

"Yes, I've seen Fairing. If his paycheck is coming out of the same pocket as ours, he shows it not."

"Oh I doubt, I doubt," Stencil said vaguely, wanting to talk about old times.

"Maijstral always sits out in front; we'll go across the street." They took seats at the Café Phoenicia, Stencil with his back to the street. Briefly, over Barcelona beer each filled the other in on the two decades between the Vheissu affair and here, voices monotone against the measured frenzy of the street.

"Odd how paths cross."

Stencil nodded.

"Are we meant to keep tabs on one another? Or were we meant to meet."

"Meant?" too quickly. "By Whitehall, of course."

"Of course."

As we get older we skew more toward the past. Stencil had thus become partially lost to the street and the yardbird across it. The ill-starred year in Florence—Demivolt having popped up again—now came back to him, each unpleasant detail quivering brightly in the dark room of his spy's memory. He hoped devoutly that Demivolt's appearance was merely chance; and not a signal for the reactivation of the same chaotic and Situational forces at work in Florence twenty years ago.

For Fairing's prediction of massacre, and its attendant politics, had all the earmarks of a Situation-in-the-process-of-becoming. He had changed none of his ideas on The Situation. Had even written an article, pseudonymous, and sent it to Punch: "The Situation as an N-Dimensional Mishmash." It was rejected.

"Short of examining the entire history of each individual participating;" Stencil wrote, "short of anatomizing each soul, what hope has anyone of understanding a Situation? It may be that the civil servants of the future will not be accredited unless they first receive a degree in brain surgery."

He indeed was visited by dreams in which he had shrunk to submicroscopic size and entered a brain, strolling in through some forehead's pore and into the cul-de-sac of a sweat gland. Struggling out of a jungle of capillaries there he would finally reach bone; down then through the skull, dura mater, arachnoid, pia mater to the fissure-floored sea of cerebrospinal fluid. And there he would float before final assault on the gray hemispheres: the soul.

Nodes of Ranvier, sheath of Schwann, vein of Galen; tiny Stencil wandered all night long among the silent, immense lightning bursts of nerve-impulses crossing a synapse; the waving dendrites, the nerve-autobahns chaining away to God knew where in receding clusters of end-bulbs. A stranger in this landscape, it never occurred to him to ask whose brain he was in. Perhaps his own. They were fever dreams: the kind where one is given an impossibly complex problem to solve, and keeps chasing dead ends, following random promises, frustrated at every turn, until the fever breaks.

Assume, then, a prospect of chaos in the streets, joined by every group on the island with a grudge. This would include nearly everyone but the OAG and his staff. Doubtless each would think only of his own immediate desires. But mob violence, like tourism, is a kind of communion. By its special magic a large number of lonely souls, however heterogeneous, can share the common property of opposition to what is. And like an epidemic or earthquake the politics of the street can overtake even the most stable-appearing of governments; like death it cuts through and gathers in all ranks of society.

☞ The poor would seek revenge against the millers, who allegedly profiteered in bread during the war.

☞ The civil servants would be out looking for a fairer shake: advance notice of open competition, higher salaries, no more racial discrimination.

☛ The tradesmen would want repeal of the Succession and Donation Duties Ordinance. This tax was meant to bring in £5000 yearly; but the actual assessments amounted to £30,000.

☛ Bolshevists among the yardbirds could only be satisfied with the abolition of all private property, sacred or profane.

☛ The anti-colonial extremists would seek of course to sweep England from the Palace forever. Damn the consequences. Though probably Italy would enter on the next crest and be even harder to dislodge. There would be blood ties, then.

☛ The Abstentionists wanted a new constitution.

☛ The Mizzists—comprising three clubs: Giovine Malta, Dante Alighieri, II Comitato Patriottico—sought (a) Italian hegemony in Malta, (b) aggrandizement for the leader, Dr. Enrico Mizzi.

☛ The Church—here perhaps Stencil's C. of E. stuffiness colored an otherwise objective view—wanted only what the Church always desires during times of political crisis. She awaited a Third Kingdom. Violent overthrow is a Christian phenomenon.

The matter of a Paraclete's coming, the comforter, the dove; the tongues of flame, the gift of tongues: Pentecost. Third Person of the Trinity. None of it was implausible to Stencil. The Father had come and gone. In political terms, the Father was the Prince; the single leader, the dynamic figure whose virtù used to be a determinant of history. This had degenerated to the Son, genius of the liberal love-feast which had produced 1848 and lately the overthrow of the Czars. What next? What Apocalypse?

Especially on Malta, a matriarchal island. Would the Paraclete be also a mother? Comforter, true. But what gift of communication could ever come from a woman. . . .

Enough, lad, he told himself. You're in dangerous waters. Come out, come out.

"Don't turn around now," Demivolt broke in conversationally, "but it's she. At Maijstral's table."

When Stencil did turn around he saw only a vague figure in an evening cape, her face shadowed by an elaborate, probably Parisian bonnet.

"That is Veronica Manganese."

"Gustavus V is ruler of Sweden. You are brimful of intelligence, aren't you."

Demivolt gave Stencil a thumbnail dossier on Veronica

444

Manganese. Origins uncertain. She'd popped up in Malta at the beginning of the war, in the company of one Sgherraccio, a Mizzist. She was now intimate with various renegade Italians, among them D'Annunzio the poet-militant, and one Mussolini, an active and troublesome anti-socialist. Her political sympathies weren't known; whatever they might be, Whitehall was less than amused. The woman was clearly a troublemaker. She was reputed to be wealthy; lived alone in a villa long abandoned by the baronage of Sant' Ugo di Tagliapiombo di Sammut, a nearly defunct branch of the Maltese nobility. The source of her income was not apparent.

"He's a double agent, then."

"It would seem so."

"Why don't I go back to London. You seem to be doing quite well—"

"Negative, negative, Sidney. You do remember Florence."

A waiter materialized with more Barcelona beer. Stencil fumbled for his pipe. "This must be the worst brew in the Mediterranean. You deserve another, for that. Can't Vheissu ever be a dead file?"

"Call Vheissu a symptom. Symptoms like that are always alive, somewhere in the world."

"Sweet Christ, we've only now concluded one. Are they quite ready, do you think, to begin this foolishness again?"

"I don't think," Demivolt smiled grimly. "I try not to. Seriously, I believe all elaborate games of this sort arise from someone in the Office—high up, of course—getting a hunch. Saying to himself, 'Look here: something is wrong, you know.' He's usually right. In Florence he was right, again only as far as we're talking about symptoms and not about any acute case of whatever the disease is.

"Now you and I are only private-soldiers. For myself, I wouldn't presume. That manner of guesswork draws from a really first-rate intuitiveness. Oh we have our own minor hunches, of course: your following Maijstral tonight. But it's a matter of level. Level of pay-grade, level of elevation above the jumble, where one can see the long-term movements. We're in it, in the thick, after all."

"And so they want us together," Stencil murmured.

"As of now. Who knows what they'll want tomorrow?"

"And I wonder who else is here."

"Look sharp. There they go." They let the two across the

street move off before they arose. "Like to see the island? They're probably on their way out to the Villa. Not that the rendezvous is apt to prove very exciting."

So they made their way down Strada Streeta, Demivolt looking like a jaunty anarchist with the black bundle under one arm.

"The roads are terrible," Demivolt admitted, "but we have an automobile."

"I'm frightened to death of automobiles."

Indeed he was. On route to the villa Stencil clutched the Peugeot's seat, refusing to look at anything but the floorboards. Autos, balloons, aeroplanes; he'd have nothing to do with them.

"Isn't this rather crude," he gritted, huddled behind the windscreen as if expecting it to vanish at any moment. "There's no one else on the road."

"At the speed she's going she'll lose us soon enough," Demivolt chirruped, all breezy. "Relax, Sidney."

They moved southwest into Floriana. Ahead Veronica Manganese's Benz had vanished in a gale of cinders and exhaust. "Ambush," Stencil suggested.

"They're not that sort." After awhile Demivolt turned right. They worked their way thus round Marsamuscetto in near-darkness. Reeds whistled in the fens. Behind them the illuminated city seemed tilted toward them, like some display case in a poor souvenir shop. And how quiet was Malta's night. Approaching or leaving other capitals one always caught the sense of a great pulse or plexus whose energy reached one by induction; broadcasting its presence over whatever arête or sea's curve might be hiding it. But Valletta seemed serene in her own past, in the Mediterranean womb, in something so insulating that Zeus himself might once have quarantined her and her island for an old sin or an older pestilence. So at peace was Valletta that with the least distance she would deteriorate to mere spectacle. She ceased to exist as anything quick or pulsed, and was assumed again into the textual stillness of her own history.

The Villa di Sammut lay past Sliema near the sea, elevated on a small prominence, facing out toward an invisible Continent. What Stencil could see of the building was conventional enough, as villas go: white walls, balconies, few windows on the landward side, stone satyrs chasing stone nymphs about dilapidated grounds; one great ceramic dol-

446

phin vomiting clear water into a pool. But the low wall surrounding the place drew his attention. Normally insensitive to the artistic or Baedeker aspect of any city he visited, Stencil was now ready to succumb to the feathery tentacles of a nostalgia which urged him gently back toward childhood; a childhood of gingerbread witches, enchanted parks, fantasy country. It was a dream-wall, swirling and curlicuing now in the light of a quarter moon, seeming no more solid than the decorative voids—some almost like leaves or petals, some almost like bodily organs not quite human— which pierced its streaked and cobbled substance.

"Where have we seen this before," he whispered.

One light in an upper story went out. "Come," said Demivolt. They vaulted the wall and crept round the villa peering in windows, listening at doors.

"Are we looking for anything particular," Stencil asked.

A lantern came on behind them and a voice said, "Turn round slowly. Hands away from your sides."

Stencil had a strong stomach and all the cynicism of a non-political career and an approaching second childhood. But the face above the lantern did give him a mild shock. It is too grotesque, too deliberately, preciously Gothic to be real, he protested to himself. The upper part of the nose seemed to have slid down, giving an exaggerated saddle-and-hump; the chin cut off at midpoint to slope concave back up the other side, pulling part of the lip up in a scarred half-smile. Just under the eye socket on the same side winked a roughly circular expanse of silver. The shadows thrown by the lantern made it worse. The other hand held a revolver.

"You are spies?" the voice inquired, an English voice twisted somehow by a mouth cavity one could only infer. "Let me see your faces." He moved the lantern closer and Stencil saw a change begin to grow in the eyes, all that had been human in the face to begin with.

"Both of you," the mouth said. "Both of you then." And tears began to squeeze from the eyes. "Then you know it is she, and why I am here." He repocketed the revolver, turned, slumped off toward the villa. Stencil started after him, but Demivolt put out an arm. At a door the man turned. "Can't you let us alone? Let her make her own peace? Let me be a simple caretaker? I want nothing more from England." The last words were spoken so weakly the

447

sea wind nearly carried them off. The lantern and its hold-
er vanished behind the door.

"Old running mate," Demivolt said, "there is a tremendous nostalgia about this show. Do you feel it? The pain of
a return home."

"Was that in Florence?"

"The rest of us were. Why not?"

"I don't like duplication of effort."

"This occupation sees nothing else." The tone was grim.
"Another one?"

"Oh hardly so soon. But give it twenty years."

Although Stencil had been face to face with her caretaker, this was the first meeting: he must have reckoned it
even then as a "first meeting." Suspecting anyway that Veronica Manganese and he had met before, why surely they
would meet again.

II

But the second meeting had to wait on the coming of a
kind of false spring, where smells of the Harbour drifted to
the highest reaches of Valletta and flocks of sea birds consulted dispiritedly down in the Dockyard country, aping
the actions of their human co-tenants.

There had been no attack on the Chronicle. On 3 February political censorship of the Maltese press was abolished.
La Voce del Popolo, the Mizzist paper, promptly began agi-
tating. Articles praising Italy and attacking Britain; excerpts
copied from the foreign press, comparing Malta to certain
Italian provinces under a tyrannical Austrian rule. The
vernacular press followed suit. None of it worried Stencil
particularly. When the freedom to criticize a government
had been suspended four years by the same government, a
great deal of pent-up resentment would obviously be released in a voluminous—though not necessarily effective—
torrent.

But three weeks later, a "National Assembly" met in Valletta to draft a request for a liberal constitution. All shades
of political opinion—Abstentionists, Moderates, the Comitato
Patriottico—were represented. The gathering met at the club
Giovine Malta, which was Mizzist-controlled.

"Trouble," Demivolt said darkly.

"Not necessarily." Though Stencil knew the difference

448

between "political gathering" and "mob" is fine indeed. Anything might touch it off.

The night before the meeting a play at the Manoel Theatre, dealing with Austrian oppression in Italy, worked the crowd into a gloriously foul humor. The actors tossed in several topical ad libs which did little to improve the general mood. Rollickers in the street sang La Bella Gigogin. Maijstral reported that a few Mizzists and Bolshevists were doing their best to drum up enthusiasm for a riot among the Dockyard workers. The extent of their success was doubtful. Maijstral shrugged. It might only be the weather. An unofficial notice had also gone out, advising merchants to close up their establishments.

"Considerate of them," Demivolt remarked next day as they strolled down Strada Reale. A few shops and cafés had been closed. A quick check revealed that the owners had Mizzist sympathies.

As the day progressed small bands of agitators, most of them with a holiday air (as if rioting were a healthy avocation like handicrafts or outdoor sports), roamed the streets, breaking windows, wrecking furniture, yelling at the merchants still open to close up their shops. But for some reason a spark was missing. Rain swept by in squalls at intervals throughout the day.

"Grasp this moment," Demivolt said, "hold it close, examine it, treasure it. It is one of those rare occasions on which advance intelligence has proved to be correct."

True: no one had been particularly excited. But Stencil wondered about that missing catalyst. Any minor accident: a break in the clouds, a catastrophic shivering at the first tentative blow to a shop window, the topology of an object of destruction (up a hill or down—it makes a difference)—anything might swell a merely mischievous humor to suddenly apocalyptic rage.

But all that came from the meeting was adoption of Mizzi's resolution calling for complete independence from Great Britain. La Voce del Popolo gibbered triumphantly. A new meeting of the Assembly was called for 7 June.

"Three and a half months," Stencil said. "It will be warmer then." Demivolt shrugged. Whereas Mizzi, an Extremist, had been secretary of the February meeting, one Dr. Mifsud, a Moderate, would be secretary next time. The Moderates wanted to sit down and discuss the constitutional question with Hunter-Blair and the Secretary of State for the Colonies, rather than make any total break with England. And the Moderates, come June, would be in the majority.

"It seems rather a good lookout," Demivolt protested. "If anything was going to happen, it would have happened while Mizzi was ascendant."

"It rained," said Stencil. "It was cold."

La Voce del Popolo and the Maltese-language papers continued their attacks on the government. Maijstral reported twice a week, giving a general picture of deepening discontent among the yardbirds, but they were afflicted by a soggy lethargy which must wait for the heat of summer to dry it, the spark of a leader, a Mizzi or equivalent, to touch it into anything more explosive. As the weeks passed Stencil came to know more about his double agent. It came out that Maijstral lived near the Dockyard with his young wife Carla. Carla was pregnant, the child was due in June.

"How does she feel," Stencil asked once with unaccustomed indiscretion, "about your being in this occupation."

"She will be a mother soon," Maijstral answered, gloomy. "That's all she thinks about or feels. You know what it is to be a mother on this island."

Stencil's boy-romanticism seized on this: perhaps there was more than a professional element to the nighttime meetings out at the Sammut villa. He was almost tempted to ask Maijstral to spy on Veronica Manganese; but Demivolt, the voice of reason, was reluctant.

"Tip our hand that way. We have an ear already in the villa. Dupiro, the ragman, who is quite genuinely in love with a kitchen maid there."

If the Dockyard were the only trouble spot to watch Stencil might have fallen into the same torpor that afflicted the yardbirds. But his other contact—Father Linus Fairing, S.J., the voice whose call for help had been heard among the mass mirth of November and set a-clattering the emotional and intuitive levers, pawls or ratchets to propel Stencil across a continent and sea for solid reasons as yet unclear to him—this Jesuit saw and heard (possibly did) enough to keep Stencil moderately hagridden.

"Being a Jesuit," said the priest, "of course there are certain attitudes . . . we do not control the world in secret, Stencil. We have no spy net, no political nerve-center at the Vatican." Oh, Stencil was unbiased enough. Though with his upbringing he could hardly have sidestepped exposure to a certain C. of E. leeriness toward the Society of Jesus. But he objected to Fairing's digressions; the fog of political opinion that crept in to warp what should have been clear-eyed reporting. At their initial meeting—shortly after the first trip out to Veronica Manganese's villa—Fairing had made a poor first impression. He'd tried to be chummy, even—good God—to talk shop. Stencil was reminded of certain otherwise competent Anglo-Indians in the civil service. "We are discriminated against," seemed to be the complaint: "we are despised by white and Asian alike. Very well, we shall play to the hilt this false role popular prejudice believes us to play." How many deliberate heightenings of dialect, breaches of conversational taste, gaucheries at table had Stencil seen dedicated to that intention?

So with Fairing. "We are all spies in this together," that was the tack he took. Stencil had been interested only in information. He wasn't about to let personality enter the Situation; this would be courting chaos. Fairing realizing soon enough that Stencil was not, after all, a No Popery man, did give up this arrogant form of honesty for more exasperating behavior. Here, seemed to be his assumption, here is a spy who has risen above the political turmoil of his time. Here is Machiavelli on the rack, less concerned with immediacy than idea. Accordingly the subjective fog crept in to obscure his weekly reports.

"Any tug in the direction of anarchy is anti-Christian," he protested once, having sucked Stencil into confessing his theory of Paracletian politics. "The Church has matured, after all. Like a young person she has passed from promiscuity to authority. You are nearly two millennia out-of-date."

An old dame trying to cover up a flaming youth? Ha!

Actually Fairing, as a source, was ideal. Malta being, after all, a Roman Catholic island, the Father was in a position to come by enough information outside the confessional to clarify (at least) their picture of every disaffected group on the island. Though Stencil was less than happy over the quality of these reports, quantity was no problem. But what had provoked his complaint to Mungo Sheaves in the first place? What was the man afraid of?

For it was not mere love of politicking and intrigue. If he did believe in the authority of the Church, of institutions, then perhaps four years of sitting sequestered, outside the suspension of peace which had lately convulsed the rest of the Old World, this quarantine might have brought him to some belief in Malta as a charmed circle, some stable domain of peace.

And then with Armistice to be exposed abruptly at every level to a daftness for overthrow among his parishioners . . . of course.

It was the Paraclete he feared. He was quite content with a Son grown to manhood.

Fairing, Maijstral, puzzlement over the identity of the hideous face above the lantern; these occupied Stencil well into March. Until one afternoon, arriving at the church early for a meeting, he saw Veronica Manganese emerge from the confessional, head bowed, face shadowed as he had seen her in Strada Stretta. She knelt at the altar rail and began to pray penance. Stencil half-knelt in the rear of the church, elbows hung over the back of the pew in front of him. Appearing to be a good Catholic, appearing to be carrying on an affair with Maijstral; nothing suspicious in either. But both at once and with (he imagined) scores of father-confessors in Valletta alone for her to choose from; it was as close to superstition as Stencil ever got. Now and again events would fall into ominous patterns.

. Was Fairing too a double agent? If so then it was actually the woman who'd brought F.O. into this. What twisted
• Italian casuistry advised revealing any plot-in-mounting to one's enemies?

She arose and left the church, passing Stencil on route. Their eyes met. Demivolt's remark came back to him: "A tremendous nostalgia about this show."

~~time~~ Nostalgia and melancholy . . . Hadn't he bridged two worlds? The changes couldn't have been all in him. It must be an alien passion in Malta where all history seemed simultaneously present, where all streets were strait with ghosts, where in a sea whose uneasy floor made and unmade islands every year this stone fish and Ghaudex and the rocks called Cumin-seed and Peppercorn had remained fixed realities since time out of mind. In London were too many distractions. History there was the record of an evolution. One-way and ongoing. Monuments, buildings, plaques were remembrances only; but in Valletta remembrances seemed almost to live.

Stencil, at home everywhere in Europe, had thus come out of his element. Recognizing it was his first step down. A spy has no element to be out of, and not feeling "at home" is a sign of weakness.

F.O. continued to be uncommunicative and unhelpful. Stencil raised the question to Demivolt: had they been turned out to pasture here?

"I've been afraid of that. We are old."

"It was different once," Stencil asked, "wasn't it?"

They went out that night and got maudlin-drunk. But nostalgic melancholy is a fine emotion, becoming blunted on alcohol. Stencil regretted the binge. He remembered rollicking down the hill to Strait Street, well past midnight, singing old vaudeville songs. What was happening?

There came, in time's fullness, One of Those Days. After a spring morning made horrible by another night of heavy drinking Stencil arrived at Fairing's church to learn the priest was being transferred.

"To America. There is nothing I can do." Again the old fellow-professional smile.

Could Stencil have sneered "God's will"; not likely. His case wasn't yet that far advanced. The Church's will, certainly, and Fairing was the type to bow to Authority. Here was after all another Englishman. So they were, in a sense, brothers in exile.

"Hardly," the priest smiled. "In the matter of Caesar and God, a Jesuit need not be as flexible as you might think. There's no conflict of interests."

"As there is between Caesar and Fairing? Or Caesar and Stencil?"

"Something like that."

"Sahha, then. I suppose your relief . . ."

"Father Avalanche is younger. Don't lead him into bad habits."

"I see."

Demivolt was out at Hamrun, conferring with agents among the millers. They were frightened. Had Fairing been too frightened to stay? Stencil had supper in his room. He'd drawn no more than a few times on his pipe when there was a timid knock.

"Oh, come. Come."

A girl, obviously pregnant, who stood, only watching him.

453

"Do you speak English, then."

"I do. I am Carla Maijstral." She remained erect, shoulderblades and buttocks touching the door.

"He will be killed, or hurt," she said. "In wartime a woman must expect to lose her husband. But now there is peace."

She wanted him sacked. Sack him? Why not. Double agents were dangerous. But now, having lost the priest . . . She couldn't know about La Manganese.

"Could you help, signor. Speak to him."

"How did you know? He didn't tell you."

"The workers know there is a spy among them. It has become a favorite topic among all the wives. Which one of us? Of course, it is one of the bachelors, they say. A man with a wife, with children, could not take the chance." She was dry-eyed, her voice was steady.

"For God's sake," Stencil said irritably, "sit down."

Seated: "A wife knows things, especially one who will be a mother soon." She paused to smile down at her belly, which upset Stencil. Dislike for her grew as the moments passed. "I know only that something is wrong with Maijstral. In England I have heard that ladies are 'confined' months before the child is born. Here a woman works, and goes out in the street, as long as she can move about."

"And you came out looking for me."

"The priest told me."

Fairing. Who was working for whom? Caesar wasn't getting a fair shake. He tried sympathy. "Was it worrying you that much? That you had to bring it all into the confessional?"

"He used to stay home at night. It will be our first child, and a first child is the most important. It is his child, too. But we hardly speak any more. He comes in late and I pretend to be asleep."

"But a child also must be fed, sheltered, protected more than a man or woman. And this requires money."

She grew angry. "Maratt the welder has seven children. He earns less than Fausto. None of them has ever gone without food, or clothing, or a home. We do not need your money."

God, she could blow the works. Could he tell her that even if he sacked her husband, there'd still be Veronica Manganese to keep him away nights? Only one answer: talk to the

454

priest. "I promise you," he said, "I will do all I can. But the Situation is more complicated than you may realize."

"My father—" curious he'd not caught that flickering edge of hysteria in her voice till now—"when I was only five also began to stay away from home. I never found out why. But it killed my mother. I will not wait for it to kill me."

Threatening suicide? "Have you talked to your husband at all?"

"It isn't a wife's place."

Smiling: "Only to talk to his employer. Very well, Signora, I shall try. But I can guarantee nothing. My employer is England: the King." Which quieted her.

When she left, he began a bitter dialogue with himself. What had happened to diplomatic initiative? They—whoever "they" were—seemed to be calling the tune.

The Situation is always bigger than you, Sidney. It has like God its own logic and its own justification for being, and the best you can do is cope.

I'm not a marriage counselor, or a priest. Don't act as if it were a conscious plot against your you. Who knows how many thousand accidents—a variation in the weather, the availability of a ship, the failure of a crop—brought all these people, with their separate dreams and worries, here to this island and arranged them into this alignment? Any Situation takes shape from events much lower than the merely human.

Oh, of course: look at Florence. A random pattern of cold-air currents, some shifting of the pack ice, the deaths of a few ponies, these helped produce one Hugh Godolphin, as we saw him. Only by the merest happenstance did he escape the private logic of that ice-world.

The inert universe may have a quality we can call logic. But logic is a human attribute after all; so even at that it's a misnomer. What are real are the cross-purposes. We've dignified them with the words "profession" and "occupation." There is a certain cold comfort in remembering that Manganese, Mizzi, Maijstral, Dupiro the ragman, that blasted face who caught us at the villa—also work at cross-purposes.

But what then does one do? Is there a way out?

There is always the way out that Carla Maijstral threatens to take.

His musings were interrupted by Demivolt, who came stumbling in the door. "There's trouble."

"Oh indeed. That's unusual."

"Dupiro the ragman."

Good things come in threes. "How."

"Drowned, in Marsamuscetto. Washed ashore downhill from Manderaggio. He had been mutilated." Stencil thought of the Great Siege and the Turkish atrocities: death's flotilla.

"It must have been I Banditti," Demivolt continued: "a gang of terrorists or professional assassins. They vie with one another in finding new and ingenious ways to murder. Poor Dupiro's genitals were found sewn in his mouth. Silk suturing worthy of a fine surgeon."

Stencil felt ill.

"We think they are connected somehow with the fasci di combattimento who've organized last month in Italy, around Milan. The Manganese has been in intermittent contact with their leader Mussolini."

"The tide could have carried him across."

"They wouldn't want it out to sea, you know. Craftsmanship of that order must have an audience or it's worthless."

What's happened, he asked his other half. The Situation used to be a civilized affair.

No time in Valletta. No history, all history at once . . .

"Sit down, Sidney. Here." A glass of brandy, a few slaps to the face.

"All right, all right. Ease off. It's been the weather." Demivolt waggled his eyebrows and retreated to the dead fireplace. "Now we have lost Fairing, as you know, and we may lose Maijstral." He summarized Carla's visit.

"The priest."

"What I thought. But we've had an ear lopped off out at the villa."

"Short of starting an affair, one of us, with La Manganese, I can't see any way to replace it."

"Perhaps she's not attracted to the mature sort."

"I didn't mean it seriously."

"She did give me a curious look. That day at the church."

"You old dog. You didn't say you'd been slipping out to secret trysts in a church." Attempting the light touch. But failing.

"It has deteriorated to the point where any move on our part would have to be bold."

"Perhaps foolish. But confronting her directly . . . I'm an optimist, as you know."

456

"I'm a pessimist. It keeps a certain balance. Perhaps I'm only tired. But I do think it is that desperate. Employing I Banditti indicates a larger move—by them—soon."

"Wait, in any event. Till we see what Fairing does."

Spring had descended with its own tongue of flame. Valletta seemed soul-kissed into drowsy complaisance as Stencil mounted the hill southeast of Strada Reale toward Fairing's church. The place was empty and its silence broken only by snores from the confessional. Stencil slipped into the other side on his knees and woke the priest rudely.

"She may violate the secrecy of this little box," Fairing replied, "but I cannot."

"You know what Maijstral is," Stencil said, angry, "and how many Caesars he serves. Can't you calm her? Don't they teach mesmerism at the Jesuit seminary?" He regretted the words immediately.

"Remember I am leaving," coldly: "speak to my successor, Father Avalanche. Perhaps you can teach him to betray God and the Church and this flock. You've failed with me. I must follow my conscience."

"What a damned enigma you are," Stencil burst out. "Your conscience is made of india rubber."

After a pause: "I can, of course, tell her that any drastic step she takes—threatening the welfare of the child, perhaps —is a mortal sin."

Anger had drained away. Remembering his "damned": "Forgive me, Father."

The priest chuckled. "I can't. You're an Anglican."

The woman had approached so quietly that both Stencil and Fairing jumped when she spoke.

"My opposite number."

The voice, the voice—of course he knew it. As the priest —flexible enough to betray no surprise—performed introductions, Stencil watched her face closely, as if waiting for it to reveal itself. But she wore an elaborate hat and veil; and the face was as generalized as that of any graceful woman seen in the street. One arm, sleeveless to the elbow, was gloved and nearly solid with bracelets.

So she had come to them. Stencil had kept his promise to Demivolt—had waited to see what Fairing would do.

"We have met, Signorina Manganese."

"In Florence," came the voice behind the veil. "Do you remember?" turning her head. In the hair visible below the

457

the comb

hat was a carved ivory comb, and five crucified faces, long-suffering beneath their helmets.

"So."

"I wore the comb today. Knowing you would be here."

Whether or not he must now betray Demivolt, Stencil suspected he'd be little use henceforth in either preventing or manipulating for Whitehall's inscrutable purposes whatever would happen in June. What he had thought was an end had proved to be only a twenty-year stay. No use, he realized, asking if she'd followed him or if some third force had manipulated them toward meeting.

voice
Riding out to the villa in her Benz, he showed none of the usual automobile-anxieties. What use? They'd come in, hadn't they, from their thousand separate streets. To enter, hand in hand, the hothouse of a Florentine spring once again; to be flayed and filleted hermetically into a square (interior? exterior?) where all art objects hover between inertia and waking, all shadows lengthen imperceptibly though night never falls, a total nostalgic hush rests on the heart's landscape. And all faces are blank masks; and spring is any drawn-out sense of exhaustion or a summer which like evening never comes.

"We are on the same side, aren't we." She smiled. They'd been sitting idly in one darkened drawing room, watching nothing—night on the sea—from a seaward window. "Our ends are the same: to keep Italy out of Malta. It is a second front, which certain elements in Italy cannot afford to have opened, now."

This woman caused Dupiro the ragman, her servant's love, to be murdered terribly.

I am aware of that.

You are aware of nothing. Poor old man.

"But our means are different."

"Let the patient reach a crisis," she said: "push him through the fever. End the malady as quickly as possible."

A hollow laugh: "One way or another."

"Your way would leave them strength to prolong it. My employers must move in a straight line. No sidetrackings. Annexationists are a minority in Italy, but bothersome."

"Absolute upheaval," a nostalgic smile: "that is your way, Victoria, of course." For in Florence, during the bloody demonstration before the Venezuelan Consulate, he had dragged her away from an unarmed policeman, whose face she was flaying with pointed fingernails. Hysterical girl, tattered velvet. Riot was her element, as surely as this dark room, almost creeping with amassed objects. The street and the hothouse; in V. were resolved, by some magic, the two extremes. She frightened him.

"Shall I tell you where I have been since our last closed room?"

"No. What need to tell me? No doubt I have passed and repassed you, or your work, in every city Whitehall has called me to." He chuckled fondly.

"How pleasant to watch Nothing." Her face (so rarely had he seen it that way!) was at peace, the live eye dead as the other, with the clock-iris. He'd not been surprised at the eye; no more than at the star sapphire sewn into her navel. There is surgery; and surgery. Even in Florence—the comb, which she would never let him touch or remove—he had noted an obsession with bodily incorporating little bits of inert matter.

"See my lovely shoes," as half an hour before he'd knelt to remove them. "I would so like to have an entire foot that way, a foot of amber and gold, with the veins, perhaps, in intaglio instead of bas-relief. How tiresome to have the same feet: one can only change one's shoes. But if a girl could have, oh, a lovely rainbow or wardrobe of different-hued, different-sized and -shaped feet . . ."

Girl? She was nearly forty. But then—aside from a body less alive, how much in fact had she changed? Wasn't she the same balloon-girl who'd seduced him on a leather couch in the Florence consulate twenty years ago?

"I must go," he told her.

"My caretaker will drive you back." As if conjured, the mutilated face appeared at the door. Whatever it felt at seeing them together didn't show in any change of expression. Perhaps it was too painful to change expression. The lantern that night had given an illusion of change: but Stencil saw now the face was fixed as any death-mask.

In the automobile, racketing back toward Valletta, neither spoke till they'd reached the city's verge.

"You must not hurt her, you know."

Stencil turned, struck by a thought. "You are young Gadrulfi—Godolphin—aren't you?"

"We both have an interest in her," Godolphin said. "I am her servant."

459

"I too, in a way. She will not be hurt. She cannot be."

III

Events began to shape themselves for June and the coming Assembly. If Demivolt detected any change in Stencil he gave no sign. Maijstral continued to report, and his wife kept silent; the child presumably growing inside her, also shaping itself for June.

Stencil and Veronica Manganese met often. It was hardly a matter of any mysterious "control"; she held no unspeakable secrets over his balding head, nor did she exert any particular sexual fascination. It could only be age's worst side-effect: nostalgia. A tilt toward the past so violent he found it increasingly more difficult to live in the real present he believed to be so politically crucial. The villa in Sliema became more and more a retreat into late-afternoon melancholy. His yarning with Mehemet, his sentimental drunks with Demivolt; these plus Fairing's protean finaglings and Carla Maijstral's inference to a humanitarian instinct he'd abandoned before entering the service, combined to undermine what virtù he'd brought through sixty years on the go, making him really no further use in Malta. Treacherous pasture, this island.

Veronica was kind. Her time with Stencil was entirely for him. No appointments, whispered conferences, hurried paper work: only resumption of their hothouse-time—as if it were marked by any old and overprecious clock which could be wound and set at will. For it came to that, finally: an alienation from time, much as Malta itself was alienated from any history in which cause precedes effect.

Carla did come to him again with unfaked tears this time; and pleading, not defiant.

"The priest is gone," she wept. "Whom else do I have? My husband and I are strangers. Is it another woman?"

He was tempted to tell her. But was restrained by the fine irony. He found himself hoping that there was indeed adultery between his old "love" and the shipfitter; if only to complete a circle begun in England eighteen years ago, a beginning kept forcibly from his thoughts for the same period of time.

Herbert would be eighteen. And probably helling it all about the dear old isles. What would he think of his father . . .

460

His father, ha.

"Signora," hastily, "I have been selfish. Everything I can do. My promise."

"We—my child and I: why should we continue to live?"

Why should any of us. He would send her husband back. With or without him the June Assembly would become what it would: blood bath or calm negotiation, who could tell or shape events that closely? There were no more princes. Henceforth politics would become progressively more democratized, more thrown into the hands of amateurs. The disease would progress. Stencil was nearly past caring.

Demivolt and he had it out the next evening.

"You're not helping, you know. I can't keep this thing off by myself."

"We've lost our contacts. We've lost more than that . . ."

"What the hell is wrong, Sidney."

"Health, I suppose," Stencil lied.

"O God."

"The students are upset, I've heard. Rumor that the University will be abolished. Conferment of Degrees law, 1915 —so that the graduating class this year is first to be affected."

Demivolt took it as Stencil had hoped: a sick man's attempt to be helpful. "Have a look into that," he muttered. They'd both known of the University unrest.

On 4 June the acting Police Commissioner requested a 25-man detachment from the Malta Composite Battalion to be quartered in the city. University students went on strike the same day, parading Strada Reale, throwing eggs at anti-Mizzists, breaking furniture, turning the street festive with a progress of decorated automobiles.

"We are for it," Demivolt announced that evening. "I'm off for the Palace." Soon after Godolphin called for Stencil in the Benz.

Out at the villa, the drawing room was lit with an unaccustomed brilliance, though occupied only by two people. Her companion was Maijstral. Others had obviously been there: cigarette stubs and teacups were scattered among the statues and old furniture.

Stencil smiled at Maijstral's confusion. "We are old friends," he said gently. From somewhere—bottom of the tank —came a last burst of duplicity and virtù. He forced himself into the real present, perhaps aware it would be his last time there. Placing a hand on the yardbird's shoulder:

461

"Come. I have private instructions." He winked at the woman. "We're still nominally opponents, you see. There are the Rules."

Outside his smile faded. "Now quickly, Maijstral, don't interrupt. You are released. We have no further use for you. Your wife's time is close: go back to her."

"The signora—" jerking his head back toward the foyer— "still needs me. My wife has her child."

"It is an order: from both of us. I can add this: if you do not return to your wife she will destroy herself and the child."

"It is a sin."

"Which she will risk." But Maijstral still shuffled.

"Very well: if I see you again, here or in my woman's company—" that had hit: a sly smile touched Maijstral's lips—"I turn your name over to your fellow workers. Do you know what they'll do to you, Maijstral? Of course you do. I can even call in the Banditti, if you prefer to die more picturesquely. . . ." Maijstral stood for a moment, eyes going numb. Stencil let the magic spell "Banditti" work for an instant more, then flashed his best—and last—diplomatic smile: "Go. You and your woman and the young Maijstral. Stay out of the blood bath. Stay inside." Maijstral shrugged, turned and left. He did not look back; his trundling step was less sure.

Stencil made a short prayer: let him be less and less sure as he gathers years. . . .

She smiled as he returned to the drawing room. "All done?"

He collapsed into a Louis Quinze chair whose two seraphim keened above a dark lawn of green velvet. "All done."

Tension grew through 6 June. Units of the civil police and military were alerted. Another unofficial notice went out, advising merchants to close up their shops.

At 3:30 P.M. on 7 June mobs began to collect in Strada Reale. For the next day and a half they owned Valletta's exterior spaces. They attacked not only the Chronicle (as promised) but also the Union Club, the Lyceum, the Palace, the houses of anti-Mizzist Members, the cafés and shops which had stayed open. Landing parties from H.M.S. Egmont, and detachments of Army and police joined the effort to keep order. Several times they formed ranks; once or twice they fired. Three civilians were killed by gunfire;

seven wounded. Scores more were injured in the general rioting. Several buildings were set on fire. Two RAF lorries with machine guns dispersed an attack on the millers at Hamrun.

A minor eddy in the peaceful course of Maltese government, preserved today only in one Board of Inquiry report. Suddenly as they had begun, the June Disturbances (as they came to be called) ended. Nothing was settled. The primary question, that of self-rule, was as of 1956 still unresolved. Malta by then had only advanced as far as dyarchy, and if anything moved even closer to England in February, when the electorate voted three to one to put Maltese members in the British House of Commons.

Early on the morning of 10 June 1919, Mehemet's xebec set sail from Lascaris Wharf. Seated on its counter, like some obsolete nautical fixture, was Sidney Stencil. No one had come to see him off. Veronica Manganese had kept him only as long as she had to. His eyes kept dead astern.

But as the xebec was passing Fort St. Elmo or thereabouts, a shining Benz was observed to pull up near the wharf and a black-liveried driver with a mutilated face to come to the harbor's edge and gaze out at the ship. After a moment he raised his hand; waved with a curiously sentimental, feminine motion of the wrist. He called something in English, which none of the observers understood. He was crying.

Draw a line from Malta to Lampedusa. Call it a radius. Somewhere in that circle, on the evening of the tenth, a waterspout appeared and lasted for fifteen minutes. Long enough to lift the xebec fifty feet, whirling and creaking, Astarte's throat naked to the cloudless weather, and slam it down again into a piece of the Mediterranean whose subsequent surface phenomena—whitecaps, kelp islands, any of a million flatnesses which should catch thereafter part of the brute sun's spectrum—showed nothing at all of what came to lie beneath, that quiet June day.

READ TOMORROW'S LITERATURE—TODAY

THE BEST OF TODAY'S WRITING BOUND FOR TOMORROW'S CLASSICS.

☐	22580	**PEACE BREAKS OUT** John Knowles	$2.95
☐	24230	**SEPARATE PEACE** John Knowles	$2.75
☐	14666	**SET THIS HOUSE ON FIRE** William Styron	$3.95
☐	24159	**SOPHIE'S CHOICE** William Styron	$4.50
☐	20290	**RAGTIME** E. L. Doctorow	$3.95
☐	13441	**ONE DAY IN THE LIFE OF IVAN DENISOVICH** Alexander Solzhenitsyn	$2.50
☐	20178	**THE END OF THE ROAD** John Barth	$3.50
☐	20850	**THE GOLDEN NOTEBOOK** Doris Lessing	$4.95
☐	22817	**MEMOIRS OF A SURVIVOR** Doris Lessing	$3.95
☐	23691	**THE CRYING OF LOT 49** Thomas Pynchon	$3.50
☐	24684	**GRAVITY'S RAINBOW** Thomas Pynchon	$5.95
☐	20580	**EVEN COWGIRLS GET THE BLUES** Tom Robbins	$3.95
☐	23246	**BEING THERE** Jerzy Kosinski	$2.95
☐	24686	**V** Thomas Pynchon	$4.95
☐	23631	**THE PAINTED BIRD** Jerzy Kosinski	$3.95

<u>Prices and availability subject to change without notice.</u>

Buy them at your local bookstore or use this handy coupon for ordering:

The Most Important Voices of Our Age

WINDSTONE BOOKS

This new line of books from Bantam brings you the most important voices and established writers of our age. Windstone. The name evokes the strong, enduring qualities of the air and the earth. The imprint represents the same qualities in literature—boldness of vision and enduring power, importance and originality of concept and statement. Windstone brings you contemporary masterpieces at affordable prices.

Windstone Books from Bantam bring you the most important voices and established writers of our age. They evoke the strong, enduring qualities of the air and the earth. Here are more Windstone titles with that same quality.

☐	23439	**THE KILLING GROUND** Mary Lee Settle	$3.95
☐	20184	**THE HOUSE ON PRAGUE STREET** Hana Demetz	$3.50
☐	23197	**AN UNKNOWN WOMAN: A JOURNEY TO SELF-DISCOVERY** Alice Koller	$3.95
☐	22604	**THE DIVINERS** M. Laurence	$3.95
☐	20850	**THE GOLDEN NOTEBOOK** D. Lessing	$4.95
☐	22817	**MEMOIRS OF A SURVIVOR** D. Lessing	$3.95
☐	20665	**THE SNOW LEOPARD** P. Matthiessen	$3.95
☐	13441	**ONE DAY IN THE LIFE OF IVAN DENISOVICH** Alexander Solzhenitsyn	$2.50
☐	23754	**DELTA OF VENUS** Anais Nin	$3.95
☐	22969	**A SPY IN THE HOUSE OF LOVE** Anais Nin	$2.95
☐	13402	**LUNAR ATTRACTIONS** Clark Blaise	$3.95

Prices and availability subject to change without notice.

THE NAMES THAT SPELL GREAT LITERATURE

Choose from today's most renowned world authors—every one an important addition to your personal library.

Hermann Hesse

☐	22973	MAGISTER LUDI	$3.95
☐	20696	DEMIAN	$2.95
☐	20855	THE JOURNEY TO THE EAST	$2.95
☐	20884	SIDDHARTHA	$2.95
☐	23837	BENEATH THE WHEEL	$3.95
☐	24413	NARCISSUS AND GOLDMUND	$3.95
☐	23812	STEPPENWOLF	$3.50

Alexander Solzhenitsyn

☐	22904	THE FIRST CIRCLE	$4.50
☐	13441	ONE DAY IN THE LIFE OF IVAN DENISOVICH	$2.50
☐	20655	CANCER WARD	$4.95

Jerzy Kosinski

☐	23386	STEPS	$2.95
☐	23631	THE PAINTED BIRD	$3.95
☐	24026	COCKPIT	$3.50
☐	23884	BLIND DATE	$3.50
☐	23246	BEING THERE	$2.95
☐	14577	THE DEVIL TREE	$2.75

Doris Lessing

☐	22811	THE FOUR-GATED CITY	$4.95
☐	22817	MEMOIRS OF A SURVIVOR	$3.95

Prices and availability subject to change without notice.

Buy them at your local bookstore or use this handy coupon for ordering:

Bantam Books, Inc., Dept. EDG, 414 East Golf Road, Des Plaines, Ill. 60016

Please send me the books I have checked above. I am enclosing $_____ (please add $1.25 to cover postage and handling). Send check or money order —no cash or C.O.D.'s please.

Mr/Mrs/Miss_____

Address_____

City_____State/Zip_____

EDG—9/84

Please allow four to six weeks for delivery. This offer expires 3/85.

BANTAM NEW AGE BOOKS

Bantam New Age Books are for all those interested in reflecting on life today and life as it may be in the future. This important new imprint features stimulating works in fields from biology and psychology to philosophy and the new physics.

☐	23564	THE PICKPOCKET AND THE SAINT	$4.50
		Sheldon B. Kopp	
☐	14146	SUPERMIND: THE ULTIMATE ENERGY	$3.95
		Barbara B. Brown	
☐	24147	CREATIVE VISUALIZATION Shatki Gawain	$3.95
☐	22511	NEW RULES: SEARCHING FOR SELF-FULFILLMENT	$3.95
		IN A WORLD TURNED UPSIDE DOWN	
		Daniel Yankelovich	
☐	22510	ZEN IN THE MARTIAL ARTS J. Hyams	$2.95
☐	23550	STRESS AND THE ART OF BIOFEEDBACK	$4.50
		Barbara Brown	
☐	24682	THE FIRST THREE MINUTES Steven Weinberg	$3.95
☐	20005	MAGICAL CHILD Joseph Chilton Pearce	$3.95
☐	24283	MIND AND NATURE: A Necessary Unity	$4.95
		Gregory Bateson	
☐	24458	ZEN/MOTORCYCLE MAINTENANCE	$4.50
		Robert Pirsig	
☐	20693	THE WAY OF THE SHAMAN Michael Hamer	$3.95
☐	23100	TO HAVE OR TO BE Fromm	$3.50
☐	23125	FOCUSING Eugene Gendlin	$3.95
☐	24562	LIVES OF A CELL Lewis Thomas	$3.95
☐	14912	KISS SLEEPING BEAUTY GOODBYE	$3.95
		M. Kolbenschlag	

Prices and availability subject to change without notice.

Buy them at your local bookstore or use this handy coupon:

Bantam Books. Inc., Dept NA, 414 East Golf Road, Des Plaines, Ill. 60016

Please send me the books I have checked above. I am enclosing $_____
(please add $1.25 to cover postage and handling). Send Check or money order—no cash or C.O.D.'s please.

Mr/Mrs/Miss _____

Address _____

City _____ State/Zip _____

NA—9/84

Please allow four to six weeks for delivery. This offer expires 3/85.

SPECIAL MONEY SAVING OFFER

Now you can have an up-to-date listing of Bantam's hundreds of titles plus take advantage of our unique and exciting bonus book offer. A special offer which gives you the opportunity to purchase a Bantam book for only 50¢. Here's how!

By ordering any five books at the regular price per order, you can also choose any other single book listed (up to a $4.95 value) for just 50¢. Some restrictions do apply, but for further details why not send for Bantam's listing of titles today!

Just send us your name and address plus 50¢ to defray the postage and handling costs.

---

old/new world : (multiple) identity

names   purgatory

church/cathedral   love

father/son   self

symbol vs. human

unknown/mythical place

situations   virginity

Fashoda   prosthetics

Protestant vs. Catholic

rational vs. irrational

the inanimate world

"humanity"   the feminine

subterranean tunnels

northern vs. southern

Judas Tree

9° 9°   Machiavelli

conspiracy   Malta

the Antarctic (224) spying

time   double agents (lives)

God   mothers

siege   Cath/Protestant

Fortune   North/South